# BENNETT CERF'S
## TAKE ALONG TREASURY

*Books by Bennett Cerf*

THE LAUGH'S ON ME

THE LIFE OF THE PARTY

GOOD FOR A LAUGH

LAUGHTER, INCORPORATED

SHAKE WELL BEFORE USING

ANYTHING FOR A LAUGH

TRY AND STOP ME

OUT ON A LIMERICK

RIDDLE-DE-DEE

*Books by Leonora Hornblow*

MEMORY AND DESIRE

THE LOVE SEEKERS

CLEOPATRA OF EGYPT

*Edited By Bennett Cerf*

READING FOR PLEASURE

AN ENCYCLOPEDIA OF MODERN AMERICAN HUMOR

# Bennett Cerf's
# TAKE ALONG
# TREASURY

*Edited by*

## LEONORA HORNBLOW

*and*

## BENNETT CERF

❧

1963

Garden City, New York

DOUBLEDAY & COMPANY, INC.

Grateful acknowledgment is made for permission to use the following copyrighted material:

Aymé, Marcel—"The Proverb" from *The Proverb and Other Stories* by Marcel Aymé, translated from the French by Norman Denny. Copyright c 1961 by The Bodley Head Ltd. Reprinted by permission of Atheneum Publishers and The Bodley Head Ltd.

Berry, John—"The Listener" from *New World Writing No. 16* by John Berry. Copyright c 1960 by John Berry. Reprinted by permission of Russell & Volkening, Inc.

Blanch, Lesley—"Aimée Dubucq de Rivery" from *The Wilder Shores of Love* by Lesley Blanch. Copyright 1954 by Lesley Blanch. Reprinted by arrangement with Simon and Schuster, Inc.

Capote, Truman—"House of Flowers" from *Breakfast at Tiffany's* by Truman Capote. Copyright 1951 by Truman Capote. Reprinted by permission of *Mademoiselle* and Random House, Inc.

Carr, John Dickson—"The Gentleman from Paris" from *The Third Bullet and Other Stories* by John Dickson Carr. Copyright 1950 by John Dickson Carr. Reprinted by permission of Harper & Row, Publishers, Incorporated.

Cather, Willa—*My Mortal Enemy* by Willa Cather. Copyright 1926 by Alfred A. Knopf, Inc. Renewed 1954 by Edith Lewis. Reprinted by permission of Alfred A. Knopf, Inc.

Cheever, John—"The Bus to St. James's" by John Cheever, from *Stories*, by Cheever, et. al. Copyright 1956 by *The New Yorker* magazine, c 1956 by Farrar, Straus & Cudahy, Inc. Reprinted by permission of Farrar, Straus & Cudahy, Inc.

Cooper, Duff—*Operation Heartbreak* by Duff Cooper. Reprinted by permission of The Executors of the late Duff Cooper.

Dahl, Roald—"The Way up to Heaven" from *Kiss Kiss* by Roald Dahl. Copyright 1954 by Roald Dahl. Reprinted by permission of Alfred A. Knopf, Inc.

Dinesen, Isak—"The Great Gesture" from *Shadows on the Grass* by Isak Dinesen. c Copyright 1960 by Isak Dinesen. Reprinted by permission of Random House, Inc., and Michael Joseph, Ltd., London.

du Maurier, Daphne—"The Birds" from *Kiss Me Again, Stranger* by Daphne du Maurier. Copyright 1952 by Daphne du Maurier. Reprinted by permission of Doubleday & Company, Inc., and Curtis Brown, Ltd.

Durrell, Lawrence—"The Ghost Train" from the book *Esprit de Corps* by Lawrence Durrell. Copyright c 1957 by Lawrence Durrell. Reprinted by permission of E. P. Dutton & Co., Inc., and Curtis Brown, Ltd.

Ellin, Stanley—"The Specialty of the House" from *Mystery Stories*. Copyright 1948 by Stanley Ellin. Reprinted by permission of Simon and Schuster, Inc. This story originally appeared in *Ellery Queen's Mystery Magazine.*

Faulkner, William—"Hell Creek Crossing" from *The Reivers*, by William Faulkner. c Copyright 1962 by William Faulkner. Reprinted by permission of Random House, Inc.

Frankau, Pamela—"The Duchess and the Smugs" from *A Wreath for the Enemy* by Pamela Frankau. Copyright 1952 by Pamela Frankau. Reprinted by permission of Harper & Row, Publishers, Incorporated.

Greene, Graham—"The End of the Party" from *Twenty-one Stories* by Graham Greene Copyright 1947 by Graham Greene. Reprinted by permission of The Viking Press, Inc., and Laurence Pollinger Limited.

Hanff, Helene—"No Legs No Jokes No Chance" from *Underfoot in Show Business* by Helene Hanff. Copyright c 1961 by Helene Hanff. Reprinted by permission of Harper & Row, Publishers, Incorporated.

Huxley, Aldous—"Sir Hercules" from *Collected Short Stories* by Aldous Huxley. Copyright 1922 by Aldous Huxley. Reprinted by permission of Harper & Row, Publishers, Incorporated.

Kerr, Jean—"How to Talk to a Man" from *The Snake Has All the Lines* by Jean Kerr. Copyright c 1958 by Jean Kerr. Reprinted by permission of Doubleday & Company, Inc.

Lambert, Gavin—"The End of the Line" from *The Slide Area* by Gavin Lambert. Copyright c 1959 by Gavin Lambert. Reprinted by permission of The Viking Press, Inc., and Harold Matson Company.

Lowry, Malcolm—*The Bravest Boat* by Malcolm Lowry. Copyright 1954 by Stuart Osborne Lowry. Reprinted by permission of J. B. Lippincott Company.

# INTRODUCTION

PEOPLE bound for a vacation necessarily set out with the assumption that they will be in a zestful, beatific mood from the moment they begin to relax. Nothing like this, of course, is the case. Comes a day of overcast skies and rain, or a disturbing long-distance call from the office or the children, and they can become on the instant just as fretful and fidgety in what the travel folders have described as a "paradise on earth" as they were before they began packing.

Today's newspapers are an added hazard to vacationers. Not only do the jets bring them to the most remote hideaways in a matter of hours, but their front-page headlines are more and more apt to scare the living daylights out of them. "Hammock reading"—light "escape" literature—clearly is no longer enough to soothe the sensitive vacationer. He should have at hand a varied fare—reading material to suit *any* mood: exalted, depressed, bored, nostalgic, impatient for a thrill.

That is the reasoning that prompted this anthology.

It is, admittedly, a mixed bag of offerings, reflecting, first, the often contrasting tastes of a woman and a man; second, the determination of two editors who not only have read, but have compiled many anthologies of their own, to introduce into this collection some very-little-known stories by writers just making their mark. Backing them up are a few older special favorites by standbys that in two conspicuous cases at least were never allowed to be reprinted in anthologies before.

There is too much "me too" reading being done in our country today. The only reason many people now buy a book is because their neighbors are reading it. It is currently "fashionable." It tops best-seller lists. This is fine for the authors of these few fortunate best-sellers—but if the trend persists, who will be left to give the promising newcomer his start? If *everybody* insists on reading already established favorites, how long will publishers be able to launch "first novels" by hopeful unknowns? We are losing at a disheartening rate the great American authors of the 1930s and 1940s. Gone in a shockingly short span of time are such greats as Willa Cather, Eugene O'Neill, Thomas

Wolfe, Sinclair Lewis, Edna Millay, Ernest Hemingway, James Thurber, and William Faulkner. We must find replacements for them! The editors of this anthology will be particularly grateful if the casual reader discovers in its pages just a few new authors whose work he will care to follow further in days to come.

The section headings of the *Take Along Treasury* will indicate very clearly what type of story the reader has in store for him. And unlike the slave of a television set, the reader of a book like this can choose his own bill of fare, decide when to pick it up, when to pause momentarily for reflection, turn back at will to reread a paragraph he particularly enjoyed—with nary a soap, beer, or cigarette endorsement from a frenetic pitchman to shatter his mood.

They never have invented—and never will invent—a machine or pastime that can provide the same joy and deep satisfaction as a fine book by a fine writer. After we had finished our explorations for this collection, we were convinced of this more than ever.

May you derive as much pleasure from these selections as we did ourselves!

LEONORA HORNBLOW

BENNETT CERF

*Mt. Kisco, Spring, 1963*

# CONTENTS

# 3. *Other Loves*

# 4. *Other Times*

# 5. *Edge-of-the-Seat Department*

## 6. *The World Today*

## 7. *Exit Laughing*

# Part I
# OTHER PEOPLE

# THE DUCHESS AND THE SMUGS

## *Pamela Frankau*

PAMELA FRANKAU (1908–   ), although English by parentage
and early background, has lived a full and lively life on both sides of
the Atlantic. Her enchanting stories deal with the bright people of
the "inner set" who find themselves at home wherever they may be.
Her autobiographical pieces and her essays on the art of putting pen
to paper are a passport to a special and fascinating world. Her early
work, done largely for the magazines and journals, was perhaps too
"popular" for her own present taste. More recent years have brought
from her some of the best writing—and most meaningful—of our time.

I SAT still at the table, with the blank paper before me. I went
back; I remembered; I thought my way in. It was the sensation
of pulling on a diver's helmet and going down deep.
Presently, on the sea-floor, I began to find lost things; to raise the
moods that were mine when I was fourteen years old, sitting in this
garden, writing my Anthology of Hates.

I would begin there.

I

There had been two crises already that day before the cook's husband
called to assassinate the cook. The stove caught fire in my presence;
the postman had fallen off his bicycle at the gate and been bitten by
Charlemagne, our sheep dog, whose policy it was to attack people only
when they were down.

Whenever there were two crises my stepmother Jeanne said, *"Jamais
deux sans trois."* This morning she and Francis (my father) had de-
bated whether the two things happening to the postman could be
counted as two separate crises and might therefore be said to have
cleared matters up. I thought that they were wasting their time. In
our household things went on and on and on happening. It was a
hotel, which made the doom worse: it would have been remarkable to

have two days without a crisis and even if we did, I doubted whether the rule would apply in reverse, so that we could augur a third. I was very fond of the word "augur."

I was not very fond of the cook. But when I was sitting on the terrace in the shade working on my Anthology of Hates, and a man with a bristled chin told me in *patois* that he had come to kill her, I thought it just as well for her, though obviously disappointing for her husband, that she was off for the afternoon. He carried a knife that did not look particularly sharp; he smelt of licorice, which meant that he had been drinking Pernod. He stamped up and down, making speeches about his wife and Laurent the waiter, whom he called a *salaud* and many other words new to me and quite difficult to understand.

I said at last, "Look, you can't do it now, because she has gone over to St. Raphael in the bus. But if you wait I will fetch my father." I took the Anthology with me in case he started cutting it up.

I went down the red rock steps that sloped from the garden to the pool. The garden looked the way it always looked, almost as brightly colored as the postcards of it that you could buy at the desk. There was purple bougainvillaea splashing down the white walls of the hotel; there were hydrangeas of the exact shade of pink blotting paper; there were huge silver-gray cacti and green umbrella-pines against a sky that was darker blue than the sky in England.

I could not love this garden. Always it seemed to me artificial, spiky with color, not quite true. My idea of a garden was a green lawn and a little apple orchard behind a gray stone house in the Cotswolds. It was my Aunt Anne's house in the village of Whiteford. I saw that garden only once a year, in September. I could conjure it by repeating inside my head,

> And autumn leaves of blood and gold
> That strew a Gloucester lane.

Then the homesickness for the place that was not my home would make a sharp pain under my ribs. I was ashamed to feel so; I could not talk about it; not even to Francis, with whom I could talk about most things.

I came to the top of the steps and saw them lying around the pool, Francis and Jeanne and the two novelists who had come from Antibes for lunch. They were all flat on the yellow mattresses, talking.

I said, "Excuse me for interrupting you, but the cook's husband has come to assassinate the cook."

Francis got up quickly. He looked like Mephistopheles. There were gray streaks in his black hair; all the lines of his face went upward and the pointed moustache followed the lines. His body was dark brown and hairy, except that the scars on his back and legs, where he was burned when the aeroplane was shot down, did not tan with the sun.

"It's a hot afternoon for an assassination," said the male novelist as they ran up the steps together.

"Perhaps," said Francis, "he can be persuaded to wait until the evening."

"He will have to," I said, "because the cook is in St. Raphael. I told him so."

"Penelope," said my stepmother, sitting up on the yellow mattress, "you had better stay with us."

"But I am working on my book."

"All right, *chérie*; work on it here."

The lady novelist, who had a sparkling, triangular face like a cat, said, "I wish you would read some of it to us. It will take our minds off the current bloodcurdling events."

I begged her to excuse me, adding that I did not anticipate any bloodcurdling events because of the battered look of the knife.

Jeanne said that the cook would have to go in any case, but that her love for Laurent was of a purely spiritual character.

I said, "Laurent is a smoothie, and I do not see how anybody could be in love with him."

"A certain smoothness is not out of place in a headwaiter," said the lady novelist.

I did not tell her my real reason for disliking Laurent; he made jokes. I hated jokes more than anything. They came first in the Anthology; they occupied whole pages; I had dozens and dozens; it was a loose-leaf book, so that new variations of hates already listed could be inserted at will.

Retiring from the conversation, I went to sit on the flat rock at the far end of the pool. Francis and the male novelist returned very soon. Francis came over to me. I shut the loose-leaf book.

"The cook's husband," he said, "has decided against it."

"I thought he would. I imagine that if you are really going to murder somebody you do not impart the intention to others."

"Don't you want to swim?" said Francis.

"No, thank you. I'm working."

"You couldn't be sociable for half an hour?"

"I would rather not."

"I'll write you down for RCI," he threatened.

RCI was Repulsive Children Incorporated, an imaginary foundation which Francis had invented a year before. It came about because a family consisting mainly of unusually spoiled children stayed at the hotel for two days, and were asked by Francis to leave on the third, although the rooms were booked for a month. According to Francis, RCI did a tremendous business and there were qualifying examinations wherein the children were tested for noise, bad manners, whining and brutal conduct. I tried to pretend that I thought this funny.

"Will you please let me work for a quarter of an hour?" I asked him. "After all, I was disturbed by the assassin."

"All right. Fifteen minutes," he said, "after which you qualify."

In fact I was not telling him the truth. I had a rendezvous at this hour every day. At four o'clock precisely I was sure of seeing the people from the next villa. I had watched them for ten days and I knew how Dante felt when he waited for Beatrice to pass him on the Ponte Vecchio. Could one, I asked myself, be in love with four people at once? The answer seemed to be "Yes." These people had become a secret passion.

The villa was called La Lézardière; a large, stately pink shape with green shutters; there was a gravel terrace, planted with orange trees and descending in tiers, to a pool that did not sprawl in a circle of red rocks as ours did, but was of smooth gray concrete. At the tip of this pool there was a real diving-board. A long gleaming speedboat lay at anchor in the deep water. The stage was set and I waited for the actors.

They had the quality of Vikings; the father and mother were tall, handsome, white-skinned and fair-haired. The boy and girl followed the pattern. They looked as I should have preferred to look. (I was as dark as Francis, and, according to the never-ceasing stream of personal remarks that seemed to be my lot at this time, I was much too thin. And not pretty. If my eyes were not so large I knew that I should be quite ugly. In Francis' opinion, my face had character. "But this, as Miss Edith Cavell said of patriotism," I told him, "is not enough.")

Oh, to look like the Bradleys; to be the Bradleys, I thought, waiting for the Bradleys. They were far, august and enchanted; they wore the halo of being essentially English. They were Dad and Mum and Don and Eva. I spied on them like a huntress, strained my ears for their words, cherished their timetable. It was regular as the clock. They swam before breakfast and again at ten, staying beside the pool all the morning. At a quarter to one the bell would ring from the villa for their lunch. Oh, the beautiful punctuality of those meals! Sometimes we did not eat luncheon until three and although Jeanne told me to go and help myself from the kitchen, this was not the same thing at all.

In the afternoon the Bradleys rested on their terrace in the shade. At four they came back to the pool. They went fishing or water-skiing.

They were always doing something. They would go for drives in a magnificent gray car with a white hood that folded back. Sometimes they played a catching game beside the pool; or they did exercises in a row, with the father leading them. They had cameras and butterfly-nets and field-glasses. They never seemed to lie around and talk, the loathèd recreation in which I was expected to join.

I took Don and Eva to be twins; and perhaps a year younger than I. I was just fourteen. To be a twin would, I thought, be a most sat-isfying destiny. I would even have changed places with the youngest member of the Bradley family, a baby in a white perambulator with a white starched nurse in charge of it. If I could be the baby, I should at least be sure of growing up and becoming a Bradley, in a white shirt and gray shorts.

Their magic linked with the magic of my early fortnight in England, when, besides having the gray skies and the green garden, I had ac-quaintance with other English children not in the least like me: solid, pink-cheeked sorts with ponies; they came over to tea at my aunt's house and it was always more fun in anticipation than in fact, because I seemed to make them shy. And I could never tell them that I yearned for them.

So, in a way, I was content to watch the Bradleys at a distance. I felt that it was hopeless to want to be friends with them; to do the things that they did. I was not only different on the outside, but dif-ferent on the inside, which was worse. On the front page of the An-thology I had written: "I was born to trouble as the sparks fly upward," one of the more consoling quotations because it made the matter seem inevitable.

Now it was four o'clock. My reverie of the golden Bradleys became the fact of the golden Bradleys, strolling down to the water. Dad and Don were carrying the water-skis. I should have only a brief sight of them before they took the speedboat out into the bay. They would skim and turn far off, tantalizing small shapes on the shiny silky sea. Up on the third tier of the terrace, between the orange trees, the neat white nurse was pushing the perambulator. But she was only faintly touched with the romance that haloed the others. I mourned.

Then a most fortunate thing happened. There was a drift of strong current around the rocks and as the speedboat moved out toward the bay, one of the water-skis slipped off astern, and was carried into the pool under the point where I sat. Don dived in after it; I ran down the slope of rock on their side, to shove it off from the edge of the pool.

"Thanks most awfully," he said. He held on to the fringed sea-weed and hooked the water-ski under his free arm. Now that he was so close to me I could see that he had freckles; it was a friendly smile and he spoke in the chuffy, English boy's voice that I liked.

"It's rather fun, water-skiing."

"It looks fun. I have never done it."

"Would you like to come out with us?" he jerked his head toward the boat: "Dad's a frightfully good teacher."

I groaned within me, like the king in the Old Testament. Here were the gates of Paradise opening and I must let them shut again, or be written down for RCI.

"Painful as it is to refuse," I said, "my father has acquired visitors and I have sworn to be sociable. The penalty is ostracism." (Ostracism was another word that appealed to me.)

Don, swinging on the seaweed, gave a gurgle of laughter.

"What's funny?" I asked.

"I'm terribly sorry. Wasn't that meant to be funny?"

"Wasn't what meant to be funny?"

"The way you talked."

"No, it's just the way I talk," I said, drooping with sadness.

"I like it awfully," said Don. This was warming to my heart. By now the speedboat was alongside the rock point. I could see the Viking heads; the delectable faces in detail. Mr. Bradley called: "Coming aboard?"

"She can't," said Don. "Her father has visitors; she'll be ostracized." He was still giggling and his voice shook.

"Oh dear, that's too bad," said Mrs. Bradley. "Why don't you ask your father if you can come tomorrow?"

"I will, most certainly," I said, though I knew that I need never ask permission of Jeanne or Francis for anything that I wanted to do.

I felt as though I had been addressed by a goddess. Don gurgled again. He flashed through the water and they pulled him into the boat.

I had to wait for a few minutes alone, hugging my happiness, preparing a kind of vizor to pull down over it when I went back to the group on the yellow mattresses.

"Making friends with the Smugs?" Francis greeted me.

"What an enchanting name," said the lady novelist.

"It isn't their name; it's what they are," said Francis.

I heard my own voice asking thinly: "Why do you call them that?" He shocked me so much that my heart began to beat heavily and I shivered. I tried to conceal this by sitting crouched and hugging my knees. I saw him watching me.

"Well, aren't they?" he said gently. I had given myself away. He had guessed that they meant something to me.

"I don't know. I don't think so. I want to know why you think so."

"Partly from observation," said Francis. "Their gift for organized leisure; their continual instructions to their children, the expressions on their faces. And the one brief conversation that I've conducted with Bradley—he congratulated me on being able to engage in a commercial enterprise on French soil. According to Bradley, you can never trust the French." He imitated the chuffy English voice.

"Isn't 'commercial enterprise' rather an optimistic description of Chez François?" asked the lady novelist, and the male novelist laughed. Francis was still looking at me.

"Why do you like them, Penelope?"

I replied with chilled dignity: "I did not say that I liked them. They invited me to go water-skiing with them tomorrow."

Jeanne said quickly: "That will be fun. You know, Francis, you are becoming too intolerant of your own countrymen: it is enough in these days for you to meet an Englishman to make you dislike him." This was comforting; I could think this and feel better. Nothing, I thought, could make me feel worse than for Francis to attack the Bradleys. It was another proof that my loves, like my hates, must remain secret, and this was loneliness.

II

I awoke next morning full of a wild surmise. I went down early to the pool and watched Francis taking off for Marseilles in his small, ramshackle seaplane. He flew in a circle over the garden as he always did, and when the seaplane's long boots pointed for the west, I saw Don and Eva Bradley standing still on the gravel terrace to watch it. They were coming down to the pool alone. Offering myself to them, I went out to the flat rock. They waved and beckoned and shouted.

"Is that your father flying the seaplane?"

"Yes."

"Does he take you up in it?"

"Sometimes."

"Come and swim with us," Don called.

I ran down the rock slope on their side. I was shy now that we stood together. I saw that Eva was a little taller than Don; that she also was freckled; and that they had oiled their skins against sunburn as the grownups did. Don wore white trunks and Eva a white swimming suit. They laughed when I shook hands with them, and Don made me an elaborate bow after the handshake. Then they laughed again.

"Are you French or English?"

That saddened me. I said, "I am English, but I live here because my stepmother is a Frenchwoman and my father likes the Riviera."

"We know that," said Don quickly. "He was shot down and taken prisoner by the Germans and escaped and fought with the Resistance, didn't he?"

"Yes. That is how he met Jeanne."

"And he's Francis Wells, the poet?"

"Yes."

"And the hotel is quite mad, isn't it?"

"Indubitably," I said. It was another of my favorite words. Eva doubled up with laughter. "Oh, that's wonderful. I'm *always* going to say indubitably."

"Is it true," Don said, "that guests only get served if your father likes the look of them, and that he charges nothing sometimes, and that all the rooms stay empty for weeks if he wants them to?"

"It is true. It does not seem to me the most intelligent way of running an hotel, but that is none of my business."

"Is he very rich?" asked Eva.

Don said quickly: "Don't, Eva, that's not polite."

"He isn't rich or poor," I said. I could not explain our finances to the Bradleys any more than I could explain them to myself. Sometimes we had money. When we had not, we were never poor in the way that other people were poor. We were "broke" which, as far as I could see, meant being in debt but living as usual and talking about money.

"Do you go to school in England?"

"No," I said, handing over my chief shame. "I am a day boarder at a convent school near Grasse. It is called Nôtre Dame les Oliviers."

"Do you like it?"

"I find it unobjectionable," I said. It would have been disloyal to Francis and Jeanne to tell these two how little I liked it.

"Do they teach the same things as English schools?"

"Roughly."

"I expect you're awfully clever," said Eva, "and top at everything."

How did she know that? Strenuously, I denied it. Heading the class in literature, composition and English poetry was just one more way of calling attention to myself. It was part of the doom of being noticeable, of not being like Other People. At Les Oliviers, Other People were French girls, strictly brought up, formally religious, cut to a foreign pattern. I did not want to be they, as I wanted to be the Bradleys: I merely envied their uniformity.

God forbid that I should tell the Bradleys about winning a special prize for a sonnet; about being chosen to recite Racine to hordes of parents; about any of it. I defended myself by asking questions in my turn. Eva went to an English boarding school in Sussex; Don would go to his first term at public school this autumn. I had guessed their ages correctly. They were just thirteen. "Home" was Devonshire.

"I would greatly love to live in England," I said.

"I'd far rather live in an hotel on the French Riviera. Lucky Penelope."

"I am not lucky Penelope; I am subject to dooms."

"How heavenly. What sort of dooms?"

"For example, getting an electric shock in science class, and finding a whole nest of mice in my desk," I said. "And being the only person present when a lunatic arrived believing the school to be Paradise."

"Go on. Go on," they said. "It's wonderful. Those aren't dooms, they are adventures."

"Nothing that happens all the time is an adventure," I said. "The hotel is also doomed."

They turned their heads to look up at it; from here, through the pines and the cactus, we could see the red crinkled tiles of its roof, the bougainvillaea, the top of the painted blue sign that announced "CHEZ FRANÇOIS."

"It can't be doomed," Don said. "Don't famous people come here?"

"Oh yes. But famous people are more subject to dooms than ordinary people."

"How?"

"In every way you can imagine. Important telegrams containing money do not arrive. Their wives leave them; they are recalled on matters of state."

"Does Winston Churchill come?"

"Yes."

"And Lord Beaverbrook and Elsa Maxwell and the Duke of Windsor and Somerset Maugham?"

"Yes. Frequently. All their signed photographs are kept in the bar. Would you care to see them?"

Here I encountered the first piece of Bradley dogma. Don and Eva, who were splashing water on each other's hair ("Dad is most particular about our not getting sunstroke") looked doubtful.

"We *would* love to."

"I'm sure it's all right, Eva; because she lives there."

"I don't know. I think we ought to ask first. It is a bar, after all."

Ashamed, I hid from them the fact that I often served in the bar when Laurent was off duty.

"Oh, do let's chance it," said Don.

"I don't believe we ought to."

Mr. and Mrs. Bradley had gone over to Nice and would not return until the afternoon, so a deadlock threatened. The white starched nurse appeared at eleven o'clock with a Thermos-flask of cold milk and a plate of buns. I gave birth to a brilliant idea; I told her that my step-mother had invited Don and Eva to lunch with us.

It was a little difficult to convince them, after the nurse had gone, that Jeanne would be pleased to have them to lunch without an invitation. When I led them up through our garden, they treated it as an adventure, like tiger-shooting.

Jeanne welcomed them, as I had foretold, and the lunch was highly successful, although it contained several things, such as *moules,* which the Bradleys were not allowed to eat. We had the terrace to ourselves. Several cars drove up and their owners were told politely that lunch could not be served to them. This delighted Don and Eva. They were even more delighted when Jeanne told them of Francis' ambition, which was to have a notice: "Keep Out; This Means You," printed in seventeen languages. One mystery about the Bradleys was that they seemed to like jokes. They thought that I made jokes. When they laughed at my phrases they did not laugh as the grownups did, but in the manner of an appreciative audience receiving a comedian. Eva would hold her stomach and cry: "Oh *stop!* It hurts to giggle like this; it really hurts."

I took them on a tour of the hotel. The salon was furnished with some good Empire pieces. The bedrooms were not like hotel bedrooms, but more like rooms in clean French farmhouses, with pale walls and dark wood and chintz. All the rooms had balconies where the guests could eat their breakfast. There were no guests.

"And Dad says people *clamor* to stay here in the season," Don said, straddled in the last doorway.

"Yes, they do. Probably some will be allowed in at the end of the week," I explained, "but the Duchess is arriving from Venice at any moment and Francis always waits for her to choose which room she wants, before he lets any. She is changeable."

Eva said, "I can't get over your calling your father Francis. Who is the Duchess?"

"The Duchessa di Terracini. She is half-Italian and half-American."

"Is she very beautiful?"

"Very far from it. She is seventy and she looks like a figure out of a waxworks. She was celebrated for her lovers but now she only loves roulette." I did not wish to be uncharitable about the Duchess, whose visit was to be dreaded, and these were the nicest things that I could make myself say. The only thing in her favor was that she had been a friend of my mother, who was American and utterly beautiful and whom I did not remember.

"*Lovers?*" Eva said, looking half-pleased and half-horrified. Don flushed and looked at his feet. I had learned from talks at school that reactions to a mention of the facts of life could be like this. I knew also that Francis despised the expression, "the facts of life," because, he said, it sounded as though all the other things that happened in life were figments of the imagination.

"A great many people loved the Duchess desperately," I said. "She was engaged to an Austrian Emperor; he gave her emeralds, but somebody shot him."

"Oh well, then, she's practically history, isn't she?" Eva said, looking relieved.

### III

I might have known that the end of the day would bring doom. It came hard upon the exquisite pleasure of my time in the speedboat with the Bradleys. This was even better than I had planned it in anticipation, a rare gift. I thought that the occasion must be under the patronage of a benign saint or what the Duchess would call a favorable aura; the only worry was Mrs. Bradley's worry about my having no dry clothes to put on after swimming; but with typical Bradley organization there were an extra white shirt and gray shorts in the boat. Dressed thus I felt like a third twin.

The sea changed color; the sea began to be white and the rocks a darker red.

"Would you like to come back and have supper with us, Penelope?"

I replied, "I can imagine nothing that I would like more."

"She *does* say wonderful things, doesn't she?" said Eva. I was drunk by now on Bradley admiration and almost reconciled to personal remarks.

"Penelope speaks very nice English," said Mrs. Bradley.

"Will you ask your stepmother then?" she added as we tied up the boat. I was about to say this was unnecessary when Don gave my ribs a portentous nudge; he said quickly, "Eva and I will walk you up there." It was obvious that the hotel exercised as much fascination for them as they for me.

When the three of us set off across the rocks Mr. Bradley called, "Seven o'clock sharp, now!" and Eva made a grimace. She said, "Wouldn't it be nice not to have to be punctual for anything?"

"I never have to be," I said, "except at school, and I think that I prefer it to having no timetable at all."

"Oh, my goodness! Why?"

"I like days to have a shape," I said.

"Can you just stay out to supper when you want to? Always? With-out telling them?"

"Oh, yes."

"What would happen if you stayed away a whole night?"

I said that I had never tried. And now we went into the bar because Don said that he wanted to see the photographs again. Laurent was there; straw-colored and supercilious in his white coat. He began to make his jokes: *"Mesdames, monsieur, bon soir.* What may I serve you? A Pernod? A champagne cocktail?" He flashed along the shelves, reading out the name of each drink, muttering under his breath, *"Mais non; c'est terrible;* we have nothing that pleases our distinguished visitors." I saw that the Bradleys were enchanted with him.

We walked all round the gallery of photographs and were lingering beside Winston Churchill when the worst thing happened. I heard it coming. One could always hear the Duchess coming. She made peals of laughter that sounded like opera; the words came fast and high be-tween the peals.

And here she was, escorted by Francis. She cried, "Ah my love, my love," and I was swept into a complicated, painful embrace, scratched by her jewelry, crushed against her stays, and choked with her scent before I got a chance to see her in perspective. When I did, I saw that there were changes since last year and that these were for the worse. Her hair, which had been dyed black, was now dyed bright red. Her powder was whiter and thicker than ever; her eyelids were dark blue; she had new false eyelashes of great length that made her look like a Jersey cow.

She wore a dress of dark blue chiffon, sewn all over with sequin stars, and long red gloves with her rings on the outside; she tilted back on her heels, small and bony, gesticulating with the gloves.

"Beautiful—beautiful—beautiful!" was one of her slogans. She said it now; she could not conceivably mean me; she just meant everything. The Bradleys had become awed and limp all over. When I introduced them they shook hands jerkily, snatching their hands away at once. Francis took from Laurent the bottle of champagne that had been on ice awaiting the Duchess; he carried it to her favorite table, the corner table beside the window. She placed upon the table a sequin bag of size, a long chiffon scarf, and a small jeweled box that held *bonbons au miel,* my least favorite sweets, reminding me of scented glue.

Francis uncorked the champagne.

"But glasses for all of us," the Duchess said. "A glass for each." The Bradleys said, "No thank you very much," so quickly that they made it sound like one syllable and I imitated them.

"But how good for you," cried the Duchess. "The vitalizing, the magnificent, the harmless grape. All children should take a little to combat the lassitude and depressions of growth. My mother used to give me a glass every morning after my fencing lesson. *Et toi,* Penelope? More than once last year you have taken your *petit verre* with me."

"Oh, didn't you know? Penelope is on the water wagon," said Francis, and the Duchess again laughed like opera. She cried, *"Santé, santé!"* raising her glass to each of us. Francis helped himself to a Pernod and perched on the bar, swinging his legs. The Bradleys and I stood in a straight, uncomfortable row.

"Of youth," said the Duchess, "I recall three things. The sensation of time seeming endless, as though one were swimming against a current; the insipid insincerity of one's teachers; and bad dreams, chiefly about giants."

Sometimes she expected an answer to statements of this character; at other times she went on talking: I had known her to continue without a break for fifteen minutes.

"I used to dream about giants," said Eva.

"How old are you, Miss?"

"Thirteen."

"At fifteen the dreams become passionate," said the Duchess, sounding lugubrious about it.

"What do you dream about now?" asked Don, who had not removed his eyes from her since she came.

"Packing; missing aeroplanes; losing my clothes," said the Duchess. "Worry—worry—worry; but one is never bored in a dream, which is more than can be said for real life. Give me your hand," she snapped at Eva. She pored over it a moment, and then said briskly, "You are going to marry very young and have three children; an honest life; always be careful in automobiles." Don's hand was already stretched out and waiting. She gave him two wives, a successful business career and an accident "involving a horse between the ages of seventeen and eighteen."

"That is tolerably old for a horse," Francis interrupted.

"Sh-h," said the Duchess, "perhaps while steeplechasing; it is not serious." She blew me a little kiss: "Penelope I already know. She is as clear to me as a book written by an angel. Let me see if there is any change," she commanded, a medical note in her voice: "Beautiful —beautiful—beautiful! Genius and fame and passion, are all here."

"Any dough?" asked Francis.

"I beg your pardon," said the Duchess, who knew perfectly well what "dough" meant, but who always refused to recognize American slang.

"I refer to cash," said Francis, looking his most Mephistophelean:

"My ambition for Penelope is that she acquire a rich husband, so that she may subsidize Papa in his tottering old age."

"Like so many creative artists, you have the soul of a fishmonger," said the Duchess. She was still holding my hand; she planted a champagne-wet kiss on the palm before she let it go. "I have ordered our dinner, Penelope. It is to be the *écrevisses au gratin* that you like, with small *goûters* of caviar to begin with and *fraises des bois* in kirsch afterward."

I had been anticipating this hurdle; she always insisted that I dine with her on her first evening, before she went to the Casino at nine o'clock.

"I am very sorry, Duchessa; you must excuse me. I am having supper with Don and Eva." I saw Francis raise one eyebrow at me. "I really didn't know you were coming tonight," I pleaded.

"No, that is true," said the Duchess, "but I am very disappointed. I have come to regard it as a regular tryst." She put her head on one side. "Why do you not all three stay and dine with me? We will make it a *partie carrée*. It could be managed, Francis? Beautiful—beautiful—beautiful! There. That is settled."

"I'm most awfully sorry; we'd love to," Eva said. "But we couldn't possibly. Supper's at seven and Mum's expecting us."

"Thank you very much, though," said Don, who was still staring at her. "Could we do it another time?"

"But of course! Tomorrow; what could be better? Except tonight," said the Duchess. "I was looking to Penelope to bring me good luck. Do you remember last year, how I took you to dine at the Carlton and won a fortune afterwards?"

"And lost it on the following afternoon," said Francis. The Duchess said an imcomprehensible Italian word that sounded like a snake hissing. She took a little ivory hand out of her bag and pointed it at him.

"I thought one never could win at roulette," said Don. "According to my father, the game is rigged in favor of the Casino."

"Ask your father why there are no taxes in Monaco," said the Duchess. "In a game of this mathematic there is no need for the Casino to cheat. The majority loses naturally, not artificially. And tell him further that all European casinos are of the highest order of probity, with the possible exception of Estoril and Bucharest. Do you know the game?"

When the Bradleys said that they did not, she took from her bag one of the cards that had upon it a replica of the wheel and the cloth. She embarked upon a roulette lesson. The Bradleys were fascinated and of course we were late for supper. Francis delayed me further, holding me back to speak to me on the terrace: "Do you have to have supper with the Smugs?"

"Please don't call them that. Yes, I do."

"It would be reasonable, I should think, to send a message saying that an old friend of the family had arrived unexpectedly."

Of course it would have been reasonable; Mrs. Bradley had expected me to ask permission. But nothing would have made me stay.

"I'm extremely sorry, Francis; I can't do it."

"You should know how much it means to her. She has ordered your favorite dinner. All right," he said, "I see that it is useless to appeal to your better nature. Tonight you qualify for RCI." He went back to the bar, calling, "The verdict can always be withdrawn if the candidate shows compensating behavior."

"Didn't you want to stay and dine with the Duchess?" asked Don, as we raced through the twilit garden.

"I did not. She embarrasses me greatly."

"I thought she was terrific. I do hope Mum and Dad will let us have dinner with her tomorrow."

"But *don't* say it's *écrevisses*, Don, whatever you do. There's always a row about shellfish," Eva reminded him.

"I wouldn't be such an ass," Don said. "And the only thing that would give it away would be if you were ill afterward."

"Why should it be me?"

"Because it usually is," said Don.

I awoke with a sense of doom. I lay under my mosquito curtain, playing the scenes of last evening through in my mind. A slight chill upon the Viking parents, due to our being late; smiles pressed down over crossness, because of the visitor. Don and Eva pouring forth a miscellany of information about the Duchess and the signed photographs; myself making mental notes, a devoted sociologist studying a favorite tribe: grace before supper; no garlic in anything; copies of *Punch* and the English newspapers; silver napkin rings; apple pie. The secret that I found in the Cotswold house was here, I told myself; the house in Devonshire took shape; on the walls there were photographs of it; a stream ran through the garden; they rode their ponies on Dartmoor; they had two wire-haired terriers called Snip and Snap. I collected more evidence of Bradley organization: an expedition tomorrow to the Saracen village near Brignoles; a Current-Affairs Quiz that was given to the family by their father once a month.

No, I said to myself, brooding under my mosquito net, nothing went wrong until after the apple pie. That was when Eva had said, "The Duchess told all our fortunes." The lines spoken were still in my head:

Don saying, "Penelope's was an absolute fizzer; the Duchess says she will have genius, fame and passion." Mr. Bradley's Viking profile becoming stony; Mrs. Bradley's smooth white forehead puckering a little as she asked me gently, "Who is this wonderful lady?"

Myself replying, "The Duchessa di Terracini," and Mrs. Bradley remarking that this was a beautiful name. But Mr. Bradley's stony face growing stonier and his officer-to-men voice saying, "Have we all finished?"; then rising so that we rose too and pushed in our chairs and bowed our heads while he said grace.

After that there was a spirited game of Monopoly. "But the atmosphere," I said to myself, "went on being peculiar." I had waited for Don and Eva to comment on it when they walked me home, but they were in a rollicking mood and appeared to have noticed nothing.

"Indubitably there is a doom," I thought while I put on my swimming suit "and since I shall not see them until this evening because of the Saracen village, I shall not know what it is."

As I crossed the terrace, the Duchess popped her head out of the corner window above me; she leaned like a little gargoyle above the bougainvillaea; she wore a lace veil fastened under her chin with a large diamond.

"Good morning, Duchessa. Did you win?"

"I lost consistently, and your friends cannot come to dine tonight, as you may know; so disappointing, though the note itself is courteous." She dropped it into my hands. It was written by Mrs. Bradley; fat, curly handwriting on paper headed

CROSSWAYS
CHAGFORD
DEVON

It thanked the Duchess and regretted that owing to the expedition, Don and Eva would not be able to accept her kind invitation to supper.

I knew that Bradleys would be back by six.

IV

I spent most of the day alone working on the Anthology. I had found quite a new Hate, which was headed "Characters." People called the Duchess a character and this was said of others who came here. I made a brief description of each and included some of their sayings and habits.

There was the usual paragraph about the Duchess in the *Conti-*

*nental Daily Mail;* it referred to her gambling and her emeralds and her *joie de vivre. Joie de vivre* seemed to me a worthy subject for Hate and I entered it on a separate page, as a subsection of Jokes.

At half past four, to my surprise, I looked up from my rock writing desk and saw the Bradleys' car sweeping in from the road. Presently Eva came running down the tiers of terrace alone. When she saw me she waved, put her finger to her lips, and signaled to me to stay where I was. She came scrambling up.

"I'm so glad to see you. There's a row. I can't stay long. Don has been sent to bed."

"Oh, dear. I was conscious of an unfavorable aura," I said. "What happened?"

Eva looked miserable. "It isn't anything against you, of course. They like you terribly. Mum says you have beautiful manners. When Don and I said we wanted you to come and stop a few days with us at Crossways in September, it went down quite *well.* Would you like to?" she asked, gazing at me. "Or would it be awfully boring?"

I was momentarily deflected from the doom and the row. "I cannot imagine anything that would give me greater pleasure," I said. She wriggled her eyebrows, as usual, at my phrases.

"That isn't just being polite?"

"I swear by yonder hornèd moon it isn't."

"But of course it may not happen now," she said in melancholy, "although it wasn't *your* fault. After all you didn't make us meet the Duchess on purpose."

"Was the row about the Duchess?"

"Mm-m."

"Because of her telling your fortunes and teaching you to play roulette? I did have my doubts, I admit."

"Apparently they were quite cross about that, but of course they couldn't say so in front of you. Daddy had *heard* of the Duchess, anyway. And they cracked down on the dinner party and sent a note. And Don kept on asking why until he made Daddy furious; and there seems to have been something in the *Continental Daily Mail,* which we are not allowed to read."

"Here it is," I said helpfully. She glanced upward over her shoulder. I said, "Have no fear. We are invisible from the villa at this angle."

She raised her head from the paper and her eyes shone; she said, "Isn't it wonderful?" I had thought it a pedestrian little paragraph, but I hid my views.

"Mummy said that the Duchess wasn't at all the sort of person she liked us to mix with, and that no lady would sit in a bar drinking champagne when there were children present, and that we shouldn't have gone into the bar again anyway. And Don lost his temper and was quite rude. So that we came home early instead of having tea out; and Dad said that Don had spoiled the day and asked him to apologize. And Don said a word that we aren't allowed to use and now he's gone to bed. Which is awful for him because he's too big to be sent to bed. And I'll have to go back. I'm terribly sorry."

"So am I," I said. "Please tell your mother that I deplore the Duchess deeply, and that I always have."

As soon as I had spoken, I became leaden inside with remorse. It was true that I deplored the Duchess because she was possessive, over-powering and embarrassing, but I did not disapprove of her in the way that the Bradleys did. I was making a desperate effort to salvage the thing that mattered most to me.

In other words, I was assuming a virtue though I had it not, and while Shakespeare seemed to approve of this practice, I was certain that it was wrong. (And I went on with it. I added that Francis would not have dreamed of bringing the Duchess into the bar if he had known that we were there. This was an outrageous lie. Francis would have brought the Duchess into the bar had the Archbishop of Canterbury been there—admittedly an unlikely contingency.)

When Eva said that this might improve matters and might also make it easier for Don to apologize, because he had stuck up for the Duch-ess, I felt lower than the worms.

Which is why I quarreled with Francis. And I knew that that was why. I had discovered that if one were feeling guilty one's instinct was to put the blame on somebody else as soon as possible.

Francis called to me from the bar door as I came up onto the ter-race. I had been freed from RCI on the grounds of having replaced Laurent before lunch at short notice. He grinned at me. "Be an angel and take these cigarettes to Violetta's room, will you, please? I swear that woman smokes two at a time."

"I am sorry," I said. "I have no wish to run errands of the Duchess just now."

Francis, as usual, was reasonable. "How has she offended you?" he asked.

I told him about the Bradleys, about the possible invitation to Dev-onshire; I said that, thanks to the Duchess cutting such a pretty figure in the bar, not to mention the *Continental Mail,* my future was being seriously jeopardized. I saw Francis' eyebrows twitching.

He said, "Penelope, you are a thundering ass. These people are te-dious *petits bourgeois,* and there is no reason to put on their act just because you happen to like their children. And I see no cause to pro-

tect anybody, whether aged seven or seventy, from the sight of Violetta
drinking champagne."

"Mrs. Bradley said that no lady would behave in such a way."

"Tell Mrs. Bradley with my love and a kiss that if she were a tenth as
much of a lady as Violetta she would have cause for pride. And I am not
at all sure," he said, "that I like the idea of your staying with them in
Devonshire."

This was, as the French said, the *comble*.

"Do you mean that you wouldn't let me go?" I asked, feeling as
though I had been struck by lightning.

"I did not say that. I said I wasn't sure that I liked the idea."

"My God, why not?"

"Do not imagine when you say, 'My God,'" said Francis, "that you
add strength to your protest. You merely add violence."

He could always make me feel a fool when he wanted to. And I
could see that he was angry; less with me than with the Bradleys. He
said, "I don't think much of the Smugs, darling, as you know. And I
think less after this. Violetta is a very remarkable old girl, and if they
knew what she went through in Rome when the Germans were there,
some of that heroism might penetrate even their thick heads. Run along
with those cigarettes now, will you please?"

I was trembling with rage; the worst kind of rage, hating me as well
as everything else. I took the cigarettes with what I hoped was a dignified gesture, and went.

The Duchess was lying on the chaise longue under her window; she
was swathed like a mummy in yards of cyclamen chiffon trimmed with
marabou. She appeared to be reading three books at once: a novel by
Ignazio Silone, Brewer's *Dictionary of Phrase and Fable* and a *Hand-
book of Carpentry for Beginners*.

The room, the best of the rooms, having two balconies, had become
unrecognizable. It worried me with its rampaging disorder. Three wardrobe trunks crowded it: many dresses, scarves and pairs of small pointed
shoes had escaped from the wardrobe trunks. The Duchess always
brought with her large unexplained pieces of material; squares of velvet,
crepe de Chine and damask, which she spread over the furniture. The
writing table had been made to look like a table in a museum; she had
put upon it a black crucifix and two iron candlesticks, a group of ivory
figures, and a velvet book with metal clasps.

Despite the heat of the afternoon the windows were shut; the room
smelled of smoke and scent.

"Beautiful—beautiful—beautiful!" said the Duchess, holding out her hand for the cigarettes. "There are the *bonbons au miel* on the bedside table. Help yourself liberally, and sit down and talk to me."

"No, thank you very much. If you will excuse me, Duchessa, I have to do some work now."

"I will not excuse you, darling. Sit down here. Do you know why I will not excuse you?"

I shook my head.

"Because I can see that you are unhappy, frustrated and restless." She joined her fingertips and stared at me over the top of them. "Some of it I can guess," she said, "and some of it I should dearly like to know. Your mother would have known."

I was silent, she was hypnotic when she spoke of my mother, but I could not make myself ask her questions.

"Genius is not a comfortable possession. What do you want to do most in the world, Penelope?"

The truthful reply would have been, "To be like other people. To live in England; with an ordinary father and mother who do not keep an hotel. To stop having dooms; never to be told that I am a genius, and to have people of my own age to play with so that I need not spend my life listening to grownups."

I said, "I don't know."

The Duchess sighed and beat a tattoo with her little feet inside the marabou; they looked like clockwork feet.

"You are, beyond doubt, crying for the moon. Everybody at your age cries for the moon. But if you will not tell me which moon, I cannot be of assistance. What is the book that you are writing?"

"It is an Anthology of Hates," I said, and was much surprised that I had told her because I had not told anybody.

"Oho," said the Duchess. "Have you enough Hates to make an anthology?"

I nodded.

"Is freedom one of your hates?"

I frowned; I did not want to discuss the book with her at all and I could not understand her question. She was smiling in a maddening way that implied more knowledge of me than I myself had.

"Freedom is the most important thing that there is. You have more freedom than the average child knows. One day you will learn to value this and be grateful for it. I will tell you why." Her voice had taken on the singsong, lecturing note that preceded a fifteen-minute monologue. I stared at the figures on the writing table. She had let her cigarette lie burning in the ash tray, and a small spiral of smoke went up like incense before the crucifix; there was this, there was the hot scented room and the sound of her voice: "It is necessary to imprison children to a certain degree, for their discipline and their protection. In schools, they are largely hidden away from life, like bees in a hive. This means that they learn a measure of pleasant untruth; a scale of simple inadequate values that resemble the true values in life only as much as a plain colored poster of the Riviera resembles the actual coastline.

"When they emerge from the kindly-seeming prisons, they meet the world of true dimensions and true values. These are unexpectedly painful and irregular. Reality is always irregular and generally painful. To be unprepared for its shocks and to receive the shocks upon a foundation of innocence is the process of growing up. In your case, Penelope, you will be spared many of those pains. Not only do you have now a wealth of freedom which you cannot value because you have not experienced the opposite, but you are also endowing yourself with a future freedom; freedom from the fear and shock and shyness which make the transition from youth to maturity more uncomfortable than any other period of existence. Francis is bringing you up through the looking-glass, back-to-front. You are learning what the adult learns, and walking through these lessons toward the lightheartedness that is usually to be found in childhood but later lost. I wonder how long it will take you to find that out." She sat up on her elbows and stared at me again. "Do you know what I think will happen to your Anthology of Hates when you do find it out? You will read it through and find that these are not Hates any more."

By this last remark she had annoyed me profoundly, and now she clapped her hands and cried, "If young people were only allowed to gamble! It takes the mind off every anxiety. If I could take you to the Casino with me tonight, Penelope! Wouldn't that be splendid? Disguised as a young lady of fashion!" She sprang off the chaise longue, snatched the square of velvet from the bed and flung it over my shoulders. Its weight almost bore me to the ground; it was heavy as a tent and it smelled musty. "Look at yourself in the mirror!" cried the Duchess. "Beautiful—beautiful—beautiful! A Principessa!" She scuttled past me. "We will place this silver girdle here." She lashed it so tightly that it hurt my stomach; I was stifled; it felt like being dressed in a carpet. "Take this fan and these gloves." They were long white kid gloves, as hard as biscuits; she forced my fingers in and cajoled the gloves up my arms as far as the shoulders.

"The little amethyst circlet for your head."

She caught some single hairs as she adjusted it and put one finger in my eye. Sweat was trickling all over me.

"Now you have a very distinct resemblance to your mother," said the Duchess, standing before me and regarding me with her head on one side.

"This is the forecast of your womanhood. Will you please go down-stairs at once and show yourself to Jeanne?"

I said that I would rather not. She was peevishly disappointed. I struggled out of the ridiculous costume; hot, dispirited, no fonder of myself than before, I got away.

V

My bedroom was on the ground-floor, with a window that opened onto the far end of the terrace. It was late, but I was still awake and I heard Francis and Jeanne talking outside. I did not mean to listen, but their voices were clear and when I heard the name "Bradley" I could not help listening.

"I agree with you," Jeanne said, "that it is all an outrageous fuss. But these Bradleys mean a great deal to Penelope."

"Wish I knew why," said Francis. "They represent the worst and dullest aspect of English 'county'; a breed that may soon become ex-tinct and no loss, either."

"They are the kind of friends that she has never had; English chil-dren of her own age."

Their footsteps ceased directly outside my window. I heard Francis sigh. "*Ought* we to send her to school in England, do you think?"

"Perhaps next year."

"That will be too late, beloved."

I had heard him call Jeanne "beloved" before, but tonight the word touched my heart, perhaps because I was already unhappy; it made me want to cry. "She will be fifteen," Francis said. "First she'll kill herself trying to fit into the pattern and if she succeeds in the task, we shall never see her again. God knows what we'll get but it won't be Penel-ope."

"She will change in any case, whether she stays or goes, darling; they always do."

"Perhaps I've done a poor job with her from the beginning," Francis said: he spoke my mother's name. And then I was so sure I must listen no more, that I covered my ears with my hands. When I took them away Jeanne was saying, "You are always sad when your back is hurting you. Come to bed. Tomorrow I'll invite the Bradley children for lunch again; on Thursday when Violetta's in Monte Carlo."

"Why should we suck up to the Smugs?" Francis grumbled, and Jeanne replied, "Only because of Penelope, *tu le sais*," and they walked away down the terrace.

I wept because they destroyed my defenses; my conscience still troubled me for the speeches of humbug that I had made to Eva, for quarreling with Francis, and for being uncivil to the Duchess. It was a weary load. If the Bradleys accepted the invitation to lunch, it would seem that God was not intending to punish me for it, but exactly the reverse, and that was a bewildering state of affairs.

By morning, however, God's plan become clear. Jeanne brought me my breakfast on the terrace. She sat with me while I ate it. I thought, as I had thought before, that she looked very young; more an elder sister than a stepmother, with her short, flying dark hair, the blue eyes in the brown face, the long slim brown legs. She smoked a Caporal cigarette.

I could hardly wait for her to tell me whether she had healed the breach with the Bradleys. But I dared not ask. Their talk on the terrace had been too intimate for me to admit that I had heard it. She said, "Penelope, the situation with your friends at La Lézardière has become a little complex."

My heart beat downward heavily and I did not want to eat any more.

"I thought that it would give you pleasure if I asked them to lunch and would perhaps clear up any misunderstanding. But I have been talking to Mrs. Bradley and apparently she would prefer them not to visit the hotel."

I did not know whether I was blushing for the hotel, for my own disappointment, or for the Bradleys; I was only aware of the blush, flaming all over my skin, most uncomfortably.

"Mrs. Bradley was friendly and polite, you must not think otherwise. She wants you to swim with them as much as you like; she said that she hoped you would go out in the speedboat again. But her exact phrase was, 'We feel that the hotel surroundings are just a little too grown-up for Don and Eva.'"

I was silent.

"So, I thought that I would tell you. And ask you not to be unhappy about it. People are entitled to their views, you know, even when one does not oneself agree with them."

"Thank you, Jeanne: I am not at all unhappy," I said, wishing that my voice would not shake. "And if the Bradleys will not come to me, I am damned if I am going to them." And I rose from the table. She came after me, but when she saw that I was near to tears she gave me a pat on the back and left me alone.

This was the point at which I discovered that hate did not cast out love, but that it was, on the contrary, possible to hate and love at the same time. I could not turn off my infatuation for the Bradleys, much as I longed to do so. They were still the desirable Vikings. The stately pink villa above the orange trees, the gray rocks where the diving-board jutted and the speedboat lay at anchor, remained the site of romance, the target of forlorn hopes. It hurt me to shake my head and retire from the flat rock when Don and Eva beckoned me. They seemed to understand quickly enough, more quickly than their parents did. Mr. Bradley still called, "Coming aboard?" and Mrs. Bradley waved to me elaborately on every possible occasion. The children turned their heads away. For two days I saw them all like figures set behind a glass screen; only the echo of their voices reached me; I gave up haunting the beach and worked in a corner of the garden; the regularity of their timetable made it easy to avoid the sight of them. I told myself that they were loathsome, that they were the Smugs, that Don and Eva were both candidates for RCI. I even considered including them in the Anthology of Hates, but I found it too difficult. Now they had indeed become the moon that the Duchess told me I cried for. I cherished dreams of saving Don's life or Eva's at great risk to myself, and being humbly thanked and praised by their parents. Then I hoped that they would all die in a fire, or better still that I would die and they would come to my funeral.

In these two days I found myself looking at my home differently; seeing it in Bradley perspective. I had been plagued by the crises and irregularities but never ashamed of them. Was I ashamed now? I could not be sure; the feeling was one of extra detachment and perception; I was more than ever aware of the garden's bright colors, of the garlic smells from the kitchen, of the dusky coolness in the bar; every time that I walked through the salon I looked at it with startled visitors' eyes; Bradleys' eyes:

"It's pretty, of course; it's like a little room in a museum, but it isn't the sort of place where one wants to *sit*." The terrace with the blue and white umbrellas above the tables, the stone jars on the balustrade, the lizards flickering along the wall, seemed as temporary as the deck of a ship on a short voyage. I felt as though I were staying here, not living here. And there was no consolation in my own room with my own books because here the saddest thoughts came and they seemed to hang in the room waiting for me, as palpable as the tented mosquito net above the bed.

I found that I was seeing Francis, Jeanne and the Duchess through a grotesque lens; they were at once complete strangers and people whom I knew intimately. I could place them in a Bradley context, thinking, "That is Francis Wells, the poet, the poet who keeps the mad hotel. He always seems to wear the same red shirt. He looks like Mephistopheles when he laughs. And that is his wife, his *second* wife; younger than he is; very gay always, isn't she? What very *short* shorts. And there goes the Duchessa di Terracini, rather a terrible old lady who gambles at the Casino and drinks champagne; doesn't she look ridiculous in all that

make-up and chiffon?" And then I would be talking to them in my own
voice and with my own thoughts and feeling like a traitor.

I knew that they were sorry for me; that Francis above all approved
my defiant refusal. I was aware of their hands held back from consoling
gestures, to spare me too much overt sympathy. Even the Duchess did
not speak to me of the Bradleys.

For once I welcomed the crises as diversion. And these two days
naturally were not free from crises; a British ambassador and his wife
found themselves *en panne* at our gates. All the entrails of their car fell
out upon the road and we were obliged to give them rooms for the
night.

This would not of itself have been other than a mechanical crisis,
because the ambassador and Francis were old friends. Unfortunately
the ambassador and the press baron from Mentone, who was dining
with the Duchess, were old enemies. So a fierce political fight was
waged in the bar, with both elderly gentlemen calling each other pol-
troon, and they would have fought a duel had not the electric current
failed and the hotel been plunged in darkness till morning. (My only
grief was that Don and Eva had missed it. All roads led to the Bradleys.)

On the third morning, which was Thursday, doom accelerated. I
woke to find Francis standing beside my bed.

"Sorry, darling; trouble," he said. "A telephone call just came through
from Aix; Jeanne's mother is very ill and I'm going to drive her over
there now. Can you take care of you for today?"

He never asked me such questions: this was like a secret signal saying
"I know you are miserable and I am sorry."

"But of course. Please don't worry."

"There are no guests, thank God. Violetta's going over to Monte
Carlo; Laurent will be in charge tonight. You might see that he locks
up, if I'm not back."

"I will do that."

"But don't let him lock Violetta out, for heaven's sake."

"I will see that he does not. Can I help Jeanne or do anything for
you?"

"No, my love. We are off now. I'll telephone you later." He ducked
under the mosquito curtain to kiss me.

"You must pray rather than worry," the Duchess said to me, standing
on the doorstep. For her expedition to Monte Carlo, she wore a coat
and skirt of white shantung, a bottle-green frilly blouse, and the usual
chiffon scarf. She was topped by a bottle-green tricorne hat with a
green veil descending from it. "Death is a part of life," she added,
pulling on her white gloves.

I could feel little emotion for my step-grandmother who loved in seclusion near Aix-en Provence, but I was sorry for Jeanne.

"The best thing that you could do, Penelope," said the Duchess, grasping her parasol like a spear, "would be to come over with me to Monte Carlo. We will lunch delightfully on the balcony of the Hôtel de Paris; then you shall eat ices while I am at the tables; then a little stroll and a little glass and we could dine on the port at Villefranche and drive home under the moon. The moon is at the full tonight and I look forward to it. *Viens, chérie, ça te changera les idées,*" she added, holding out her hand.

I thanked her very much and said that I would rather stay here.

When she was placed inside the high purple Isotta-Fraschini, I thought that she and her old hooky chauffeur looked like a Punch-and-Judy show. The car was box-shaped with a fringed canopy under the roof and they swayed as it moved off. I waved goodbye.

The first part of the day seemed endless. I sat in the garden on a stone bench under the largest of the umbrella pines. That way I had my back to La Lézardière, I could hear their voices and that was all. When the bell rang for their lunch, I went down to the pool and swam. I swam for longer than usual; then I climbed to the flat rock and lay in the sun. I was almost asleep when I heard Eva's voice. "Penelope!"

She was halfway up the rock; she said, "Look; we are so miserable we've written you this note. I have to go back and rest now." She was like a vision out of the long past; the freckles, the sunburn and the wet hair. I watched her scuttle down and she turned to wave to me from the lowest tier of the terrace. I gave her a half-wave and opened the note.

It said:

DEAR PENELOPE,

Please don't be cross with us. Mum and Dad are going out to supper tonight. Don't you think that you could come? They have asked us to ask you.

*Always your friends,*
DON AND EVA

I wrote my reply at the *écritoire* in the salon. I wrote:

Much as I appreciate the invitation, I am unable to accept it. Owing to severe illness in the family my father and stepmother have left for Aix. I feel it necessary to stay here and keep an eye on things.

PENELOPE

To run no risk of meeting them, I went into the bar and asked Laurent if he would be so kind as to leave this note at La Lézardière.

Laurent was in one of his moods; he replied sarcastically that it gave him great pleasure to run errands and do favors for young ladies who had not the energy to perform these for themselves. I echoed the former cook's husband, the assassin, and said, "*Salaud,*" but not until he was gone.

After I had answered the note, I alternated between wishing that I had accepted and wishing that I had given them more truthful reasons for my refusal.

Later, I sought comfort by writing to my Aunt Anne in England; I sat there conjuring the fortnight as it would be and putting in the letter long descriptions of the things that I wanted to see and do again. It helped. I had covered twelve pages when the telephone rang.

Francis' voice spoke over a bad line: "Hullo, Child of Confusion. Everything all right?"

"Yes, indeed. Nothing is happening at all. What is the news?"

"Better," he said, "but Jeanne will have to stay. I may be very late getting back. See that Laurent gives you the cold lobster. Jeanne sends her love."

Nothing would have induced me to ask Laurent for my dinner, but I was perfectly capable of getting it myself and the reference to cold lobster had made me hungry. No reason why I should not eat my dinner at six o'clock. I was on my way to the kitchen by way of the terrace when I heard a voice calling me:

"Penelope!"

I turned, feeling that horrible all-over blush begin. Mrs. Bradley stood at the doorway from the salon onto the terrace. She looked golden and statuesque in a white dress with a scarlet belt. The sight of her was painful. It seemed as though I had forgotten how lovely she was.

"May I talk to you a moment, my dear?"

"Please do," I said, growing hotter and hotter.

"Shall we sit here?" She took a chair beneath one of the blue and white umbrellas. She motioned to me to take the other chair. I said, "Thank you, but I prefer to stand."

She smiled at me. I could feel in my heart the alarming collision of love and hate and now I could see her in two contexts; as a separate symbol, the enemy; as a beloved haunting of my own mind, the Mrs. Bradley of the first days, whom I had made my private possession. Her arms and hands were beautifully shaped, pale brown against the white of her dress.

"Can't we be friends, Penelope? I think we can, you know, if we try. Don and Eva are so sad and it all seems such a pity."

I said, "But, Mrs. Bradley, you made it happen."

"No, dear. That is what I want to put right. When I talked to your stepmother, I made it quite clear that we all hoped to see much more of you."

"But," I said, "that Don and Eva couldn't come here. As though it were an awful place."

She put her hand on mine; she gave a soft low laugh. "Penelope, how foolish of you. Of course it isn't an awful place. You have just imagined our thinking that, you silly child."

"Did I imagine what you said about the Duchess?"

Still she smiled and kept her hand on mine. "I expect that what I said about the Duchess was quite a little exaggerated to you by Eva and Don. That was an uncomfortable day for all of us. We don't often quarrel in our family; I don't suppose that you do, either. Quarrels are upsetting to everybody and nobody likes them."

"Certainly," I said, "I don't like them."

"Let's try to end this one, Penelope."

Did she guess how badly I wanted to end it? I could not tell.

"Supposing," she said, "that you let me put my point of view to you, as one grown-up person to another. You are very grown-up for your age, you know."

"I do know, and I deplore it."

She gave another little low laugh. "Well, I shouldn't go on deploring it if I were you. Think what a dull world it would be if we were all made alike."

I winced at the cliché because Francis had taught me to wince at clichés. But I pretended that she had not said it. She went on: "Listen, dear. Just because you are so grown-up and this place is your home, you have a very different life from the life that Don and Eva have. I'm not saying that one sort of life is right and the other wrong. They just happen to be different. Now, my husband and I have to judge what is good for Don and Eva, don't we? You'll agree? Just as your father and stepmother have to judge what is good for you."

"Yes. I agree to that." It sounded reasonable; the persuasion of her manner was beginning to work.

"Well, we think that they aren't quite grown-up enough yet to understand and appreciate all the things that you understand and appreciate. That's all. It's as though you had a stronger digestion and could eat foods that might upset them. Do you see?"

When I was still silent, she added, "I think you should. Your stepmother saw perfectly."

"I suppose I see."

"Do try."

In fact I was trying hard; but the struggle was different from the struggle that she imagined. I felt as though I were being pulled over the line in a tug of war. Inside me there was a voice saying, "No, no. This is wrong. Nothing that she says can make it right. It is not a matter of seeing her point of view; you *can* see it; she has sold it to you. But you mustn't surrender." Oddly, the voice seemed to be the voice of the Duchess. I felt as though the Duchess were inside me, arguing.

I looked into the lovely, smiling face. "Do try," Mrs. Bradley repeated. "And do please come and have supper with the children tonight. Let's start all over again; shall we?"

When she held out both hands to me, she had won. I found myself in her arms and she was kissing my hair. I heard her say, "Poor little girl."

VI

Only the smallest shadow stayed in my heart and I forgot it for long minutes. We talked our heads off. It was like meeting them again after years. I found myself quoting in my head: *"And among the grass shall find the golden dice wherewith we played of yore."* They still loved me; they still laughed at everything I said. When I ended the description of the ambassador fighting the press baron and the failure of the electric lights, they were sobbing in separate corners of the sofa.

"Go on; go on. What did the Duchess do?"

"I think she enjoyed it mightily. She had an electric torch in her bag and she flashed it over them both like a searchlight."

"You do have the loveliest time," said Eva.

"Where is the Duchess tonight?" asked Don.

"In fact I think I heard her car come back about ten minutes ago." I began to describe the car and the chauffeur.

"*Older* than the Duchess? He can't be. I'd love to see them bouncing away under the fringe. Let's go out and look."

"Too late," I said. "At night he takes the car to the garage in Théoule."

"Hark, though," Don said. "There's a car now." He ran to the window; but I knew that it wasn't the Isotta-Fraschini. It was the putt-putt noise of Laurent's little Peugeot.

"How exactly like Laurent," I said. "As soon as the Duchess gets home, he goes out for the evening. And Francis has left him in charge."

It occurred to me now that I should go back. I reminded myself that Charlemagne was an effective watchdog. But I was not comfortable about it.

"D'you mean you ought to go and put the Duchess to bed? Undo her stays; help her off with her wig?"

"It isn't a wig; it's her own hair, and she requires no help. But I do think I should go back. The telephone may ring."

"Well then, the Duchess will answer it."

"She will not. She claims that she has never answered a telephone in her life. She regards them as an intrusion upon privacy."

"Isn't there anybody else in the hotel?"

"No."

"Oh, you *can't* go yet," said Eva.

I sat on a little longer. Then I knew that it was no good. "I shall have remorse if I don't," I said, "and that is the worst thing."

"All right, then. We'll go with you."

"Oh, Don—" said Eva.

"Mum and Dad won't be back yet awhile," said Don, "and we'll only stay ten minutes."

"They'll be furious."

"We won't tell them."

Eva looked at me. I said, "I cannot decide for you. I only know I must go."

"Of course if you want to stay behind," Don said to Eva.

"Of course I don't. What shall we say to Nanny?"

"We can say we went down to the beach."

We crept out, silent in the spirit of adventure. The moon had risen, the full moon, promised by the Duchess, enormous and silver and sad; its light made a splendid path over the sea; the palms and the orange trees, the rock shapes on the water, were all sharp and black.

"Here we go on Tom Tiddler's ground," Eva sang. We took the short cut, scrambling through the oleander hedge instead of going round by the gate. I could hear Don panting with excitement beside me. Almost, their mood could persuade me that the hotel was an enchanted place. We came onto the terrace and darted into the empty bar; Laurent had turned off the lights; I turned them up for the Bradleys to look at the photographs.

"What'll we drink?" said Don facetiously, hopping onto a stool.

"Champagne," said Eva.

"If the Duchess was still awake, she'd give us some champagne."

"You wouldn't drink it," said Eva.

"I would."

"You wouldn't."

"I jolly well would."

"She's probably in the salon," I said. "She never goes to bed early."

I put out the lights again and led them to the salon by way of the terrace. The salon lights were lit. We looked through the windows.

"There she is," said Don. "She's lying on the sofa."

They bounded in ahead of me. I heard Don say, "Good evening, Duchessa," and Eva echoed it. There was no reply from the Duchess. With the Bradleys, I stood still staring at her. She was propped on the Empire sofa, her red head had fallen sideways on the stiff satin cushion. Her little pointed shoes and thin ankles stuck out from the hem of her shantung skirt and the skirt, which was of great width, drooped down over the edge of the sofa to the floor. On the table beside her she had placed the green tricorne hat, the green scarf and her green velvet bag. A bottle of champagne stood in an ice pail; the glass had fallen to the floor; since one of her arms dangled limply, I thought that she must have dropped the glass as she went off to sleep.

"Please wake up, Duchessa; we want some champagne," said Don.

He took a step forward and peered into her face, which was turned away from us.

"She looks sort of horrid," he said; "I think she's ill."

For no reason that I could understand I felt that it was impertinent of him to be leaning there so close to her. When he turned back to us, I saw that his face was pale; the freckles were standing out distinctly on the bridge of his nose.

"She is ill, I'm sure," he said. "She's unconscious." He looked at the bottle of champagne. "She must be—" He stopped. I saw that he thought that the Duchess was intoxicated and that he could not bring himself to say so.

"Let's go," Eva said in a thin scared voice. She grabbed Don's hand. "Come on, Penelope. Quick."

"But of course I'm not coming."

They halted. "You can't stay here," Don said. Eva was shivering. There was no sound nor movement from the figure on the sofa. I said, "Certainly I can stay here. What else can I do? If she is ill, I must look after her."

I saw them straining against their own panic. Suddenly they seemed like puppies, very young indeed.

"But *we* can't stay here," Eva said. "Oh, please, Penelope, come with us."

"No indeed. But you go," I said. "It's what you want to do, isn't it?"

"It's what we ought to do," Eva stammered through chattering teeth. Don looked a little more doubtful. "Look here, Penelope, you needn't stay with her. When they—they get like that, they sleep it off."

Now I was angry with him. "Please go at once," I said. "This is my

affair. And I know what you mean and it isn't true." I found that I had
clapped my hands to shoo them off; they went; I heard the panic rush
of their feet on the terrace. I was alone with the Duchess.

Now that they were gone, I had no hesitation in approaching her.
I said softly, "Hullo, Duchessa. It's only me," and I bent above her as
Don had done. I saw what he had seen; the shrunken look of the white
face with the false eyelashes. Indeed she looked shrunken all over, like a
very old doll.

I lowered my head until my ear touched the green frilled chiffon at
her breast. I listened for the beat of her heart. When I could not hear it,
I lifted the little pointed hand and the felt the wrist. There was no
pulse here that I could find.

I despised myself because I began to shiver as Eva Bradley had
shivered. My fingers would not stay still; it was difficult to unfasten the
clasp of the green velvet bag. I thought that there would be a pocket
mirror inside and that I must hold this to her lips. Searching for the
mirror I found other treasures; the ivory hand that she had aimed at
Francis, a cut-glass smelling-bottle, some colored plaques from the Casino, a chain holding a watch, and a cluster of seals.

The mirror, when I found it, was in a folding morocco case with
visiting cards in the pocket on the other side. I said, "Excuse me, please,
Duchessa," as I held it in front of her face. I held it there a long time;
when I took it away the bright surface was unclouded. I knew that the
Duchess was dead.

A profound curiosity took away my fear. I had never seen a person
lying dead before. It was so strange to think of someone I knew well,
as having stopped. But the more I stared at her, the less she looked as
though she had stopped; rather, she had gone. This was not the Duchess
lying here; it was a little old doll, a toy thing of which the Duchess
had now no need. Where, I wondered, had she gone? What had
happened to all the things that she remembered, the fencing lessons,
and the child's dreams, and the Emperor? What happened, I wondered,
to the memories that you carried around in your head? Did they go on
with your soul or would a soul not want them? What did a soul want?
Did the Duchess' soul like roulette? Theology had never been my
strongest subject and I found myself baffled by the rush of abstract
questions flowing through my mind.

Then I became aware of her in relation to me. It was impossible to
believe that I would not talk to her again. I was suddenly deeply sorry
that I had not dined with her on the first evening, that I had not gone
down in the fancy-dress to show myself to Jeanne. She had asked me to

do this; she had asked me to come to Monte Carlo with her. *"Viens, chérie, ça te changera les idées."* Always she had been kind. I had not. I had never been nice to her because she embarrassed me and now I should never have another chance to be nice to her.

Automatically I began to perform small meaningless services. I covered her face with the green scarf, drawing it round her head so that it made a dignified veil. I fetched a rug and laid it across her feet; I did not want to see the little shoes. I carried the untouched champagne back to the bar. I lifted her tricorne hat, her bag and gloves off the table; I took them up to her room. It was more difficult to be in her room, with the bed turned down and the nightclothes laid there, than it was to be in the salon with her body. I put the hat, bag and gloves down on the nearest chair and I was running out when I saw the crucifix on the table. I thought that she might be pleased to have this near her ("Although," I said to myself, "she isn't there any more, one still goes on behaving as if she is"), and I carried it down; I set it on the table beside her. There seemed to be too many lights here now. I turned off all but one lamp; this room became a suitable place for her to lie in state, the elegant little shell of a room with the Empire furnishings. I pulled a high-backed chair from the wall, set it at the foot of the sofa, and sat down to watch with her.

Outside the windows the moonlight lay in the garden. I heard her saying, "The moon is at the full tonight. I look forward to it." I heard her saying, "Naturally, you cry for the moon." I heard her saying, "Death is a part of life," as she pulled on her white gloves.

At intervals I was afraid again; the fear came and went like intermittent seasickness. I did not know what brought it. She was so small and still and gone that I could not fear her. But I felt as though I were waiting for a dreadful thing to walk upon the terrace, and the only poem that would stay in my head was one that had always frightened me a little, "The Lykewake Dirge":

> This ae nighte, this ae nighte,
> Everye nighte and alle,
> Fire and sleet and candlelyte,
> And Christe receive thy saule.

It made shivers down my back. I would have liked to fetch Charlemagne from his kennel, but I had heard that dogs howled in the presence of the dead and this I did not want.

Sitting there so stiffly I became terribly tired: "But it is a vigil," I said to myself, "and it is all that I can do for her." It was not much. It was no true atonement for having failed her in kindness; it could not remit my having betrayed her to the Bradleys. It seemed hours since I had thought of the Bradleys. Now I wondered whether the parents had returned, and with the question there came incredulity that Don and Eva should not have come back. They had simply run off and left me, because they were afraid. The memory of their scared faces made them small and silly in my mind. Beside it, I uncovered the memory of my talk with Mrs. Bradley: the talk that had left a shadow. I admitted the shadow now: it was the note of patronage at the end of all the spellbinding. She had called me "poor little girl."

"You never called me 'poor little girl,'" I said in my thoughts to the Duchess. She had called me fortunate and a genius. She had spoken to me of the world, of freedom and maturity. That was truly grown-up conversation. In comparison the echo of Mrs. Bradley saying, "As one grown-up person to another," sounded fraudulent. Some of the magic had left the Bradleys tonight.

I was so tired. I did not mean to sleep, because this was a vigil. But I found my head falling forward and the moonlight kept vanishing and the Duchess' voice was quite loud in my ears. "Of death," she said, "I remember three things: being tired, being quiet and being gone. That's how it is, Penelope." She seemed to think that I could not hear her. She went on calling, "Penelope! Penelope!"

I sat up with a start. Somebody was in fact calling "Penelope": a man's voice from the terrace. I climbed down stiffly from the chair. "Who's that?" I asked, my voice sounding cracked and dry. Mr. Bradley stood against the moonlight.

"Are you there, child? Yes, you are. Come along out of this at once." He looked large and golden and worried; he seized my hand; then he saw the Duchess on the sofa.

"Lord," he said. "She's still out, is she?" He started again. "Did you cover her up like that?"

"Yes. Please talk quietly," I said. "She is dead."

He dropped my hand, lifted the scarf a little way from her face, and put it back. I saw him looking at the crucifix.

"I put it there. I thought that she would like it. I am watching by her," I said.

He looked pale, ruffled, not the way, I thought, that grown-up people should look. "I'm terribly sorry," he said in a subdued voice. "Terribly sorry. Young Don came along to our room, said he couldn't sleep for knowing you were over here with her. Of course he didn't think—"

"I know what he thought, Mr. Bradley," I said coldly. "Don and Eva are only babies really. Thank you for coming, just the same."

He said, in his officer-to-men voice, "Out of here now. There's a good girl."

"I beg your pardon?"

"You're coming to our house. I'll telephone the doctor from there." He took my hand again; I pulled it free.

"I'll stay with her, please. You telephone the doctor."

He looked down at me, amazed, almost smiling. He dropped his voice again. "No, no, no, Penelope. You mustn't stay."

I said, "I must."

"No, you mustn't. You can't do her any good."

"It is a vigil."

"That's just morbid and foolish. You're coming over to our house now."

"I am not."

"Yes, you are," he said, and he picked me up in his arms. To struggle in the presence of the Duchess would have been unseemly. I remained tractable, staying in his arms until he had carried me onto the terrace. He began to put me down and at once I twisted free.

"I'm not coming with you. I'm staying with her. She is my friend and she is not your friend. You were rude about her, and stupid," I said to him.

He grabbed me again and I fought: he imprisoned me with my arms to my sides. For the moment he did not try to lift me. He simply held me there.

"Listen, Penelope, don't be hysterical. I'm doing what's best for you. That's all. You can't possibly sit up all night alone with the poor old lady; it's nearly three o'clock now."

"I shall stay with her till dawn; and she is not a poor old lady, just because she is dead. That is a ridiculous cliché."

I was aware of his face close to mine, the stony, regular features, the blue eyes and clipped moustache in the moonlight. The face seemed to struggle for speech. Then it said, "I don't want insolence any more than I want hysteria. You just pipe down and come along. This is no place for you."

"It is my home," I said.

He shook me gently. "Have some sense, will you? I wouldn't let my kids do what you're doing and I won't let you do it."

"Your children," I said, "wouldn't want to do it anyway; they are, in vulgar parlance, a couple of sissies."

At this he lifted me off my feet again and I struck at his face. I had the absurd idea that the Duchess had come to stand in the doorway and was cheering me on. And at this moment there came the miracle. The noise of the car sweeping in from the road was not the little noise of

Laurent's car, but the roaring powerful engine that meant that Francis
had come home.

The headlights swung yellow upon the moonlit garden. Still aloft in
Mr. Bradley's clutch I said, "That is my father, who will be able to
handle the situation with dignity."

He set me down as Francis braked the car and jumped out.

"That you, Bradley?" said Francis. "What, precisely, are you doing?"

Mr. Bradley said, "I am trying to make your daughter behave in a
sensible manner. I'm very glad to see you."

Francis came up the steps onto the terrace. He sounded so weary that
I knew his back hurt him: "Why should it be your concern to make my
daughter behave in any manner whatsoever?"

"Really, Wells, you'll have to know the story. There's been a tragedy
here tonight, I'm afraid. Just doing what I could to help."

"I will tell him," I said. I was grateful for Francis' arm holding me;
my legs had begun to feel as though they were made of spaghetti.

"You let me do the talking, young woman," said Mr. Bradley.

"If you don't mind, I'd prefer to hear it from Penelope," said Francis.

I told him. I told him slowly, leaving out none of it; there seemed less
and less breath in my lungs as I continued. "And Mr. Bradley called it
morbid and foolish and removed me by force," I ended.

"Very silly of you, Bradley," said Francis.

"Damn it, look at the state she's in!"

"Part of which might be due to your methods of persuasion, don't you
think? All right, Penelope, easy now." I could not stop shivering.

"Leaving her alone like that in a place like this. You ought to be
ashamed of yourself," Mr. Bradley boomed.

"Quiet, please," said Francis in his most icy voice.

"Damned if I'll be quiet. It's a disgrace and I don't want any part of
it."

"Nobody," I said, "asked you to take any part in it, Mr. Bradley."

"Hush," said Francis. "Mr. Bradley meant to be kind and you must
be grateful."

"I am not in the least."

"Fine manners you teach her," said Mr. Bradley.

"Quiet, please," said Francis again. "Penelope has perfect manners,
mitigated at the moment by perfect integrity and a certain amount of
overstrain." Looking up at him, I could see the neat Mephistophelean
profile, the delicate shape of his head. I loved him more than I had ever
loved him. Mr. Bradley, large and blowing like a bull, was outside this
picture, nothing to do with either of us.

Suddenly he looked as though he realized this. He said: "I don't
want my wife or my kids mixed up in it either."

"Mixed up in what, precisely?" Francis asked.

I said, "It is possible that he is referring to the inquest. Or do you mean mixed up with me? Because if you do, no problem should arise. After tonight I have not the slightest wish to be mixed up with them or you."

It would have been more effective had I been able to stop shivering; I was also feeling rather sick, never a help when attempting to make dignified speeches.

Mr. Bradley faded away in the moonlight.

Francis said gently, "Did you mean it? It is easy to say those things in anger."

"I think I meant it. Was the vigil, in your opinion, the right thing to do?"

"It was. I am very pleased with you."

I said, "But I am not sure that I can continue with it for a moment. I feel funny."

Francis took me into the bar; he poured out a glass of brandy and a glass of water, making me drink them in alternate swallows.

"Of course," he said gloomily, "it may make you sick. In which event the last state will be worse than the first."

But it did not; it made me warm.

"They can't *help* being the Smugs, can they?" I said suddenly, and then for the first time I wanted to cry.

"They're all right," said Francis. "They are merely lacking in imagination."

I managed to say, "Sorry," and no more. I knew that he disliked me to cry. This time he said, watching me, "On some occasions it is better to weep."

I put my head down on the table and sobbed, "If only she could come back; I would be nice."

Francis said, "You gave her great pleasure always."

"Oh, not enough."

"Nobody can give anybody enough."

"Not ever?"

"No, not ever. But one must go on trying."

"And doesn't one ever value people until they are gone?"

"Rarely," said Francis.

I went on weeping; I saw how little I had valued him; how little I had valued anything that was mine. Presently he said, "Do you think that you can cry quite comfortably by yourself for a few minutes because I must telephone the doctor?"

Though I said, "Yes, indeed," I stopped crying immediately. As I sat waiting for him, I was saying goodbye, to my first dead, to a love that was ended, and to my dream of being like other people.

The next day I tore the Anthology of Hates into pieces and cast the pieces into the sea. I did not read through the pages first, so certain was I that I had done with hating.

# THE MAN IN THE TOOLHOUSE

*Harvey Swados*

HARVEY SWADOS (1920– ) stands out as one of the most talented and prolific of the post World War II writers. He was born in Buffalo, New York, graduated from the University of Michigan, and after a period of seafaring has taught at colleges all over the United States from New York University to San Francisco State. Three of his novels as well as a collection of exceptional short stories have been published. Many articles by him on many subjects, literary and otherwise, have appeared in leading magazines. The story that follows is an example of his special concern with man and his place in the modern scene.

Not any more, but once upon a time, I used to travel to Buffalo with the kind of exhilaration that children have on the way to a long-awaited circus. It had nothing to do with Buffalo, since the orchestras with which I have been performed in dozens of similar places; but even though I will probably never go there again, the mere mention of Buffalo by a stranger on a street corner can set to rattling in my mind the whole chain of recollections of Rita Conway and Ralph Everett, so that I find myself once again reviewing each link in the chain that will bind me for the rest of my life not only to Rita, but to Ralph and to the Everett home, which exists now only in the imperfect memories of a handful of people like myself.

I think I fell in love with Rita the first time we met, one dark winter afternoon in a rehearsal room of the Eastman School of Music in Rochester. She was seated at a harp, her head bent forward, listening intently to the octaves that she was rapidly plucking as she tuned the instrument, her face so hidden by her long blonde hair that when she looked up at the clicking of the heavy door which I closed behind me, I was stunned by her beauty, and I shifted my violin case from one hand to the other, stammering an apology. She laughed, and I introduced myself.

Rita made it very clear that she respected my musical ability, my metropolitan background, even my poverty. And I adored her hardy delicacy that always reminded me of a wildflower, and her small-town temperament mixing matter of factness with romanticism in a way that charmed me completely.

As I think back now, the years at Eastman seem to me like one of those intense dreams which end so abruptly that you can't remember, try as you may, whether its essential quality was one of frustration or fulfillment. Rita and I played duets together, picnicked together, and worried together about our separate futures. She always knew that I loved her and she was shrewd enough to realize that, since the whole thing was impossible, it was her responsibility to keep everything pitched on a comradely plane so that the inevitable break would not be too painful.

But Rita flattered me by intimating that I was more adventurous than she, as well as more talented (which I knew anyway), and that it was I and not she who faced the exciting prospect of conquering poverty with my music; while she would eventually have to relegate her harp to its proper corner in the parlor, and find a suitable husband.

My impossible dreams ended brutally with an invitation to Rita's wedding, which took place the September after our graduation. Fortunately I was touring that year with a dance band, and I was able to express both congratulations and regrets by mail.

I had met Ralph Everett just once, before I knew that Rita would accept him, and I remembered him only as an engineering student at the University of Rochester, with a shock of black hair. Rita's explanation, made one June evening shortly before Commencement, had hurt me. "You see," she said, "Ralph already has a job lined up in Buffalo, with the Water Department. So that we'll be able to have an apartment, and everything . . . and really, even my parents are quite pleased."

I would have preferred to hear that they were displeased; I suspected that her parents must always have feared that she would run off with someone like me. "And Ralph? Do you love him?"

"I've just never met anyone like him. He's as solid as a rock, and yet he's the most talented person I've ever known."

"In engineering?"

"He writes. I have faith in him, Harry. I'm going to help him become a great writer."

"Is that what he's going to be?"

"Engineering is just a financial crutch for Ralph. He wants to make his father happy, and he knows that it will be years before he makes a living from his writing, anyway."

"When is he going to get all this done?"

"You don't know Ralph. Nothing will stop him."

"Not even a family?"

Rita laughed. "No."

I don't think that Rita really knew what she was saying. I don't think that she knew Ralph at all in those early days, before their marriage; she could hardly have guessed his extraordinary powers of concentration. But his attractiveness, coupled with the security that he could immediately offer, must have impelled her not only to accept him, but to make herself believe in his future greatness.

When I came to Buffalo for the first time after their marriage, I found that they were happy with each other. Rita invited me to dinner; her voice was breathless and warm, and I played through the afternoon rehearsal (I was with the Indianapolis Symphony that year) in a haze of romantic reminiscence.

Rita and Ralph had a flat in a huge old house on Humboldt Parkway. Almost every home along the pleasant street had a large front lawn with an elm tree shading the porch, and a large back yard, with an occasional stable in the rear. The houses looked as though people had been born in them in the days before women went to hospitals to give birth, as though people had grown old in them, died in them, and left the furnishings to their children. It wasn't the kind of street that I would have envisioned for Rita and her golden harp—it struck me that I could have done almost as well for her myself.

"I'm so glad, Harry!" she cried when she answered the doorbell. "I was hoping though that you'd bring your fiddle. Maybe we could have tried one little duet." She led me forward by the hand.

"Rehearsals in the afternoon, a concert in the evening . . ." I almost fell over the harp and the music stand in the living room.

"Care for a drink?" Rita was a little nervous. "Ralph will be home any minute."

"Anything will do."

She smiled shyly. "You can congratulate me—I'm going to have a baby." She turned away and began to make a drink.

"I think that's wonderful."

"I want a houseful. Ralph is agreeable, as long as he can go on with his writing. That way we'll both be able to—well, fulfill ourselves."

I would have said something inappropriate in reply, but Ralph's Ford pulled into the driveway at that moment.

Ralph had grown an aggressive bushy moustache which, together with his straw hat, made him look considerably older than I had remembered him. But as soon as he had removed his hat and accepted my congratulations on his impending fatherhood, he relaxed and grew extremely agreeable. Rita had told me that Ralph didn't have much of an ear for music (about which he apologized deferentially but firmly, like a man asserting that he cannot abide olives, while protesting that he realizes he must be missing something special), but at the dinner table he asked me a number of questions about the relationships between guest artists and orchestra members.

He wanted to know, with a modest air that made me feel as though I were doing him a great favor, all sorts of technical details about the mechanics of touring orchestras.

"You know, Harry," he said, bringing his jaws together on a stalk of celery with a loud snap, "it's my theory that a man can compensate for a lack of imagination in a given field, say in music, by an extra expenditure of effort."

"Do you mean that a fiddler can become a Heifetz simply because he's willing to work harder than the average musician?"

Ralph laughed good-naturedly. "What I mean is that you can learn to do almost anything well if you organize your learning process and utilize every minute of the time you've dedicated to it."

"You may be right."

"Of course he's right!" Rita turned to me vivaciously. "That's how Ralph became a good engineer, even though he didn't care for it."

"Don't mind us, Harry. We don't usually waste time on abstract discussions like this."

Rita and Ralph had tickets for the concert, so we left together in their car, and after the concert they came backstage for me. Rita turned pink when I introduced her to our conductor as a talented classmate; Ralph stood stolidly at her side, his eyes darting in every direction as if to make sure that he would miss nothing.

Later I teased him about it. "You looked like you were soaking up atmosphere."

"The important thing is to observe, isn't it, and to practice at being a writer even when you're not writing? Besides," he added with some hesitation, "I lead a pretty sedentary life. The music business is new to me."

I was impressed and baffled. Rita, wedged between us in the narrow front seat of the car, was tired, but sat contentedly with her head on her husband's shoulder and her hand in mine, unaware of how disturbed I was.

"It's been a wonderful evening," she murmured as we drew up to the house. "Didn't you like it, Ralph?"

"It was a very fruitful experience." In the dark I couldn't tell whether he was being grim or merely funny.

But when we were sipping cold beer on the front porch and watching the Canadian flies slapping restlessly at the yellow lamp, I felt that Ralph was quite humble, and that it was Rita who was sustained by an unquestioning confidence in her husband's secret genius. After a while she arose from the creaking glider and said, "I get worn out early these days." She kissed us both. "Don't talk too late. We all have to get up early."

When she had gone inside Ralph said, "I suppose you envy me."

"Why yes," I replied, a little embarrassed, "I guess I do."

He gestured at the house. "This is the life I've marked out for myself, but only because I can envision something different, something better, for Rita and me."

I suspected that he was thinking primarily of another kind of life for himself, as he teetered back and forth in the rocker and stared moodily at me. And I was startled into a kind of wary wakefulness, because I had been wondering drowsily of the way Rita had cheated herself, or had been cheated by Ralph, somehow, out of the glamorous and exciting life that should have been hers. It appeared obvious to me that it was Ralph who had chosen this quiet humdrum routine, and who was better fitted for it.

I threw my cigarette onto the front lawn, and said rather coldly, "What kind of life do you think you'd like, Ralph?"

He laughed with sudden eagerness. "Oh, I can tell you that. I'd like to travel with Rita, to take her to the places she'd like to see—"

"But how about you?"

"Only because it would give me a chance to meet people, to talk to people. I don't mind living in Buffalo. Any city is interesting, if you take the trouble to learn it. But I do resent having to spend precious time behind a desk checking blueprints that don't mean a damn thing to me."

"You must have known you wouldn't like it, even before you started."

"Of course I knew. I've never had any alternative. Even during high school and college I had to hustle every summer, driving a milk truck or working on a lake boat. And when I graduated—well, there was Rita . . ."

"But if you were writing in a garret you'd probably wish you were leading a normal life."

"Oh, I could never be a starving artist. I think most of those guys are phonies, don't you? Anyway, I have Rita. And it won't be too long before I have my success."

I wasn't sure of what he meant by that, so I said vaguely, "I wish you all the luck in the world."

"Thanks Harry." He grasped my hand. "Too bad we can't get together more often. Sometimes I feel cut off from the people I need— like a spy with nobody to report to."

"Don't you have friends here?"

"One or two. But I don't belong, don't have any connection with

other writers—haven't even got time to read their books!" He drained
his glass and wiped his mouth with the back of his hand. "Let's turn
in, shall we?"

Rita and Ralph had more room than they needed at the time. I had
accepted Rita's eager invitation to sleep there rather than at the hotel;
but I hadn't foreseen that I would be bedded down in the nursery-to-be,
next to their own room. I lay there quietly in the dark, hardly breathing, listening to Ralph removing his shoes (thunk, thunk) and hanging
up his trousers (jingle, jingle) and clambering into bed with his wife
(a squeak, several murmurs, and a grunt). And after that I wrapped
the pillow about my ears. But still I slept very poorly that night.

So it was that, even before the sun came up, I was standing at the
window that overlooked the back yard, staring down vacantly at the
dewy lawn and at a pair of dungarees flapping mournfully from the
clothesline, when I caught sight of Ralph.

He was walking across the damp grass with his trousers rolled up
over the ankles, chomping hungrily on the buttered heel of a rye bread
and carrying a couple of looseleaf notebooks in the crook of his arm.
His shock of black hair stood up angrily, as if someone had used it as
a handle to yank him out of bed. He moved purposefully across the
yard until he had gained a small frame building adjoining the barn-
garage. The rickety door closed behind him with a cool clatter, a light
snapped on in the one window beyond the door, and then there was
silence.

I shuffled over to the bed and lay down, exhausted. Eventually I fell
asleep, thinking of Ralph working alone in the little building and of
Rita beyond the wall, a few feet from me, curled into a ball like her
unborn baby, her hair unbound on the pillow and her hands clasped
warmly between her knees.

It was Rita who woke me. Ralph had already gone to work, but
she was waiting to have her coffee with me, her eyes still swollen with
sleep.

"I saw Ralph crossing the yard," I said to her, "oh, it must have been
hours ago."

"He gets up every morning at four to write. We fixed up the toolhouse so he can work undisturbed."

"I wouldn't have the stamina for that routine."

Rita nodded calmly. "He says sleep is a matter of habit. I only wish
he had people to discuss his work with. It's going to be a kind of history of Buffalo, you know, in story form."

"A historical novel?"

"Ralph hates that expression! He's doing a lot of research."

"It's fine, that he knows what he wants to make of his life."

"He'll get out of the Water Department some day. We'll both be free. I know we will!"

When I turned at the porch to shake Rita's hand in farewell I felt a sudden ruefulness like a sharp physical pain in the pit of my stomach. Rita was young and fragile in her dressing gown, and it seemed to me that the outline of her pregnancy was just becoming visible. Her hand felt small and warm in mine. "The neighbors must be wondering who the tall dark stranger is."

"I'd better leave now, before you're ruined up and down Humboldt Parkway."

Rita laughed out loud. As I stood on the porch in the pleasant morning sunlight, holding her hand, I realized (more than realized: I had known it all along) that I was not cut out to be a tall dark stranger, in her life or in any other girl's. I had always known it, but nevertheless it was brutal, the way we stood there and joked about it. And then we said goodbye.

Six months later I received an announcement of the birth of a daughter to Ralph and Rita Everett. I must have gone to five or six stores before I found a silver fork and spoon set that seemed suitable. When I dropped the little package down the mail chute, I felt that a chapter of my life had been finished, and that while I was purged now of the anxious desire that had run its course like a long and serious illness, I would never again be really young. A few days later I got one of those little thank-you notes from Rita. It was enclosed with a copy of *Harper's* that contained a poem by Ralph (about the burning of Buffalo in 1812, I think). "Ralph wants you to know," Rita added, "that you're the kind of reader he had in mind. He says it's not so much, just one poem, but I feel as though it's the beginning of a new life for us."

Six or eight months later, Ralph sent me a reprint of a brief article that had been accepted by the *American Historical Review*, entitled (I still have it) "Some Neglected Aspects of the Early Rivalry Between Black Rock and Buffalo." It wasn't the kind of information that you'd go out of your way to learn, but I thought it had more verve than the usual scholarly monograph. And it was proof that Ralph was organizing his time, as he would have said, digging away at the raw material for his book.

By the time I got to Buffalo again, Rita had had another baby, and Ralph's father had come to live with them.

The first thing I noticed when Ralph opened the front door was that the harp was gone.

"You shouldn't have taken a cab," Ralph said. "I would have been only too glad to pick you up."

I put my armful of presents on the couch. At the far end of the room, barricaded behind a baby's play pen, Ralph's father was seated in the easy chair, studying the want ad pages of the *Buffalo Evening News.* The oval peak of his bald head shone under the floor lamp and his high-top black shoes caught the light.

"Father, this is our friend Harry."

The old man arose. "You went to school with Rita."

"That's right." While we were shaking hands I could hear Rita cooing to an infant who suddenly burst into an angry wail. Ralph moved uneasily, but the old man stood still and erect, like a steel engraving out of an old American history book.

He was taller than his son, with a reddish closely shaven face on which time had worn two vertical grooves between his eyes and on either side of his thin mouth. His left arm was missing just above the elbow, and his empty shirt sleeve (he wore only an unbuttoned vest) was pinned neatly back. On his right arm he wore an elastic garter to shorten the sleeve. Despite his complexion and the almost combative cast of his features, there was an aura of death about him that affected me most unpleasantly. He looked as though he were relaxing after having served as a pallbearer at a friend's funeral; and yet he gave the impression that his own end could not be far off. Perhaps the anger in his face, in his whole stringy body, even in his gnarled, veiny, and trembling hand, was that of a man who hated and cursed the idea of death.

Ralph said, "Would you like to see the kids before they go to sleep?"

"By all means. Excuse me, Mr. Everett. I'll let you finish your paper."

He looked at me sourly. "Nothing but bad news anyway."

Rita was diapering the infant, a safety pin between her lips, while the older child stood in her crib, silently watching her mother. "Harry! Give us all a kiss."

I kissed Rita first. Her lips were hot and dry, and the infant squirmed uncomfortably between us as we embraced briefly. I made the appropriate remarks about the children, who were friendly enough; but I cannot remember now what they looked like that evening, except that neither of them seemed to take after their mother. We closed the door quietly behind us and stood in the hall for a moment talking softly.

"You must be working like a dog."

"Ralph gets up with the babies at night. And he *still* manages to write. That's something, isn't it?"

"The harp is gone."

Rita flushed. "Impossible, with the children underfoot. And with father here . . . it's stored in the attic . . . Come, tell me about yourself while I fix the grapefruit."

Dinner was not a happy meal. Rita had to jump up twice to go in to the babies. She and Ralph wanted to talk about New York, music, books, but the table was dominated by Mr. Everett. The old man hated the world, and he wanted as many people as possible to know before he took reluctant leave if it. He spooned up his grapefruit carefully with his one hand, disposing of as much juice as he possibly could, and wiped his mouth with the back of his hand, using the same gesture as his son. Throughout the meal he stared hard at me, as though waiting for me to make a social error. "I understand you're on the road a lot, with that orchestra." His eyes narrowed calculatingly. "How are conditions?"

I hesitated. He went on quickly. "I'll tell you something. This country is going to hell in a basket."

Rita and Ralph were very absorbed in their food. I said, "I think we're better off than we were a few years ago."

"You wouldn't talk that way if you had to struggle along on a pension. What *are* you anyway," he said with rising aggressiveness, "another Roosevelt New Dealer?"

"Father," Ralph said, "don't you think it would be better if we discussed politics later and let our guest finish his supper now?"

"Later?" He said the word with such anguish that we all looked up, taken aback by his vehemence. "When is that? I might not wake up tomorrow. This is still a free country, isn't it? Well, isn't it?"

"Of course, Father. I just don't want to spoil Harry's dinner."

"I'm only a fiddler," I said. "In politics I vote for the man and not for the party."

The old man's eyes lit up. "That's just the kind of thinking that's softening up the country."

Rita's hand shook as she ladled noodles onto my plate. "Isn't that a little extreme, Father?"

"Extreme? What do you call those professors in Washington? I just hope none of you ever have to exist on a miserable pittance. I went to work when I was eight years old, after my father lost his farm." He glared insanely at me. "Worked hard, saved, all my life, to the day I lost my arm. But they don't encourage thrift and hard work any more. Suckers, that's what we were, suckers."

"More noodles, Father?"

The old man hooked a finger inside his mouth and drew forth a piece of gristle on which he had been chewing as he talked. He put it on the edge of his plate and stared at it somberly. "Now Roosevelt wants a law that a man can't make more than twenty-five thousand dollars a year. What do you say to that?"

"I haven't thought much about it."

"That's how the public gets fooled. They don't think."

"I never expect to earn that kind of money. Or anybody I know."

Ralph raised his eyes and looked at me coolly. "I do, Harry."

"Who cares how much money you're going to make?" Ralph's father chewed savagely on a pickle. "If you had mouths to feed, the incentive would be there, wouldn't it?"

"The opportunities—"

"Don't tell me about opportunities. I've lived longer than you. Rubinoff and *his* violin, on Eddie Cantor's program—I bet *he* makes more than twenty-five thousand a year. There's no reason for the government to confiscate the wealth of those who did make good, just to provide cake and circuses for the ones that didn't. It's high time we quit thinking of ourselves and started thinking about principles."

"I respect your principles, Father," Ralph said, "but Harry hasn't come here to talk politics. Besides he's got a hard evening ahead of him."

"You hear that?" the old man cried out to me. "He respects me—isn't that a hot one? I'll tell you something. To this day he doesn't know what I sacrificed in order to put him through the University of Rochester. He doesn't know the policies I borrowed on, the friends I—"

Ralph's nostrils were dilated. "I must insist—"

"I'm talking."

Ralph subsided, after giving Rita (who was desperatley spooning cream into the hollow cavern of her baked apple) and me an odd glance, at once beseeching and encouraging.

His father went on inexorably, "It makes me sick to my stomach to watch a boy with your education wasting his time, getting up at four every morning to write that junk."

"Say it all. You might as well."

"Respect? You don't even respect your wife and children, or you'd try to make that expensive education pay off. You'd try to get someplace in your profession and provide some security for your family."

The old man bent his right hand back against the edge of the table until the knuckles whitened. In the hot silence his swollen finger joints cracked loudly, one after the other. Suddenly he cried out in an agonized voice, like an old minister appealing to his wicked flock, "How do you suppose I feel that the few miserable dollars of my savings has to go to you? You'll piss it away, fooling yourself and Rita into thinking you're a genius. I just wish I could live long enough—"

"You will live long enough." Rita flung her head back challengingly. Her eyes were damp and pained, but I sensed that she had been through crises like this before. "I have faith in Ralph, and I know that you're going to be—"

"I'm going to be dead, that's what. And I wish I could take my money with me." He looked impassively at Rita. "You let him make a fool out of you."

"But I'm happy." Her voice rose dangerously. "I'm happy, won't you believe me?"

At that moment the clear little voice of her older child came floating through the open doorway. "I want a glass of water."

Rita jumped up. The three of us were left at the table in a mist of heavy breathing and tobacco smoke. The old man actually looked pleased with himself, but now it was Ralph who could not let matters dispose themselves so easily; he seemed to have been bitten by a bug of misery which inflamed his entire being with a desire to justify himself to his father. I don't know whether he remembered, or even cared that I was sitting there—or perhaps everything that he said was really directed to me, as the one person who could judge his manner of life against the claims pressed against it by his father. I am not very perceptive about such things—I only know that Ralph spoke to his father like a despairing man.

I heard him say, "I'm trying the best I know to make something worthwhile of my life."

The old man didn't move. His voice was unexpectedly gentle. "I haven't got any future left, Ralph. Maybe that's why I'm so anxious about yours."

Ralph turned pale. "I'm sorry." He made no effort to deny his father's statement; perhaps there was an unspoken agreement between them not to bluff about the older man's life expectations. "I can only ask you to have faith in me."

"You talk like a preacher!" The old man's sudden sneer was shocking. I think now that he was trying to conceal his emotions, but at the time I was angered and embarrassed. "If you had any ability it would have come out by now."

"You're not competent to judge."

"Who is? All I ever saw was one poem in a highbrow magazine that nobody reads anyway."

"So that's it. You'll never be proud of me, because you won't let yourself. If I made a fortune and was praised by all the critics, you'd say it was a fluke."

The old man knocked his pipe into the dessert dish and stared down at the charred fragments of tobacco floating slowly in the remains of his baked apple. "I don't know if they told you. I've got a bad heart condition. I'm apt to go almost any time."

Ralph did not return my glance. He was staring at his father with an expression of concentrated loathing, and in the first stunning instant the thought flashed through my mind that he was disgusted with his father's inability to keep his secret to himself; but then I felt that Ralph hated his father because he was going to die too soon, and so cheat him of his eventual triumph.

"No point in going to my grave," the old man said, "without getting everything off my chest."

"You're not going yet. And you're not going to rush me, you hear? I've got my schedule laid out, I won't let you scare me out of it."

Rita came back into the dining room then. She had put on make-up and tied her hair behind her ears with a ribbon. "I didn't hear any dishes breaking," she said pleasantly.

Ralph said heavily, "We'd better get going. It's not early."

"You won't have to worry about the children, Father, they won't get up."

"Oh, the children. They'll be in good hands—" the old man spoke slowly, so that no one should mistake his meaning . . . "—as long as I'm here."

We went out to the car and then we all turned around, as if by a common impulse. The old man was standing at the parlor window, holding the curtain back with his one arm and staring out blindly at the darkening street.

I was already committed to spending the night at the Everetts'. Now although there was nothing I would have liked more than to have gone off to a hotel, I could not bring myself to decline the invitation which I had already accepted for fear of hurting Ralph and Rita.

After the concert we were joined by two high-school classmates of Ralph's, Jim Bagby, a tall cadaverous fellow, and Ed Herlands, who was fat, well dressed, and had the kind of self-assurance that comes only with inherited money. We spent the evening drinking beer and talking about the cultural sterility of Buffalo. It seemed that it was only this common grievance which still bound Ralph to his old friends, for he held hands with Rita as if to assert his basic separateness from the rest of us.

We were driving home when Rita said, "Harry, I know you're ill at ease about staying with us tonight. But you're one of us . . . maybe you could consider it as a favor to us."

There was an uncomfortable silence—I could think of absolutely no reply—and we finally made our way up the steps to the silent house. The old man was sitting sideways in the easy chair, asleep, his forehead glistening in the lamplight, his stump pressed tight against his chest. His lean mouth had gone slack and his legs were folded sharply at the knees as though they had finally snapped from the long task of holding his body erect. He did not stir when the door closed behind us.

Rita tiptoed across the room, turned off the bridge lamp, and kissed him on the forehead. He stirred and raised his wrinkled lids, and Rita said gently, "I've brought the morning paper."

"That's fine." He cleared his throat. "The children didn't stir. How was the concert?" He looked amiably at me, as though there had been no words between us at all.

"We played pretty well. I hope they enjoyed it."

"All you can do is your best." He arose and clapped his son on the back. "Eh, Ralphie? Then if they don't like what you've done, it's tough, that's all." He chuckled as he waved his good nights and stalked off to the bedroom, the morning paper tucked obliquely under his stump and the white waxy cast of death on his narrow farmer's face.

Ralph stared expressionlessly after him until Rita said gaily, "You see, darling? It's all right."

"You don't understand," he replied slowly. "You don't understand at all."

"Well, I understand that I've got to make up the couch for Harry." She set to work briskly, brushing aside my offer to help, and not quite looking me in the eye as she tucked in the sheets. When it was done I sat down on the temporary bed and looked up at my tired friends. They stood arm in arm, their minds already turned inward to their dark bedroom and their common life. Even the most bitter recriminations bound them closer to each other than I could ever be to anyone.

That night I was untroubled by intimations of my nearness to Rita and Ralph. Before I fell into a heavy sleep, I wondered only whether old man Everett lay in the little bedroom that had once been mine for a night, with the rumpled morning paper lying where his weary hand had dropped it, listening to his son's lively ardent useless movements beyond the thin wall, and cursing his inability either to fall asleep or to die and leave those whom he had given his curse to their damned stupidity.

It seemed to me that I had been sleeping for only a few minutes when I was awakened by a light shining in my eyes. I raised myself on my elbow and peered into the kitchen, where Ralph was outlined before the open refrigerator, whose bare bulb sprayed light rays around his disheveled figure. I called out to him softly.

"Oh, I'm sorry." He turned quickly, digging his fingers through his stiff uncombed hair. "Didn't mean to disturb you."

"How do you do it? An earthquake couldn't get me out of bed after two hours of sleep."

Ralph advanced towards me through the dark dining room, hitching at his half-buttoned trousers, over which his shirttails still hung, and squeezing together a thick sandwich with his other hand. As he reached the couch where I lay with my hands behind my head, I looked up into his red-rimmed unsmiling eyes and realized perhaps for the first time how profound were the differences between us.

"It's just a matter of habit," he said quietly.

"Tell me, Ralph. I don't mean to be rude, but is it really worth it, this kind of life, just to do some writing?"

The circles under his eyes were violet in the pale glow of the street lamp. "Rita would have been willing to make any sacrifice, to go without children, to go out to work to support us, so that I could write. But I couldn't do that to her."

Yes, I thought, that's all very well, but would she? As Ralph talked on about his book, speaking of the sacrifice of sleep, and of the eventual freedom it would bring them, my sleepy mind wandered to Rita, whose smooth cheek even now was buried in her warm soft pillow, and whom some part of me would always love; and I felt that at last I was seeing her through disenchanted eyes. Looking up into Ralph's haggard fanatic's face, I felt that he was crazy, that he was driven by an utterly unrealizable obsession to punish himself day after day, year after year, with this gruelling schedule for something which was, after all, just another book.

"My father," he was saying, "hates creative work. He persists in acting the betrayed parent in front of Rita, although he knows that I can't stand to see her upset on my account."

"Maybe Rita's right about him."

"In any case my work will go on, and he knows it." He smiled and extended his hand. "So long, Harry."

I never saw Ralph's father again. He must have been a terrible problem, for not long after my departure he had a stroke which left him bedridden and helpless, a burden to Ralph and Rita and even more so to himself.

In addition to telling me about Ralph's father Rita wrote me that she was pregnant again, and that the doctor had told her to expect twins. She mentioned nothing at all about Ralph, which more than anything else led me to suspect that he had reached the limits of his financial and physical endurance.

I sat in my mother's living room in the Bronx (I never thought of it as my living room), with both my 4-F notice and the letter from Rita in my hand, thinking of old man Everett lying stiff and moribund, cursing the world because he could not be quit of it, and listening to his son tiptoeing off in the middle of the night to his fantastic labors; of Rita, heavy and tired, struggling to keep the two little girls from disturbing the old man; and of Ralph, still adding pages to his endless novel and silently looking through his red-rimmed eyes at his dying father and his taut wife. I was glad that I would not be going to Buffalo that year.

It was Ralph who sent me the next letter from Buffalo, some time later. "My father died peacefully yesterday afternoon," he wrote. "I thought you would want to know although you only met him once. It is just as well that he is gone from this unhappy world . . ." The twins had arrived, and they were both girls: counting Rita, Ralph now had a household of five females.

Old man Everett had left them his pittance, apparently, for they had been able to take over the remainder of the big house in which they lived. There was plenty of space now, even with the children, and when I arrived in Buffalo the following year, it was taken for granted that I should stay with them.

I was very much taken with the children. The older girls resembled their father in physique, in their stern little faces, and in their slow and thoughtful speech. Penny, the oldest, held out her hand as soon as she saw me and said gravely, "Hello, Uncle Harry. Have you got a nice present for me?"

It was fun, in spite of the war. I even took Rita canoeing in Delaware Park one fine afternoon, with Penny and her younger sister Daisy. Rita stretched out before me, trailing her fingertips in the dusty quiet water as I paddled slowly around the margin of the lake. We reminisced about school, and then I think we chatted about Ralph, but when I asked about his writing, she smiled nervously, reached back to stroke her silent little girls' legs with her wet fingertips, and changed the subject.

But Ralph did not want to change the subject. When he learned at supper where we had been, he said, "Rita and I never have the opportunity to do anything like that. But I'm going to make it possible for Rita to float around in a canoe all day long."

"What do you mean?"

He looked at me in genuine surprise. "There's no contradiction between writing a good book and writing a profitable one. Isn't that one of the reasons why this country is the envy of the world—the fact that excellence is rewarded?"

"Do you believe your book will be a bestseller?"

Ralph didn't even smile. "With all my heart."

How like his father he looked at that moment!

That evening Ed Herlands rolled up to the house in his fine convertible, escorting a frightened showgirl with long legs and a nervous smile. Rita had also invited her brother, who was at the time an Army captain stationed at Fort Niagara for the duration, and his wife. We were a very mixed company.

Rita's brother Fred was a sandy-haired small-town lawyer with a pompous drawl and a way of uttering commonplace statements as though they were new and important. He seemed very pleased with his uniform. His wife was a clubwoman with fluttering fingers and a harassed air who regarded Rita and Ralph as her social equals and me as her superior, apparently simply because I was a New Yorker associated with "the arts." Her deferential manner did not extend to Ed Herlands, despite his obvious wealth, and certainly not to his girl friend, who sat in a corner of the couch with her wonderful legs tightly crossed, chain smoking and trying desperately to look as though she was used to spending her evenings chatting about T. S. Eliot.

Ed was determined to shock the yokels. Obviously Captain Fred Conway and his wife had never mixed with showgirls, and were making an earnest effort to regard Ellie as a girl with a "different" and "interesting" occupation, despite Ed's chuckling assurances that she was just someone whom he was fortunate (or wealthy) enough to be sleeping with. "Ellie and I were having breakfast the other day," he said genially, "and we got involved in a heated discussion—even before we'd brushed our teeth—on the relation of homosexuality to artistic creation." Then he looked around to observe the effect of his statement.

Fred sat with his freckled fingers linked across his officer's jacket, his eyes blinking rapidly and expressionlessly, as if he were listening to a client outlining a legal problem; his wife looked as though she wished with all her heart that she were back home in Fredonia; and Ellie herself, breathing deeply, perhaps from nervousness, perhaps to call attention to her excellent bosom, smiled defiantly, waiting for us to challenge this preposterous account of a conversation that could never have taken place.

But Rita was grinning happily, why I couldn't tell; it might have been that she was not even listening, but was only smiling at the pleasure of relaxing after a long day. Ralph however was nibbling angrily and nervously at his stiff moustache.

"Where's your friend Bagby?" I said to Ed. "I'd half expected to see him tonight."

"He's in New York, studying the dance on a Herlands fellowship."

"Oh?"

"Nothing princely, you understand. But whenever he gets hungry, he manages to let me know, and I send on a check. If you can't accomplish anything yourself, it's nice to know that you can do it vicariously."

Mrs. Conway was delighted that the conversation was being diverted into safer channels. "That's wonderful of you. If only more people of means—"

"It's not wonderful at all. I take it off my taxes. Besides, it gives me a feeling of power." He laughed soundlessly. "I've made the same offer to Ralph, but he's afraid."

"Afraid?" Fred cocked his head with judicial caution, scenting some new buffoonery on Ed's part.

"I told him to go off someplace where he wouldn't be bothered by the kids, where he could write all day and talk all night—for a year, or longer if he needed . . . and I would foot the bills. But as you see he's never taken me up on it."

Out of the corner of my eye I could see Ellie's bust rising and falling, rising and falling. Ralph sat with his lips tightly pressed together.

"But you could hardly expect—" Fred's wife began indignantly.

"That he'd leave his family? Not if he were an ordinary ungifted person like me—or like your husband . . . But don't we always have other expectations of artistic people?"

Rita said sharply, "Ed, I think—" but he cut in swiftly:

"I'll tell you why he turns me down. He's afraid that if I gave him his real chance he'd write a couple tons of junk, or even worse that he wouldn't write at all without the spur of a lousy job and the dream of getting loose from it by making a million bucks.

"But we mustn't forget that Ralph is a very moral man. And if he failed to produce he figured he'd have to come back with his tail between his legs and spend the rest of his life working, like a character out of Balzac or DeMaupassant, to pay me back the money I'd given him, and that I wouldn't particularly want anyway, except for his peculiar standards of rectitude."

Ralph stood up. "Are you all through?"

"Hell, no. Now I've got a good idea for a novel myself, and I suspect that I could really get it done and make a name for myself if I was broke and had your incentive to get at it. By the way, am I monopolizing the conversation?"

Rita said: "Tell us about your novel—I hope it's funny."

"It's deadly serious. My hero is a man who is obsessed by one strange fear, which forces him to change his entire pattern of life."

"Oh, that sounds fascinating." Mrs. Conway looked around hopefully, as if she still expected that somehow the evening could be salvaged.

"My hero has heart trouble. He has to avoid overeating and overexertion. He's grown terrified that one day he'll strain too hard—he also suffers from constipation—and will have a heart attack in the bathroom. This fear of dying at stool is particularly repugnant to him because he is a sensitive man. He has visions, nightmares, of himself dead in an ignominious position, his trousers crumpled around his ankles, his suspenders dangling on the floor, his face pressed against his bare hairy knees, and his thin hair hanging forward so that his bald spot, usually decently concealed, is immediately apparent to the firemen who break open the door and discover his lifeless body. Sometimes he is horrified by the thought that his body will remain undiscovered for many hours, and will stiffen in its ridiculous and ungainly position. He visualizes burly policemen with faces as red as his is purple, trying to straighten out his corpse and draw his trousers up over his flanks. The irony of it is that this fastidious man must go to the most degrading lengths in order to avoid the necessity of evacuating alone. He searches out bathrooms without locks, and uses those primitive arrangements where men relieve themselves publicly in long rows, military style. He—"

"That's enough, Ed."

"More than enough. A compulsive writer could make a powerful thing out of it, couldn't he? Subtly bringing out the symbolism of the man who wants to create alone but can't take a chance." He winked at Ellie, who was nervously rearranging her back hair with arms upraised so that her taut bust, covered with sequins, seemed to blink back at him. "But I enjoy myself so much that I've never gotten past the first chapter."

"Don't play dumb," Ralph snapped. "You're determined to make me look a fool, with this coarse and vulgar—"

"If you're going to be stuffy, old man, I'll withdraw my standing offer of a Herlands fellowship."

"I'd never take a dime from you for a share in my stock. When it comes, my success is going to be my own."

Ralph's brother-in-law nodded approvingly. With his professional smile turned on, he looked like a death's-head. "Your book will be all the better for that attitude."

"I doubt if it will satisfy either you or me," Ed put in blandly. "Ralph operates under the illusion that he can produce a real work of art and make a fortune with it. Mark Twain had reason to believe in himself as a businessman-artist, in his time a Buffalo boy could still make his pile with his pen. But not any more, Ralphie, not any more."

Rita put her hand to her mouth and turned blindly away, fumbling for a candy dish. At that moment I hated Ed with all my heart.

"I think Ralph is entitled to a hobby without being teased about it, don't you?" Fred's wife asked me, as if I could become her ally in averting disaster.

But Ralph turned on her bitterly. "I have no hobbies. I despise people with hobbies. Someday you'll brag that you're my relative."

The three of us were a little constrained at the end of the evening, after Fred and his wife had left, coldly declining Ed's offer of a lift. Ed stayed on long enough to offer to fix me up with Ellie's younger sister (I declined not without regret) and to apologize perfunctorily to Rita.

"He was a monster tonight," she said tiredly, as she stood at the sink in her stocking feet, washing the cake dishes.

"Oh, I don't think so," Ralph replied slowly. "It wasn't an unusual performance. I happened to be handy, so he used me. I don't really care. What the hell, the proof will be in the eating."

Ralph's pudding wasn't ready when I met him next, several years later, but the circumstances of our meeting were so unusual that I didn't think much about his book at first. I was totally unprepared to see him advancing towards me in the bar of the Mark Hopkins in San Francisco, dressed in the uniform of a Naval lieutenant, and without his moustache.

"Great to see you, Harry! Got time for a drink?"

"You seem less surprised to see me than I am to see you."

"I read about the orchestra in the paper." He took off his white officer's hat, and I saw that his stiff shock of black hair had been cropped quite short. He looked ten years younger. "I'd planned to look you up tonight. Didn't you know I was in the Navy? Didn't Rita write you?"

"I've had only one postal from her in the last year."

"I expect she wasn't too anxious to tell you about it. That was the biggest row we've ever had, when she learned that I'd applied for a commission. She'd gotten to like the kind of life we were leading, and she couldn't bear to have anything disrupt it, even though it was inevitable. Probably she'd have been just as upset if I'd allowed myself to be drafted."

"I doubt that."

Ralph turned red. "You're right, of course. What bothered her most was the idea that I was willing, even anxious, to get away. The night I left for indoctrination school—" he hesitated, toying with his glass of beer, "—Rita accused me of deliberately setting out to commit suicide, the way children fantasy themselves dead in their coffins, surrounded by weeping and repentant parents."

"She was overwrought."

"Of course."

"But you look happier now than in years."

"I am. And I think Rita is too. She had visions of me being torpedoed, *spurlos versenkt*, or blown to pieces by a Kamikaze. But here I am safe and sound in San Francisco, presumably doing naval research because I'm a hydraulic engineer, and with leisure to read and meet people for the first time in my life. I suspect Rita's enjoying a vacation from the old routine herself."

"Do you still get up in the middle of the night?"

Ralph smiled shyly, "Only writing I can do is letters to Rita. There'll be time for the book when I get back." He stood up and glanced at his watch. "Rita's expecting a long-distance call from me in a few minutes. Would you like to say hello?"

"I'd love to."

I stood next to the phone booth and watched Ralph drumming his fingers while he waited for the connection. I thought of his father, whom he never mentioned any more, and as I looked at Ralph I observed for the first time that two vertical furrows were grooving into his cheeks, just like the old man's. He looked young in his uniform, but he was not really young.

Suddenly he stuck his head out of the door and said, apropos of nothing at all, "You must know what it means to get some recognition for your work. If only the war was over and I could *finish,* I know in my bones that people like—" he looked into the telephone as though he could not meet my eyes, "—well, like Edmund Wilson, would take me seriously. If they didn't, I don't think I could go on living." His eyes were burning. "But right now I'm concentrating on finding out what the man in the street wants. I want to do a new final draft that will insure me a really big audience. That's why I've been reading a lot of good histories and talking to all kinds of people."

Then he laughed and said, "You must think I'm an egomaniac. What about you? You don't have a wife or anything yet, do you?"

"I was engaged for a while to an OPA economist, but she got sick of waiting for me to make up my mind, so she joined the Waves."

Ralph disconcerted me by laughing out loud. "Tell you what," he said. "Why don't you talk to Rita first? We'll surprise her. Go on, go ahead." He stepped out and extended the earphone to me.

I stood in the little metal chamber, listening to the sharp inhuman voices of switchboard girls all over the country. *Yes Des Moines, The exchange is Linden, L as in Love,* and suddenly I did not want to speak to Rita at all, I wanted to be quit of the Everetts and their crumbling dream world.

But suddenly Rita's voice, clear and yet infinitely small, as though she were speaking from another world, filled me with such anguished nostalgia that I could not bring myself to look through the glass door as I listened. She was frightened and lonely, and she insisted that with Ralph gone, there was no one in Buffalo to talk to. That had been

Ralph's old complaint. I clung to the telephone and I wondered. Why must there be someone to talk to? Does it really mean someone to listen, like the audiences I have had all my adult life—so that I have never deeply felt the need of a listener—or does it imply that the listener will answer, that he will say not the things that are better left unsaid, like Ed Herlands, but the things that one needs desperately to hear?

Ralph's smile had faded to a shadow by the time he replaced me in the phone booth, for I had managed to get Rita to say goodbye only by promising to come to Buffalo at the earliest opportunity.

Actually I had no such opportunity until after the Japanese had quit and Ralph had returned from the West Coast. When I did get to Buffalo it seemed to me that Rita must have been overwrought during that feverish telephone conversation, for the Everetts' lives appeared hardly to have been affected by the war. Rita and the older girls had been thrilled by their one visit to the West Coast, and Ralph himself said to me briefly, after he had greeted me at the station and helped me into his car, "Well, I had a very pleasant vacation too—" (this in reply to my remark about a trip to Nova Scotia I had just taken with my brother and his family) "—but it's over now, and I'm satisfied. If the war had lasted much longer, I would have had trouble getting back my work habits."

He had gotten back his moustache too. It was peppered with gray, and I wondered why he felt that he needed it, but that was the kind of question you could never ask of Ralph even if you put it as a joke. Almost as soon as we had reached his home, Ralph excused himself and headed back for the toolhouse, saying over his shoulder, "See you at the supper table."

The girls greeted me with shrieks of delight and led me to the kitchen, where Rita stood with her head bent forward over a mixing bowl, her blonde hair hanging full across her face. When she looked up her eyes were brimming with tears: I was startled and frightened, and for one instant I felt like bolting.

But then she laughed, and as she brushed the back of her hand across her face I saw that the tears had been caused by onions which she was slicing into a bowl of chopped meat. I was overcome with such enormous relief that I stepped forward and kissed her damp cheek.

"Are we going to play some duets while I'm here?" I asked.

"Don't tease me. If it wasn't for our record collection, which is mostly albums you've brought us, there wouldn't be any music in my life at all—except for the girls."

"Are you happy?"

"I'm busy. Ralph has been writing ten hours a day, trying to finish before his terminal leave runs out. I take his lunch out to the toolhouse so he won't break his train of thought."

"And now you're satisfied. I was never really sure."

Rita's hand came down on the kitchen table so sharply that the silverware jumped in the air and fell with a clatter. "Don't you see, Harry? He's almost finished. Suppose it's a failure? What will we do?"

"What you've been doing for ten years. It depends on what you mean by failure, doesn't it?"

"For ten years Ralph has been living for the day when the critics will cheer him. He talks about the money and independence, but it's recognition he's after. Suppose he doesn't get it? Do you think he'll be able to say, Better luck next time? Do you?" Her voice rose dangerously. "Do you?"

"His book might sell moderately well and get some nice reviews, enough to make Ralph feel that he had made a good start."

"A start?" she laughed scornfully. "And then what—back to the Water Department and the toolhouse? We're not kids any more, Harry, neither of us . . . I hate melodrama, don't you? Would you do me a favor— tell Ralph it's time to knock off? You can go right out the kitchen door."

So I followed the little trampled path that Ralph had made in the grass in his years of crossing back and forth; when I reached the sagging frame toolhouse I hesitated, still uncertain whether I should intrude. Finally I raised my fist and pounded on the iron-barred old door.

But Ralph's voice said "Yup," and I entered his headquarters. The walls of his spotless workroom were whitewashed and covered with old maps of the Niagara Frontier. Ralph was seated at a roll-top desk with his shirt sleeves turned back halfway to his elbows. He got up when he saw me. "You've never been in here before, have you? Let me show you my stuff."

"Rita suggested that it's time to knock off. I didn't want to intrude."

"Let me show you my layout."

His wooden filing cabinets were a marvel of precision. Ralph had cross-filed all of his material the way his engineering reports must have been indexed at his office, so that you could open any drawer and find references to the downtown scene in Buffalo of the 1850s, the clothing of the men, the manners of the women, the shape of the buildings.

The novel itself was in a series of looseleaf notebooks, one chapter to a notebook, and they were stacked head-high on the roll-top desk. "I would have asked you to read it, as a favor to me," Ralph said, "but every time I got a draft out it needed a little more work. After all these years, I'm almost through. I'm sure that if I hadn't had to go downtown to work every day I could have gotten it out in a year or two of concentrated effort."

"Don't you think you're more mature now than when you started?"

"I'm older, that's all I know. Believe me, there's something wrong about grubbing away so slowly in secret, like a hermit crab. I often think how much better it would have been if I had been able to publish regularly years ago, with each book maybe improving a little."

"Haven't you enjoyed it?"

Ralph rubbed his knuckles across his eyelids. "I suppose you're happiest when you don't have time to think about what you're doing. But even if I don't make a dime on my book, even if no one reads it but the critics, they'll recognize that my very best is in it. That's something to be able to say, isn't it, that you've given everything that you have? And that you've done it without stimulation or encouragement, in the lonely hours of the night? . . . . You go on, I'll be in shortly."

As I turned on Ralph's lawn to look back at him standing in the toolhouse doorway, caught by the waning rays of the late afternoon sun, I was filled with envy and admiration. Rita was wrong about him—of that I was sure.

Only a few months (perhaps a year) later, I came home to the Bronx one evening from Philadelphia, put down my valise and fiddle in the foyer, and found my mother waiting up for me, lying on the sofa with a newspaper and a bowl of grapes. She had a way of popping the pulp into her mouth so that the skin remained between her fingers—it always made me nervous. She shoved aside the bowl, unable to divide her attention between me and the grapes, and said in a voice at once sad and accusing, "You said you'd be home early."

"I had to catch a later train. What's new?"

She sighed, hauling herself upright with a groan, to register her resentment against being treated as merely a messenger service.

"What should be new? A boy (all of my friends were boys to my mother) called up this afternoon. He *said* his name was Ralph Edwards," she added, as if she was perfectly aware that he had been lying.

"But I don't know any Ralph Edwards."

"From Rochester."

"From—Ralph Everett you mean, from Buffalo!"

"So it was Everett. He said to tell you he was at a cocktail party. He sounded drunk."

"Where? In New York?" Gradually I pieced together from my mother's grudging answers the information that Ralph's book had been accepted by a publisher who had already begun an intensive promotional campaign with a cocktail party. I dialed the Algonquin, but the operator would not put me through to Ralph. Probably passed out cold, I thought, and asked for his wife; but she wasn't registered.

So he had come to New York alone for his first moment of triumph. It was a masculine enough action, and I knew that if the situation had been reversed Rita would surely have taken her husband and children along, like a lady ambassador. But I called the next morning and Ralph insisted that I meet him for lunch. He sounded frightened.

I had to join him in an out-of-the-way spot on Eighth Avenue, and although I was early, Ralph was already waiting when I arrived. "Hell of a thing," he said. "I had to sneak off, or they would have dragged me to lunch too."

"Are you that popular?"

"I need advice," he replied obliquely. "Never realized what I was getting into. Look here." He opened a heavy old-fashioned briefcase and pulled out a bundle of papers. "They've promised me lecture tours —personal appearances in bookstores—radio quiz programs—interviews with columnists I never heard of—"

"That sounds wonderful!"

"There's a catch to it."

"There always is. But it looks like your book is going to be a big thing!"

Ralph looked up, surprised. "Of course. But I didn't figure on a bunch of editors, agents, press agents, book club representatives, and I don't know what the hell the rest of them are, all nagging me to jazz up the manuscript."

"I don't understand, Ralph."

"Probably I'm naïve. I didn't expect to be told I'd written a great book, and then have a bunch of plumbers go to work on it, not paying any more attention to me than if I had been just a yokel, sightseeing in the publisher's office."

"Apparently they want to make sure it will sell."

"But what are they going to make out of me? Yesterday they threw graphs at me to prove they know what makes a book sell. I said, Won't it sell if it's good? And then they gave me reader involvement."

"What's that?"

"They've got figures that show how long people read a book before putting it down. Somebody has even found out what catches people's eyes when they're browsing in bookstores. And my book hasn't got it. My editor says—" Ralph's voice was scornful, and yet uncertain, and he spoke without looking at me, "—I've got to make it longer."

"Longer?"

"I've been thinking about telling them to go to hell. But they're nice people, Harry. They can't understand why I'm not more cooperative, when all that they're interested in is me and my career and seeing that I reach the big public I'm entitled to. All I can say in answer is Yes, but what about the book? It's shaken down now to where they've turned the job over to a girl named Doris. A Wellesley girl, out of Butte, Montana . . . I need your advice."

"If I can only help—"

"They want to send Doris back to Buffalo with me to advise me on a new draft. Doris has the proposed changes lined up in a card index. She's very efficient—used to work for Gallup. Should I go through with it? I've been up all night trying to make up my mind."

"What does Rita say?"

"She thinks it's the chance of a lifetime."

"It is your first book," I said. "And it isn't as if you didn't want it to be popular. I remember in San Francisco you were trying to find out what the average man wants to read."

"Sure, but I've already gone as far as I can, maybe even too far, in that direction. Will it still be my book when that Wellesley girl gets through with it?"

"She can't make you do anything you don't want to."

"Somehow I didn't think you'd agree with Rita about this." Ralph began to stuff the papers back into his briefcase. "But I know what you mean. I suppose I have the obligation to listen. I can always say No."

Ralph flew back to Buffalo, and the Wellesley girl went with him. I still have a letter from Rita that describes, with a mixture of fear and mounting excitement, how Doris with her statistics on reader involvement was succeeding in persuading Ralph, despite himself, to broaden his story, work in material that he had previously scrapped, simplify his prose, and inject additional romance. It was on the last point, though, that Ralph balked. Doris explained very carefully, as I gathered, that the firm had had the manuscript mimeographed and pretested: there had been strong indications that the reading public would be happier if an aged Iroquois squaw were made out to be eighteen, in order that she might be involved in a romance.

Although he had been going along with Doris's judgment, something about this suggestion made Ralph become really stubborn: he informed his publishers that he was calling the whole thing off. Doris turned to Rita for help, and it was at this point that Rita used a weapon which she had never, in all the years of their marriage, turned on her husband. "It hurt me to do it," she wrote me, "in fact it went against the grain, but I felt that in this instance it was for his own good. I told him that I hadn't skimped and sacrificed all these years just so that he could throw everything away in one quixotic gesture. Of course when

I said this I was thinking of Ralph, and of what was best for him, but he took it to mean that I was hurt about the past and frightened about the future—and as a result he has promised at least to think it over."

Ralph's resistance was weakened, but not completely destroyed, by Rita's declaration that if it continued it could only make their years together seem a terrible, useless waste. He wanted, she told me, some assurance from a disinterested person, an artist. "He doesn't *know* anybody. Whom can he turn to, Ed Herlands? It has to be you, Harry. Please call him on the phone and talk to him."

I was very reluctant. I didn't know anything about fiction, or about the merits of the proposal that had so disturbed Ralph. Nevertheless I did feel that I had a responsibility, as a family friend, if nothing more. So I called Ralph. I didn't attempt to pressure him. I simply asked: "What will you gain if you persist? Will you change the manuscript back to what it was?"

"Maybe part-way."

"Supposing you start all over with another publisher, assuming you can get out of your contract. What makes you so sure you wouldn't run into the same thing again? What makes you sure that your way is the right way, or the only way? You've never published a book before, and these people have been doing it all their lives."

"So if you were me, you'd give in."

"I'm not saying that. I'm just asking you what the alternatives are, and whether you've thought them all through."

Ralph didn't say much to that; I think Rita was at his side while he talked. He thanked me most warmly for having phoned, and within a day or two he was back at work on the manuscript. Very shortly thereafter the job was done.

Doris was right, of course. No matter how reasonable Ralph's objections may have seemed to him, the immediate astonishing success of the book was proof that the Wellesley girl (as he persisted in calling her) knew her business.

It seems to me now that before I was actually aware of what was happening, "Queen City" became a national catch phrase. The papers were full of it, I listened to the speculation in Pullman washrooms, backstage at concerts, in restaurants, everywhere, about which Hollywood stars would play the leading roles in the movie version of Ralph's book, and for a while you couldn't turn on the radio without hearing a pun on the book's title or on Ralph's name, to the accompaniment of roars and applause.

In a matter of months Ralph and his book achieved the status of an institution, and I grew used to the feature articles on Ralph's long ordeal and the photographs of Ralph—smiling rather grimly, it seemed to me—seated with Rita and their four famous daughters in the living room, as though he had just been elected Governor. From time to time I thought that I should salute in some practical way my friends' great good fortune, but all I could think of was something ridiculously inappropriate like sending a basket of fruit or a box of flowers. So I did nothing.

The excitement about the book was at its peak when Rita wrote extending me a feverish invitation to spend at least part of my vacation with them at their new summer place in Canada. She made it sound as if I would be doing a great favor by coming up and helping them to enjoy their success. I was flattered and I accepted.

In the club car I picked up a copy of *Life;* it seemed inevitable that there should be a story about Ralph and his novel. The article itself was full of statistics on the number of hours Ralph had spent in the toolhouse, the number of pounds that his manuscript weighed, and the marks that his public school teachers remembered giving him, but there was an omission which struck me with special force: while Ralph's mother, who had died during his teens, was adequately and conventionally described, there was absolutely no mention of his father. And in addition to this there was one sentence that leaped up at me and that I immediately committed to memory, like a musical phrase that would have to recur in my life: "While the final verdict on Ralph Everett's work is not yet in, it must be obvious to the author by now that sophisticates will ignore any work which celebrates the American dream in a manner acceptable to the general public. But their disdain will surely be counterbalanced by the shower of gold now raining down on Ralph Everett as a reward for his long years of solitary labor."

I was intercepted at the station by Penny, who ran into my arms breathless and excited.

"Mom couldn't find a place to park and she's driving back and forth, back and forth!"

We found Rita cruising slowly down the street in a handsome green convertible. I tossed my bag in the back.

"The car goes well with your hair, Rita."

"I hope you won't tease me about all our new belongings. Prosperity has brought more problems than we ever had before."

"What's wrong?"

"I'm terribly worried about Ralph. He's working like a dog fixing the summer place—" she waved up ahead, along the river road on which we were driving, "—and yet he can't sleep nights. He wanders around all night, and the whole routine starts again in the morning."

"Perhaps he can't break his old habits."

"It's more than that. He says the money is a trap for us, and that we'll wind up living like rich people. For a while he talked about our being too provincial, and what Europe could do for us, and how we could sink our roots when we came back, oh I don't know, in South Dakota or some such place. Imagine sinking roots in the Black Hills with four daughters!"

"But now?"

"He's like a man who suspects he has cancer and sits in the doctor's office laughing and joking, and waiting to hear the worst. Ralph has been waiting and waiting for the verdict of the important critics. The more the book sells, the worse their silence is." Rita indicated a pile of magazines that lay between us on the leather seat. "These are mostly quarterlies, college magazines and such. Some of them I never heard of. I'm afraid to look and see if there's anything about the book in them. It sounds crazy but sometimes he acts as though he was ashamed that the book is so successful."

We had turned off the highway and were driving down a narrow sandy road, at the end of which stood a rambling bungalow, half concealed by scrub pines and oaks. As we neared the house I could see Lake Erie glimmering through the trees, perhaps an eighth of a mile away. Daisy, swinging slowly and seriously on an old tire hanging from a tree on the front lawn, raised her arm gravely in a formal greeting. Behind her I could hear Robin and Laura playing jacks on the screened porch.

As we drove to the back of the house I caught sight of Ralph, stripped to the waist and straightening up stiffly from a barbecue pit which he had been plastering. He too waved to us, trowel in hand, and came slowly to the car, sweating heavily and scowling into the sunlight.

I hauled out my bag. "You look twice as tired as when you used to work for an honest living, Ralph."

"I am! But they tell me I'm living the way a successful writer should. Quit my job, you know—I'm an ex-engineer." Suddenly he caught sight of the magazines. His nostrils dilated above the tough moustache and I could see his fine rib cage expand as he wiped his sweaty palms on his dungarees. "Excuse me," he said politely. He reached over and plucked up the magazines from the car seat, then riffled them quickly.

"I've struck gold," he exclaimed. "Not just a review, a whole article. The Problem of the American Writer: Ralph Everett, A Case in Point."

"Couldn't it wait till after supper? I'm sure that Harry—"

"I bet Harry wants to know what this twenty-one year old prodigy from Savannah thinks of old Ralph's first book. All Harry's seen is praise from the hacks so far." There was something menacing in his tone. We stood there helplessly in the driveway while Ralph flipped the pages of the journal. "A Case in Point—did you ever think of me in that way, Rita?" Ralph began to walk toward the porch, reading as he moved; Rita and I followed him like two nervous retainers, uncertain whether to follow the master into the bath. But in an instant Ralph turned on us savagely.

"This kid knows more than the old men. 'What can one do but weep,' he says, 'when one examines the career of Ralph Everett? Here is a man, as we are told, who gave his all for his art. He made the accepted sacrifices, cut himself off from fun and frolic, practiced his craft in silence in a drafty toolhouse in the worst hours of the early morning, did not compromise by publishing prematurely, and . . . made a tidy fortune with a book which can only be called a *production.*'"

Ralph looked up from the magazine, his face expressionless. "The boy resents my money. That's the only false note so far. Doesn't he know that it's fashionable for writers to be well off these days?"

"Let's drop it for now, Ralph."

"'*Queen City,*'" he read on, ignoring us, "'can be viewed in two ways, either as the labored effort of a serious but essentially untalented man, or as a striking example of the effect of the corruption of American culture on its worst victim, the creative man.'"

Rita stared very hard at the keys that she still clasped in her fingers, her brows contracted as though they had suddenly become a mysterious object. Finally she said, "I just don't see why you should be so affected by a youngster, a mere boy, when you've been praised by—"

"Because writing means more to this kid than it does to those old fakers who make a living by patting people like me on the back. I know he gets a childish kick out of sniping at success, but he believes what he's saying. 'The very smell of big money,' he says, 'is on every page of Mr. Everett's novel, and while it would be unfair to conclude from the text that his years of selfless labor were spent with one eye on the eventual reproduction of his story in more popular media, his triumphant reliance on stock situations for characters on whose details of speech and dress he has obviously lavished untiring research would point to the fact that Ralph Everett is a captive, bound not hand and foot, but body and soul, to the culture from which he thought to liberate himself by an intense but hopelessly insincere act of will.' That's what the people I've been waiting for would have said, if they had felt like taking the trouble." Ralph tossed the magazine on a porch chair. "I want a copy of this sent to the Wellesley girl."

"Is that necessary?"

"She deserves a better souvenir than the inscribed book I gave her. If you won't do it, I will. I believe that consciences should be kept functioning. Right now I'm going for a swim."

"Ralph, it's much too chilly—" Rita started to protest, but I put my hand on her arm. Ralph strode swiftly away, down the narrow path to the lake, and Rita and I mounted the porch steps together.

Not long after, he returned to the cottage with a towel draped around his neck and his shock of thick hair standing defiantly on end. "Had a good swim. Did some thinking too—I've made up my mind."

Rita looked at him with fear in her eyes. "What do you mean?"

"I'm driving into town right after supper—going to start work on a new book."

Rita leaped up like a young girl and threw her arms around his neck. "I knew those rotten articles wouldn't get you down!"

At that moment I felt like an intruder. Fortunately I remembered that my mother's only brother, a notions salesman, was in Buffalo on business and that I had half-promised to spend an evening with him, so I said to Ralph, "Would you mind if I drove in with you?"

He and Rita were startled by my request, and I had to explain about Uncle Louis. "But couldn't it keep until later in the week?" Rita asked. I was on the point of yielding when Daisy came running in to announce that Uncle Ed had arrived.

"Leave it to Herlands," Ralph said. "He always manages to show up at suppertime. But as long as he's staying, I'd like to have you along. I was a little worried about leaving Rita and the kids alone this evening."

Supper was difficult, mostly because of Ralph's abstractedness and Rita's wary desire that the children should not disturb their father; and the dull badinage between Ed and me didn't help much. Ed was just as well pleased to keep Rita company for the evening, since he was obviously anxious to rebuild his friendship with Ralph. "Just make a start, Ralph," Rita pleaded, "and then bring Harry back. After all, you have so much time now."

"I do, don't I?" He kissed Rita fondly, and at such length that even Ed turned away with me in embarrassment; but Penny and Daisy began to laugh, and the spell was broken, and Ralph and I clambered into the convertible. He didn't forget to take the magazine with him.

The evening was cool, but Ralph didn't appear to notice it, and I was hesitant to ask him to put up the top. At old Fort Erie the road swerves sharply and suddenly you come upon the Niagara River and the shallow skyline of Buffalo; seeing it at twilight as we did, it seemed very beautiful. "I see why you've been fascinated by Buffalo," I said.

"We're looking at it now from another country. That makes a difference."

"I think I understand how you can spend your entire life writing about a place."

"Somebody else, not me."

"Then what's your next book going to be about?"

Ralph looked at me dazedly, as if I had been speaking too fast.

"The one you're going to start tonight."

At last he said slowly, "That was just a lie I told Rita."

I hesitated, but finally I asked, "Why are you going into town?"

"I have to get back to the toolhouse. I have to get back there. It's the only place where I've ever had any peace of mind."

"Maybe I shouldn't have come out to visit just at this time."

"I was the one who urged Rita to invite you. I'm glad for Rita's sake, not just for mine, that you're here now."

"When I think of the pleasure you've given so many people, and the pride that your family has—"

"The wrong kind of pleasure, the wrong kind of pride."

"You're very tired, aren't you, Ralph?"

"Why wasn't I tired during all the years I was working on the book? If you can understand that, you'll know how I feel now."

Ralph brought the car to a stop at the American end of the Peace Bridge; the immigration man leaned forward and said to me, "Where were you born?" and then he recognized Ralph. "Hello, Mr. Everett. Back to town, eh?"

Ralph nodded curtly. From the other side of the car the customs inspector said solicitously, "Better put up the top, Mr. Everett. It's turning cold."

"You see," Ralph said, without looking at me as he drove ahead, "I'm even a celebrity for the wrong reasons. They're going to go home and gossip about me."

"That's nothing to be upset about, is it?"

The street lamps winked on as we rolled downtown. "At least there's money," Ralph murmured. "If I never did anything but build barbecue pits for the rest of my life, there'd still be enough for Rita and the girls. Why work? To grind out a shelf full of second-rate books?"

"Just the same," I protested, "your father would have been proud of you."

"Luckiest thing that happened was the old man's dying when he did. He would have laughed his head off at all this publicity. Oh, he would have been pleased for Rita, I suppose. He was very fond of her—just as you are. That makes things easier for me."

He came to a stop in front of my uncle's hotel. "Here you are. You don't mind picking me up when you're through with your uncle, do you?"

"Not at all."

"Just hop in a cab and come over. You'll find me in the toolhouse. Goodbye, Harry." He leaned out of the car and extended his hand. "I've always enjoyed your company. You've been a good friend to us."

I went up to my Uncle Louis's room and we spent a desultory few hours trading jokes and playing cribbage. At last we had bored each other to the point where we were both relieved when I excused myself. I was glad when my cab reached Humboldt Parkway.

But the street was blocked, and when I smelled smoke and saw children running towards Ralph's house, I jumped out of the taxi. The sky suddenly reddened before me, and I felt my heart constrict.

I was much too late, of course. The firemen had kept the blaze confined to the toolhouse, but that was enough. A spaniel-faced old inspector pointed at the flaming shack and said, "We have to figure that he's inside. His car is still out front with the key in the ignition. It's a terrible thing."

It was a terrible thing. They made me identify Ralph when it was all over. I got sick and had to go outside, but the night air revived me—or maybe it was the feeling that Ralph had died in a way that had more dignity than the ugly deathbed scenes with which so many of us reluctantly let go our grip on life. They found him leaning forward over the typewriter as though he were hard at work, and they surmised that when he was sickened by smoke and unable to make his way to the blackened windows or the latched door (which he had locked from the inside apparently to make sure that he would not be disturbed) he returned to his typewriter to await the end with tranquillity and courage. Everyone seemed to agree that while Ralph had been inexcusably careless in dozing off with a lighted cigarette in a wooden shed piled high with papers, what was more important was that he had finished his masterpiece *before* the tragic accident, which could have taken place at any time during the previous decade. As for his files and records, which he had maintained with such scrupulous devotion, they were utterly destroyed. Nothing remained, not his notes, not even the cabinets themselves, nor the framed pictures of Rita and his daughters.

I took Ralph's car and drove back to Canada. The night was cold and I had to concentrate on the unfamiliar road; somehow I found my way to the summer house, where Rita and Ed were sitting on the porch and waiting for Ralph and me. Without any preliminaries I told them what had happened. Rita looked at me uncomprehendingly, then brushed past me and ran down the steps to the empty car, as though I had perpetrated some kind of hideous joke. I stood stupidly staring after her, and it was Ed Herlands who lumbered down and caught her as she fell.

Rita refused ever to return to the house on Humboldt Parkway. The funeral was held from the cottage in Canada—we buried Ralph next to his father—and Rita stayed on there with the children and the nursemaid while her sister-in-law and Ed and I disposed of everything in the house, which we also sold at her request.

I took a room in an ugly boardinghouse in the nearby resort town of Crystal Beach, and I passed my entire summer vacation with Rita. The girls, as children will, were soon playing happily, unaware of what their gaiety was costing their mother.

"If only they didn't forget so quickly, Harry."

"It would be worse. Life would be unbearable if children lived in the past. And as for us, we have to live in the future, don't we?"

"Ralph did, and for what? I can bear everything else but the thought that he had to die just at the beginning of the kind of life he deserved."

"He fulfilled himself in his children and his book. And he lived long enough to reap the reward for his work. Isn't that more than most artists can say?"

Rita took my hand. "You're very comforting. I know it's hard for you to sit here all summer and listen to me. But who else can I talk to about Ralph? You understood him so well."

At the end of the season I arranged for Rita to take a cruise with her sister-in-law. It seemed only natural for me to meet her at the pier with the children upon her return. By the beginning of the winter I didn't feel too much constraint about asking her to marry me, and I was overjoyed when she accepted.

We have a lovely home in Westchester now, and the children seem very fond of me. When we moved in I surprised Rita by having her harp (which she thought I had sold, along with everything else) placed in the living room. Naturally she approached it with some diffidence, but soon she began to practice regularly, and now our friends enjoy dropping in and listening to our duets.

We often speak of Ralph, and I make a point of impressing upon the girls that their comfortable standard of life is due largely to his unremitting and unselfish labors. The movie made from *Queen City* was released recently, and we all went to see it. Rita cried a little—she says that the stars realized their roles just as Ralph would have wanted —and the girls were thrilled. I like to think that Ralph would have been pleased to see us at the première, which represented in a way the culmination of all his striving. And if he is watching, wouldn't he be happy now to know that not only his great public but his wife and children too revere his memory and respect the fruits of his genius?

# THE PROVERB

## *Marcel Aymé*

MARCEL AYMÉ (1902–  ) The son of a blacksmith, born and
raised in small towns in the heart of France, this author has long
occupied a leading position in the literary life of that country. With
little schooling but with an early passion for the works of Villon and
Balzac, he published his first novel before he was twenty. Then,
living in Paris on the small return of such jobs as movie extra,
bank clerk, and insurance agent, he pressed on with his writing and
won a major literary prize for his fourth novel, *Table aux Creves*.
But it was not until after World War II that he came to the general
notice of American readers. Typically French in its satire and wit,
well blended with charm and occasional tenderness, his writing has
been turned with great facility into every form. His own life,
whether as a boy in Burgundy or in wartime Paris, has provided him
with endless material. For those who have never read him, the story
that follows will be in the nature of a pleasant discovery.

By the light of the hanging bulbs in the kitchen M. Jacotin
surveyed his assembled family, who sat with their heads bowed
over their plates, betraying by sidelong glances their mistrust of
the master's mood. A profound consciousness of his own devotion and
self-abnegation, together with an acute sense of domestic justice, did
indeed render M. Jacotin both unjust and tyrannical, and his choleric
explosions, always unpredictable, created in his household an atmosphere of constraint which in its turn had an irritating effect upon him.

Having learned during the afternoon that his name had been put
forward for the *palmes académiques,* he had resolved to await the
ending of the meal before informing his nearest and dearest; and now,
after drinking a glass of wine with his cheese, he was ready to make
the pronouncement. But the general tone of the gathering seemed to
him not altogether propitious to the reception of the great news. His
gaze went slowly round the table, pausing first at his wife, whose
sickly aspect and timid, melancholy expression did him so little credit
with his colleagues. He turned next to Aunt Julie, who was seated by
the fireside in manifestation of her advanced age and several incurable

maladies, and who in the past seven years must certainly have cost him more than was to be looked for under her will. Then came his two daughters, aged seventeen and sixteen, shop assistants at five hundred francs a month but dressed like film-stars, with wrist-watches, gold brooches at the bosom of their blouses, a general look of being above their station so that one wondered where the money came from and was amazed. M. Jacotin had a sudden intolerable feeling that his substance was filched from him, that the sweat of his labours was sucked dry, and that he was long-suffering to the point of absurdity. The wine rose in a wave to his head, suffusing his broad face, which was noteworthy for its redness even in repose.

And while he was in the grip of this emotion his gaze fell upon his thirteen-year-old son, Lucien, who since the beginning of supper had been doing his best to escape notice. There was something suspect in the pallor of the boy's face. He did not look up, but feeling his father's eyes upon him he twisted a corner of his black, schoolboy's overall with both hands.

'Trying to tear it, are you?' said M. Jacotin in a voice filled with gloating. 'You seem to be doing your best to destroy it.'

Lucien let go his apron and put his hands on the table. He bent over his plate without daring to seek the comfort of his sisters' glance, lonely in the face of approaching calamity.

'Do you hear me speaking to you? Can't you answer? I'm beginning to think you aren't quite easy in your mind.'

Lucien replied with a look of apprehension, not from any hope of disarming suspicion but because he knew his father would be disappointed not to see alarm in his eyes.

'No, your conscience is certainly not clear. Will you please tell me what you've been doing this afternoon?'

'I was with Pichon. He said he'd come and fetch me at two. Then we met Chapusot, who had to go to the doctor because his uncle's ill. The day before yesterday his uncle started having a pain on his liver and—'

But realising that the anecdote was designed to divert his attention, M. Jacotin cut it short.

'Never mind about other people's livers. Nobody bothers about my liver. Tell me what you did this morning.'

'I went with Fourmont to see the house in the Avenue Poincaré that was burnt down the other night.'

'In fact, you've been out all day, from first thing in the morning until this evening. Well, if you can afford to spend the whole of your Thursday amusing yourself, I take it that means you've done all your homework.'

M. Jacotin uttered these words in a voice of mildness that caused all his hearers to hold their breath.

'My homework?' murmured Lucien.

'Yes, your homework.'

'I worked yesterday evening when I got back from school.'

'I'm not asking whether you worked yesterday evening. I'm asking if you have done your homework for tomorrow.'

The others felt the crisis approaching and longed to avert it, but experience had taught them that any intervention in these circumstances would only make things worse, transforming the choleric man's ill-temper into fury. Lucien's sisters tactfully pretended to ignore the scene, while his mother, preferring not to be too close a witness, got up and went to a cupboard. M. Jacotin himself, not yet launched upon his wrath, was reluctant to postpone the news of the *palmes académiques*. But Aunt Julie, moved to sympathy, could not hold her tongue.

'The way you always go on at the poor boy! He told you he worked yesterday evening. He has to play sometimes.'

M. Jacotin replied with dignity:

'I must ask you kindly not to interfere with my efforts to assist my son's education. Being his father, I act as such, and I shall continue to supervise his activities as I think fit. When you have children of your own you will be at liberty to indulge them in any way you choose.'

Aunt Julie, being seventy-three, seemed to detect a hint of irony in this reference to her future offspring. Greatly offended, she rose and left the kitchen. Lucien, apprehensively watching her departure, saw her for an instant groping for the switch in the half-light of the spotlessly clean living-room. When she had shut the door behind her M. Jacotin called the family to witness that he had said nothing to warrant her withdrawal, and he went on to protest at a scheming manoeuvre designed to show him in an unfavourable light. But neither his daughters, who had begun to clear the table, nor his wife could bring themselves to acquiesce, although by doing so they might have relieved the tension. Their silence did him further outrage and he returned furiously to Lucien:

'I'm still waiting for your answer. Have you finished your homework or not?'

Realising that he had nothing to gain by prolonging the agony, Lucien threw in his hand.

'I haven't done my French.'

A gleam of thankfulness appeared in M. Jacotin's eyes. It was agreeable to tackle this boy.

'And why not, may I ask?'

Lucien raised his shoulders in token of ignorance and even of astonishment, as though the question had taken him by surprise.

'I'm waiting,' said M. Jacotin, gazing intently at him.

For a moment longer he sat meditating in silence upon the iniquity and abject state of this graceless son, who for no avowable reason and with no appearance of remorse had failed to do his French homework.

'It's as I thought,' he said, his voice gradually rising with his eloquence. 'Not only do you neglect your work, but you do so deliberately. This French homework was set last Friday, to be shown up tomorrow. That is to say, you had a week to do it in, but you haven't done it. And if I had said nothing you would have gone to school tomorrow with it still not done. Worst of all, you have spent the whole of today idling and loafing. And with whom? With Pichon, Fourmont, Chapusot—boys as lazy as yourself, all at the bottom of the class! Birds of a feather flock together. It would naturally never have occurred to you to visit Béruchard. You would think it a disgrace, I suppose, to go and play with a good boy. But in any case Béruchard wouldn't want you. I'm sure he doesn't waste his time playing. He's not an idler, like you. Béruchard is a worker, and the result is he's always near the top. Only last week he was nine places above you. You can imagine how pleasant that is for me, seeing that I have to spend all day at the office with his father. A man, I may add, who is less well thought of than I am. A hard-working fellow, no doubt, but lacking in ability. And as limited in his political outlook as he is in his work. He has never had any imagination and he knows it. When we're discussing general topics, the other men and I, he keeps pretty quiet. But that doesn't stop him scoring over me whenever he mentions his son. And it puts me in a very awkward position. I'm not lucky enough to have a son like Béruchard's, always first in French and maths, a boy who walks off with all the prizes. Lucien, kindly stop fiddling with that napkin-ring. I will not tolerate impertinence. Are you listening, or do you want a box on the ears to remind you that I'm your father? Idle, useless oaf that you are! Your French homework was set a week ago. You can't pretend that this would have happened if you had any feeling for me or any sense of the burden you are to me. When I think of all the work I have to do, and my worries and anxieties, both for the present and the future! There'll be no one to keep me when I have to retire. One has to rely upon oneself in this world, not on other people. I've never asked a halfpenny of anyone, or expected any help from my neighbour when I was in trouble. I got nothing from my family either. My father didn't let me stay at school. I started my apprenticeship when I was twelve. Out in all weathers pulling the barrow, chilblains in winter and the shirt clinging to my back in summer. But you just loaf your time away because by

good luck you have an over-indulgent father. But don't imagine it will
last for ever. The more I think of it—your French homework utterly neglected! Lazy young lout! It never pays to be kind, people mistake it for
weakness. And just when I was planning to take you all to the theatre
on Wednesday, to see "Les Burgraves". Little did I think what I should
find when I got home! It's always the same—when I'm not here the
place is in a state of chaos, homework not done, nothing done properly.
And of course you had to choose the very day when . . .'

Here M. Jacotin made a pause. A sense of delicacy, of coyness and
modesty, caused him to lower his eyes.

'. . . the day when I learnt that my name has been put forward for
the *palmes académiques*. That is the day you have chosen!'

He paused again, awaiting the effect of these words. But, following
so abruptly upon the lengthy exordium, they seemed not to have been
understood. The others had heard the sound, as they had heard the rest
of his discourse, without grasping the sense. Only Mme. Jacotin, who
knew that for two years her husband had been hoping for some recognition of his services as Honorary Treasurer of the local Musical
Society, had the impression that something of importance had fallen
from his lips. The words '*palmes académiques*' reached her ears with a
sound at once familiar and exotic, evoking in her mind an image of her
husband, in his honorary musician's cap, seated astride the topmost
branches of a coconut palm. Her fear of having been inattentive
caused her at length to grasp the meaning of this poetic vision, and she
opened her mouth, prepared to utter sounds of deferent rejoicing. But it
was too late. M. Jacotin, taking an acid pleasure in his family's indif-
ference, and fearing lest a word from his wife might soften the effect of
their heavy silence, hastened to forestall her.

'To continue,' he said with a mirthless laugh. 'I was saying that you
have had a week in which to do this French homework. A week! I
should like to know when Béruchard did his. I'm quite sure it didn't
take him a week, or even half a week. I've no doubt Béruchard got it
done next day. And now will you tell me what the homework consists
of?'

Lucien, who was not listening, let slip the interval for a reply. His
father called him to attention in a voice that could be heard three doors
away, startling Aunt Julie in her bedroom. In her night attire and with
a woebegone countenance she came to inquire the cause of the disturb-
ance.

'What's the matter? What are you doing to that child? I insist upon
knowing!'

Misfortune willed it that at this moment M. Jacotin's mind was
principally occupied with the thought of his *palmes académiques*, and

for this reason his patience failed him. Even at the height of his rages he was accustomed to express himself with moderation. But that an old woman taken into his home from charitable motives should thus browbeat a man on the verge of being decorated, seemed to him a provocation warranting extreme language.

'As for you,' he said, 'I can tell you what you are in five letters.'

Aunt Julie gaped, round-eyed and unbelieving, and when he stated specifically what the five letters spelt she swooned. There were cries of alarm and a prolonged, dramatic hubbub filled with the clatter of kettles, bottles and cups and saucers. Lucien's mother and sisters busied themselves about the sufferer with words of sympathy and consolation, each one a dart in M. Jacotin's flesh. They avoided looking at him, and when by chance their heads turned his way their eyes were hard. Conscious of his guilt, and feeling sorry for the old girl, he genuinely regretted his coarseness. Indeed, he would have liked to apologise, but in face of this ostentatious condemnation his pride hardened. As Aunt Julie was being led back to her room he said in a loud, clear voice:

'For the third time, will you tell me what your French homework is?'

'It's an essay,' said Lucien. 'I have to illustrate the proverb, "Nothing is gained by running: it is better to start in time."'

'Well? That doesn't sound very difficult.'

Lucien nodded as though in agreement but with a noncommittal expression.

'Anyway, get your books and start work. I want to see it finished.'

Lucien fetched his satchel, which was lying in a corner of the kitchen, got out his rough notebook and wrote at the head of a virgin page. 'Nothing is gained by running: it is better to start in time.' Slowly though his hand moved, he could not make this take more than a minute or two. He then sucked the end of his pen while he brooded over the words with a hostile and sulky air.

'I can see you aren't really trying,' said his father. 'Well, please yourself. I'm in no hurry. I'm quite prepared to sit up all night.'

He had settled himself comfortably and in an attitude of calm resolution that filled Lucien with despair. He tried to think about the proverb, 'Nothing is gained by running: it is better to start in time.' The thing seemed to him too obvious to call for demonstration, and he thought with scorn of La Fontaine's fable about the Hare and the Tortoise. Meanwhile his sisters, after getting Aunt Julie to bed, had begun to put the dishes and plates back in the dresser. Despite their attempts to do so silently they made rattling sounds that irritated M. Jacotin, who suspected them of trying to provide their brother with an excuse for doing nothing. And suddenly there was a hideous clatter. His wife had let fall an iron saucepan over the sink so that it rebounded on to the floor.

'Be careful, can't you?' snapped M. Jacotin. 'It's really very trying. How do you expect the boy to work with this racket going on? Go away and don't disturb him. You've finished washing up. Go to bed.'

The women left the kitchen at once. Lucien was left defenceless, at the mercy of his father and the night, and conjuring up a vision of death in the dawn, strangled by a proverb, he burst into tears.

'A lot of good that's going to do you,' said his father. 'Don't be a little ass!'

Although he spoke roughly there was now a hint of compassion in his voice, for M. Jacotin, still upset by the crisis he had provoked, hoped to redeem himself by showing some clemency in his treatment of his son. Perceiving the change, Lucien's self-pity deepened and he wept the more. His father, genuinely touched, came round the table bringing a chair with him and seated himself at the boy's side.

'That'll do. Get out your handkerchief and stop crying. At your age you ought to understand that if I'm hard on you it's for your own good. Later on you'll see that I was right. There's nothing better for a boy than a father who knows how to be stern. Oddly enough, Béruchard was saying the same thing to me only the other day. He makes no bones about beating his lad. Sometimes he'll just give him a clout or a kick in the pants, but at other times it's the cane. And he gets good results, what's more. He knows the boy's on the right road and that he'll go far. But I could never bring myself to strike a child, except of course just now and then, on the spur of the moment. We all have our own methods, as I said to Béruchard. Personally I think it's better to use persuasion.'

Disarmed by these soothing words, Lucien had stopped crying, a fact which caused his father to feel certain misgivings.

'Mind you, you mustn't mistake it for weakness on my part if I talk to you as though you were grown up!'

'Oh, no!' said Lucien in a voice of profound conviction.

Reassured, M. Jacotin mellowed again. As he considered the proverb on the one hand and his son's distress on the other, it seemed to him that he could afford to be generous, and he said amiably:

'I can see that if I don't lend you a hand we shall be here till breakfast. We'd better get started. We have to show that "Nothing is gained by running: it is better to start in time." Well, now let me see. Nothing is gained by running . . .'

Until this moment the subject of the essay had appeared to M. Jacotin almost ludicrously simple; but now that he had taken over the job he began to see it in a different light. With a somewhat worried expression he re-read the sentence several times and then murmured:

'It's a proverb.'

'Yes,' said Lucien, and sat confidently awaiting further enlightenment.

His innocent trustfulness touched M. Jacotin's heart, while at the same time the thought that his prestige as a father was at stake occasioned in him a certain dismay.

'Did your master say anything when he set the subject?' he asked.

'He said, "Whatever else you do, don't quote the fable of the Hare and the Tortoise. You must find an example of your own." That's what he said.'

'Ha!' said M. Jacotin. 'I must say, the Hare and the Tortoise is an excellent illustration. I hadn't thought of that.'

'But it's forbidden.'

'Yes, of course—forbidden. But good God, if everything's forbidden——!'

His face a little suffused, M. Jacotin groped round for some other idea, or at the very least for a phrase which would serve as a point of departure. His imagination did not prove helpful. He began to consider the proverb with feelings of alarm and exasperation, and by degrees his face assumed the same expression of boredom that Lucien's had worn a short time before.

Finally a notion occurred to him arising out of a newspaper headline that had caught his eye only that morning—'The Armaments Race.' It promised well. A certain country has for a long time been preparing for war, producing guns, tanks, bombs and aircraft, while its neighbour has been sluggish in its preparations, so that when war breaks out it is by no means ready and struggles in vain to catch up. Here was the material for an admirable essay.

But then M. Jacotin's countenance, which had momentarily lightened, again grew sombre. He had recalled that his political creed did not permit him to choose an example so tendentious in its nature. He was too high-minded to do injury to his principles, but it was a great pity. Despite the firmness of his convictions he could not help slightly regretting that he was not the helot of one of the parties of reaction, which would have allowed him to develop the idea with the approval of his conscience. He consoled himself with the thought of the *palmes académiques*, but gloomily, none the less.

Lucien sat placidly awaiting the outcome of his meditations. Having, as he considered, been relieved of the task of elucidating the proverb, he was no longer even thinking about it. But his father's protracted silence made the time seem slow in passing. His lids drooped and he

yawned widely several times. To M. Jacotin, tight-lipped with the effort
of concentration, these yawns were a reproach, and his state of nervous
tension increased. Rack his brains as he would, he could think of nothing else. The armaments race had become a hindrance. It seemed to
have attached itself to the proverb, and his very attempts to dismiss it
brought it the more vividly to his mind. From time to time he glanced
covertly and anxiously at his son.

At length, when he had almost given up hope and was on the verge
of admitting failure, he had another idea. It came to him as a sort of off-
shoot of the armaments race, dispelling that obsession from his mind.
This time it was a sporting contest—two crews of oarsmen in training,
the one going about it methodically, the other with a negligent air.

'Right,' said M. Jacotin. 'Take this down.'

Lucien, who was dozing, started and reached hastily for his pen.
'What! Do you mean to say you were asleep?'

'Oh, no. I was thinking. I was thinking about the proverb. But I
couldn't think of anything.'

M. Jacotin chuckled indulgently. Then his gaze became fixed and he
began slowly to dictate.

'On this glorious Sunday afternoon, comma, what are those long,
comma, slender, comma, green objects that present themselves to our
gaze? Seen at a distance one might suppose them to possess long arms,
but those arms are none other than oars, and the green objects are in
reality racing-boats rocking gently upon the waters of the Marne . . .'

Lucien at this point raised his head and looked at his father in some
alarm, but M. Jacotin, absorbed in polishing a transitional phrase which
would enable him to introduce the rival crews, paid no attention. With
mouth half-open and eyes half-closed he was contemplating his oarsmen
and grouping them within the structure of his argument. His hand
groped for his son's pen.

'Give that to me. I'll write it myself. It's better than dictating.'

He began to write feverishly and copiously. Thoughts and words
came in an effortless flow, and in a sequence that was at once convenient and exhilarating, lending itself to lyrical treatment. He felt rich,
master of a fruitful and abundant domain. For a few more moments,
and still with apprehension, Lucien watched the inspired pen travelling
rapidly across the page of his exercise book, and then he fell asleep
with his head on the table. At eleven o'clock his father woke him and
handed the book back.

'Now you must copy it out carefully. I'll go over it when you've
finished. Take particular care with the punctuation.'

'It's rather late,' said Lucien. 'Perhaps it would be better if I got up
early in the morning.'

'No, no. One must strike while the iron's hot. And there's another proverb for you!' M. Jacotin smiled delightedly and added: "What's more, it's another that I should have no difficulty in illustrating. I'd be quite ready to tackle it, if I could spare the time. A splendid subject. I could do you a dozen pages on it. Well, at least I hope you understand what it means.'

'What?'

'I'm asking you if you know the meaning of the proverb, "Strike while the iron's hot."'

Lucien nearly gave way to despair. He pulled himself together and said very gently:

'Yes, father, I understand it. But now I must copy this one.'

'That's right, copy it out,' said M. Jacotin in the tone of one who disdains the humbler activities.

A week later Lucien's form master returned the corrected essays.

'Taking them all round,' he said, 'they're a poor lot. Apart from Béruchard, who gets thirteen, and three or four others, none of you has understood the subject.'

He went on to explain what should have been done, and then selected for comment three out of the pile of exercise books with their red ink markings. The first was Béruchard's, which he praised. The third was Lucien's.

'When I read your essay, Jacotin, I was startled by a literary manner to which you have not accustomed me, and which I found so distasteful that I had no hesitation in giving you only three. If I have often in the past had occasion to complain of your flatfootedness, this time you have gone to the opposite extreme. You have managed to fill six pages with matter that is entirely beside the point. And what is most intolerable is the odiously florid style you have seen fit to adopt.'

The master talked for some time about Lucien's essay, offering it to the class as a model of what not to do. He read out certain passages which he thought especially instructive. There were grins and titters and even one or two bursts of prolonged laughter. Lucien turned very pale, deeply wounded in his sense of filial piety no less than in his self-esteem.

And at the same time he was furious with his father for having brought this mockery upon him. Indifferent scholar though he was, neither his negligence nor his ignorance had hitherto exposed him to ridicule. Whether the subject was French, Latin or algebra, he contrived in his very inadequacy to show a regard for the scholastic proprieties and even for scholastic elegance. When he had copied his father's text, his eyes half-closing with sleep, he had had little doubt as to how the essay would be received. In the morning, with his wits about him, he had been half-inclined not to show it up, being more than ever conscious of its many discordances and false notes in terms of what was acceptable in the classroom. But at the last moment an instinctive trust in his father's infallibility had decided the matter.

When he came home at midday he was still angrily brooding over that impulse of almost religious faith which had caused him to go against his better judgement. What business had his father to do his home-work for him? It served him right that he had only got three out of twenty, and perhaps this would cure him of trying to write essays. And Béruchard had got thirteen. Father would find that hard to swallow. That would teach him!

As they sat down to lunch M. Jacotin appeared gay and almost amiable his looks and words invested with a slightly feverish liveliness. He coyly refrained from at once asking the question which was upper-most in his mind and his son's. The atmosphere round the table was not much different from that of other days. The father's high spirits, far from putting the rest at ease, were rather an added source of discom-fort. Mme. Jacotin and her daughters struggled in vain to adapt their manner to his own, while Aunt Julie made a point of emphasizing, by her sulky demeanour and air of offended surprise, how strange this display of good humour appeared in the eyes of the family. M. Jacotin evidently felt it himself, because his mood rapidly darkened.

'Well,' he said abruptly, 'and what about the proverb?'

His voice betrayed an emotion more akin to nervousness than to mere impatience. And in that instant Lucien perceived that he had the power to do lasting injury to his father. He saw him suddenly with a detach-ment that delivered him into his hands. He realised that for many years the unhappy man had lived on the sense of his infallibility as head of the household, and that when he had set out to elucidate the proverb he had exposed his principle to a dangerous hazard. Not only was the domestic tyrant about to lose face in the eyes of his family, but the con-sideration in which he held himself would also be undermined. It would be a disaster. In the familiar setting of the kitchen, the group round the table, Aunt Julie ever-watchful for the chance to score a point, the crisis that a single word might provoke assumed a shattering reality. Con-fronted by the startling discovery of his father's weakness, Lucien's heart melted in generous commiseration.

'Have you gone to sleep? I'm asking you if your master has returned my essay,' said M. Jacotin.

'Your essay? Yes, he gave it back.'

'And how many marks did we get?'

'Thirteen.'

'Well, that's not bad. How about Béruchard?'

'He got thirteen too.'

'And what was the most anyone got?'

'Thirteen.'

M. Jacotin was radiant. He turned to gaze fixedly at Aunt Julie, as though the thirteen marks had been awarded in her despite. Lucien had lowered his eyes and was communing with himself in secret gratification. M. Jacotin laid a hand on his shoulder and said kindly:

'You see, my dear boy, the most important thing, when one starts on a piece of work, is to think it over carefully. Thoroughly to understand one's task is more than half the battle. That is what I want to get firmly into your head. I shall succeed in the end. I shall spare no pains. From now on we will do all your essays together.'

# THE GREAT GESTURE

## Isak Dinesen

---

ISAK DINESEN (1885–1962) was Karen Dinesen, the Baroness Blixen, a Danish aristocrat by birth, by marriage and by personal quality. Her recent death provoked deep sorrow all over the many lands in which her work is read. There will be regret as well that her ability to find the time to write did not match the singular gift she brought to the task. Her prose, written in English, has a jewel-like refinement, her evocations of people and places have poetical power, and she was, above all, a rare story teller. In *The Great Gesture* the reader shares with her a mood and moment of the African life that was so precious to her and that has gone forever.

I was a fairly famous doctor to the squatters of the farm, and it happened that patients came down from Limoru or Kijabe to consult me. I had been, in the beginning of my career, miraculously lucky in a few cures, which had made my name echo in the manyattas. Later I had made some very grave mistakes, of which I still cannot think without dismay, but they did not seem to affect my prestige; at times I felt that the people liked me better for not being infallible. This trait in the Africans comes out in other of their relations with the Europeans.

My consultation hour was vaguely from nine to ten, my consultation room the stone-paved terrace east of my house.

On most days my activity was limited to driving in the sick people to the hospital in Nairobi or up to that of the Scotch Mission at Kikuyu, both of which were good hospitals. There would almost always be plague about somewhere in the district; with this you were bound to take the sufferers to Nairobi plague hospital, or your farm would be put in quarantine. I was not afraid of plague, since I had been told that one would either die from the disease or rise from it as fit as ever, and since, besides, I felt that it would be a noble thing to die from an illness to which popes and queens had succumbed. There would likewise almost always be smallpox about, and gazing at old and young faces round me, stamped for life like thimbles, I was afraid of smallpox, but Government regulations strictly kept us to frequent inoculations against the illness. As to other diseases like meningitis or typhoid fever, whether I drove the patients into Nairobi or tried to cure them myself out on the farm, I was always convinced that I should not catch the sickness—my faith may have been due to an instinct, or may have been in itself a kind of protection. The first *sais* that I had on the farm, Malindi—who was a dwarf, but a great man with horses—died from meningitis actually in my arms.

Most of my own practice was thus concerned with the lighter accidents of the place—broken limbs, cuts, bruises and burns—or with coughs, children's diseases and eye diseases. At the start I knew but little above what one is taught at a first-aid course. My later skill was mostly obtained through experiments on my patients, for a doctor's calling is demoralizing. I arrived at setting a broken arm or ankle with a splint, advised all through the operation by the sufferer himself, who very likely might have performed it on his own, but who took pleasure in setting me to work. Ambition a few times made me try my hand at undertakings which later I had to drop again. I much wanted to give my patients Salvarsan—which in those days was a fairly new medicine and was given in big doses—but although my hand was steady with a rifle I was nervous about it with a syringe for intravenous injections. Dysentery I could generally keep in check with small, often-repeated doses of Epsom salt, and malaria with quinine. Yet it was in connection with a case of malaria that I was nearest to becoming a murderer.

On a day in the beginning of the long rains Berkeley Cole came round the farm from up-country, on his way to Nairobi. A little while after, Juma appeared to report that an old Masai Chief with his followers was outside, asking for medicine for a son of his who had been taken ill, evidently—from the symptoms reported—with malaria.

The Masai were my neighbours; if I rode across the river which formed the border of my farm I was in their Reserve. But the Masai themselves were not always there. They trekked with their big herds of cattle from one part of the grass-land—which was about the size of Ireland—to another, according to the rains and the condition of the grazing. When again they came round my way and set to patch up their huts of cow-hide for a sojourn of some time, they would send over to notify me, and I would ride over to call on them.

If I had been alone this afternoon, I should have gone outside to talk the case over with the old Chief, to hand him the quinine and altogether to get Masai news. But Berkeley, dried after his drive and revived by a glass or two, was in one of his sweet, dazzling moods and entertaining me on old Ireland memories of his, so that I sat on with him. I just handed over the keys of the medicine chest to Kamante, who was the skilled and deep amanuensis to my doctor and had dealt out quinine to our patients a hundred times, telling him to count up the tablets to the father of the sick boy and to instruct him to give his son two of them in the evening and six in the course of the next day. But after dinner, while Berkeley and I by the fireside were listening to my records of Petrouchka just out from Europe, Juma once more stood in the door, an ominous spectre in his long white *kansu,* to inform me that the old Masai was back with a small lot of his people. For his son, after having taken my medicine, had got very ill indeed, with terrible pains in his stomach. I called in the Masai Chief, and found that he was an old acquaintance of mine. I knew his son well too, his name was San-doa; like the big Masai Chief, he was a Moran of two years ago, and it was he who had taught me to shoot with a bow and arrow. Calling to mind that the most inexplicable fits of idiocy might occur even in the most intelligent Natives, I had Kamante woken up and ordered him to show me the box from which he had taken the quinine. And it was Lysol.

Berkeley said: "We had better go out there at once." But it was rain-ing heavily; the road round Mbagathi Bridge was impassable, so that it would be useless to think of starting a car, and we should have to take the shorter cut across the river on foot. I collected the bicarbonate and oil which I used against accidents with corrosives, and we took two boys with hurricane lamps with us. The Masai also had brought lamps. The descent to the river, in the tall wet bush and long wet grass, was steep and stony, but the Masai knew of a better way than my riding-path, and when we came to the river itself, which had swelled high with the rain, they carried me across.

On the way none of us had spoken. As now, to the other side of the river, we were ascending the long slope of the Masai Reserve, I said to Berkeley: "If Sandoa is dead by the time we get there, I shall not go back to the farm. I shall stay on with the Masai. If they will have me." I had no answer from Berkeley, only, the next moment, a sudden, wild, extremely rude curse straight in my face. For he had in that second put his foot into the long marching column of an army of Siafu. The Siafu are the universally dreaded, man-eating ants of Africa, the which, left to themselves, will eat you up alive. My dogs in their hut at night when they had got the Siafu on them would yell out miserably in their agony, until you rushed out to save them. My friend Ingrid Lindström of Njoro at one time had her whole flock of turkeys devoured by the killers. They are about mostly at night, and in the rainy season. If you happen to get the Siafu on you, there is nothing for you but to tear off your clothes and have the person nearest at hand pluck them out of your flesh. Now, turning round to see what was happening to Berkeley, I saw him, in the midst of the infinite black African night and of the Masai plain, his trousers at his heels, changing feet as if he were treading water, with one toto holding up a hurricane lamp and another picking out the burning, ferocious creatures from his strangely white legs.

When we came to the Masai manyatta we found Sandoa still alive. By a stroke of luck, or by some kind of intuition, he had taken but one tablet of Kamante's medicine—possibly also the intestines of Masai Morani are hardier than those of other human beings. I administered the bicarbonate and oil to him, feeling that I ought to be on my knees with gratitude, and I saw him well on his way to recovery before, in the grey light of dawn, Berkeley and I returned to my house.

Snake-bites were frequent, but although I lost oxen and dogs from snake-bite I never lost a human patient from them. The spitting cobra caused pain and distress; I still have before me the picture of an old squatter woman staggering up to the house wailing and blind after having her face spat in while cutting wood in the forest—she must have been chopping with her mouth wide open, for her tongue and gums were swollen to suffocation and had turned a deadly pale blue. But the effect of the poison could be relieved with bicarbonate and oil and would pass after a while.

Fashion—the ambition to be *comme il faut*—made itself felt in the ailments on the farm, as in other departments of Native life. At one time the truly chic thing was to come to the house for worm-medicine. I did not myself taste the mixture, which looked very nasty in its bottle, like green slime, but the people, old and young, drank it down with pride. After a while I warned my patients that I had no faith in their need of worm-medicine, and that if they wanted to go on taking it as an apéritif they would in the future have to pay for it themselves—and I thereby put an end to that particular kind of dandyism. A very old squatter a couple of years later presented himself at the house and begged to have the "green medicine." His wife, he informed me, had got a *nyoka* —which word really means a snake—in her stomach, and at night it would roar so loudly that neither he nor she could sleep. On my doorstep he looked *démodé*, the last adherent to a fashion of the past.

My patients and I thus worked together in good understanding. Only one shadow lay over the terrace: that of the hospital. During my early days in Africa, till the end of the First World War, the shadow was light like that of trees in spring; later on it grew and darkened.

For some of my years on the farm I had been holding the office of *fermier général* there—that is, in order to save the Government trouble I collected the taxes from my squatters locally and sent in the sum total to Nairobi. In this capacity I had many times had to listen to the Kikuyu complaining that they were made to pay up their money for things which they would rather have done without: roads, railways, street lighting, police—and hospitals.

I wished to understand them and to know how deep was their reluctance against the hospital, and to what it was really due, but it was not easy, for they would not let me know; they closed up when I questioned them, they died before my eyes, as Africans will. One must wait and be patient in order to find the right moment for putting salt on the tail of the timid, dark birds.

It fell to Sirunga, in one of his little quicksilver movements, to give me a kind of information.

Sirunga was one of the many grandchildren of my big squatter Kaninu, but his father was a Masai. His mother had been among those pretty young girls whom Kaninu had sold across the river, but she had come back again to her father's land with her baby son. He was a small, slightly built child with a sudden, wild, flying gracefulness in all his movements and a corresponding, incalculable, crazy imagination of a kind which I have not met in any other Native child, and which maybe will have been due to the mixture of blood. The other boys kept back from Sirunga, they called him "Sheitani"—the Devil—and at first I laughed at it—for even with a good deal of mischief in him Sirunga could be nothing but a very small devil—but later on I realized that in the boys' eyes he was possessed by the Devil, and his smallness then made the fact the more tragic. Sirunga suffered from epilepsy.

I did not know of it until I happened to see him under an attack. I was lying on the lawn in front of the house talking with him and some other totos when all at once he rose up straight and announced: "Na taka kufa"—I am dying, or literally, I want to die, as they say in Swahili. His face grew very still, the mouth so patient. The boys round him at once spread to all sides. The attack, when it came upon him, was indeed terrible to watch, he stiffened in cramp and foamed from the mouth. I sat with my arms round him; I had never till then seen an epileptic attack and did not know what to do about it. Sirunga's amazement as he woke up in my arms was very deep, he was used to seeing everybody run away when he was seized with a fit, and his dark gaze at my face was almost hostile. All the same after this he kept close to me—I have before written about him that he held the office of an inventive fool or jester and followed me everywhere like a small, fidgety, black shadow. His mighty uncontrolled fantasies and whims were totally confused and highly confusing to listen to. Sirunga, at a time when we had an epidemic on the farm, explained to me that once—long long long ago— all people had been very ill. It was, Msabu, when the sun was pregnant with the moon—walked with the moon in the stomach—but as the moon jumped out and was born, they grew well again. I did not connect his fantasy with hospitals, from which no such universal cure could rightly be expected; it was the words "long long long ago" which gave me my perspective.

At the time when the Natives of the Highlands were free to die as they liked, they would follow the ways of their fathers and mothers. When a Kikuyu fell ill, his people carried him out of his hut on his bedstead of sticks and hides, since a hut in which a person had died must not again be lived in but had to be burned down. Out here under the tall fringed trees his family sat round him and kept him company, squatter friends came up to give the news and gossip of the farm, at night small charcoal fires were made up on the ground round the bed. If the sick man got well he was carried back into the hut. If he died he was brought across the river out on the plain, and was left there to the quick and neat cleaning and polishing of jackals and vultures, and of the lions coming down from the hills.

I myself was in sympathy with the tradition of the Natives, and I instructed Farah—who showed himself deeply averse to the idea, for the Mohammedans wall up the graves of their dead and perform solemn rites by the side of them—if I died on the farm to let me travel in the track of my old squatters across the river. There were so many of the true qualities of the Highland country in the *castrum doloris* out there under the big firmament, with its wild, free, gluttonous undertakers: silent drama, a kind of silent fun—at which after a day or two the main character himself would be smiling—and silent nobility. The silent, all-embracing genius of consent.

The Government prohibited and put an end to the funeral custom of old days, and the Natives gave it up unwillingly. The Government and the Missions then undertook to build hospitals, and, seeing the reluctance of the people of the land to go into them, were surprised and indignant, and blamed them for being ungrateful and superstitious, or for being cowards.

The Africans, though, feared pain or death less than we ourselves did, and life having taught them the uncertainty of all things, they were at any time ready to take a risk. An old man with a headache once asked me if I might not be able to cut off his head, take out the evil from it, and set it back in its right place, and if I had consented I think that he would have let me make the experiment. It was other things in us which at times set their nerves on edge.

For they had had our civilization presented to them piecemeal, like incoherent parts of a mechanism which they had never seen functioning, and the functioning of which they could not on their own imagine. We had been transforming, to them, Rite into Routine. What by now most of all they feared from our hands was boredom, and on being taken into hospital they may well have felt that they were in good earnest being taken in to die from boredom.

They had deep roots to their nature as well, down in the soil and back in the past, the which, like all roots, demanded darkness. When, in his small confused Kikuyu-Masai mind, Sirunga had given me a small contorted key, the reference to a past—"long long long ago"—an African past of a thousand years, I took it into my course of thought. We white people, I reflected, were wrong when in our intercourse with the people of the ancient continent we forgot or ignored their past or did indeed decline to ackowledge that they had ever existed before their meeting with us. We had deliberately deprived our picture of them of a dimension, thus allowing it to become distorted to our eyes and blurred in its Native harmony and dignity, and our error of vision had caused deep and sad misunderstandings between us and them. The view to me later on was confirmed as I observed the fact that white people to whom the past was still a reality—in whose minds the past of their country, their name and blood or their home was naturally alive—would get on easier with the Africans and would come closer to them than others, to whom the world was created yesterday, or upon the day when they got their new car.

The dark people, then, as the clever doctor from Volaia approached, may well have gone through the kind of agony which one will imagine a tree to be suffering at the approach of a zealous forester intending to pull up her roots for inspection. Their hearts in an instinctive deadly nausea turned from the medical examinations of the hospitals, such as they did from the *kipanda,* the passport giving the name and data of its bearer, which some years later the Government made compulsory to each individual Native of the Highlands.

We Nations of Europe, I thought, who do not fear to floodlight our own inmost mechanisms, are here turning the blazing lights of our civilization into dark eyes, fitly set like the eyes of doves by the rivers of waters (Song of Solomon 5:12), essentially different to ours. If for a long enough time we continue in this way to dazzle and blind the Africans, we may in the end bring upon them a longing for darkness, which will drive them into the gorges of their own, unknown mountains and their own, unknown minds.

We may, if we choose to, I thought further, look forward to the day when we shall have convinced them that it be a meritorious and happy undertaking to floodlight a whole continent. But for that they will have to get other eyes. The intelligent, efficient and base Swahili of the coast have got such eyes.

The outcome of these various circumstances was this: that I would from time to time find myself unemployed as a doctor, and my consulting room empty.

It would most often happen after I had been taking a patient into hospital. But it might be brought about, suddenly, by reasons unknown to me and probably unknowable, like the sudden pause which may occur amongst labourers in the field. They would then, after a week, bring me up a patient or two with a high fever or a broken limb, too far gone for treatment. I would feel that I was being made a fool of, and lose patience with my people, I would speak to them without mercy:

"Why," I asked them, "must you wait to come to me with your broken arms and legs until they are gangrenous, and the stench, as I am driving you to Nairobi, makes me myself sick?—or with a festering eye until the ball of it has shrunk and withered so that the cleverest doctor of Volaia will not be able to cure it? The old fat Msabu matron in the Nairobi hospital will be angry with me once more and will tell me that I do not mind whether my people on the farm live or die—and in the future she shall be right. You are more obstinate than your own goats and sheep, and I am tired of working for you, and from now on I shall bandage and dose your goats and sheep and leave you yourself to be one-legged and one-eyed, such as you choose to be."

Upon this they would stand for some time without a word, and then, very sullenly, let me know that they would in the future bring me up their injuries in good time, if on my side I would promise not to take them into hospital.

During the last few months that I was still on the farm, at the time when very slowly it was being made clear to me that my fight of many years was lost, and that I should have to leave my life in Africa and go home to Europe, I had as a patient a small boy of six or seven named Wawerru, who had got bad burns on both legs. Burns are an ailment which you would often get to treat in the Kikuyu, for they built up piles of charcoal in their huts and slept round them, and it happened that in the course of the night the coals slid down on top of the sleepers.

In the midst of a strangely non-real existence, unconnected with past or future; the moments that I spent in doctoring Wawerru were sweet to me, like a breeze on a parched plain. The French Fathers had presented me with a new kind of ointment for burns, just out from France. Wawerru was a slight, slant-eyed child, late-born in his family and spoilt, in so far as he believed that nobody would do him anything but good. He or his elder brothers who carried him up to the house had managed to grasp the idea of a treatment every third day, and his sores were yielding to my cure. Kamante as my amanuensis was aware of the happiness that the task gave me, his lynx eyes every third day would seek out the small group amongst the patients on the terrace, and one

time, when they had missed a day, he gave himself the trouble to walk
down to Wawerru's manyatta and to admonish his family about their
duties. Then suddenly Wawerru did not appear, he vanished out of my
existence. I questioned another toto about him; "Sejui"—I know not—he
answered. A few days later I rode down to the manyatta, my dogs running with me.

The manyatta lay at the foot of a long, green grass-slope. It contained
a large number of huts, for Wawerru's father had got several wives,
with a hut to each of them and—in the way of most wealthy Kikuyu—a
central hut of his own, into which he could retire from the world of
femininity to meditate in peace, and there was also an irregular suburb
of bigger and smaller granaries to the settlement.

As I rode down the slope, I saw Wawerru himself sitting on the grass,
playing with a couple of other totos. One of his play-fellows caught sight
of me and notified him, and he at once, without so much as a glance in
my direction, set off into the maze of the huts and disappeared to my
eyes. His legs were still too weak to carry him, he scuttled along with
wondrous quickness on all fours like a mouse. I quite suddenly was
thrown into a state of flaming anger at the sight of such ingratitude. I
set Rouge into a canter to catch up with him, and at the moment when,
in the exact way of a mouse with its hole, he slipped into a hut, I
jumped from the saddle and followed him. Rouge was a wise horse; if
I left him, the reins loose round his neck, he would stand still and wait
for me till I came back. I had my riding whip in my hand.

The hut to my eyes, as I came into it from the sunlight of the plain,
was almost dark; there were a few dim figures in it, old men or women.
Wawerru, when he realized that he had been run to earth, without a
sound rolled over on his face. Then I saw that long bandages, with
which I had taken so much trouble, had been unwound, and that from
heel to hip his legs were smeared with a thick coat of cow-dung. Now
cow-dung is not actually a bad remedy for burns, since it coagulates
quickly and will keep the air out. But at the moment the sight and
smell of it to me were nauseating, as if deadly—in a kind of self-preservation I tightened my grip on the whip.

I had not, till now, in my mind associated my success or failure in
curing Wawerru's legs with my own fate, or with the fate of the farm.
Standing here in the hut, adjusting my eyes to the twilight of it, I saw
the two as one, and the world round me grew infinitely cheerless, a place
of no hope. I had ventured to believe that efforts of mine might defeat
destiny. It was brought home to me now how deeply I had been mistaken; the balance-sheet was laid before me, and proved that whatever I
took on was destined to end up in failure. Cow-dung was to be my
harvest. I bethought myself of the old Jacobite song:

*Now all is done that could be done.*
*And all is done in vain.*

I spoke no word, I do not think that I gave out any sound at all. But the tears all at once welled out from behind my eyelids, and I could not stop them. In a few moments I felt my face bathed in tears. I kept standing like that for what seemed to me a long time, and the silence of the hut to me was deep. Then, as the situation had to end somehow, I turned and went out, and my tears still flowed abundantly, so that twice I missed the door. Outside the hut I found Rouge waiting; I got into the saddle and rode away slowly.

When I had ridden ten yards, I turned round to look for my dogs. I then saw that a number of people had come out from the huts and were gazing after me. Riding on another ten or twenty yards, I was struck by the thought that this in my squatters was an unusual behaviour. In general, unless they wanted something from me and would shout for it—as the totos, popping from the long grass, screeched out for sugar—or wanted just to send off a friendly greeting: "Jambu, Msabu!" they let me pass fairly unnoticed. I turned round again to have another look at them. This second time there were still more people standing on the grass, immovable, following me with their eyes. Indeed the whole population of the manyatta would have got on their legs to watch Rouge and me slowly disappearing across the plain. I thought: "They have never till now seen me cry. Maybe they have not believed that a white person ever did cry. I ought not to have done it."

The dogs, having finished their investigation of the various scents of the manyatta and their chasing of its hens, were coming with me. We went home together.

Early next morning, before Juma had come in to draw the curtains of my windows, I sensed, by the intensity of the silence round me, that a crowd was gathered at short distance. I had had the same experience before and have written about it. The Africans have got this to them—they will make their presence known by other means than eyesight, hearing or smell, so that you do not tell yourself: "I see them," "I hear them," or "I smell them," but: "They are here." Wild animals have got the same quality, but our domestic animals have lost it.

"They have come up here, then," I reflected. "What are they bringing me?" I got up and went out.

There were indeed a great many people on the terrace. As I kept standing silent, looking at them, they, silent too, formed a circle round me; they obviously would not have let me go away had I wanted to. There were old men and women here, mothers with babies on their

back, impudent Morani, coy Nditos—maidens—and lively, bright-eyed
totos. Gazing from one face to another I realized what in our daily life
together I never thought of: that they were dark, so much darker than I.
Slowly they thronged closer to me.

Confronted with this kind of dumb, deadly determination in the
African, a European in his mind will grope for words in which to
formulate and fix it—in the same way as that in which, in the fairy-
tale, the man pitting his strength against the troll must find out the
name of his adversary and pin him down to a word, or be in a dark,
trollish manner, lost. For a second my mind, running wildly, responded
to the situation in a wild question: "Do they mean to kill me?" The
moment after I struck on the right formula. My people of the farm had
come up to tell me: "The time has come." "It has, I see," in my mind I
assented. "But the time for what?"

An old woman was the first to open her mouth to me.

The old women of the farm were all good friends of mine. I saw less
of them than of the small restless totos, who were ever about my house,
but they had agreed to assume the existence of a particular understanding and intimacy between them and me, as if they had all been aunties
of mine. Kikuyu women with age shrink and grow darker; seen beside
the cinnamon-colored Nditos, sap-filled, sleek lianas of the forest, they
look like sticks of charcoal, weightless, desiccated all through, with a
kind of grim jocosity at the core of them, noble, high-class achievements of the skilled charcoal-burner of existence.

This old woman of the terrace now, in the grip of her left hand, held
forth her right hand to me, as if she were making me a present of it.
Across the wrist ran a scarlet burn. "Msabu," she whimpered into my
face. "I have got a sick hand, sick. It needs medicine." The burn was but
superficial.

An old man with a cut in the leg from his wood-chopper's axe came
up next, then a couple of mothers with feverish babies, then a Moran
with a split lip and another with a sprained ankle, and an Ndito with
a bruise in one round breast. None of the injuries were serious. I was
even pressed upon to examine a collection of splinters in the palm of a
hand, from a climb for honey in a tree.

Slowly I took in the situation. My people of the farm, I realized,
today, in a common great resolution had agreed to bring me what,
against all reason and against the inclination of their own hearts, I
had wanted from them. They must have been grappling with, imparting
to one another and discussing between them the fact: "We have been
trying her too hard. She clearly is unable to bear any more. The time
has come to indulge her."

It could not be explained away that I was being made a fool of. But I was being made so with much generosity.

After a minute or two I could not help laughing. And as, scrutinizing my face, they caught the change in it, they joined me. One after another all faces round me lightened up and broke in laughter. In the faces of toothless old women a hundred delicate wrinkles screwed up cheeks and chin into a baroque, beaming mask—and they were no longer scars left by the warfare of life, but the traces of many laughters.

The merriment ran along the terrace and spread to the edge of it like ripples on water. There are few things in life as sweet as this suddenly rising, clear tide of African laughter surrounding one.

> *Legend has it that a Gaul*
> *seeing wild, fierce Gallic courage*
> *mowed down round him by the rigid*
> *discipline of Roman legions,*
>
> *heavenwards shot his last arrow,*
> *at the God whom he had worshipped,*
> *at the God who had betrayed him.*
> *And then fell with cloven forehead.*
>
> *From the bones of fallen Gauls*
> *peasants of the land built fences*
> *round their fair and fruitful vineyards.*
> *No one had a nobler burial.*

# SIR HERCULES

*Aldous Huxley*

---

ALDOUS HUXLEY (1894– ) had his origins in Surrey from a line on both sides of distinguished writers and thinkers. His wish to enter medicine was thwarted by an early near-blindness which has beset him throughout his long and active literary life. With his early novels such as *Point, Counterpoint* and *Antic Hay* he found expression in bright satirical delineation of his time and society, while with *Brave New World* he plunged into the future and depicted all human problems as solved at last by science. More an intellectual and essayist than a novelist, his talent carries over into other forms, including short stories and screenplays. Indeed, he has long been one of Hollywood's most distinguished—and appreciative—residents. His novels, a form in which he has shown declining interest, have gradually moved from satire to the meditative and mystical.

THE infant who was destined to become the fourth baronet of the name of Lapith was born in the year 1740. He was a very small baby, weighing not more than three pounds at birth, but from the first he was sturdy and healthy. In honour of his maternal grandfather, Sir Hercules Occam of Bishop's Occam, he was christened Hercules. His mother, like many other mothers, kept a notebook, in which his progress from month to month was recorded. He walked at ten months, and before his second year was out he had learnt to speak a number of words. At three years he weighed but twenty-four pounds, and at six, though he could read and write perfectly and showed a remarkable aptitude for music, he was no larger and heavier than a well-grown child of two. Meanwhile, his mother had borne two other children, a boy and a girl, one of whom died of croup during infancy, while the other was carried off by smallpox before it reached the age of five. Hercules remained the only surviving child.

On his twelfth birthday Hercules was still only three feet and two inches in height. His head, which was very handsome and nobly shaped, was too big for his body, but otherwise he was exquisitely proportioned and, for his size, of great strength and agility. His parents, in the hope of making him grow, consulted all the most eminent physicians of the time. Their various prescriptions were followed to the letter, but in vain. One ordered a very plentiful meat diet; another exercise; a third constructed a little rack, modelled on those employed by the Holy Inquisition, on which young Hercules was stretched, with excruciating torments, for half an hour every morning and evening. In the course of the next three years Hercules gained perhaps two inches. After that his growth stopped completely, and he remained for the rest of his life a pigmy of three feet and four inches. His father, who had built the most extravagant hopes upon his son, planning for him in his imagination a military career equal to that of Marlborough, found himself a disappointed man. "I have brought an abortion into the world," he would say, and he took so violent a dislike to his son that the boy dared scarcely come into his presence. His temper, which had been serene, was turned by disappointment to moroseness and savagery. He avoided all company (being, as he said, ashamed to show himself, the father of a *lusus naturae,* among normal, healthy human beings), and took to solitary drinking, which carried him very rapidly to his grave; for the year before Hercules came of age his father was taken off by an apoplexy. His mother, whose love for him had increased with the growth of his father's unkindness, did not long survive, but little more than a year after her husband's death succumbed, after eating two dozen of oysters, to an attack of typhoid fever.

Hercules thus found himself at the age of twenty-one alone in the world, and master of a considerable fortune, including the estate and mansion of Crome. The beauty and intelligence of his childhood had survived into his manly age, and, but for his dwarfish stature, he would have taken his place among the handsomest and most accomplished young men of his time. He was well read in Greek and Latin authors, as well as in all the moderns of any merit who had written in English, French, or Italian. He had a good ear for music, and was no indifferent performer on the violin, which he used to play like a bass viol, seated on a chair with the instrument between his legs. To the music of the harpsichord and clavichord he was extremely partial, but the smallness of his hands made it impossible for him ever to perform upon these instruments. He had a small ivory flute made for him, on which, whenever he was melancholy, he used to play a simple country air or jig, affirming that this rustic music had more power to clear and raise the spirits than the most artificial productions of the masters. From an early age he practised the composition of poetry, but, though conscious of his great powers in this art, he would never publish any specimen of his writing. "My stature," he would say, "is reflected in my verses; if the public were to read them it would not be because I am a poet, but because I am a dwarf." Several MS. books of Sir Hercules's poems survive. A single specimen will suffice to illustrate his qualities as a poet.

In ancient days, while yet the world was young,
Ere Abram fed his flocks or Homer sung;
When blacksmith Tubal tamed creative fire,
And Jabal dwelt in tents and Jubal struck the lyre;
Flesh grown corrupt brought forth a monstrous birth
And obscene giants trod the shrinking earth,
Till God, impatient of their sinful brood,
Gave rein to wrath and drown'd them in the Flood.
Teeming again, repeopled Tellus bore
The lubber Hero and the Man of War;
Huge towers of Brawn, topp'd with an empty Skull,
Witlessly bold, heroically dull.
Long ages pass'd and Man grown more refin'd,
Slighter in music but of vaster Mind,
Smiled at his grandsire's broadsword, bow and bill,
And learn'd to wield the Pencil and the Quill.
The glowing canvas and the written page
Immortaliz'd his name from age to age,
His name emblazon'd on Fame's temple wall;
For Art grew great as Humankind grew small.
Thus man's long progress step by step we trace;
The Giant dies, the hero takes his place;
The Giant vile, the dull heroic Block:
At one we shudder and at one we mock.
Man last appears. In him the Soul's pure flame
Burns brightlier in a not inord'nate frame.
Of old when Heroes fought and Giants swarmed,
Men were huge mounds of matter scarce inform'd;
Wearied by leavening so vast a mass,
The spirit slept and all the mind was crass.
The smaller carcase of these later days
Is soon inform'd; the Soul unwearied plays
And like a Pharos darts abroad her mental rays.
But can we think that Providence will stay
Man's footsteps here upon the upward way?
Mankind in understanding and in grace
Advanc'd so far beyond the Giants' race?
Hence impious thought! Still led by GOD'S own Hand,
Mankind proceeds towards the Promised Land.
A time will come (prophetic, I descry
Remoter dawns along the gloomy sky),
When happy mortals of a Golden Age
Will backward turn the dark historic page,

*And in our vaunted race of Men behold*
*A form as gross, a Mind as dead and cold,*
*As we in Giants see, in warriors of old.*
*A time will come, wherein the soul shall be*
*From all superfluous matter wholly free:*
*When the light body, agile as a fawn's,*
*Shall sport with grace along the velvet lawns.*
*Nature's most delicate and final birth,*
*Mankind perfected shall possess the earth.*
*But ah, not yet! For still the Giants' race,*
*Huge, though diminish'd, tramps the Earth's fair face;*
*Gross and repulsive, yet perversely proud,*
*Men of their imperfections boast aloud.*
*Vain of their bulk, of all they still retain*
*Of giant ugliness absurdly vain;*
*At all that's small they point their stupid scorn*
*And, monsters, think themselves divinely born.*
*Sad is the Fate of those, ah, sad indeed,*
*The rare precursors of the nobler breed!*
*Who come man's golden glory to foretell,*
*But pointing Heav'nwards live themselves in Hell.*

As soon as he came into the estate, Sir Hercules set about re-modelling his household. For though by no means ashamed of his deformity—indeed, if we may judge from the poem quoted above, he regarded himself as being in many ways superior to the ordinary race of man—he found the presence of full-grown men and women embarrassing. Realizing, too, that he must abandon all ambitions in the great world, he determined to retire absolutely from it and to create, as it were, at Crome a private world of his own, in which all should be proportionable to himself. Accordingly, he discharged all the old servants of the house and replaced them gradually, as he was able to find suitable successors, by others of dwarfish stature. In the course of a few years he had assembled about himself a numerous household, no member of which was above four feet high and the smallest among them scarcely two feet and six inches. His father's dogs, such as setters, mastiffs, greyhounds, and a pack of beagles, he sold or gave away as too large and too boisterous for his house, replacing them by pugs and King Charles spaniels and whatever other breeds of dog were the smallest. His father's stable was also sold. For his own use, whether riding or driving, he had six black Shetland ponies, with four very choice piebald animals of New Forest breed.

Having thus settled his household entirely to his own satisfaction, it only remained for him to find some suitable companion with whom to share this paradise. Sir Hercules had a susceptible heart, and had more than once, between the ages of sixteen and twenty, felt what it was to love. But here his deformity had been a source of the most bitter humiliation, for, having once dared to declare himself to a young lady of his choice, he had been received with laughter. On his persisting, she had picked him up and shaken him like an importunate child, telling him to run away and plague her no more. The story soon got about—indeed, the young lady herself used to tell it as a particularly pleasant anecdote—and the taunts and mockery it occasioned were a source of the most acute distress to Hercules. From the poems written at this period we gather that he meditated taking his own life. In course of time, however, he lived down this humiliation; but never again, though he often fell in love, and that very passionately, did he dare to make any advances to those in whom he was interested. After coming to the estate and finding that he was in a position to create his own world as he desired it, he saw that, if he was to have a wife—which he very much desired, being of an affectionate and, indeed, amorous temper—he must choose her as he had chosen his servants—from among the race of dwarfs. But to find a suitable wife was, he found, a matter of some difficulty; for he would marry none who was not distinguished by beauty and gentle birth. The dwarfish daughter of Lord Bemboro he refused on the ground that besides being a pigmy she was hunchbacked: while another young lady, an orphan belonging to a very good family in Hampshire, was rejected by him because her face, like that of so many dwarfs, was wizened and repulsive. Finally, when he was almost despairing of success, he heard from a reliable source that Count Titimalo, a Venetian nobleman, possessed a daughter of exquisite beauty and great accomplishments, who was but three feet in height. Setting out at once for Venice, he went immediately on his arrival to pay his respects to the count, whom he found living with his wife and five children in a very mean apartment in one of the poorer quarters of the town. Indeed, the count was so far reduced in his circumstances that he was even then negotiating (so it was rumoured) with a travelling company of clowns and acrobats, who had had the misfortune to lose their performing dwarf, for the sale of his diminutive daughter Filomena. Sir Hercules arrived in time to save her from this untoward fate, for he was so much charmed by Filomena's grace and beauty, that at the end of three days' courtship he made her a formal offer of marriage, which was accepted by her no less joyfully than by her father, who perceived in an English son-in-law a rich and unfailing source of revenue. After an unostentatious marriage, at which the English ambassador acted as one of the witnesses, Sir Hercules and his bride returned by sea to England, where they settled down, as it proved, to a life of uneventful happiness.

Crome and its household of dwarfs delighted Filomena, who felt herself now for the first time to be a free woman living among her equals in a friendly world. She had many tastes in common with her husband, especially that of music. She had a beautiful voice, of a power surprising in one so small, and could touch A in alt without effort. Accompanied by her husband on his fine Cremona fiddle, which he played, as we have noted before, as one plays a bass viol, she would sing all the liveliest and tenderest airs from the operas and cantatas of her native country. Seated together at the harpsichord, they found that they could with their four hands play all the music written for two hands of ordinary size, a circumstance which gave Sir Hercules unfailing pleasure.

When they were not making music or reading together, which they often did, both in English and Italian, they spent their time in healthful outdoor exercises, sometimes rowing in a little boat on the lake, but more often riding or driving, occupations in which, because they were entirely new to her, Filomena especially delighted. When she had become a perfectly proficient rider, Filomena and her husband used often to go hunting in the park, at that time very much more extensive than it is now. They hunted not foxes nor hares, but rabbits, using a pack of about thirty black and fawn-coloured pugs, a kind of dog which, when not overfed, can course a rabbit as well as any of the smaller breeds. Four dwarf grooms, dressed in scarlet liveries and mounted on white Exmoor ponies, hunted the pack, while their master and mistress, in green habits, followed either on the black Shetlands or on the piebald New Forest ponies. A picture of the whole hunt—dogs, horses, grooms, and masters—was painted by William Stubbs, whose work Sir Hercules admired so much that he invited him, though a man of ordinary stature, to come and stay at the mansion for the purpose of executing this picture. Stubbs likewise painted a portrait of Sir Hercules and his lady driving in their green enamelled calash drawn by four black Shetlands. Sir Hercules wears a plum-coloured velvet coat and white breeches; Filomena is dressed in flowered muslin and a very large hat with pink feathers. The two figures in their gay carriage stand out sharply against a dark background of trees; but to the left of the picture the trees fall away and disappear, so that the four black ponies are seen against a pale and strangely lurid sky that has the golden-brown colour of thunder-clouds lighted up by the sun.

In this way four years passed happily by. At the end of that time Filomena found herself great with child. Sir Hercules was overjoyed. "If God is good," he wrote in his day-book, "the name of Lapith will be preserved and our rarer and more delicate race transmitted through the generations until in the fullness of time the world shall recognize

the superiority of those beings whom now it uses to make mock of." On
his wife's being brought to bed of a son he wrote a poem to the same
effect. The child was christened Ferdinando in memory of the builder
of the house.

With the passage of the months a certain sense of disquiet began to
invade the minds of Sir Hercules and his lady. For the child was
growing with an extraordinary rapidity. At a year he weighed as much
as Hercules had weighed when he was three. "Ferdinando goes
*crescendo*," wrote Filomena in her diary. "It seems not natural." At
eighteen months the baby was almost as tall as their smallest jockey,
who was a man of thirty-six. Could it be that Ferdinando was destined
to become a man of the normal, gigantic dimensions? It was a thought
to which neither of his parents dared yet give open utterance, but in
the secrecy of their respective diaries they brooded over it in terror and
dismay.

On his third birthday Ferdinando was taller than his mother and not
more than a couple of inches short of his father's height. "To-day for
the first time," wrote Sir Hercules, "we discussed the situation. The
hideous truth can be concealed no longer: Ferdinando is not one of us.
On this, his third birthday, a day when we should have been rejoicing
at the health, the strength, and beauty of our child, we wept together
over the ruin of our happiness. God give us strength to bear this cross."

At the age of eight Ferdinando was so large and so exuberantly
healthy that his parents decided, though reluctantly, to send him to
school. He was packed off to Eton at the beginning of the next half. A
profound peace settled upon the house. Ferdinando returned for the
summer holidays larger and stronger than ever. One day he knocked
down the butler and broke his arm. "He is rough, inconsiderate, un-
amenable to persuasion," wrote his father. "The only thing that will
teach him manners is corporal chastisement." Ferdinando, who at this
age was already seventeen inches taller than his father, received no
corporal chastisement.

One summer holidays about three years later Ferdinando returned to
Crome accompanied by a very large mastiff dog. He had bought it from
an old man at Windsor who found the beast too expensive to feed. It
was a savage, unreliable animal; hardly had it entered the house when it
attacked one of Sir Hercules's favourite pugs, seizing the creature in its
jaws and shaking it till it was nearly dead. Extremely put out by this
occurrence, Sir Hercules ordered that the beast should be chained up in
the stable-yard. Ferdinando sullenly answered that the dog was his, and
he would keep it where he pleased. His father, growing angry, bade
him take the animal out of the house at once, on pain of his utmost
displeasure. Ferdinando refused to move. His mother at this moment

coming into the room, the dog flew at her, knocked her down, and in a twinkling had very severely mauled her arm and shoulder; in another instant it must infallibly have had her by the throat, had not Sir Hercules drawn his sword and stabbed the animal to the heart. Turning on his son, he ordered him to leave the room immediately, as being unfit to remain in the same place with the mother whom he had nearly murdered. So awe-inspiring was the spectacle of Sir Hercules standing with one foot on the carcase of the gigantic dog, his sword drawn and still bloody, so commanding were his voice, his gestures, and the expression of his face, that Ferdinando slunk out of the room in terror and behaved himself for all the rest of the vacation in an entirely exemplary fashion. His mother soon recovered from the bites of the mastiff, but the effect on her mind of this adventure was ineradicable; from that time forth she lived always among imaginary terrors.

The two years which Ferdinando spent on the Continent, making the Grand Tour, were a period of happy repose for his parents. But even now the thought of the future haunted them; nor were they able to solace themselves with all the diversions of their younger days. The Lady Filomena had lost her voice and Sir Hercules was grown too rheumatical to play the violin. He, it is true, still rode after his pugs, but his wife felt herself too old and, since the episode of the mastiff, too nervous for such sports. At most, to please her husband, she would follow the hunt at a distance in a little gig drawn by the safest and oldest of the Shetlands.

The day fixed for Ferdinando's return came round. Filomena, sick with vague dreads and presentiments, retired to her chamber and her bed. Sir Hercules received his son alone. A giant in a brown travelling-suit entered the room. "Welcome home, my son," said Sir Hercules in a voice that trembled a little.

"I hope I see you well, sir." Ferdinando bent down to shake hands, then straightened himself up again. The top of his father's head reached to the level of his hip.

Ferdinando had not come alone. Two friends of his own age accompanied him, and each of the young men had brought a servant. Not for thirty years had Crome been desecrated by the presence of so many members of the common race of men. Sir Hercules was appalled and indignant, but the laws of hospitality had to be obeyed. He received the young gentlemen with grave politeness and sent the servants to the kitchen, with orders that they should be well cared for.

The old family dining-table was dragged out into the light and dusted (Sir Hercules and his lady were accustomed to dine at a small table twenty inches high). Simon, the aged butler, who could only just

look over the edge of the big table, was helped at supper by the three
servants brought by Ferdinando and his guests.

Sir Hercules presided, and with his usual grace supported a conversation on the pleasures of foreign travel, the beauties of art and nature
to be met with abroad, the opera at Venice, the singing of the orphans
in the churches of the same city, and on other topics of a similar nature.
The young men were not particularly attentive to his discourses; they
were occupied in watching the efforts of the butler to change the plates
and replenish the glasses. They covered their laughter by violent and
repeated fits of coughing or choking. Sir Hercules affected not to notice, but changed the subject of the conversation to sport. Upon this
one of the young men asked whether it was true, as he had heard, that
he used to hunt the rabbit with a pack of pug dogs. Sir Hercules
replied that it was, and proceeded to describe the chase in some detail.
The young men roared with laughter.

When supper was over, Sir Hercules climbed down from his chair
and, giving as his excuse that he must see how his lady did, bade them
good-night. The sound of laughter followed him up the stairs. Filomena
was not asleep; she had been lying on her bed listening to the sound of
enormous laughter and the tread of strangely heavy feet on the stairs
and along the corridors. Sir Hercules drew a chair to her bedside and sat
there for a long time in silence, holding his wife's hand and sometimes
gently squeezing it. At about ten o'clock they were startled by a violent
noise. There was a breaking of glass, a stamping of feet, with an
outburst of shouts and laughter. The uproar continuing for several
minutes, Sir Hercules rose to his feet and, in spite of his wife's en-
treaties, prepared to go and see what was happening. There was no light
on the staircase, and Sir Hercules groped his way down cautiously,
lowering himself from stair to stair and standing for a moment on each
tread before adventuring on a new step. The noise was louder here;
the shouting articulated itself into recognizable words and phrases. A
line of light was visible under the dining-room door. Sir Hercules
tiptoed across the hall towards it. Just as he approached the door there
was another terrific crash of breaking glass and jangled metal. What
could they be doing? Standing on tiptoe he managed to look through
the keyhole. In the middle of the ravaged table old Simon, the butler,
so primed with drink that he could scarcely keep his balance, was
dancing a jig. His feet crunched and tinkled among the broken glass,
and his shoes were wet with spilt wine. The three young men sat
round, thumping the table with their hands or with the empty wine
bottles, shouting and laughing encouragement. The three servants leaning against the wall laughed too. Ferdinando suddenly threw a handful of walnuts at the dancer's head, which so dazed and surprised the

little man that he staggered and fell down on his back, upsetting a decanter and several glasses. They raised him up, gave him some brandy to drink, thumped him on the back. The old man smiled and hic-coughed, "To-morrow," said Ferdinando, "we'll have a concerted ballet of the whole household." "With father Hercules wearing his club and lion-skin," added one of his companions, and all three roared with laughter.

Sir Hercules would look and listen no further. He crossed the hall once more and began to climb the stairs, lifting his knees painfully high at each degree. This was the end; there was no place for him now in the world, no place for him and Ferdinando together.

His wife was still awake; to her questioning glance he answered, "They are making mock of old Simon. To-morrow it will be our turn." They were silent for a time.

At last Filomena said, "I do not want to see to-morrow."

"It is better not," said Sir Hercules. Going into his closet he wrote in his day-book a full and particular account of all the events of the eve-ning. While he was still engaged in this task he rang for a servant and ordered hot water and a bath to be made ready for him at eleven o'clock. When he had finished writing he went into his wife's room, and preparing a dose of opium twenty times as strong as that which she was accustomed to take when she could not sleep, he brought it to her, saying, "Here is your sleeping-draught."

Filomena took the glass and lay for a little time, but did not drink immediately. The tears came into her eyes. "Do you remember the songs we used to sing, sitting out there *sulla terrazza* in summer-time?" She began singing softly in her ghost of a cracked voice a few bars from Stradella's "*Amor, amor, non dormir più.*" "And you playing on the violin. It seems such a short time ago, and yet so long, long, long. *Addio, amore. A rivederti.*" She drank off the draught and, laying back on the pillow, closed her eyes. Sir Hercules kissed her hand and tip-toed away, as though he were afraid of waking her. He returned to his closet, and having recorded his wife's last words to him, he poured into his bath the water that had been brought up in accordance with his orders. The water being too hot for him to get into the bath at once, he took down from the shelf his copy of Suetonius. He wished to read how Seneca had died. He opened the book at random. "But dwarfs," he read, "he held in abhorrence as being *lusus naturae* and of evil omen." He winced as though he had been struck. This same Augustus, he remembered, had exhibited in the amphitheatre a young man called Lucius, of good family, who was not quite two feet in height and weighed seventeen pounds, but had a stentorian voice. He turned over the pages. Tiberius, Caligula, Claudius, Nero: it was a tale of growing horror. "Seneca his preceptor, he forced to kill himself." And there was Petronius, who had called his friends about him at the last, bidding them talk to him, not of the consolations of philosophy, but of love and gallantry, while the life was ebbing away through his opened veins. Dipping his pen once more in the ink he wrote on the last page of his diary: "He died a Roman death." Then, putting the toes of one foot into the water and finding that it was not too hot, he threw off his dressing-gown and, taking a razor in his hand, sat down in the bath. With one deep cut he severed the artery in his left wrist, then lay back and composed his mind to meditation. The blood oozed out, floating through the water in dissolving wreaths and spirals. In a little while the whole bath was tinged with pink. The colour deepened; Sir Hercules felt himself mastered by an invincible drowsiness; he was sinking from vague dream to dream. Soon he was sound asleep. There was not much blood in his small body.

# Part II
# OTHER PLACES

# PARIS! PARIS!

## *Irwin Shaw*

IRWIN SHAW (1913–   ) It was his one-act play *Bury the Dead* that brought this Bronx born and Brooklyn bred writer to wide public notice. Before that, his had been the typical city life of a boy of small means who on leaving school tried many ways of making a living, as a furniture salesman, childrens' tutor, even small-time pro baseball player. Then he returned to school and after graduating from Brooklyn College became a staff writer for radio shows like *Dick Tracy* and *The Gumps*. Soon began the succession of brilliant short stories which have made his name a by-word in that field, occasionally interrupted in more recent years by novels which have invariably commanded attention. Among these was *The Young Lions* which helped to bring Mr. Shaw an international reputation. All his work is marked by a deep social awareness and by dialogue and characterizations that are vividly real and touching. Above all, per-haps, is his ability to convey the passing joy of the moment. This is richly manifest in the piece that follows about the city where he now lives.

You start at a café table because everything in Paris starts at a café table. You are waiting for the girl you love.

She is young and American and perfect. She has straight legs and an enormous appetite and solid low-heeled shoes and she likes to walk and she has just arrived in the city for the first time in her life and she likes to listen to you talk and she is imaginary. She is late, of course, because you have been so conditioned by the women you have known that even the ones you invent can't meet you on time. You have in-vented her because you have been daydreaming; you have been playing with the idea of pleasure and it has occurred to you that there could be few things more pleasurable in this sad world than to roam Paris for a day hand-in-hand with such a girl.

You sit there, glowing with the prospect of unfolding Paris for the first time to this superb, unreal and uninitiated creature.

It is summer or autumn or winter or spring and it is sunny and raining and there is snow on the statues and bits of ice in the Seine and the trees are all in full blossom and the swimmers are diving into the purified water in the wooden pools along the riverbanks and it is early in the morning and late at night and the President is giving a ball and the Garde Republicaine is out in breastplates and horsehair tails and the North Africans are rioting for autonomy at the Place de la République and all the policemen have dents in their shining steel helmets.

Mass is being celebrated at St.-Sulpice and they are burying an actor in Père Lachaise. There are long lines outside the mail windows at the American Express. The young lieutenants are leaving for Indo-China. There is a fair on the Esplanade des Invalides and the phrenologists are doing well next to the shooting galleries. They are selling perfume on the Rue de la Paix and the wine merchants are worried about this year's Burgundy and a thousand deep baskets of water cress are being stacked at Les Halles. The busses are coming in from the Orly airfield to the Gare des Invalides with the passengers from New York and South Africa and Warsaw and the trains going south have whole cars filled with bicycles for the vacationers en route to the Côte d'Azur. It is August and half the shops are closed, with their iron shutters down, and it is February and the porters wait with wheel chairs at the Gare de l'Est for the skiers with broken legs.

On the gray islands in the river, they are turning out 450 buglike, four-horsepower Renaults a day and the communists are painting *Americans Go Home* on the iron bridges. They are selling canaries near the Hôtel de Ville and putting out newspapers on the Rue Réaumur and the headlines show that the Premier is worried about the price of butter, that French football has suffered another catastrophe at Colombes, and that a young woman with an Algerian lover has walled up her landlady in the cellar. The butchers are putting lilacs in their windows and everybody at the Flea Market is guaranteeing that everything is over a hundred years old. A carrousel calliope is playing under the elevated structure on the Boulevard Garibaldi and children are getting rides in goat carts near the American Embassy. There is a new middleweight fighting at the Palais des Sports who will never make anyone forget Marcel Cerdan. A pensioner has committed suicide because he was afraid the inflation would deprive him of his tobacco, and there is a banquet planned for the millers who are accused of driving a whole town mad with flour tainted by ergot.

It is Sunday and the couples are sprawled all over the Bois and the lions are roaring for the crowds across the deep moats in the Vincennes zoo. It is the fourteenth of July, and there are parades and the placing of wreaths in the memory of the dead and the memory of the Bastille and the memory of the unfortunate Foullon, whose head was carried on a pike up the Rue St.-Martin in 1789, his mouth stuffed with grass because he had said of the people of Paris, *"Eh bien. If this riffraff has no bread, they'll eat hay."* There is also the sound of jets flying in formation over the city, and there is dancing in the streets and in the gardens of the great houses, and there are fireworks in the sky behind the cathedral and marshals of France standing at attention while the bands play the anthem, whose words include, "To arms, citizens!"

It is a workday and the open platforms of the busses are crowded with people who breathe deeply of the gasoline fumes on their way to their offices. It is market day and the housewives push through the stalls under the trees at the Place de l'Alma, next to the Salon Nautique, looking at the prices of the chickens and the cheeses and the celery root and complaining that life is too expensive.

There is the smell of freshly baked bread in the air and the streets are full of people hurrying home with long, unwrapped loaves under their arms. In the crowded *charcuteries* there are a dozen different kinds of *pâté* on the counters and Alsatian *choucroute* and *gnocchi* and snails and *coquilles* St.-Jacques, ready to be put into the oven, and the salesgirls sound like a cageful of flutes as they call out the prices to the customers. In the Métro, there is an experimental train that runs on rubber tires, to alleviate the nervous agony of being alive in the 20th Century. In the Berlitz classrooms the activities of the family Dupont are carefully followed as they say good morning to each other, open and close doors and lay various objects on a table. On the Ile St.-Louis, the owner of a convertible finds its top slashed for the seventh time and decides he will have to buy a closed car.

In the lobbies of the big hotels, sharp-eyed men are whispering to each other, making deals to import and export vital materials, and an American at the bar of the George Cinq says to his business associates, "I don't like to boast, but I am very close to the Virginia tobacco industry."

The all-girl orchestras are tuning up for their afternoon programs of waltzes in the big, bare cafés on the Boulevard Clichy and in the *bals musettes* shopgirls dance with clerks under the paintings of thugs and apaches. There are thousands of people lined up at the Porte Saint-Cloud to watch a bicycle race and everybody is going to Deauville for the week end.

The fountains are playing at the Rond-Point, casting a fine spray over the flower borders and Notre-Dame is illuminated and looks as light as a dream on its stone island and the streets are empty and the traffic heavy and you sit there planning this limitless, all-seasoned, per-

fect day with your perfect girl in the city which is the Jerusalem of
many strange pilgrimages and the capital of nostalgia and which you
can never leave without tasting a faint, bitter flavor of exile.

You sit at the table on land that has been rented from the munici-
pality for 4000 francs a square meter a year and you remember that
there is a rumor that the government, in a typically indirect and tactful attempt to limit alcoholism, is going to raise the price of its sidewalks
to make drinking less general or at least more expensive. You are sipping
a Cinzano because gin is so dear and it is too early for brandy. Behind
you, on the wall of the café, there is a yellowed copy of the law to suppress public drunkenness. The law was passed during World War I but
is still in effect and you admire the men who could worry about things
like that with the Germans only a few miles away and dropping shells
every twenty minutes into the city from the long-range gun which
they called Big Bertha and which was trained on Paris from the St.
Gobain Forest, eighty-two miles distant.

You lift your eyes above the rim of your glass and read that anyone
who is found for the first time in a state of manifest drunkenness in
the streets, roads, cafés, cabarets or other public places can be fined between one and five francs, which at the present rate would range between one quarter of a cent and about a penny. But if you get caught
manifestly drunk twice, the results, according to the proclamation, promise to be more grave: For two years you lose the right to vote, the
right to serve as a juror or in the administration of the government and
the right to carry arms, and you are deprived, according to the small
print, of you paternal powers over your children and your descendants.

You sip soberly at your drink and peer out among the passers-by for
the bright American head which is bound to look a little artless and
unpremeditated among the clever, artificially streaked, short hair of
the Parisian women on the boulevard. The girl you love has not yet
arrived, and you half-close your eyes and plan the first step.

First, there should be a general, bird's-eye view of the city, and the
best place for that is the top of the Eiffel Tower. From there, the city
lies embraced by its winding river and flows in a silvery haze over its
moderate hills and its central plain. You can look out over the homes
and the shops and the cemeteries and places of worship of three million
people and you can see the hill in Montmartre where the Temple of
Mercury used to stand and where St. Denis was beheaded. You can
trace the course of the river and see where the canals join it and the
Marne, and you can tell the girl about the Norsemen who sailed up
the river in their oared galleys in the 9th Century, jovially axing the

farmers and the city dwellers along the banks, as was the custom of travelers in that time.

There is one drawback about the Tower, though: the elevator makes you nervous. You know that you are unreasonable. You know that since it opened for business in 1889, it has carried millions of people safely up to the top. But you suffer a little from vertigo, and every time you get into the creaking, slightly tilted car you regret, with unreasonable chauvinism, being that high in the air and dependent for your life on French machinery. You would depend unhesitatingly upon French courage to get you out of danger, on French medicine to cure a stomach ache, upon French wit to make you laugh or a French wife to make you happy—but all that cable, all those girders, all those grinding gears. . . . You decide to settle for a more moderate eminence; the top of the Arch of Triumph is quite high enough for a young girl's first view of Paris and its elevator is comfortably enclosed in a stone shaft.

Anyway, you will tell her, Paris is not a city of heights. Its architects, out of a respect for man, have made certain that man is not dwarfed by his works here. It is a city built to human scale, so that no man should feel pygmied here. Parisians are devoted to their sky and have passed a set of complicated laws designed to keep the height of buildings at a modest level, so that the sky—soft, streaked, gentle, beloved by painters—can be a constant, intimate presence above the roofs and the treetops. In defense of their sky, Parisians can be outlandishly fierce. Recently, a builder in Neuilly put up an apartment house taller than the legal limit and was ordered by the court to tear down the top two stories, although they had been leased in advance and there is a crucial housing shortage. In addition the builder was forced to pay a whopping fine for every day that the offending twenty feet of construction loomed above the skyline. And then, as an aesthetic afterthought, the judge sentenced him to jail. Oh, you think, remembering the caged and distant sky above your native city, if only there were more builders in Sing Sing.

From the top of the monument, staring out at the city, your girl doesn't say anything because she is perfect. The great avenues, which Baron Haussmann, Napoleon III's prefect of police, created to get the mob of Paris out into the open where he could use cavalry on them when they wanted a raise in salary or wished to murder a minister, sweep out to all points of the compass.

The boulevards are named after victories and soldiers and on the Arch itself are the names of one hundred and seventy-two battles chiseled into the stone. Many of the streets of Paris are labeled for battlefields on which Frenchmen have conquered and you wonder what it

must do to the spirit of the citizens of a city to have the sound of triumph on their lips every time they give an address to a taxi driver, and
if they would be different today if, along with the Avenue de Wagram
and the Avenue de Friedland, there were a Boulevard Sedan, a Rue
Waterloo and a Place of the Surrender.

There are so many trees that when they are in foliage and seen from
above, much of the city seems to be built in a giant park. Close by,
the city leans against the green escarpments of Saint-Cloud and Saint-
Germain, across the bending river, reminding you that Paris is more intimate with and more accessible to the countryside than any other great
city in the world. The slate, jumbled world of the rooftops is pewter
and lavender, Paris' own colors, and there is the gleam of innumerable studio windows, facing to the north. The pinkish Carrousel past
the other end of the Champs-Élysées is like a distant and frivolous reflection of the Arch, on whose peak you are standing, and the wind
up here carries a frail leaf-and-mold smell of the river with it. The
white dome of Sacré-Coeur speaks of 19th Century religion on the
heights of Montmartre and you can see the gray, medieval stone tower
of Saint-Germain-des-Prés rising on the opposite bank from its nest of
cafés.

Standing there, with the whole city spread around you, its palaces
and spires and statues glistening in the damp sunlight, you reflect aloud
to the girl on how wise Parisians are to have had ancestors who were
ruled over by tyrants, because tyrants are egotists with an itch to build
monuments to themselves. Then after a while you get rid of the tyrants
and are left with the Louvre and the Tuileries and the obelisk and the
Place Vendôme and the brave, sculptured horses and the great boulevards that were built because someone was ruthless enough and powerful enough to tear down acre after acre of people's homes and pave what
used to be somebody's kitchen and plant chestnut trees in somebody
else's bedroom. You reflect on the selfishness of being alive in your own
time. You are delighted with what Louis XIV did to the city with the
taxes he squeezed from the poor, and with what Napoleon built on
the blood of a generation of young Frenchmen, though you would
struggle to the death against a new Louis or a later Napoleon, no matter how many arches and palaces he guaranteed for your descendants to
enjoy on their visit from America a hundred years from now.

You remember the first time you climbed to the top of the Arch,
which was just after the Liberation, when the 28th Division marched
past to show Paris the Americans were really here. You remember the
noise the tanks made on the Champs-Elysées, and the massed, weary,
pleasant young faces of the soldiers, and the absence of music because
they were all going to fight that night at Saint-Denis and they had no

time for bands. And you realize that every time you think of the city, there is something of that time in your feeling for it.

It is difficult not to love a city you have seen for the first time on the day it was liberated. And Paris was liberated in just the right way. It hadn't been bombed, except on the outskirts, and all the bridges were still standing and the inhabitants themselves had spent the last five days firing off small arms and feeling heroic and the weather was sunny and warm and all the girls wore their best dresses and there were enough Germans left to put up a show of war, and give the local boys an opportunity to behave martially in front of good audiences before the final surrender.

Everybody was thin from the war, but not starving, and you kept hearing the *Marseillaise,* and the smoke from a few small fires rose unimportantly here and there and for an afternoon it felt as though the war had ended and it couldn't have ended in a better place. The word was that von Sholtitz had spared the city, against Hitler's orders, and the Parisians felt, of course, who could have the heart to blow up Paris? There was blood against some of the walls and the next day they were piling flowers there for the dead and everybody was kissing everybody else and there was a considerable amount of free wine.

Travelers are always telling you their favorite times for seeing a city for the first time: Rome at Easter, London in June, New York in October, Pittsburgh at five o'clock in the morning. And you tell the girl to make sure to see Paris the next afternoon it is liberated. It is a city which takes gratefully to a mixture of riot, celebration and bloodshed. The citizens are experts at putting up and tearing down barricades, at killing each other, and at greeting and firing upon troops. The streets are admirably arranged for mass demonstrations, parades and the maneuvering of armor. The buildings are solid and made of stone and merely chip when hit by shells and in a year or two the damp, benevolent air ages the scars so that they are indistinguishable from the precious marks of the centuries before. There are monuments everywhere which lend an atmosphere of significance to acts performed in their vicinity and when people die in front of them in the belief that they are preserving civilization, civilization takes on a tangible and satisfactory presence.

You tell something of this to the girl whose hair is blowing and whose eyes are shining here above the jumble of stone and memory and history and she squeezes your hand and says, "Isn't it time for lunch? I'm *dying.*"

Then you begin a ritual which is one of the most pleasant in the world—deciding slowly and carefully which place in all the city of Paris is the one place you wish to lunch that day. You can go to the run-down old hotel on the hill at Saint-Cloud, which has a terrace over-looking some tennis courts, with the river down at the bottom of the slope and the city lost beyond its trees just three hundred yards away on the opposite bank, and you can sit out there getting sunburned, feeding off the tableful of hors d'oeuvres, watching the French play tennis. (The French play a crafty, deft game, slow and full of lobs and chops and angles, and unless you're Sedgman or McGregor it is less tantalizing to eat lunch and watch them than play against them.) The hotel used to be a club for American airborne officers in the hi-larious summer just after the war and cognac used to be ten cents a glass and everybody used to mix it with Coca-Cola and there was a pretty waitress there who decided one night she was wildly in love with an airborne major who weighed a hundred and thirty-five pounds and who was working for the National Broadcasting Company in Chi-cago the last time you heard about him.

Or, since it is the girl's first day in town and you feel limitlessly wealthy in her presence, you might take a taxi out to the Bois and eat in the restaurant under the glass chandeliers that are swung from the trees and order trout and a bottle of white wine and take a walk later and watch the ceremonious ladies and gentlemen cantering around the bridle paths as though nothing had happened since 1900. And you could walk in the forest, which is amazingly like a real forest for a tract of land so close to a large city, and imagine how it must have looked when the troops of Wellington and the Czar were encamped there in 1815 after Napoleon had had his final bad time.

If it is a gray, autumnal day, you can walk on over to Auteil with her and wander around the almost empty stands and watch the steeplechase races, buying the odds from dusty men in the paddock who have them written down on flimsy strips of yellow paper, and putting your bets down, as usual, on the horse that falls at the last hedge, but enjoying the stretching deep green field and the inconsequent way the horses vanish behind trees, carrying your money with them into obscurity. And you can regret the decline of jump racing in America and the lack of variety in the dirt tracks of Saratoga and Arlington and Santa Anita, where the horses always run the same way, like wooden horses on a merry-go-round and where your money is always painfully visible as it is being lost.

But if your girl doesn't feel like open air her first afternoon, you can be less enterprising and walk through the 8th, or American, *arrondisse-ment,* because at certain moments it looks as though the French had moved out and the Americans moved in, and go to a small restaurant which has grape vines planted all along its sliding glass windows, so that everyone is reflected in shimmering green above the tablecloths. It is not your favorite restaurant, but you were the witness there to a meal that was not so much a lunch as a ceremony, an act of devotion, a celebration of the mystic nature of food, a reverent wallowing in gluttony that erased for two hours all memory of the drugstore sandwiches and hasty milk shakes of your native land.

The meal was eaten by four grave-faced businessmen, obviously men of importance and economic power, and they started with *pâté de foie gras,* pink and fatty, and went on to *quenelles de brochet*—river fish, flaked and mixed with soaked bread and crumbs, kidney fat and eggs, and covered with a sauce of mushrooms and cream. The four gentlemen—talking in subdued, polite voices of taxes, labor policies, import difficulties and the necessity for expanding plants—ate solidly and industriously, washing the *quenelles* down with a half bottle of Chablis apiece. Then they moved on to slablike Chateaubriands, blue and bloody and complete with fried potatoes and *Bordelaise* sauce and two bottles of Nuits St. Georges. Then, of course, there was salad and cheese Brie and Camembert and plump chunks of pale Gruyère, with another bottle of Nuits St. Georges, and fruit and *crêpes,* flaming with liqueurs, and finally coffee and two brandies apiece, after which they solemnly rose from the table, shook hands and went back to their offices to oversee the manufacture of automobiles or the transfer of stock.

You walk past the shop where you can buy an umbrella for ninety dollars and past the doorway where a ragged, shapeless old lady, wrapped in newspapers, slept all winter, as though she had a lease on the space, past the big hotels where the Hollywood people stay and in front of which there are the parked Cadillacs and the taxis that have signs in their windows, "English Spoken." You go past the corner where a squarely built, rubber-booted, peasantlike flower girl, with bright red cheeks and wearing a fluttering apron, offers lilacs and violets and gladiolas, which she brings each morning in a taxi, whose driver she tips handsomely. You skirt the religious school behind its wall, where the eight-year-old boys arrive bare-legged and chilled each morning and gravely shake hands with each other before going in to their catechism. You walk past the café with the inviting name of The Beautiful Ironworker, at whose tables sit the mannequins from the nearby fashion houses, and American soldiers, and a number of Rumanians and Hungarians speaking in their native tongues. The café is dominated by a coffee machine only a little smaller than a locomotive boiler, and the man who tends it leaps from lever to lever and wheel to wheel like a nervous engineer trying to run a dynamo that is slightly out of order. The coffee is black and, contrary to the usual slander, delicious; and if you want it *au lait,* the man behind the counter pours some milk into a copper pitcher and shoots steam into it with a roaring hoarse noise and serves your coffee frothy and bubbled.

You arrive at the restaurant, but the four heroes are not there that afternoon and you decide to prolong the ecstasy of choosing a place to eat and you saunter down toward the river and if it is spring the chestnuts are in bloom, pink and white, and even if your girl has never been to Paris before she has read enough about the chestnut trees of Paris so that you don't have to say anything about *them*. But if it is late spring, the blossoms drift thickly along the curbs, swirling up in pink and white clouds with the wind of passing automobiles, and the young girls float across the streets in leafy light and shadow, going to and coming from First Communion in their trailing white veils, like frail, light-footed, grave-eyed brides.

Tied up at the stone riverbanks are the oil barges and the pleasure craft, which can be berthed by payment of a nominal rental to the city and which then can boast what must certainly be the most attractive address in the world, "The River Seine, just a little east of the Pont Alexander III."

You pass the Grand Palais, where the big exhibitions are held and where there was the scandal of the Salon d'Automne, when some propaganda paintings by communists were hung, then taken down, then hung again, and you remember one in particular, which was called *The Good Health of Comrade Thorez*. Comrade Thorez is the head of the French Communist Party and he was in Moscow at the time being treated for a stroke and the painting showed a band of uniformly smiling workers dancing and registering pleasure while a rosy young workman held up, in the foreground, a newspaper which carried a headline announcing Comrade Thorez' recovery and it was hard to see whom the picture could damage, except possibly Comrade Thorez and then only if he were an art critic.

You cross the Bridge of the Concorde and stare at the Chambre des Députés. There seem to be dozens of policemen on duty there, in front of the statues, as though the legislators half expected a rush of citizens to flood past the gates in a berserk desire to vote. Inside, the government is probably falling, and deputies are almost certainly making speeches denouncing each other for their behavior at the time of Munich, or at the signing of the Nazi-Soviet Pact, or during the Occupation, and the right and the left are insulting each other and voting together against the government on every proposal. The deputies, in their red-plush amphitheater, do not have the look of ponderous, fleshy well-being of our own Congressmen. They seem small, quick, intellectual, and poised for flight, and they have an air of restrained ir-

ritation with each other, like passengers in a crowded elevator that has
been stuck between floors for a long time. And you remember what a
French friend said to you about the then current premier. "If that man
is to be a success," he said, "he must make the French eat worse next
year. Anyone can demand austerity in England and get away with it.
But in France it takes character."

It was in this chamber that Clemenceau, when he was premier, came
out with one of the most invigoratingly candid statements ever pronounced by the head of a state. "I am against all governments," he
growled, "including my own."

You wonder how far the old man would have gotten in an American
election with talk like that.

Poised there, in the middle of the city, before the seat of troubled
democracy, looking across the bridge at the immense stone stretch of the
Place de la Concorde, you can go in a dozen different, inviting directions. Because it is lunchtime, there is not much traffic, since all
Paris declares a profound truce with business between the hours of
twelve and two. You would not be surprised if you heard that the
underworld had an unwritten agreement with the police not to pick a
pocket or knife an associate at lunchtime.

Back across the bridge there is the restaurant in which each year
the jury meets and has lunch while they vote the Prix Goncourt to
the best novel of the year. After reading about the Prize lunch in the
papers, you went to the restaurant the day following such a meeting on
the intelligent assumption that any place good enough for ten middle-
aged, successful French writers deserved your patronage.

Or you could wander down along the riverside, past the Beaux-Arts,
which has been responsible for so much fine painting, since almost
every good French artist has studied there at one time or another and
has left swearing to violate every principle he was taught within its
walls. And, sticking to the river, you could go to the restaurant on the
corner of the Place St.-Michel and sit at a window on the second floor
and look across at Notre-Dame while you eat wild duck with blood
sauce or you can go to the restaurant on the Quai de la Tournelle
which is decorated with large jars of pickles and photographs of wres-
tlers being hurled through the air. On the way, you can look at the
paintings in the windows or fuss around the bookstalls and pick up
magazines that were printed under the Germans during the Occupation
and which are ostensibly banned, or buy an ornately printed card which
contains an invocation to Paris by Victor Hugo and which reads in
part:

Cities are bibles of stone. This city possesses no single dome, roof or pavement which does not convey some message of alliance and of union, and which does not offer some lesson, example or advice. Let the people of all the world come to this prodigious alphabet of monuments, of tombs and of trophies to learn peace and to unlearn the meaning of hatred. Let them be confident. For Paris has proven itself. To have once been Lutece and to have become Paris—what could be a more magnificent symbol! To have been mud and to have become spirit!

At lunch you can remember that Victor Hugo also said "Paris is the ceiling of the human race," after which he was forced to flee to the islands of Jersey and Guernsey where he remained for the eighteen years of Napoleon III's reign. When he returned they began naming streets and squares after him and they have scarcely stopped since. Parisians seem to have a habit of exiling their heroes, or guillotining them, and making up for it later with street markers. Voltaire spent a good deal of his life in Germany and Switzerland and when in due course they came to bury him in the Panthéon they discovered that his heart was missing and the rumor is that it was mislaid in a desk drawer which was sold by a junkman. Danton paid with his head for his activities in the city, but the city replaced it for the bronze statue of him on the Place de l'Odéon. Poor Courbet, too, who painted women's breasts so well, took down the statue of Napoleon from its pedestal on the Vendôme Column during the Commune, on the grounds that it was a warlike and inartistic creation. Then, when the tide of government changed, he was put in jail and had to turn into a painter of fruits and vegetables because they wouldn't allow his models into the jail. And, much later, the government demanded that he pay the costs of restoring the monument, which came to 323,000 francs. His paintings were seized as partial payment and with the balance staring him in the face, he fled to Switzerland, where he died, and now, of course, there is a Passage Courbet in Passy.

Replete with lunch and praising the wine, and happy that you will be hungry again in six hours, you and your girl leave the restaurant and find the Rue de Seine, where the little art galleries, the antique shops and the butcher shops stand side by side. There are larks in boxes on the butchers' marble tables, and partridge and wild doves flutter dead and head down, their wings outspread, in long strings across the open fronts of the stores and the butchers in their sweaters and aprons look ruddy and frozen and keep blowing on their hands all winter. You buy a snuffbox and price some silver and haggle over a candlestick and notice the influence of Picasso on everybody and go into a tiny gallery which is having a *vernissage* of the works of a young painter who makes a specialty of lonely, moonlit cold walls around abandoned, dreamlike ports. The little room is crowded with people who are not looking at the pictures. There is a great deal of conversation and the young painter is standing alone in a corner, looking lonely and moonlit and abandoned.

You walk toward the Rodin Museum, which is not too far away, because you want to show your girl the thirty-nine statues of Balzac which the sculptor produced out of his relentless energy and disatisfaction, when he was commissioned to create a monument of the novelist to be erected at the angle of the Boulevards Raspail and Montparnasse. On the way you pass a horsemeat shop, under its sign of a gilded equine head, and you peer into a pharmacy window and see a celluloid contraption, equipped with a movable disk, with lines and dates and numbers drawn on it and which is advertised as a fecundity meter in this country which frowns on more direct methods of birth control.

There is also a rolling pin with rubber spikes which is guaranteed to work off excess fat and a preparation for the skin which is supposed to ward off old age. The prescription desk is usually busy, because French doctors rarely carry medicines with them, and if they are to inject you with anything, send you to the nearest drugstore to buy it yourself before their next visit.

There is a dressmaker's shop which advertises mourning outfits in twelve hours, convenient to an undertaker's which has photographs in its window of some of its better funerals, and a furniture shop which offers Provençal and bourgeois furniture and an electrical-appliance shop which offers for sale a refrigerator which makes only enough ice every forty-eight hours for one long glass of lemonade.

There are placards and posters and signs on all the walls. The communists are calling a meeting to denounce American activities in Korea and in Italy and in Greece, and the anticommunists have made a list of all the leaders of the Russian revolution, politicians, artists, writers and scientists, who have been purged since 1917. There is a small, neat sign advertising the address of a gentleman who deals professionally in occultism, palm reading, cards, horoscopes and the return of affection. His hours are from ten to five, except on Sundays, and by appointment. At the bottom of the advertisement, he guarantees serious work.

Wood and coal can be ordered at the counters of many of the bars and you can bet on the horses in the bars that advertise that they represent the Pari-Mutuel Urbain. Tickets for the national lottery are also being sold from little gaily decorated stands and you buy a chance and hope you are going to win five hundred thousand francs. You have bought a ticket every week, but you have not yet won five hundred thousand.

Many of the older women you pass are in black, giving the street a village air, and you notice a new provocative style of black jeans and tennis shoes for the young girls who live in the Quarter, studying art or posing for artists or just living in the Quarter. There is a bar nearby where they serve Martinique rum punch, almost exclusively, hot or cold, sirupy and deathly sweet, but the bar is always crowded just the same with people who are planning a magazine or criticizing a writer or wiring home for money.

The Rodin Museum, close to the martial austerities of the Invalides and the École de Guerre, is in two buildings—the old Hôtel Biron and the chapel, which at one time was consecrated to the devotions of the nuns of the Sacred Heart. The nuns were dispossessed in one of the surges of anticlericalism that have left their mark on French history, and Rodin bought the property and moved his blocks of stone into the vaulted, high, lead-windowed chapel, and even now, after so many years of being at home there, the oversized, passionate bare figures seem strange in their invincibly religious surroundings.

You go out into the gallery where, among the thirty-nine studies, stands your favorite statue of a literary man: Balzac, in bronze, glaring at the Paris which he memorialized as a jungle of rapacity, betrayal, greed, ambition and intrigue, to the applause of generations of Parisions. He stands there, fat, big-bellied, powerful, mustached, aging, defiant, forbidding, with a hint of almost-madness in his metal eyes, and he stands there naked. It is as though the sculptor had said to himself, Well, you have told everything about us, you deserve to have everything told about you.

Your girl blinks, because she is not used to such complete tributes to literature and you speculate on what would happen in America if the custom spread there and some devout society established a similar statue of Mark Twain in Hannibal, Missouri, or a full-length bronze, sans fig leaf, of Emerson, in Concord, Massachusetts.

You drift away from Rodin and hail a taxi in front of the bronze cannons of Napoleon's wars and the two tanks of our own war which stand in front of the Invalides. Geared for the moment to museums you say, "The Louvre," to the driver and he starts frantically toward the right bank. The taxi was built in the 1930's and smells of twenty-year-old leather and the perfume of the lady who has just been delivered to a great mansion nearby in Proust's territory, the Faubourg St.-Germain. The driver hurls himself into traffic like a small boy jumping into a haystack from the second story of a barn, and snarls insults at other drivers of an obscenity which would start a blood feud in Tennessee.

The traffic policemen you pass on corners wave impatiently for you to go faster and you shudder as you swerve down on bicyclists, pedestrians, and ladies with baby carriages. Motorcyclists pass you, with their wives riding behind them, both of them wearing padded leather helmets, as though before starting out, they always assumed, with debonair pessimism, that they would be thrown on their heads at least once on each trip. Neatly dressed business gentlemen putt-putt alongside on small Vespas, with brief cases between their legs and miniature plastic windshields strapped to their foreheads.

There is a cynical joke drivers repeat about the law of the road in Paris. "To hit a pedestrian in the street—that is sport. But to hit him in the *clou*—that is sadism." The *clou* is the crossing between curbs that is marked by iron buttons for the use of people on foot, and you have a feeling that thousands of Parisians have met their end in these deceptive sanctuaries. Somewhere you have heard a dark apocryphal statistic—that one driver out of every twelve in Paris has killed his man. On foot, the Parisian is as courteous as the citizen of any other city. But mounted, he is merciless. Racial memories of the Bourbon era, when the coaches of nobles clattered heedlessly through the narrow streets, crushing pedestrians unlucky enough to be in their path, must seethe through a Parisian's brain as soon as he has a wheel in his hands.

Charging across the Pont Alexander III, the driver grumbles about the usual natural enemies of taxi drivers anywhere—the police. The police, it seems, have proposed that all taxi drivers take a physical examination every five years to determine their fitness to continue in their profession. "For me," the driver said, "it is nothing. I am a young man of fifty. But what of the drivers who are eighty years old who started driving hansom cabs sixty years ago and know nothing else? They have no livers left, no eyes, no kidneys. How can they be expected to pass a physical examination? It is inhuman."

There is nothing you can do but agree—and hope, silently, that whatever eighty-year-old taxi pilots ply their trade in Paris are partial to neighborhoods you rarely visit.

In the museum you are firm in forbidding a general tour, from which you would only come out stunned, foot-worn, adrift in the looted centuries. You go dutifully to the Mona Lisa, behind its glass and its little velvet rope, because your girl wants to see her, but you have seen so many prints and read about the picture so often that the smile is just a faint, fogged glimmer behind its mist of associations.

You leave the great paintings for another day, because they transcend Paris, transcend France, and stand in front of the enormous
battle pieces of Delacroix, which find an echo in the voices of all the
French generals who still keep saying today, "Glory!" and "Attack!"
As you look at the brightly colored tunics, the pretty smoke, the rearing horses, the clean, unreal dying, you regret the disappearance of the
sword and the horse from the battlefield, the discovery of neutral khaki
and gray, and the ubiquitous presence of photographers at our own
wars.

You leave the Louvre and pass Joan of Arc, gold on her gilt horse,
and enter your favorite museum in all the world, the *Musée du Jeu de
Paume*, where the great impressionists have been collected and where,
even on the grayest winter afternoon, sunshine seems to be pouring
from the walls. Here Cézanne and Renoir and Monet and Manet and
Degas and Pissarro announce that air is good to breathe, that women
are delightful to look at, that food is good to eat, that wine is good to
drink, that the world, be it a Paris street or a garden in Chatou or a
village in the Midi, is worthy to be lived in. In this small, clean building, with the roar of traffic coming in through the windows from the
crowded Place de la Concorde outside, you find a robust and delicious
corrective to our times and a powerful antidote to suicide.

Many of the pictures are superb, but there are two that you could
look at forever. There is the huge, mischievous *Lunch on the Grass*, of
Manet, with the comfortable, bearded gentlemen seated at their ease
beneath the trees, and the picnic lunch, and the long, magnificent nude
girl, staring gravely out at you in troubling contrast to her fully dressed
gentlemen friends. The girl seems to be saying, "Do you see anything
wrong? *I* don't." And over the entire thing there hangs a mocking air
of repletion, health and rakish innocence that makes whatever picnics
you have had in your own life seem, in retrospect, discouragingly incomplete.

The other picture is by Degas and it is simply of two laundresses,
ironing. They are both young women with careless hair and round,
solid arms and one of them is stretching and yawning, but there is a
pink, golden late-afternoon light on them and a sense of the cheerful
celebration of the homely, holy, sensual everyday and when you go out
once more into the street the people of the second half of the 20th
Century who throng past seem inexcusably wan and dun-colored.

You pause at the corner and look down at the Church of the Made-
leine and congratulate yourself for being in a city where a copy of the
Parthenon stands, surrounded by flower stalls and delicatessens. You go
to Hediard, the most famous of the delicatessens, which has been there
at the same spot since 1851, and which smells peppery and fragrant,

and you order a basket of cumquats and a kilo of sweet potatoes, which are a rarity in Paris, and an avocado, which is seldom seen in the markets, and a jar of black English marmalade and a small, dry, spiced sausage and a great jar of sweet stewed raspberries and some preserved ginger root and a pound of litchi nuts.

You walk up the Rue Faubourg-St.-Honoré, which is a dangerous thing to do with a girl on any day but Sunday, when the shops are closed, because here are the most expensive windows in the world. You admire a polished side saddle and a pair of silvery spurs and a suède jacket and a silk scarf printed with the flags of the ancient baronies and fine lisle socks with clocks more brilliant than any you would dare wear and you pass the English Embassy, where the MP's, with the red bands around their caps, stand at attention, looking overdisciplined and British.

You tell your girl that if she is very rich she will dress more handsomely here in Paris than anywhere else in the world, but otherwise will do better at any department store in the United States, because in France there is none of the mass production of pretty clothes which is Seventh Avenue's gift to America and which has made American women of all classes so generally pleasing to the eye. But you promise to look for someone who knows somebody else who has her dresses made by a copyist to whom the mannequins of several important houses smuggle out models overnight and who, with blithe immorality, will make you a reasonable facsimile for less than a third the price of the original.

You also tell your girl to beware of French shoes, because all the American women you know are constantly complaining that French feet are different from American feet and you have seen the look of pain produced on the face of an American lady who had been to a Parisian bootmaker when it was suggested that she walk three blocks to a theater.

You think of going to the Museum of Modern Art, on the hill of Chaillot, where there is an exhibition of Mexican art—which is a kind of point-by-point denial of every brushstroke you have seen in the *Jeu de Paume*. There everything is oversize, distorted, tragic, violent, rebellious; there a monstrous painted figure with a head that is not human, but which looks as though it had been made of flesh which has turned to stone, stretches out two grotesque hands in agony, supplication and threat.

But you decide to be frivolous for a little while longer and take your girl instead to a couturier's, which is having a final rehearsal of its new show before the grand opening the next day. You are early and you seat yourself in the newly painted oblong room with the narrow raised platform running down the middle, as the room fills with the heads of the various departments, the woman in charge of the buying of material, the woman in charge of the hats, the woman in charge of furs, the *vendeuses*. Around the entrance stand the seamstresses, modest and birdlike, to watch their glorious sisters parade in their finery.

The owner-designer comes out and everybody stands up for him like war correspondents honoring a three-star general in a press conference. He makes a graceful little speech, praising his co-workers for their loyalty in the past and assuring himself of their loyalty in the future. He tells them all to notice the elliptical motif of the skirts this season and reminds them that what was called raw silk last year, will be called *soie sauvage*, wild silk, during this. There is a little nervous hush while everybody prays that the designer, from whose quick hands come all their livelihoods, will not have lost his touch this time.

All through the fashionable district, where the grand couturiers have their mansions, on the Avenue Montaigne, on the Avenue George Cinq, on the Place Vendôme, in all the busy, nerve-wracked establishments where Paris erects, twice each year, its most glittering monument to frivolity, the same scene is being enacted during this week.

The first girl comes out, swinging slowly along the ramp in that arrogant walk which has cost so many men so much money, and the show is on, interrupted from time to time by bursts of applause for a particular dress.

A plumpish girl comes out in a flashy pencil-striped white suit and the woman next to you says, "That's for the Spaniards."

"Don't forget the South Americans," says the woman sitting next to her.

"And the Portuguese," says a lady across the room.

There are seven girls to show 110 dresses in one hour and a half and there are scenes of frantic zippering and buttoning behind the dressing-room door, but there is no delay and each girl comes sauntering out radiant, perfectly accoutered, and not breathing hard, a living rebuke to all wives who keep their husbands waiting the last bitter half hour while they get themselves up for the evening.

The last dress you see before you have to leave is a "court dress." It is white, with glass pendants in glittering diagonal lines on the skirt and bosom. The girl who wears it is tall and blond and has a tiara in her hair and a choker of pearls around her throat and in her regal, extravagant, top-heavy, and slightly ludicrous dress, she shines as princesses should, yet rarely do, and you hope she is not living in a single disordered room on the Left Bank with a drunken photographer who takes her money and makes passes at all her friends.

Now you have to go to a cocktail party. It is a kind of housewarming, being given by a friend who waited for fifteen years to get this apartment. His old apartment, which was one floor above, had only three rooms, and this one has four. He really needs five rooms. On the floor below there is a five-room apartment. He inquires politely about the health of the tenant and looks forward patiently to the next fifteen years.

One pretty dark girl is never applauded, although as far as you can tell, her dresses are on a level with the others. "She doesn't *sell* the dresses any more," the woman next to you whispers. "Last year, they applauded her all the time. But she's engaged to be married now, her fiancé gave her a ring big enough to choke a horse, and she isn't interested any more."

A girl comes out in a plain blue suit and the woman next to you says, "That will sell to all the bourgeoisie. It's a bourgeois suit and we put it on the girl with a bourgeois face."

For a moment you're glad you're not a girl, glad you're not French, and glad you're not modeling clothes in the abattoir-efficient atmosphere of a great fashion house.

At the cocktail party there is gin, expensively imported from England, which shows that the host is serious about this collection of guests. People are standing in groups, smoking French cigarettes, which make your mouth smell like a small industrial town after you have gone through half a pack. Three or four of the guests have rosettes of the Legion of Honor and a plump, intelligent-looking lawyer is defending the ancient practice of dueling.

"There are arguments," he says, "which cannot be taken to law and which can only be settled by the duel. Otherwise they go on and on forever, with people cutting each other at dinners and in offices and making everybody uncomfortable and bored. A duel has the quality of a period at the end of a paragraph and civilized life has need of such periods."

In a corner, a group of Frenchmen are talking: "Americans," one of them says, "Americans may think they come to Paris for a number of reasons: To be artists, to be restless, to be young, to be free . . . but, essentially, they are all here in the same capacity. As archaeologists. To study antiquity. Nobody comes to the Paris of today, because Paris is a city of the past. Everybody visits a Paris which no longer exists except in ruins and memory."

"Paris is the only real city," adds another. "New York is four villages, London an industry, Rio de Janeiro a place where you have the feeling you must behave as though you are a schoolboy in a religious institution. Everything is possible in Paris, everything can be said, everybody can be met, often on the same day. It is the one city in the world which is not provincial."

And a sixty-year-old painter, looking back on his career and all the invitations he had accepted, says, "In Paris, fame is a telephone call."

Another guest has just come from a cocktail party which is a monthly feature given by a great publishing house for all its authors. "You could tell whose books weren't selling this season," the guest says. "They brought their wives and they never moved away from the hors d'oeuvres table."

"Let me explain about our government," a little round man with enormous glasses is saying to an American lady. "It is always falling and it is always Radical Socialist."

"There is only one country in the world," a journalist is saying, "which is rich enough to permit capitalism to work—and that is America. In France, capitalism cannot work." He pauses for a moment, reflecting on what he has said, then smiles happily. "In fact," he adds, "in France socialism cannot work. In fact, in France, nothing can work."

A handsome white-haired politician, who is being baited by some young intellectuals, turns brick red and moves to the attack. "Why don't you just drink Coca-Cola and get it over with?" he demands. "All you young people are secretly Americans at heart. All you want is security."

The editor of a publishing house is introduced to a successful writer. The editor bows and says, "When you feel yourself on the verge of committing an infidelity to your publisher, I trust you will come and visit me."

A smartly dressed woman of a certain age is standing in a corner with her arm affectionately around the shoulders of a well-known young author. "Darling," she is saying, "why don't you write the way you really are? Rosy and funny and healthy. Why are you always writing those long, sad books, full of the *saloperies* of youth, with all the people going to bed with everybody else?"

You leave because you want to go to the theater and there is just time for dinner before the curtain.

You go to the restaurant opposite the Odéon, where you can sit on the glassed-in terrace and look across the little square to the Greek-styled theater, now taken over by the Comédie-Française, and whose columns are illuminated each night by marvelously theatrical blue floodlights. Just after the Liberation you could meet Jean Cocteau at that restaurant, and Christian Bérard, bearded and carrying a tawny, long-furred cat. You could also get a fluffy chocolate mousse there, made with American Army chocolate whose availability was no doubt connected with the nightly presence of the smiling, well-fed American soldier at the bar who must have been a mess sergeant.

Now it is crowded and fashionable and there is a rich smell of bouillabaisse in the air and you can eat your favorite oysters there, the enormous, deep-sea tasting *fines de claires,* which are scorned by the epicures who favor the subtler Belons and Marennes, and who call the *claire,* or Portugaise, the workingman's oyster. The *sommelier,* who has an almost incomprehensible Midi accent, carries a cork screw with an obscene device on it, but the wines are good and it is pleasant to sit there looking across at the floodlit columns and watching the polite people arriving for *Cyrano.*

You can see *Antigone* tonight or a dozen plays whose central theme is that of the cuckolded husband, including one in which the cuckolded husband is the magistrate who condemns to death for murder the man who was cozily tucked away in a hotel with the magistrate's wife on the afternoon on which the crime was committed. This last play, not unnaturally, drew some pained letters from the company of magistrates, who are overworked and underpaid and who feel sorry enough for themselves as it is.

You can even see a play which was put on at a little art theater and became a great success largely because it was a comedy which was not about cuckolded husbands.

You can see Molière or Racine or Bernstein or Sartre or Anouilh, a kind of one-man trust who pours out a seemingly inexhaustible stream of bitter, witty, elegant, slightly constructed popular plays, which follow so quickly on the heels of one another that there is a jealous legend about him that he writes all day every day and and whenever he reaches twenty thousand words, sends them down to the nearest theater to be produced immediately.

The acting is generally of a high quality and gives evidence of solid, plays that are brilliantly mounted and directed to a makeshift level of protracted training. The productions vary enormously, ranging from scenic improvisation far below the standard of the most mediocre Broadway offering.

In the theater, at even the gravest plays, you are likely to be distracted between acts by magic-lantern slides advertising silk stockings, raincoats, shampoos, and studios which make a specialty of photographing infants.

There is a movement on foot to attract the tourist trade by installing earphones into which will be poured a running English translation of the script, as it is being played. Some of the language of the Paris stage, which is remarkably free, may have explosive effects on unaccustomed American ears when it is put into plain Anglo-Saxon English.

It is midnight by the time you get out of the theater. In St.-Germain, the ugliest bars in the world are jammed with the young unwashed of half a dozen countries and a lanky, recent graduate of Yale is announcing to the crowded sidewalk tables that his girl is deceiving him inside with the second son of an Indian prince. Nobody sympathizes with him and he laughs, showing the good old Yale spirit, and sits down and has a glass of beer.

On the Champs-Elysées the girls are prowling like jaguars, twitching their fur neckpieces under the cold, controlled stares of the police. The movies are letting out and everybody has been to see *Un Américain à Paris* and the couples are kissing frankly in the side streets. A young man, slightly drunk, comes up to an American group and bows and says, "You are Americans. Naturally, you are not communists. You do not have to work at the lathe. I, however, have to work at the lathe, so you must forgive me if I would do everything in my power to force you to the lathe." He says, "Thank you," and wanders politically and incoherently off in the direction of Passy.

In the night clubs, sad girls are singing that they hate Sunday, and there is a dancing horse and young men who sing that the Seine flows and flows and flows and sings and sings and sings and is a mistress in whose bed Paris sleeps. Off the Place Pigalle dark figures whisper out of the shadows, asking if you want to see a show, and in the big cafés, devoted to the almost-nude female body, parade all shapes of girls, bare from the waist up, but conforming to police regulations below that. After their turn, the girls line up, demure in ball gowns, on the staircase, and you can dance with them, if you will, by buying a ticket. Like most French women, they dance so tightly clasped to you that you feel like an infant strangling in his crib under blankets that have been tucked in too well.

In a Russian night club, where all the talent is over fifty years old, they play guitars and dance gypsy dances and sit around candles in a group and sing sorrowful winter songs and come to your table and drink your health in your own champagne, after which you have to drain your glass and break it on the table in honor of the czar, or in honor of yourself, or in honor of the price of champagne.

Needing air, you and your girl walk to the river and step onto a tiny, crowded floating bar which is attached to a launch, and with a glass in your hand, and feeling, No, this is too romantic, chug off down the black river toward the cathedral. The city is quiet on both sides of you, the river wind is cool, the trees on the banks are fitfully illuminated by the headlights of occasional automobiles crossing the bridges. The bums are sleeping on the quais, waiting to be photographed at dawn by the people who keep turning out the glossy picture books on Paris;

a train passes somewhere nearby, blowing its whistle, which sounds like a maiden lady who has been pinched, surprisingly, by a deacon; the buildings of the politicians and the diplomats are dark; the monuments doze; the starlit centuries surround you on the dark water. . . .

You turn, hesitantly, toward the girl at your side. . . .

You blink. It is daylight and you are still at the same café table. Your girl has never arrived, of course. At the table next to you a woman is saying, "I have a friend on *Figaro*. He says the war will start in September. What do you think will happen in Paris?"

"Paris," says the man who is sitting with her, "Paris will be spared."

"Why?"

"Because Paris is always spared," the man says, and orders a coffee.

# THE GHOST TRAIN

## *Lawrence Durrell*

LAWRENCE DURRELL (1912– ), a British citizen of Irish parentage, was born in the high Himalayas and when still young was taken by his mother to live on the Island of Corfu. This Byronian pattern of travel has pursued him to the present day and, in between, he has had romantic and dramatic experiences in many colorful parts of the world, a background strongly woven into his writing. Although his early work was versatile and abundant and much praised by critics and other writers, among them T. S. Eliot, success in a large international sense did not come to him until completion of his magnum opus. This, of course, was *The Alexandria Quartet*, four sensuous, baroque novels with entwined story lines, almost classical in form but modern in their irony and in their decadent sun-drenched characters. Today he lives in France, his happiest landfall.

I LIKE Antrobus. I can't really say why—I think it is because he takes everything so frightfully seriously. He is portentous—always dropping into a whisper, clicking his tongue, making a po-face, pursing his lips, turning the palms of his hand outwards and making "what-would-you" gestures.

We've served together in a number of foreign capitals, he as a regular of the career, I as a contract officer: which explains why he is now a heavily padded senior in Southern while I am an impoverished writer. Nevertheless, whenever I'm in London he gives me lunch at his club and we talk about the past—those happy days passed in foreign capitals "lying abroad" for our country.

"The Ghost Train episode", said Antrobus, "was a bit before your time. I only mention it because I can think of nothing which illustrates the peculiar hazards of Diplomatic Life so well. In fact it throws them into Stark Relief.

"Every nation has its particular *idée fixe*. For the Yugoslavs it is trains. Nothing can compare for breathtaking romance with the railway train. Railway engines have to be put under armed guard when not in motion or they would be poked to pieces by the enquiring peasantry. No other object arouses the concupiscence of the Serb like a train. They drool over it, old boy, positively drool. *Ils bavent.*

"You twig this the minute you alight from the Orient Express at Belgrade because there is something queer about the station building itself. It leans to one side. It is neatly cracked from platform level to clock-tower. Moreover there are several distinct sets of ruts in the concrete of the platform which are highly suggestive. The first porter you engage will clear up the mystery. Apparently every fifteenth train or so leaps the buffers, grinds across the Freight Section and buries itself in the booking office. No one is ever hurt and the whole town joyfully bands together to dig the engine out. Everyone is rather proud of this particular idiosyncrasy. It is part of the Serbian way of life.

"Well, being aware of this as I was, I could not help being a bit concerned when Nimic in the Protocol hinted that the Diplomatic Corps was to be sent to Zagreb for Liberation Day in a special train which would prove once and for all that the much-vaunted Yugoslav heavy industry was capable of producing machinery every bit as good as the degenerate Capitalist West. This tip was accompanied by dark looks and winks and all efforts to probe the mystery further proved vain. A veil of secrecy (one of the seven veils of Communist diplomacy) was drawn over the subject. Naturally we in the Corps were interested, while those who had served for some time in the Balkans were perturbed. *'Mon Dieu,'* said Du Bellay the French Minister gravely, *'si ces animaux veulent jouer aux locos avec le Corps Diplomatique . . .'* He was voicing the Unspoken Thoughts of many of us.

"There was no further information forthcoming about the Ghost Train as we jokingly called it, so we sat back and waited for Liberation Day. Sure enough the customary fat white envelope appeared ten days before from the Protocol. I opened mine with a troubled curiosity. It announced that the Corps would be travelling by a Special Train which would be placed at its disposal. The train itself was called 'The Liberation-Celebration Machine'.

"Even Polk-Mowbray looked a bit grave. 'What sort of Devil-Car do you think it will be?' he said apprehensively. I couldn't enlighten him, alas. 'It's probably a chain-drive Trojan with some carriages built around it in plywood.'

"There was a short-lived movement among the Corps to go by road instead and thus sidestep the 'Liberation-Celebration Machine' but the Doyen put his foot down. Such a defection would constitute a grave slight. The Yugoslav heavy industry would be hurt by our refusal to allow it to unveil the marvels of modern science to us. Reluctantly we all accepted. 'Butch' Benbow, the naval attaché, who was clairvoyant and who dabbled in astrology, took the omens. Apparently they were not propitious. 'All I can see is clouds of smoke,' he said hoarsely, looking up from the progressed chart on his desk. 'And someone gets a severe scalp wound—probably you, sir.'

"Polk-Mowbray started. 'Now, look here,' he said, 'let's have no alarm and despondency on this one. If the Yugoslav heavy industry gives me even a trifling scalp wound I'll see that there is an International Incident over it.'

"The day drew inexorably nearer. The Special Train, we learned, was to be met in a siding just outside Belgrade. There is a small station there, the name of which I forget. Here at the appointed time, which was dusk, we duly presented ourselves in full *tenue*. There were to be flowers and speeches by representatives of the Yugoslav Heavy Industry. Most of the representatives looked nearly as heavy as their industry. But I couldn't take my eyes off the train.

"I'm not saying it was gaudy. It was absolutely breathtaking. The three long coaches were made of painted and carved timber; flowers, birds, liberation heroes, *cache-sexes,* emblematic devices, post-horns— everything you can imagine, all carved and painted according to the peasant fancy. The general effect was that of a Sicilian market-cart with painted and carved side-boards—or the poop of some seventeenth- century galleon. Every blacksmith, wheelwright and cartwright in Serbia must have had a hand in it. '*C'est un chalet Tyroléan ou quoi?*' I heard Du Bellay say under his breath. His scepticism was shared by us all.

"We entered and found our reserved carriages which seemed normal enough. The band played. We accepted a wreath or two. Then we set off in the darkness to the braying of donkeys and cocks and the rasping of trombones. We were off across the rolling Serbian plains.

"Two things were immediately obvious. All this elaborate woodwork squeaked and groaned calamitously, ear-splittingly. How were we to get any sleep? But more serious still was the angle of inclination of the second coach with the Heads of Mission in it. It was about thirty de- grees out of centre and was only, it seemed, held upright by the one immediately before and behind it. It was clear that the Yugoslav heavy industry had mislaid its spirit-level while it was under construction. People who looked out of the windows on one side had the illusion that the ground was coming up to hit them. I paid Polk-Mowbray a visit to see if he was all right and found him looking rather pale, and drawn up on the higher elevation of the coach like someone on a sinking ship. The noise was so great that we couldn't speak—we had to shout: 'My God,' I heard him cry out, 'what is to become of us all?' It was a little difficult to say. We were now gathering speed. The engine was a very old one. It had been abandoned before the war by an American film company and the Yugoslavs had tied it together with wire. Its gaping furnace, which was white hot, was being passionately fed by some very hairy men in cloth caps who looked like Dostoevsky's publishers. It seemed to me that the situation had never looked graver. Despite its age, however, it had managed to whip up a good forty-five. And every five hundred yards it would groan and void a bucketful of white clinker into the night which set fire to the grass on either side of the track. From far off we must have looked like an approaching forest fire.

"Another feature of the 'Liberation-Celebration Machine' was an ingenious form of central heating which could not be turned off, and as none of the windows opened, the temperature inside the coaches rapidly mounted into the hundreds. People were fanning themselves with their tall hats. Old man, never have I seen the Corps subjected to such a strain. Sleep was impossible. The lights would not turn off. The wash basins appeared to empty into each other. And all the time we had the ghastly thought of all the Heads of Mission in the Hanging Coach, drinking brandy and gibbering with fright as we sped onwards through the night.

"The chance of some frightful accident taking place was far from remote and consequently nobody was able to relax. We did not even dare to get into pyjamas but sat about in that infernal racket staring desperately at one another and starting at every regurgitation of the engine, every shiver and squeak of the coaches. The American Ambassador was so overcome that he spent the night singing 'Nearer My God To Thee'. Some said that he had had the forethought to take a case of rye into his compartment with him. Madame Fawzia, the Egyptian Ambassadress, spent the night on the floor of her compartment deep in prayer. I simply did not dare to think of Polk-Mowbray. From time to time when the wind changed the whole train was enveloped in a cloud of rich dense smoke containing fragments of half-digested coal the size of hailstones. But still the ghoulish crew in the engine-cab plied their grisly shovels and on we sped with mournful shrieks and belches.

"At two in the morning there was a ghastly rending noise as we entered the station of Slopsy Blob, named after the famous Independence fighter. The Hanging Coach somehow got itself engaged with the tin dado which ran along the roof of the station and ripped it off as clean as a whistle, by the same token almost decapitating one of the drivers. The noise was appalling and the whole Corps let out a unified shriek of terror. I have never heard diplomats scream like that before or since—and I never want to. A lot of cherubs and floral devices were ripped off the Hanging Coach in the encounter and the people in the rear coaches found themselves assailed by a hail of coloured fragments of wood which made them shriek the louder. It was all over in a moment.

"Then we were out in the night once more racing across the dark plain, the brothers Karamazov still plying the engine with might and main. It is possible that, in the manner of Serbs, they had heard nothing. We spent the rest of the night in Sleepless Vigil, old man. The guardian angel of the Yugoslav Heavy Industry must have been with us for nothing much worse happened. But it was a pretty dispirited and shaken dip corps that was finally dragged into Zagreb station on that Liberation morning. I can tell you, never was liberation so much in the forefront of everyone's thoughts.

"It must have been about six o'clock when we stormed into Zagreb squealing and blowing out an Etna of steam. The brakes had been applied some three miles outside the station and their ear-splitting racket had to be heard to be believed.

"But this was not the end. Though we missed the red carpet by a quarter of a mile, and though the waiting dignitaries and the Zagreb Traction and Haulage Workers' Band padded down the platform after us our troubles were not yet at an end. It was found that the doors of the coaches on the platform side were fast shut and could not be opened. I suppose Zagreb Station must have been on the opposite side of the track from Belgrade Station and consequently nobody dreamed that we should need more than one exit from the train. It was, of course, fearfully humiliating. We leaned against the windows making inarticulate gestures of goodwill and vague grimaces in the direction of the Traction Haulage Workers' Band and the Liberation Reception Committee.

"We must have looked like a colony of dispossessed fairground apes pining for the old life of the trees. After a good deal of mopping and mowing there was nothing for it but to climb out of the Zagreb Flyer on to the permanent way and walk round the train to the reception point. This we somewhat shamefacedly did. But when all was said and done it was good to feel terra firma under our feet once more. Drawn up in order of precedence on Zagreb platform we submitted to the Liberation anthem sung by the Partisan choir in a register so low that it could not drown the merry cries of self-congratulation with which the Karamazov brothers were greeting the morn. Their observations were punctuated by blasts of hot steam and whiffs of sound from the whistle of the Liberation-Celebration Machine which looked even more improbable in the cold morning light than it had done the evening before.

"All this went off as well as such things can be expected to do; but sleepy as we were a sudden chill struck our hearts at a phrase in the Speech of Welcome which plainly indicated that the authorities were expecting us to make the return journey in the Liberation-Celebration Machine on the following day. This gave us all food for thought. Madame Fawzia made an involuntary retching noise which was interpreted by our hosts as an expression of joy. Several other ladies in the Corps showed a disposition to succumb to the vapours at this piece of intelligence. But the old training dies hard. There was many a tight lip and beady eye but not a word was said until we were assembled for breakfast in the card room of the Slopsy Blob Hotel. Then the pent-up floodwaters of emotion overflowed. Ambassadors, Ministers, Secretaries of Embassy and their wives began as one man to gesticulate and gabble. It was a moving scene. Some called upon the Gods to witness that they would never travel by train again; others spoke wonderingly of the night they had just spent when the whole of their past life flashed before them as if on a screen; the wife of the Spanish Republican Minister, by far the most deeply shaken by events, fell upon the Doyen, the Polish Ambassador, and named him as responsible before God for our safety and well-being. It was an interesting study in national types. The Egyptians screamed, the Finns and Norwegians snarled, the Slav belt pulled at each other's lapels as if they were milking goats. The Greeks made Promethean gestures at everyone. (They could afford to take the Balanced View since they had already hired the only six taxis in Zagreb and were offering seats for the return journey at a thousand dinars each.)

"One thing emerged clearly from all this. The Corps was in a state of open mutiny and would not easily be persuaded to entrain once more with the Brothers Karamazov. The Doyen pleaded in vain. We struck various national attitudes all round the room. The Italian Ambassadress who looked as if her anger would succeed in volatilizing her went so far as to draw up her dress and show the company a bruise inflicted on her during the journey. As for Polk-Mowbray, he did indeed have a scalp wound—an egg-shaped protuberance on the crown of his head where he had doubtless been struck by a passing railway station. It was clear that the journey had aged him.

"Well, that day most of us spent the time in bed with cold compresses and aspirin. In the evening we attended a performance of the Ballet and a Torchlight Tattoo. Liberation Day was at an end. That night the Doyen convened another meeting in the hotel at which he harangued us about diplomatic procedure in general and our obligations to the Service in particular. In vain. We were determined not to travel back on the Ghost Train. He pleaded with us but we were adamant. That evening a flock of telegrams fluttered into the Protocol Department of the Ministry of Foreign Affairs—telegrams pleading sudden illness, pressure of work, unforeseen political developments, migraine, influenza, neuritis or Events Beyond the Writer's Control. At dawn a convoy of taxis set out on the homeward track bearing the shattered remnants of the Corps, unshaven, unhonoured, but still alive, still breathing. . . . In a way I was sorry for the Brothers Karamazov and the Liberation-Celebration Machine. God knows, one did not wish them ill. But I must confess I was not surprised to read in the paper a week later that this latest triumph of the Yugoslav Heavy Industry had jumped the points at Slopsy Blob and finished the good work it had begun by carrying away most of the station buildings. No one was hurt. No one ever is in Serbia. Just badly shaken and frightened out of one's wits. It is all, when you come to think of it, part of the Serbian Way of Life. . . ."

# THE TREE

## *Dylan Thomas*

DYLAN THOMAS (1914–1953) This poet's death in New York at
the age of thirty-nine brought to an abrupt end a career that was at-
tracting attention throughout the English-speaking world. Educated
in the grammar schools of his native Wales, he followed the familiar
path of young writers into journalism. But it was with his verse
that he first showed his gift for rich language employed with intense
feeling. A prize awarded by the American magazine *Poetry* set him
wholly on his way as a writer. The beauty and color of his verse and
the power and wit of his prose brought him a large and eager public
whom he also served both in England and in America with readings
of his work. His flamboyance and good-natured wildness never de-
tracted from his position as an artist. The following tender and tragic
short story gives evidence of his magical ability to bring poetry to prose.

RISING from the house that faced the Jarvis hills in the long distance, there was a tower for the day-birds to build in and for
the owls to fly around at night. From the village the light of
the tower window shone like a glowworm through the panes; but the
room under the sparrows' nests was rarely lit; webs were spun over its
unwashed ceilings; it stared over twenty miles of the up-and-down
county, and the corners kept their secrets where there were claw marks
in the dust.

The child knew the house from roof to cellar; he knew the irregular
lawns and the gardener's shed where flowers burst out of their jars; but
he could not find the key that opened the door of the tower.

The house changed to his moods, and a lawn was the sea or the shore
or the sky or whatever he wished it. When a lawn was a sad mile of
water, and he was sailing on a broken flower down the waves, the
gardener would come out of his shed near the island of bushes. He,
too, would take a stalk, and sail. Straddling a garden broom, he would
fly whenever the child wished. He knew every story from the beginning
of the world.

In the beginning, he would say, there was a tree.

What kind of a tree?

A hawk, a hawk, cried the child.

The gardener would look up at the tree seeing a monstrous hawk perched on a bough or an eagle singing in the wind.

The gardener loved the Bible. When the sun sank and the garden was full of people, he would sit with a candle in his shed, reading of the first love and the legend of apples and serpents. But the death of Christ on a tree he loved most. Trees made a fence around him, and he knew of the changing of the seasons by the hues on the bark and the rushing of sap through the covered roots. His world moved and changed as spring moved along the branches, changing their nakedness; his God grew up like a tree from the apple-shaped earth, giving bud to His children and letting His children be blown from their places by the breezes of winter; winter and death moved in one wind. He would sit in his shed and read of the crucifixion, looking over the jars on his window-shelf into the winter nights. He would think that love fails on such nights, and that many of its children are cut down.

The child transfigured the blowsy lawns with his playing. The gardener called him by his mother's name, and seated him on his knee, and talked to him of the wonders of Jerusalem and the birth in the manger.

In the beginning was the village of Bethlehem, he whispered to the child before the bell rang for tea out of the growing darkness.

Where is Bethlehem?

Far away, said the gardener, in the East.

To the east stood the Jarvis hills, hiding the sun, their trees drawing up the moon out of the grass.

The child lay in bed. He watched the rocking horse and wished that it would grow wings so that he could mount it and ride into the Arabian sky. But the winds of Wales blew at the curtains, and crickets made a noise in the untidy plot under the window. His toys were dead. He started to cry and then stopped, knowing no reason for tears. The night was windy and cold, he was warm under the sheets; the night was as big as a hill, he was a boy in bed.

Closing his eyes, he stared into a spinning cavern deeper than the darkness of the garden where the first tree on which the unreal birds had fastened stood alone and bright as fire. The tears ran back under his lids as he thought of the first tree that was planted so near him, like a friend in the garden. He crept out of bed and tiptoed to the door. The rocking horse bounded forward on its springs, startling the child into a noiseless scamper back to bed. The child looked at the horse and the horse was quiet; he tiptoed again along the carpet, and reached the door, and turned the knob around, and ran on to the landing. Feeling blindly in front of him, he made his way to the top of the stairs; he looked down the dark stairs into the hall, seeing a host of shadows curve in and out of the corners, hearing their sinuous voices, imagining the pits of their eyes and their lean arms. But they would be little and secret and bloodless, not cased in invisible armour but wound around with cloths as thin as a web; they would whisper as he walked, touch him on the shoulder, and say S in his ear. He went down the stairs; not a shadow moved in the hall, the corners were empty. He put out his hand and patted the darkness, thinking to feel some dry and velvet head creep under the fingers and edge, like a mist, into the nails. But there was nothing. He opened the front door, and the shadows swept into the garden.

Once on the path, his fears left him. The moon had lain down on the unweeded beds, and her frosts were spread on the grass. At last he came to the illuminated tree at the long gravel end, older even than the marvel of light, with the woodlice asleep under the bark, with the boughs standing out from the body like the frozen arms of a woman. The child touched the tree; it bent as to his touch. He saw a star, brighter than any in the sky, burn steadily above the first birds' tower, and shine on nowhere but on the leafless boughs and the trunk and the travelling roots.

The child had not doubted the tree. He said his prayers to it, with knees bent on the blackened twigs the night wind fetched to the ground. Then, trembling with love and cold, he ran back over the lawns towards the house.

There was an idiot to the east of the county who walked the land like a beggar. Now at a farmhouse and now at a widow's cottage he begged for his bread. A parson gave him a suit, and it lopped round his hungry ribs and shoulders and waved in the wind as he shambled over the fields. But his eyes were so wide and his neck so clear of the country dirt that no one refused him what he asked. And asking for water, he was given milk.

Where do you come from?

From the east, he said.

So they knew he was an idiot, and gave him a meal to clean the yards.

As he bent with a rake over the dung and the trodden grain, he heard a voice rise in his heart. He put his hand into the cattle's hay, caught a mouse, rubbed his hand over its muzzle, and let it go away.

All day the thought of the tree was with the child; all night it stood up in his dreams as the star stood above its plot. One morning towards the middle of December, when the wind from the farthest hills was rushing around the house, and the snow of the dark hours had not dissolved from lawns and roofs, he ran to the gardener's shed. The gardener was repairing a rake he had found broken. Without a word, the child sat on a seedbox at his feet, and watched him tie the teeth, and knew that the wire would not keep them together. He looked at the gardener's boots, wet with snow, at the patched knees of his trousers, at the undone buttons of his coat, and the folds of his belly under the patched flannel shirt. He looked at his hands as they busied themselves over the golden knots of wire; they were hard, brown hands, with the stains of the soil under the broken nails and the stains of tobacco on the tips of the fingers. Now the lines of the gardener's face were set in determination as time upon time he knotted the iron teeth only to feel them shake insecurely from the handle. The child was frightened of the strength and uncleanliness of the old man; but, looking at the long, thick beard, unstained and white as fleece, he soon became reassured. The beard was the beard of an apostle.

I prayed to the tree, said the child.

Always pray to a tree, said the gardener, thinking of Calvary and Eden.

I pray to the tree every night.

Pray to a tree.

The wire slid over the teeth.

I pray to that tree.

The wire snapped.

The child was pointing over the glasshouse flowers to the tree that, alone of all the trees in the garden, had no sign of snow.

An elder, said the gardener, but the child stood up from his box and shouted so loud that the unmended rake fell with a clatter on the floor.

The first tree. The first tree you told me of. In the beginning was the tree, you said. I heard you, the child shouted.

The elder is as good as another, said the gardener, lowering his voice to humour the child.

The first tree of all, said the child in a whisper.

Reassured again by the gardener's voice, he smiled through the window at the tree, and again the wire crept over the broken rake.

God grows in strange trees, said the old man. His trees come to rest in strange places.

As he unfolded the story of the twelve stages of the cross, the tree waved its boughs to the child. An apostle's voice rose out of the tarred lungs.

So they hoisted him up on a tree, and drove nails through his belly and his feet.

There was the blood of the noon sun on the trunk of the elder, staining the bark.

The idiot stood on the Jarvis hills, looking down into the immaculate valley from whose waters and grasses the mists of morning rose and were lost. He saw the dew dissolving, the cattle staring into the stream, and the dark clouds flying away at the rumour of the sun. The sun turned at the edges of the thin and watery sky like a sweet in a glass of water. He was hungry for light as the first and almost invisible rain fell on his lips; he plucked at the grass, and, tasting it, felt it lie green on his tongue. So there was light in his mouth, and light was a sound at his ears, and the whole dominion of light in the valley that had such a curious name. He had known of the Jarvis hills; their shapes rose over the slopes of the county to be seen for miles around, but no one had told him of the valley lying under the hills. Bethlehem, said the idiot to the valley, turning over the sounds of the word and giving it all the glory of the Welsh morning. He brothered the world around him, sipped at the air, as a child newly born sips and brothers the light. The life of the Jarvis valley, steaming up from the body of the grass and the trees and the long hand of the stream, lent him a new blood. Night had emptied the idiot's veins, and dawn in the valley filled them again.

Bethlehem, said the idiot to the valley.

The gardener had no present to give the child, so he took out a key from his pocket and said, This is the key to the tower. On Christmas Eve I will unlock the door for you.

Before it was dark, he and the child climbed the stairs to the tower, the key turned in the lock, and the door, like the lid of a secret box, opened and let them in. The room was empty. Where are the secrets? asked the child, staring up at the matted rafters and into the spiders' corners and along the leaden panes of the window.

It is enough that I have given you the key, said the gardener, who believed the key of the universe to be hidden in his pocket along with the feathers of birds and the seeds of flowers.

The child began to cry because there were no secrets. Over and over again he explored the empty room, kicking up the dust to look for a colourless trap-door, tapping the unpanelled walls for the hollow voice of a room beyond the tower. He brushed the webs from the window, and looked out through the dust into the snowing Christmas Eve. A world of hills stretched far away into the measured sky, and the tops of the hills he had never seen climbed up to meet the falling flakes.

Woods and rocks, wide seas of barren land, and a new tide of mountain
sky sweeping through the black beeches, lay before him. To the east
were the outlines of nameless hill creatures and a den of trees.

Who are they? Who are they?

They are the Jarvis hills, said the gardener, which have been from
the beginning.

He took the child by the hand and led him away from the window.
The key turned in the lock.

That night the child slept well; there was power in snow and darkness; there was unalterable music in the silence of the stars; there was a
silence in the hurrying wind. And Bethlehem had been nearer than he
expected.

On Christmas morning the idiot walked into the garden. His hair
was wet and his flaked and ragged shoes were thick with the dirt of the
fields. Tired from the long journey from the Jarvis hills, and weak for
the want of food, he sat down under the elder-tree where the gardener
had rolled a log. Clasping his hands in front of him, he saw the desolation of the flower-beds and the weeds that grew in profusion on the
edges of the paths. The tower stood up like a tree of stone and glass
over the red eaves. He pulled his coat-collar round his neck as a fresh
wind sprang up and struck the tree; he looked down at his hands and
saw that they were praying. Then a fear of the garden came over him,
the shrubs were his enemies, and the trees that made an avenue down
to the gate lifted their arms in horror. The place was too high, peering
down on to the tall hills; the place was too low, shivering up at the
plumed shoulders of a new mountain. Here the wind was too wild,
fuming about the silence, raising a Jewish voice out of the elder boughs;
here the silence beat like a human heart. And as he sat under the cruel
hills, he heard a voice that was in him cry out: Why did you bring me
here?

He could not tell why he had come; they had told him to come and
had guided him, but he did not know who they were. The voice of a
people rose out of the garden beds, and rain swooped down from
heaven.

Let me be, said the idiot, and made a little gesture against the sky.
There is rain on my face, there is wind on my cheeks. He brothered
the rain.

So the child found him under the shelter of the tree, bearing the
torture of the weather with a divine patience, letting his long hair blow
where it would, with his mouth set in a sad smile.

Who was the stranger? He had fires in his eyes, the flesh of his neck under the gathered coat was bare. Yet he smiled as he sat in his rags under a tree on Christmas Day.

Where do you come from? asked the child.

From the east, answered the idiot.

The gardener had not lied, and the secret of the tower was true; this dark and shabby tree, that glistened only in the night, was the first tree of all.

But he asked again:

Where do you come from?

From the Jarvis hills.

Stand up against the tree.

The idiot, still smiling, stood up with his back to the elder.

Put out your arms like this.

The idiot put out his arms.

The child ran as fast as he could to the gardener's shed, and, returning over the sodden lawns, saw that the idiot had not moved but stood, straight and smiling, with his back to the tree and his arms stretched out.

Let me tie your hands.

The idiot felt the wire that had not mended the rake close round his wrists. It cut into the flesh, and the blood from the cuts fell shining on to the tree.

Brother, he said. He saw that the child held silver nails in the palm of his hand.

# THE LISTENER

## John Berry

---

JOHN BERRY (1915– ) is one of the few Americans writing of India today with an intimate knowledge of his subject. After a period of teaching at the University of Southern California he became an instructor for several years at Bharat University in Bengal, one hundred miles inland from Calcutta. Speaking Bengali, and with an ardent wish to find the secrets of the "ancient wisdom," he has achieved a personal relationship with all the classes and castes of that teeming country. His novel *Krishna Fluting,* set in India with Hindu and American characters, won the Macmillan Fiction Award for 1959. His present writing, both prose and verse, also embraces other matters and themes, much influenced by the subtlety of the East. He is again living and working in Southern California where he was born.

ONCE there was a puny little Zech concert violinist named Rudolf, who lived in Sweden. Some of his friends thought he was not the best of musicians because he was restless; others thought he was restless because he was not the best of musicians. At any rate, he hit upon a way of making a living, with no competitors. Whether by choice or necessity, he used to sail about Scandinavia in his small boat, all alone, giving concerts in little seaport towns. If he found accompanists, well and good; if not, he played works for unaccompanied violin; and it happened once or twice that he wanted a piano so badly that he imagined one, and then he played whole sonatas for violin and piano, with no piano in sight.

One year Rudolf sailed all the way out to Iceland and began working his way around that rocky coast from one town to another. It was a hard, stubborn land; but people in those difficult places do not forget the law of hospitality to the stranger—for their God may decree that they too shall become strangers on the face of the earth. The audiences were small, and even if Rudolf had been really first-rate, they would not have been very demonstrative. From ancient times their energy had gone, first of all, into earnest toil. Sometimes they were collected by

the local schoolteacher, who reminded them of their duty to the names
of Beethoven and Bach and Mozart and one or two others whose music
perhaps was not much heard in those parts. Too often people sat
stolidly watching the noisy little fiddler, and went home feeling gravely
edified. But they paid.

As Rudolf was sailing from one town to the next along a sparsely
settled shore, the northeast turned black and menacing. A storm was
bearing down upon Iceland. Rudolf was rounding a bleak, dangerous
cape, and his map told him that the nearest harbor was half a day's
journey away. He was starting to worry when he saw, less than a mile
off shore, a lighthouse on a tiny rock island. At the base of the lighthouse was a deep, narrow cove, protected by cliffs. With some difficulty,
in the rising seas, he put in there and moored to an iron ring that hung
from the cliff. A flight of stairs, hewn out of the rock, led up to the
lighthouse. On top of the cliff, outlined against the scudding clouds,
stood a man.

"You are welcome!" the voice boomed over the sound of the waves
that were already beginning to break over the island.

Darkness fell quickly. The lighthouse keeper led his guest up the
spiral stairs to the living room on the third floor, then busied himself
in preparation for the storm. Above all, he had to attend to the great
lamp in the tower, that dominated the whole region. It was a contin-
uous light, intensified by reflectors, and eclipsed by shutters at regular
intervals. The duration of light was equal to that of darkness.

The lighthouse keeper was a huge old man with a grizzled beard
that came down over his chest. Slow, deliberate, bearlike, he moved
without wasted motion about the limited world of which he was the
master. He spoke little, as if words had not much importance compared
to the other forces that comprised his life. Yet he was equable, as those
elements were not.

After the supper of black bread and boiled potatoes, herring, cheese
and hot tea, which they took in the kitchen above the living room,
the two men sat and contemplated each other's presence. Above them
was the maintenance room, and above that the great lamp spoke majestic, silent messages of light to the ships at sea. The storm hammered like a battering ram on the walls of the lighthouse. Rudolf offered tobacco, feeling suddenly immature as he did so. The old man
smiled a little as he declined it by a slight movement of the head; it
was as if he knew well the uses of tobacco and the need for offering
it, and affirmed it all, yet—here he, too, was halfway apologetic—was
self-contained and without need of anything that was not already
within his power or to which he did not relinquish his power. And he

sat there, gentle and reflective, his great workman hands resting on outspread thighs.

It seemed to Rudolf that the lighthouse keeper was entirely aware of all the sounds of the storm and of its violent impact upon the lighthouse, but he knew them so well that he did not have to think about them: they were like the involuntary movements of his own heart and blood. In the same way, beneath the simple courtesy that made him speak and listen to his guest in specific ways, he was already calmly and mysteriously a part of him, as surely as the mainland was connected with the little island, and all the islands with one another, so commodiously, under the ocean.

Gradually Rudolf drew forth the sparse data of the old man's life: He had been born in this very lighthouse eighty-three years before, when his father was the lighthouse keeper. His mother—the only woman he had ever known—had taught him to read the Bible, and he read it daily. He had no other books.

As a musician, Rudolf had not had time to read much either—but then, he had lived in cities. He reached down and took his beloved violin out of its case.

"What do you make with that, sir?" the old man asked.

For a second Rudolf thought his host might be joking; but the serenity of the other's expression reassured him. There was not even curiosity about the instrument, but rather a whole interest in him, the person, that included his "work." In most circumstances Rudolf would have found it hard to believe that there could exist someone who did not know what a violin was; yet now he had no inclination to laugh. He felt small and inadequate.

"I make—music with it," he stammered in a low voice.

"Music," the old man said ponderously. "I have heard of it. But I have never seen music."

"One does not see music. One hears it."

"Ah, yes," the lighthouse keeper consented, as it were with humility. This too was in the Nature of Things wherein all works were wonders, and all things were known eternally and were poignant in their transiency. His wide gray eyes rested upon the little fiddler and conferred upon him all the importance of which any individual is capable.

Then something in the storm and the lighthouse and the old man exalted Rudolf, filled him with compassion and love and a spaciousness infinitely beyond himself. He wanted to strike a work of fire and stars into being for the old man. And, with the storm as his accompanist, he stood and began to play—the Kreutzer Sonata of Beethoven.

The moments passed, moments that were days in the creation of that world of fire and stars: abysses and heights of passionate struggle, the

Idea of Order, and the resolution of these in the greatness of the human spirit. Never before had Rudolf played with such mastery—or with such an accompanist. Waves and wind beat the tower with giant hands. Steadily above them the beacon blazed in its sure cycles of darkness and light. The last note ceased and Rudolf dropped his head on his chest, breathing hard. The ocean seethed over the island with a roar as of many voices.

The old man had sat unmoving through the work, his broad, gnarled hands resting on his thighs, his head bowed, listening massively. For some time he continued to sit in silence. Then he looked up, lifted those hands calmly, judiciously, and nodded his head.

"Yes," he said. "That is true."

# THE WILD GOAT'S KID

*Liam O'Flaherty*

LIAM O'FLAHERTY (1897–    ). It was in 1925 that world-wide attention was drawn to this Irish writer by his novel *The Informer*, later made into a celebrated film by John Ford. Until then he had lived the life of a man of action, which included wartime service in France with the Irish Guards, travels around the world as stoker and beachcomber and finally the dangers and difficulties of Irish civil war. It was not until he reached the relative quiet of London some time later that he undertook to write. Oddly enough and quite contrary to the usual course, none of the excitements and adventures of his past had any place in his stories. His novels dwell on man's plight in a difficult world and the injustice that besets him; his background usually the Aran Islands where Mr. O'Flaherty was born or the dingy back streets of Dublin. Into this drabness he brings a kind of poetic beauty, and in his short stories his fusion of the dramatic with the idyllic is memorable. A superb example follows.

HER nimble hoofs made music on the crags all winter, as she roamed along the cliff-tops over the sea.

During the previous autumn, when goats were mating, she had wondered away, one of a small herd that trotted gaily after a handsome fellow, with a splendid grey-black hide and winding horns. It was her first mating. Then, with end of autumn, peasant boys came looking for their goats. The herd was broken up. The gallant buck was captured and slain by two hungry dogs from the village of Drumranny. The white goat alone remained. She had wandered too far away from her master's village. He couldn't find her. She was given up as lost.

So that she became a wild one of the cliffs, where the sea-gulls and the cormorants were lords, and the great eagle of Mohur soared high over the thundering sea. Her big, soft, yellow eyes became wild from looking down often at the sea, with her long chin whiskers swaying gracefully in the wind. She was a long, slender thing, with short, straight horns and ringlets of matted hair trailing far down on either haunch.

With her tail in the air, snorting, tossing her horns, she fled when anybody approached. Her hoofs would patter over the crags until she was far away. Then she would stand on some eminence and turn about to survey the person who had disturbed her, calmly, confident in the power of her slender legs to carry her beyond pursuit.

She roamed at will. No stone fence however high could resist her long leap, as she sprang on muscular thighs that bent like silk. She was so supple that she could trot on the top of a thin fence, carelessly, without a sound except the gentle tapping of her delicate hoofs. She hardly ever left the cliff-tops. There was plenty of food there, for the winter was mild, and the leaves and grasses that grew between the crevices of the crags were flavoured by the strong, salt taste of the brine carried up on the wind. She grew sleek and comely.

Towards the end of winter a subtle change came over her. Her hearing became more acute. She took fright at the least sound. She began to shun the sea except on very calm days, when it did not roar. She ate less. She grew very particular about what she ate. She hunted around a long time before she chose a morsel. She often went on her knees, reaching down into the bottom of a crevice to nibble at a briar that was inferior to the more accessible ones. She became corpulent. Her udder increased.

Winter passed. Green leaves began to sprout. Larks sang in the morning. There was sweetness in the air and a great urge of life. The white goat, one morning a little after dawn, gave birth to a grey-black kid.

The kid was born in a tiny, green glen under an overhanging ledge of low rock that sheltered it from the wind. It was a male kid, an exquisite, fragile thing, tinted delicately with many colours. His slender belly was milky white. The insides of his thighs were of the same colour. He had deep rings of grey, like bracelets, above his hoofs. He had black knee-caps on his forelegs, like pads, to protect him when he knelt to take his mother's teats into his silky, black mouth. His back and sides were grey-black. His ears were black, long, and drooping with the weakness of infancy.

The white goat bleated over him, with soft eyes and shivering flanks, gloating over the exquisite thing that had been created within her by the miraculous power of life. And she had this delicate creature all to herself, in the wild solitude of the beautiful little glen, within earshot of the murmuring sea, with little birds whistling their spring songs around her, and the winds coming with their slow murmurs over the crags. The first tender hours of her first motherhood were undisturbed by any restraint, not even by the restraint of a mate's presence. In absolute freedom and quiet, she watched with her young.

How she manoeuvred to make him stand! She breathed on him to warm him. She raised him gently with her forehead, uttering strange, soft sounds to encourage him. Then he stood up, trembling, staggering, swaying on his curiously long legs. She became very excited, rushing around him, bleating nervously, afraid that he should fall again. He fell. She was in agony. Bitter wails came from her distended jaws and she crunched her teeth. But she renewed her efforts, urging the kid to rise, to rise and live . . . to live, live, live.

He rose again. Now he was steadier. He shook his head. He wagged his long ears as his mother breathed into them. He took a few staggering steps, came to his padded knees, and rose again immediately. Slowly, gently, gradually, she pushed him towards her udder with her horns. At last he took the teat within his mouth, he pushed joyously, sank to his knees and began to drink.

She stayed with him all day in the tiny glen, just nibbling a few mouthfuls of the short grass that grew around. Most of the time she spent exercising her kid. With a great show of anxiety and impor- tance, she brought him on little expeditions across the glen to the opposite rock, three yards away and back again. At first he staggered clumsily against her sides, and his tiny hoofs often lost their balance on tufts of grass, such was his weakness. But he gained strength with amazing speed, and the goat's joy and pride increased. She suckled and caressed him after each tiny journey.

When the sun had set he was able to walk steadily, to take little short runs, to toss his head. They lay all night beneath the shelter of the ledge, with the kid between his mother's legs, against her warm udder.

Next morning she hid him securely in a crevice of the neighbouring crag, in a small groove between two flags that were covered with a withered growth of wild grass and ferns. The kid crawled instinctively into the warm hole without any resistance to the gentle push of his mother's horns. He lay down with his head towards his doubled hind legs, and closed his eyes. Then the goat scraped the grass and fern- stalks over the entrance hole with her fore feet, and she hurried away to graze, as carelessly as if she had no kid hidden.

All the morning, as she grazed hurriedly and fiercely around the crag, she took great pains to pretend that she was not aware of her kid's nearness. Even when she grazed almost beside the hiding-place, she never noticed him, by look or by cry. But still, she pricked her little ears at every distant sound.

At noon she took him out and gave him suck. She played with him on a grassy knoll and watched him prance about. She taught him how to rear on his hind legs and fight the air with his forehead. Then she put him back into his hiding-place and returned to graze. She continued to graze until nightfall.

Just when she was about to fetch him from his hole and take him to the overhanging ledge to rest for the night, a startling sound reached her ears. It came from afar, from the south, from beyond a low fence that ran across the crag on the skyline. It was indistinct, barely audible, a deep, purring sound. But to the ears of the mother-goat, it was loud and ominous as a thunderclap. It was the heavy breathing of a dog sniffing the wind.

She listened stock-still, with her head in the air and her short tail lying stiff along her back, twitching one ear. The sound came again. It was nearer. Then there was a patter of feet. Then a clumsy, black figure hurtled over the fence and dropped on to the crag, with awkward secrecy. The goat saw a black dog, a large, curly fellow, standing by the fence in the dim twilight, with his fore paw raised and his long, red tongue hanging. Then he shut his mouth suddenly, and raising his snout upwards sniffed several times, contracting his nostrils as he did so, as if in pain. Then he whined savagely, and trotted towards the goat sideways.

She snorted. It was a sharp, dull thud, like a blow from a rubber sledge. Then she rapped the crag three times with her left fore foot, loudly and sharply. The dog stood still and raised his fore paw again. He bent down his head and looked at her with narrowed eyes. Then he licked his breast and began to run swiftly to the left. He was running towards the kid's hiding-place, with his tail stretched out straight and his snout to the wind.

With another fierce snort the goat charged him at full speed, in order to cut him off from his advance on the kid's hiding-place. He stopped immediately when she charged. The goat halted too, five yards from the hiding-place, facing the dog.

The dog stood still. His eyes wandered around in all directions, with the bashfulness of a sly brute, caught suddenly in an awkward position. Then slowly he raised his bloodshot eyes to the goat. He bared his fangs. His mane rose like a fan. His tail shot out. Picking his steps like a lazy cat, he approached her without a sound. The goat shivered along her left flank, and she snorted twice in rapid succession.

When he was within six yards of her he uttered a ferocious roar—a deep, rumbling sound in his throat. He raced towards her, and leaped clean into the air, as if she were a fence that he was trying to vault. She parried him subtly with her horns, like a swordthrust, without moving her fore feet. Her sharp horns just grazed his belly as he whizzed past her head. But the slight blow deflected his course. Instead of falling on his feet, as he had intended cunningly to do, between the goat and the kid, he was thrown to the left and fell on his side, with a thud. The goat whirled about and charged him.

But he had arisen immediately and jerked himself away, with his haunches low down, making a devilish scraping and yelping and growling noise. He wanted to terrify the kid out of his hiding-place. Then it would be easy to overpower the goat, hampered by the task of hiding the kid between her legs.

The kid uttered a faint, querulous cry, but the goat immediately replied with a sharp, low cry. The kid mumbled something indistinct, and then remained silent. There was a brushing sound among the ferns that covered him. He was settling himself down farther. The goat trotted rigidly to the opposite side of the hiding-place to face the dog again.

The dog had run away some distance, and lay on his belly, licking his paws. Now he meant to settle himself down properly to the prolonged attack, after the failure of his first onslaught. He yawned lazily and made peculiar mournful noises, thrusting his head into the air and twitching his snout. The goat watched every single movement and sound, with her ears thrust forward past her horns. Her great, soft eyes were very wild and timorous in spite of the valiant posture of her body, and the terrific force of the blows she delivered occasionally on the hard crag with her little hoofs.

The dog remained lying for half an hour or so, continuing his weird pantomime. The night fell completely. Everything became unreal and ghostly under the light of the distant myriads of stars. An infant moon had arisen. The sharp rushing wind and the thunder of the sea only made the silent loneliness of the night more menacing to the white goat, as she stood bravely on the limestone crag defending her newborn young. On all sides the horizon was a tumultuous line of barren crag, dented with shallow glens and seamed with low, stone fences that hung like tattered curtains against the rim of the sky.

Then the dog attacked again. Rising suddenly, he set off at a long, swinging gallop, with his head turned sideways towards the goat, whining as he ran. He ran around the goat in a wide circle, gradually increasing his speed. A white spot on his breast flashed and vanished as he rose and fell in the undulating stretches of his flight. The goat watched him, fiercely rigid from tail to snout. She pawed the crag methodically, turning around on her own ground slowly to face him.

When he passed his starting-point, he was flying at full speed, a black ball shooting along the gloomy surface of the crag, with a sharp rattle of claws. The rattle of his claws, his whining and the sharp tapping of the goat's fore feet as she turned about, were the only sounds that rose into the night from this sinister engagement.

He sped round and round the goat, approaching her imperceptibly each round, until he was so close that she could see his glittering eyes and the white lather of rage on his half-open jaws. She became slightly dizzy and confused, turning about so methodically in a confined space, confused and amazed by the subtle strategy of the horrid beast. His whining grew louder and more savage. The rattle of his claws was like the clamour of hailstones driven by a wind. He was upon her.

He came in a whirl on her flank. He came with a savage roar that deafened her. She shivered and then stiffened in rigid silence to receive him. The kid uttered a shrill cry. Then the black bulk hurtled through the air, close up, with hot breathing, snarling, with reddened fangs and . . . smash.

He had dived for her left flank. But as he went past her head she turned like lightning and met him again with her horns. This time she grazed his side, to the rear of the shoulder. He yelped and tumbled sideways, rolling over twice. With a savage snort she was upon him. He was on his haunches, rising, when her horns thudded into his head. He went down again with another yelp. He rolled over and then suddenly, with amazing speed, swept to his feet, whirled about on swinging tail and dived for her flank once more. The goat uttered a shriek of terror. He had passed her horns. His fangs had embedded themselves in the matted ringlet that trailed along her right flank. The dog's flying weight, swinging on to the ringlet as he fell, brought her to her haunches.

But she was ferocious now. As she wriggled to her feet beside the rolling dog that gripped her flank, she wrenched herself around and gored him savagely in the belly. He yelled and loosed his hold. She rose on her hind legs in a flash, and with a snort she gored him again. Her sharp, pointed horns penetrated his side between the ribs. He gasped and shook his four feet in the air. Then she pounded on him with her fore feet, beating his prostrate body furiously. Her little hoofs pattered with tremendous speed for almost a minute. She beat him blindly, without looking at him.

Then she suddenly stopped. She snorted. The dog was still. She shivered and looked down at him curiously. He was dead. Her terror was passed. She lifted her right fore foot and shook it with a curious movement. Then she uttered a wild, joyous cry and ran towards her kid's hiding-place.

Night passed into a glorious dawn that came over a rippling sea from the east. A wild, sweet dawn, scented with dew and the many perfumes of the germinating earth. The sleepy sun rose brooding from the sea, golden and soft, searching far horizons with its concave shafts of light. The dawn was still. Still and soft and pure.

The white goat and her kid were travelling eastwards along the cliff-tops over the sea. They had travelled all night, flying from the horrid carcass of the beast that lay stretched on the crag beside the little glen. Now they were far away, on the summit of the giant white Precipice of Cahir. The white goat rested to give suck to her kid, and to look out over the cliff-top at the rising sun.

Then she continued her flight eastwards, pushing her tired kid gently before her with her horns.

# THE END OF THE LINE

*Gavin Lambert*

---

GAVIN LAMBERT (1924–    ) is a young Englishman who lives in Los Angeles where he is engaged in writing for the screen. This is an interesting turn as for some years he was a film critic in Great Britain as well as the editor of *Sight and Sound*. His first book, *The Slide Area*, is a group of linked short stories about Hollywood, its environs and its inhabitants; a crisp and witty mixture of the factual and the fantastic. *The End of the Line*, from that collection, impresses the editors as one of the most original pieces of short fiction in recent years.

COUNTESS MARGUERITE OSTERBERG-STEBLECHI lives in a big grey patrician house in the Hollywood hills. Steep and narrow roads twist through these hills, where living was fashionable in the twenties. Valentino and Nazimova built homes here. Stateliness hangs in the air. Most of the houses are large, but you have the impression half their rooms are closed now, furniture draped with old sheets and blinds pulled down.

A flight of stone steps leads up to the heavy oak door of the Countess's house, and two old yucca trees put out thin white blossoms each year. The fine spacious living-room with fake panelling has an open fireplace at one end, two 'French Provincial' arches at the other, and its windows open out to a high-walled patio. It seems odd there is no door from the living-room to the patio, but this is because the patio was added later. It was the first of a series of miscalculations. The man who added the patio liked to sunbathe in the nude and ordered a high wall so he shouldn't be overlooked, but the wall is so high the patio gets only an hour or two of sun each day in summer, and none in winter. The sun never gets through to the living-room at all.

A door in the patio wall leads to a neglected garden, the ground slopes down to a swimming pool shaped like a half moon. There are usually a few hundred eucalyptus leaves floating on the water, and a faint sour-sweet perfume haunts the air. A chipped stone cupid with a broken arrow presides over the deep end.

Portraits painted by the Countess thirty and forty years ago hang everywhere in the house. Jean Cocteau, Mistinguette, Somerset Maugham and Queen Marie of Rumania are side by side as you go upstairs. The Countess herself looks down at different ages from different walls. In the 1900's she is delicate and unreal, everything white except her long coppery hair: a soft slender figure in a white dress, white parasol in one hand and white hat in the other, behind her a mountain peak covered in snow. The last portrait is in 1933, when she is rather sternly middle-aged, still handsome but putting on weight against a background of the Grand Canal in Venice.

The Countess has been blind and fairly deaf for more than a year. Through a strange error for which she cannot be held responsible, she believes her house is in the Arab quarter of Marrakech. She is convinced she came to Morocco after an extensive European tour more than a year ago, and liked it so much she decided to settle there. And when she sits out in the patio she can hear strange flutes and drums, Arab cries from the seething market-place called Djema el Fnaa. These sounds are weak and blurred as they reach her failing ears, but she finds that distance increases their allure. Sometimes, she says, they seem to be beckoning.

She will tell you she is the only European in the Medina who can bear the terrible hot season from June to September when a fiery wind blows from the desert and the sky turns blood red. It seems no worse than California at the height of summer. Every Thursday night she eats couscous.

Except for her two unmarried nieces, myself and Mark Cusden, who first introduced me to her, everyone in Hollywood who knows the Countess also believes she is in North Africa. They send greetings at Christmas and occasionally remark how they miss her Sunday teas. They wonder how she fared during the recent political disturbances, and some feel she would be safer in Tangier.

For a long time I couldn't see any way out of the situation. I felt I should have done. I used to think that if a story about the Countess appeared in print, something was bound to happen. The nieces would receive a visit from the police, most likely. But that would have made a rather feeble ending and solved very little. I decided to wait and see if life itself couldn't provide something better; after all, it had already provided so much. In a way this was an immoral decision, though now it is all over I can't see that any harm has been done, or that much has been lost. The nieces have certainly gained. They have changed their names and are among the richest women in Florida.

It is a strange thought, too, that if I hadn't decided to do nothing, quite a few people whom none of us has ever met might have died in Budapest during the uprising against the Soviets, or at least still be in prison there.

The Countess arrived in America in December 1939. Before this she spent five years of widowhood in a Venetian palace, last of several great houses bought by her husband.

Count Gabriele was the only son of two noble families. An Osterberg of Budapest married a Steblechi of Rome and they made their home on the vast Osterberg estates near Cracow. Their son Gabriele showed signs of financial genius at school in Lucerne, and by the time he was twenty-five it was clear he would turn the bank founded by his grandfather into a great international corporation.

Spanish and Belgian blood excellent on both sides flowed in Marguerite's veins. Like Gabriele she was sent to school in Switzerland. She fell into his arms while ski-ing at St. Moritz in 1901.

Their life together was cosmopolitan from the start. The Countess once showed me her collection of cuttings from *Vogue*, *The Tatler*, *Harpers* and so on, with photographs of herself and the Count together in their various beautiful homes all over the world. They were always elegant, smiling, arm-in-arm, and the captions praised their dinner parties, their clothes, their antiques and their patronage of the arts. After the marriage they went to live on the Osterberg estates, but Gabriele travelled a great deal, opening new branches in new capitals. They sat out the first world war in Geneva. The Austro-Hungarian Empire fell and the estates became part of a new country called Poland. This involved years of litigation, never brought to a head. They moved to Paris. Marguerite loved the arts, she bought some early Picassos and Matisses, commissioned a ballet from Diaghilev and gave a masked ball for the young Cocteau. One of the guests was Gertrude Stein, who later wrote *Portrait of Marguerite Osterberg-Steblechi at the Villa Tricorne*.

The Countess began painting, but her style was much more conservative than her subjects. The portraits now in her Hollywood home are surprisingly flat and literal. Soon after she arrived in Hollywood a small gallery held an exhibition of her work, which was enthusiastically reviewed by Elsa Maxwell.

In 1926 they moved to London and took a beautiful Georgian house in Curzon Street. Marguerite gave dinner parties reported in the society columns, but hated the climate. Unfortunately she arrived in the year of the General Strike and near Notting Hill Gate a group of workmen threw potatoes at her Daimler.

They left to visit New York, then bought a castle in Provence. After three years Count Gabriele remarked that the Riviera had somehow lost its charm, and in Venice they found a vacant palazzo which they cleared of damp and neglect, hung with pictures, furnished with antique pieces collected all over Europe, and warmed with acres of carpets. Only Gabriele didn't live to enjoy it long. He had taken up flying as a hobby and piloted his own plane. On New Year's Day 1934 it crashed over the Dalmatian coast.

The Count's death was reported in newspapers all over the world. Most of them added in smaller type the fact that a passenger was killed with him, describing her simply as Mrs. Thelma Brighouse of Canterbury, England. Recently I wrote to Carlotta, eldest of Marguerite's two nieces, and asked what she could tell me about this. She replied from Florida in her dry, factual and peculiar English:

This is ancient history and Pia and I is not very good at it. 23 years has passed now and memory is not so sharp. Will you have guessed that Mrs. Brighouse was last of a very long line? Naturally we cannot remember all names of ladies favored by the attention of our late Uncle the Count, and send you only an incomplete list representing our best efforts.

The list contained fourteen names, of Spanish, French, Italian, American, English and Rumanian women. In some cases Carlotta added a date in brackets. She went on:

We can be sure these ladies caused poor Marguerite much pain. She *never* favored no one else and all rumors to contrary is disgusting. She was devoted to the Count, though Pia agrees *he* would not have minded.

After Gabriele's death the Countess continued to live alone at the palazzo with six servants and a personal maid. She was fifty now and a little stout. Gabriele's death seemed to hasten a physical decay. She grew bloated; her hair greyed and her eyes dulled; she began to wear the hideous flowered prints I knew so well in California. She gave up painting and shuffled round her sixteen beautiful and opulent rooms in a pair of frayed old mules. When Gabriele was alive there were always guests at the palazzo, rich or titled or brilliant. Now people still came to stay, but they were mediocre and grasping. Servants sometimes reported the loss of ornaments or silverware.

Dictators were growing powerful in Europe now, but the Countess seldom read a newspaper. She preferred to start writing her memoirs and leafed endlessly through photographs of the old life in half a dozen different countries. If she heard predictions of war, she shook her head wisely or gave a faint wheeze of laughter. On September 3rd 1939 she sent Hitler a telegram: PLEASE MAKE EVERY EFFORT AVOID WAR STOP AM CONVINCED YOU DO NOT WISH BRING DISASTER ON CIVILIZED WORLD—MARGUERITE OSTERBERG-STEBLECHI.

By the time it arrived, Warsaw was burning. Two weeks later the Cracow estates had been overrun.

The bank's funds in Germany, Austria and Czechoslovakia had already been confiscated by the Nazis, and Marguerite felt poverty dreadfully near. She decided to leave the palazzo, but couldn't sell it. She dismissed her servants and managed to dispose of her Picassos and Matisses, most of her furniture and carpets. As she watched all the beautiful things being taken away on a steamer, she fainted. Afterwards she told her doctor it was a most extraordinary feeling. The ground had seemed to open up under her feet, and she had a vision of all Europe falling down the crack.

She travelled to America with her jewels and the portraits she had painted; about a hundred knick-knacks; a bedroom suite and a few pieces of furniture she particularly liked; only two trunks of clothes but eleven of letters, newspaper cuttings and photograph albums.

Water lapped at a shuttered palace until the end of the war. When they opened it up in 1946, they found it full of dead cats. Today it is a hotel. Wealthy tourists sit in a dining-room where the famous long table used to be laid with crested silver and china bearing the two crowned eagles of the Austro-Hungarian Empire. An oil painting of Count Gabriele Osterberg-Steblechi, suffocated with varnish, hangs in a shadowy part of the hall.

Alone in California, Marguerite sat out the second world war. Her banks fell in country after country, but like the Cracow estates seemed too far away to worry about. She took up her memoirs, abandoned them again. Memory was failing. Was it the Queen of the Belgians or the Grand Duchess of Luxembourg who had entertained her to tea at La Panne when the news of Jutland arrived? Or was she confusing this with a picnic lunch on the shores of Lake Geneva when reports of the armistice came through and she danced with the Count of Klausenburg? The old life that had always seemed so vivid and certain began to elude her. She went to the movies and read a great many mystery stories.

Although she had lost a good deal of money, people said the Countess was still 'worth' between two and three million dollars. But in her own eyes she was threatened with ruin. Money was the only thing left for her to preserve. In one of her albums is a photograph taken during a dinner party given by herself and Gabriele in 1907. The guests included international royalty and society figures. By the time Marguerite reached California, everyone at that table at the Ritz in Paris, except herself, was dead. 'If the rest of my money goes,' she said once, 'I am finished. I am like Warsaw. Razed to the ground, dear child.' So she scoured remote second-hand stores to furnish her new home, and would bring back an old rocking chair, a dressing-table with a cracked mirror, as if it were a priceless bargain. Apart from the furniture she had brought with her, and occasionally hired to film companies for historical productions—she once went without her own bed for a month—there was nothing in the house that didn't look worn or makeshift.

Remains of her Venetian period were concentrated in the hall and living-room. Here nothing matched but everything was graceful and distinguished. Any vacant space was filled with Dresden figurines, little Indian buddhas, Lowestoft China, lacquered boxes from Japan, all kinds of glass and silver. Down in the cellars were crates and trunks that had never been opened. She couldn't remember what was in them, and grew tired of unpacking.

The Countess didn't lack new acquaintances. Snobs took her up very quickly and pumped her for anecdotes of royalty. At one dinner party in her honour she exposed the host as a false Papal Knight. The Sunday afternoon teas at which there was nothing to eat and the tea was made in bags were an attempt, I suppose, to create a *salon*. Decorators came to bargain for her antiques—she was always willing to sell anything—and she could hold expatriates spellbound with a fairly rambling account of the first performance of *The Rite of Spring*.

A popular rumour at one time was that she had secretly married her houseboy to get American nationality. Another was that she had bought a burlesque house in down-town Los Angeles. I know she always drove eight miles to buy food at a market in the San Fernando Valley because prices were a few cents lower there. And Mark Cusden assured me, the first time he brought me to see her, that she was wearing a linen dress he had helped her choose from a rack marked 'Factory Rejects' at the Hollywood Bargain Centre.

I didn't want to kiss her hand. It was a limp speckled claw ringed with emerald, topaz and garnet. I touched a knuckle with my lips, and it seemed to satisfy her. 'You look like a dear child to me,' she said.

'As it's not Sunday,' Mark suggested, 'why don't you bring out something more interesting than tea?' He had wanted to avoid a Sunday reception for our first meeting and show me the Countess in private.

'The most interesting thing in this house is already brought out!' The Countess jabbed herself in the stomach and winked a hawkish eye. 'However, I will confess the ice-box also holds it charms.'

'A bottle of Dubonnet?'

She chuckled. 'He knows all my little secrets. Fetch it, sweet one.'

Breathing deeply, she wedged herself into a chair as Mark went to the kitchen. Behind her, on the wall, hung her first self-portrait. I went to look at it.

'It's charming, isn't it?' the Countess said. 'A very exact likeness, as a matter of fact.'

Eyes looked out softly from a pale fragile face. I glanced at the ancient hulk in the chair and said: 'You were a great beauty.'

The chair trembled under her wheeze. 'So what do you expect me to do about it? Sit here and remember it?'

Mark returned with the Dubonnet and three glasses on a tarnished silver tray. The Countess got up, walked very slowly to another chair and seated herself in it. 'It's my birthday,' she said.

We congratulated her. She waved a hand. 'It's a melancholy occasion, really. More like a funeral. But I've been wondering how old I am.'

'Do you know when you were born, Marguerite?' asked Mark, pouring the Dubonnet.

She nodded. 'Eighteen seventy-eight. But it's too much to count.'

'You're seventy-nine,' I said.

She gave a chuckle. 'You bring me good news. I thought I was eighty.' She raised her glass to herself. '*Bonne fête!*' she said, then got up again and moved to another chair. 'I've been doing this all afternoon. I have a great many chairs. I move about from one to the other. It's a depressing way to spend one's birthday, but I can't think of anything else to do.'

'You're looking well,' Mark said.

She patted her hair. 'Yes, I think so. I'm glad you didn't see me yesterday. Yesterday was bad; I thought I mightn't get through it.'

'What happened?' I asked.

'Nothing, dear child. That's exactly it. It was one of those days without pain, without pleasure. Hour after hour of appalling nothingness.' She licked her lips. 'I finally cheered myself up by eating six éclairs. It's not a very healthy diet, éclairs and Dubonnet, but sometimes one is driven to extremes. I shall try and eat nothing except boiled eggs tomorrow.'

With a sudden convulsive movement she got up and directed herself towards the kitchen.

'Where are you going now?' Mark asked.

'Surprise, surprise!' She propped herself against the purple velvet couch for a moment. 'Don't help me. I usually get there in the end.'

Finally she disappeared into the kitchen. After what seemed a very long time, she came back with a large coffee éclair on a cracked antique plate. She handed it to Mark. 'Divide this into three, sweet one.'

Mark did so.

'*Bonne fête!*' the Countess wished herself again, swallowing her piece at one go.

'You only brought one napkin,' Mark said.

'It's enough for the three of us. Divide it also!' She watched sharply while he tore it into strips, then turned to me. 'Who do you know in England?' She muttered a few names under her breath, and ended clearly: 'Sir Harry Lauder.'

'He's dead,' I told her.

'I painted him.' She took a pair of spectacles from a mother-of-pearl case hanging on a chain round her neck, and perched them on the end of her nose. 'But I can't remember where I put him.' Looking up suddenly at Mark, she went on: 'You can't stay long, my lawyer's coming about the Cracow estates.'

I asked if there were any chance of getting them back.

'Getting them back?' She laughed until she gasped. 'They don't *exist*, dear child. During the war they were a concentration camp, now they're a collective farm.'

Mark yawned and switched on the little portable radio which stood beside an Indian buddha on a satinwood table.

'The first time it happened, Gabriele didn't worry because he said Poland would never last. I suppose if we wait . . .' The lids drooped over Marguerite's eyes. 'But isn't there so little left of Europe now?'

'You'd find it very changed.'

She scratched her nose and let her hand drop slackly to her lap. Everything about her became vague and slow, like clockwork running down.

'Dear child, have you ever stayed at the Hotel d'Altri Tempi in Venice?'

'Much too expensive,' I said.

'It was ours.' She gave a sigh. 'Before everything stopped.'

*Just One of Those Things* came from the radio. The Countess made curious rhythmic sounds in her throat, I supposed she was humming. 'Sinatra is still the best,' she said quietly. She looked at Mark. 'We loved Sinatra, didn't we?' She hummed again. 'I would like to go back to Europe, you know. Only I'm too tired.'

Then she yawned and fell asleep with the spectacles still on the end of her nose. We thought it better not to wake her.

As we went out through the hall, I noticed another portrait of the

Countess. She must have painted it in the twenties. Slightly askew, it hung next to Nijinsky. I straightened it, sending up a thick cloud of dust.

I first met the nieces at a Sunday tea about two months later. In fact they weren't nieces at all, but the daughters of some remote Steblechi connection whose mother had died and left them penniless in Naples. 'Really it is impossible to decide what they are,' the Countess said, 'but we agree they shall be considered nieces.' Anyway, apart from Marguerite herself, they were the last surviving Steblechis. The Osterberg line had come to an end with Gabriele's death.

The nieces were both in their early forties, tall and bony in black silk dresses and long low-heeled shoes shaped like gondolas. They had sallow Latin complexions and faint moustaches, sharp chins and long anxious necks. As I came into the room I heard Carlotta say:

'Tea in bags is horrible and must be stopped.'

Pia, who was the younger, made a knowing grimace. Then both assumed ghastly hypocritical smiles as the Countess brought me over. 'These are my poor dear girls, they miss their mother.'

They watched the Countess move slowly away, then Carlotta seized my wrist. 'Everything is mad and ridiculous!'

'You should see my bedroom,' Pia hissed. 'Like a market.'

'There is eighteen dresses with flowers in her cupboards.'

'There is nothing but old pictures and chairs that fall down.'

'On Sundays there is tea in bags.' The tea bags seemed to obsess Carlotta. She glanced round the room. 'Either these people is worth nothing, or is worth more than tea in bags.'

'There should be cookies,' I suggested.

The nieces considered this, then Pia asked: 'How much is cookies?'

'We ask because expenses is terrible here,' Carlotta explained. 'Aunt Marguerite thinks she is clever to drive eight miles to a market with lower prices. But she is not clever, because that big old car does only seven miles to the gallon.'

'Typical false economy,' said Pia.

I was wondering how naturally mean they were, or whether the Countess had already convinced them of her poverty, when Carlotta asked: 'You think Aunt Marguerite is nearer two or three million dollars?'

In what I hoped was a discouraging tone, I said I didn't know. Its only effect was to make Carlotta ask another question. 'You think she got a good price for that old palazzo?'

'Why don't you ask her?'

They muttered to each other in Italian, then Carlotta answered: 'You think we want to create a bad impression?'

Two weeks later they put a stop to the Sunday afternoons. They announced the Countess was unwell and had been ordered to rest completely for a while, but we knew it was really because they had decided we were all worth nothing.

Then I met Carlotta in a supermarket. She was buying yesterday's bread at reduced prices, and told me the Countess had gone blind. I asked if nothing could be done, and Carlotta shook her head. 'Even if operations was not doubtful, Aunt Marguerite is too old for them.' She went on to tell me that they'd dismissed the houseboy. 'Nothing has been dusted for years, and he never waters the garden, so everything is dirty or dead.'

She advised me not to go and see the Countess, but I decided to pay a call. I couldn't tell Mark about it, for this was one of the periods when he disappeared and no one could find him.

'Two minutes is all,' Carlotta announced, admitting me reluctantly. She seemed to include time in her stringent economies. The Countess lay on the purple couch in the living-room, nibbling a banana. She wore a bright flowered print and a lot of jewellery. The red dye was beginning to grow out of her hair.

'Dear child,' she said when Carlotta told her loudly who had come. 'I am in the dark.'

She raised her face and gave me a blind unblinking look. I noticed Pia on a canvas swing-seat in the patio, taking sun. She wore an old-fashioned black bathing suit, nodded rather curtly and didn't come in.

The Countess appeared in good spirits but her responses were alternately vague and sharp. She was also growing deaf. Once she couldn't remember who I was, a moment later she stretched out a hand and closed her fingers over the little buddha on the satinwood table by her side.

'Do you like this little treasure?'

'Yes,' I said.

'You can have it for three dollars.'

Carlotta watched disapprovingly while I paid for it. 'Such robbery,' she said and forced her lips into a smile. Without a word, I put the buddha in her hand. 'Excuse me please,' she said and went out to the patio, presumably to tell Pia.

The Countess asked me to light a cigarette for her. She smoked thin brown Havanas. She took a puff, then sniffed the smoke as it curled away from her nose. 'I cannot taste much,' she said. 'It takes away the pleasure of tobacco. However, I can smell a little.' Then she ran her hand along my arm, up to my shoulder. 'Dear child, you will have to be my mirror. My mirror that speaks. Tell me, mirror, is the dye running out of my hair?'

'Yes, a little.'

'I knew it!' She gave a grunt of satisfaction. 'Carlotta and Pia lied to me, as usual. You know, I am sad when I cannot see my beautiful antiques, I miss them very much. But I am not so sad,' she began to shake with laughter, 'when I cannot see my nieces. It helps, if you will pardon the expression, to look on the brighter side of things . . .'

Carlotta returned and said it was time for me to leave.

'You must come again soon,' the Countess said, 'and I'll show you my memoirs. Did you know I'd started them again?'

'They will never be finished!' Carlotta hissed at me as I left. 'We have to sit for an hour each morning while she dictates ridiculous nonsense. She gets all the names and dates wrong, no one can make anything of it.'

Opening the front door, she saw my battered Chevrolet parked on the opposite side of the street.

'Your car?' I nodded. 'Will you please tell me how much it cost?' 'Seventy dollars,' I said 'You spend much money on it since?' 'No,' I said. 'You spoil the front yourself?' 'No,' I said, 'that's the way I bought it.'

Carlotta became almost friendly. 'Most economical.' We shook hands. She held out her left hand, which had been hidden behind her back. The little buddha lay in it.

'Pia and I discussed this matter. We decided,' she gave a little sigh, 'what is paid for, *belongs*.'

I thanked her gravely. She stood at the top of the steps, plucking a flower from the yucca tree and sniffing it as she watched me drive off. I thought that the Countess had gone as far away as any human being can without actually dying. Cut off from seeing, soon without sounds to hear, and confused by her memories, she seemed scarcely more part of the world than the little buddha in my pocket.

Not long after this, Carlotta telephoned.

'Good-bye! We have to take Aunt Marguerite round the world.'

'What on earth for?'

'It cannot be stopped. She is bored and refuses to go on with her memoirs. She wants a last look round.'

'But she can't see.'

'This is unnecessary. She can hear a little. She will know all the places and wants just to be in them again.'

'I think you should dissuade her.'

'Impossible. There is trunks and bags already in the hall. She packs all those dresses herself.'

'What did the doctor say?'

'She has the strongest heart of any old lady he ever listened to.'

'Then I suppose there's nothing you can do.'

'Such expenses is bad for *my* heart!'

'You'll have to make the best of it, Carlotta. After all, you complain you never get out of the house. When do you leave?'

'Tomorrow . . .' A long thin sigh. 'We take a train to New York and then a Greek boat to France. It saves a little.'

For a while I hardly thought of the Countess again, except to hope for a postcard from time to time; but I knew Carlotta and Pia would be too mean to send any.

One afternoon I was buying records at a store on Hollywood Boulevard. A woman wearing a black silk dress and funereal hat with thick veiling hurried out through the swing doors. I followed her into the street, and glimpsed a pair of gondola-shaped shoes as she disappeared into a cab and it drove quickly away.

It must have been Carlotta. Nobody else dressed that way, except Pia. Then was the Countess back already? I telephoned the house that evening and a recorded voice informed me that I had reached a disconnected number.

Still convinced I had seen Carlotta, I drove up to the house next day. It looked neglected and aloof, shutters drawn across the windows, tall weeds sprouting in crevices on the stone steps and one of the yucca trees dying. But as I stood looking at it, I heard an extraordinary sound. I couldn't believe it, and listened again. No doubt of it, loud bursts of flamenco music were coming from somewhere.

From the house next door? No, the music faded when I went over there. Tracing the sound of mandolins and castanets and a gipsy voice, I went past the yucca trees, up the stone steps to the shuttered windows. I rang the doorbell. Waiting, I noticed that a little peephole had been cut in the door. The music seemed very loud now and underneath it I thought I detected the rattle of a train.

Nobody answered the bell. I was about to ring again, when I saw a pair of eyes on the other side of the peephole. They met close and level with mine in a fixed alarming stare. It was a fantastic moment, as if two dreams had collided. At last the eyes went away, the door opened a few inches and Carlotta peered furiously round the crack. When I moved a step closer she gave a piercing scream and slammed the door in my face.

I could see her watching me again through the peephole, glassily.

This wouldn't do at all. I moved off towards my car with a deliberate saunter, got in and ran the engine for a minute. Then I walked round to the back of the house and inspected the patio wall for footholds. Luckily there were flying buttresses too and I managed to scale it.

Carlotta was not expecting an attack from this quarter. Staying close to the wall, I moved up to the windows without being seen. Venetian blinds had been added now, but they were half open. Bars of shadow lay across the living-room.

A space had been cleared in the centre of the room, and was occupied by part of a railway carriage. There was a seat with a luggage rack above it, a window on one side and sliding glass doors on the other, opening directly to the fireplace. In a sable coat and a pink straw hat topped with artificial fruit, the Countess was settled on the window seat. Sightless eyes were raised to her own patio; but in her mind, I suppose, she saw strange distances. There must have been a mechanical device under the seat, because it rocked slightly.

With ungainly flamenco movements, Pia circled the carriage. She clicked a pair of castanets, stretched her long neck and flapped her arms like a hungry distracted bird. From the couch Carlotta clapped her hands and shouted an occasional 'Olé!' Three record-players stood side by side on a long table against the wall, issuing music and the sounds of a train. The performance continued for about two minutes, Pia grew breathless and rolled her eyes in supplication at her sister, who took no notice but clapped her hands and shouted in sharp implacable rhythm. Sometimes the Countess smiled and nodded, beating time with her foot. Then the sound of the train slowed down.

Carlotta stopped the flamenco music. She put a record on the third player and filled the room with trains whistling and steaming out of a station, crowds of people bustling and muttering, carriage doors being opened and heavy trolleys passing. Pia threw away her castnets with relief, leaned over the Countess and pulled her to her feet. Each taking an arm, the sisters led the old woman out of the room.

After a moment, Carlotta came back. She silenced the last record player. I tapped on the window. She looked across at me, stiff with fright at first; then she shrugged. She let me in through the dining-room door. I noticed a wind machine standing in the corner.

'Where's Marguerite?' I asked.

Rather wearily she pointed down the cellar stairs. 'She'll be back in a minute.' From below I heard faint sounds of an engine whirring. A horn blew, a door slammed.

'Excuse me a moment,' Carlotta said.

I followed her. Pia was helping the Countess up the stairs from the cellar. She gave me a nervous glance and said loudly in her aunt's ear: 'Only eleven more!' The Countess appeared suddenly dazed, and asked: 'More what?' 'Steps,' said Pia. 'Where to?' 'The hotel.' 'Oh,' said the Countess, 'then what time is it?'

They had reached the top, and 'Buenos dias, Senora!' came in a deep bass voice which I realized had been assumed by Carlotta. The Countess seemed happy and vivacious now. 'Pia, is our luggage all right?' she asked as they led her along the hall. 'Tell Carlotta to count it, last time I was in Madrid . . .' She broke off again, dazed. 'I can't remember when it was.'

'Nineteen ten, you told us yesterday,' Pia said.

'No, it wasn't. It was nineteen nine. Anyway, the porter lost a hat-box.'

'Senora, I regret to announce the elevator is temporarily not working,' said Carlotta in her deep Spanish voice.

A shadow of irritation darkened her aunt's face. 'Pia, you have a genius for finding hotels with broken elevators.'

'Only seventeen stairs to the first floor,' Pia said cheerfully.

On the way up, the Countess asked again: 'What time is it? Is it night?'

'No, it's day.'

They took her to her own bedroom and sat her in an armchair. 'You'd better rest,' Carlotta advised. 'It's been a long journey.'

'Is the window open?'

'Yes,' said Pia, closing it.

The Countess frowned. 'Why did you tell me I lost a hat-box in Madrid?'

'It was *you* who told *me*.'

'Impossible. Anyway, it was in Amsterdam. In nineteen six. We must look for it.' She scratched her nose. 'Is it Sunday?'

'Yes.'

'Then there's a band concert in the Retiro.' The Countess started to get out of her chair.

'Band concerts is on Saturdays now,' Carlotta said quickly, pushing her down.

'Are you sure?'

'I saw a notice in the hall.' Her niece's voice was firm. 'It said, all band concerts on Saturdays until further notice.'

The Countess sighed. 'Everything's changing. Ring for tea.'

'Wouldn't you rather sleep first?'

'No.'

With a look of exasperation, Pia left the room.

'It's not worth waiting another six days for a band concert. Careless girls.' The Countess sounded peevish. 'We'll leave tomorrow.'

'So soon? Where do you wish to go?' Carlotta asked brokenly.

'Rome. No, Rome may be too cold.'

'In July?'

'Is it July?' With a look of alarm the Countess stroked her sables. 'But I'm wearing my sables, in July in Madrid one should swelter in sables!'

'Exceptionally cool summer, everyone is talking about it here!'

After a pause the Countess asked: 'Is there something on my head?'

'Your hat.'

'Take it off, please.' As Carlotta did so, the Countess added: 'We go to Venice, see about the tickets.' An uncertain look came over her face. 'Where am I now?'

'How tired you get after long journeys, you really should sleep. You're in Madrid,' Carlotta said with a touch of impatience.

Her aunt smiled. 'I haven't been in Madrid since——'

'Nineteen nine!'

'Much longer ago than that. What a bad memory you have, Carlotta. In nineteen nine I was near Cracow.'

'Shouldn't you take off your coat?'

'Not in an exceptionally cool summer,' said the Countess and yawned. 'Tell them to hurry with the tea.'

I followed Carlotta downstairs. She sank exhausted to the living-room couch. As Pia passed through the hall with a tea-tray, she called: 'We leave for Venice in the morning!'

'Doesn't she like it here?' Pia asked.

'It was my fault.' Carlotta sighed. 'For telling lies about band concerts. But we had no music.'

'Couldn't we find out there is special concerts on Mondays and get records tomorrow?'

'Cheaper to go to Venice.'

Pia took the tray upstairs.

I watched Carlotta. She lay back on the purple couch and stared at the ceiling. Presently she said: "Gipsy flamenco music on Spanish trains is possible?'

'In the third class, anyway,' I agreed.

She pointed to the railway carriage. 'This is all we got. Long journeys is impossible, we cannot describe landscapes and stations for ever. To-day we said a gipsy is on the train and passengers ask her to dance.' Carlotta tapped my wrist. 'This kind of thing is very good because it excites her, then she is tired out and now she sleeps a little.'

'Fraud? Oh, that is not a word I should use,' Carlotta was saying a few minutes later, when Pia came back with the news that their aunt was asleep. 'What we are doing is economy.'

'The cost of living rises all over the world,' Pia remarked. 'Extravagances must be stopped.'

'Old ladies of seventy-nine must not start travelling everywhere when they cannot even see where they are going!'

When the Countess decided to revisit Europe, her nieces had been appalled. It would cost a fortune, and they couldn't bear to think of their aunt's remaining millions shrinking away. After all, she had no one else to whom to leave them. 'Have we no rights?' Carlotta said. 'Are we to return to the slums of Naples?' What they had been allowed to see of California had begun to please them, especially the boom in real estate; already they were making plans to buy apartment houses and rent them out when the Countess died. They tried everything to dissuade their aunt from the trip, until she threatened to cut them out of her will. Two days before they were due to leave, they sat complaining as usual and Carlotta said again:

'She is blind and does not hear well. She will hardly know where she is!'

And in the silence that followed, these words held a new meaning. Next morning Carlotta and Pia got up early. They had a list of what they needed, and by lunchtime had ordered everything, from guidebooks to wind machines, electric fires for heat and fans for cold. When the time for departure came, they settled the Countess in the Rolls and Carlotta drove it very slowly down the hill, along Hollywood Boulevard, then turned round and arrived back at the house. For the next three days the Countess sat and slept in the railway carriage in the living-room, under the impression she was in a Pullman bound for New York.

The ship to Europe had a state-room rigged up in the dining-room and a record of ocean sounds, the surge of waves and the cry of gulls, played incessantly under her berth. An occasional walk in the patio with the wind machine gently blowing served as a stroll on deck. The Countess could take the sun there too, on the swing-seat carefully adjusted to suggest a steady rolling movement. As she lost all sense of time on long journeys, they cut down the tedium of an Atlantic crossing to two days.

'We had three weeks in London,' Carlotta said, 'a month in Paris, a few days on the Riviera and now we arrive in Madrid.' The Countess had stood in her patio running her finger along a wall that she believed was part of her house in Curzon Street. She had attended Mass at Notre-Dame, the living-room sprayed with incense and Pia tinkling a bell in her ear. She had been to the Opéra-Comique, sitting between her nieces in a box overlooking a beautiful sideboard she had brought with her from the palazzo. She had gambled at Monte Carlo, with Carlotta and Pia taking it in turns to be croupier, and making sure she didn't lose too much.

The only thing that distressed the Countess was that everyone she knew was dead.

'We have to be firm about this,' Carlotta said. 'Impersonating old barons or princesses is really too difficult.'

'And most of them is dead anyway,' Pia added.

After a moment, I burst out laughing. The nieces stared at me, reproachful and unamused. I laughed more wildly, and they looked a little frightened. Finally, wiping the tears from my eyes, I managed to say: 'I'd like to talk to Marguerite.'

'He is still joking,' Carlotta said disapprovingly to Pia.

I shook my head. 'And I'll tell you how it's going to be done. The day after tomorrow, I shall be on holiday in Venice.'

The Countess had never cared about her garden. You opened the door from the patio and looked down a steep slope overgrown with shrubs and long dry grass. There were no flowers, only laurel bushes, banks of yellowing ivy and tall slanting eucalyptus trees that dripped their leaves. A path with cracked crazy paving led to the swimming pool at the end of the slope.

This morning, rubbish was burning in the incinerator and a twist of smoke sidled towards the pool. Sunlight made the leafy water gleam, and played on the bright artificial fruit of the Countess's hat. She was sitting among cushions in a rowing boat, moored off the deep end. She trailed her fingers absently in the water, and a gondolier's song came from the distance.

Carlotta and Pia were side by side in deck chairs, near the stone cupid, as I arrived. 'Aunt Marguerite!' exclaimed Carlotta, pulling the boat a little nearer the edge with a rope. 'How extraordinary, here is someone we know!'

The Countess looked up at me with her blind eyes and extended a hand to be kissed. 'Dear child,' she said vaguely.

'Such a coincidence!' Carlotta insisted. She seemed nervous about it. 'He was coming out of the hotel——'

'I haven't the courage to go in,' the Countess said. 'I am trying to find it, but I haven't got it.'

'You know the Altri Tempi was Aunt Marguerite's palazzo before they converted it?' Pia said.

'I thought I had the courage.' The Countess spoke in a low voice. 'But then I asked the gondolier to tie us up and let me sit and . . .

and think about it.' In a whisper she asked: 'Is it completely changed?'
'I'm afraid so.'

'But Gabriele's portrait is still in the hall,' Carlotta said.

The Countess smiled faintly. 'And the chandeliers in the dining-room?'

'Still there!' said Pia loudly.

The Countess trailed her hand in the water again and asked Carlotta for a piece of chocolate. 'You stayed here when you were children,' she said. 'Don't you remember the day your mother brought you?' I noticed a tear welling in Carlotta's left eye. 'There was piccata for dinner,' the Countess continued with one of her surprisingly exact flashes of memory.

'Very good piccata.' Pia sniffed. 'But we wasn't children, Aunt Marguerite. I was nearly twenty.'

A heavy truck rumbled down the hill. Carlotta wiped her eye and looked up sharply to see whether its sound might disconcert the Countess, but she was deep in memory. 'I thought I sold the chandeliers,' she said at last. 'But perhaps . . . When you have lived in so many great houses, it grows confusing. Is the portrait in good condition?'

'Yes,' I said. 'They take good care of it.'

'I made a stipulation in the contract, you know. People haven't much respect nowadays.' She frowned. 'Is this a good hat?'

'It suits you.'

'Sometimes it feels good, sometimes it feels like a mistake. But when there are no more mirrors, what does it matter?' She turned her blind sharp old face to the sky. 'Everything I knew is gone. It's all stone walls and flattering voices. Did you know it's easier to believe voices when you can't see faces?' Her head drooped, she was growing tired. 'Gabriele,' she murmured. 'I could see Gabriele's face, and I could never believe his voice.' A sigh that seemed to come from the bottom of a deep dry well. 'What a pity, such a handsome face!'

'Are you all right, Aunt Marguerite?' asked Carlotta.

She shook her head irritably. 'Those girls are idiots,' she whispered. 'Give them ten million and their world will be no more beautiful. Their values are all wrong. I knew this when they told me the dye wasn't coming out of my hair. It would have cost so little and looked so much better to dye it again, but they didn't mind looking at it, day after day, running out!'

She brooded. A sad wheeze escaped her. Then she said rather loudly: 'It sinks . . .'

'What sinks, Aunt Marguerite?' the nieces asked in chorus.

'Venice . . . Idiots!' she muttered at them, then turned to me. 'Year after year it is slowly drowning, sinking into the water. And one day . . .' She turned back to Carlotta and Pia. 'Take me home. Slowly.'

Carlotta loosened the rope. The boat drifted towards the centre of the pool.

'Too fast!' The Countess clutched her hat. 'Where are you, Carlotta? Where are you, Pia?'

'We're here,' they said, Carlotta holding on to the rope so the boat shouldn't drift too far.

'Facts is facts,' said Carlotta. 'You have seen her in her own swimming pool and she thinks it's the Grand Canal. She misses nothing. Would it make her more happy to be really in Venice?'

'If she really went to Europe, it might be fatal,' said Pia. 'This way she travels so comfortably.'

'Maybe so.' I glanced from one to the other. 'But what's your profit?'

Carlotta made a little clicking sound of disapproval. 'I have no time to count such things, I work my fingers to the bone.'

'Cooking is worst,' said Pia. 'We have to learn dishes of every country.'

'Making money out of blind old women was never our object.' Carlotta's tone was almost self-righteous. 'We only wish to stop Aunt Marguerite wasting her fortune.'

'And invest in real estate for the future,' added Pia.

'All the same,' I said, 'it's a fraud. A confidence trick. You're just helping yourselves to the old woman's money.'

Carlotta's eyes grew suddenly fierce. 'What is this money? Osterberg money!' She stood up, and began pacing the room. 'Money made by the genius of our late Uncle the Count! Most of it gone because of wars and countries changing hands—and the rest will go too, if we leave it to Aunt Marguerite! She has no values for this kind of thing. Pia and I is only poor girls from the slums of Naples, but we have business flair. Aunt Marguerite is past, we is future. We think it is time for Osterberg money to grow again, not shrink. That is our purpose!'

She sat down, rather flushed, in the railway carriage. I had never seen her so passionate before. She seemed to have gained a new dimension, I almost respected her.

Before I could answer, she had an afterthought. 'You think Pia and I is funny girls. People tell us the sense of humour is not our strong point, but we find nothing funny. We are *serious*.'

'If I could think of anything to do, I'd do it,' I said. 'But I can't. I suppose I'll just have to be an accomplice after the fact.'

'What is that?' Pia asked.

A bell rang upstairs and Carlotta frowned. 'Aunt Marguerite has woken, she wants to go over to the Lido tonight. But it's too difficult. Pia, we'll have to make another storm.'

Pia went into the dining-room and beat the thunder sheet.

'Not loud enough! Take it upstairs and beat it outside her door. And try a little wind.' Carlotta watched her sister hoist the contraption over her shoulders, than turned to me with a complacement joyless smile. 'Aunt Marguerite will never go out in weather like this!'

In Vienna, said Carlotta, the Countess wept a great deal and grew very confused. Sitting in her sunless patio which she imagined was a terrace at the Belevedere, she listened to records of old waltzes and conjured up the Danube at her feet. Once she was convinced they would be late for a parade in honour of the Emperor Franz Josef's birthday, another time she wouldn't leave the café and sipped weak coffee for five hours. When Carlotta complained, she said: 'The Count of Klausenburg promised to come by.'

They were supposed to go on to St. Moritz, but the Countess changed her mind. 'I begin to hate my memories,' she said. 'It's time to go somewhere where I haven't any.'

'We are in Marrakech and cannot get out!' Carlotta announced over the telephone about three weeks later. 'It is a horrible blow.'

'You mean she wants to stay there?'

'She is infatuated with the East, it becomes a new lease of life!' Carlotta's voice trembled. 'She has taken a house in the native quarter and drinks mint tea. She likes the sounds of the market place and listens to ridiculous flutes and drums all day.'

'At least it means less work if she stays in one place.'

'But not this place, listening to horrible music! Are we to be stuck in an Arab city for the rest of her life?'

It seemed nothing would move the Countess. Carlotta and Pia warned her about the hot season, announced it had come, closed all the windows and filled her room with electric fires. 'It's not as bad as I expected,' the Countess said. Carlotta would add another fire. 'Makes me a little sleepy,' the Countess said.

They told her the climate was unreliable and arranged a terrific storm one night. Pia banged the thunder sheet for hours and turned the wind machine on her aunt as directly as she dared. They slammed and rattled windows and claimed the house next door had been struck by lightning. 'Ask them if there is anything we can do,' the Countess said.

They read her reports of terrorism from the newspapers. Machine-gun fire rang through the house one morning and Carlotta said all the windows had been broken. 'Mend them,' ordered the Countess. 'And don't forget to sweep up carefully.'

Desperate, they switched off the record-players and said all the musicians in the market place had gone away. 'Nomads I suppose,' the Countess said. 'But there'll be others.'

There was nothing they could do but agree, and start the record-players again next day. The Countess lay on her purple couch and listened and fell asleep. After six months she was still charmed by the sounds, but physically weaker. On many days she never got out of bed. She started her memoirs again, dictated an anecdote or two to Pia. 'It's all going further and further away,' she said once. There was regret and satisfaction in her voice. 'I can hardly remember California now.'

I saw her once in her Marrakech period. Carlotta and Pia had cleared all the furniture out of her bedroom and made it completely Moroccan. The Countess reclined on a mattress on the floor, covered by a sheepskin rug. She was asleep; I didn't want to wake her. Her hair was white as the sheepskin now, her skin very lined and mottled, yet she gave an impression of calm and strength. Beside her was a low table with a silver pot of mint tea on a tray. Flutes and drums were gently piped through a loudspeaker.

'We think Morocco must be quite agreeable,' Pia said. 'In fact, Carlotta and I would like to go there ourselves.'

Just before he left California, Mark and I discussed the situation and tried to find a way of resolving it. It seemed a pity to try and bring the Countess home; we were only frightened she might somehow find out the deception and never recover from the shock. Mark had an idea that Carlotta and Pia should be kidnapped. He would impersonate the American Consul and inform the Countess that lustful sheikhs had carried off her nieces. Under the circumstances she would have to agree to go home.

'But who will look after her then?' I asked.

'We'll have Carlotta and Pia rescued, naturally.'

'I think she'd suspect it. Besides, you and I would have to spend eight days in that house pretending it's a boat.'

'Couldn't they rush up the gangway, just as it's leaving?'

'It won't do.'

After a silence, Mark said: 'Odd to think I used to dance with her.'

'To Sinatra?'

He nodded, then asked me for a cigarette. His usual gesture for closing a subject.

And later that night the telephone rang.

'We are back!' Carlotta's voice shivered with elation. 'Since an hour we are back in California, thank God!'

'How on earth did it happen?'

One could never have predicted the reason. The Countess received letters from time to time, mainly circulars, which she imagined had been forwarded from California. Most of them didn't interest her, unless they contained offers of free samples, which she applied for on principle. A few days after the October rising in Budapest, there was a letter inviting her to a Victims of Oppression Dinner in Hollywood. The idea of the dinner was to raise funds for refugees from Hungary, and a telegram had already been sent to the State Department urging relaxation of the laws for immigrants. In view of the late Count Oster-berg-Steblechi's connection with Hungary, the letter suggested, wouldn't the Countess like to lend her support?

When the news of the rising came through, there was a good deal of activity in Hollywood. An émigré Hungarian producer joined with an émigré Hungarian composer to write a nostalgic song about Budapest, which they had both left over twenty years ago. It was played quite often on the radio. A Hungarian actress who had once appeared in a film with the Marx Brothers presided at a Help Hungary Cocktail. Somebody announced a film to be called *Beast of Budapest*. The Countess, too, was stirred. She ordered Carlotta to cable her lawyer to watch for news of the Cracow estates, ignoring reminders that they were in Poland, and sent Pia to buy tickets for the earliest possible plane.

'We think to attend this dinner is ridiculous,' Carlotta said, 'but it brings her home. We think if we say no more about it, she will forget.'

She didn't, however, and was determined to go. Carlotta asked me to accompany them, and on the night of the dinner I went round to the house to pick them up. They were still dressing the Countess, who stood erect in the centre of her bedroom in a rich blue velvet evening gown that she hadn't worn since the days of Venice. The nieces were worried it would be too heavy for her, and she finally allowed them to cut off the train. Pia was on her knees now, stitching the hem. Carlotta had opened the jewel box, the entire contents of which Marguerite had decided to wear. Rigid as an effigy in her magnificent blue velvet, she directed the diamond tiara to be placed on her head with its newly dyed hair; had three bracelets slipped on her arms, one above the elbow; seven rings on her fingers; five strings of pearls, and a sapphire clasp at her waist.

When I asked if she'd had a good journey, the Countess only gave a short disinterested nod. She seemed strangely indifferent to all of that now. 'I have returned just in time,' she said, then grimaced. 'The Sleeping Beauty has been awakened by a strange Prince!'

It took her a long time to walk downstairs. She wouldn't use a stick.

We drove out in the Rolls. Sitting very upright, occasionally patting her tiara, she talked about the revolution. Although it had failed by now, she was not discouraged. 'They are stirring, everywhere they are stirring. They want us back and we mustn't abandon them.' But a little later she asked anxiously: 'Have they asked the Count of Klausenburg tonight?'

About thirty people came to dinner, held in the banqueting hall of a restaurant near Hollywood Boulevard. The hall was plain and gloomy, walls of chipped sky blue with lifesize palms painted on them. The floor was bare, we sat at a long table in the centre amd there was no other furniture except for a grand piano at one end. All the guests except the Countess and her party were originally immigrants from Hungary who had come to America thirty or more years ago. The organizer owned a canning factory down-town. Most of the others were business people, an oil producer, a hotel owner, a raw cotton dealer who had come up from the San Joaquin Valley. There was also a once famous playwright, now almost eighty and ending his days at a beach house in Malibu, and an old actress who ran a dramatic school.

Everyone wore tuxedos, and the actress had a red rose pinned to her low-cut black evening dress. Glowing with jewels and bright velvet, flanked by her tall nieces, the Countess made a striking entrance but was unaware of it. Advancing down the room with slow difficult steps, the sapphire clasp glittering in the centre of her enormous stomach, she looked like an exotic potentate arriving for some secret ritual. The organizer introduced himself and made a little speech to the others at table, saying how honoured they were by her presence. We guided her to a chair next to the old playwright, who burst into tears. He had been a week-end guest at Cracow before the first world war. 'Are you Ferenc Molnar?' the Countess asked. "No, he is dead. But I knew him well.' 'Did you know the Count of Klausenburg?' 'Slightly,' said the old playwright. 'Is he coming tonight?'

The main dish was goulash and we drank imperial Tokay. Conversation was sporadic and uneasy at first, then suddenly everyone began talking about profits, new installations, and taking a trip to Hawaii. It grew very hot, this was an old room without air-conditioning, and with only one fan. After dessert the organizer stood up, mopped his forehead with a paper napkin and proposed toasts: to the liberty of free peoples everywhere, to the spirit of Budapest, to the United States of America. Then came speeches. The factory owner told of his arrival in New York just as the Depression started. Hard days and broken hopes, but he won through. 'This is a wonderful country, and I am proud to

be a citizen of it. But I can never forget the land of my birth. Today,'
he said, 'I am shedding tears for it.' It was true.

'Bravo!' the Countess exclaimed as he sat down. 'They are stirring,'
she repeated, her blind eyes fixed on the painted palms. 'They want us
back, they are begging us to return.'

I realized that in her mind everyone at the table was part of a
vanished aristocratic world. Somehow she believed this dinner was dedicated to its rebirth.

The old playwright spoke of Budapest at the turn of the century.
'Those were golden days, those days before nineteen fourteen.' He
evoked the memory of his friend Molnar and told some whimsical
stories about the neighbours in the little street where he used to live.
'The Danube,' he said, 'is the most beautiful river in the world. And it
is most beautiful, and most blue, at Budapest. Alas, our river is no longer
blue. Our beautiful river is stained with red . . .'

Guttural and hierarchic, the actress spoke of Hungary's contribution
to the theatre. In 1912 she played in Ibsen's *Ghosts*, later she had a
theatre named after her. She described her country first under the
jackboot, then the hammer and sickle. When the Russians occupied
Hungary, they changed the name of her theatre. 'But in secret they
still call it *my* theatre,' she finished proudly. 'I know. I have information.'

'I have never heard of this woman,' the Countess said. 'Is she famous?'

A malicious expression came over the playwright's face and he whispered something to her in Hungarian.

At the end of the speeches, came a long silence. We all seemed to be
staring at the blue wall and the palms. The air felt heavy and stale. The
Countess was still napping when the organizer took a cheque book from
his pocket, laid it solemnly on the table, and asked us all to be generous.

For the first time, Carlotta and Pia stopped looking bored. Carlotta
nudged her aunt. 'How much is it to be?' she asked in a nervous
whisper.

The Countess awoke with a start. 'We mustn't abandon them,' she
said. 'They are stirring.'

'Twenty dollars?' Pia suggested in a hoarse undertone.

'Idiot girls! What do you know of life as it really was?' The Countess
sighed. 'I should give them everything I have!'

For a moment I thought the nieces were going to faint.

'A cheque has no poetry, no passion,' the Countess said. 'My gift
must be symbolic.'

Slowly, her hands began to caress her jewels. They stroked her rings
and bracelets, then groped up to her head. They removed the tiara.

Wheezing, she laid it on the table. 'Cartier valued it at a hundred thousand, in nineteen twenty-eight, I think.'

A spot of colour tinged each cheek. She didn't know who she was giving it to, or what she was giving it for; it was a blessing on the old world that, too late for her, was struggling to come back. Her blind eyes stared at the ceiling while staid business faces gazed at her from each side of the table. Then the playwright took her hand and kissed it. 'When you see a thing like this, you feel all is not yet lost.'

The others clapped. Then the cheques were collected and the total announced: over thirty thousand dollars, plus the tiara. They thanked the Countess again, but she had fallen asleep. A final toast was drunk, Carlotta woke up her aunt, and we straggled out into Hollywood Boulevard and the parking lot where all the cars were massed. *Wrap Your Troubles in Dreams* was coming from a radio at a hamburger stand. Groups of adolescents wandered by in the warm airless evening, boys in jeans and sweat shirts, girls in vividly-coloured shirts and tight pants. A few turned to stare at the Countess, as Pia and Carlotta helped her into the crested Rolls. A little further up the street, crowds were leaving a theatre after a première. Lights tinted the night sky a harsh yellowy pink.

Now the only thing left is to bury her. The Countess died in her sleep a few hours after the dinner. The nieces didn't find out till morning, when they went into her bedroom to wake her. The radio was still playing and Marguerite sat tightly wedged in a chair, a half-eaten peach in her hand. Carlotta supposed she had sat up to listen for news reports from Hungary.

Pia has saved a brochure pushed under the front door of the house some weeks ago, and now she brings it out. It is called the Boomtower Pictorial. Boomtower Mortuaries offer funerals at six different price ranges, from $52 to $282, they are rapidly expanding and have built two new Chapels this year to serve, as the Pictorial says, 'the community's ever-increasing needs.' Carlotta is interested in their scheme for buying coffins on the instalment plan.

After long arguments they decide on a $92 funeral.

On the morning of the funeral, Mrs. Leota Sperling from Boomtower Mortuaries calls to advise on costume and make-up. She is a cheerful lady with tight brown curls and a brisk manner. She has a husband and two children, and when the time comes for each one to pass on, she is happy to think it will be 'through Boomtower'. She thinks it would be nice to bury the Countess in her blue velvet, which is so much more dignified than the flowered prints in the wardrobe. She will rouge the old lady's lips, rub some colour into her cheeks, and touch up her hair.

Carlotta asks her opinion of the $92 funeral and is delighted when

Mrs. Sperling says in her view it's the best value of them all. She puts it this way: 'Not drab, but not ostentatious either. We at the Mortuaries never encourage extravagance at a time of emotional stress.'

A black Boomtower Cadillac takes the body to the Chapel. Carlotta and Pia and I follow in the Rolls. The sun beats down on slow lines of traffic, and we are all perspiring slightly. The outside of the Chapel is calm and secular, it looks like a residential hotel. In a sense, I suppose, it is. An awning stretches above the entrance with BOOMTOWER in slanting letters across the fringe. On one side of the Chapel is a laundromat, on the other a restaurant.

Inside, it is cool. Attendants lay the Countess in an air-conditioned Slumber Room. It looks like any living-room in a comfortable Californian house, with a corpse on the couch.

There are armchairs with restful patterns, soothing lights and flower paintings on the wall. Music comes from a concealed loudspeaker like sweet religious scent. This is our last communion. Standing by the Countess with her painted cheeks and splendid gown, I can only think there is something horribly fitting about this final pretence of many pretences. The last journey is the only real one, yet more fantastic than any the Countess imagined.

It is time to begin the service. Through the Chapel windows we can see a patio garden brilliant with flowers. A fountain plays and sparkles in the sun. It is all so beautiful, we hardly notice when a panel in the wall slides away and the coffin disappears down a chute. The panel slides back and the music is still coming from all sides, reverent and soft.

In a minute the Countess will be burning.

Everything seems illusion; all troubles have been finally wrapped in dreams. Carlotta and Pia bring out their handkerchiefs. Each will soon have a million dollars in the bank, and later much more out of real estate in Florida. As we go out, Carlotta suddenly looks very white. She leans on Pia's arm and holds the handkerchief to her mouth. A moment later she is all right again, turns to me and says quietly:

'We heard this morning the tiara fetched ninety thousand. I wonder how many refugees that will bring in?'

'It was a birthday present,' Pia remarks in a reflective tone. 'From Gabriele.'

I watch them drive off in the imperial Rolls, and think of them back in that living-room in the hills.

The earliest portrait of Marguerite is still hanging there, the girl in a white dress in Switzerland more than fifty years ago. I believe it was painted a few days before she fell into Count Österberg-Steblechi's arms.

# Part III
# OTHER LOVES

# MY MORTAL ENEMY

## *Willa Cather*

WILLA CATHER (1876–1947) Born in Virginia but raised in
the West, Miss Cather found much of her finest material on the
deserts and prairies of her younger years. Writing with great sen-
sitivity and rare literary quality, it may be said that she achieved
the promise of immortality in her own lifetime. Her later books embraced other fields, among them music, always a passion with her,
all done with a curious, indefinable atmosphere of timelessness.
The West remained her spiritual home, but she wrote of New York
as well and was living there at the time of her death. It is a privilege
to be able to present here the following story of a fatal attraction
which has never before been included in an anthology.

I

I FIRST met Myra Henshawe when I was fifteen, but I had known
about her ever since I could remember anything at all. She and
her runaway marriage were the theme of the most interesting, indeed the only interesting, stories that were told in our family, on
holidays or at family dinners. My mother and aunts still heard from
Myra Driscoll, as they called her, and Aunt Lydia occasionally went to
New York to visit her. She had been the brilliant and attractive figure
among the friends of their girlhood, and her life had been as exciting
and varied as ours was monotonous.

Though she had grown up in our town, Parthia, in southern Illinois,
Myra Henshawe never, after her elopement, came back but once. It
was in the year when I was finishing High School, and she must then
have been a woman of forty-five. She came in the early autumn, with
brief notice by telegraph. Her husband, who had a position in the New
York offices of an Eastern railroad, was coming West on business, and
they were going to stop over for two days in Parthia. He was to stay at
the Parthian, as our new hotel was called, and Mrs. Henshawe would
stay with Aunt Lydia.

I was a favourite with my Aunt Lydia. She had three big sons, but no daughter, and she thought my mother scarcely appreciated me. She was always, therefore, giving me what she called "advantages," on the side. My mother and sister were asked to dinner at Aunt Lydia's on the night of the Henshawes' arrival, but she had whispered to me: "I want you to come in early, an hour or so before the others, and get acquainted with Myra."

That evening I slipped quietly in at my aunt's front door, and while I was taking off my wraps in the hall I could see, at the far end of the parlour, a short, plump woman in a black velvet dress, seated upon the sofa and softly playing on Cousin Bert's guitar. She must have heard me, and, glancing up, she saw my reflection in a mirror; she put down the guitar, rose, and stood to await my approach. She stood markedly and pointedly still, with her shoulders back and her head lifted, as if to remind me that it was my business to get to her as quickly as possible and present myself as best I could. I was not accustomed to formality of any sort, but by her attitude she succeeded in conveying this idea to me.

I hastened across the room with so much bewilderment and concern in my face that she gave a short, commiserating laugh as she held out to me her plump, charming little hand.

"Certainly this must be Lydia's dear Nellie, of whom I have heard so much! And you must be fifteen now, by my mournful arithmetic—am I right?"

What a beautiful voice, bright and gay and carelessly kind—but she continued to hold her head up haughtily. She always did this on meeting people—partly, I think, because she was beginning to have a double chin and was sensitive about it. Her deep-set, flashing grey eyes seemed to be taking me in altogether—estimating me. For all that she was no taller than I, I felt quite overpowered by her—and stupid, hopelessly clumsy and stupid. Her black hair was done high on her head, à la Pompadour, and there were curious, zigzag, curly streaks of glistening white in it, which made it look like the fleece of a Persian goat or some animal that bore silky fur. I could not meet the playful curiosity of her eyes at all, so I fastened my gaze upon a necklace of carved amethysts she wore inside the square-cut neck of her dress. I suppose I stared, for she said suddenly: "Does this necklace annoy you? I'll take it off if it does."

I was utterly speechless. I could feel my cheeks burning. Seeing that she had hurt me, she was sorry, threw her arm impulsively about me, drew me into the corner of the sofa and sat down beside me.

"Oh, we'll get used to each other! You see, I prod you because I'm certain that Lydia and your mother have spoiled you a little. You've been overpraised to me. It's all very well to be clever, my dear, but you mustn't be solemn about it—nothing is more tiresome. Now, let us get acquainted. Tell me about the things you like best; that's the short cut to friendship. What do you like best in Parthia? The old Driscoll place? I knew it!"

By the time her husband came in I had begun to think she was going to like me. I wanted her to, but I felt I didn't have half a chance with her; her charming, fluent voice, her clear light enunciation bewildered me. And I was never sure whether she was making fun of me or of the thing we were talking about. Her sarcasm was so quick, so fine at the point—it was like being touched by a metal so cold that one doesn't know whether one is burned or chilled. I was fascinated, but very ill at ease, and I was glad when Oswald Henshawe arrived from the hotel.

He came into the room without taking off his overcoat and went directly up to his wife, who rose and kissed him. Again I was some time in catching up with the situation; I wondered for a moment whether they might have come down from Chicago on different trains; for she was clearly glad to see him—glad not merely that he was safe and had got round on time, but because his presence gave her lively personal pleasure. I was not accustomed to that kind of feeling in people long married.

Mr. Henshawe was less perplexing than his wife, and he looked more as I had expected him to look. The prominent bones of his face gave him a rather military air; a broad, rugged forehead, high cheek-bones, a high nose, slightly arched. His eyes, however, were dark and soft, curious in shape—exactly like half-moons—and he wore a limp, drooping moustache, like an Englishman. There was something about him that suggested personal bravery, magnanimity, and a fine, generous way of doing things.

"I am late," he explained, "because I had some difficulty in dressing. I couldn't find my things."

His wife looked concerned for a moment, and then began to laugh softly. "Poor Oswald! You were looking for your new dress shirts that bulge in front. Well, you needn't! I gave them to the janitor's son."

"The janitor's son?"

"Yes. To Willy Bunch, at home. He's probably wearing one to an Iroquois ball to-night, and that's the right place for it."

Mr. Henshawe passed his hand quickly over his smooth, iron-grey hair. "You gave away my six new shirts?"

"Be sure I did. You shan't wear shirts that give you a bosom, not if we go to the poorhouse. You know I can't bear you in ill-fitting things."

Oswald looked at her with amusement, incredulity, and bitterness. He turned away from us with a shrug and pulled up a chair. "Well, all I can say is, what a windfall for Willy!"

"That's the way to look at it," said his wife teasingly. "And now try to talk about something that might conceivably interest Lydia's niece. I promised Liddy to make a salad dressing."

I was left alone with Mr. Henshawe. He had a pleasant way of giving his whole attention to a young person. He "drew one out" better than his wife had done, because he did not frighten one so much. I liked to watch his face, with its outstanding bones and languid, friendly eyes—that perplexing combination of something hard and something soft. Soon my mother and uncle and my boy cousins arrived. When the party was complete I could watch and enjoy the visitors without having to think of what I was going to say next. The dinner was much gayer than family parties usually are. Mrs. Henshawe seemed to remember all the old stories and the old jokes that had been asleep for twenty years.

"How good it is," my mother exclaimed, "to hear Myra laugh again!"

Yes, it was good. It was sometimes terrible, too, as I was to find out later. She had an angry laugh, for instance, that I still shiver to remember. Any stupidity made Myra laugh—I was destined to hear that one very often! Untoward circumstances, accidents, even disasters, provoked her mirth. And it was always mirth, not hysteria; there was a spark of zest and wild humour in it.

## II

THE big stone house, in its ten-acre park of trees and surrounded by a high, wrought-iron fence, in which Myra Driscoll grew up, was still, in my time, the finest property in Parthia. At John Driscoll's death it went to the Sisters of the Sacred Heart, and I could remember it only as a convent. Myra was an orphan, and had been taken into this house as a very little girl and brought up by her great-uncle.

John Driscoll made his fortune employing contract labour in the Missouri swamps. He retired from business early, returned to the town where he had been a poor boy, and built a fine house in which he took great pride. He lived in what was considered great splendour in those days. He kept fast horses, and bred a trotter that made a national record. He bought silver instruments for the town band, and paid the salary of the bandmaster. When the band went up to serenade him on his birthday and on holidays, he called the boys in and treated them to his best whisky. If Myra gave a ball or a garden-party, the band furnished the music. It was, indeed, John Driscoll's band.

Myra, as my aunt often said, had everything: dresses and jewels, a fine riding horse, a Steinway piano. Her uncle took her back to Ireland with him, one summer, and had her painted by a famous painter. When they were at home, in Parthia, his house was always open to the young people of the town. Myra's good looks and high spirits gratified the old man's pride. Her wit was of the kind that he could understand, native and racy, and none too squeamish. She was very fond of him, and he knew it. He was a coarse old codger, so unlettered that he made a poor showing with a pen. It was always told of him that when he became president of our national bank, he burned a lot of the treasury notes sent up to his house for him to sign, because he had "spoiled the sig-nay-ture." But he knew a great deal about men and their motives. In his own way he was picturesque, and Myra appreciated it—not many girls would have done so. Indeed, she was a good deal like him; the blood tie was very strong. There was never a serious disagreement between them until it came to young Henshawe.

Oswald Henshawe was the son of a German girl of good family, and an Ulster Protestant whom Driscoll detested; there was an old grudge of some kind between the two men. This Ulsterman was poor and impractical, a wandering schoolmaster, who had charge for a while of the High School in Parthia, and afterwards taught in smaller towns about. Oswald put himself through Harvard with very little help from his parents. He was not taken account of in our town until he came home from college, a handsome and promising young man. He and Myra met as if for the first time, and fell in love with each other. When old Driscoll found that Oswald was calling on his niece, he forbade him the house. They continued to meet at my grandfather's, however, under the protection of my Aunt Lydia. Driscoll so persecuted the boy that he felt there was no chance for him in Parthia. He roused himself and went to New York. He stayed there two years without coming home, sending his letters to Myra through my aunt.

All Myra's friends were drawn into the web of her romance; half a dozen young men understudied for Oswald so assiduously that her uncle might have thought she was going to marry any one of them. Oswald, meanwhile, was pegging away in New York, at a time when salaries were small and advancement was slow. But he managed to get on, and in two years he was in a position to marry. He wrote to John Driscoll, telling him his resources and prospects, and asked him for his niece's hand. It was then that Driscoll had it out with Myra. He did not come at her in a tantrum, as he had done before, but confronted her with a cold, business proposition. If she married young Henshawe, he would cut her off without a penny. He could do so, because he had never adopted her. If she did not, she would inherit two-thirds of his property—the remaining third was to go to the church. "And I advise ye to think well," he told her. "It's better to be a stray dog in this world than a man without money. I've tried both ways, and I know. A poor man stinks, and God hates him."

Some months after this conversation, Myra went out with a sleighing party. They drove her to a neighbouring town where Oswald's father had a school, and where Oswald himself had quietly arrived the day before. There, in the presence of his parents and of Myra's friends, they were married by the civil authority, and they went away on the Chicago express, which came through at two in the morning.

When I was a little girl my Aunt Lydia used to take me for a walk along the broad stone flagging that ran all the way around the old Driscoll grounds. Through the high iron fence we could see the Sisters, out for recreation, pacing two and two under the apple-trees. My aunt would tell me again about that thrilling night (probably the most exciting in her life), when Myra Driscoll came down that path from the house, and out of those big iron gates, for the last time. She had wanted to leave without taking anything but the clothes she wore—and indeed she walked out of the house with nothing but her muff and her *porte-monnaie* in her hands. My prudent aunt, however, had put her toilet articles and some linen into a travelling-bag, and thrown it out of the back window to one of the boys stationed under an apple-tree.

"I'll never forget the sight of her, coming down that walk and leaving a great fortune behind her," said Aunt Lydia. "I had gone out to join the others before she came—she preferred to leave the house alone. We girls were all in the sleighs and the boys stood in the snow holding the horses. We had begun to think she had weakened, or maybe gone to the old man to try to move him. But we saw by the lights behind when the front door opened and shut, and here she came, with her head high, and that quick little bouncing step of hers. Your Uncle Rob lifted her into the sleigh, and off we went. And that hard old man was as good as his word. Her name wasn't mentioned in his will. He left it all to the Catholic Church and to institutions."

"But they've been happy, anyhow?" I sometimes asked her.

"Happy? Oh, yes! As happy as most people."

That answer was disheartening; the very point of their story was that they should be much happier than other people.

When I was older I used to walk around the Driscoll place alone very often, especially on spring days, after school, and watch the nuns pacing so mildly and measuredly among the blossoming trees where Myra used to give garden-parties and have the band to play for her. I thought of the place as being under a spell, like the Sleeping Beauty's palace; it had been in a trance, or lain in its flowers like a beautiful corpse, ever since that winter night when Love went out of the gates and gave the dare to fate. Since then, chanting and devotions and discipline, and the tinkle of little bells that seemed forever calling the Sisters in to prayers.

I knew that this was not literally true; old John Driscoll had lived on there for many years after the flight of his niece. I myself could remember his funeral—remember it very vividly—though I was not more than six years old when it happened. I sat with my parents in the front of the gallery, at the back of the church that the old man had enlarged and enriched during the latter days of his life. The high altar blazed with hundreds of candles, the choir was entirely filled by the masses of flowers. The bishop was there, and a flock of priests in gorgeous vestments. When the pall-bearers arrived, Driscoll did not come to the church; the church went to him. The bishop and clergy went down the nave and met that great black coffin at the door, preceded by the cross and boys swinging cloudy censers, followed by the choir chanting to the organ. They surrounded, they received, they seemed to assimilate into the body of the church, the body of old John Driscoll. They bore it up to the high altar on a river of colour and incense and organ-tone; they claimed it and enclosed it.

In after years, when I went to other funerals, stark and grim enough, I thought of John Driscoll as having escaped the end of all flesh; it was as if he had been translated, with no dark conclusion to the pageant, no "night of the grave" about which our Protestant preachers talked. From the freshness of roses and lilies, from the glory of the high altar, he had gone straight to the greater glory, through smoking censers and candles and stars.

After I went home from that first glimpse of the real Myra Henshawe, twenty-five years older than I had always imagined her, I could not help feeling a little disappointed. John Driscoll and his niece had suddenly changed places in my mind, and he had got, after all, the more romantic part. Was it not better to get out of the world with such pomp and dramatic splendour than to linger on in it, having to take account of shirts and railway trains, and getting a double chin into the bargain?

The Henshawes were in Parthia three days, and when they left, it was settled that I was to go on to New York with Aunt Lydia for the Christmas holidays. We were to stay at the old Fifth Avenue Hotel, which, as Myra said, was only a stone's throw from their apartment, "if at any time a body was to feel disposed to throw one, Liddy!"

### III

My aunt Lydia and I arrived at the Jersey City station on the day before Christmas—a soft, grey December morning, with a little snow falling. Myra Henshawe was there to meet us; very handsome, I thought, as she came walking rapidly up the platform, her plump figure swathed in furs—a fur hat on her head, with a single narrow garnet feather sticking out behind, like the pages' caps in old storybooks. She was not alone. She was attended by a tall, elegant young man in a blue-grey ulster. He had one arm through hers, and in the other hand he carried a walking-stick.

"This is Ewan Gray," said Mrs. Henshawe, after she had embraced us. "Doubtless you have seen him play in Chicago. He is meeting an early train, too, so we planned to salute the morn together, and left Oswald to breakfast alone."

The young man took our hand-luggage and walked beside me to the ferryboat, asking polite questions about our trip. He was a Scotchman, of an old theatrical family, a handsome fellow, with a broad, fair-skinned face, sand-coloured hair and moustache, and fine grey eyes, deep-set and melancholy, with black lashes. He took us up to the deck of the ferry, and then Mrs. Henshawe told him he had better leave us. "You must be there when Esther's train gets in—and remember, you are to bring her to dine with us to-morrow night. There will be no one else."

"Thank you, Myra." He stood looking down at her with a grateful, almost humble expression, holding his soft hat against his breast, while the snow-flakes fell about his head. "And may I call in for a few moments to-night, to show you something?"

She laughed as if his request pleased her. "Something for her, I expect? Can't you trust your own judgment?"

"You know I never do," he said, as if that were an old story.

She gave him a little push. "Do put your hat on, or you'll greet Esther with a sneeze. Run along."

She watched him anxiously as he walked away, and groaned: "Oh, the deliberation of him! If I could only make him hurry once. You'll hear all about him later, Nellie. You'll have to see a good deal of him, but you won't find it a hardship, I trust!"

The boat was pulling out, and I was straining my eyes to catch, through the fine, reluctant snow, my first glimpse of the city we were approaching. We passed the *Wilhelm der Grosse* coming up the river under tug, her sides covered with ice after a stormy crossing, a flock of sea gulls in her wake. The snow blurred everything a little, and the buildings on the Battery all ran together—looked like an enormous fortress with a thousand windows. From the mass, the dull gold dome of the *World* building emerged like a ruddy autumn moon at twilight.

From the Twenty-third Street station we took the crosstown car—people were economical in those days—to the Fifth Avenue Hotel. After we had unpacked and settled our things, we went across the Square to lunch at Purcell's, and there Mrs. Henshawe told us about Ewan Gray. He was in love with one of her dearest friends, Esther Sinclair, whose company was coming into New York for the holidays. Though he was so young, he had, she said, "a rather spotty past," and Miss Sinclair, who was the daughter of an old New England family and had been properly brought up, couldn't make up her mind whether he was stable enough to marry. "I don't dare advise her, though I'm so fond of him. You can see; he's just the sort of boy that women pick up and run off into the jungle with. But he's never wanted to marry before; it might be the making of him. He's distractedly in love—goes about like a sleep-walker. Still, I couldn't bear it if anything cruel happened to Esther."

Aunt Lydia and Myra were going to do some shopping. When we went out into Madison Square again, Mrs. Henshawe must have seen my wistful gaze, for she stopped short and said: "How would Nellie like it if we left her here, and picked her up as we come back? That's our house, over there, second floor—so you won't be far from home. To me this is the real heart of the city; that's why I love living here." She waved to me and hurried my aunt away.

Madison Square was then at the parting of the ways; had a double personality, half commercial, half social, with shops to the south and residences on the north. It seemed to me so neat, after the raggedness of our Western cities; so protected by good manners and courtesy—like an open-air drawing-room. I could well imagine a winter dancing party being given there, or a reception for some distinguished European visitor.

The snow fell lightly all the afternoon, and friendly old men with brooms kept sweeping the paths—very ready to talk to a girl from the country, and to brush off a bench so that she could sit down. The trees and shrubbery seemed well-groomed and sociable, like pleasant people. The snow lay in clinging folds on the bushes, and outlined every twig of every tree—a line of white upon a line of black. Madison Square Garden, new and spacious then, looked to me so light and fanciful, and Saint Gaudens' Diana, of which Mrs. Henshawe had told me, stepped out freely and fearlessly into the grey air. I lingered long by the intermittent fountain. Its rhythmical splash was like the voice of the place. It rose and fell like something taking deep, happy breaths; and the sound was musical, seemed to come from the throat of spring. Not far away, on the corner, was an old man selling English violets, each bunch wrapped in oiled paper to protect them from the snow. Here, I felt, winter brought no desolation; it was tamed, like a polar bear led on a leash by a beautiful lady.

About the Square the pale blue shadows grew denser and drew closer. The street lamps flashed out all along the Avenue, and soft lights began to twinkle in the tall buildings while it was yet day—violet buildings, just a little denser in substance and colour than the violet sky. While I was gazing up at them I heard a laugh close beside me, and Mrs. Henshawe's arm slipped through mine.

"Why, you're fair moon-struck, Nellie! I've seen the messenger boys dodging all about you!" It was true, droves of people were going through the Square now, and boys carrying potted plants and big wreaths. "Don't you like to watch them? But we can't stay. We're going home to Oswald. Oh, hear the penny whistle! They always find me out." She stopped a thin lad with a cap and yarn comforter but no overcoat, who was playing *The Irish Washerwoman* on a little pipe, and rummaged in her bag for a coin.

The Henshawes' apartment was the second floor of an old brown-stone house on the north side of the Square. I loved it from the moment I entered it; such solidly built, high-ceiled rooms, with snug fire-places and wide doors and deep windows. The long, heavy velvet curtains and the velvet chairs were a wonderful plum-colour, like ripe purple fruit. The curtains were lined with that rich cream-colour that lies under the blue skin of ripe figs.

Oswald was standing by the fire, drinking a whisky and soda while he waited for us. He put his glass down on the mantel as we opened the door, and forgot all about it. He pushed chairs up to the hearth for my aunt and me, and stood talking to us while his wife went to change her dress and to have a word with the Irish maid before dinner.

"By the way, Myra," he said, as she left us, "I've put a bottle of champagne on ice; it's Christmas eve."

Everything in their little apartment seemed to me absolutely individual and unique, even the dinner service; the thick grey plates and the soup tureen painted with birds and big, bright flowers—I was sure there were no others like them in the world.

As we were finishing dinner the maid announced Mr. Gray. Henshawe went into the parlour to greet him, and we followed a moment later. The young man was in evening clothes, with a few sprays of white hyacinth in his coat. He stood by the fire, his arm on the mantel. His clean, fair skin and melancholy eyes, his very correct clothes, and something about the shape of his hands, made one conscious of a cool, deliberate fastidiousness in him. In spite of his spotty past he looked, that night, as fresh and undamaged as the flowers he wore. Henshawe took on a slightly bantering tone with him, and seemed to be trying to cheer him up. Mr. Gray would not sit down. After an interval of polite conversation he said to his host: "Will you excuse me if I take Myra away for a few moments? She has promised to do something kind for me."

They went into Henshawe's little study, off the parlour, and shut the door. We could hear a low murmur of voices. When they came back to us Mrs. Henshawe stood beside Gray while he put on his caped cloak, talking encouragingly. "The opals are beautiful, but I'm afraid of them, Ewan. Oswald would laugh at me, but all the same they have a bad history. Love itself draws on a woman nearly all the bad luck in the world; why, for mercy's sake, add opals? He brought two bracelets for me to decide between them, Oswald, both lovely. However did they let you carry off two, Ewan?"

"They know me there. I always pay my bills, Myra. I don't know why, but I do. I suppose it's the Scotch in me."

He wished us all good-night.

"Give a kiss to Esther for me," said Mrs. Henshawe merrily at the door. He made no reply, but bent over her hand and vanished.

"What he really wanted was to show me some verses he's made for her," said Mrs. Henshawe, as she came back to the fire. "And very pretty ones they are, for sweet-heart poetry."

Mr. Henshawe smiled. "Maybe you obliged him with a rhyme or two, my dear? Lydia—" he sat down by my aunt and put his hand on hers—"I'd never feel sure that I did my own courting, if it weren't that I was a long way off at the time. Myra is so fond of helping young men along. We nearly always have a love affair on hand."

She put her hand over his lips. "Hush! I hate old women who egg on courtships."

When Oswald had finished his cigar we were taken out for a walk. This was primarily for the good of her "figger," Myra said, and incidentally we were to look for a green bush to send to Madame Modjeska. "She's spending the holidays in town, and it will be dismal at her hotel."

At the florist's we found, among all the little trees and potted plants, a glistening holly-tree, full of red berries and pointed like a spire, easily the queen of its companions. "That is naturally hers," said Mrs. Myra.

Her husband shrugged. "It's naturally the most extravagant."

Mrs. Myra threw up her head. "Don't be petty, Oswald. It's not a woollen petticoat or warm mittens that Madame is needing." She gave careful instructions to the florist's man, who was to take the tree to the Savoy; he was to carry with it a box of cakes, "of my baking," she said proudly. He was to ask for Mrs. Hewes, the housekeeper, and under her guidance he was to carry the tree up to Madame Modjeska's rooms himself. The man showed a sympathetic interest, and promised to follow instructions. Then Mrs. Henshawe gave him a silver dollar and wished him a Merry Christmas.

As we walked home she slipped her arm through mine, and we fell a little behind the other two. "See the moon coming out, Nellie—behind the tower. It wakens the guilt in me. No playing with love; and I'd sworn a great oath never to meddle again. You send a handsome fellow like Ewan Gray to a fine girl like Esther, and it's Christmas eve, and they rise above us and the white world around us, and there isn't anybody, not a tramp on the park benches, that wouldn't wish them well—and very likely hell will come of it!"

IV

THE next morning Oswald Henshawe, in a frock-coat and top-hat, called to take Aunt Lydia and me to church. The weather had cleared before we went to bed, and as we stepped out of our hotel that morning, the sun shone blindingly on the snow-covered park, the gold Diana flashed against a green-blue sky. We were going to Grace Church, and the morning was so beautiful that we decided to walk.

"Lydia," said Henshawe, as he took us each by an arm, "I want you to give me a Christmas present."

"Why, Oswald," she stammered.

"Oh, I have it ready! You've only to present it." He took a little flat package from his pocket and slipped it into her muff. He drew both of us closer to him. "Listen, it's nothing. It's some sleeve-buttons, given me by a young woman who means no harm, but doesn't know the ways of the world very well. She's from a breezy Western city, where a rich girl can give a present whenever she wants to and nobody questions it. She sent these to my office yesterday. If I send them back to her it will hurt her feelings; she would think I had misunderstood her. She'll get hard knocks here, of course, but I don't want to give her any. On the other hand—well, you know Myra; nobody better. She would punish herself and everybody else for this young woman's questionable taste. So I want you to give them to me, Lydia."

"Oh, Oswald," cried my aunt, "Myra is so keen! I'm not clever enough to fool Myra. Can't you just put them away in your office?"

"Not very well. Besides," he gave a slightly embarrassed laugh, "I'd like to wear them. They are very pretty."

"Now, Oswald . . ."

"Oh, it's all right, Lydia, I give you my word it is. But you know how a little thing of that sort can upset my wife. I thought you might give them to me when you come over to dine with us to-morrow night. She wouldn't be jealous of you. But if you don't like the idea . . . why, just take them home with you and give them to some nice boy who would appreciate them."

All through the Christmas service I could see that Aunt Lydia was distracted and perplexed. As soon as we got back to the hotel and were safe in our rooms she took the brown leather case from her muff and opened it. The sleeve-buttons were topazes, winy-yellow, lightly set in crinkly gold. I believe she was seduced by their beauty. "I really think he ought to have them, if he wants them. Everything is always for Myra. He never gets anything for himself. And all the admiration is for her; why shouldn't he have a little? He has been devoted to a fault. It isn't good for any woman to be humoured and pampered as he has humoured her. And she's often most unreasonable with him—most unreasonable!"

The next evening, as we were walking across the Square to the Henshawes, we glanced up and saw them standing together in one of their deep front windows, framed by the plum-coloured curtains. They were looking out, but did not see us. I noticed that she was really quite a head shorter than he, and she leaned a little towards him. When she was peaceful, she was like a dove with its wings folded. There was something about them, as they stood in the lighted window, that would have discouraged me from meddling, but it did not shake my aunt.

As soon as we were in the parlour, before we had taken off our coats, she said resolutely: "Myra, I want to give Oswald a Christmas present. Once an old friend left with me some cuff-links he couldn't keep—unpleasant associations, I suppose. I thought of giving them to one of my own boys, but I brought them for Oswald. I'd rather he would have them than anybody."

Aunt Lydia spoke with an ease and conviction which compelled my admiration. She took the buttons out of her muff, without the box, of course, and laid them in Mrs. Henshawe's hand.

Mrs. Henshawe was delighted. "How clever of you to think of it, Liddy, dear! Yes, they're exactly right for him. There's hardly any other stone I would like, but these are exactly right. Look, Oswald, they're the colour of a fine Moselle." It was Oswald himself who seemed disturbed, and not overpleased. He grew red, was confused in his remarks, and was genuinely reluctant when his wife insisted upon taking the gold buttons out of his cuffs and putting in the new ones. "I can't get over your canniness, Liddy," she said as she fitted them.

"It's not like me, is it, Myra?" retorted my aunt; "not like me at all to choose the right sort of thing. But did it never occur to you that anyone besides yourself might know what is appropriate for Oswald? No, I'm sure it never did!"

Mrs. Myra took the laugh so heartily to herself that I felt it was a shame to deceive her. So, I am sure, did Oswald. During dinner he talked more than usual, but he was ill at ease. Afterwards, at the opera, when the lights were down, I noticed that he was not listening to the music, but was looking listlessly off into the gloom of the house, with something almost sorrowful in his strange, half-moon eyes. During an *entr'acte* a door at the back was opened, and a draught blew in. As he put his arm back to pull up the cloak which had slipped down from his wife's bare shoulders, she laughed and said: "Oh, Oswald, I love to see your jewels flash!"

He dropped his hand quickly and frowned so darkly that I thought he would have liked to put the topazes under his heel and grind them up. I thought him properly served then, but often since I have wondered at his gentle heart.

v

DURING the week between Christmas and New Year's day I was with Mrs. Henshawe a great deal, but we were seldom alone. It was the season of calls and visits, and she said that meeting so many people would certainly improve my manners and my English. She hated my careless, slangy, Western speech. Her friends, I found, were of two kinds: artistic people—actors, musicians, literary men—with whom she was always at her best because she admired them; and another group whom she called her "moneyed" friends (she seemed to like the word), and these she cultivated, she told me, on Oswald's account. "He is the sort of man who does well in business only if he has the incentive of friendships. He doesn't properly belong in business. We never speak of it, but I'm sure he hates it. He went into an office only because we were young and terribly in love, and had to be married."

The business friends seemed to be nearly all Germans. On Sunday we called at half-a-dozen or more big houses. I remember very large rooms, much upholstered and furnished, walls hung with large paintings in massive frames, and many stiff, dumpy little sofas, in which the women sat two-and-two, while the men stood about the refreshment tables, drinking champagne and coffee and smoking fat black cigars. Among these people Mrs. Myra took on her loftiest and most challenging manner. I could see that some of the women were quite afraid of her. They were in great haste to rush refreshments to her, and looked troubled when she refused anything. They addressed her in German and profusely complimented her upon the way she spoke it. We had a carriage that afternoon, and Myra was dressed in her best—making an especial effort on Oswald's account; but the rich and powerful irritated her. Their solemnity was too much for her sense of humour; there was a biting edge to her sarcasm, a curl about the corners of her mouth that was never there when she was with people whose personality charmed her.

I had one long, delightful afternoon alone with Mrs. Henshawe in Central Park. We walked for miles, stopped to watch the skating, and finally had tea at the Casino, where she told me about some of the singers and actors I would meet at her apartment on New Year's Eve. Her account of her friends was often more interesting to me than the people themselves. After tea she hailed a hansom and asked the man to drive us about the park a little, as a fine sunset was coming on. We were jogging happily along under the elms, watching the light change on the crusted snow, when a carriage passed from which a handsome woman leaned out and waved to us. Mrs. Henshawe bowed stiffly, with a condescending smile. "There, Nellie," she exclaimed, "that's the last woman I'd care to have splashing past me, and me in a hansom cab!"

I glimpsed what seemed to me insane ambition. My aunt was always thanking God that the Henshawes got along as well as they did, and worrying because she felt sure Oswald wasn't saving anything. And here Mrs. Myra was wishing for a carriage—with stables and a house and servants, and all that went with a carriage! All the way home she kept her scornful expression, holding her head high and sniffing the purple air from side to side as we drove down Fifth Avenue. When we alighted before her door she paid the driver, and gave him such a large fee that he snatched off his hat and said twice: "Thank you, thank you, my lady!" She dismissed him with a smile and a nod. "All the same," she whispered to me as she fitted her latchkey, "it's very nasty, being poor!"

That week Mrs. Henshawe took me to see a dear friend of hers, Anne Aylward, the poet. She was a girl who had come to New York only a few years before, had won the admiration of men of letters, and was now dying of tuberculosis in her early twenties. Mrs. Henshawe had given me a book of her poems to read, saying: "I want you to see her so that you can remember her in after years, and I want her to see you so that we can talk you over."

Miss Aylward lived with her mother in a small flat overlooking the East River, and we found her in a bathchair, lying in the sun and watching the river boats go by. Her study was a delightful place that morning, full of flowers and plants and baskets of fruit that had been sent her for Christmas. But it was Myra Henshawe herself who made that visit so memorably gay. Never had I seen her so brilliant and strangely charming as she was in that sunlit study up under the roofs. Their talk quite took my breath away; they said such exciting, such fantastic things about people, books, music—anything; they seemed to speak together a kind of highly flavoured special language.

As we were walking home she tried to tell me more about Miss Aylward, but tenderness for her friend and bitter rebellion at her fate choked her voice. She suffered physical anguish for that poor girl. My aunt often said that Myra was incorrigibly extravagant; but I saw that her chief extravagance was in caring for so many people and in caring for them so much. When she but mentioned the name of someone whom she admired, one got an instant impression that the person must be wonderful, her voice invested the name with a sort of grace. When she liked people she always called them by name a great many times in talking to them, and she enunciated the name, no matter how commonplace, in a penetrating way, without hurrying over it or slurring it; and this, accompanied by her singularly direct glance, had a curious effect. When she addressed Aunt Lydia, for instance, she seemed to be speaking to a person deeper down than the blurred, taken-for-granted image of my aunt that I saw every day, and for a moment my aunt became more individual, less matter-of-fact to me. I had noticed this peculiar effect of Myra's look and vocative when I first met her, in Parthia, where her manner of addressing my relatives had made them all seem a little more attractive to me.

One afternoon when we were at a matinée I noticed in a loge a young man who looked very much like the photographs of a story-writer popular at that time. I asked Mrs. Henshawe whether it could be he. She looked in the direction I indicated, then looked quickly away again.

"Yes, it's he. He used to be a friend of mine. That's a sad phrase, isn't it? But there was a time when he could have stood by Oswald in a difficulty—and he didn't. He passed it up. Wasn't there. I've never forgiven him."

I regretted having noticed the man in the loge, for all the rest of the afternoon I could feel the bitterness working in her. I knew that she was suffering. The scene on the stage was obliterated for her; the drama was in her mind. She was going over it all again; arguing, accusing, denouncing.

As we left the theatre she sighed: "Oh, Nellie, I wish you hadn't seen him! It's all very well to tell us to forgive our enemies; our enemies can never hurt us very much. But oh, what about forgiving our friends?"—she beat on her fur collar with her two gloved hands—"that's where the rub comes!"

The Henshawes always gave a party on New Year's Eve. That year most of the guests were stage people. Some of them, in order to get there before midnight, came with traces of make-up still on their faces. I remember old Jefferson de Angelais arrived in his last-act wig, carrying his plumed hat—during the supper his painted eyebrows spread and came down over his eyes like a veil. Most of them are dead now, but it was a fine group that stood about the table to drink the New Year in. By far the handsomest and most distinguished of that company was a woman no longer young, but beautiful in age, Helena Modjeska. She looked a woman of another race and another period, no less queenly than when I had seen her in Chicago as Marie Stuart, and as Katharine in *Henry VIII*. I remember how, when Oswald asked her to propose a toast, she put out her long arm, lifted her glass, and looking into the blur of the candlelight with a grave face, said: "To my coun-n-try!"

As she was not playing, she had come early, some time before the others, bringing with her a young Polish woman who was singing at the Opera that winter. I had an opportunity to watch Modjeska as she sat talking to Myra and Esther Sinclair—Miss Sinclair had once played in her company. When the other guests began to arrive, and Myra was called away, she sat by the fire in a high-backed chair, her head resting lightly on her hand, her beautiful face half in shadow. How well I remember those long, beautifully modelled hands, with so much humanity in them. They were worldly, indeed, but fashioned for a nobler worldliness than ours; hands to hold a sceptre, or a chalice—or, by courtesy, a sword.

The party did not last long, but it was a whirl of high spirits. Everybody was hungry and thirsty. There was a great deal of talk about Sarah Bernhardt's *Hamlet,* which had been running all week and had aroused hot controversy; and about Jean de Reszke's return to the Metropolitan that night, after a long illness in London.

By two o'clock everyone had gone but the two Polish ladies. Modjeska, after she put on her long cloak, went to the window, drew back the plum-coloured curtains, and looked out. "See, Myra," she said with that Slav accent she never lost, though she read English verse so beautifully, "the Square is quite white with moonlight. And how still all the ci-ty is, how still!" She turned to her friend; "Emelia, I think you must sing something. Something old . . . yes, from *Norma*." She hummed a familiar air under her breath, and looked about for a chair. Oswald brought one. "Thank you. And we might have less light, might we not?" He turned off the lights.

She sat by the window, half draped in her cloak, the moonlight falling across her knees. Her friend went to the piano and commenced the *Casta Diva* aria, which begins so like the quivering of moonbeams on the water. It was the first air on our old music-box at home, but I had never heard it sung—and I have never heard it sung so beautifully since. I remember Oswald, standing like a statue behind Madame Modjeska's chair, and Myra, crouching low beside the singer, her head in both hands, while the song grew and blossomed like a great emotion.

When it stopped, nobody said anything beyond a low good-bye. Modjeska again drew her cloak around her, and Oswald took them down to their carriage. Aunt Lydia and I followed, and as we crossed the Square we saw their cab going up the Avenue. For many years I associated Mrs. Henshawe with that music, thought of that aria as being mysteriously related to something in her nature that one rarely saw, but nearly always felt; a compelling, passionate, overmastering something for which I had no name, but which was audible, visible in the air that night, as she sat crouching in the shadow. When I wanted to recall powerfully that hidden richness in her, I had only to close my eyes and sing to myself: *"Casta diva, casta diva!"*

## VI

On Saturday I was to lunch at the Henshawes' and go alone with Oswald to hear Bernhardt and Coquelin. As I opened the door into the entry hall, the first thing that greeted me was Mrs. Henshawe's angry laugh, and a burst of rapid words that stung like cold water from a spray.

"I tell you, I will know the truth about this key, and I will go through any door your keys open. Is that clear?"

Oswald answered with a distinctly malicious chuckle: "My dear, you'd have a hard time getting through that door. The key happens to open a safety deposit box."

Her voice rose an octave in pitch. "How dare you lie to me, Oswald? How dare you? They told me at your bank that this wasn't a bank key, though it looks like one. I stopped and showed it to them—the day you forgot your keys and telephoned me to bring them down to your office."

"The hell you did!"

I coughed and rapped at the door . . . they took no notice of me. I heard Oswald push back a chair. "Then it was you who took my keys out of my pocket? I might have known it! I never forget to change them. And you went to the bank and made me and yourself ridiculous. I can imagine their amusement."

"Well, you needn't! I know how to get information without giving any. Here is Nellie Birdseye, rapping at the gates. Come in, Nellie. You and Oswald are going over to Martin's for lunch. He and I are quarrelling about a key ring. There will be no luncheon here to-day."

She went away, and I stood bewildered. This delightful room had seemed to me a place where light-heartedness and charming manners lived—housed there just as the purple curtains and the Kiva rugs and the gay water-colours were. And now everything was in ruins. The air was still and cold like the air in a refrigerating-room. What I felt was fear; I was afraid to look or speak or move. Everything about me seemed evil. When kindness has left people, even for a few moments, we become afraid of them, as if their reason had left them. When it has left a place where we have always found it, it is like shipwreck; we drop from security into something malevolent and bottomless.

"It's all right, Nellie." Oswald recovered himself and put a hand on my shoulder. "Myra isn't half so furious with me as she pretends. I'll get my hat and we'll be off." He was in his smoking-jacket, and had been sitting at his desk, writing. His inkwell was uncovered, and on the blotter lay a half-written sheet of note paper.

I was glad to get out into the sunlight with him. The city seemed safe and friendly and smiling. The air in that room had been like poison. Oswald tried to make it up to me. We walked round and round the Square, and at Martin's he made me drink a glass of sherry, and pointed out the interesting people in the dining-room and told me stories about them. But without his hat, his head against the bright window, he looked tired and troubled. I wondered, as on the first time I saw him, in my own town, at the contradiction in his face: the strong bones, and the curiously shaped eyes without any fire in them. I felt that his life had not suited him; that he possessed some kind of courage and force which slept, which in another sort of world might have asserted themselves brilliantly. I thought he ought to have been a soldier or an explorer. I have since seen those half-moon eyes in other people, and they were always inscrutable, like his; fronted the world with courtesy and kindness, but one never got behind them.

We went to the theatre, but I remember very little of the performance except a dull heartache, and a conviction that I should never like Mrs. Myra so well again. That was on Saturday. On Monday Aunt Lydia and I were to start for home. We positively did not see the Henshawes again. Sunday morning the maid came with some flowers and a note from Myra, saying that her friend Anne Aylward was having a bad day and had sent for her.

On Monday we took an early boat across the ferry, in order to breakfast in the Jersey station before our train started. We had got settled in our places in the Pullman, the moment of departure was near, when we heard an amused laugh, and there was Myra Henshawe, coming into the car in her fur hat, followed by a porter who carried her bags.

"I didn't plot anything so neat as this, Liddy," she laughed, a little out of breath, "though I knew we'd be on the same train. But we won't quarrel, will we? I'm only going as far as Pittsburgh. I've some old friends there. Oswald and I have had a disagreement, and I've left him to think it over. If he needs me, he can quite well come after me."

All day Mrs. Myra was jolly and agreeable, though she treated us with light formality, as if we were new acquaintances. We lunched together, and I noticed, sitting opposite her, that when she was in this mood of high scorn, her mouth, which could be so tender—which cherished the names of her friends and spoke them delicately—was entirely different. It seemed to curl and twist about like a little snake. Letting herself think harm of anyone she loved seemed to change her nature, even her features.

It was dark when we got into Pittsburgh. The Pullman porter took Myra's luggage to the end of the car. She bade us good-bye, started to leave us, then turned back with an icy little smile. "Oh, Liddy dear, you needn't have perjured yourself for those yellow cuff-buttons. I was sure to find out, I always do. I don't hold it against you, but it's disgusting in a man to lie for personal decorations. A woman might do it, now, . . . for pearls!" With a bright nod she turned away and swept out of the car, her head high, the long garnet feather drooping behind.

Aunt Lydia was very angry. "I'm sick of Myra's dramatics," she declared. "I've done with them. A man never *is* justified, but if ever a man was . . ."

## PART II

### I

TEN years after that visit to New York I happened to be in a sprawling overgrown West-coast city which was in the throes of rapid development —it ran about the shore, stumbling all over itself and finally tumbled untidily into the sea. Every hotel and boarding-house was overcrowded, and I was very poor. Things had gone badly with my family and with me. I had come West in the middle of the year to take a position in a college—a college that was as experimental and unsubstantial as everything else in the place. I found lodgings in an apartment-hotel, wretchedly built and already falling to pieces, although it was new. I moved in on a Sunday morning, and while I was unpacking my trunk, I heard, through the thin walls, my neighbour stirring about; a man, and, from the huskiness of his cough and something measured in his movements, not a young man. The caution of his step, the guarded consideration of his activities, let me know that he did not wish to thrust the details of his housekeeping upon other people any more than he could help.

Presently I detected the ugly smell of gasolene in the air, heard a sound of silk being snapped and shaken, and then a voice humming very low an old German air—yes, Schubert's *Frühlings-glaube*; ta ta te-ta | ta–ta ta–ta ta–ta | ta. In a moment I saw the ends of dark neckties fluttering out of the window next mine.

All this made me melancholy—more than the dreariness of my own case. I was young, and it didn't matter so much about me; for youth there is always the hope, the certainty, of better things. But an old man, a gentleman, living in this shabby, comfortless place, cleaning his neckties of a Sunday morning and humming to himself . . . it depressed me unreasonably. I was glad when his outer door shut softly and I heard no more of him.

There was an indifferent restaurant on the ground floor of the hotel. As I was going down to my dinner that evening, I met, at the head of the stairs, a man coming up and carrying a large black tin tray. His head was bent, and his eyes were lowered. As he drew aside to let me pass, in spite of his thin white hair and stooped shoulders, I recognised Oswald Henshawe, whom I had not seen for so many years—not, indeed, since that afternoon when he took me to see Sarah Bernhardt play *Hamlet*.

When I called his name he started, looked at me, and rested the tray on the sill of the blindless window that lighted the naked stairway.

"Nellie! Nellie Birdseye! Can it be?"

His voice was quite uncertain. He seemed deeply shaken, and pulled out a handkerchief to wipe his forehead. "But, Nellie, you have grown up! I would not know you. What good fortune for Myra! She will hardly believe it when I tell her. She is ill, my poor Myra. Oh, very ill! But we must not speak of that, nor seem to know it. What it will mean to her to see you again! Her friends always were so much to her, you remember? Will you stop and see us as you come up? Her room is thirty-two; rap gently, and I'll be waiting for you. Now I must take her dinner. Oh, I hope for her sake you are staying some time. She has no one here."

He took up the tray and went softly along the uncarpeted hall. I felt little zest for the canned vegetables and hard meat the waitress put before me. I had known that the Henshawes had come on evil days, and were wandering about among the cities of the Pacific coast. But Myra had stopped writing to Aunt Lydia, beyond a word of greeting at Christmas and on her birthday. She had ceased to give us any information about their way of life. We knew that several years after my memorable visit in New York, the railroad to whose president Oswald had long been private secretary, was put into the hands of a receiver, and the retiring president went abroad to live. Henshawe had remained with the new management, but very soon the road was taken over by one of the great trunk lines, and the office staff was cut in two. In the reorganization Henshawe was offered a small position, which he indignantly refused—his wife wouldn't let him think of accepting it. He went to San Francisco as manager of a commission house; the business failed, and what had happened to them since I did not know.

I lingered long over my dismal dinner. I had not the courage to go upstairs. Henshawe was not more than sixty, but he looked much older. He had the tired, tired face of one who has utterly lost hope.

Oswald had got his wife up out of bed to receive me. When I entered she was sitting in a wheel-chair by an open window, wrapped in a Chinese dressing-gown, with a bright shawl over her feet. She threw out both arms to me, and as she hugged me, flashed into her old gay laugh.

"Now wasn't it clever of you to find us, Nellie? And we so safely hidden—in earth, like a pair of old foxes! But it was in the cards that we should meet again. Now I understand; a wise woman has been coming to read my fortune for me, and the queen of hearts has been coming up out of the pack when she had no business to; a beloved friend coming out of the past. Well, Nellie, dear, I couldn't think of any old friends that weren't better away, for one reason or another, while we are in temporary eclipse. I gain strength faster if I haven't people on my mind. But you, Nellie . . . that's different." She put my two hands to her cheeks, making a frame for her face. "That's different. Somebody young, and clear-eyed, chock-full of opinions, and without a past. But you may have a past, already? The darkest ones come early."

I was delighted. She was . . . she was herself, Myra Henshawe! I hadn't expected anything so good. The electric bulbs in the room were shrouded and muffled with coloured scarfs, and in that light she looked much less changed than Oswald. The corners of her mouth had relaxed a little, but they could still curl very scornfully upon occasion;

her nose was the same sniffy little nose, with its restless, arched nostrils, and her double chin, though softer, was no fuller. A strong cable of grey-black hair was wound on the top of her head, which, as she once remarked, "was no head for a woman at all, but would have graced one of the wickedest of the Roman emperors."

Her bed was in the alcove behind her. In the shadowy dimness of the room I recognised some of the rugs from their New York apartment, some of the old pictures, with frames peeling and glass cracked. Here was Myra's little inlaid tea-table, and the desk at which Oswald had been writing that day when I dropped in upon their quarrel. At the windows were the dear, plum-coloured curtains, their cream lining streaked and faded—but the sight of them rejoiced me more than I could tell the Henshawes.

"And where did you come from, Nellie? What are you doing here, in heaven's name?"

While I explained myself she listened intently, holding my wrist with one of her beautiful little hands, which were so inexplicably mischievous in their outline, and which, I noticed, were still white and well cared for.

"Ah, but teaching, Nellie! I don't like that, not even for a temporary expedient. It's a cul-de-sac. Generous young people use themselves all up at it; they have no sense. Only the stupid and the phlegmatic should teach."

"But won't you allow me, too, a temporary eclipse?"

She laughed and squeezed my hand. "Ah, *we* wouldn't be hiding in the shadow, if we were five-and-twenty! We were throwing off sparks like a pair of shooting stars, weren't we, Oswald? No, I can't bear teaching for you, Nellie. Why not journalism? You could always make your way easily there."

"Because I hate journalism. I know what I want to do, and I'll work my way out yet, if only you'll give me time."

"Very well, dear." She sighed. "But I'm ambitious for you. I've no patience with young people when they drift. I wish I could live their lives for them; I'd know how! But there it is; by the time you've learned the short cuts, your feet puff up so that you can't take the road at all. Now tell me about your mother and my Lydia."

I had hardly begun when she lifted one finger and sniffed the air. "Do you get it? That bitter smell of the sea? It's apt to come in on the night wind. I live on it. Sometimes I can still take a drive along the shore. Go on; you say that Lydia and your mother are at present in disputation about the possession of your late grandfather's portrait. Why don't you cut it in two for them, Nellie? I remember it perfectly, and half of it would be enough for anybody!"

While I told her any amusing gossip I could remember about my family, she sat crippled but powerful in her brilliant wrappings. She looked strong and broken, generous and tyrannical, a witty and rather wicked old woman, who hated life for its defeats, and loved it for its absurdities. I recalled her angry laugh, and how she had always greeted shock or sorrow with that dry, exultant chuckle which seemed to say: "Ah-ha, I have one more piece of evidence, one more, against the hideous injustice God permits in this world!"

While we were talking, the silence of the strangely balmy February evening was rudely disturbed by the sound of doors slamming and heavy tramping overhead. Mrs. Henshawe winced, a look of apprehension and helplessness, a tortured expression, came over her face. She turned sharply to her husband, who was resting peacefully in one of their old, deep chairs, over by the muffled light. "There they are, those animals!"

He sat up. "They have just come back from church," he said in a troubled voice.

"Why should I have to know when they come back from church? Why should I have the details of their stupid, messy existence thrust upon me all day long, and half the night?" she broke out bitterly. Her features became tense, as from an attack of pain, and I realised how unable she was to bear things.

"We are unfortunate in the people who live over us," Oswald explained. "They annoy us a great deal. These new houses are poorly built, and every sound carries."

"Couldn't you ask them to walk more quietly?" I suggested.

He smiled and shook his head. "We have, but it seems to make them worse. They are that kind of people."

His wife broke in. "The palavery kind of Southerners; all that slushy gush on the surface, and no sensibilities whatever—a race without consonants and without delicacy. They tramp up there all day long like cattle. The stalled ox would have trod softer. Their energy isn't worth anything, so they use it up gabbling and running about, beating my brains into a jelly."

She had scarcely stopped for breath when I heard a telephone ring overhead, then shrieks of laughter, and two people ran across the floor as if they were running a foot-race.

"You hear?" Mrs. Henshawe looked at me triumphantly. "Those two silly old hens race each other to the telephone as if they had a sweetheart at the other end of it. While I could still climb stairs, I hobbled up to that woman and implored her, and she began gushing about 'mah sistah' and 'mah son,' and what 'rahfined' people they were. . . . Oh, that's the cruelty of being poor; it leaves you at the mercy of such pigs! Money is a protection, a cloak; it can buy one quiet, and some sort of dignity." She leaned back, exhausted, and shut her eyes.

"Come, Nellie," said Oswald, softly. He walked down the hall to my door with me. "I'm sorry the disturbance began while you were there. Sometimes they go to the movies, and stay out later," he said mournfully. "I've talked to that woman and to her son, but they are very unfeeling people."

"But wouldn't the management interfere in a case of sickness?"

Again he shook his head. "No, they pay a higher rent than we do—occupy more rooms. And we are somewhat under obligation to the management."

## II

I soon discovered the facts about the Henshawes' present existence. Oswald had a humble position, poorly paid, with the city traction company. He had to be at his desk at nine o'clock every day except Sunday. He rose at five in the morning, put on an old duck suit (it happened to be a very smart one, with frogs and a military collar, left over from prosperous times), went to his wife's room and gave her her bath, made her bed, arranged her things, and then got their breakfast. He made the coffee on a spirit lamp, the toast on an electric toaster. This was the only meal of the day they could have together, and as they had it long before the ruthless Poindexters overhead began to tramp, it was usually a cheerful occasion.

After breakfast Oswald washed the dishes. Their one luxury was a private bath, with a large cupboard, which he called his kitchen. Everything else done, he went back to his own room, put it in order, and then dressed for the office. He still dressed very neatly, though how he managed to do it with the few clothes he had, I could not see. He was the only man staying in that shabby hotel who looked well-groomed. As a special favour from his company he was allowed to take two hours at noon, on account of his sick wife. He came home, brought her her lunch from below, then hurried back to his office.

Myra made her own tea every afternoon, getting about in her wheelchair or with the aid of a cane. I found that one of the kindest things I could do for her was to bring her some little sandwiches or cakes from the Swedish bakery to vary her tinned biscuit. She took great pains to get her tea nicely; it made her feel less shabby to use her own silver tea things and the three glossy English cups she had carried about with her in her trunk. I used often to go in and join her, and we spent some of our pleasantest hours at that time of the day, when the people overhead were usually out. When they were in, and active, it was too painful to witness Mrs. Henshawe's suffering. She was acutely sensitive to sound and light, and the Poindexters did tramp like cattle—except that their brutal thumping hadn't the measured dignity which the step of animals always has. Mrs. Henshawe got great pleasure from flowers, too, and during the late winter months my chief extravagance and my chief pleasure was in taking them to her.

One warm Saturday afternoon, early in April, we went for a drive along the shore. I had hired a low carriage with a kindly Negro driver. Supported on his arm and mine, Mrs. Henshawe managed to get downstairs. She looked much older and more ill in her black broadcloth coat and a black taffeta hat that had once been smart. We took with us her furs and an old steamer blanket. It was a beautiful, soft spring day. The road, unfortunately, kept winding away from the sea. At last we came out on a bare headland, with only one old twisted tree upon it, and the sea beneath.

"Why, Nellie!" she exclaimed, "it's like the cliff in *Lear*, Gloucester's cliff, so it is! Can't we stay here? I believe this nice darkey man would fix me up under the tree there and come back for us later."

We wrapped her in the rug, and she declared that the trunk of the old cedar, bending away from the sea, made a comfortable back for her. The Negro drove away, and I went for a walk up the shore because I knew she wanted to be alone. From a distance I could see her leaning against her tree and looking off to sea, as if she were waiting for something. A few steamers passed below her, and the gulls dipped and darted about the headland, the soft shine of the sun on their wings. The afternoon light, at first wide and watery-pale, grew stronger and yellower, and when I went back to Myra it was beating from the west on her cliff as if thrown by a burning-glass.

She looked up at me with a soft smile—her face could still be very lovely in a tender moment. "I've had such a beautiful hour, dear; or has it been longer? Light and silence: they heal all one's wounds—all but one, and that is healed by dark and silence. I find I don't miss clever talk, the kind I always used to have about me, when I can have silence. It's like cold water poured over fever."

I sat down beside her, and we watched the sun dropping lower towards his final plunge into the Pacific. "I'd love to see this place at dawn," Myra said suddenly. "That is always such a forgiving time. When that first cold, bright streak comes over the water, it's as if all our sins were pardoned; as if the sky leaned over the earth and kissed it and gave it absolution. You know how the great sinners always came home to die in some religious house, and the abbot or the abbess went out and received them with a kiss?"

When we got home she was, of course, very tired. Oswald was waiting for us, and he and the driver carried her upstairs. While we were getting her into bed, the noise overhead broke out—tramp, tramp, bang! Myra began to cry.

"Oh, I've come back to it, to be tormented again! I've two fatal maladies, but it's those coarse creatures I shall die of. Why didn't you leave me out there, Nellie, in the wind and night? You ought to get me away from this, Oswald. If I were on my feet, and you laid low, I wouldn't let you be despised and trampled upon."

"I'll go up and see those people to-morrow, Mrs. Henshawe," I promised. "I'm sure I can do something."

"Oh, don't, Nellie!" She looked up at me in affright. "She'd turn a deaf ear to you. You know the Bible says the wicked are deaf like the adder. And, Nellie, she has the wrinkled, white throat of an adder, that woman, and the hard eyes of one. Don't go near her!"

(I went to see Mrs. Poindexter the next day, and she had just such a throat and just such eyes. She smiled, and said that the sick woman underneath was an old story, and she ought to have been sent to a sanatorium long ago.)

"Never mind, Myra. I'll get you away from it yet. I'll manage," Oswald promised as he settled the pillows under her.

She smoothed his hair. "No, my poor Oswald, you'll never stagger far under the bulk of me. Oh, if youth but knew!" She closed her eyes and pressed her hands over them. "It's been the ruin of us both. We've destroyed each other. I should have stayed with my uncle. It was money I needed. We've thrown our lives away."

"Come, Myra, don't talk so before Nellie. You don't mean it. Remember the long time we were happy. That was reality, just as much as this."

"We were never really happy. I am a greedy, selfish, worldly woman; I wanted success and a place in the world. Now I'm old and ill and a fright, but among my own kind I'd still have my circle; I'd have courtesy from people of gentle manners, and not have my brains beaten out by hoodlums. Go away, please, both of you, and leave me!" She turned her face to the wall and covered her head.

We stepped into the hall, and the moment we closed the door we heard the bolt slip behind us. She must have sprung up very quickly. Oswald walked with me to my room. "It's apt to be like this, when she has enjoyed something and gone beyond her strength. There are times when she can't have anyone near her. It was worse before you came."

I persuaded him to come into my room and sit down and drink a glass of cordial.

"Sometimes she has locked me out for days together," he said. "It seems strange—a woman of such generous friendships. It's as if she had used up that part of herself. It's a great strain on me when she shuts herself up like that. I'm afraid she'll harm herself in some way."

"But people don't do things like that," I said hopelessly.

He smiled and straightened his shoulders. "Ah, but she isn't people! She's Myra Driscoll, and there was never anybody else like her. She can't endure, but she has enough desperate courage for a regiment."

### III

THE next morning I saw Henshawe breakfasting in the restaurant, against his custom, so I judged that his wife was still in retreat. I was glad to see that he was not alone, but was talking, with evident pleasure, to a young girl who lived with her mother at this hotel. I had noticed her respectful admiration for Henshawe on other occasions. She worked on a newspaper, was intelligent and, Oswald thought, promising. We enjoyed talking with her at lunch or dinner. She was perhaps eighteen, overgrown and awkward, with short hair and a rather heavy face; but there was something unusual about her clear, honest eyes that made one wonder. She was always on the watch to catch a moment with Oswald, to get him to talk to her about music, or German poetry, or about the actors and writers he had known. He called her his little chum, and her admiration was undoubtedly a help to him. It was very pretty and naïve. Perhaps that was one of the things that kept him up to the mark in his dress and manner. Among people he never looked apologetic or crushed. He still wore his topaz sleeve-buttons.

On Monday, as I came home from school, I saw that the door of Mrs. Henshawe's room was slightly ajar. She knew my step and called to me: "Can you come in, Nellie?"

She was staying in bed that afternoon, but she had on her best dressing-gown, and she was manicuring her neat little hands—a good sign, I thought.

"Could you stop and have tea with me, and talk? I'll be good to-day, I promise you. I wakened up in the night crying, and it did me good. You see, I was crying about things I never feel now; I'd been dreaming I was young, and the sorrows of youth had set me crying!" She took my hand as I sat down beside her. "Do you know that poem of Heine's, about how he found in his eye a tear that was not of the present, an old one, left over from the kind he used to weep? A tear that belonged to a long dead time of his life and was an anachronism. He couldn't account for it, yet there it was, and he addresses it so prettily: 'Thou old, lonesome tear!' Would you read it for me? There's my little Heine, on the shelf over the sofa. You can easily find the verse, *Du alte, einsame Thräne!"*

I ran through the volume, reading a poem here and there where a leaf had been turned down, or where I saw a line I knew well. It was a fat old book, with yellow pages, bound in tooled leather, and on the fly-leaf, in faint violet ink, was an inscription, "To Myra Driscoll from Oswald," dated 1876.

My friend lay still, with her eyes closed, and occasionally one of those anachronistic tears gathered on her lashes and fell on the pillow, making a little grey spot. Often she took the verse out of my mouth and finished it herself.

"Look for a little short one, about the flower that grows on the suicide's grave, *die Arme-sünderblum'*, the poor-sinner's-flower. Oh, that's the flower for me, Nellie; *die Arme—sünder—blum'!"* She drew the word out until it was a poem in itself.

"Come, dear," she said presently, when I put down the book, "you don't really like this new verse that's going round, ugly lines about ugly people and common feelings—you don't really?"

When I reminded her that she liked Walt Whitman, she chuckled slyly. "Does that save me? Can I get into your new Parnassus on that dirty old man? I suppose I ought to be glad of any sort of ticket at my age! I like naughty rhymes, when they don't try to be pompous. I like the kind bad boys write on fences. My uncle had a rare collection of such rhymes in his head that he'd picked off fences and out-buildings. I wish I'd taken them down; I might become a poet of note! My uncle was a very unusual man. Did they ever tell you much about him at home? Yes, he had violent prejudices; but that's rather good to remember in these days when so few people have any real passions, either of love or hate. He would help a friend, no matter what it cost him, and over and over again he risked ruining himself to crush an enemy. But he never did ruin himself. Men who hate like that usually have the fist-power to back it up, you'll notice. He gave me fair warning, and then he kept his word. I knew he would; we were enough alike for that. He left his money wisely; part of it went to establish a home for aged and destitute women in Chicago, where it was needed."

While we were talking about this institution and some of the refugees it sheltered, Myra said suddenly: "I wonder if you know about a clause concerning me in that foundation? It states that at any time the founder's niece, Myra Driscoll Henshawe, is to be received into the institution, kept without charge, and paid an allowance of ten dollars a week for pocket money until the time of her death. How like the old Satan that was! Be sure when he dictated that provision to his lawyer, he thought to himself: 'She'd roll herself into the river first, the brach!'

And then he probably thought better of me, and maybe died with some decent feeling for me in his heart. We were very proud of each other, and if he'd lived till now, I'd go back to him and ask his pardon; because I know what it is to be old and lonely and disappointed. Yes, and because as we grow old we become more and more the stuff our forebears put into us. I can feel his savagery strengthen in me. We think we are so individual and so misunderstood when we are young; but the nature our strain of blood carries is inside there, waiting, like our skeleton."

It had grown quite dusk while we talked. When I rose and turned on one of the shrouded lights, Mrs. Henshawe looked up at me and smiled drolly. "We've had a fine afternoon, and Biddy forgetting her ails. How the great poets do shine on, Nellie! Into all the dark corners of the world. They have no night."

They shone for her, certainly. Miss Stirling, "a nice young person from the library," as Myra called her, ran in occasionally with new books, but Myra's eyes tired quickly, and she used to shut a new book and lie back and repeat the old ones she knew by heart, the long declamations from *Richard II* or *King John*. As I passed her door I would hear her murmuring at the very bottom of her rich Irish voice:

*Old John of Gaunt, time-honoured Lan-cas-ter . . .*

## IV

ONE afternoon when I got home from school I found a note from Mrs. Henshawe under my door, and went to her at once. She greeted me and kissed me with unusual gravity.

"Nellie, dear, will you do a very special favour for me to-morrow? It is the fifteenth of April, the anniversary of Madame Modjeska's death." She gave me a key and asked me to open an old trunk in the corner. "Lift the tray, and in the bottom, at one end, you will find an old pair of long kid gloves, tied up like sacks. Please give them to me."

I burrowed down under old evening wraps and dinner dresses and came upon the gloves, yellow with age and tied at both ends with corset lacings; they contained something heavy that jingled. Myra was watching my face and chuckled. "Is she thinking they are my wedding gloves, piously preserved? No, my dear; I went before a justice of the peace, and married without gloves, so to speak!" Untying the string, she shook out a little rain of ten- and twenty-dollar gold pieces.

"All old Irish women hide away a bit of money." She took up a coin and gave it to me. "Will you go to St. Joseph's Church and inquire for

Father Fay; tell him you are from me, and ask him to celebrate a mass to-morrow for the repose of the soul of Helena Modjeska, Countess Bozenta-Chlapowska. He will remember; last year I hobbled there myself. You are surprised, Nellie? Yes, I broke with the Church when I broke with everything else and ran away with a German free-thinker; but I believe in holy words and holy rites all the same. It is a solace to me to know that to-morrow a mass will be said here in heathendom for the spirit of that noble artist, that beautiful and gracious woman."

When I put the gold back into the trunk and started making the tea, she said: "Oswald, of course, doesn't know the extent of my resources. We've often needed a hundred dollars or two so bitter bad; he wouldn't understand. But that is money I keep for unearthly purposes; the needs of this world don't touch it."

As I was leaving she called me back: "Oh, Nellie, can't we go to Gloucester's cliff on Saturday, if it's fine? I do long to!"

We went again, and again. Nothing else seemed to give her so much pleasure. But the third time I stopped for her, she declared she was not equal to it. I found her sitting in her chair, trying to write to an old friend, an Irish actress I had met at her apartment in New York, one of the guests at that New Year's Eve party. Her son, a young actor, had shot himself in Chicago because of some sordid love affair. I had seen an account of it in the morning paper.

"It touches me very nearly," Mrs. Henshawe told me. "Why, I used to keep Billy with me for weeks together when his mother was off on tour. He was the most truthful, noble-hearted little fellow. I had so hoped he would be happy. You remember his mother?"

I remembered her very well—large and jovial and hearty she was. Myra began telling me about her, and the son, whom she had not seen since he was sixteen.

"To throw his youth away like that, and shoot himself at twenty-three! People are always talking about the joys of youth—but, oh, how youth can suffer! I've not forgotten; those hot southern Illinois nights, when Oswald was in New York, and I had no word from him except through Liddy, and I used to lie on the floor all night and listen to the express trains go by. I've not forgotten."

"Then I wonder why you are sometimes so hard on him now," I murmured.

Mrs. Henshawe did not reply to me at once. The corners of her mouth trembled, then drew tight, and she sat with her eyes closed as if she were gathering herself for something.

At last she sighed, and looked at me wistfully. "It's a great pity, isn't it, Nellie, to reach out a grudging hand and try to spoil the past for anyone? Yes, it's a great cruelty. But I can't help it. He's a sentimentalist, always was; he can look back on the best of those days when we were young and loved each other, and make himself believe it was all like that. It wasn't. I was always a grasping, worldly woman; I was never satisfied. All the same, in age, when the flowers are so few, it's a great unkindness to destroy any that are left in a man's heart." The tears rolled down her cheeks, she leaned back, looking up at the ceiling. She had stopped speaking because her voice broke. Presently she began again resolutely. "But I'm made so. People can be lovers and enemies at the same time, you know. We were. . . . A man and woman draw apart from that long embrace, and see what they have done to each other. Perhaps I can't forgive him for the harm I did him. Perhaps that's it. When there are children, that feeling goes through natural changes. But when it remains so personal . . . something gives way in one. In age we lose everything; even the power to love."

"He hasn't," I suggested.

"He has asked you to speak for him, my dear? Then we have destroyed each other indeed!"

"Certainly he hasn't, Mrs. Myra! But you are hard on him, you know, and when there are so many hard things, it seems a pity."

"Yes, it's a great pity." She drew herself up in her chair. "And I'd rather you didn't come any more for the time being, Nellie. I've been thinking the tea made me nervous." She was smiling, but her mouth curled like a little snake, as I had seen it do long ago. "Will you be pleased to take your things and go, Mrs. Casey?" She said it with a laugh, but a very meaning one.

As I rose I watched for some sign of relenting, and I said humbly enough: "Forgive me, if I've said anything I shouldn't. You know I love you very dearly."

She mockingly bowed her tyrant's head. "It's owing to me infirmities, dear Mrs. Casey, that I'll not be able to go as far as me door wid ye."

## V

FOR days after that episode I did not see Mrs. Henshawe at all. I saw Oswald at dinner in the restaurant every night, and he reported her condition to me as if nothing had happened. The short-haired newspaper girl often came to our table, and the three of us talked together. I could see that he got great refreshment from her. Her questions woke pleasant trains of recollection, and her straightforward affection was dear to him. Once Myra, in telling me that it was a pleasure to him to have me come into their lives again thus, had remarked: "He was always a man to feel women, you know, in every way." It was true. That crude little girl made all the difference in the world to him. He was generous enough to become quite light-hearted in directing her inexperience and her groping hunger for life. He even read her poor little "specials" and showed her what was worst in them and what was good. She took correction well, he told me.

Early in June Mrs. Henshawe began to grow worse. Her doctors told us a malignant growth in her body had taken hold of a vital organ, and that she would hardly live through the month. She suffered intense pain from pressure on the nerves in her back, and they gave her opiates freely. At first we had two nurses, but Myra hated the night nurse so intensely that we dismissed her, and, as my school was closed for the summer, I took turns with Oswald in watching over her at night. She needed little attention except renewed doses of codeine. She slept deeply for a few hours, and the rest of the night lay awake, murmuring to herself long passages from her old poets.

Myra kept beside her now an ebony crucifix with an ivory Christ. It used to hang on the wall, and I had supposed she carried it about because some friend had given it to her. I felt now that she had it by her for a different reason. Once when I picked it up from her bed to straighten her sheet, she put out her hand quickly and said: "Give it to me. It means nothing to people who haven't suffered."

She talked very little after this last stage of her illness began; she no longer complained or lamented, but toward Oswald her manner became strange and dark. She had certain illusions; the noise overhead she now attributed entirely to her husband. "Ah, there, he's beginning it again," she would say. "He'll wear me down in the end. Oh, let me be buried in the king's highway!"

When Oswald lifted her, or did anything for her now, she was careful to thank him in a guarded, sometimes a cringing tone. "It's bitter enough that I should have to take service from you—you whom I have loved so well," I heard her say to him.

When she asked us to use candles for light during our watches, and to have no more of the electric light she hated, she said accusingly, at him rather than to him: "At least let me die by candlelight; that is not too much to ask."

Father Fay came to see her almost daily now. His visits were long, and she looked forward to them. I was, of course, not in her room when he was there, but if he met me in the corridor he stopped to speak to me, and once he walked down the street with me talking of her. He was a young man, with a fresh face and pleasant eyes, and he was deeply interested in Myra. "She's a most unusual woman, Mrs. Henshawe," he said when he was walking down the street beside me. Then he added, smiling quite boyishly: "I wonder whether some of the saints of the early Church weren't a good deal like her. She's not at all modern in her make-up, is she?"

During those days and nights when she talked so little, one felt that Myra's mind was busy all the while—that it was even abnormally active, and occasionally one got a clue to what occupied it. One night when I was giving her her codeine she asked me a question.

"Why is it, do you suppose, Nellie, that candles are in themselves religious? Not when they are covered by shades, of course—I mean the flame of a candle. Is it because the Church began in the catacombs, perhaps?"

At another time, when she had been lying like a marble figure for a long while, she said in a gentle, reasonable voice:

"Ah, Father Fay, that isn't the reason! Religion is different from everything else; *because in religion seeking is finding.*"

She accented the word "seeking" very strongly, very deeply. She seemed to say that in other searchings it might be the object of the quest that brought satisfaction, or it might be something incidental that one got on the way; but in religion, desire was fulfillment, it was the seeking itself that rewarded.

One of those nights of watching stands out in my memory as embracing them all, as being the burden and telling the tale of them all. Myra had had a very bad day, so both Oswald and I were sitting up with her. After midnight she was quiet. The candles were burning as usual, one in her alcove. From my chair by the open window I could see her bed. She had been motionless for more than an hour, lying on her back, her eyes closed. I thought she was asleep. The city outside was as still as the room in which we sat. The sick woman began to talk to herself, scarcely above a whisper, but with perfect distinctness; a voice that was hardly more than a soft, passionate breath. I seemed to hear a soul talking.

"I could bear to suffer . . . so many have suffered. But why must it be like this? I have not deserved it. I have been true in friendship; I have faithfully nursed others in sickness. . . . Why must I die like this, alone with my mortal enemy?"

Oswald was sitting on the sofa, his face shaded by his hand. I looked at him in affright, but he did not move or shudder. I felt my hands grow cold and my forehead grow moist with dread. I had never heard a human voice utter such a terrible judgment upon all one hopes for. As I sat on through the night, after Oswald had gone to catch a few hours of sleep, I grew calmer; I began to understand a little what she meant, to sense how it was with her. Violent natures like hers sometimes turn against themselves . . . against themselves and all their idolatries.

## VI

On the following day Mrs. Henshawe asked to be given the Sacrament. After she had taken it she seemed easier in mind and body. In the afternoon she told Henshawe to go to his office and begged me to leave her and let her sleep. The nurse we had sent away that day at her urgent request. She wanted to be cared for by one of the nursing Sisters from the convent from now on, and Father Fay was to bring one to-morrow.

I went to my room, meaning to go back to her in an hour, but once on my bed I slept without waking. It was dark when I heard Henshawe knocking on my door and calling to me. As I opened it, he said in a despairing tone: "She's gone, Nellie, she's gone!"

I thought he meant she had died. I hurried after him down the corridor and into her room. It was empty. He pointed to her empty bed. "Don't you see? She has gone, God knows where!"

"But how could she? A woman so ill? She must be somewhere in the building."

"I've been all over the house. You don't know her, Nellie. She can do anything she wills. Look at this."

On the desk lay a sheet of note paper scribbled in lead pencil: *Dear Oswald: my hour has come. Don't follow me. I wish to be alone. Nellie knows where there is money for masses."* That was all. There was no signature.

We hurried to the police station. The chief sent a messenger out to the men on the beat to warn them to be on the watch for a distraught woman who had wandered out in delirium. Then we went to Father Fay. "The Church has been on her mind for a long while," said Henshawe. "It is one of her delusions that I separated her from the Church. I never meant to."

The young priest knew nothing. He was distressed, and offered to help us in our search, but we thought he had better stay at home on the chance that she might come to him.

When we got back to the hotel it was after eleven o'clock. Oswald said he could not stay indoors; I must be there within call, but he would go back to help the police.

After he left I began to search Mrs. Henshawe's room. She had worn her heavy coat and her furs, though the night was warm. When I found that the pair of Austrian blankets was missing, I felt I knew where she had gone. Should I try to get Oswald at the police station? I sat down to think it over. It seemed to me that she ought to be allowed to meet the inevitable end in the way she chose. A yearning strong enough to lift that ailing body and drag it out into the world again should have its way.

At five o'clock in the morning Henshawe came back with an officer and a Negro cabman. The driver had come to the station and reported that at six last night a lady, with her arms full of wraps, had signalled him at the side door of the hotel, and told him to drive her to the boat landing. When they were nearing the landing, she said she did not mean to stop there, but wanted to go farther up the shore, giving him clear directions. They reached the cliff she had indicated. He helped her out of the cab, put her rugs under the tree for her, and she gave him a ten-dollar gold piece and dismissed him. He protested that the fare was too much, and that he was afraid of getting into trouble if he left her there. But she told him a friend was going to meet her, and that it would be all right. The lady had, he said, a very kind, coaxing way with her. When he went to the stable to put up his horse, he heard that the police were looking for a woman who was out of her head, and he was frightened. He went home and talked it over with his wife, who sent him to report at headquarters.

The cabman drove us out to the headland, and the officer insisted upon going along. We found her wrapped in her blankets, leaning against the cedar trunk, facing the sea. Her head had fallen forward; the ebony crucifix was in her hands. She must have died peacefully and painlessly. There was every reason to believe she had lived to see the dawn. While we watched beside her, waiting for the undertaker and Father Fay to come, I told Oswald what she had said to me about longing to behold the morning break over the sea, and it comforted him.

## VII

ALTHOUGH she had returned so ardently to the faith of her childhood, Myra Henshawe never changed the clause in her will, which requested that her body should be cremated, and her ashes buried "in some lonely and unfrequented place in the mountains, or in the sea."

After it was all over, and her ashes sealed up in a little steel box, Henshawe called me into her room one morning, where he was packing her things, and told me he was going to Alaska.

"Oh, not to seek my fortune," he said, smiling. "That is for young men. But the steamship company have a place for me in their office there. I have always wanted to go, and now there is nothing to hold me. This poor little box goes with me; I shall scatter her ashes somewhere in those vast waters. And this I want you to keep for remembrance." He dropped into my hands the necklace of carved amethysts she had worn on the night I first saw her.

"And, Nellie——" He paused before me with his arms folded, standing exactly as he stood behind Modjeska's chair in the moonlight on that New Year's night; standing like a statue, or a sentinel, I had said then, not knowing what it was I felt in his attitude; but now I knew it meant indestructible constancy . . . almost indestructible youth. "Nellie," he said, "I don't want you to remember her as she was here. Remember her as she was when you were with us on Madison Square, when she was herself, and we were happy. Yes, happier than it falls to the lot of most mortals to be. After she was stricken, her recollection of those things darkened. Life was hard for her, but it was glorious, too; she had such beautiful friendships. Of course, she was absolutely unreasonable when she was jealous. Her suspicions were sometimes —almost fantastic." He smiled and brushed his forehead with the tips of his fingers, as if the memory of her jealousy was pleasant still, and perplexing still. "But that was just Molly Driscoll! I'd rather have been clawed by her, as she used to say, than petted by any other woman I've ever known. These last years it's seemed to me that I was nursing the mother of the girl who ran away with me. Nothing ever took that girl from me. She was a wild, lovely creature, Nellie. I wish you could have seen her then."

Several years after I said good-bye to him, Oswald Henshawe died in Alaska. I have still the string of amethysts, but they are unlucky. If I take them out of their box and wear them, I feel all evening a chill over my heart. Sometimes, when I have watched the bright beginning of a love story, when I have seen a common feeling exalted into beauty by imagination, generosity, and the flaming courage of youth, I have heard again that strange complaint breathed by a dying woman into the stillness of night, like a confession of the soul: "Why must I die like this, alone with my mortal enemy!"

# THE WEEPING CHILDREN

*Frank O'Connor*

---

FRANK O'CONNOR (Michael Donovan) (1903– ) is today regarded as heading the long list of distinguished Irish story tellers. Born in Cork of poor parents, he had even before his teens started to write poetry and historic tales of the homeland. His education was acquired, by his own account, "haphazard in a public library," and later he sought technique and experience as a writer for the Abbey Theatre in Dublin. But pure story telling came closest to his heart; the Russian writers influenced him strongly and in this regard Yeats once said of him "O'Connor is doing for Ireland what Chekhov did for Russia." Typically one feels a sense of deep compassion as well as wonderful native humor in his every story. *The Weeping Children* is a recent example; at its close the reader may find that not only the children are weeping.

J OE Saunders and his wife, Brigid, had been married a year and were living in a development about twenty miles outside London when they had their first baby, a little girl they called Nance, after Brigid's mother. Brigid was Irish, and Joe, who was a Cockney, had always had a feeling that there was some affinity between the Irish and himself. She was a Catholic, and though he had never been able to believe in anything himself, he liked it in her and encouraged her to put up holy pictures and statues about the house. He even went to Mass with her occasionally, but she said mockingly that he put her off her prayers by his airs of devotion. She made him laugh, and he liked to be made to laugh, because he had a natural gravity that turned easily to melancholy and even to tears. She had good breeding as well, and Joe liked that, too, though she sometimes upset him by the way she unconsciously patronized his mother and sisters. She had kept her youthful gaiety and her delight in flirting in the most abandoned way with any man who fancied her. It amused Joe, because for all her charm he knew the innocent, chaste streak in her, and realized that the wide boys had very little chance with her.

After Nance's birth Joe felt that life had done him well. There were times when he saw everything with a sort of double vision, as though he were not only doing whatever he was at the moment—like pushing the pram round the development, or creeping into the back room at night to make sure the baby was covered—but was observing himself do it. And the conjunction of the two visions gave the experience an intense stereoscopic quality. He was sure this must be what they meant by happiness.

But he realized that it was different for Brigid. Though she could forget herself and play with the baby like a little girl with a doll, she was often gloomy, tearful, and irritable. This wasn't like her. Joe's great friend, Jerry Cross, called it something like post-partum psychosis, and though Joe had no great faith in the long names Jerry loved to tag on to things, he took Brigid for a week to Brighton. This did her good but the effect didn't last. Joe thought he knew how she felt—a wild girl with a vivacious temperament, who loved outings and parties, trapped by a morsel of humanity that took everything and gave nothing. He was attentive to the point of officiousness, seeing that she went to the cinema and visited friends and had them to the house. But even to old friends she had changed, and she took a positive dislike to Jerry Cross. Jerry was the only man who came to the house who was always circumspect with her, and now she chose to interpret this as resentment. With a sort of schoolgirl pertness that drove Joe to despair she jeered Cross on his overheated bachelor flat, his expensive gramophone and collection of records, and his liquor cabinet that always seemed to contain some new exotic drink, which Jerry plied them with in his effusive, enthusiastic way, rubbing his hands and saying modestly, "It isn't bad, is it? I mean, it really isn't bad." Twice, to protect Cross, Joe had had to reprove her, and though he did it gently, it cut him to the heart to have to do it at all.

"Why in God's name can't you be nice to Jerry?" he asked when they were going home. "He hasn't so many friends."

"He has none at all, if you ask me," Brigid replied coolly. "He's too bloody selfish to afford them."

"Selfish?" Joe exclaimed, stopping dead. "Haven't I told you how when I was going bust he waited till I was out of the room to put a check for two hundred quid on the mantelpiece?"

"You told me often enough," Brigid said contemptuously. "Damn well he knew you wouldn't take it!"

"He knew more than I did," said Joe, resuming his walk. "Anyway, it's not the money that mattered. It was Jerry's confidence in me. It gave me confidence in myself. I tell you, girl, there's things between men you'll never understand, not till the day you die."

But reasoning had no effect on Brigid except perhaps to give her fresh grounds for spite. One evening at Joe's house, Cross was boasting innocently about some shady deal he had refused to be connected with, and Brigid with an air of mock admiration drew him out skillfully. It was one of Cross's little weaknesses that he liked to think himself a really shrewd businessman.

"You always play it safe, Jerry, don't you?" she asked at last.

"What's that, Brigid?" Cross asked eagerly, too surprised to be aware of her malice.

"Brigid!" Joe said warningly.

"Anyone that had anything to do with you would want to watch out," she said.

Cross got up and clutched the lapels of his coat as though he were going to make a speech. It suddenly struck Joe that he was a little man who lived in the expectation of having to make speeches—unpleasant ones.

"I can assure you, Brigid," Cross said overloudly, "that nobody who had anything to do with me ever had to watch out, as you put it. I do play it safe, though. You're right there. I do. And for the future I'll play it safe by not calling here, the way I've been doing."

Then he made for the door, and Joe, holding his coat for him, realized that he was shivering. He opened the door, put his hand round Cross's shoulder, and walked down to the gate with him. The estate road went uphill to the bus stop on the tree-shaded suburban road, and the two men went together like that till they reached it. Then Joe took Cross's hand in his own two.

"Try to forget it, Jerry," he said in a low voice. "You know she doesn't mean what she says. The girl is sick in her mind."

"She is, Joe, she is, she is," Cross said eagerly. "I thought it from the first, but now I'm sure."

It was only when he had waved good-bye to Cross from the pavement that Joe gave way to tears. He walked slowly up and down the ill-lit suburban road till the fit had passed. As he entered the house, Brigid was waiting for him in the sitting room, exactly as she was when he left.

"Come in, Joe," she said quietly. "We have to talk."

"I'm sorry, Brigid, but I don't want to talk," he said, feeling sure that if he did he would weep again.

"I do," she said in a flat tone. "It may be the last chance we'll get. I'm going to clear out."

"What's that?"

"I have to clear out," she said, and he knew that she meant it.

"Clear out, dear?" he asked mildly, taking a seat inside the door and

joining his hands before him. It was at moments like this that all the
wise passivity in Joe came to the top. He knew you had to give in to
things. "Why?" he asked.

"I don't want to ruin your life the way I ruined my own," she said.

"Well, I've got something to say to that," he said. "So has the baby,
of course. Or were you planning to take Nance with you?"

"I wasn't," she said with artificial casualness. "I daresay your mother
can look after her."

"I daresay. But I don't suppose that's what any of us wants."

"At least your mother won't insult your friends," Brigid said bitterly.
He knew then that she had no illusions about her behavior to Cross,
and his heart softened.

"You mean more to me than any of my friends, dear," he said steadily.
"Even Jerry—and Heaven knows he means quite a lot. What is it,
Brigid? Why don't you trust me? Is it another man?"

For a moment Joe thought she was going to strike him. Then she
gave a weak grin. "Ah, for God's sake don't be a bloody fool!" she said
in the brisk, good-humored tone that was most characteristic of her.
"Sure I never looked at the side of the road a man walked on since I
married you."

There was no mistaking the truthfulness of that, and again he felt
a sense of relief, and with it the old tenderness and admiration.

"Naturally that was what I'd hoped, dear," he said evenly. "And I
don't see that anything else matters."

"Not even the ones I met before I did marry you?" she asked mockingly.

"I see," he said after a moment. "You mean there was someone else?"

"I do," she replied. And then, as though reading his thoughts, she
reverted to her tone of exasperated amusement. "And, for God's sake,
if you think he's waiting for me this minute in London and that I'm
crazy to get back to him, forget it, boy! I hope to God I never lay my
eyes on him again—and I wish I could say the same about his daughter."

"His daughter?" Joe repeated stupidly. "You mean you had a child
already?"

"What do you think brought me over to London in the first place?"

"I don't know," Joe said with simple dignity. "I just thought you
might have been telling me the truth when you said you came over to
get a job. I suppose you're right to think I'm a bit simple-minded."

"I never thought you were simple-minded," she replied furiously. "I
thought you were too bloody good to be true, if you want to know
what I thought."

"How old is this child?"

"She's two."

"And you have her here?"

"No. At home, outside Cork. I suppose I wanted her as far away as possible. And, as I'm about it, there's another thing. I pinched some of the housekeeping money to support her. After I left the job I had nothing of my own."

"You could scarcely have left the child to starve," he said. "That doesn't count beside the other things."

"What other things?"

"All the lies you've told me," he said sternly. "Look, Brigid, it's no use pretending I'm not hurt. Not by what you've just told me. That was your business. But you might have told me that before you married me."

"So that you needn't have married me?" she asked.

"I mean nothing of the sort," said Joe. "I mean you might have trusted me. As I trusted you."

"As if the two things were alike!" she retorted. "I told you I thought you were too good to be true. You weren't. But for a girl to get to know you that way she has to marry you, and to marry you she has to tell lies. At least, that's what I thought then. And a hell of a lot of good it did me!"

Joe sighed. "Anyway," he said, "we have to think what we're going to do about this kid, and that's something that can't be decided tonight."

"There's only one thing to do, Joe," she said. "I'll have to go back to London and get a job."

"No," he said. "We don't have to break up this house. At the worst, we can still bring her to live with us."

"But I don't want to bring her to live with us. Can't you understand? It was all a miserable bloody mistake, and I don't want to have to live with it for the rest of my life. It's just that I feel such a bitch, having every damn thing in the world I want while she has nothing."

"I see that," Joe said gently. "We'll have to think of something, that's all."

He thought about it a lot that night, but less of what they were to do with Brigid's child than of the disaster that had overtaken his beautiful world. Again he could see himself acting, doing whatever he finally decided was necessary, but beyond that he could see it all as though it were happening to someone in a book or a movie, only this time it wasn't happiness but grief. Yet when Brigid waked him, bringing him a cup of tea in bed, it seemed to have taken nothing out of her. Unburdening herself of the secret seemed to have given her back all her native liveliness.

When he got home that evening, he was astonished to see Cross waiting for him in the front room, and he knew from Cross's manner that, however she had managed it, Brigid had made her peace with him. At any other time this would have made him happy, but now it didn't seem to matter. As he saw Cross off, Cross said urgently, "You won't think I'm interfering, Joe, but Brigid came to the office and told me about your little trouble. I only want to say how sorry I am."

Joe was amused at Cross's delicacy, and touched that Brigid, for all her fierce pride, had humiliated herself so abjectly before him, but that no longer seemed to matter, either. "I know, Jerry, I know," he said, squeezing his friend's arm, but Cross was full of the subject.

"It's going to be terrible, however you arrange things," he said, "and I only want you to know that if there's anything I can do I'll be delighted. Delighted! Because I have a great admiration for Brigid, Joe. You know that."

Joe realized that by ways that could have been no great pleasure to her Brigid had at last managed to pierce Cross's defenses. Being Cross, he was doing more than intercede; he was hiding the check on the mantelpiece.

After supper Joe said to Brigid, "I've been thinking this thing over, dear, and I can see only one way out of it. We have to bring the child here."

"I've been thinking it over, too," she said hastily, "and I don't see the necessity for that at all. To tell you the truth, I think 'twould be impossible."

Joe could see what she was thinking. Now that the burden of the secrecy had been lifted, she had fled to the opposite extreme of self-confidence. Only a wild outburst of self-confidence could have given her the courage to go to Cross's office like that. But with self-confidence she had regained all her old personality, and was planning how much she could retrieve from the wreck and how she could avoid humiliating herself before the neighbors and Joe's decent working-class family.

"Not impossible," he said. "Difficult, I grant you. We've made a good many friends on the development and it's going to take some explaining. But others have had to do that and worse."

"It's easier for a man than for a woman," Brigid said ruefully.

"It's not easy for anybody, but it doesn't count compared with a child's life."

"And there's your mother," she said.

"Exactly. There's Mother, and there's Barbara and Coralie, and we know what they'll say. And that's not the worst. We may get the kid too late for her to be able to fit in. But at least it will be easier now than it would be in ten or fifteen years' time."

"I don't know, Joe," Brigid said earnestly. "I cracked up on you because I was trying to handle the whole thing on my own. I won't do that on you again, and I think there are a lot of things I can do without making the pair of us miserable."

"Such as?"

"Well, it was really Jerry who suggested it—getting her over here to someplace where I can keep an eye on her; maybe taking her away on holidays with Nance and seeing that she goes to a decent school when she's old enough."

"And I suppose Jerry offered to help?"

"He did," she said slowly. "He's damn decent."

"He is, but he's wrong," said Joe. Like many gentle souls he had a streak of iron in him, and when he made up his mind about something he could be very obstinate. "Jerry is a bachelor. He doesn't know what he's talking about. You can cut off a man or a woman as a loss and feel that maybe they'll keep afloat, but you can't do that to a child. A child is too helpless. And this time it isn't only you who have to live with the consequences. If anything happened to that child, you and I would both be murderers."

A FORTNIGHT later as they were flying in over Dublin from the sea, Joe asked, "Feeling frightened?" and Brigid said, "Wouldn't you be?" He squeezed her hand. When they travelled into the city on the tall, bumpy, swaying bus, she kept silent, and when they reached their hotel room she broke down.

"Look, Joe, I can't face it," she said.

"Now, Brigid, you've done things a great deal more difficult than this," he said comfortingly.

"I haven't, Joe," she said. "You don't understand. I can't go down to Cork tomorrow and meet people I used to know and start inventing explanations for coming back."

"You don't have to invent explanations. You're just there with your husband on a holiday. What's wrong with that?"

"And carry a two-year-old baby through the town in my arms!" she said bitterly. "I tell you, Joe, I don't care what happens to her, I'm not going down."

"Do you think they're going to come after you with knives?"

"There are worse things than knives."

"Like what?"

She didn't answer.

"Very well, dear," he said. "I'll go. I daresay your family can direct me."

"I suppose they can," she said doubtfully. "But if you have any consideration for them you'll keep as far away from them as you can."

He knew it was unsafe to argue with her. She was too close to hysteria.

"Very well," he said. "If you say so, I will."

The trip on the train to Cork was pleasant, and his only regret was that he hadn't Brigid with him to tell him about the places of interest he passed. It seemed like the waste of a good excursion. The city itself looked pleasant enough, too, and he had a good view of the river from his bedroom window. Downstairs, he talked to the hotel manager, who was big-boned, deep-voiced, and amiable, and who seemed to throw himself into the business of getting Joe to his destination as though he had no other aim in life. He heaved himself across the desk, looking at a map and studying a timetable, bellowed softly to members of the staff who might help, and even called to casual passersby. This rather scared Joe, because he didn't want his business made public at once. It would be time enough for explanations when he returned with a child. But the last ten miles of his journey seemed to be the most difficult of all.

"It's all right, Mr. Coleman," Joe said. "I'll hire a car."

The hotel manager glanced at a clock in the hall and said in his deep voice, "You won't hire any car. I'll take an hour off after dinner and drive you."

"That's very kind of you," said Joe, "but it might be better if I ordered a car. You see, it's rather a delicate matter."

"Oh, I'm sorry. I didn't mean to be inquisitive," Coleman said.

"No, no, you're not being inquisitive," said Joe. "I haven't anything to hide, and anyhow I'd have had to tell you. Sit down for a moment and let me explain."

The two men sat in a corner of the lounge and Joe explained. The hotel manager listened with a vague smile.

"So far as I'm concerned," he said, "I can keep my mouth shut, but don't be surprised if a lot of the staff know who you are already. If they don't know it tonight, they'll know it tomorrow. This may seem a big city to you, but it doesn't seem so big to those who have to live in it. Mind you," he added with a fat chuckle, "I wouldn't let that disturb me too much, either. Will I get a cot into your room?"

"Not just now," said Joe. "I've tried to think this thing out. I don't feel it would be fair to the kid to bring her back tonight. Even if my wife was here it would still be a shock. I thought I'd go to this house and let the kid get to know me and then bring her back tomorrow."

"Tomorrow I have the whole morning clear," said Coleman.

"No, I didn't mean it that way," Joe protested. "I can hire a car. Damn it, having come all this way, I can afford to hire a car."

"No reason you should unless you want to," said Coleman gruffly.

"I agree that you're right not to bring her tonight. I'll see you in the lounge after dinner. I'd try the roast beef, if I were you."

After dinner the two men set off down the quiet street in Coleman's old car. After a few moments Coleman spoke. "This isn't an aspect of life you get much advice on when you go into the hotel business," he said in his bluff, good-humored way. "But if you'll excuse my being personal, Mr. Saunders, you seem to me a rather unusual sort of man."

"Do I?" asked Joe in surprise. "I should have said in my circumstances most men would have felt the same."

"Felt the same I've no doubt," said Coleman. "I'm not so sure that they'd have acted the same, though. Naturally, the first thing I did when you told me your story was to ask myself what I'd have done in your place."

"Yes?" said Joe.

"I decided that I'd think twice about it, that's all," said Coleman.

"Don't worry, old man," Joe said with a laugh. "I did. I thought about it three or four times, as a matter of fact."

They had passed the city boundaries and were driving along a river-bank with a river walk at the other side of the water, lined with old trees. The main road led along another river, with trees down to its banks. Finally they reached a little village with a church and pub, where they went off on a byroad that wound uphill giving views of the river and harbor. They stopped to inquire their way, and drove for several miles along a deserted upland road far above the development that fringed the harbor. It was darkening, and Coleman drove slowly. There was a cottage on their right, and a small boy and girl with bare feet were playing in the roadway outside it. He stopped the car.

"I fancy this is the place we want," he said, and bellowed to the children, "Is this Mrs. Ryan's?"

"What's that, sir?" asked the little boy.

"Mrs. Ryan's, I said."

" 'Tis, sir," said the little boy.

"And is this Marie?" Coleman asked, pointing to the little girl who accompanied him.

"No, sir," said the little boy.

"Then where *is* Marie?" Coleman asked, and suddenly a tall, rough-looking countrywoman with rosy cheeks appeared by the white gate-post. Afterward, Joe thought he would never forget that first impression of her with the white gatepost and dark fuchsia bushes, cut out against the sky.

"Is this the gentleman from England?" she called. "Marie is inside, gentlemen. Won't ye come in?"

Joe got out first and held out his hand. "I'm Joe Saunders, Brigid

Healy's husband," he said. "And this is Mr. Coleman, the hotel manager. He was kind enough to give me a lift."

"I was after giving up expecting ye," she said, showing her teeth, which, like her face, were big and rough. "Come in, let ye. I'm afraid the house is in a mess, but 'tis only the children."

"Oh, you don't have to apologize, Mrs. Ryan," said Joe. "I come of a large family myself."

But even Joe's large London family had not prepared him for the little cottage, even if the shadows inside gave small opportunity for deciding whether or not it was in a mess. An open door into the bedroom suggested that the big bed hadn't been made, and the walls of the kitchen were bare except for a grocer's calendar inside the door. Sitting round the open fire were three other children, whose faces he could barely see, but it was clear enough that the little barelegged girl who toasted her feet before it was Brigid's child.

"This is Miss Healy's little girl," said Mrs. Ryan. "She's the spit of her, but ye can't see. I'll light the lamp. I suppose ye'd like a cup of tea after yeer journey?"

"No, thanks, Mrs. Ryan," said Joe. "We've only just finished dinner. Besides, we're not staying long. We thought we'd come back tomorrow for Marie, just to give you time to get her ready. . . . Hullo, Marie," he said, taking the child's hand. "I bet you don't know who I am."

"Hullo, Marie," Coleman said with casual amiability, and he, too, took the child's cold and dirty hand. She looked up at them without expression, and Joe suddenly recognized the resemblance with Brigid.

"Run out and play with Martha and Michael," Mrs. Ryan shouted. "And bring Kitty with you." Silently the two children got up and went out, closing the half door behind them. They did not act as though they were frightened but as though they saw no reason for disobeying, and for some reason this impressed Joe even more than if they had showed fear. Mrs. Ryan lit the lamp.

"Wisha, sit down, let ye," she said, pulling up two chairs and wiping the seats vaguely with her apron. "And how is Miss Healy? You'll have to frogive me. I forget her married name."

"Saunders," said Joe, sitting down and opening the little case he had brought with him. "She's fine, Mrs. Ryan. She probably told you that we have a little girl of our own now. She wasn't well when we got to Dublin or she'd have been here herself. As I say, I don't want to rush you. These are a few clothes I brought, and perhaps you can tell me if they'll fit."

He passed the frock, the overcoat, and the hat to her, and she held them to the light with a vague smile.

"Wisha, aren't they lovely?" she said. "Aha, Marie, aren't you the lucky girl? Ye're sure ye won't have tea? 'Twouldn't take me a minute to boil the kettle."

"Certain, thanks," said Joe, crossing to the half door. Again he got an image that he felt he would not forget, of the lamplight on the hedge and gatepost, where four children were crowded together, talking in whispers. "You'd better come in now," he said with a laugh. "I bet you heard every word we said. Are these all yours, Mrs. Ryan?"

"Ah, no, sir," she replied almost reproachfully. "We had none of our own."

The four children came in and stood fidgeting by the dresser, two little boys and two little girls, apparently well fed if not well dressed or clean, but somehow lacking all the spontaneity of other children. Joe took out a fistful of coins and distributed them. The children took the money meekly.

"Well, Marie," he asked, stooping over the child on the stool, "how do you think you're going to like me for a daddy?"

"She's strange," Mrs. Ryan said apologetically when the child said nothing. "Most of the time she have plenty to say for herself."

"That's right," said Joe. "And in a couple of days she'll be giving me cheek as well. I know that young lady."

They sat and talked for a few minutes longer. Then Joe said good night, kissed Marie, and patted the other children on the head. On the road it was already dark, and he was glad of the headlights, which made the green banks seem theatrical.

"Well," said Coleman, "I don't know how you feel, but I'm ready for a drink."

"What I should like is to buy a few toys for the other kids," said Joe.

"Too late for that, I'm afraid," said Coleman. "The shops are shut till Monday. You might be able to pick up a few cheap toys in a sweet-shop, and maybe a couple of bags of sweets. If you mean they won't have the money long, I'm inclined to agree with you."

As they entered the hotel, the tall night porter looked up from his evening paper and said, "Night, sir. Night, Mr. Saunders," and something in his manner revealed to Joe that already his business there was being discussed. The waiter who brought them their drinks in the lounge seemed to know as well, and Joe thought he approved. The waiter might even have known Brigid. She and Marie's father might have sat in this very lounge, like any of the couples who sat here now under the bright lights. It was only the other side of the picture he had been looking at that evening in a lonesome cottage on the hills.

He felt more cheerful next morning. He woke to the sound of the bells. He had never heard so many bells, or else they sounded louder in the hollow of the city. As they drove out of town they saw the

well-dressed crowds on their way to Mass. In the little village there was
a large group outside the church and a smaller one outside the public
house. The four elder children were waiting for them in the roadway,
and as the car approached, two of them rushed in to give warning.
They had all been washed, and two of them wore boots. When the two
men went in, Marie was sitting stiffly on a low chair by the kitchen
door, as though she had been glued there to keep her from soiling her
new dress, and she looked up at them blankly and pointed to her shoes.
"Look! Shoes!" she said shrilly, and Joe, stooping to admire them, saw
that they were too big.

He distributed the few presents he had managed to buy, shook hands
with Mrs. Ryan, and carried Marie out to the car. The other children
followed, and he shook hands with each in turn. Over the low
wooden gate he could see the tall figure of Mrs. Ryan holding the
doorpost and gazing up and down the deserted road. As the car started,
he turned to wave to the little group of children. They stood in the
roadway, their presents clutched in their hands, and he saw that they
were all weeping quietly. It seemed to him that they weren't weeping
as real children weep, with abandonment and delight, but hopelessly,
as old people weep whom the world has passed by. His first thought
was to shut the sight off from Marie, but he needn't have worried. She
was leaning forward, trying to touch her shoes. Coleman was driving
with his eyes fixed on the winding roadway across the hills, and his fat
face was expressionless.

"I wonder if you saw what I did," Joe said at last, and Coleman
stared at him.

"I'm in dread I'll never forget it," he said.

# HOUSE OF FLOWERS

## *Truman Capote*

---

TRUMAN CAPOTE (1924–    ) was born in New Orleans. By
the time he was seventeen he had sold his first story to a national
magazine. At twenty-two he was working on *The New Yorker*
magazine staff, had won the O. Henry Memorial Prize, and was
hailed as "the most remarkable new literary talent of the year." From
this point forward, his skill and reputation have grown apace. A match-
less stylist, he is equally at home in the realms of comedy, fantasy,
tragedy, and straight reportage. *House of Flowers*, the love story
presented here, is as sunny and inviting as its Haitian setting; it is
Capote at his witty best.

OTTILIE should have been the happiest girl in Port-au-Prince. As
Baby said to her, look at all the things that can be put to your
credit. Like what? said Ottilie, for she was vain and preferred
compliments to pork or perfume. Like your looks, said Baby: you have
a lovely light color, even almost blue eyes, and such a pretty, sweet
face—there is no girl on the road with steadier customers, every one of
them ready to buy you all the beer you can drink. Ottilie conceded that
this was true, and with a smile continued to total her fortunes: I have
five silk dresses and a pair of green satin shoes, I have three gold teeth
worth thirty thousand francs, maybe Mr. Jamison or someone will give
me another bracelet. But, Baby, she sighed, and could not express her
discontent.

Baby was her best friend; she had another friend too: Rosita. Baby
was like a wheel, round, rolling; junk rings had left green circles on
several of her fat fingers, her teeth were dark as burnt tree stumps,
and when she laughed you could hear her at sea, at least so the sailors
claimed. Rosita, the other friend, was taller than most men, and
stronger; at night, with the customers on hand, she minced about, lisp-
ing in a silly doll voice, but in the daytime she took spacious, loping
strides and spoke out in a military baritone. Both of Ottilie's friends
were from the Dominican Republic, and considered it reason enough
to feel themselves a cut above the natives of this darker country. It

did not concern them that Ottilie was a native. You have brains, Baby told her, and certainly what Baby doted on was a good brain. Ottilie was often afraid that her friends would discover that she could neither read nor write.

The house where they lived and worked was rickety, thin as a steeple, and frosted with fragile, bougainvillaea-vined balconies. Though there was no sign outside, it was called the Champs Elysées. The proprietress, a spinsterish, smothered-looking invalid, ruled from an upstairs room, where she stayed locked away rocking in a rocking chair and drinking ten to twenty Coca-Colas a day. All counted, she had eight ladies working for her; with the exception of Ottilie, no one of them was under thirty. In the evening, when the ladies assembled on the porch, where they chatted and flourished paper fans that beat the air like delirious moths, Ottilie seemed a delightful dreaming child surrounded by older, uglier sisters.

Her mother was dead, her father was a planter who had gone back to France, and she had been brought up in the mountains by a rough peasant family, the sons of whom had each at a young age lain with her in some green and shadowy place. Three years earlier, when she was fourteen, she had come down for the first time to the market in Port-au-Prince. It was a journey of two days and a night, and she'd walked carrying a ten-pound sack of grain; to ease the load she'd let a little of the grain spill out, then a little more, and by the time she had reached the market there was almost none left. Ottilie had cried because she thought of how angry the family would be when she came home without the money for the grain; but these tears were not for long: such a jolly nice man helped her dry them. He bought her a slice of coconut, and took her to see his cousin, who was the proprietress of the Champs Elysées. Otillie could not believe her good luck; the jukebox music, the satin shoes and joking men were as strange and marvelous as the electric-light bulb in her room, which she never tired of clicking on and off. Soon she had become the most talked-of girl on the road, the proprietress was able to ask double for her, and Ottilie grew vain; she could pose for hours in front of a mirror. It was seldom that she thought of the mountains; and yet, after three years, there was much of the mountains still with her: their winds seemed still to move around her, her hard, high haunches had not softened, nor had the soles of her feet, which were rough as lizard's hide.

When her friends spoke of love, of men they had loved, Ottilie became sulky: How do you feel if you're in love? she asked. Ah, said Rosita with swooning eyes, you feel as though pepper has been sprinkled on your heart, as though tiny fish are swimming in your veins. Ottilie shook her head; if Rosita was telling the truth, then she had never been in love, for she had never felt that way about any of the men who came to the house.

This so troubled her that at last she went to see a *Houngan* who lived in the hills above town. Unlike her friends, Ottilie did not tack Christian pictures on the walls of her room; she did not believe in God, but many gods: of food, light, of death, ruin. The Houngan was in touch with these gods; he kept their secrets on his altar, could hear their voices in the rattle of a gourd, could dispense their power in a potion. Speaking through the gods, the Houngan gave her this message: You must catch a wild bee, he said, and hold it in your closed hand . . . if the bee does not sting, then you will know you have found love.

On the way home she thought of Mr. Jamison. He was a man past fifty, an American connected with an engineering project. The gold bracelets chattering on her wrists were presents from him, and Ottilie, passing a fence snowy with honeysuckle, wondered if after all she was not in love with Mr. Jamison. Black bees festooned the honeysuckle. With a brave thrust of her hand she caught one dozing. Its stab was like a blow that knocked her to her knees; and there she knelt, weeping until it was hard to know whether the bee had stung her hand or her eyes.

It was March, and events were leading toward carnival. At the Champs Elysées the ladies were sewing on their costumes; Ottilie's hands were idle, for she had decided not to wear a costume at all. On rah-rah week ends, when drums sounded at the rising moon, she sat at her window and watched with a wandering mind the little bands of singers dancing and drumming their way along the road; she listened to the whistling and the laughter and felt no desire to join in. Somebody would think you were a thousand years old, said Baby, and Rosita said: Ottilie, why don't you come to the cockfight with us?

She was not speaking of an ordinary cockfight. From all parts of the island contestants had arrived bringing their fiercest birds. Ottilie thought she might as well go, and screwed a pair of pearls into her ears. When they arrived the exhibition was already under way; in a great tent a sea-sized crowd sobbed and shouted, while a second crowd, those who could not get in, thronged on the outskirts. Entry was no problem to the ladies from the Champs Elysées: a policeman friend cut a path for them and made room on a bench by the ring. The country people surrounding them seemed embarrassed to find themselves in such stylish company. They looked shyly at Baby's lacquered nails, the rhinestone combs in Rosita's hair, the glow of Ottilie's pearl earrings. However, the fights were exciting, and the ladies were soon forgotten; Baby was annoyed that this should be so, and her eyes rolled about searching for glances in their direction. Suddenly she nudged Ottilie. Ottilie, she said, you've got an admirer: see that boy over there, he's staring at you like you were something cold to drink.

At first she thought he must be someone she knew, for he was looking at her as though she should recognize him; but how could she know him when she'd never known anyone so beautiful, anyone with such long legs, little ears? She could see that he was from the mountains: his straw country hat and the worn-out blue of his thick shirt told her as much. He was a ginger color, his skin shiny as a lemon, smooth as a guava leaf, and the tilt of his head was as arrogant as the black and scarlet bird he held in his hands. Ottilie was used to boldly smiling at men; but now her smile was fragmentary, it clung to her lips like cake crumbs.

Eventually there was an intermission. The arena was cleared, and all who could crowded into it to dance and stamp while an orchestra of drums and strings sang out carnival tunes. It was then that the young man approached Ottilie; she laughed to see his bird perched like a parrot on his shoulder. Off with you, said Baby, outraged that a peasant should ask Ottilie to dance, and Rosita rose menacingly to stand between the young man and her friend. He only smiled, and said: Please, madame, I would like to speak with your daughter. Ottilie felt herself being lifted, felt her hips meet against his to the rhythm of music, and she did not mind at all, she let him lead her into the thickest tangle of dancers. Rosita said: Did you hear that, he thought I was her mother? And Baby, consoling her, grimly said: After all, what do you expect? They're only natives, both of them: when she comes back we'll just pretend we don't know her.

As it happened, Ottilie did not return to her friends. Royal, this was the young man's name, Royal Bonaparte, he told her, had not wanted to dance. We must walk in a quiet place, he said, hold my hand and I will take you. She thought him strange, but did not feel strange with him, for the mountains were still with her, and he was of the mountains. With her hands together, and the iridescent cock swaying on his shoulder, they left the tent and wandered lazily down a white road, then along a soft lane where birds of sunlight fluttered through the greenness of leaning acacia trees.

I have been sad, he said, not looking sad. In my village Juno is a champion, but the birds here are strong and ugly, and if I let him fight I would only have a dead Juno. So I will take him home and say that he won. Ottilie, will you have a dip of snuff?

She sneezed voluptuously. Snuff reminded her of her childhood, and mean as those years had been, nostalgia touched her with its far-reaching wand. Royal, she said, be still a minute, I want to take off my shoes.

Royal himself did not have shoes; his golden feet were slender and airy, and the prints they left were like the track of a delicate animal. He said: How is it that I find you here, in all the world here, where nothing is good, where the rum is bad and the people thieves? Why do I find you here, Ottilie?

Because I must make my way, the same as you, and here there is a place for me. I work in a—oh, kind of hotel.

We have our own place, he said. All the side of a hill, and there at the top of the hill is my cool house. Ottilie, will you come and sit inside it?

Crazy, said Ottilie, teasing him, crazy, and she ran between the trees, and he was after her, his arms out as though he held a net. The bird Juno flared his wings, crowed, flew to the ground. Scratchy leaves and fur of moss thrilled the soles of Ottilie's feet as she lilted through the shade and shadows; abruptly, into a veil of rainbow fern, she fell with a thorn in her heel. She winced when Royal pulled out the thorn; he kissed the place where it had been, his lips moved to her hands, her throat, and it was as though she were among drifting leaves. She breathed the odor of him, the dark, clean smell that was like the roots of things, of geraniums, of heavy trees.

Now that's enough, she pleaded, though she did not feel that this was so: it was only that after an hour of him her heart was about to give out. He was quiet then, his thickly haired head rested above her heart, and shoo she said to the gnats that clustered about his sleeping eyes, shush she said to Juno who pranced around crowing at the sky.

While she lay there, Ottilie saw her old enemy, the bees. Silently, in a line like ants, the bees were crawling in and out of a broken stump that stood not far from her. She loosened herself from Royal's arms, and smoothed a place on the ground for his head. Her hand was trembling as she lay it in the path of the bees, but the first that came along tumbled onto her palm, and when she closed her fingers it made no move to hurt her. She counted ten, just to be sure, then opened her hand, and the bee, in spiraling arcs, climbed the air with a joyful singing.

The proprietress gave Baby and Rosita a piece of advice: Leave her alone, let her go, a few weeks and she will be back. The proprietress spoke in the calm of defeat: to keep Ottilie with her, she'd offered the best room in the house, a new gold tooth, a Kodak, an electric fan, but Ottilie had not wavered, she had gone right on putting her belongings in a cardboard box. Baby tried to help, but she was crying so much that Ottilie had to stop her: it was bound to be bad luck, all those tears falling on a bride's possessions. And to Rosita she said: Rosita, you ought to be glad for me instead of standing there wringing your hands.

It was only two days after the cockfight that Royal shouldered Ottilie's cardboard box and walked her in the dusk toward the mountains. When it was learned that she was no longer at the Champs Elysées many of the customers took their trade elsewhere; others, though remaining loyal to the old place, complained of a gloom in the atmosphere: some evenings there was hardly anyone to buy the ladies a beer. Gradually it began to be felt that Ottilie after all would not come back; at the end of six months the proprietress said: She must be dead.

Royal's house was like a house of flowers; wisteria sheltered the roof, a curtain of vines shaded the windows, lilies bloomed at the door. From the windows one could see far, faint winkings of the sea, as the house was high up a hill; here the sun burned hot but the shadows were cold. Inside, the house was always dark and cool, and the walls rustled with pasted pink and green newpapers. There was only one room; it contained a stove, a teetering mirror on top a marble table, and a brass bed big enough for three fat men.

But Ottilie did not sleep in this grand bed. She was not allowed even to sit upon it, for it was the property of Royal's grandmother, Old Bonaparte. A charred, lumpy creature, bowlegged as a dwarf and bald as a buzzard, Old Bonaparte was much respected for miles around as a maker of spells. There were many who were afraid to have her shadow fall upon them; even Royal was wary of her, and he stuttered when he told her that he'd brought home a wife. Motioning Ottilie to her, the old woman bruised her here and there with vicious little pinches, and informed her grandson that his bride was too skinny: She will die with her first.

Each night the young couple waited to make love until they thought Old Bonaparte had gone to sleep. Sometimes, stretched on the straw moonlit pallet where they slept, Ottilie was sure that Old Bonaparte was awake and watching them. Once she saw a gummy, star-struck eye shining in the dark. There was no use complaining to Royal, he only laughed: What harm was there in an old woman who had seen so much of life wanting to see a little more?

Because she loved Royal, Ottilie put away her grievances and tried not to resent Old Bonaparte. For a long while she was happy; she did not miss her friends or the life in Port-au-Prince; even so, she kept her souvenirs of those days in good repair: with a sewing basket Baby had given her as a wedding gift she mended the silk dresses, the green silk stockings that now she never wore, for there was no place to wear

them: only men congregated at the café in the village, at the cockfights.
When women wanted to meet they met at the washing stream. But
Ottilie was too busy to be lonesome. At daybreak she gathered eucalyptus leaves to start a fire and begin their meals; there were chickens to
feed, a goat to be milked, there was Old Bonaparte's whining for attention. Three and four times a day she filled a bucket of drinking water
and carried it to where Royal worked in the cane fields a mile below
the house. She did not mind that on these visits he was gruff with her:
she knew that he was showing off before the other men who worked in
the fields, and who grinned at her like split watermelons. But at night,
when she had him home, she'd pull his ears and pout that he treated
her like a dog until, in the dark of the yard where the fireflies flamed,
he would hold her and whisper something to make her smile.

They had been married about five months when Royal began doing
the things he'd done before his marriage. Other men went to the café
in the evenings, stayed whole Sundays at a cockfight—he couldn't
understand why Ottilie should carry on about it; but she said he had
no right behaving the way he did, and that if he loved her he wouldn't
leave her alone day and night with that mean old woman. I love you,
he said, but a man has to have his pleasures too. There were nights
when he pleasured himself until the moon was in the middle of the
sky; she never knew when he was coming home, and she would lie
fretting on the pallet, imagining she could not sleep without his arms
around her.

But Old Bonaparte was the real torment. She was about to worry
Ottilie out of her mind. If Ottilie was cooking, the terrible old woman
was sure to come poking around the stove, and when she did not like
what there was to eat she would take a mouthful and spit it on the
floor. Every mess she could think of she made: she wet the bed, insisted
on having the goat in the room, whatever she touched was soon
spilled or broken, and to Royal she complained that a woman who
couldn't keep a nice house for her husband was worthless. She was
underfoot the whole day, and her red, remorseless eyes were seldom
shut; but the worst of it, the thing that finally made Ottilie threaten to
kill her, was the old woman's habit of sneaking up from nowhere and
pinching her so hard you could see the fingernail marks. If you do that
one more time, if you just dare, I'll snatch that knife and cut out your
heart! Old Bonaparte knew Ottilie meant it, and though she stopped
the pinching, she thought of other jokes: for instance, she made a
point of walking all over a certain part of the yard, pretending she did
not know that Ottilie had planted a little garden there.

One day two exceptional things happened. A boy came from the
village bringing a letter for Ottilie; at the Champs Elysées postcards

had once in a while arrived from sailors and other traveling men who had spent pleasant moments with her, but this was the first letter she'd ever received. Since she could not read it, her first impulse was to tear it up: there was no use having it hang around to haunt her. Of course there was a chance that someday she would learn to read; and so she went to hide it in her sewing basket.

When she opened the sewing basket, she made a sinister discovery: there, like a gruesome ball of yarn, was the severed head of a yellow cat. So, the miserable old woman was up to new tricks! She wants to put a spell, thought Ottilie, not in the least frightened. Primly lifting the head by one of its ears, she carried it to the stove and dropped it into a boiling pot: at noon Old Bonaparte sucked her teeth and remarked that the soup Ottilie had made for her was surprisingly tasty.

The next morning, just in time for the midday meal, she found twisting in her basket a small green snake which, chopping fine as sand, she sprinkled into a serving of stew. Each day her ingenuity was tested: there were spiders to bake, a lizard to fry, a buzzard's breast to boil. Old Bonaparte ate several helpings of everything. With a restless glittering her eyes followed Ottilie as she watched for some sign that the spell was taking hold. You don't look well, Ottilie, she said, mixing a little molasses in the vinegar of her voice. You eat like an ant: here now, why don't you have a bowl of this good soup?

Because, answered Ottilie evenly, I don't like buzzard in my soup; or spiders in my bread, snakes in the stew: I have no appetite for such things.

Old Bonaparte understood; with swelling veins and a stricken, powerless tongue, she rose shakily to her feet, then crashed across the table. Before nightfall she was dead.

Royal summoned mourners. They came from the village, from the neighboring hills and, wailing like dogs at midnight, laid siege to the house. Old women beat their heads against the walls, moaning men prostrated themselves: it was the art of sorrow, and those who best mimicked grief were much admired. After the funeral everyone went away, satisfied that they'd done a good job.

Now the house belonged to Ottilie. Without Old Bonaparte's prying and her mess to clean she had more spare time, but she did not know what to do with it. She sprawled on the great brass bed, she loafed in front of the mirror; monotony hummed in her head, and to drive away its fly-buzz sound she would sing the songs she'd learned from the jukebox at the Champs Elysées. Waiting in the twilight for Royal she would remember that at this hour her friends in Port-au-Prince were gossiping on the porch and waiting for the turning headlights of a car; but when she saw Royal ambling up the path, his cane cutter swinging at his side like a crescent moon, she forgot such thoughts and ran with a satisfied heart to meet him.

One night as they lay half-drowsing, Ottilie felt suddenly another presence in the room. Then, gleaming there at the foot of the bed, she saw, as she had seen before, a watching eye; thus she knew what for some time she had suspected: that Old Bonaparte was dead but not gone. Once, when she was alone in the house, she'd heard a laugh, and once again, out in the yard, she'd seen the goat gazing at someone who was not there and twinkling his ears as he did whenever the old woman scratched his skull.

Stop shaking the bed, said Royal, and Ottilie, with a finger raised at the eye, whisperingly asked him if he could not see it. When he replied that she was dreaming, she reached for the eye and screamed at feeling only air. Royal lighted a lamp; he cuddled Ottilie on his lap and smoothed her hair while she told him of the discoveries she'd made in her sewing basket, and of how she had disposed of them. Was it wrong what she'd done? Royal did not know, it was not for him to say, but it was his opinion that she would have to be punished; and why? because the old woman wanted it, because she would otherwise never leave Ottilie in peace: that was the way with haunts.

In accordance with this, Royal fetched a rope the next morning and proposed to tie Ottilie to a tree in the yard: there she was to remain until dark without food or water, and anyone passing would know her to be in a state of disgrace.

But Ottilie crawled under the bed and refused to come out. I'll run away, she whimpered. Royal, if you try to tie me to that old tree I'll run away.

Then I'd have to go and get you, said Royal, and that would be the worse for you.

He gripped her by an ankle and dragged her squealing from under the bed. All the way to the yard she caught at things, the door, a vine, the goat's beard, but none of these would hold her, and Royal was not detained from tying her to the tree. He made three knots in the rope, and went off to work sucking his hand where she had bit him. She hollered to him all the bad words she'd ever heard until he disappeared over the hill. The goat, Juno and the chickens gathered to stare at her humiliation; slumping to the ground, Ottilie stuck out her tongue at them.

Because she was almost asleep, Ottilie thought it was a dream when, in the company of a child from the village, Baby and Rosita, wobbling on high heels and carrying fancy umbrellas, tottered up the path calling her name. Since they were people in a dream, they probably would not be surprised to find her tied to a tree.

My God, are you mad? shrieked Baby, keeping her distance as though she feared that indeed this must be the case. Speak to us, Ottilie!

Blinking, giggling, Ottilie said: I'm just happy to see you. Rosita, please untie me so that I can hug you both.

So this is what the brute does, said Rosita, tearing at the ropes. Wait till I see him, beating you and tying you in the yard like a dog.

Oh no, said Ottilie. Royal never beats me. It's just that today I'm being punished.

You wouldn't listen to us, said Baby. And now you see what's come of it. That man has plenty to answer for, she added, brandishing her umbrella.

Ottilie hugged her friends and kissed them. Isn't it a pretty house? she said, leading them toward it. It's like you picked a wagon of flowers and built a house with them: that is what I think. Come in out of the sun. It's cool inside and smells so sweet.

Rosita sniffed as though what she smelled was nothing sweet, and in her well-bottom voice declared that yes, it was better that they stay out of the sun, as it seemed to be affecting Ottilie's head.

It's a mercy that we've come, said Baby, fishing inside an enormous purse. And you can thank Mr. Jamison for that. Madame said you were dead, and when you never answered our letter we thought it must be so. But Mr. Jamison, that's the loveliest man you'll ever know, he hired a car for me and Rosita, your dearest loving friends, to come up here and find out what had happened to our Ottilie. Ottilie, I've got a bottle of rum here in my purse, so get us a glass and we'll all have a round.

The elegant foreign manners and flashing finery of the city ladies had intoxicated their guide, a little boy whose peeking black eyes bobbed at the window. Ottilie was impressed, too, for it was a long time since she'd seen painted lips or smelled bottle perfume, and while Baby poured the rum she got out her satin shoes, her pearl earrings. Dear, said Rosita when Ottilie had finished dressing up, there's no man alive that wouldn't buy you a whole keg of beer; to think of it, a gorgeous piece like you suffering far away from those who love you.

I haven't been suffering so much, said Ottilie. Just sometimes.

Hush now, said Baby. You don't have to talk about it yet. It's all over anyway. Here, dear, let me see your glass again. A toast to old times, and those to be! Tonight Mr. Jamison is going to buy champagne for everybody: Madame is letting him have it at half-price.

Oh, said Ottilie, envying her friends. Well, she wanted to know, what did people say of her, was she remembered?

Ottilie, you have no idea, said Baby; men nobody ever laid eyes on before have come into the place asking where is Ottilie, because they've heard about you way off in Havana and Miami. As for Mr. Jamison, he doesn't even look at us other girls, just comes and sits on the porch drinking by himself.

Yes, said Ottilie wistfully. He was always sweet to me, Mr. Jamison.

Presently the sun was slanting, and the bottle of rum stood three-quarters empty. A thunderburst of rain had for a moment drenched the hills that now, seen through the windows, shimmered like dragon-fly wings, and a breeze, rich with the scent of rained-on flowers, roamed the room rustling the green and pink papers on the walls. Many stories had been told, some of them funny, a few that were sad; it was like any night's talk at the Champs Elysées, and Ottilie was happy to be a part of it again.

But it's getting late, said Baby. And we promised to be back before midnight. Ottilie, can we help you pack?

Although she had not realized that her friends expected her to leave with them, the rum stirring in her made it seem a likely assumption, and with a smile she thought: I told him I would go away. Only, she said aloud, it's not like I would have even a week to enjoy myself: Royal will come right down and get me.

Both her friends laughed at this. You're so silly, said Baby. I'd like to see that Royal when some of our men got through with him.

I wouldn't stand for anybody hurting Royal, said Ottilie. Besides, he'd be even madder when we got home.

Baby said: But, Ottilie, you wouldn't be coming back here with him.

Ottilie giggled, and looked about the room as though she saw something invisible to the others. Why, sure I would, she said.

Rolling her eyes, Baby produced a fan and jerked it in front of her face. That's the craziest thing I've ever heard, she said between hard lips. Isn't that the craziest thing you've ever heard, Rosita?

It's that Ottilie's been through so much, said Rosita. Dear, why don't you lie down on the bed while we pack your things?

Ottilie watched as they commenced piling her possessions. They scooped her combs and pins, they wound up her silk stockings. She took off her pretty clothes, as if she were going to put on something finer still; instead, she slipped back into her old dress; then, working quietly, and as though she were helping her friends, she put everything back where it belonged. Baby stamped her foot when she saw what was happening.

Listen, said Ottilie. If you and Rosita are my friends, please do what

I tell you: tie me in the yard just like I was when you came. That way no bee is ever going to sting me.

Stinking drunk, said Baby; but Rosita told her to shut up. I think, said Rosita with a sigh, I think Ottilie is in love. If Royal wanted her back, she would go with him, and this being the way things were they might as well go home and say that Madame was right, that Ottilie was dead.

Yes, said Ottilie, for the drama of it appealed to her. Tell them that I am dead.

So they went into the yard; there, with heaving bosoms and eyes as round as the daytime moon scudding above, Baby said she would have no part in tying Ottilie to the tree, which left Rosita to do it alone. On parting, it was Ottilie who cried the most, though she was glad to see them go, for she knew that as soon as they were gone she would not think of them again. Teetering on their high heels down the dips of the path, they turned to wave, but Ottilie could not wave back, and so she forgot them before they were out of sight.

Chewing eucalyptus leaves to sweeten her breath, she felt the chill of twilight twitch the air. Yellow deepened the daytime moon, and roosting birds sailed into the darkness of the tree. Suddenly, hearing Royal on the path, she threw her legs akimbo, let her neck go limp, lolled her eyes far back into their sockets. Seen from a distance, it would look as though she had come to some violent, pitiful end; and, listening to Royal's footsteps quicken to a run, she happily thought: This will give him a good scare.

# THE BUS TO ST. JAMES'S

## John Cheever

JOHN CHEEVER (1912– ) signaled his start as a notable writer of short stories when he was seventeen by writing for *The New Republic* about his expulsion from Thayer Academy. Since that time his active pen has produced over a hundred highly original stories which have had success in England and France as well as at home. Turning to the longer form, his first novel *The Wapshot Chronicle*, full of fun and warmth, won the National Book Award for Fiction in 1957. Born in Massachusetts, Mr. Cheever lives today with his wife and their three children in Ossining, New York. The following is one of the most moving love stories of our time.

THE BUS to St. James's—a Protestant Episcopal school for boys and girls—started its round at eight o'clock in the morning, from a corner of Park Avenue in the Sixties. The earliness of the hour meant that some of the parents who took their children there were sleepy and still without coffee, but with a clear sky the light struck the city at an extreme angle, the air was fresh, and it was an exceptionally cheerful time of day. It was the hour when cooks and doormen walk dogs, and when porters scrub the lobby floor mats with soap and water. Traces of the night—the parents and children once watched a man whose tuxedo was covered with sawdust wander home—were scarce.

When the fall semester began, five children waited for the school bus at this stop, and they all came from the limestone apartment houses of the neighborhood. Two of the children, Louise and Emily Sheridan, were newcomers. The others—the Pruitt boy, Katherine Bruce, and the little Armstrong girl—had met the bus for St. James's the year before.

Mr. Pruitt brought his son to the corner each morning. They had the same tailor and they both tipped their hats to the ladies. Although Katherine Bruce was old enough to walk to the bus stop by herself, she was nearsighted and her father made the trip with her unless he was out of town on business, in which case a maid brought her. Stephen Bruce's first wife, Katherine's mother, had died, and he was more painstakingly attentive to his daughter than fathers usually are.

She was a large girl, but he took her hand tenderly and led her across the street and sometimes stood on the corner with his arm around her shoulders. The second Mrs. Bruce had no children. Mrs. Armstrong took her daughter to the bus stop only when her maid or her cook refused. Like Mrs. Armstrong, Mrs. Sheridan shared this chore with a maid, but she was more constant. At least three mornings a week she came to the corner with her daughters and with an old Scotch terrier on a leash.

St. James's was a small school, and the parents, waiting on the street corner until the bus arrived, spoke confidently to one another. Mr. Bruce knew Mr. Pruitt's brother-in-law and was the second cousin of a woman who had roomed with Mrs. Armstrong in boarding school. Mrs. Sheridan and Mr. Pruitt had friends in common. "We saw some friends of yours last night," Mr. Pruitt said one morning. "The Murchisons?" "Oh yes," Mrs. Sheridan said, *"yes."* She never gave a simple affirmative; she always said "Oh yes, *yes,"* or "Oh yes, *yes,* yes."

Mrs. Sheridan dressed plainly and her hair was marked with gray. She was not pretty or provocative, and compared to Mrs. Armstrong, whose hair was golden, she seemed plain; but her features were fine and her body was graceful and slender. She was a well-mannered woman of perhaps thirty-five, Mr. Bruce decided, with a well-ordered house and a perfect emotional digestion—one of those women who, through their goodness, can absorb anything. A great deal of authority seemed to underlie her mild manner. She would have been raised by solid people, Mr. Bruce thought, and would respect all the boarding-school virtues: courage, good sportsmanship, chastity, and honor. When he heard her say in the morning "Oh yes, *yes!,"* it seemed to him like a happy combination of manners and spirit.

Mr. Pruitt continued to tell Mrs. Sheridan that he had met her friends, but their paths never seemed to cross directly. Mr. Bruce, eavesdropping on their conversation, behind his newspaper, was gratified by this because he disliked Mr. Pruitt and respected Mrs. Sheridan; but he knew they were bound to meet somewhere other than on the street, and one day Mr. Pruitt took his hat off to Mrs. Sheridan and said, "Wasn't it a delightful party?" "Oh yes," Mrs. Sheridan said, "yes." Then Mr. Pruitt asked Mrs. Sheridan when she and her husband had left, and she said they had left at midnight. She did not seem anxious to talk about the party, but she answered all of Mr. Pruitt's questions politely.

Mr. Bruce told himself that Mrs. Sheridan was wasting her time; Pruitt was a fool and she deserved better. His dislike of Pruitt and his respect for Mrs. Sheridan seemed idle, but he was pleased, one morning, to get to the corner and find that Mrs. Sheridan was there with her two daughters and the dog, and that Pruitt wasn't. He wished her a good morning.

"Good morning," she said. "We seem to be early."

Katherine and the older Sheridan girl began to talk together.

"I think I knew Katherine's mother," Mrs. Sheridan said politely. "Wasn't your first wife Martha Chase?"

"Yes."

"I knew her in college. I didn't know her well. She was in the class ahead of me. How old is Katherine now?"

"She was eight last summer," Mr. Bruce said.

"We have a brother," the younger Sheridan girl said, standing beside her mother. "He's eight."

"Yes, dear," Mrs. Sheridan said.

"He was drowned," the little girl said.

"Oh, I'm sorry," Mr. Bruce said.

"He was quite a good swimmer," the little girl went on, "but we think that he must have gotten a cramp. You see, there was a thunderstorm, and we all went into the boathouse and we weren't looking and—"

"That was a long time time ago, dear," Mrs. Sheridan said gently.

"It wasn't so long ago," the little girl said. "It was only last summer."

"Yes, dear," her mother said. "Yes, yes."

Mr. Bruce noticed that there was no trace of pain, or of the effort to conceal it, on her face, and her composure seemed to him a feat of intelligence and grace. They continued to stand together, without talking, until the other parents arrived with their children, just as the bus came up the street. Mrs. Sheridan called to the old dog and went down Park Avenue, and Mr. Bruce got into a taxi and went to work.

Toward the end of October, on a rainy Friday night, Mr. and Mrs. Bruce took a taxi to St. James's School. It was Parents' Night. One of the senior boys ushered them into a pew at the rear of the chapel. The altar was stripped of its mysteries, and the rector stood on the raised floor between the choir stalls, waiting for the laggard parents to be seated. He tucked and pulled nervously at his clericals, and then signalled for silence by clearing his throat.

"On behalf of the faculty and the board of trustees," he said, "I welcome the parents of St. James's here this evening. I regret that we have such inclement weather, but it doesn't seem to have kept any of you at home." This was said archly, as if the full attendance reflected his powers of intimidation. "Let us begin," he said, "with a prayer for the welfare of our school: Almighty Father, Creator of Heaven and earth! . . ." Kneeling, and with their heads bowed, the congregation looked indestructible and as if the permanence of society depended and could always depend on them. And when the prayer ended, the rector spoke to them about their durability. "I have some very interesting statistics for you all tonight," he said. "This year we have sixteen children enrolled in the school whose parents *and* whose grandparents were St. James's children. I think that's a very impressive number. I doubt that any other day school in the city could equal it."

During the brief speech in defense of conservative education that followed, Mr. Bruce noticed that Mrs. Sheridan was seated a few pews in front of him. With her was a tall man—her husband, presumably— with a straight back and black hair. When the talk ended, the meeting was opened for questions. The first question was from a mother who wanted advice on how to restrict her children's use of television. While the rector was answering this question, Mr. Bruce noticed that the Sheridans were having an argument. They were whispering, and their disagreement seemed intense. Suddenly, Mrs. Sheridan separated herself from the argument. She had nothing further to say. Mr. Sheridan's neck got red. He continued, in a whisper, to press his case, bending toward his wife, and shaking his head. Mrs. Sheridan raised her hand.

"Yes, Mrs. Sheridan," the rector said.

Mr. Sheridan picked up his coat and his derby, and, saying "Excuse me, please," "Thank you," "Excuse me," passed in front of the other people in the pew, and left the chapel.

"Yes, Mrs. Sheridan?" the rector repeated.

"I wonder, Dr. Frisbee," Mrs. Sheridan said, "if you and the board of trustees have ever thought of enrolling Negro children in St. James's?"

"That question came up three years ago," the rector said impatiently, "and a report was submitted to the board of trustees on the question. There have been very few requests for it, but if you would like a copy, I will have one sent to you."

"Yes," Mrs. Sheridan said, "I would like to read it."

The rector nodded and Mrs. Sheridan sat down.

"Mrs. Townsend?" the rector asked.

"I have a question about science and religion," Mrs. Townsend said. "It seems to me that the science faculty stresses science to the detriment of religious sentiment, especially concerning the Creation. It seems to me . . ."

Mrs. Sheridan picked up her gloves and, smiling politely and saying "Excuse me," "Thank you," "Please excuse me," she brushed past the others in the pew. Mr. Bruce heard her heels on the paved floor of the hall and, by craning his neck, was able to see her. The noise of traffic and of the rain grew louder as she pushed open one of the heavy doors, and faded as the door swung to.

Late one afternoon the following week, Mr. Bruce was called out of a stockholders' meeting to take a telephone call from his wife. She wanted him to stop at the stable where Katherine took riding lessons and bring her home. It exasperated him to have been called from the meeting to take this message, and when he returned, the meeting itself had fallen into the hands of an old man who had brought with him Robert's Rules of Order. Business that should have been handled directly and simply dragged, and the meeting ended in a tedious and heated argument. Immediately afterward, he took a taxi up to the Nineties, and went through the tack room of the riding stable into the ring. Katherine and some other girls, wearing hunting bowlers and dark clothes, were riding. The ring was cold and damp, its overhead lights burned whitely, the mirrors along the wall were fogged and streaked with moisture, and the riding mistress spoke to her pupils with an elaborate courteousness. Mr. Bruce watched his daughter. Katherine wore glasses, her face was plain, and her light hair was long and stringy. She was a receptive and obedient girl, and her exposure to St. James's had begun faintly to show in her face. When the lesson ended, he went back into the tack room. Mrs. Sheridan was there, waiting for her daughters.

"Can I give you a lift home?" Mr. Bruce said.

"You most certainly can," Mrs. Sheridan said. "We were going to take a bus."

The children joined them and they all went out and waited for a cab. It was dark.

"I was interested in the question you asked at the Parents' meeting," Mr. Bruce said. This was untrue. He was not interested in the question, and if Negroes had been enrolled in St. James's, he would have removed Katherine.

"I'm glad someone was interested," she said. "The Rector was wild."

"That's principally what interested me," Mr. Bruce said, trying to approach the truth.

A cab came along, and they got into it. He let Mrs. Sheridan off at the door of her apartment house, and watched her walk with her two daughters into the lighted lobby.

Mrs. Sheridan had forgotten her key and a maid let her in. It was late and she had asked people for dinner. The door to her husband's room was shut, and she bathed and dressed without seeing him. While she was combing her hair, she heard him go into the living room and turn on the television set. In company, Charles Sheridan always spoke contemptuously of television. "By Jove," he would say, "I don't see how anyone can look at that trash. It must be a year since I've turned our set on." Now his wife could hear him laughing uproariously.

She left her room and went down the hall to the dining room to check on everything there. Then she went through the pantry into the kitchen. She sensed trouble as soon as the door closed after her. Helen, the waitress, was sitting at a table near the sink. She had been crying. Anna, the cook, put down the pan she had been washing, to be sure of hearing everything that was said.

"What's the matter, Helen?" Mrs. Sheridan asked.

"From my pie he took twelff dollars, Mrs. Seridan," Helen said. She was Austrian.

"What for, Helen?"

"The day I burn myself. You told me to go to the doctor?"

"Yes."

"For that he took from my pie twelff dollars."

"I'll give you a check tomorrow, Helen," Mrs. Sheridan said. "Don't worry."

"Yes, Ma'am," Helen said. "Thank you."

Mr. Sheridan came through the pantry into the kitchen. He looked handsome in his dark clothes. "Oh, here you are," he said to his wife. "Let's have a drink before they come." Then, turning to the waitress, he asked, "Have you heard from your family recently?"

"No, Mr. Seridan," Helen said.

"Where is it your family lives?" he asked.

"In Missigan, Mr. Seridan." She giggled, but this joke had been made innumerable times in the past few years and she was tired of it.

"Where?" Mr. Sheridan asked.

"In Missigan, Mr. Seridan," she repeated.

He burst out laughing. "By Jove, I think that's funny!" he said. He put his arm around his wife's waist and they went in to have a drink.

Mr. Bruce returned to a much pleasanter home. His wife, Lois, was a pretty woman, and she greeted him affectionately. He sat down with her for a cocktail. "Marguerite called me this morning," she said, "and told me that Charlie's lost his job. When I heard the phone ring, I sensed trouble; I *sensed* it. Even before I picked up the receiver, I knew that something was wrong. At first, I thought it was going to be poor Helen Luckman. She's had so many misfortunes recently that she's been on my mind a lot of the time. Then I heard Marguerite's voice. She

said that poor Charlie had been a wonderful sport about the whole
thing and that he was determined to get an even better job. He travelled
all over the United States for that firm and now they're just letting him
go. *She* called while I was in bed, and the reason I stayed in bed this
morning is because my back's been giving me a little trouble again. It's
nothing serious—it's nothing serious at all—but the pain's excruciating
and I'm going to Dr. Parminter tomorrow and see if he can help me."

Lois had been frail when Mr. Bruce first met her. It had been one of
her great charms. The extreme pallor and delicacy of her skin could be
accounted for partly by a year of her life when, as she said, the doctors
had given her up for dead. Her frailness was a fact, a mixture of chance
and inheritance, and she could not be blamed for her susceptibility to
poison oak, cold germs, and fatigue.

"I'm very sorry to hear about your back, dear," Mr. Bruce said.

"Well, I didn't spend the whole day in bed," she said. "I got up
around eleven and had lunch with Betty and then went shopping."

Lois Bruce, like a great many women in New York, spent a formidable amount of time shopping along Fifth Avenue. She read the advertisements in the newspapers more intently than her husband read the
financial section. Shopping was her principal occupation. She would get
up from a sickbed to go shopping. The atmosphere of the department
stores had a restorative effect on her disposition. She would begin her
afternoon at Altman's—buy a pair of gloves on the first floor, and then
travel up on the escalator and look at andirons. She would buy a purse
and some face cream at Lord & Taylor's, and price coffee tables, upholstery fabrics, and cocktail glasses. "Down?" she would ask the elevator operator when the doors rolled open, and if the operator said "Up,"
Lois would board the car anyhow, deciding suddenly that whatever it
was that she wanted might be in the furniture or the linen department.
She would buy a pair of shoes and a slip at Saks', send her mother some
napkins from Mosse's, buy a bunch of cloth flowers at De Pinna's, some
hand lotion at Bonwit's, and a dress at Bendel's. By then, her feet and
her head would be pleasantly tired, the porter at Tiffany's would be
taking in the flag, the lamps on the carriages by the Plaza would be
lighted. She would buy a cake at Dean's, her last stop, and walk home
through the early dark like an honest workman; contented and weary.

When they sat down to dinner, Lois watched her husband taste his
soup and smiled when she saw that he was pleased. "It is good, isn't it?"
she said. "I can't taste it myself—I haven't been able to taste anything
for a week—but I don't want to tell Katie, bless her, because it would
hurt her feelings, and I didn't want to compliment her if it wasn't right.
Katie," she called, through the pantry, "your soup is delicious."

Mrs. Sheridan did not come to the corner all the next week. On Wednesday afternoon, Mr. Bruce stopped by for Katherine at her dancing class, on the way home from his office. The Sheridan girls were in the same class, and he looked for Mrs. Sheridan in the lobby of the Chardin Club, but she wasn't there. He didn't see her again, actually, until he went, on Sunday afternoon, to bring Katherine home from a birthday party.

Because Lois sometimes played cards until seven o'clock, it often fell to Mr. Bruce to call for Katherine at some address at the end of the day, to see her through the stiff thanks and goodbyes that end a children's party. The streets were cold and dark; the hot rooms where the parties were smelled of candy and flowers. Among the friends and relatives there he was often pleased to meet people with whom he had summered or been to school. Some of these parties were elaborate, and he had once gone to get Katherine at an apartment in the Waldorf Towers where six little girls were being entertained by a glass blower.

In the hallway that Sunday afternoon, an Irish maid was taking up peanut shells with a carpet sweeper, lost balloons were bunched on the ceiling above her white head, and Mr. Bruce met a dwarf, dressed as a clown, who had entertained at parties in his own childhood. The old man had not changed his stock of tricks or his patter, and he was proud that he was able to remember the names and faces of most of the generations of children he had entertained. He held Mr. Bruce in the hall until, after several wrong guesses, he came up with his name. In the living room a dozen friends and relatives were drinking cocktails. Now and then, a weary child, holding a candy basket or a balloon, would wander through the crowd of grown people. At the end of the living room, a couple who worked a marionette show were dismantling their stage. The woman's hair was dyed, and she smiled and gesticulated broadly while she worked, like a circus performer, though no one was watching her.

While Mr. Bruce was waiting for Katherine to put her coat on, Mrs. Sheridan came in from the foyer. They shook hands. "Can I take you home?" he asked.

She said, "Yes, *yes,*" and went in search of her older daughter.

Katherine went up to her hostess and dropped a curtsy. "It was nice of you to ask me to your party, Mrs. Howells," she said, without mumbling. "And thank you very much."

"She's such a dear. It's such a joy to have her!" Mrs. Howells said to Mr. Bruce, and laid a hand absent-mindedly on Katherine's head.

Mrs. Sheridan reappeared with her daughter. Louise Sheridan curtsied and recited her thanks, but Mrs. Howells was thinking about something else and did not hear. The little girl repeated her thanks, in a louder voice.

"Why, thank you for coming!" Mrs. Howells exclaimed abruptly.

Mr. Bruce and Mrs. Sheridan and the two children went down in the elevator. It was still light when they came out of the building onto Fifth Avenue.

"Let's walk," Mrs. Sheridan said. "It's only a few blocks."

The children went on ahead. They were in the lower Eighties and their view was broad; it took in the Avenue, the Museum, and the Park. As they walked, the double track of light along the Avenue went on with a faint click. There was a haze in the air that made the lamps give off a yellow light, and the colonnades of the Museum, the mansard roof of the Plaza above the trees, and the multitude of yellow lights reminded Stephen Bruce of many pictures of Paris and London ("Winter Afternoon") that had been painted at the turn of the century. This deceptive resemblance pleased him, and his pleasure in what he could see was heightened by the woman he was with. He felt that she saw it all very clearly. They walked along without speaking most of the way. A block or two from the building where she lived, she took her arm out of his.

"I'd like to talk with you some day about St. James's School," Mr. Bruce said. "Won't you have lunch with me? Could you have lunch with me on Tuesday?"

"I'd love to have lunch with you," Mrs. Sheridan said.

The restaurant where Mrs. Sheridan and Mr. Bruce met for lunch on Tuesday was the kind of place where they were not likely to see anyone they knew. The menu was soiled, and so was the waiter's tuxedo. There are a thousand places like it in the city. When they greeted one another, they could have passed for a couple that had been married fifteen years. She was carrying bundles and an umbrella. She might have come in from the suburbs to get some clothes for the children. She said she had been shopping, she had taken a taxi, she had been rushed, she was hungry. She took off her gloves, rattled the menu, and looked around. He had a whiskey and she asked for a glass of sherry.

"I want to know what you really think about St. James's School," he said, and she began, animatedly, to talk.

They had moved a year earlier from New York to Long Island, she said, because she wanted to send her children to a country school. She had been to country schools herself. The Long Island school had been unsatisfactory, and they had moved back to New York in September. Her husband had gone to St. James's, and that had determined their choice. She spoke excitedly, as Mr. Bruce had known she would, about the education of her daughters, and he guessed that this was something she couldn't discuss with the same satisfaction with her husband. She was excited at finding someone who seemed interested in her opinions, and she put herself at a disadvantage, as he intended she should, by talking too much. The deep joy we take in the company of people with whom we have just recently fallen in love is undisguisable, even to a purblind waiter, and they both looked wonderful. He got her a taxi at the corner. They said goodbye.

"You'll have lunch with me again?"

"Of course," she said, "of course."

She met him for lunch again. Then she met him for dinner—her husband was away. He kissed her in the taxi, and they said good night in front of her apartment house. When he called her a few days later, a nurse or a maid answered the telephone and said that Mrs. Sheridan was ill and could not be disturbed. He was frantic. He called several times during the afternoon, and finally Mrs. Sheridan answered. Her illness was not serious, she said. She would be up in a day or two and she would call him when she was well. She called him early the next week, and they met for lunch at a restaurant in an uptown apartment house. She had been shopping. She took off her gloves, rattled the menu, and looked around another failing restaurant, poorly lighted and with only a few customers. One of her daughters had a mild case of measles, she said, and Mr. Bruce was interested in the symptoms. But he looked, for a man who claimed to be interested in childhood diseases, bilious and vulpine. His color was bad. He scowled and rubbed his forehead as if he suffered from a headache. He repeatedly wet his lips and crossed and recrossed his legs. Presently, his uneasiness seemed to cross the table. During the rest of the time they sat there, the conversation was about commonplace subjects, but an emotion for which they seemed to have no words colored the talk and darkened and enlarged its shapes. She did not finish her dessert. She let her coffee get cold. For a while, neither of them spoke. A stranger, noticing them in the restaurant, might have thought that they were a pair of old friends who had met to discuss a misfortune. His face was gray. Her hands were trembling. Leaning toward her, he said, finally, "The reason I asked you to come here is because the firm I work for has an apartment upstairs."

"Yes," she said. "Yes."

For lovers, touch is metamorphosis. All the parts of their bodies seem to change, and they seem to become something different and better. That part of their experience that is distinct and separate, the totality of the years before they met, is changed, is redirected toward this moment. They feel they have reached an identical point of intensity, an ecstasy of rightness that they command in every part, and any recollection that occurs to them takes on this final clarity, whether it be a sweep hand on an airport clock, a snow owl, a Chicago railroad station on Christmas Eve, or anchoring a yawl in a strange harbor while all along the stony coast strangers are blowing their horns for the yacht-club tender, or running a ski-trail at that hour when, although the sun is still in the sky, the north face of every mountain lies in the dark.

"Do you want to go downstairs alone? The elevator men in these buildings—" Stephen Bruce said, when they had dressed.

"I don't care about the elevator men in these buildings," she said lightly.

She took his arm, and they went down in the elevator together. When they left the building, they were unwilling to part, and they decided on the Metropolitan Museum as a place where they were not likely to be seen by anyone they knew. The nearly empty rotunda looked, at that hour of the afternoon, like a railroad station past traintime. It smelled of burning coal. They looked at stone horses and pieces of cloth. In a dark passage, they found a prodigal representation of the Feast of Love. The god—disguised now as a woodcutter, now as a cowherd, a sailor, a prince—came through every open door. Three spirits waited by a holly grove to lift the armor from his shoulders and undo his buckler. A large company encouraged his paramour. The whole creation was in accord—the civet and the bear, the lion and the unicorn, fire and water.

Coming back through the rotunda, Mr. Bruce and Mrs. Sheridan met a friend of Lois's mother. It was impossible to avoid her and they said How-do-you-do and I'm-happy-to-meet-you, and Stephen promised to remember the friend to his mother-in-law. Mr. Bruce and Mrs. Sheridan walked over to Lexington and said goodbye. He returned to his office and went home at six. Mrs. Bruce had not come in, the maid told him. Katherine was at a party, and he was supposed to bring her home. The maid gave him the address and he went out again without taking off his coat. It was raining. The doorman, in a white raincoat, went out into the storm, and returned riding on the running board of a taxi. The taxi had orange seats, and as it drove uptown, he heard the car radio playing a tango. Another doorman let him out and he went into a lobby that, like the one in the building where he lived, was meant to resemble the hall of a manor house. Upstairs, there were peanut shells on the rug, balloons on the ceiling; friends and relatives were drinking cocktails in the living room, and at the end of the room, the marionette stage was again being dismantled. He drank a Martini and talked with a friend while he waited for Katherine to put her coat on. "Oh yes, *yes!*" he heard Mrs. Sheridan say, and then he saw her come into the room with her daughters.

Katherine came between them before they spoke, and he went, with his daughter, over to the hostess. Katherine dropped her curtsy, and said brightly, "It was very nice of you to ask me to your party, Mrs. Bremont, and thank you very much." As Mr. Bruce started for the elevator, the younger Sheridan girl dropped her curtsy and said, "It was a very nice party, Mrs. Bremont. . . ."

He waited downstairs, with Katherine, for Mrs. Sheridan, but something or someone delayed her, and when the elevator had come down twice without bringing her, he left.

Mr. Bruce and Mrs. Sheridan met at the apartment a few days later. Then he saw her in a crowd at the Rockefeller Center skating rink, waiting for her children. He saw her again in the lobby of the Chardin Club, among the other parents, nursemaids, and chauffeurs who were waiting for the dancing class to end. He didn't speak to her, but he heard her at his back, saying to someone: "Yes, Mother's very well, thank you. Yes, I will give her your love." Then he heard her speaking to someone farther away from him and then her voice fell below the music. That night, he left the city on business and did not return until Sunday, and he went Sunday afternoon to a football game with a friend. The game was slow and the last quarter was played under lights. When he got home, Lois met him at the door of the apartment. The fire in the living room was lighted. She fixed their drinks and then sat across the room from him in a chair near the fire. "I forgot to tell you that Aunt Helen called on Wednesday. She's moving from Gray's Hill to a house nearer the shore."

He tried to find something to say to this item of news and couldn't. After five years of marriage he seemed to have been left with nothing to say. It was like being embarrassed by a shortage of money. He looked desperately back to the football game and the trip to Chicago for something that might please her, and couldn't find a word. Lois felt his struggle and his failure. She stopped talking herself. I haven't had anyone to talk to since Wednesday, she thought, and now he has nothing to say. "While you were away, I strained my back again, reaching for a hatbox," she said. "The pain is excruciating, and Dr. Parminter doesn't seem able to help me, so I'm going to another doctor, named Walsh, who—"

"I'm terribly sorry your back is bothering you," he said. "I hope Dr. Walsh will be able to help."

The lack of genuine concern in his voice hurt her feelings. "Oh, and I forgot to tell you—there's been some *trouble*," she said crossly. "Katherine spent the afternoon with Helen Woodruff and some other children. There were some boys. When the maid went into the playroom to call them for supper, she found them all undressed. Mrs. Woodruff was very upset and I told her you'd call."

"Where is Katherine?"

"She's in her room. She won't speak to me. I don't like to be the one to say it, but I think you ought to get a psychiatrist for that girl."

"I'll go and speak to her," Mr. Bruce said.

"Well, will you want any supper?" Lois asked.

"Yes," he said, "I would like some supper."

Katherine had a large room on the side of the building. Her furniture had never filled it. When Mr. Bruce went in, he saw her sitting on the edge of her bed, in the dark. The room smelled of a pair of rats that she had in a cage. He turned on the light and gave her a charm bracelet that he had bought at the airport, and she thanked him politely. He did not mention the trouble at the Woodruffs', but when he put his arm around her shoulders, she began to cry bitterly.

"I didn't want to do it this afternoon," she said, "but *she* made me, and she was the hostess, and we always have to do what the hostess says."

"It doesn't matter if you wanted to or not," he said. "You haven't done anything terribly wrong."

He held her until she was quiet, and then left her and went into his bedroom and telephoned Mrs. Woodruff. "This is Katherine Bruce's father," he said. "I understand that there was some difficulty there this afternoon. I just wanted to say that Katherine has been given her lecture, and as far as Mrs. Bruce and I are concerned, the incident has been forgotten."

"Well, it hasn't been forgotten over here," Mrs. Woodruff said. "I don't know who started it, but I've put Helen to bed without any supper. Mr. Woodruff and I haven't decided how we're going to punish her yet, but we're going to punish her severely." He heard Lois calling to him from the living room that his supper was ready. "I suppose you know that immorality is sweeping this country," Mrs. Woodruff went on. "Our child has never heard a dirty word spoken in her life in this household. There is no room for filth here. If it takes fire to fight fire, that's what I'm going to do!"

The ignorant and ill-tempered woman angered him, but he listened helplessly to her until she had finished, and then went back to Katherine.

Lois looked at the clock on the mantelpiece and called to her husband sharply, a second time. She had not felt at all like making his supper. His lack of concern for her feelings and then her having to slave for him in the kitchen had seemed like an eternal human condition. The ghosts of her injured sex thronged to her side when she slammed open the silver drawer and again when she poured his beer. She set the tray elaborately, in order to deepen her displeasure in doing it at all. She heaped cold meat and salad on her husband's plate as if they were poisoned. Then she fixed her lipstick and carried the heavy tray into the living room herself, in spite of her lame back.

Now, smoking a cigarette and walking around the room, she let five minutes pass. Then she carried the tray back to the kitchen, dumped the beer and coffee down the drain, and put the meat and salad in the icebox. When Mr. Bruce came back from Katherine's room he found her sobbing with anger—not at him but at her own foolishness. "Lois?" he asked, and she ran out of the room and into her bedroom and slammed the door.

During the next two months, Lois Bruce heard from a number of sources that her husband had been seen with a Mrs. Sheridan. She confided to her mother that she was losing him and, at her mother's insistence, employed a private detective. Lois was not vindictive; she didn't want to trap or intimidate her husband; she had, actually, a feeling that this maneuver would somehow be his salvation.

The detective telephoned her one day when she was having lunch at home, and told her that her husband and Mrs. Sheridan had just gone upstairs in a certain hotel. He was telephoning from the lobby, he said. Lois left her lunch unfinished but changed her clothes. She put on a hat with a veil, because her face was strained, and she was able because of the veil to talk calmly with the doorman, who got her a taxi. The detective met her on the sidewalk. He told her the floor and the number of the apartment, and offered to go upstairs with her. She dismissed him officiously then, as if his offer was a reflection on her ability to handle the situation competently. She had never been in the building before, but the feeling that she was acting on her rights kept her from being impressed at all with the building's strangeness.

The elevator man closed the door after her when she got off at the tenth floor, and she found herself alone in a long, windowless hall. The twelve identical doors painted dark red to match the dusty carpet, the dim ceiling lights, and the perfect stillness of the hall made her hesitate for a second, and then she went directly to the door of the apartment, and rang the bell. There was no sound, no answer. She rang the bell several times. Then she spoke to the shut door. "Let me in, Stephen. It's Lois. Let me in. I know you're in there. Let me in."

She waited. She took off her gloves. She put her thumb on the bell and held it there. Then she listened. There was still no sound. She looked at the shut red doors around her. She jabbed the bell. "Stephen!" she called. "Stephen. Let me in there. Let me in. I know you're in there. I saw you go in there. I can hear you. I can hear you moving around. I can hear you whispering. Let me in, Stephen. Let me in. If you don't let me in, I'll tell her husband."

She waited again. The silence of the early afternoon filled the interval. Then she attacked the door handle. She pounded on the door with the frame of her purse. She kicked it. "You let me in there, Stephen Bruce!" she screamed. "You let me in there, do you hear! Let me in, let me in, let me in!"

Another door into the hallway opened, and she turned and saw a man in his shirtsleeves, shaking his head. She ran into the back hall and, crying, started down the fire stairs. Like the stairs in a monument, they seemed to have no beginning and no end, but at last she came down into a dark hall where tricycles and perambulators were stored, and found her way into the lobby.

When Mr. Bruce and Mrs. Sheridan left the hotel, they walked through the Park, which, in the late-winter sunshine, smelled faintly like a wood. Crossing a bridle path, they saw Miss Prince, the children's riding mistress. She was giving a lesson to a fat little girl whose horse was on a lead. "Mrs. Sheridan!" she said. "Mr. Bruce! Isn't this fortunate!" She stopped the horses. "I wanted to speak to both of you," she said. "I'm having a little gymkhana next month, and I want your children to ride in it. I want them all three to ride in the good-hands class. . . . And perhaps next year," she said, turning to the fat little girl, "you too may ride in the good-hands class."

They promised to allow their children to take part in the gymkhana, and Miss Prince said goodbye and resumed her riding lesson. In the Seventies they heard the roaring of a lion. They walked to the southern edge of the Park. It was then late in the afternoon. From the Plaza he telephoned his office. Among the messages was one from the maid; he was to stop at the Chardin Club and bring Katherine home.

From the sidewalk in front of the dancing school they could hear the clatter of the piano. The Grand March had begun. They moved through the crowd in the vestibule and stood in the door of the ballroom, looking for their children. Through the open door they could see Mrs. Bailey, the dancing teacher, and her two matrons curtsying stiffly as the children came to them in couples. The boys wore white gloves. The girls were simply dressed. Two by two the children bowed, or curtsied, and joined the grown people at the door. Then Mr. Bruce saw

Katherine. As he watched his daughter doing obediently what was expected of her, it struck him that he and the company that crowded around him were all cut out of the same cloth. They were bewildered and confused in principle, too selfish or too unlucky to abide by the forms that guarantee the permanence of a society, as their fathers and mothers had done. Instead, they put the burden of order onto their children and filled their days with specious rites and ceremonies.

One of the dancing teachers came up to them and said, "Oh, I'm so glad to see you, Mrs. Sheridan. We were afraid that you'd been taken sick. Very soon after the class began this afternoon, Mr. Sheridan came and got the two girls. He said he was going to take them out to the country, and we wondered if you were ill. He seemed very upset."

The assistant smiled and wandered off.

Mrs. Sheridan's face lost its color and got dark. She looked very old. It was hot in the ballroom, and Mr. Bruce led her out the door into the freshness of a winter evening, holding her, supporting her really, for she might have fallen. "It will be all right," he kept saying, "it will be all right, my darling, it will be all right."

# GOODBYE AND GOOD LUCK

## Grace Paley

GRACE PALEY (1922–    ) is well equipped to write about New York. Born in the Bronx, she was educated in the schools and colleges of the city and today lives with her husband and two children in West Manhattan. Her first book, *The Little Disturbances of Man*, drew praise from critics and writers alike. She employs a direct, gravelly prose to tell stories full of compassion and feeling. *Goodbye and Good Luck* may not be a love story in the usual sense but the reader will find it an authentic one.

I WAS popular in certain circles, says Aunt Rose. I wasn't no thinner then, only more stationary in the flesh. In time to come, Lillie, don't be surprised—change is a fact of God. From this no one is excused. Only a person like your mama stands on one foot, she don't notice how big her behind is getting and sings in the canary's ear for thirty years. Who's listening? Papa's in the shop. You and Seymour, thinking about yourself. So she waits in a spotless kitchen for a kind word and thinks—poor Rosie. . . .

Poor Rosie! If there was more life in my little sister, she would know my heart is a regular college of feelings and there is such information between my corset and me that her whole married life is a kindergarten.

Nowadays you could find me any time in a hotel, uptown or downtown. Who needs an apartment to live like a maid with a dustrag in the hand, sneezing? I'm in very good with the bus boys, it's more interesting than home, all kinds of people, everybody with a reason. . . .

And my reason, Lillie, is a long time ago I said to the forelady, "Missus, if I can't sit by the window, I can't sit." "If you can't sit, girlie," she says politely, "go stand on the street corner." And that's how I got unemployed in novelty wear.

For my next job I answered an ad which said: "Refined young lady, medium salary, cultural organization." I went by trolley to the address, the Russian Art Theater of Second Avenue where they played only the best Yiddish plays. They needed a ticket seller, someone like me, who

likes the public but is very sharp on crooks. The man who interviewed
me was the manager, a certain type.

Immediately he said: "Rosie Lieber, you surely got a build on you!"

"It takes all kinds, Mr. Krimberg."

"Don't misunderstand me, little girl," he said. "I appreciate, I appreciate. A young lady lacking fore and aft, her blood is so busy warming the toes and the finger tips, it don't have time to circulate where it's
most required."

Everybody likes kindness. I said to him: "Only don't be fresh, Mr.
Krimberg, and we'll make a good bargain."

We did: Nine dollars a week, a glass of tea every night, a free ticket
once a week for Mama, and I could go watch rehearsals any time I
wanted.

My first nine dollars was in the grocer's hands ready to move on already, when Krimberg said to me, "Rosie, here's a great gentleman, a
member of this remarkable theater, wants to meet you, impressed no
doubt by your big brown eyes."

And who was it, Lillie? Listen to me, before my very eyes was
Volodya Vlashkin, called by the people of those days the Valentino of
Second Avenue. I took one look, and I said to myself: Where did
a Jewish boy grow up so big? "Just outside Kiev," he told me.

How? "My mama nursed me till I was six. I was the only boy in the
village to have such health."

"My goodness, Vlashkin, six years old! She must have had shredded
wheat there, not breasts, poor woman."

"My mother was beautiful," he said. "She had eyes like stars."

He had such a way of expressing himself, it brought tears.

To Krimberg, Vlashkin said after this introduction: "Who is responsible for hiding this wonderful young person in a cage?"

"That is where the ticket seller sells."

"So, David, go in there and sell tickets for a half hour. I have something in mind in regards to the future of this girl and this company.
Go, David, be a good boy. And you, Miss Lieber, please, I suggest
Feinberg's for a glass of tea. The rehearsals are long. I enjoy a quiet
interlude with a friendly person."

So he took me there, Feinberg's, then around the corner, a place so
full of Hungarians, it was deafening. In the back room was a table of
honor for him. On the tablecloth embroidered by the lady of the house
was "Here Vlashkin Eats." We finished one glass of tea in quietness,
out of thirst, when I finally made up my mind what to say.

"Mr. Vlashkin, I saw you a couple weeks ago, even before I started
working here, in *The Sea Gull*. Believe me, if I was that girl, I wouldn't
look even for a minute on the young bourgeois fellow. He could fall out

of the play altogether. How Chekhov could put him in the same play as
you, I can't understand."

"You liked me?" he asked, taking my hand and kindly patting it.
"Well, well, young people still like me . . . so, and you like the theater
too? Good. And you, Rose, you know you have such a nice hand, so
warm to the touch, such a fine skin, tell me, why do you wear a scarf
around your neck? You only hide your young, young throat. These are
not olden times, my child, to live in shame."

"Who's ashamed?" I said, taking off the kerchief, but my hand right
away went to the kerchief's place, because the truth is, it really was
olden times, and I was still of a nature to melt with shame.

"Have some more tea, my dear."

"No, thank you, I am a samovar already."

"Dorfmann!" he hollered like a king. "Bring this child a seltzer with
fresh ice!"

In weeks to follow I had the privilege to know him better and better
as a person—also the opportunity to see him in his profession. The time
was autumn; the theater full of coming and going. Rehearsing without
end. After *The Sea Gull* flopped *The Salesman from Istanbul* played, a
great success.

Here the ladies went crazy. On the opening night, in the middle of
the first scene, one missus—a widow or her husband worked too long
hours—began to clap and sing out, "Oi, oi, Vlashkin." Soon there was
such a tumult, the actors had to stop acting. Vlashkin stepped forward.
Only not Vlashkin to the eyes . . . a younger man with pitch-black hair,
lively on restless feet, his mouth clever. A half a century later at the end
of the play he came out again, a gray philosopher, a student of life from
only reading books, his hands as smooth as silk. . . . I cried to think
who I was—nothing—and such a man could look at me with interest.

Then I got a small raise, due to he kindly put in a good word for me,
and also for fifty cents a night I was given the pleasure together with
cousins, in-laws, and plain stage-struck kids to be part of a crowd scene
and to see like he saw every single night the hundreds of pale faces
waiting for his feelings to make them laugh or bend down their heads in
sorrow.

The sad day came, I kissed my mama goodbye. Vlashkin helped me
to get a reasonable room near the theater to be more free. Also my
outstanding friend would have a place to recline away from the noise of
the dressing rooms. She cried and she cried. "This is a different way of
living, Mama," I said. "Besides, I am driven by love."

"You! You, a nothing, a rotten hole in a piece of cheese, are you
telling me what is life?" she screamed.

Very insulted, I went away from her. But I am good-natured—you know fat people are like that—kind, and I thought to myself, poor Mama . . . it is true she got more of an idea of life than me. She married who she didn't like, a sick man, his spirit already swallowed up by God. He never washed. He had an unhappy smell. His teeth fell out, his hair disappeared, he got smaller, shriveled up little by little, till goodbye and good luck he was gone and only came to Mama's mind when she went to the mailbox under the stairs to get the electric bill. In memory of him and out of respect for mankind, I decided to live for love.

Don't laugh, you ignorant girl.

Do you think it was easy for me? I had to give Mama a little something. Ruthie was saving up together with your papa for linens, a couple knives and forks. In the morning I had to do piecework if I wanted to keep by myself. So I made flowers. Before lunch time every day a whole garden grew on my table.

This was my independence, Lillie dear, blooming, but it didn't have no roots and its face was paper.

Meanwhile Krimberg went after me too. No doubt observing the success of Vlashkin, he thought, "Aha, open sesame . . ." Others in the company similar. After me in those years were the following: Krimberg I mentioned. Carl Zimmer, played innocent young fellows with a wig. Charlie Peel, a Christian who fell in the soup by accident, a creator of beautiful sets. "Color is his middle name," says Vlashkin, always to the point.

I put this in to show you your fat old aunt was not crazy out of loneliness. In those noisy years I had friends among interesting people who admired me for reasons of youth and that I was a first-class listener.

The actresses—Raisele, Marya, Esther Leopold—were only interested in tomorrow. After them was the rich men, producers, the whole garment center; their past is a pincushion, future the eye of a needle.

Finally the day came, I no longer could keep my tact in my mouth. I said: "Vlashkin, I hear by carrier pigeon you have a wife, children, the whole combination."

"True, I don't tell stories. I make no pretense."

"That isn't the question. What is this lady like? It hurts me to ask, but tell me, Vlashkin . . . a man's life is something I don't clearly see."

"Little girl, I have told you a hundred times, this small room is the convent of my troubled spirit. Here I come to your innocent shelter to refresh myself in the midst of an agonized life."

"Ach, Vlashkin, serious, serious, who is this lady?"

"Rosie, she is a fine woman of the middle classes, a good mother to my children, three in number, girls all, a good cook, in her youth handsome, now no longer young. You see, could I be more frank? I entrust you, dear, with my soul."

It was some few months later at the New Year's ball of the Russian Artists Club, I met Mrs. Vlashkin, a woman with black hair in a low bun, straight and too proud. She sat at a small table speaking in a deep voice to whoever stopped a moment to converse. Her Yiddish was perfect, each word cut like a special jewel. I looked at her. She noticed me like she noticed everybody, cold like Christmas morning. Then she got tired. Vlashkin called a taxi and I never saw her again. Poor woman, she did not know I was on the same stage with her. The poison I was to her role, she did not know.

Later on that night in front of my door I said to Vlashkin, "No more. This isn't for me. I am sick from it all. I am no home breaker."

"Girlie," he said, "don't be foolish."

"No, no, goodbye, good luck," I said. "I am sincere."

So I went and stayed with Mama for a week's vacation and cleaned up all the closets and scrubbed the walls till the paint came off. She was very grateful, all the same her hard life made her say, "Now we see the end. If you live like a bum, you are finally a lunatic."

After this few days I came back to my life. When we met, me and Vlashkin, we said only hello and goodbye, and then for a few sad years, with the head we nodded as if to say, "Yes, yes, I know who you are."

Meanwhile in the field was a whole new strategy. Your mama and your grandmama brought around—boys. Your own father had a brother, you never even seen him. Ruben. A serious fellow, his idealism was his hat and his coat. "Rosie, I offer you a big new free happy unusual life." How? "With me, we will raise up the sands of Palestine to make a nation. That is the land of tomorrow for us Jews." "Ha-ha, Ruben, I'll go tomorrow then." "Rosie!" says Ruben. "We need strong women like you, mothers and farmers." "You don't fool me, Ruben, what you need is dray horses. But for that you need more money." "I don't like your attitude, Rose." "In that case, go and multiply. Goodbye."

Another fellow: Yonkel Gurstein, a regular sport, dressed to kill, with such an excitable nature. In those days—it looks to me like yesterday—the youngest girls wore undergarments like Battle Creek, Michigan. To him it was a matter of seconds. Where did he practice, a Jewish boy? Nowadays I suppose it is easier, Lillie? My goodness, I ain't asking you nothing—touchy, touchy. . . .

Well, by now you must know yourself, honey, whatever you do, life don't stop. It only sits a minute and dreams a dream.

While I was saying to all these silly youngsters "no, no, no," Vlashkin went to Europe and toured a few seasons . . . Moscow, Prague, London, even Berlin—already a pessimistic place. When he came back he wrote a book, you could get from the library even today, *The Jewish Actor Abroad*. If someday you're interested enough in my lonesome years, you could read it. You could absorb a flavor of the man from the book. No, no, I am not mentioned. After all, who am I?

When the book came out I stopped him in the street to say congratulations. But I am not a liar, so I pointed out, too, the egotism of many parts—even the critics said something along such lines.

"Talk is cheap," Vlashkin answered me. "But who are the critics? Tell me, do they create? Not to mention," he continues, "there is a line in Shakespeare in one of the plays from the great history of England. It says, 'Self-loving is not so vile a sin, my liege, as self-neglecting.' This idea also appears in modern times in the moralistic followers of Freud. . . . Rosie, are you listening? You asked a question. By the way, you look very well. How come no wedding ring?"

I walked away from this conversation in tears. But this talking in the street opened the happy road up for more discussions. In regard to many things. . . . For instance, the management—very narrow-minded —wouldn't give him any more certain young men's parts. Fools. What youngest man knew enough about life to be as young as him?

"Rosie, Rosie," he said to me one day, "I see by the clock on your rosy, rosy face you must be thirty."

"The hands are slow, Vlashkin. On a week before Thursday I was thirty-four."

"Is that so? Rosie, I worry about you. It has been on my mind to talk to you. You are losing your time. Do you understand it? A woman should not lose her time."

"Oi, Vlashkin, if you are my friend, what is time?"

For this he had no answer, only looked at me surprised. We went instead, full of interest but not with our former speed, up to my new place on Ninety-fourth Street. The same pictures on the wall, all of Vlashkin, only now everything painted red and black, which was stylish, and new upholstery.

A few years ago there was a book by another member of that fine company, an actress, the one that learned English very good and went uptown—Marya Kavkaz, in which she says certain things regarding Vlashkin. Such as, he was her lover for eleven years, she's not ashamed to write this down. Without respect for him, his wife and children, or even others who also may have feelings in the matter.

Now, Lillie, don't be surprised. This is called a fact of life. An actor's soul must be like a diamond. The more faces it got the more shining is his name. Honey, you will no doubt love and marry one man and have a couple kids and be happy forever till you die tired. More than that, a person like us don't have to know. But a great artist like Volodya Vlashkin . . . in order to make a job on the stage, he's got to practice. I understand it now, to him life is like a rehearsal.

Myself, when I saw him in *The Father-in-law*—an older man in love with a darling young girl, his son's wife, played by Raisele Maisel—I cried. What he said to this girl, how he whispered such sweetness, how all his hot feelings were on his face . . . Lillie, all this experience he had with me. The very words were the same. You can imagine how proud I was.

So the story creeps to an end.

I noticed it first on my mother's face, the rotten handwriting of time, scribbled up and down her cheeks, across her forehead back and forth—a child could read—it said, old, old, old. But it troubled my heart most to see these realities scratched on Vlashkin's wonderful expression.

First the company fell apart. The theater ended. Esther Leopold died from being very aged. Krimberg had a heart attack. Marya went to Broadway. Also Raisele changed her name to Roslyn and was a big comical hit in the movies. Vlashkin himself, no place to go, retired. It said in the paper, "an actor without peer, he will write his memoirs and spend his last years in the bosom of his family among his thriving grandchildren, the apple of his wife's doting eye."

This is journalism.

We made for him a great dinner of honor. At this dinner I said to him, for the last time, I thought, "Goodbye, dear friend, topic of my life, now we part." And to myself I said further: Finished. This is your lonesome bed. A lady what they call fat and fifty. You made it personally. From this lonesome bed you will finally fall to a bed not so lonesome, only crowded with a million bones.

And now comes? Lillie, guess.

Last week, washing my underwear in the basin, I get a buzz on the phone. "Excuse me, is this the Rose Lieber formerly connected with the Russian Art Theater?"

"It is."

"Well, well, how do you do, Rose? This is Vlashkin."

"Vlashkin! Volodya Vlashkin?"

"In fact. How are you, Rose?"

"Living, Vlashkin, thank you."

"You are all right? Really, Rose? Your health is good? You are working?"

"My health, considering the weight it must carry, is first-class. I am back for some years now where I started, in novelty wear."

"Very interesting."

"Listen, Vlashkin, tell me the truth, what's on your mind?"

"My mind? Rosie, I am looking up an old friend, an old warm-hearted companion of more joyful days. My circumstances, by the way, are changed. I am retired, as you know. Also I am a free man."

"What? What do you mean?"

"Mrs. Vlashkin is divorcing me."

"What come over her? Did you start drinking or something from melancholy?"

"She is divorcing me for adultery."

"But, Vlashkin, you should excuse me, don't be insulted, but you got maybe seventeen, eighteen years on me, and even me, all this nonsense—this daydreams and nightmares—is mostly for the pleasure of conversation alone."

"I pointed all this out to her. My dear, I said, my time is past, my blood is as dry as my bones. The truth is, Rose, she isn't accustomed to have a man around all day, reading out loud from the papers the interesting events of our time, waiting for breakfast, waiting for lunch. So all day she gets madder and madder. By nighttime a furious old lady give me my supper. She has information from the last fifty years to pepper my soup. Surely there was a Judas in that theater, saying every day, 'Vlashkin, Vlashkin, Vlashkin . . .' and while my heart was circulating with his smiles he was on the wire passing the dope to my wife."

"Such a foolish end, Volodya, to such a lively story. What is your plans?"

"First, could I ask you for dinner and the theater—uptown, of course? After this . . . we are old friends. I have money to burn. What your heart desires. Others are like grass, the north wind of time has cut out their heart. Of you, Rosie, I recreate only kindness. What a woman should be to a man, you were to me. Do you think, Rosie, a couple of old pals like us could have a few good times among the material things of this world?"

My answer, Lillie, in a minute was altogether. "Yes, yes, come up," I said. "Ask the room by the switchboard, let us talk."

So he came that night and every night in the week, we talked of his long life. Even at the end of time, a fascinating man. And like men are, too, till time's end, trying to get away in one piece.

"Listen, Rosie," he explains the other day. "I was married to my wife, do you realize, nearly half a century. What good was it? Look at the bitterness. The more I think of it, the more I think we would be fools to marry."

"Volodya Vlashkin," I told him straight, "when I was young I warmed your cold back many a night, no questions asked. You admit it, I didn't make no demands. I was softhearted. I didn't want to be

called Rosie Lieber, a breaker up of homes. But now, Vlashkin, you are
a free man. How could you ask me to go with you on trains to stay in
strange hotels, among Americans, not your wife? Be ashamed."

So now, darling Lillie, tell this story to your mama from your young
mouth. She don't listen to a word from me. She only screams, "I'll
faint, I'll faint." Tell her after all I'll have a husband, which, as everybody knows, a woman should have at least one before the end of the
story.

My goodness, I am already late. Give me a kiss. After all, I watched
you grow from a plain seed. So give me a couple wishes on my
wedding day. A long and happy life. Many years of love. Hug Mama,
tell her from Aunt Rose, goodbye and good luck.

# THE BRAVEST BOAT

## Malcolm Lowry

MALCOLM LOWRY (1909–1957) This English writer might have
stepped out of a Conrad novel. A seagoing, adventuring man who
sailed the oceans and fought adversity in many other forms, he came
slowly to recognition as a writer. But, persisting despite such discour-
agements as losing the entire manuscript of a novel of which he had
no copy and the burning down of his house when he was writing another, Mr. Lowry was suddenly rewarded by important critical
acclaim. At this point death came to him in Vancouver at the age
of forty-eight. Some of his most striking work has been published
posthumously, revealing remarkable qualities of complexity and power.

I T was a day of spindrift and blowing sea-foam, with black clouds
presaging rain driven over the mountains from the sea by a wild
March wind.

But a clean silver sea light came from along the horizon where the
sky itself was like glowing silver. And far away over in America the
snowy volcanic peak of Mount Hood stood on high, disembodied, cut
off from earth, yet much too close, which was an even surer presage of
rain, as though the mountains had advanced, or were advancing.

In the park of the seaport the giant trees swayed, and taller than any
were the tragic Seven Sisters, a constellation of seven noble red cedars
that had grown there for hundreds of years, but were now dying,
blasted, with bare peeled tops and stricken boughs. (They were dying
rather than live longer near civilization. Yet though everyone had forgotten they were called after the Pleiades and thought they were named
with civic pride after the seven daughters of a butcher, who seventy
years before when the growing city was named Gaspool had all danced
together in a shop window, nobody had the heart to cut them down.)

The angelic wings of the seagulls circling over the tree tops shone
very white against the black sky. Fresh snow from the night before lay
far down the slopes of the Canadian mountains, whose freezing sum-
mits, massed peak behind spire, jaggedly traversed the country north-

ward as far as the eye could reach. And highest of all an eagle, with
the poise of a skier, shot endlessly down the world.

In the mirror, reflecting this and much besides, of an old weighing
machine with the legend *Your weight and your destiny* encircling its
forehead and which stood on the embankment between the streetcar
terminus and a hamburger stall, in this mirror along the reedy edge of
the stretch of water below known as Lost Lagoon two figures in mack-
intoshes were approaching, a man and a beautiful passionate-looking
girl, both bare-headed, and both extremely fair, and hand-in-hand, so
that you would have taken them for young lovers, but that they were
alike as brother and sister, and the man, although he walked with
youthful nervous speed, now seemed older than the girl.

The man, fine-looking, tall, yet thick-set, very bronzed, and on approaching still closer obviously a good deal older than the girl, and
wearing one of those blue belted trenchcoats favored by merchant
marine officers of any country, though without any corresponding cap
—moreover the trenchcoat was rather too short in the sleeve so that you
could see some tattooing on his wrist, as he approached nearer still it
seemed to be an anchor—whereas the girl's raincoat was of some sort of
entrancing forest-green corduroy—the man paused every now and then
to gaze into the lovely laughing face of his girl, and once or twice they
both stopped, gulping in great draughts of salty clean sea and mountain
air. A child smiled at them, and they smiled back. But the child belonged elsewhere, and the couple were unaccompanied.

In the lagoon swam wild swans, and many wild ducks: mallards and
buffleheads and scaups, golden eyes, and cackling black coots with
carved ivory bills. The little buffleheads often took flight from the
water and some of them blew about like doves among the smaller trees.
Under these trees lining the bank other ducks were sitting meekly on
the sloping lawn, their beaks tucked into their plumage rumpled by the
wind. The smaller trees were apples and hawthorns, some just opening
into bloom even before they had foliage, and weeping willows, from
whose branches small showers from the night's rain were scattered on
the two figures as they passed.

A red-breasted merganser cruised in the lagoon, and at this swift and
angry sea bird, with his proud disordered crest, the two were now gazing
with a special sympathy, perhaps because he looked lonely without his
mate. Ah, they were wrong. The red-breasted merganser was now joined
by his wife and on a sudden duck's impulse and with immense fuss the
two wild creatures flew off to settle on another part of the lagoon. And
for some reason this simple fact appeared to make these two good people
—for nearly all people are good who walk in parks—very happy again.

Now at a distance they saw a small boy, accompanied by his father who was kneeling on the bank, trying to sail a toy boat in the lagoon. But the blustery March wind soon slanted the tiny yacht into trouble and the father hauled it back, reaching out with his curved stick, and set it on an upright keel again for his son.

*Your weight and your destiny.*

Suddenly the girl's face, at close quarters in the weighing machine's mirror, seemed struggling with tears: she unbuttoned the top button of her coat to readjust her scarf, revealing, attached to a gold chain around her neck, a small gold cross. They were quite alone now, standing on top of the embankment by the machine, save for a few old men feeding the ducks below, and the father and his son with the toy yacht, all of whom had their backs turned, while an empty tram abruptly city-bound trundled around the minute terminus square; and the man, who had been trying to light his pipe, took her in his arms and tenderly kissed her, and then pressing his face against her cheek, held her a moment closely.

The couple, having gone down obliquely to the lagoon once more, had now passed the boy with his boat and his father. They were smiling again. Or as much as they could while eating hamburgers. And they were smiling still as they passed the slender reeds where a northwestern redwing was trying to pretend he had no notion of nesting, the northwestern redwing who like all birds in these parts may feel superior to man in that he is his own customs official, and can cross the wild border without let.

Along the far side of Lost Lagoon the green dragons grew thickly, their sheathed and cowled leaves giving off their peculiar animal-like odor. The two lovers were approaching the forest in which, ahead, several footpaths threaded the ancient trees. The park, seagirt, was very large, and like many parks throughout the Pacific Northwest, wisely left in places to the original wilderness. In fact, though its beauty was probably unique, it was quite like some American parks, you might have thought, save for the Union Jack that galloped evermore by a pavilion, and but for the apparition, at this moment, passing by on the carefully landscaped road slightly above, which led with its tunnels and detours to a suspension bridge, of a posse of Royal Canadian Mounted Policemen mounted royally upon the cushions of an American Chevrolet.

Nearer the forest were gardens with sheltered beds of snowdrops and here and there a few crocuses lifting their sweet chalices. The man and his girl now seemed lost in thought, breasting the buffeting wind that blew the girl's scarf out behind her like a pennant and blew the man's thick fair hair about his head.

A loudspeaker, enthroned on a wagon, barked from the city of Enochvilleport composed of dilapidated half-skyscrapers, at different levels, some with all kinds of scrap iron, even broken airplanes, on their roofs, others being moldly stock exchange buildings, new beer parlors crawling with verminous light even in mid-afternoon and resembling gigantic emerald-lit public lavatories for both sexes, masonries containing English tea-shoppes where your fortune could be told by a female relative of Maximilian of Mexico, totem pole factories, drapers' shops with the best Scotch tweed and opium dens in the basement (though no bars, as if, like some hideous old roué shuddering with every unmentionable secret vice this city without gaiety had cackled "No, I draw the line at that.—What would our wee laddies come to then?"), cerise conflagrations of cinemas, modern apartment buildings, and other soulless behemoths, housing, it might be, noble invisible struggles, of literature, the drama, art or music, the student's lamp and the rejected manuscript; or indescribable poverty and degradation, between which civic attractions were squeezed occasional lovely dark ivy-clad old houses that seemed weeping, cut off from all light, on their knees, and elsewhere bankrupt hospitals, and one or two solid-stoned old banks, held up that afternoon; and among which appeared too, at infrequent intervals, beyond a melancholy never-striking black and white clock that said three, dwarfed spires belonging to frame façades with blackened rose windows, queer grimed onion-shaped domes, and even Chinese pagodas, so that first you thought you were in the Orient, then Turkey or Russia, though finally, but for the fact that some of these were churches, you would be sure you were in hell: despite that anyone who had ever really been in hell must have given Enochvilleport a nod of recognition, further affirmed by the spectacle, at first not unpicturesque, of the numerous sawmills relentlessly smoking and champing away like demons, Molochs fed by whole mountainsides of forests that never grew again, or by trees that made way for grinning regiments of villas in the background of "our expanding and fair city," mills that shook the very earth with their tumult, filling the windy air with their sound as of a wailing and gnashing of teeth: all these curious achievements of man, together creating as we say "the jewel of the Pacific," went as though down a great incline to a harbor more spectacular than Rio de Janeiro and San Francisco put together, with deep-sea freighters moored at every angle for miles in the roadstead, but to whose heroic prospect nearly the only human dwellings visible on this side of the water that had any air of belonging, or in which their inhabitants could be said any longer to participate, were, paradoxically, a few lowly little self-built shacks and floathouses, that might have been driven out of the city altogether, down to the water's edge into the sea itself, where they stood on piles, like fishermen's huts (which several of them apparently were), or on rollers, some dark and tumbledown, others freshly and prettily painted, these last quite evidently built or placed with some human need for beauty in mind, even if under the permanent threat of eviction, and all standing, even the most somber, with their fluted tin chimneys smoking here and there like toy tramp steamers, as though in defiance of the town, before eternity. In Enochville-port itself some ghastly-colored neon signs had long since been going through their unctuous twitchings and gesticulations that nostalgia and love transform into a poetry of longing: more happily one began to flicker: PALOMAR, LOUIS ARMSTRONG AND HIS ORCHESTRA. A huge new gray dead hotel that at sea might be a landmark of romance, belched smoke out of its turreted haunted-looking roof, as if it had caught fire, and beyond that all the lamps were blazing within the grim courtyard of the law courts, equally at sea a trysting place of the heart, outside which one of the stone lions, having recently been blown up, was covered reverently with a white cloth, and inside which for a month a group of stainless citizens had been trying a sixteen-year-old boy for murder.

Nearer the park the apron lights appeared on a sort of pebble-dashed Y.M.C.A.-Hall-cum-variety-theater saying TAMMUZ *The Master Hypnotist, To-nite 8:30*, and running past this the tramlines, down which another parkwise streetcar was approaching, could be seen extending almost to the department store in whose show window Tammuz' subject, perhaps a somnolent descendant of the seven sisters whose fame had eclipsed even that of the Pleiades, but whose announced ambition was to become a female psychiatrist, had been sleeping happily and publicly in a double bed for the last three days as an advance publicity stunt for tonight's performance.

Above Lost Lagoon on the road now mounting toward the suspension bridge in the distance much as a piece of jazz music mounts toward a break, a newsboy cried: "LASH ORDERED FOR SAINT PIERRE! SIXTEEN YEAR OLD BOY, CHILD-SLAYER, TO HANG! Read all about it!"

The weather too was foreboding. Yet, seeing the wandering lovers, the other passers-by on this side of the lagoon, a wounded soldier lying on a bench smoking a cigarette, and one or two of those destitute souls, the very old who haunt parks—since, faced with a choice, the very old will sometimes prefer, rather than to keep a room and starve, at least in such a city as this, somehow to eat and live outdoors—smiled too.

For as the girl walked along beside the man with her arm through his and as they smiled together and their eyes met with love, or they paused, watching the blowing seagulls, or the ever-changing scene of the snow-freaked Canadian mountains with their fleecy indigo chasms, or to listen to the deep-tongued majesty of a merchantman's echoing roar (these things that made Enochvilleport's ferocious aldermen imagine that it was the city itself that was beautiful, and maybe they were half right), the whistle of a ferryboat as it sidled across the inlet northward, what memories might not be evoked in a poor soldier, in the breasts of the bereaved, the old, even, who knows, in the mounted policemen, not merely of young love, but of lovers, as they seemed to be, so much in love that they were afraid to lose a moment of their time together?

Yet only a guardian angel of these two would have known—and surely they must have possessed a guardian angel—the strangest of all strange things of which they were thinking, save that, since they had spoken of it so often before, and especially, when they had opportunity, on this day of the year, each knew of course that the other was thinking about it, to such an extent indeed that it was no surprise, it only resembled the beginning of a ritual when the man said, as they entered the main path of the forest, through whose branches that shielded them from the wind could be made out, from time to time, suggesting a fragment of music manuscript, a bit of the suspension bridge itself:

"It was a day just like this that I set the boat adrift. It was twenty-nine years ago in June."

"It was twenty-nine years ago in June, darling. And it was June twenty-seventh."

"It was five years before you were born, Astrid, and I was ten years old and I came down to the bay with my father."

"It was five years before I was born, you were ten years old, and you came down to the wharf with your father. Your father and grandfather had made you the boat between them and it was a fine one, ten inches long, smoothly varnished and made of wood from your model airplane box, with a new strong white sail."

"Yes, it was balsa wood from my model airplane box and my father sat beside me, telling me what to write for a note to put in it."

"Your father sat beside you, telling you what to write," Astrid laughed, "and you wrote:

"Hello.

"My name is Sigurd Storlesen. I am ten years old. Right now I am sitting on the wharf at Fearnought Bay, Clallam County, State of Washington, U.S.A., 5 miles south of Cape Flattery on the Pacific side, and my Dad is beside me telling me what to write. Today is June 27, 1922. My Dad is a forest warden in the Olympic National Forest but my Granddad is the lighthouse keeper at Cape Flattery. Beside me is a small shiny canoe which you now hold in your hand. It is a windy day and my Dad said to put the canoe in the water when I have put this in and glued down the lid which is a piece of balsa wood from my model airplane box.

"Well must close this note now, but first I will ask you to tell the Seattle Star that you have found it, because I am going to start reading the paper from today and looking for a piece that says, who when and where it was found.

"Thanks. Sigurd Storlesen."

"Yes, then my father and I put the note inside, and we glued down the lid and sealed it and put the boat on the water."

"You put the boat on the water and the tide was going out and away it went. The current caught it right off and carried it out and you watched it till it was out of sight!"

The two had now reached a clearing in the forest where a few gray squirrels were scampering about on the grass. A dark-browed Indian in a windbreaker, utterly absorbed by his friendly task, stood with a sleek black squirrel sitting on his shoulder nibbling popcorn he was giving it from a bag. This reminded them to get some peanuts to feed the bears, whose cages were over the way.

*Ursus Horribilis:* and now they tossed peanuts to the sad lumbering sleep-heavy creatures—though at least these two grizzlies were together, they even had a home—maybe still too sleepy to know where they were, still wrapped in a dream of their timberfalls and wild blueberries in the Cordilleras Sigurd and Astrid could see again, straight ahead of them, between the trees, beyond a bay.

But how should they stop thinking of the little boat?

Twelve years it had wandered. Through the tempests of winter, over sunny summer seas, what tide rips had caught it, what wild sea birds, shearwaters, storm petrels, jaegers, that follow the thrashing propellers, the dark albatross of these northern waters, swooped upon it, or warm currents edged it lazily toward land—and blue-water currents sailed it after the albacore, with fishing boats like white giraffes—or glacial drifts tossed it about fuming Cape Flattery itself. Perhaps it had rested, floating in a sheltered cove, where the killer whale smote, lashed, the deep clear water; the eagle and the salmon had seen it, a baby seal stared with her wondering eyes, only for the little boat to be thrown aground, catching the rainy afternoon sun, on cruel barnacled rocks by the waves, lying aground knocked from side to side in an inch of water like a live thing, or a poor old tin can, pushed, pounded ashore, and swung around, reversed again, left high and dry, and then swept another yard up the beach, or carried under a lonely salt-gray shack, to drive a seine fisherman crazy all night with its faint plaintive knocking, before it ebbed out in the dark autumn dawn, and found its way afresh, over the deep, coming through thunder, to who will ever know what fierce and desolate uninhabited shore, known only to the dread Wendigo, where not even an Indian could have found it, unfriended there, lost, until it was borne out to sea once more by the great brimming black tides of January, or the huge calm tides of the midsummer moon, to start its journey all over again——

Astrid and Sigurd came to a large enclosure, set back from a walk, with two vine-leaved maple trees (their scarlet tassels, delicate precursors of their leaves, already visible) growing through the top, a sheltered cavernous part to one side for a lair, and the whole, save for the barred front, covered with stout large-meshed wire—considered sufficient protection for one of the most Satanic beasts left living on earth.

Two animals inhabited the cage, spotted like deceitful pastel leopards, and in appearance like decorated, maniacal-looking cats: their ears were provided with huge tassels and, as if this were in savage parody of the vine-leaved maples, from the brute's chin tassels also depended. Their legs were as long as a man's arm, and their paws, clothed in gray fur out of which shot claws curved like scimitars, were as big as a man's clenched fist.

And the two beautiful demonic creatures prowled and paced endlessly, searching the base of their cage, between whose bars there was just room to slip a murderous paw—always a hop out of reach an almost invisible sparrow went pecking away in the dust—searching with eternal voraciousness, yet seeking in desperation also some way out, passing and repassing each other rhythmically, as though truly damned and under some compelling enchantment.

And yet as they watched the terrifying Canadian lynx, in which seemed to be embodied in animal form all the pure ferocity of nature, as they watched, crunching peanuts themselves now and passing the bag between them, before the lovers' eyes still sailed that tiny boat, battling with the seas, at the mercy of a wilder ferocity yet, all those years before Astrid was born.

Ah, its absolute loneliness amid those wastes, those wildernesses, of rough rainy seas bereft even of sea birds, between contrary winds, or in the great dead windless swell that comes following a gale; and then with the wind springing up and blowing the spray across the sea like rain, like a vision of creation, blowing the little boat as it climbed the highlands into the skies, from which sizzled cobalt lightnings, and then sank down into the abyss, but already was climbing again, while the whole sea crested with foam like lambs' wool went furling off to leeward, the whole vast moon-driven expanse like the pastures and valleys and snow-capped ranges of a Sierra Madre in delirium, in ceaseless motion, rising and falling, and the little boat rising, and falling into a paralyzing sea of white drifting fire and smoking spume by which it seemed overwhelmed: and all this time a sound, like a high sound of singing, yet as sustained in harmony as telegraph wires, or like the unbelievably high perpetual sound of the wind where there is nobody to listen, which perhaps does not exist, or the ghost of the wind in the rigging of ships long lost, and perhaps it was the sound of the wind in its toy rigging, as again the boat slanted onward: but even then what further unfathomed deeps had it oversailed, until what birds of ill omen turned heavenly for it at last, what iron birds with saber wings skimming forever through the murk above the gray immeasurable swells, imparted mysteriously their own homing knowledge to it, the lonely buovant little craft, nudging it with their beaks under golden sunsets in a blue sky, as it sailed close in to mountainous coasts of clouds with stars over them, or burning coasts at sunset once more, as it rounded not only the terrible spume-drenched rocks, like incinerators in sawmills, of Flattery, but other capes unknown, those twelve years, of giant pinnacles, images of barrenness and desolation, upon which the heart is thrown and impaled eternally! —And strangest of all how many ships themselves had threatened it, during that voyage of only some three score miles as the crow flies from its launching to its final port, looming out of the fog and passing by harmlessly all those years—those years too of the last sailing ships, rigged to the moonsail, sweeping by into their own oblivion—but ships cargoed with guns or iron for impending wars, what freighters now at the bottom of the sea he, Sigurd, had voyaged in for that matter, freighted with old marble and wine and cherries-in-brine, or whose engines even now were still somewhere murmuring: *Frère* Jacques! *Frère* Jacques!

What strange poem of God's mercy was this?

Suddenly across their vision a squirrel ran up a tree beside the cage and then, chattering shrilly, leaped from a branch and darted across the top of the wire mesh. Instantly, swift and deadly as lightning, one of the lynx sprang twenty feet into the air, hurtling straight to the top of the cage toward the squirrel, hitting the wire with a twang like a mammoth guitar, and simultaneously flashing through the wire its scimitar claws: Astrid cried out and covered her face.

But the squirrel, unhurt, untouched, was already running lightly along another branch, down to the tree, and away, while the infuriated lynx sprang straight up, sprang again, and again and again and again, as his mate crouched spitting and snarling below.

Sigurd and Astrid began to laugh. Then this seemed obscurely unfair to the lynx, now solemnly washing his mate's face. The innocent squirrel, for whom they felt such relief, might almost have been showing off, almost, unlike the oblivious sparrow, have been taunting the caged animal. The squirrel's hairbreadth escape—the thousand-to-one chance—that on second thought must take place every day, seemed meaningless. But all at once it did not seem meaningless that they had been there to see it.

"You know how I watched the paper and waited," Sigurd was saying, stooping to relight his pipe, as they walked on.

"The Seattle *Star*," Astrid said.

"The Seattle *Star* . . . It was the first newspaper I ever read. Father always declared the boat had gone south—maybe to Mexico, and I seem to remember Granddad saying no, if it didn't break up on Tatoosh, the tide would take it right down Juan de Fuca Strait, maybe into Puget Sound itself. Well, I watched and waited for a long time and finally, as kids will, I stopped looking."

"And the years went on——"

"And I grew up. Granddad was dead by then. And the old man, you know about him. Well, he's dead too now. But I never forgot. Twelve years! Think of it—! Why, it voyaged around longer than we've been married."

"And we've been married seven years."

"Seven years today—"

"It seems like a miracle!"

But their words fell like spent arrows before the target of this fact.

They were walking, as they left the forest, between two long rows of Japanese cherry trees, next month to be an airy avenue of celestial bloom. The cherry trees behind, the forest reappeared, to left and right of the wide clearing, and skirting two arms of the bay. As they approached the Pacific, down the gradual incline, on this side remote from the harbor the wind grew more boisterous: gulls, glaucous and raucous, wheeled and sailed overhead, yelling, and were suddenly far out to sea.

And it was the sea that lay before them, at the end of the slope that changed into the steep beach, the naked sea, running deeply below, without embankment or promenade, or any friendly shacks, though some prettily built homes showed to the left, with one light in a window, glowing warmly through the trees on the edge of the forest itself, as of some stalwart Columbian Adam, who had calmly stolen back with his Eve into Paradise, under the flaming sword of the civic cherubim.

The tide was low. Offshore, white horses were running around a point. The headlong onrush of the tide of beaten silver flashing over its crossflowing underset was so fast the very surface of the sea seemed racing away.

Their path gave place to a cinder track in the familiar lee of an old frame pavilion, a deserted tea house boarded up since last summer. Dead leaves were slithering across the porch, past which on the slope to the right picnic benches, tables, a derelict swing, lay overturned, under a tempestuous grove of birches. It seemed cold, sad, inhuman there, and beyond, with the roar of that deep low tide. Yet there was that between the lovers which moved like a warmth, and might have thrown open the shutters, set the benches and tables aright, and filled the whole grove with the voices and children's laughter of summer. Astrid paused for a moment with a hand on Sigurd's arm while they were sheltered by the pavilion, and said, what she too had often said before, so that they always repeated these things almost like an incantation:

"I'll never forget it. That day when I was seven years old, coming to the park here on a picnic with my father and mother and brother. After lunch my brother and I came down to the beach to play. It was a fine summer day, and the tide was out, but there'd been this very high tide in the night, and you could see the lines of driftwood and seaweed where it had ebbed. . . . I was playing on the beach, and I found your boat!"

"You were playing on the beach and you found my boat. And the mast was broken."

"The mast was broken and shreds of sail hung dirty and limp. But your boat was still whole and unhurt, though it was scratched and weatherbeaten and the varnish was gone. I ran to my mother, and she saw the sealing wax over the cockpit, and, darling, I found your note!"

"You found our note, my darling."

Astrid drew from her pocket a scrap of paper and holding it between them they bent over (though it was hardly legible by now and they knew it off by heart) and read:

Hello.

My name is Sigurd Storlesen. I am ten years old. Right now I am sitting on the wharf at Fearnought Bay, Clallam County, State of Washington, U.S.A., 5 miles south of Cape Flattery on the Pacific side, and my Dad is beside me telling me what to write. Today is June 27, 1922. My Dad is a forest warden in the Olympic National Forest but my Granddad is the lighthouse keeper at Cape Flattery. Beside me is a small shiny canoe which you now hold in your hand. It is a windy day and my Dad said to put the canoe in the water when I have put this in and glued down the lid which is a piece of balsa wood from my model airplane box.

Well must close this note now, but first I will ask you to tell the Seattle Star that you have found it, because I am going to start reading the paper from today and looking for a piece that says, who when and where it was found.

Thanks.

SIGURD STORLESEN.

They came to the desolate beach strewn with driftwood, sculptured, whorled, silvered, piled everywhere by tides so immense there was a tideline of seaweed and detritus on the grass behind them, and great logs and shingle-bolts and writhing snags, crucificial, or frozen in a fiery rage—or better, a few bits of lumber almost ready to burn, for someone to take home, and automatically they threw them up beyond the sea's reach for some passing soul, remembering their own winters of need—and more snags there at the foot of the grove and visible high on the sea-scythed forest banks on either side, in which riven trees were growing, yearning over the shore. And everywhere they looked was wreckage, the toll of winter's wrath: wrecked hencoops, wrecked floats, the wrecked side of a fisherman's hut, its boards once hammered together, with its wrenched shiplap and extruding nails. The fury had extended even to the beach itself, formed in hummocks and waves and barriers of shingle and shells they had to climb up in places. And everywhere too was the grotesque macabre fruit of the sea, with its exhilarating iodine smell, nightmarish bulbs of kelp like antiquated motor horns, trailing brown satin streamers twenty feet long, sea wrack like demons, or the discarded casements of evil spirits that had been cleansed. Then more wreckage: boots, a clock, torn fishing nets, a demolished wheelhouse, a smashed wheel lying in the sand.

Nor was it possible to grasp for more than a moment that all this was its feeling of death and destruction and barrenness was only in appearance, that beneath the flotsam, under the very shells they crunched, within the trickling overflows of winterbournes they jumped over, down at the tide margin, existed, just as in the forest, a stirring and stretching of life, a seething of spring.

When Astrid and Sigurd were almost sheltered by an uprooted tree on one of these lower billows of beach they noticed that the clouds had lifted over the sea, though the sky was not blue but still that intense silver, so that they could see right across the Gulf and make out, or thought they could, the line of some Gulf Islands. A lone freighter with upraised derricks shipped seas on the horizon. A hint of the summit of Mount Hood remained, or it might have been clouds. They remarked too, in the southeast, on the sloping base of a hill, a triangle of storm-washed green, as if cut out of the overhanging murk there, in which were four pines, five telegraph posts, and a clearing resembling a cemetery. Behind them the icy mountains of Canada hid their savage peaks and snowfalls under still more savage clouds. And they saw that the sea was gray with whitecaps and currents charging offshore and spray blowing backwards from the rocks.

But when the full force of the wind caught them, looking from the shore, it was like gazing into chaos. The wind blew away their thoughts, their voices, almost their very senses, as they walked, crunching the shells, laughing and stumbling. Nor could they tell whether it was spume or rain that smote and stung their faces, whether spindrift from the sea or rain from which the sea was born, as now finally they were forced to a halt, standing there arm in arm. . . . And it was to this shore, through that chaos, by those currents, that their little boat with its innocent message had been brought out of the past finally to safety and a home.

But ah, the storms they had come through!

# Part IV
# OTHER TIMES

# AIMÉE DUBUCQ DE RIVERY

## MESSAGE FROM A GHOST

### *Lesley Blanch*

LESLEY BLANCH An artist and explorer in many fields, Miss Blanch has in turn been painter, theatrical designer, caricaturist and drama critic, mostly in London where she was born. More recently she has traveled extensively throughout the world, making notes for the biographical essays to which she is now turning her artist's viewpoint. She has a particular talent for writing about interesting and highly romantic women of the past. The story which follows presents one of her favorite ladies, a cousin of the Empress Josephine, who was seized by pirates and made the captive of a royal Turkish harem.

WHEN the Corsairs led Aimée Dubucq de Rivery through the teeming lanes of Constantinople towards the Seraglio, a path was cleared for her by the slashing hippopotamus-hide whips of the Sultan's Eunuchs. She was a present from the Dey of Algiers to his master, the Padishah, or Sultan of Turkey, Allah's Shadow upon Earth. She had been on her way home to Martinique from her convent schoolroom in Nantes, where she was a special favorite with the Sisters. She was a beautiful, intelligent, pious and charming young creature. There had been tears and prayers when she set sail, and even the Mother Superior had been on the jetty, to wave farewell. How many more tears, how many more prayers, if they could have foreseen her fate!

But Aimée, now swaddled in sumptuous brocades and bundled in veils, must have remembered the prophecies of the old Negress Euphemia David, in Martinique, when Aimée and her cousin, a dark, skinny little girl, Joséphine Tascher de la Pagerie, whom the world was to know as Joséphine Bonaparte, crept through the sugar canes at dusk to cross the old sibyl's palm with silver. At the time, her mumblings had seemed a wild farrago of crowns, thrones and pirate ships. The children had listened breathlessly—they did not believe her, but they remem-

bered. . . . Now, with a thud of terror in her heart, Aimée saw an
enormous figure waddling towards her, his ermine-lined pelisse sweeping behind him, his towering turban nodding with flamingo plumes. It
was the Chief Black Eunuch, the Kizlar Agha, a princely Nubian, *Son
Altesse Noir,* come to the Gate of Felicity to inspect the Dey's offering
to his Sublime master. Beside him Aimée saw a great pyramid of heads,
some so newly severed that they reeked and steamed with blood. The
future seemed to close round her. It was not a nightmare! It was her
destiny, and she could not escape! Her large blue eyes stared out wildly
over the yashmak, and then closed. Aimée had fainted.

Very little has ever been known or written about Aimée Dubucq de
Rivery, "the French Sultana," mother of the Sultan Mahmoud II, The
Reformer, whose sweeping changes laid the first foundations of the new
Turkey. But once we know of her existence, her influence can be traced
in many ways, from vast sweeps of international policy to salon revolu-
tions such as the introduction of a French dancing master to the
Harem, or the Sultan Mahmoud's predilection for champagne. By nature the Turks are secretive and withdrawn, especially concerning their
homes and their women. Significant Turkish intrigues, particularly
those centered round, or originating in the Seraglio, as so many of them
did, have remained veiled through the centuries. Since Aimée Dubucq
de Rivery lived in the Seraglio as an infidel, a *Giaour,* she was a thousand times stranger, more suspect than all the other odalisques, the
Georgians and Circassians. As a Frenchwoman, she had every need to
remain a shadowy figure; not only was her own life threatened, but that
of her son, who, if he was to inherit the throne she coveted for him
(and which had been predicted for him, too) must never appear to be
tainted by dangerous European influences.

Thus she has remained a romantic cipher, a ghost, sensed rather than
seen, flitting through the kiosks and pavilions of the Seraglio, a baffling
phantom. Her beauty was acknowledged by the whole Seraglio; but
to a small inner group of statesmen and courtiers she became a symbol
of horizons breathlessly new to the ingrown world of Ottoman administration; a symbol of justice and liberty and gentleness far removed from
the passions and corruption of the decaying oligarchy that ruled the
Turkish Empire from the inner fastnesses of the Seraglio.

In Aimée Dubucq de Rivery we see a remarkable illustration of the
saying "character plus opportunity equals fortune." The only known
portrait of the French Sultana, made when she was about sixteen, shows
a face full of spirit. It has nothing placid, or resigned. It is likely that
once she accepted the impossibility of struggling against her lot, she
made the best of it, extracting the maximum from its fabulous resources.

The nose is witty, delicately upturned; the brows strongly arched; the mouth small and pouting, the perfect cupid's bow so much admired at that time. The eyes are large, a clear blue, we are told, and seem to have at once a lanquishing and quizzical regard. It is a determined, self-contained face; softened, no doubt, by her fair Norman complexion. In the Harem she was known as *Naksh,* The Beautiful One, which must be taken as high tribute from a world where the odalisques and slaves were of unparalleled beauty.

She was born in Martinique, at Pointe Royale, in 1763. Her family was of noble Norman stock. An ancestor, the Sieur Pierre Dubucq, had been a young officer in Cardinal Richelieu's own regiment, exiled for dueling and killing his adversary. At that time dueling was rigorously proscribed, punishable by death. The boy had fled the country, joined a ship sailing for the West Indies and took service under the Governor of Saint Kitts. He did well, and presently was sent as aide-de-camp to the new Governor of Martinique, where he settled, subdued the natives, built a sugar mill, the first on the island, and ran a large, flourishing plantation at La Trinité. Settling down is a comparative term, however; he continued to see much active service, thrusting and parrying his way from one swashbuckling engagement to the next, several times wounded, but always emerging victoriously. In 1701 he was granted letters of nobility, in recognition of his services to France and her Colonial expansion. His sons remained on Martinique, continuing to cultivate the family estates, and to marry among the daughters of the other settlers. One of Pierre Dubucq's descendants, François Henri Dubucq de Rivery, was to become the father of the French Sultana. He died the same year she was born, and when his widow, Marie-Victoire Menant, died six years later, their daughter, the little Marie-Marthe Aimée, was adopted by her guardian, a relative, Monsieur Dubucq de Sainte Preuve.

There were a lot of relatives, uncles and aunts, greataunts and cousins of first, second and third degree. The child was loved and petted by them all, and adored by her *da,* the fiercely loving mulatto nurse who reared her. Among her favorite playmates was her cousin Maria-Joseph (or Joséphine) Rose Tascher de la Pagerie. There seems to have been something in the air of Martinique which bred a race of queens. Joséphine, who was to become Empress of the French, her daughter Hortense, who became Queen of Holland, Madame de Maintenon, morganatic wife of Louis XIV, and Aimée, the Sultan Valideh, or Queen Mother, of Turkey—all these seductive women were Creoles from Martinique.

It was an agreeable way of life for the big French families. The days slid by, the months merged together, year after year, without any per-

ceptible break. Only the hurricanes, and, rarely, the muttered threats of
Mount Pelée, the volcano, ever threatened the calm. Everywhere, tropic
vegetation coiled overwhelmingly, that scarlet flamboyant tree, purple
bougainvillea, palms, breadfruit, calabash and papaya. The plunging
gorges and mountain slopes seemed choked in luxuriance. Over all, the
trade winds wafted their spicy breezes from one bay to the next. The
island was dotted with the spacious but simple white houses of the plantation owners, such as that belonging to Aimée's guardian, at La Trinité.
The slaves were, on the whole, well treated; they were gay and child-
like, passionately devoted to the fripperies of dress peculiar to Martinique, the madras muslins, the checked and striped foulard handkerchiefs they wore like shawls, and the countless variations of starched
turbans, *tête calendée,* set so coquettishly on their blue-black heads. Beneath all this, however, ran a deep strain of superstition; there were tales
of prophecies, and black magic, of hauntings, incantations and zombis;
a dark breath of poison behind the frangipani.

The strange story of the prophecy told to the young Joséphine is too
well authenticated to be dismissed as a mere legend. There is a detailed
account left by Mlle. Lenormand, herself the most famous of all French
fortunetellers, who was to become an intimate friend of the Empress
Joséphine. It is from Joséphine herself that Mlle. Lenormand claims to
have obtained the details. Mlle. Lenormand, who had been consulted by
such as Talleyrand, Napoleon, Marat and Alexander of Russia, published her *Mémoires historiques et secrètes de l'Impératrice Joséphine*
in 1820, six years after Joséphine's death, and it is easy to dismiss the
prophecies she records as opportunist fabrication. But they are attested
by many; indeed, the Empress herself sometimes spoke, in her hey-
day, of the tragic end predicted for her by Euphemia David. Sir Walter Scott, too, claimed that the prophecies were related to a friend during
Napoleon's Italian campaign, long before either Joséphine's rise or fall.

About fifteen miles from the Dubucq estates at Pointe Royale, was
Trois Islets, belonging to the Tascher de la Pagerie family. Aimée and
Joséphine were often together and one day the two children, then about
twelve, decided to visit a celebrated old fortuneteller, who lived near
Trois Islets. The seer lived in a tumble-down shack, the path bordered
by huge lilies, *amaryllis gigantea,* to which Joséphine, always of a horti-
cultural bent, took a great fancy. In later years she cultivated them at
Malmaison, and it is said she would often sigh over them, recalling the
Pythoness of Martinique.

When Joséphine and Aimée entered the shack, they found her
crouched on a mat, muttering. Mumbo jumbo and abracadabra, all of
it; sharpened, no doubt, by Mlle. Lenormand, who, herself, lived by
such abracadabras. The two girls crossed the plum-pink paw with silver

and watched her as she peered intently at their hands. Together, the future Empress of France at the apogee of its glory, and the future French Sultana, mother of the Grand Turk, Allah's Shadow upon Earth, stood gaping at history.

After outlining, in detail, the chequered opening to Joséphine's life of adventure, touching on her loves, the disastrous marriage with Beauharnais, the Revolution, her widowhood and her two children, Euphemia predicted that Joséphine's second husband would be a dark, apparently insignificant man; nevertheless, he would fill the world with his glory. Many nations would bow before him as a mighty conqueror. Joséphine would become a great lady, a queen—but having been the wonder of the world, she would die unhappy, repudiated, and often regretting the free, peaceful life of Martinique. One statement has never been disputed, for many witnessed the phenomenon. She told of a strange meteor, or light, which would appear out of the heavens, on the moment of Joséphine's departure from Martinique. And, as is well known, on the day Joséphine sailed, a glowing light appeared overhead; it was the phosphoric flame, known as St. Elmo's fire, and, in Mlle. Lenormand's words, "seemed to attach itself to the ship, forming a sort of wreath around it." The young Joséphine, sailing to unknown worlds and an unknown husband, was hardly consoled by this strange augury of fortune. She preferred the dolls with which she still played.

Aimée approached the old witch with some coffee grounds, one of the methods of divination she used, and again the prophecies appear to have been equally exact. *"You will be sent to Europe to complete your schooling,"* she told Aimée. *"Your ship will be seized by Corsairs. You will be taken captive and placed in a Seraglio. There you will give birth to a son. This son will reign gloriously, but the steps of his throne will be dyed with the blood of his predecessor. As to you, you will never taste the outward honors of the Court, but you will live in a great and splendid palace where you will reign supreme. At the very hour when you know your happiness is won, that happiness will fade like a dream, and a lingering illness will carry you to the tomb."*

It can be imagined how the cousins hung on her words. Such a future was to be both dreaded and desired. It was nothing if not romantic. Were they to believe it or not? In any case, it seemed best kept away from family mockery, at present. However, such a pronouncement was not likely to be forgotten, and when, a few years later, it was decided Aimée should complete her education in France, she must have recalled the warning note on Algerian Corsairs, and trembled. Or was it, rather, a tremor of excitement? For a thirteen-year-old beauty, life at Sainte Rose would soon pall. If she had any doubts about the voyage she said nothing, and so, in 1776 she sailed for Nantes, accompanied by her

devoted *da*. At Fort de France—then Fort Royale—the brightly clad
crowds of slaves gathered at the harbor to wave farewell. *Adieu madras,
adieu foulards*, the traditional song of the Martinique girls to their
sailor lovers, sounded faintly across the gathering distance. The ship set
its course—eastward.

The convent of the Dames de la Visitation, at Nantes, where Aimée
was bound, was then regarded in the light of an elegant finishing
school for the daughters of the nobility. While living a cloistered life, its
inmates were not subjected to the rigors of a nunnery. Not that they
enjoyed the license associated with some eighteenth-century convents,
such as that in Venice, which, if we are to believe Casanova, was little
more than a *maison de renedezvous*; nor that of the convent at Beja,
from which the immortal Portuguese nun wrote these burning evocations of her lover's visits. At the convent of the Dames de la Visitation,
the pensionnaires spent their time in light studies, needlework and
polite accomplishments. This sojourn, it was thought, would fit Aimée
for her future life. And perhaps it did: perhaps it succeeded better
than anyone could know. It is likely that after such an austere regime,
the voluptuous tenor of life in the Seraglio may have seemed particularly agreeable. Seated in the refectory, eating wholesome fare,
her eyes cast meeky down, at her devotions, or lying stiffly in her
narrow bed, did she ever recall the prophecy? At her embroidery, or
helping Soeur Angélique with the conserves, she must have remembered the episode, as fantastic as a fairy tale, as remote as *La Belle
aux bois dormant*. But perhaps, being a Creole, and accepting the
superstitions of Martinique, she accepted the prophecy too, and secretly
cherished her fearful and wonderful destiny. It is recorded that she
was a pupil of exceptional abilities, with a wide range of interests.
As children, she and Joséphine had both played the guitar; now she
studied singing, the harpsichord, choosing, perhaps, with a little secret
smile, the quasi-Orientalisms of Couperin's *Sultane*. Perhaps she
showed an extra animation, an added application for geography, "the
uses of the globe," with a leaning towards the Eastern hemisphere.
And Racine, having had a century or more in which to become a
classic, was probably allowed as light reading in the Convent. If so,
she must have pored over the noble sorrows of *Bajazet*.

Aimée spent nearly eight years at the Convent; far longer than had
been anticipated, for the war between France and England, over the
American Colonies, had broken out in 1778, and it was thought unsafe
for her to risk the return voyage at a time when the high seas raged
with battles. Aimée said nothing: what would be, would be. She would
return home safely, God willing, marry, and follow the placid, cradle-

dull pattern of her kind. In 1784, when she was twenty-one, the war being over, Aimée set sail from Nantes for Martinique; she took with her the prayers of the whole Convent, where she was much loved, a number of books to relieve the tedium of a two months' voyage, and the company of her dragon, the old *da*.

A few days out, in the Bay of Biscay, a fearful storm broke. The vessel was small and leaky—it could not stand up to the violence of the waves. Soon its seams were gaping. At nightfall, all hope was abandoned as the ship listed and began to sink. But miraculously, a sail was sighted. It was a large Spanish trader, speeding to the rescue. In inky darkness, with waves breaking over them, the sodden passengers and crew were transferred to the Spanish ship, which was heading for the Balearic Isles. Next day, the sun blazed down. Nature had been vanquished. The rescued passengers preened themselves dry, and were in a mood to savor the smooth roll of the ship as it sailed towards land. But not for long. After nature, man. As they were congratulating each other, in full sight of their destination, the pink spires of Palma de Majorca, they perceived that they were pursued by Algerian Corsairs. No sooner sighted than overhauled; there was no escape, no defense. Pirates! Even the bellying sails seemed to sag. Soon the pirate galley was alongside, and Aimée, now doubtless resigned to her fate, and perhaps buoyed by the ultimate splendors foreseen by Euphemia, caught her first glimpse of the dreaded Corsairs. Swarthy, red-capped, and grinning derisively, they scarcely bothered to draw their cutlasses. It was child's play to overcome the Spanish trader's resistance, and the ship, with all on board, was taken to Algiers in triumph.

During the eighteenth century, piracy was on the decline, but Tunis and Algiers were still the Corsairs' lair. Algiers, in particular, by its natural formation, had become a towering fortress, dominating the snug harbor, offering a hideout for both men and ships. It was under Turkish domination, but all along the Barbary Coast, pirates of every race knew they would be protected and encouraged by the Turkish Governor. The dazzling white cubes of the Kasbah piled up the hillside, under the shelter of Turkish cannons menacing any unwelcome newcomers. In the labyrinthine climb, where overhanging eaves left only a slit of sky to pierce the sinister depths, all races were congregated, Spanish, Italian, Berber, Nubian, Greek and Arab, eating, sleeping, loving, thieving and brawling together. The uneven cobbled alleys were slimy with filth; rats fattened on the refuse; entrails glowed red on the butchers' stalls, beside the bouquets of carnations or jasmine with which the Arabs love to surround themselves. Sometimes, behind a tattered calico curtain, a blue tiled courtyard could be glimpsed, with a fig tree, or a fountain, and a group of Negro slaves fanning a charcoal brazier. The old bawds squatted in their doorways shouting their wares, and sometimes the sound of a flute, or a sudden scream, echoed across the flat roofs where the women gathered at sunset. The sinister reputation of the Kasbah had grown with the centuries. Even the pirates trod warily, there.

We have no record of Aimée's emotions, as she was led, a captive, through these mazes, up and up, to the palace of the Dey, an inner fortress, set deep in the Kasbah, more protected there than the original Governor's palace, the Djanina, in the lower part of the town. At this moment, Algiers was commanded by Baba Mohammed Ben Osman, a foxy septuagenarian, and worthy successor to Barbarossa the Terrible, who first captured Algiers for the Turks, and now dead two hundred years or more, lying in a splendid tomb beside the Bosphorus. Baba Mohammed, too, was the terror of the Mediterranean. As master of the Barbary pirates, he defended his men and ships against all comers—his raiding expeditions went unrevenged, and although all Europe set a price on his head, he continued to taunt the world from his Algerian stronghold. Only that year, he had defeated a force of three hundred Spanish men-o'-war with his handful of ships. The old tiger was adored by his men, and their finest plunder was always brought first to him.

Thus it happened that when the Corsairs boarded the Spanish ship where Aimée and her *da* were standing on deck, their captain, realizing her beauty, set her apart as prize booty, to be reserved for Baba Mohammed. Slave trading flourished all along the African coast, there was a constant stream of ebony flesh being shipped to Turkey alone. Those unfortunate boys designed to supply the demand for Eunuch guards were a trade in themselves. So few survived the operation, from which they were left to recover, or die, plunged up to their waists in the burning sands. White Eunuchs, mostly recruited from eastern Europe, were also in steady demand, white female slaves, especially the beautiful Circassian or Spanish women, fetched high prices. If the pirates could come by the comparative rarity of a blond young European, they earned their chief's particular approval. Aimée was a splendid haul. Useless for her distracted *da* to plead and curse. The captain merely locked Aimée in his cabin and ordered that she be treated with respect. What happened to the rest of the ladies on board, we do not know. Nor do we know the fate of the *da*. Was she allowed to accompany her young mistress, was she sent packing (in view of the tale she could tell, it is unlikely she was returned to Europe), or did she simply vanish into the shadows of the Kasbah? We have no records, but it seems that when Baba Mohammed Ben Osman saw Aimée, he at once realized she would be a rare and worthy offering to the Sultan himself; a really sumptuous present, reflecting a lasting luster on the giver. He ordered that she be kept apart, inviolate, and heavily guarded. Aimée was not consulted, of course, but by now she can have had no doubts as to the workings of Destiny. The pirates fitted out a splendid ship, a vessel of state, worthy of future favorite of the Sultan, and presently, adorned in the most lavish Oriental style, and heavily veiled, Aimée set sail for Constantinople.

She was now committed irrevocably to her fate. Another voyage began, and she sailed away from all she had ever known, from last echoes of France, or Martinique. Now there were no handkerchiefs waving fond farewell; no pious prayers, no soft voices singing . . . *Adieu madras, adieu foulards* . . . henceforth she was to be quite alone . . . as she remained, ghostly and apart. But sometimes it seems as if the ghost beckons, or signals to us from the obscurity of history. The signs take many strange forms: the fantastic balloons of Montgolfier floating over the minarets of Santa Sophia; Prince Selim's letter of friendship to King Louis XVI; the introduction of a system of quarantine; even an expression in the eyes of her son the Sultan Mahmoud, The Reformer, when he greeted a Western European . . . an expression which was to culminate, one day, in the massacre of twenty-six thousand Janissaries, the arch enemies of all that progress along Western lines which she craved, and for which she worked; as well as being the embodiment of the cruel and tyrannous system of which she, the captured, enslaved French girl was a victim. Of all the signals so long ignored by the outside world, the most unmistakable is the sudden, inexplicable manner in which the Sultan Mahmoud II was to turn against Napoleon, turning the tide of history, to bring about his downfall. This can perhaps be attributed to a purely personal motive, one of family revenge: the loyalty of one little French girl from Martinque defending another—her cousin Joséphine—whom Napoleon by his divorce was to repudiate so ruthlessly.

The Corsairs' ship skirted the last of Africa. The ruins of Carthage and the little white huddle of Sidi Bou Säid were visible in a line of red earth that was Tunis. Far away, inland, rose the lovely blue silhouette of the Bou Kornëin, and behind it, faintly, the phantom of another peak, Djebel Ressas. . . . Africa faded.

The voyage was long; it seemed an eternal moment, becalmed between past and future. Sicily, Greece, the Aegean islands, the Syrian coast, and then, one day, the forlorn wastes of the Dardanelles, widening at last to the milky blueness of the Marmora, dotted with frisking dolphins and little islands. As they drew near to Constantinople, there were busy lanes of shipping, galleys and *mahouns,* and gilded caïques, all converging on the Porte. The ship rounded the point, and Stamboul rose before them, its thousand domes and minarets lit by the westering sun. It was the capital of the Ottoman Empire, home of the Caliph of the Faithful, Padishar of the Barbary States, Shadow of the Prophet upon Earth, the Sultan Abd ül Hamid I—Aimée's fate.

As they anchored, and all the tumult of the harbor rose from below, Aimée could see the great mass of the Seraglio, the Royal Palace, set on its promentory between Asia and Europe, lapped by the waters of the Bosphorus and the Golden Horn. This fabulous conglomeration of palaces and kiosks, stables, kitchens, barracks, prisons, torture chambers, pleasure gardens and mosques was capable of housing twenty thousand souls. The cypresses rose black and chill beside its battlemented walls—it was at once menacing and fabulous—like nothing else. And so Aimée came at last to the Gate of Felicity, and being received by the Chief Eunuch, fainted away.

When Aimée Dubucq de Rivery came to herself she was in the heart of the Harem, one of the hundreds of odalisques who entered it like convent novices to acquire a new name, a new personality, and to live there, according to rule, immured, for the rest of their lives. To Aimée, it must have seemed almost as if her school days at Nantes were all to do again. The same strict surveillance, the same crowds of girls, giggling, childish and silly, with their petty feuds, secrets and gushing friendships. Their ages ranged from twelve upwards; none of them spoke French, and Aimée could not understand a word they said to her. They might have been mocking her, tormenting her, proffering friendship or criticism. There was only the tone of the voice to go by: but jealousy is unmistakable. Such a striking newcomer must inevitably find it a hard school.

If the girls seemed much the same as those at Nantes, everything else was wildly different. The food was neither plain nor wholesome. As to the hours spent lolling in Turkish baths, naked and sleek, ladling perfumed water over each other, twisting pearls and peacock feathers in their long hair, nibbling sugary comfits, gossiping, idling away the hours, becalmed in the dreamy, steamy limbo-land, nothing could have been a more violent contrast. Aimée recalled the convent's views on baths; dangerous reminders of the flesh, and only to be permitted if the body was shrouded in a voluminous calico robe. Yes; it was very different in the Seraglio. Slowly, she began to accustom herself to her new life and its strange mixture of luxury and restraint, etiquette, ritual and abandon.

The Seraglio has always represented mystery in its most absolute form, and remained, through the centuries, an impenetrable legend. Few outsiders ever crossed its threshold, or were privileged to penetrate further than the Second Courtyard. On rare occasions an Envoy Extraordinary would be granted audience, and has left accounts of as much as he was able to see around him; but for the most part, until the fall of the Osmanli dynasty in 1909, the inner life of the Seraglio was almost unknown. Few who had entered ever escaped, or lived to tell of their experiences. The Turkish passion for concealment amounted to a fetish —their homes, their women, and their monarch, all were shrouded, not only from the foreigner, but from each other, too. When the Sultan rode abroad in his capital he was surrounded by guards who carried large banners, pearl-fringed umbrellas, and even wore helmets topped by forests of waving ostrich plumes, the better to screen their master from curious eyes. Those persons granted an audience found it quite an ordeal (though in no degree approaching the severity imposed by one Byzantine Emperor who used to put out the eyes of visiting emissaries, as a precaution against prying). The foreign visitors were first submitted to a ritual bath, and then, being clothed in magnificent robes, they were lifted bodily into the presence of Allah's Vice Regent, supported on each side by high court dignitaries, lest, it was supposed, the overwhelming honor should paralyze them. After which introductory flourish, they were seldom vouchsafed more than one jeweled finger, extended for salutation through the drawn curtains of the throne. This was like a gigantic four-poster bed, its framework silver-gilt, and encrusted with a blinding array of precious stones, slabs of emerald, rubies the size of farmhouse eggs, its brocaded hangings stiff with pearls and bullion.

The Seraglio is variously referred to as the Sarail, Le Grand Serai, the Serayi or the Harem, though this latter is incorrect, to describe the whole palace, since it applies only to the women's quarters, the core, within the whole. The word "Harem" derives from the Arabic *haram*, forbidden, unlawful. A certain area of land centered round the Holy Cities of Mecca and Medina were considered as set apart, inviolate, and so described as *haram*. The word came to be applied, in its secular sense, to the women's quarters of a Moslem household—it was their *haram*, or sanctuary, territory apart, inviolate to all but the master of the household. The Selamlik, or men's quarters, derived from the word *selam*, a greeting, the Selamlik being the one part of the house where it is permitted to receive visitors.

Although the Seraglio has always remained shrouded in an aura of mystery, there have been, through the centuries, a few eyewitness accounts. In the fifteenth and sixteenth century those foreigners admitted were mostly physicians or craftsmen. The Italian doctor, Domenico Hierosolimitano, has left a detailed account of his visit during the reign of Murad III; and an Englishman, Thomas Dallam, went there in 1599 to install an organ specially commanded by the Sultan. He did not see very much: "At everie gate of the surralia there always sittethe a stoute Turke . . . the gathes ar faste shut, for thare pasethe none in or oute at their owne pleasures. . . ." He speaks of the pavilion where he was ordered to set up the organ as being "no dwellinge house, but a house of pleasure, and lykewyse a house of slaughter; for in that house . . . the emperor that rained when I was there had nynteene brothers put to deathe in it and it was bulte for no other use but for the stranglings of everie emperors bretherin." Perhaps he had seen enough.

In the early eighteenth century, a daring French traveler, Aubry de La Motraye, succeeded in persuading a Swiss clockmaker of Galata to take him as assistant when he went to repair some pendulums in the Seraglio. La Motraye prudently donned Turkish clothing, and tried to note all that he saw, as a black Eunuch hurried them from one time-piece to the next, through perspectives of overwhelming grandeur. They visited part of the Harem, though the women were absent, and La Motraye closes his observations on a censorious note. *"In comparing the Chambers of the Grand Seigniors Women to the Cells of Nuns, we must except the Richness of the Furniture, as well as the Use they are put to; the Difference of which is easy enough to be imagin'd without Explication."*

In the heart of the Seraglio was the Harem and the Selamlik. Between the two, dominating both, and focal point of all, where the apartments of the Sultan Valideh: the Veiled Crown, or mother of the Sultan, who, next the Sultan, occupied a supreme position. The layers of walls and courtyards encircling the center were a warren of subterranean passages leading to prisons or treasure vaults; or stairways giving on to unexpected terraces and pavilions set in tulip gardens, with distant vistas of the Bosphorus and the mosques of Scutari, on the far Asiatic shore. There was the Corridor of the Bath, or Hamam, the pivot-point of daily life; the Golden Path, down which the chosen odalisque was led to the Sultan's bed; the aviaries and libraries, laundries and hospitals; the kitchens occupied almost the whole of the southeastern side of the enclosure. There were great ice pits, too, where snow, wrapped in flannel, was brought on muleback some seventy miles from Mount Olympus, was stored for the making of sherbets and other cooling delicacies.

There was the Confectioner's Mosque, the Black Eunuchs' quarters and those of the White Eunuchs, too. The slaves' lodgings, the guard-houses of the six hundred Janissaries, with their line of "kettle drums" ever muttering threats. There was the Divan, or Council Chamber, the Pavilion of the Holy Mantle, dormitories of the dwarfs, mutes and buffoons, as well as the place of execution and the Chief Eunuch's suite. There were, too, such necessary adjuncts to Moslem life as the Hall of

Circumcision, the Place of Consultation of the Djinns, and the Kefess, or Cage (which was described by Thomas Dallam), where the heir to the throne was immured until his accession or slaughter by rival claimants. Added to all this there were such personages as the Keeper of the Pedigree of the Prophets' Descendants; the Chief Turban-Winder, Nightingale Keeper, and Tent-Pitcher, and myriads of gardeners, pages, waiting-women, grooms, scribes, apothecaries, astronomers and messengers, besides.

Over all, ranking with the Grand Vizier, ruled the Chief Black Eunuch, the Kizlar Agha. His power was absolute. Aimée soon realized that he was the most important person in this new world around her. He alone had the right to speak directly to the Sultan. He was at once Comptroller of the Household, Master of Ceremonies and the Sultan's confidant. He was in supreme control of the Harem and the odalisques, and in consequence ranked higher than the Chief White Eunuch, the Kapi Agha, who controlled the Selamlik. Between the two Chiefs lay centuries of rivalry: the corruption of the White Eunuchs had gradually led to a decline in their authority and the concentration of power being invested in the Black Eunuchs. Like most of the Seraglio's personnel, both black and white Eunuchs were imported from afar. It was held that coming to the palace as children, knowing no country, no master other than the Grand Turk, they would be more likely to be loyal, less swayed by internal politics and the intrigues which exercised so galvanic an effect on the otherwise supine Turks.

At the time of Aimée's arrival, the Kizlar Agha represented a moderate and humane influence within the Seraglio. He was not to be bought, and the Sultan was known to like and respect him. Therefore, when she remembered that he had been waiting at the Gate of Felicity to receive her, she knew it was proof of the prestige she enjoyed, as an offering from the Dey of Algiers. Perhaps the attitude of the other odalisques, or the deference of the Eunuchs who guarded them, had already made her sense she was set apart. It was then, in all probability, that she first began to regain her courage, and try to calculate, with shrewd French common sense, just how much she could rely on the Kizlar Agha's support, steering her solitary way. She may have hoped, wildly, innocently, that he would take pity on her awful fate. We imagine her, the calm, reserved French girl, flung down among the cushions, her long golden hair falling in confusion around her tear-stained face, sobbing tears of rage and misery . . . and then, raising those large blue eyes which were to prove so compelling, to fix them, thoughtfully, on the majestic figure of the Kizlar Agha, who had come to pay his daily visit to his protégée, the Dey's offering. Perhaps she thought that through him she might be able to send a letter to her uncle at Nantes; and then he would hasten to Versailles, to the all-powerful King Louis, who would personally appeal to the Sultan for her release. . . . But perhaps there were also a few appraising glances at the opulent setting in which she found herself. To her thrifty French mind, especially after those eight convent years, the Seraglio must have been dazzling, calling Euphemia David's mumbling prophecies to mind again, sharply. *You will live in a great and splendid palace where you will reign supreme. . . .*

There is no doubt that the Kizlar Agha, too, was eyeing her speculatively. Like Baba Mohammed Ben Osman, he was aware of her exceptional quality; here was a young woman who had grown to maturity in the outside world, who could offer perspectives of which they were ignorant; who breathed the air of liberty which was in itself a new and heady perfume not only in the Seraglio but to all Turkey, too. By which it will be seen that the Chief Eunuch was of a progressive nature.

In the inner factions which revolved around the throne with the slow, ritualistic cunning of a chessboard, moves and countermoves of life, death, the Kizlar Agha was allied to a small group of liberally minded statesmen and courtiers headed by the Mufti Vely-Zadé, and a beautiful Circassian Kadine, once the favorite of the late Sultan Mustapha III, the father of her son Selim, now heir apparent. Turkish succession did not go direct from father to son, but went by age, the eldest surviving Osmanli always succeeding. This explains the holocausts by which ambitious mothers of younger sons would murder any elder claimants standing between their sons and the throne. Selim's life was in constant danger from the jealousy of other Kadine, the reigning Sultan Abd ül Hamid's favorite. She was a cruel and treacherous woman in the scheming manner of the Seraglio, where violence as much as *volupté* was the tradition. It was her son Mustapha, Abd ül Hamid's sole surviving child, who would succeed, were Selim removed. Not only did Mustapha's mother covet the throne for her son, but even more she coveted the position which would then be hers, one of supreme power, as Sultan Valideh, the Sultan's mother, or crown of the Veiled Heads, or all Moslem women, throughout the Empire.

The history of the Ottoman Empire is a long testimony to the power wielded by women—by the Harem. This Oriental state, where women are generally believed to have no place or status and to be submissive playthings, to be petted or abandoned at will, was, in fact, governed for centuries at a time by the secret influence of the Harem, and the intrigues which originated in the kiosks and alcoves of the Seraglio. Capricious, cruel and cunning, ruthless and ambitious . . . such were many of the Kadines who enslaved their Lord and Master, and virtually ruled the country. Women such as Roxelana, the unscrupulous Russian, who in Turkey was known as Khurrem, the Joyous, and whose influence was such that she persuaded Suleiman the Magnificent to murder his eldest son, thus clearing the way for her own child. For the most part these scheming voluptuaries contented themselves with internal policies, material acquisitions and the advancement of their protégés: above all, the accession of their sons. Foreign policy was of less consequence to them.

But now, since the middle of the eighteenth century, there had been a more progressive group within the Seraglio who were beginning to be conscious of a world outside its walls and of horizons of thought and progress which must come from the West, and which it was folly to ignore. Such were the views of this inner, liberal group headed by the Kizlar Agha and the Circassian Kadine; and as such they were opposed violently by the Janissary Corps who feared their own powers might be wrested from them. This Corps centered round the heir apparent, Mustapha, who could be their puppet were he to reign in Selim's place. Together, the Janissaries and Mustapha's mother were of a mind. Nothing must be allowed to stand in the way of Mustapha's accession.

The Janissaries were an age-old institution: this dread body, a sort of Praetorian guard, had come to represent all that was most reactionary and corrupt. They were recruited from the numbers of Christian children levied from the provinces, who were forcibly removed, and converted to the Moslem faith. They underwent a rigorous military training, but always enjoyed certain privileges. Some of them became the Sultan's picked troops, but for the most part they were mercenaries, and moved from one battle zone to the next. They were expected to live austere lives, the better to harden them. Celibacy was the rule. They were also forbidden to wear the beards that were almost universally worn by the Turks. Instead, they cultivated long mustachios, hanging to their waists, which, it was held, increased the ferocity of their appearance.

Their dress was curious; the color of their boots, red, yellow or black, proclaimed their rank, as did certain enormous paradise plumes, falling from their turbans in an arc, nearly to their knees. Their titles all derived from the kitchen—the Chief was called the Chorbaji-Bashi, or Head Soup-Distributor; next came the Head Cook, and so on. Their standard displayed a vast caldron, or kettle. In time, these kettles came to have a special signficance, and were used by the corps as a symbol of revolt. When the Janissaries were in camp, their kettles were piled before the tent doors in the manner of regimental drums. And in the same manner, beating upon them furiously was a call to battle or revolt. Each week, their rations were fetched from the Seraglio kitchens in these kettles. If they were dissatisfied, they would reverse the kettles and begin drumming on them ominously with the long ladlelike spoons each man wore fixed into his cap. So terrible were their uprisings that the whole Seraglio, the Sultan, too, would listen for the dreaded sound. Some Sultans stayed to argue, others acted swiftly. Ringleaders were seized and executed on the spot, the decapitated heads piled up in a huge silver dish, for all to take warning. But as time went on, the Janissaries became more puissant, the Sultans less decisive: at least six Sultans were dethroned or slaughtered by their orders. This decay in loyalty is supposed to have originated with the decline in successive Sultans' military prowess. When they were a picked guard, campaigning with their Padishah, a fine military morale prevailed—but as the Sultans waxed fat, never venturing beyond their harem, so the Janissaries began to abuse their power, grew lax in turn, and thrived on corruption and intrigue. They looted the city, terrorized its citizens, extorted money, sold preferment to their favorites and opposed all progressive measures on principle. In the beginning of the nineteenth century there were around one hundred thousand of them. They were often to be seen issuing forth on plundering forays in the bazaars. They thought nothing of trying out a new scimitar blade on a passing infidel, and brooked no discipline, or remonstrances on the part of either the Grand Vizier or the Sultan himself.

While the Janissaries muttered, their kettle drums sounding ominously, it was obvious to the Chief Eunuch that they were only biding their time, before rising, to dethrone Abd ül Hamid and install Mustapha. On that day his head would no longer be safe: a reign of terror and reaction would set in. But he was not altogether without hope: he thought he saw a new way to outmaneuver his enemies; and so, hurried off to the apartments of his friend the Circassian Kadine, to recount his impressions of the new French slave, and to air his theories as to how best she could be used to their advantages. This Circassian woman was the daughter of a Christian priest in Georgia. She had been abducted into the Seraglio as a child, and was a woman of brilliant intellect, and kindness, too. All her force was directed towards saving her son Selim from his enemies, and, while avoiding the terroristic methods adopted by so many other Seraglio mothers, yet see him placed upon the Osmanli throne. She listened to the Kizlar Agha attentively. Yes, she agreed: this new French odalisque, *Giaour* or no, might be used to their advantage. Gaining the Sultan's favor, she might well become the decisive factor in their game. Was she really so lovely? Yes . . .? It might work out very well, then. . . . We can imagine them, the Chief Eunuch, *Son Altesse Noir,* his gigantic sugarloaf turban nodding, as both of them puffed contentedly at their jeweled *techibouks,* while the hanging lamps cast a swaying shadow on the cushioned alcove where they sat, two old friends, planning the next move in the eternal game of life and death.

At the moment when Aimée was first pitched into this sinister game, a pawn who was to become a Queen, there was no Sultan Valideh, for the Sultan Abd ül Hamid's mother was long dead. Mustapha's mother, the favorite Kadine, retained her rank and influence, not so much by her charms as by the lassitude of the Sultan. All these things Aimée was only learning by degrees; from someone who had a smattering of French to answer her questions, perhaps, or as she began to pick up some Turkish, herself. The Sultan's four wives, or Kadines, were always known by their distinct titles, taking precedence accordingly. The Bach-kadine, or first wife, the Skindji-kadine, or second wife, the Artanie-kadine, or middle-kadine, and the Kutchuk-kadine, or little-Kadine. It was this latter title which Aimée was to assume, on the birth of her son. But at first, although singled out for the Royal alcove, she merely ranked as one of the novices. First, she must be put through the school for odalisques, to perfect her in every seductive art her Royal Master's jaded palate might demand. There was so much to learn; to accept; and as she bagan to look about her with that shrewd French eye, intensely practical for all its languorous blue depths, it must have been clear to her that the heir apparent, the young prince Selim, was worth cultivating. The Sultan Abd ül Hamid was her master —the present. But Selim was the future. He was said to be gentle, and good; perhaps he could be persuaded to help her smuggle out a letter? The thought must have given her renewed courage, fresh hope in her solitary battle.

The first months which Aimée spent in the Harem must have been a shattering experience: her whole way of life, even her name was changed. The women were known by descriptive titles—the Lily, Moon-Face, Nightingale, and such, and it is a tribute to Aimée's loveliness that in this paradise of houris she became *Naksh*—The Beautiful One.

The Seraglio has been described as a kind of huge monastery whose religion was pleasure and whose God the Sultan: but although this might apply to the Seraglio as a whole, it is by no means applicable to the Harem, where a disciplinary tone prevailed. There are those who imagine it to have been a temple of unbridled license, one long riot of indulgence conducted on the lines of Scheherazade's revels as presented by the *Ballets Russes,* where unleashed slaves bound from one inviting bosom to the next. But however licentious or indulgent the principle, in practice the Harem was maintained on lines of the strictest formality.

It was a hierarchy, with its own protocol and etiquette. Some of the inmates never saw the Sultan, and spent their whole lives inventing ways of passing the time . . . consoling themselves with useful works, bookkeeping, jam making, overeating, other people's babies, or distractions of a Lesbian nature. Once incorporated, they could never leave; those few who were discovered to have been unfaithful were executed, or dumped in the Bosphorus in weighted sacks. The Sultan Ibrahim, being of a particularly self-indulgent nature, once dispatched his whole harem, three hundred strong, for the pleasure of being able to restock it with refreshing newcomers. A diver off Seraglio Point came up with tales of dead bodies all standing upright, weighted by their feet, swaying and bowing in the underwater swell with a sort of ghastly *politesse*.

The odalisques were bored, and disillusioned, too, perhaps, by the rigidity of life beside the legends that had lured them there. All of them lived for the moment when, perhaps, they would attract the Padishah's eye, and then . . . Some of them contrived to establish a sort of relationship with the Eunuchs, for it was well known that not all the mutilations were effective, although the Seraglio doctors were ever-watchful on this score. For the most part, the Eunuchs were, as may be imagined, a resentful lot, full of malice and envy, lashing out with their hippopotamus-hide whips. The women took a delight in tormenting them. They were known ironically as "Keeper of the Rose," or "Guardian of Delights." Occasionally it happened that a Eunuch loved and was loved by an odalisque. The Harem is reported to have admitted, on occasion, the "marriage" of Eunuchs; in which case the Eunuch was generally appointed to another palace, further down the Bosphorus, or at Broussa, or Adrianople.

All this regiment of ungratified creatures existed for the sole pleasure of the Grand Turk. He had absolute power over them, in life, in death. Sometimes it happened that a Sultan preferred boys; many of the White Eunuchs, when young, were beautiful creatures, we are told, slim and smooth, their faces lavishly painted, their rich costumes smothered in attar of roses. Sometimes the Sultan would pass on one of his odalisques to a minister he wished to favor, or perhaps liquidate. No man could refuse, even if he suspected it to be his death warrant. This was one of the accepted techniques by which the Seraglio disposed of their enemies. The favorite would install herself in her husband's house and proceed to spy on the outside world, reporting back to the Seraglio. Or else, she would proceed to remove her husband, in her own way. Her task accomplished, she was reintegrated into the Royal household and rewarded for her services. In the argot of the Seraglio, this was known as "earning a passport."

The hierarchy of the Harem was founded on the law that there could be no liaison between a Sultan and his subjects. The Harem was therefore always recruited from outside—from Circassia, Georgia, Syria, Roumania, with an occasional Italian or Spaniard to vary the menu. Thus the succeeding Sultans were always the sons of slave-mothers, and only half Turkish, themselves. Agents from the Porte scoured eastern Europe and the Levant for recruits—Circassians ranked first, on account of their beauty. Dramatic stories of the kidnaping of young children are not to be altogether believed, for large numbers of girls grew up with the fixed intention of entering a Turkish harem—if not the Seraglio itself—much as, fifty years ago, country girls decided on domestic service in the big cities. (And, strangely, there were also numbers of voluntary Eunuchs, both black and white). The odalisques were usually well treated, as one of the family; and if they were chosen for the Seraglio, there was always the glittering possibility of Royal favors. Even without, it promised a life of luxury, which many girls preferred to the hard toil of a peasant's lot. There was never any question of dishonor—a moral Mason-Dixon Line might be said to have divided Europe over the question of white slavery. The Sultan's concubines, so shocking, so pitiable to the West, were congratulated and envied by the East. Aimée, being groomed and schooled for the Sultan's favors, found that she had to change her viewpoint considerably. Useless, now, to cast backward glances to Martinique, or Nantes, or to view the intricacies of Seraglio living through European, let alone convent, eyes. Useless to cling to the notion that she was a sacrificial lamb, being decked for the slaughter, when it was obvious that everyone around her, from the Wardrobe Mistress to the Chief Eunuch, felt she was singled out for glory.

Like all the other slaves, Aimeé must pass through the *Academie de l'Amour,* or school for odalisques, where they were instructed in the finer shades of pleasing. The young candidates for the Imperial alcove had to pass an examining board, usually presided over by the Sultan Valideh (who, as mothers, were nothing if not thorough). Nothing was left to chance. It was really a very sensible arrangement, and saved the Sultan many a disappointment. When the newcomer was pronounced perfect, she passed into the ranks of ladies-in-waiting. . . . Around her would be at least two or three hundred more, all lovely, all voluptuous, jealous, bored; all specialists in those arts they could so seldom practice; all waiting for their chance to prove themselves.

In general, this came when the Sultan paid a state visit to his Harem. It was announced by the Eunuchs, who rang a big golden bell. Then followed a feverish rush for the grandest toilettes, the most brilliant *maquillage.* The Chief Treasurer of the Harem, together with the Sultan Valideh, received the Sultan in state, at the entrance to the Harem, and conducted him, with the Chief Eunuch, to the reception, held either in the apartments of the Sultan Valideh or those of the reigning favorite. A Eunuch walked before, magnificently dressed, chanting in a nasal voice: "Behold our Sovereign, Emperor of the True Believers, Shadow of Allah upon Earth, The Prophet's Successor, The Master of Masters, Chosen among the Chosen, our Padishah, our Sultan! Long live our Sultan! Let us admire Him who is the glory of the house of Osman!"

The Sultan would then pass between the breathless ranks of beauty, each slave holding herself in the prescribed Court pose, head thrown back, hands crossed on the breast. The reception room would be crowded with the more favored members of the hierarchy, past favorites, the family, daughters, or Sultanas, the Kadines, or wives by whom the Sultan had children, the Ikbals, those who had already enjoyed the Royal attentions, and the Guzdehs, "those who had caught the eye," odalisques who had already been remarked, but not yet been tried. The Sultan then knelt before his mother, who raised him, and signified that the long ceremony of obeisance might begin. When all the rituals were at last over, the Sultan took his place on the divan, flanked by the Chief Eunuch and the Treasurer. The Sultan Valideh sat on an opposite divan. To this rigid setting, the young odalisques were now admitted. The Sultan would eye them speculatively. Such ceremony, such protocol, especially when under maternal supervision, must have been dampening to spontaneous desires. But perhaps it was an artificial barrier, cunningly contrived, to stimulate a jaded palate. While the youngest slaves, little newcomers of eight or ten years old, skipped about with silver trays of coffee, or sweetmeats, the older ones gathered round the Sultan; perhaps not quite "the rosebud garden of girls" which Tennyson had in mind, but still, a flowerbed of lovely faces, all turned towards him as to the sun. Hundreds of charmers, each yearning for a chance to charm! All of them twittering round in fevered efforts to catch the Royal eye. O! happiest of men! No competition! No rebuffs! All of them hanging on his word, applauding his every quip . . . while in the background, the professional laughers tinkled with discreet but festive gaiety, the caged nightingales outvied each other, the perfumed breezes (reinforced by incense burners) wafted through the pavilions, and over all, unseen, but powerful, brooded the reassuring presence of the Court Abortionist.

Sometimes a Sultan would take a malicious pleasure in ending the revels abruptly by stalking out in dudgeon. In which case there were reproaches and nerve-storms, tears, dramas, and extra doses of opium all round. (Opium, it must be remembered, was the aspirin of the East.)

But if the Grand Turk singled out a charmer, he would ask the Valideh Sultan her name, and the odalisque would be then authorized to approach the dais, and kiss the cushion of his Majesty's divan. This was an official consecration—now she became a Guzdeh, and from that moment set apart from the rest, installed in a special apartment, where, pampered, polished and perfected, she waited the summons to the Imperial alcove, while all around, her rivals strove to spoil her chances by any mischief they could devise.

Nor must it be supposed that formality and protocol ceased at the doors of the Royal alcove. When the Sultan received a favorite, the date and duration of the nuptials were meticulously entered in a special register. If, nine months later, a child was born, it was attributed to the Sultan, and the fortunate Ikbal passed into the ranks of the Kadines, with all the privileges attached: a larger establishment, more slaves, jewels and money. Those Kadines who had sons were at once placed in the highest rank of the hierarchy; all of them lived in the hope of seeing their son as Sultan, themselves as Sultan Valideh. Those who had daughters were also ranked as Kadines, but without any special privileges. Throughout the Moslem world, daughters were always at a discount.

That the Seraglio was not overflowing with children was due not only to violent methods of liquidating any possible claimants to the throne, but also to the strict surveillance of the calfas, old slaves who watched over the girls minutely, and at the first signs of pregnancy informed the Court Abortionist, who was empowered to exercise her calling at once. For a slave to become a mother, it was necessary that the Sultan be so enraptured with her charms that he prove his fondness by thus permitting her to acquire Kadine's rank. Occasionally, a determined Ikbal, aided by her companions, succeeded in disguising her condition until the accouchement, in which case the child became the adored and petted plaything of all the other thwarted odalisques, or was strangled, drowned or otherwise removed.

Sometimes the Sultans themselves, surfeited by plenty, and the tedium of etiquette attendant on selecting a new favorite, preferred to live austerely; or, fearing for their lives, would not risk an unknown newcomer who might be the instrument of vengeance; whose very kiss might be poisoned. Sultan Selim III (who was a gentle young prince at the time of Aimée's arrival) was so horror-struck by the fate awaiting so many infant and possible claimants to the throne, that, we are told by Lady Craven (who was then visiting the capital), "as soon as he knew the horrid custom of strangling every infant which is born in the Seraglio not the child of the reigning Sultan, he declared he would never be the cause of a human creature's death, and has constantly avoided any opportunities of becoming a father." This attitude must have seemed to undermine the very foundations of the Harem.

Like all the visitors to Constantinople, Lady Craven was eager for every scrap of information regarding the Seraglio. She was staying with the French Ambassador, in 1785, and from his windows at Galata, used to follow the ceremonial comings and goings on Seraglio Point, across the Golden Horn, by means of the Ambassador's telescope. *"Yesterday I saw the Sultan (Abd ül Hamid) sitting on a silver sofa, while his boats and many of the people who were to accompany him were lining the banks of the garden. We had a large telescope and saw the Ottoman splendors very distinctly. The Sultan dyes his beard black to give himself a young look; he is known at a considerable distance by that, which contrasts singularly with his face, that is extremely livid and pale."*

Lady Craven was an insatiable traveler and gossip. She had driven the length of Europe to Moscow, and from there to Turkey by way of the Crimea, staying, en route, with the governors or princes of each province. She noted everything with lively interest, in a series of letters to the Margrave of Brandenburg and Anspach, whom later she was to marry. The letters were published in book form in 1787. From them we have a vivid picture of Constantinople at its last truly magnificent moment. She describes a rambling city, an extraordinary jumble of marble and wood: of luxury and waste lands where gypsies and beggars camped in the shadow of the glorious Suleimanyé Mosque, much as they do today. She conveys something of its sinistry too: for it must not be imagined that Constantinople basked in the refulgent gaiety of sun and song; there was nothing Mediterranean about this city, at once fierce, voluptuous and squalid; a dramatic atmosphere peculiarly its own; like nothing else.

It has been said that the history of Constantinople is a costume drama, and it is certain that with the decline of the ceremonial and specialized clothing which was reserved for each rank and each occasion, much of the city's splendor and unique interest vanished. Alas! It was Aimée's westernizing influence upon her son that may be said to have brought about many of these lesser, sartorial reforms. Today's cloth cap is a poor substitute for yesterday's fez, which, in its turn, is a miserable object, beside the towering turban (in Turkish *dulbend,* from which "tulip" derives, the flower being fancifully likened to a turban). Its various forms, height and color, like the width of a fur edging, or the length of a train, were all Imperial edicts—law. Admirals wore scarlet and gold; the Tressed Halberdiers were so named because of two locks of false hair falling from their helmets, on each side of their face (its purpose being, originally, to prevent the wearer's casting glances at the odalisques whom they might encounter during their duties of stacking firewood in the Harem). Furs, too, had a hieratical significance. While the Janissaries wore splendid robes trimmed with lynx, sable was reserved for the Master of the Stirrup. Many costumes were copied *in toto* from the conquered Byzantine Court. Splendor was the prevailing note throughout the Seraglio. Even as late as the last days of the Sultanate, in 1909, we are told of solid silver dustpans, and real diamond buttons sewed onto the modern kid boots imported from Paris to assuage the Harem's craving for Western chic.

When Aimée Dubucq de Rivery entered the Seraglio, its spendors were still unshadowed by restraint; indeed many of the subsequent reforms probably originated in her thrifty French brain, as we shall see. But in 1784, we read of umbrellas with gold ribs studded in sapphires, patterns for the bath inlaid with pearls, and hand towels stiff with gold embroidery. No favorite ever appeared before the Sultan in the same dress twice. The first visit was an occasion of unparalleled grandeur, and Aimée must have felt herself very fat from the convent, as they robed her in the innumerable gauze chemises, velvet and fur caftans, the vast pantaloons, or *chalvari*, and the three-trained overdress tradition demanded. There are no portraits of her, thus adorned, but there is one eyewitness description which has been preserved: she was remarked above the other three black-haired Kadines for the beauty of her coloring, her fair skin, and pale golden hair. It seems she was always dressed resplendently, *à la Turque*. On her head, and tilted to one side, she wore a tiny, flat pillbox cap, blazing with jewels. Her flowing hair fell to her waist, and was powdered with diamonds which trembled among the gold and seemed scattered carelessly, but were, in fact, cunningly attached by fine golden chains. Her hands and feet were hennaed, though she had little need of the paint so much a part of the other women's toilette, and an essential part of Turkish tradition.

But before Aimée had arrived at this point of acceptance, of total integration, there were some scenes unparalleled in the history of the Seraglio, where no woman ever questioned her lot, much less repulsed the Sultan's favor. When the Kizlar Agha announced to Aimée that she was singled out for the Royal alcove, and that he would conduct her, personally, along the Golden Road, she resisted with violence. Shrewd and ambitious as she was, and carefully as she had planned her line of conduct, it is likely that she had not envisaged this decisive moment with all its implications. She must have realized that there was no other way for her to obtain power; but it was the spontaneous reaction of a young convent-bred girl, terrified of her fate. Through her birth and

privilege in Martinique, she was proud, still unbroken in spirit. A Dubucq was not to be intimidated by the Turks. But this was a terrible
moment: a point of no return. Her outbreak was perhaps the reflex of a
slaveowner's daughter, now being led, herself, to the couch of a man she
must have regarded in the light of a savage. For all her strategies, the
outburst was uncontrollable: it was the last of all that remained of that
girlish, perhaps childish creature who could still recall so clearly, her
home, her family, and her old *da*.

The Kizlar Agha had never seen such a display of resistance. At all
costs he must avoid an uproar in the Harem; his Royal Master's appetite was whetted by descriptions of Baba Mohammed's French catch;
it would never do to disappoint him. Aimée's fury and independence
were such that the Kizlar Agha feared she might be not only unco-opera-
tive but downright dangerous. The more she stormed, the more the
other odalisques regarded her with astonishment . . . a crazy creature
. . . if only *they* could be in her place, summoned by the Sultan!
. . . The Chief Eunuch recalled some old story of a *tzigane* who had
bitten a Sultan to the bone. . . . Well might he shudder, imagining
the sort of tortures, culminating in the silken bowstring, that would be
his lot, were he to sponsor another such wildcat. He left Aimée storm-
ing and padded off to be soothed and advised by his old friend, the
Circassian Kadine. She listened sympathetically, and then, being a
woman of great tact, her wits sharpened even more by the atmosphere
danger which was now concentrated round her son, she thought she
saw a way to aid the Chief Eunuch, calm Aimée, and further her own
plans too. She sent for Aimée, and had the sense to speak frankly.
Again, we wonder, in what language these two women talked together?
Aimée cannot, at this stage, have acquired much Turkish; it seems
unlikely that the Circassian Kadine, who had entered the Harem at the
age of eight, had learned to speak French, or Italian, but perhaps she
had. Some of the women obtained all sorts of cultivated graces, studying astronomy, languages or even medicine; though it must be admitted
that they were usually the less successful members of the Seraglio,
those who had never succeeded in catching the Royal eye, and who
thus fell back on learning, in the long interval between their integration
and retirement to the Old Seraglio, a sort of almshouse, or old ladies'
home, down by the water on the Seraglio Point.

The Circassian woman played on the French girl's good sense, her
emotion, and her vanity. She impressed on her that all thoughts of escape were hopeless. It was for life: then why not accept the honors
offered to her? She could be the first—the favorite, and, perhaps, mother
of a son who would one day rule. (There was a striking precedent in
Saladin's mother, Berengeria, though it is unlikely that this was known

to either of them.) Then, reassuring Aimée as to the character of the Sultan, she spoke of the part Aimée could play influencing him towards the reforms Turkey needed so urgently. Lastly, she painted a fearful picture of the dangers to which she, her son, Selim, and all her adherents, the liberally minded, progressive group, were exposed by the enmity of the present favorite, Mustapha's reactionary mother. They looked to Aimée to protect them: the way led down the Golden Road.

Aimée was before else of a practical nature. Her innate common sense told her that the Circassian Kadine spoke the truth. There were no more rebellious outbreaks. Resigned to her fate, Aimée was to become, in time, its master. In triumph, the Chief Eunuch, *Son Altesse Noir,* conducted Mlle. Dubucq de Rivery to the Sultan Abd ül Hamid I.

The Sultan was no Terrible Turk, but a cultivated voluptuary, a patriarchal figure to whom the intrigues and violence of the Harem were abhorrent. Aimée seemed a creature apart; her blond beauty, her Western intellect, her Frankish background. . . . He was delighted with her. Very soon, as the Circassian Kadine had forseen, she had supplanted Mustapha's mother in his affections. *Naksh,* The Beautiful One, was formally installed as the new favorite.

One year later, on July 20, 1785, her son Mahmoud, was born. Thus Aimée Dubucq de Rivery found herself a key figure in the succession to the Ottoman throne, and the words of the old Euphemia David must have echoed in her ears again. . . . *You will be taken captive and placed in a Seraglio. There you will give birth to a son. This son will reign gloriously.* . . .

The whole Seraglio was illuminated to celebrate the birth of the Sultan's son. The aging Abd ül Hamid felt himself reborn. None of the other favorites were so enchanting; and none, except the shrewish woman who was Mustapha's mother, had given him a son. It is said that Mustapha and Mahmoud were the only fruits of all his five hundred wives. There seems to have been no question that the Sultan was as delighted with Aimée's child as with Aimée herself. There was no talk of strangling this newborn infant (except by Mustapha's mother, in secret longing). The Sultan ordered a magnificent fête. There were fireworks and wrestling matches, and a pavilion made entirely of spun sugar, decorated with palms, to symbolize the fertility of the union. Cages of nightingales (the bulbul of Oriental literature) were hung in the boxwood thickets. To crown the celebration there was a tulip festival, where decorative arrangements of the flowers were illuminated by colored lights, set between glass globes of colored water which reflected the lanterns and fountains. The Turks were particularly fond of such displays; they liked to set off the beauty of tulips or roses in illuminated booths, a sort of floral theater, where bird-song and the soft notes of a rebeck were a background to the aesthetic spectacle.

While the nightingales sang and the fountains plashed and the great showers of fireworks sparked across the night sky, Mustapha's mother probably skulked in her apartments. The new baby was next in succession to Selim, after her son Mustapha. She must see to it that both Selim and the baby were disposed of; it would simplify things. But Aimée, hanging over the ruby-studded cradle, must have felt complete confidence in her child's future. Euphemia David had predicted his glory—and so far, all she had foretold had come true.

At the time of Aimée's entrance into the Harem of the Sultan Abd ül Hamid, Selim, his nephew, was about the same age as Aimée. He had been brought up almost as a son by the Sultan, who, after spending forty-five years in the Prince's Cage himself, did not wish to impose this cruel incarceration upon his heir. Abd ül Hamid showed the greatest indulgence towards Selim, who had grown into a scholarly, sweet-tempered youth, passionately devoted to the ideals of his mother's liberal faction. He was in hourly danger from the assaults of Mustapha's mother, who had already succeeded in having him poisoned once, and awaited a second chance. Selim's life was only saved by the resourcefulness of his mother, who, anticipating such attacks, kept a skilled toxologist at hand, day and night. Although she had saved Selim by this promptitude, he was considerably enfeebled.

He was of that pallid delicacy seen in the Persian miniatures; one of those sighing Princes, whose vellum-toned features have a feminine cast, at odd variance with their blue-black beards, thick and trim as a yew hedge. Their long, almond eyes gaze sidelong in liquid pathos, and are emphasized by a thick sweep of painted brows, often meeting across. The Oriental manuscripts depict them, poetic and languid, riding their steeds across a barren landscape, locked in heroic but unconvincing combat with leopards or Asiatic hordes; or surrounded by courtiers, playing the lute, in fountain courts or tulip gardens. Lamartine tells us Selim's face was beautiful, his character gentle, his enthusiasm ardent; his mother had insisted that his education should befit him for his duties as Sultan. If he was to rule, it would be his strength; if he was doomed to remain vegetating in the eternal captivity of the Seraglio, then it would be his consolation. Turkish poets and philosophers surrounded his youth: as he grew older, greatly daring, he sometimes talked with an Italian doctor, Lorenzo, accredited to the Seraglio, and would interrogate him minutely on that strange faraway Western life outside the frontiers of Turkey. He was sensitive, shy and abstracted, seeming more suited to the mosque than the palace. We are told that he was faintly pitted with smallpox, very tall, and stooped slightly, from long years of study. Gossip substantiated Lady Craven's claims that he neglected his Harem and even declined to assume the responsibilities of parenthood, being so revolted by the Seraglio's general practice of strangling new-born infants. This, then, was the lonely, dreamy young prince who was to fall under Aimée Dubucq de Rivery's spell when she first appeared in the Seraglio so dazzlingly fair, so extraordinarily different to all the rest.

Aimée was now in the bloom of her northern beauty, which had nothing of the Creole exoticism so marked in her cousin Joséphine Bonaparte. Hers was the fresh silvery beauty of her Norman ancestry, so remarkable among the sultry inmates of the Seraglio. (And it must not be forgotten that she had also been through that celebrated school for odalisques where all the Oriental arts of seduction were taught.) It is therefore not surprising that as she gained in ascendancy over the Sultan Abd ül Hamid, so Mustapha's mother dropped from power, until she became a dispossessed malefic force, biding her time—that moment when her weakling son would succeed to the throne, and she would become Sultan Valideh. The Janissaries, confident of her future support, continued to center round her, a reactionary clot. But it was Aimée and her immediate circle who now had the Sultan's ear. Aimée was of the Seraglio—and yet, she always retained something of the West, quite unchanged by the ritual, costume and language she had adopted. However meltingly pink and white and gold she appeared, a steely steak remained. It was probably about this time that she first began to work at something which can be regarded as her most striking, most powerful message to the outside world of which she was born—the education of her son. The little Prince Mahmoud was a robust child, strangely independent, yet disciplined, compared to the fretful princelings who only struggled to maturity in spite of overpetting and indulgence or abortive attempts upon their lives. Aimée succeeded in imposing Western nursery restraints along with certain hygienic and dietetic measures unknown to the Seraglio. Beneath the great cypress trees that fringed the gardens, she could be seen, all summer long, playing with the child. . . . The loved, lost echoes of France sounded round her once more.

*Sur le Pont d'Avignon on y danse, on y danse . . .*
*Les beaux monsieurs font comme ça. . . .*

The little boy must have listened delightedly, watching his mother as she went through the pantomime of curtsies and courtly bows, hand on heart, toe pointed with a classic flourish. She could never return to

France, but she was slowly contriving, within the Ottoman Empire, a breach through which the Western air would one day pour.

She spoke French with Mahmoud in secret. As he grew older, she steeped him in the legends of France: in the high deeds of Charlemagne and le Vert Galant, no doubt, though she probably respected the Turkish tradition which forbade any mention of defeat at the hands of the Crusaders, so that Richard Coeur de Lion was not likely to have been a nursery hero. With his mother, the little Prince lisped the fables of La Fontaine, and entered into the enchanted kingdom of Perrault; but with the rest of the Seraglio, he enjoyed the antics of Nas-reddin, the Moslem Tyl Eulenspiegel, and all the bare-faced audacities of Karageuz, the Turkish *polichinelle.* His profound love of all things French or Western, an atavistic force, was to remain with him all his life. The formation of his character was Western: its restraints and purpose, its energy, overlaid the Orient. Behind all his most decisive actions we sense the French girl from Martinique. Her influence in the Seraglio, too, was extreme. It is even said that she succeeded in converting the Sultan Abd ül Hamid to Catholicism, though this does not seem probable to the present writer. On this point, as on so many others regarding Aimée Dubucq de Rivery, all is conjecture and reconstruction. But it is certain she was loved and respected, even by her rivals in the Harem (all save Mustapha's mother) and among the high dignitaries of the Porte, those few privileged ones who were familiar with the Seraglio, she was a respected, if veiled, figure.

Behind the outward semblance of a pampered Kadine we see that Aimée was, in fact, the inspiration and guiding force behind various significant political intrigues stretching far beyond the Seraglio's walls, or even Turkish frontiers. Behind the unprecedented letter which Selim, as heir apparent, wrote to Louis XVI, in 1786, we sense Aimée Dubucq de Rivery. It was the first of a long series of pro-French gestures she was to engender. To understand the whole significance of this letter, it must be remembered that until that time there had been no regular diplomatic exchange between Turkey and the West: a French ambassador was suffered, rather than encouraged, to reside in Constantinople, but no Turkish ambassador had been appointed to Paris. Any negotiations that were made were circuitous affairs, conducted by temporary agents, recalled to the Porte as soon as their mission was completed. The Sultan and his Grand Vizier remained legendary and remote. Therefore, when the French Foreign Minister received a letter addressed to Louis XVI, proffering friendship and admiration, signed by Selim, the heir apparent to the Turkish Empire, he was nonplused. It was a departure from both protocol and procedure; highly unorthodox, very suspect.

The Foreign Minister could not be expected to see, behind the inept overtures, a convent miss. Up to that time, no one in France knew of Aimée's fate. Her family had given her up for dead. No one, not even her cousin Joséphine, who must have recalled the prophecy, could imagine she was now not only the reigning favorite of the Seraglio, but a potential influence in international affairs. Then, too, a letter from the Turkish heir apparent was in itself curious, since the Princes were by tradition always immured in the Kefess, from the age of seven onwards. And even though Selim had not been so immured, he still lived sequestered, playing no part in the policies of the Porte. By custom, the Princes saw no one from the outside world. The majority of mothers preferred to act as filters; it kept their sons more dependent and gave them greater power, themselves. Only their immediate family and their tutors ever visited them; though at fourteen they had the right to claim their own slaves and odalisques to share their confinement. Such distractions apart, these unfortunate Princes lived in absolute stagnation, awaiting their summons to rule, or die.

Why, then, did Selim, if not a prisoner, still of no acknowledged power, suddenly decide to write such a letter? What was his motive? Who was the motivating force behind such an extraordinary step? But the answer is obvious. This clumsy, naïve overture was not really addressed to Louis XVI—to France, but, rather, to the beautiful French odalisque, Aimée Dubucq de Rivery. It proves how ably Aimée had played her part; not only that assigned her by the Kizlar Agha and his faction around the throne, but also that which she had chosen to play for herself. It shows unmistakably the power that this twenty-three-year old French girl now exercised over the young heir apparent. However strong Aimée's influence over the Sultan Abd ül Hamid I may have been, she can hardly have hoped to persuade this tired, conservative old ruler to take so drastic a step. But Selim was young and idealistic. He had fallen completely under Aimée's spell, and believed in her judgment. They were of an age; to him, she appeared the incarnation of all that liberty and civilization he sought in vain around him. There were a few happy hours when Aimée visited his mother's apartments, and they could be together. In secret, no doubt, for Aimée, as the Sultan's favorite, the youngest Kadine, was not permitted, officially, to meet even the heir apparent. But the complicity of the Kizlar Agha must have smoothed the way to many such stolen meetings. After all, if the young creatures enjoyed it, so much the better; it was to the advantage of the Kizlar Agha, and all the liberal faction, too, that Aimée should enslave the heir apparent. Selim must have seized his chance to talk to Aimée of the West, and of her ideas and hopes, so similar to his own; and eager to please her, he needed no persuasion to write the French monarch. No doubt Aimée dictated the simple phrases —too artless to seem other than madness or extreme Oriental cunning, to the stilted circle of diplomats who received it.

This message from a ghost reached Versailles in October, 1786. But nothing came of it. The King did not trouble to reply until the following May, and then only by empty phrases. Aimée was not discredited by the failure, however. Her supporters accepted the rebuff fatalistically, and went on with their efforts to reorganize an army which should be modeled on the French system, disciplined, loyal, and uncorrupted by the Janissaries.

Even though Aimée's influence on Turkish foreign policy has never been established, and must always remain a matter of conjecture, there is strong evidence that she was behind Selim's letter, for the same messenger to whom the letter was entrusted also carried one from Aimée to her uncle, Monsieur Dubucq of Havre. At last she had achieved the dreamed-of letter. But now it was too late to think of escape. Everything was changed. There was the little Mahmoud, who could never leave. He must stay there, to meet his destiny, and she must stay beside him, to help him meet it well. The letter was her first communication with her family since leaving the convent. They had probably given her up for dead. Her news must have been at once reassuring and disquieting. We have no record of how the Dubucqs viewed their lost Aimée: whether they were disinterested, proud or horrified by her exotic fate. Did they hush up the whole matter, speaking of it in whispers, and never before the servants or children? *A fate worse than death* . . . but that is probably a Victorian attitude: theirs would have been robustly eighteenth century; and since they were French, tinged by a worldly approbation. Viewed that way, Aimée had done rather well for herself, ensnaring no less a person than the Grand Turk. Though, on the other hand, the Osmanli were not perhaps quite the family the Dubucqs would have chosen for an alliance. We do not know if they replied to Aimée, but we can imagine with what longing the ghost waited for an answer from that living world to which she had once belonged.

In April, 1789, the Sultan Abd ül Hamid died, and was succeeded by his nephew, Selim, who became the Sultan Selim III, Allah's Vice Regent upon Earth. He was twenty-seven years old, and the nation rallied round him, confident that his youthful eagerness could overcome the abuses of government and taxation under which they now labored. But for all his enthusiasm, his bold resolves, and Aimée's support behind the scenes, Selim was not strong enough for such a monumental task.

At every turn he was harassed: at home by the Janissaries; abroad by his enemies, the Russians. Everything depended on achieving a new army, disciplined along French lines, and loyal to the Sultan, alone. He set about creating such a body, called the Nizam-Djedid, or new troops. This was a blow aimed directly at the Janissaries: and following it up by another, he decreed that the pick of the youngest Janissaries should now be incorporated into his Nizam-Djedid. The Janissaries were thunderstruck. Evidently this weakling meant business. The Agha sent for his captains and they began to plot their countermoves. But it was not so easy. Selim was proving himself firmer than they had thought; and the people were on his side, too. It was a stalemate. Once more, both factions drew back, waiting. . . .

When the Revolution swept France in 1793 Aimée followed events as well as she could, from behind the Seraglio's high crenelated walls. It was discouraging to have to admit that such a great country as hers was now gripped by a violent mob displaying a positively Oriental savagery. But Selim was not shaken: he agreed with her; it was the terrible outbreak of a misguided minority. France as a whole was sound. It is likely that from time to time she had news of her family; of her cousin Joséphine, too, now the mother of two children, now Beauharnais' widow, and now wife of a dynamic little Corsican general. News traveled slowly, then. Perhaps the gossip of the Paris salons reached the French Embassy at Pera. But no further. That last mile, across the caïques that bridged the Golden Horn, past the spices and serpent skins and perfumed roots piled along the Egyptian Bazaar, news from Europe faded, and was lost. It was said that ten thousand people crossed the bridge daily—but not one idea. This was the East, enclosed, remote. Time, like Western thought, flowed past the bubble-domed roofs of the Great Bazaar, past the minarets of the Suleimanyé, on past the gates of the Seraglio. The East had its own rumors, its own dramas. No echoes of Paris reached so far. Within the courtyards of the Seraglio, where a strange, oppressive silence was always remarked, no such small talk reached Aimée. Only the barest outlines of her cousin's story were known to her, over the years; the more spirited episodes in Joséphine's life during the Terror; but after, Joséphine, *la femme galante*, Barras, the mirrored bedroom in the Rue Chantereine—all this was certainly unknown to her, until—marvelous justification of all Euphemia David's most extravagant claims—Joséphine was crowned Empress of the French.

There was no record that the cousins ever corresponded; although it is known that much later, during Selim's reign, when Aimée enjoyed almost as much authority as the Sultan Valideh, she was able to dispatch magnificent presents to the Emperor and his family; diamond aigrettes, pearls, and a hundred of the delicate *cachemires* that Joséphine wore so

incomparably. But beyond this formal gesture there is no record of any
personal exchange. They were very different characters. One, a frivolous, cynical, calculating, extravagant charmer. The other, serious, idealistic, practical and sentimental. Only ambition and a sense of adventure
seem to have been common to both these beautiful Creoles.

But Aimée cherished a special affection for the memory of her cousin.
She had been cut off from France for so long; all that she remembered
of her childhood and home in Martinique was now embodied in Joséphine. It was a lonely life within the Seraglio; there can have been so
few outsiders that she could ever meet. It was only some thirty or forty
years after her death that the stream of distinguished French visitors
began to arrive. We can imagine with what delight Aimée would have
welcomed the state visit of the Empress Eugénie, on her way to the
Suez Canal, and for whom Aimée's grandson, Abd ül Medjuel, decorated the sugary little palace on the Bosphorus.

Even such an austerely dedicated woman as Florence Nightingale
would have been welcomed: indeed, she would have probably found
the practical and energetic temperament of the French Sultana a great
help in her struggles to establish the hospital at Scutari, just across the
water from Aimée's kiosk. Gérard de Nerval, too, wandering giddily
about the Levant, collecting material for his *Voyage en Orient*, how
welcome a guest he would have been! And how much he would have
enjoyed her story: his book is full of such vignettes, blazing with
color. But of all of them it is really Pierre Loti who should have been
there in Aimée's day, instead of sixty years later. Would he have written
*Aziyadé*, if he could have feasted on the drama and mystery and pathos
of the French Sultana's story? How Loti would have luxuriated in the
delicious melancholy of it all . . . and set within the fastness of the
Seraglio, too! *Pauvre petit fantôme . . . chère petite Sultane.* . . . We
imagine them, sitting together in some shadowy pavilion; Aimée, the
ghost, trying, through him, to return to the West; and Loti, the writer,
the Turcophil, trying, through her, to become one with the East; each
aching with voluptuous nostalgia . . . talking at cross purposes, but
still, talking in French, the language of Aimée's heart.

Selim had a positively childish enthusiasm for all that was French. He
must have had unlimited confidence, revolution or no, in a land from
which the incomparable Aimée sprang. During the early years of his
reign, after the peace of Jassy in 1792, by which Russia was ceded the
Crimea, Turkey withdrew to lick its wounds, and Selim concentrated a
new and powerful army on completely French lines. French and
Swedish engineers were employed. The cannon foundry at Top Hané
was under French command. French artillery officers were employed to

effect a series of drastic changes in army administration. Next there were translations of French manuals on mathematics and military tactics. French naval officers trained the navy; French shipbuilders organized the shipyards. In 1705 Selim sanctioned a French weekly, *Le Moniteur de l'Orient*, to be published in Constantinople. We have no doubt why it was sanctioned, or for whom. Selim himself had only the barest smattering of French, but no doubt he enjoyed the extracts Aimée read him. Most significant of all, the first permanent ambassador was appointed to France in 1797. He became the sensation of Directoire Paris, where everything was *à la Turque* for a few weeks. Napoleon received him warmly. He had long had his eye on Constantinople as the greatest strategic prize Europe could offer. Perhaps he remembered how, in 1793, when the Porte had first sent for French military experts, he had been one of the officers who had volunteered; but his application had been turned down, and he had stayed behind, to become First Consul, to conquer Europe, and aspire to becoming Emperor of the world, Turkey as part of the spoils.

When news reached the Seraglio that General Bonaparte, the First Consul, had married none other than Aimée's cousin, the Vicomtesse de Beauharnais, Selim must have felt confident of French interest and support in his progressive dreams. But Napoleon was less interested in dreams than schemes. It was a severe shock to the Sultan to learn, in July, 1798, and after all Napoleon's professions of amity, that a French army thirty thousand strong had landed in Egypt intending to wrest it from Turkish rule. However, Napoleon's mirage of Oriental conquest (of which this was the first step) faded. In 1801 there were a flurry of treaties and a general, though brief, era of peace was established. Napoleon acknowledged the sovereignty of the Porte in Egypt and the Sultan, in return, favored French interest in Turkey. No doubt Aimée rejoiced that this painful breach had been healed. She must have had to employ all her arts, persuading Selim, the proud, the just, to overlook so many unprovoked acts of aggression at Napoleon's hands. And so, one by one, sharper, more distinct each time, signs were coming from the fastness of the Seraglio, signaling to the world, of the mysterious presence of a *French* mind behind the close-latticed window of the Divan, where, by custom, the Sultan could watch, unobserved, from a secret gallery, the workings of his Divan, or ministerial conferences.

During these years, there was one man who went between Paris and the Porte, and was becoming a revered figure among the Turks. The name of Pierre Ruffin recurs over a wide span of time. He was born at Salonika in 1742, the son of a dragoman who represented French interests in the Levant. He grew up to become an Orientalist of high attainments. He was six times Chargé d'Affaires in Constantinople,

and had become so influential with the Turks, so much loved by the
successive Sultans, who addressed him as *Père*, that on his retirement,
his mere presence in the city enfeebled the authority of the succeeding
Ambassador, who asked for him to be removed elsewhere. Ruffin must
have come to know Aimée well; he probably helped her to form the
Francophile tendencies of both Selim and Mahmoud. With his scholarly interests, his knowledge of European and Oriental literature, it was
probably he who guided Aimée in the daring innovation of a new library containing enormous numbers of French books, the classics, the
Encyclopaedists, many of them translated into Turkish. When we consider that the first Turkish press was only established permanently in
1784, the year of Aimée's arrival, it seems likely that her influence was
already at work here, for it needed the direct encouragement and protection of the Sultan, the *ulemas,* or priests, being opposed to any dif-
fusion of knowledge. The Koran was only authorized to be printed and
sold publicly as late as 1850. Between them, Selim, Ruffin and Aimée
were beginning to open windows onto the world.

At this time Selim's reforms had not yet aggravated the people.
Whatever the Janissaries felt, it was wiser to wait. The Sultan's faction
was both purposeful and powerful. Behind Selim stood the puissant
Pasha of Rustchuk, governor of a province in the north of Bulgaria, a
loyal and devoted servant; there was the Kizlar Agha, the Sultan
Valideh, the Mufti Vely-Zadé, and, it now seemed, French support.
No; it was not yet time to strike. Across the courts, the two factions
watched each other implacably. Sometimes, in the dusk, the scuttling
figure of a dwarf, or one of the mutes could be glimpsed, carrying a
message between the pavilion of Mustapha's mother and the Court of
the Janissaries. There were eyes and ears everywhere. Nothing passed
unobserved. As the atmosphere became increasingly tense, the Janissaries would break out with some fresh piece of insolence or cruelty,
which Selim was not powerful enough to quell. When their kettle
drums sounded, even the bravest quailed, and Aimée, knowing the price
she and her son might one day have to pay for her years of hostility to
the Corps, and her influence over the Sultan, must have closed the
shutters and stopped her ears against the sinister beat. And in the morning there would be fresh tales of violence and anarchy, and some loyal
member of the Sultan's party would be discovered hanging from the
great plane tree outside their quarters; or another head would be added
to the pyramid beside the Gate of Felicity. During those years Aimée's
hatred was forming into that implacable force which one day was to
overthrow the whole Corps and all the violence they represented.

But that day was still far away; now, there were golden interludes,
when Aimée and her son enjoyed an almost serene family life beside

Selim and his mother. Selim loved his young cousin Mahmoud devotedly. It was Aimée's child; he loved him like his own; or, perhaps, as a younger brother. The Circassian Kadine and "the French Sultana" had violated all the traditions of the Seraglio when they joined forces to foster loyalty and affection between their children, the rival claimants. From the beginning Selim had shown a devoted interest in the child. As the baby grew into the boy, and boy into the young man, the gap in their ages seemed to dwindle, until, by the time Mahmoud was twenty to Selim's forty and Aimée's forty-one years, there were times when they all seemed of an age. Serene and golden days, when they picnicked in the hyacinth gardens overlooking the Golden Horn; or made expeditions to one of the Royal *yalis,* or summer palaces reflected in the blue waters of the Bosphorus, lapping below its windows. Sometimes the Sultan Selim would hold an archery tournament, beyond the city's walls, and a splendid tented-pavilion would be pitched; wherever it had stood remaining, ever afterwards, as free land—a gift to the people. Often, Selim sat beside Aimée in her kiosk as she worked at her embroidery frame. The needle flashed in and out of the petit point garlands, hung poised, and then plunged; her long hair fell over her face like a burnished golden veil; the diamonds glittered and trembled on their invisible chains. Selim thought her the most beautiful creature in the world: he would have done anything for her—anything. He drank in her words; and all the while she was talking about France . . . the West; the world outside the Seraglio . . . the world she had known before she became a ghost.

Sometimes she showed a naïve, and rather touching nostalgia for odd aspects of her French past. Within the Seraglio, anything she commanded was hers. Selim gratified her every whim: yet she harked back to her youthful memories. The Montgolfier brothers and their marvelous balloon had been the rage when Aimée was at Nantes. All France talked of their extraordinary invention; there were pictures and prints, and even wallpapers of "Montgolfiers," as the striped and decorated balloons were called. First the balloons had been tested with goats sent aloft as victim-passengers, rather in the manner they are now used for atomic experiments. Later, it became fashionable to make an ascent, several hundred feet up, in a beribboned basket: Aimée must have recounted it all to Selim and Mahmoud many times over. So one day, and probably to gratify the wish of *Naksh,* The Beautiful One, a Montgolfier rose from the fields of Dolma Bagtché. Not only that, the Sultan himself proved to the French Kadine that he was as fearless as her Western men, by making an ascent himself, and there was the astonishing spectacle of the Padishah of the Faithful, Allah's Shadow upon Earth, soaring over the five thousand domes and minarets of his capital, while far below, pandemonium reigned among the caïques that crammed the Sweet Waters of Asia, as their occupants craned skywards in delicious apprehension, cheering wildly. And at sunset, the mosques filled with the Faithful, all gathered together to hear the *ulemas* rendering thanks to Allah for the safe return of their Sultan. These gaily striped balloons were like so many airy bubbles of frivolity and elegance, gigantic *articles de Paris,* soaring in the blue skies of Turkey. Yes; it was evident in many ways that there was a French woman behind the throne, and her power was perhaps even more striking than that exercised by her cousin Joséphine, in France.

Under Selim's protection, Aimée found much to enjoy. She was of a sanguine nature and did not anticipate disaster. There were many agreeable aspects of life now. Her son; Selim's love and admiration; considerable liberty; increasing power and the most seducing luxury. There were her gardens, her study of Oriental culture, her French books, her music, and her warm friendship with the Sultan Valideh, who had helped to make her path easier. But on October 16, 1805, the Circassian woman died, and with her Aimée's carefree days. She was buried in one of the sumptuous Imperial Turbehs, as befitted her state, and Selim and Aimée and Mahmoud, the Kizlar Agha and all her friends mourned her loss. But the Janissaries knew that one of their keenest adversaries had gone: they began to take stock. Now Aimée stood alone between them and the two Princes, Mahmoud, her son, and Selim, the gentle Sultan, so unfitted to oppose them, and for whom she felt, perhaps, more than a protective love.

The sixteen years of Selim's reign had not given him the authority he required, surrounded by such enemies. His wars had weakened the country, as his reforms had weakened his popularity. Napoleon's invasion of Egypt had proved a weapon in the hands of the anti-French faction. Mahmoud was barely twenty, without any claims to the throne while Mustapha lived, but he had grown into a self-reliant, withdrawn character, bound up in the secret world of all things French, which he shared with his mother. He had studied military tactics with the French officers, learned to ride his horse with a European saddle, and to read everything of the West he could come by; but he had no place in official life. He could do no more than encourage Selim.

It was a Turkish tradition that every Prince of the blood must have a profession. Mahmoud chose to be a scribe, and spent long hours perfecting the graceful arabesques. The beauty of his calligraphy was such that he was often asked to inscribe the prayers or verses on public monuments about the city; many of them are still to be seen, great sweeps of black and gold, decorative and splendid, an ironic monument for a Sultan who had the force to break away from the bondage of his ancestors, and who was to pass into history as The Reformer.

Between 1805 and 1806, Selim, actuated by Aimée, had made two more overtures to the French. Friendship at all costs. Their need for a powerful ally was desperate, now. Not only was anarchy spreading within the country, reaching outward from the very Seraglio itself, but Russia was waiting to pounce on the weakened country. Selim's cry for help sounded a desperate note. Ruffin's reports enlightened Napoleon as to the urgency. For Mustapha's supporters were closing in. They, too, had been making outside overtures—to Russia, Turkey's traditional enemy, and to the English, too. The Tzar's troops were marching south. The British fleet was sailing east. Selim sent another, more agonized appeal for support, and now Napoleon acted quickly. He appointed one of his young staff officers, General, later Marshal, Sebastiani, as his special envoy to the Porte. Sebastiani, like Napoleon, was a Corsican. He was a brilliant soldier, capable of conceiving and executing the boldest schemes. He traveled fast, driving on, through the plains of central and southern Europe, blinding white in the dust of midsummer. He reached Constantinople on August 10, 1806, to the fury of Mustapha's faction. They were outmaneuvered.

The British Ambassador was in a great taking too. Under his very nose, General Sebastiani was being received in private audience by the Sultan, an honor not accorded their Ambassador, even under great stress. There was no stopping the General. French officers commanded Turkish ships—Good God! even the sailors' turban badge was a tricolor beside the Crescent! Colonel Sebastiani was in daily conference with the Seraglio; he was arming them, advising them, organizing them, *running* them in a most irregular fashion. It was not diplomacy . . . it was unheard of—it amounted to an act of war! Thus the outraged British Ambassador to his Government.

The British fleet sailed up the Dardanelles, their object being to demand Sebastiani's recall. Under threat of their guns, Selim weakened. But Aimée stood firm. There must be no negotiation, unless the fleet withdrew beyond the Dardanelles. Meanwhile, Sebastiani must be invested with absolute power. The Turkish people, now roused to the danger, flung themselves into preparations for defense, dragging their few cannons into the positions Sebastiani chose. They closed their ranks for battle. Selim pitched his tent next to that of Sebastiani and ordered his ministers to establish themselves beside the various batteries along the walls. For many of the Seraglio sycophants this was a most disagreeable order, but they knew better than to question it, then. Sebastiani's presence was both galvanic and reassuring. Under his orders the city was turned into an arsenal and fortress. The people were now ranged solidly behind him: neither the Janissaries nor Mustapha's party could turn them in favor of the English. While the foundries were contriving clumsy grapeshot and cannon balls made of rough stone, the British men o'war lay becalmed off Prinkipo Island, in sight of the city. The wind had turned against them, and for several days they were helpless. Those few days were crucial. They gave Sebastiani the time he needed to consolidate his defense. He achieved miracles, was everywhere at once; in the foundries, at the Seraglio, in conference with the Divan, about the city, at the Arsenal, on the Galata Tower, scanning the city's outer defenses. Even the Corps Diplomatique were fired—young attachés helped drag the guns; the Dutch Chargé d'Affaires flung gold coins right and left, to encourage the mob. The secretaries from the French Embassy, in lace-edged shirts, toiled beside ragged brigades of Armenians or Greeks. When at last the wind changed, Constantinople had been transformed into a fortress, commanded by a daring General, supported by the entire population. Admiral Duckworth decided discretion was the wisest course, and sailed for home. Aimée had won the first round.

The pro-French element around the throne could breathe easier, now. They foresaw a period of security and more progress along French lines. But progress, like beauty, is apt to lie in the eye of the beholder. "Orthodoxy is my doxy—heterodoxy is the other man's doxy." The mere word "reform" sounded ominous to many. The Janissaries smoldered with resentment. But while Sebastiani, representing Napoleonic force, was in control, there was no chance of gaining power. Their puppet, Mustapha, and his mother waited, too. . . .

In Aimée's apartments, safe from prying ears, there were many conferences. The atmosphere must have seemed dazzlingly European to Selim. Some years earlier Aimée had refurnished a suite of rooms in the French style, delicate Louis XVI chairs, satinwood commodes and curtains of *toile de Jouy*. The bold silhouette of Directoire or Empire furniture was unknown to her. She had recreated the salons of her youth, of the few visits she had made to her friends outside the convent. There were mirrors with swagged and gilded frames. Porcelain bowls full of potpourri stood on spindle-legged little satinwood tables. The love seats and *bergères* were plump with pale striped satin cushions; but they were unmistakably strict in form; they were for sitting, in the formal, European style; no lolling, as on the Turkish *minder*, or couch. A harp stood in one corner, though Aimée preferred to play the guitar. Sometimes Selim persuaded to her to sing, and Lully or Couperin sounded across the courtyards of the Seraglio, tinkling, ghostly music, sung by a ghost, scarcely heard, above the clanking of the Janissary guard, patroling below the latticed windows.

In this frivoulous setting, Selim loved to savor the West (not a *tchibouk* or divan in sight!). He liked to listen to Aimée's clear voice.

> *Nous n'irons plus au bois*
> *Les lauriers sont coupés . . .*

Even her saddest songs seemed gay, beside the minor *mélopées* of the East. Sometimes the Sebastianis came to join them and then there was champagne, a taste Aimée was much criticized for fostering in the young Mahmoud, who, like all Moslems, defied the Koran with every sip. Selim would sit silent, listening to the many plans which, in the light of Sebastiani's experience and Aimée's enthusiasm, seemed feasible. Sometimes there were more frivolous exchanges; Sebastiani would recount life at the Tuileries, and his wife, the charming Fanny de Coigny, would give Aimée accounts of the day-to-day doings of cousin Joséphine, and elegant Paris. Before that there had only been Monsieur Ruffin, who had represented a rather arid aspect of France, and was, besides, so much of an Orientalist that he preferred to speak Turkish. Aimée herself, although long established in the Turkish way of life and dress, was still undeniably French; while Mahmoud's upbringing and ancestry left no doubt as to his sympathies. He had a strong conviction of his duty towards his people. They *must* be westernized. Then, once more, the pashas would be shaken out of their habits of graft and inertia; flail-like, the reforms struck right and left, and across the inner courtyards of the Seraglio, Mustapha's mother noted everything, the Sultan's visits to *Naksh*, The Beautiful One, the infidel; Sebastiani's comings and go-ings—nothing escaped her: everything was noted and reported to her masters, the Janissaries. But when their kettle drums sounded, not all Selim's devotion, not all the brocaded *bergères* and harps could give Aimée a feeling of ease. To her, the drums were the pulse of that hateful Orient which had enslaved her; to her they symbolized all the savagery of the East; the very cannons of the pirates who had dragged her, a captive, through the alleys of the Kasbah.

Not only in the Sultan's immediate entourage, but throughout the city, among the people, Sebastiani's popularity was enormous. He was the savior of Constantinople, the hero of the hour. But then he usually was. He had formed the pattern of success early. Throughout his long and vivid life he went from glory to glory. He was, besides, fitted by nature to be at once a compelling and alluring figure. He charmed everyone by his magnificent physique and romantic good looks: "A creature who caused drawing-room riots." The Abbé de Pradt described him as *le Cupidon de l'Empire*. He must have been the perfect type of Napoleonic Marshal. Today, all that is left to us of this dashing band is the line of stone figures in their grimy niches along the façade of the Louvre beside the Rue de Rivoli. They stand there, the stone Marshals of France, while the buses grind past and the pigeons perch on cocked hat and flourished saber.

Sebastiani is a particularly highly colored figure. We imagine him galloping across Europe, looking like one of Gros' equestrian portraits, his charger rearing, a leopard-skin saddlecloth flung over the dappled rump, his plumed shako set rakishly, his uniform smothered in soutache, his hussar's jacket falling from one shoulder, his drawn saber gleaming as he spurs forward into the smoke of battle. Onward! Eastward! To Vienna! To Belgrade! To the walls of Constantinople! To glory!

He was born in Corsica in 1772. His father was a shoemaker, comfortably well off, and said to be related to the Bonaparte family. The young Horace François Bastien Sebastiani was destined for the church, but having other ideas, he left Corsica for France, where he joined the army. His rise was spectacular. He saw much fighting, played a conspicuous part in the Coup d'Etat of 18 Brumaire, after which Bonaparte marked him out for success and appointed him to his staff. After fighting at Marengo and Austerlitz, he was created a Colonel, then Count of the Empire; presently Bonaparte entrusted him with a delicate mission in the East. He was to go to Egypt and discover the relations between Turkey and the Mamelukes: he was to sound the Arab chiefs, reassure the Christian Syrians as to French support, and return by way of Constantinople, where he was to flatter and reassure the Padishah on Bonaparte's behalf. All this Sebastiani executed with his customary adroitness; so that when Selim's second desperate cry for help reached Bonaparte, Sebastiani was the obvious choice of envoy extraordinary, a diplomat and soldier, already familiar with the Levant, and fit to meet whatever emergency he might find at the Porte.

That he succeeded brilliantly, we know; had it not been for his wife's sudden death, he would have probably stayed beside Selim indefinitely, and Aimée's cherished dreams of progress might have been achieved in full. But when Fanny died giving birth to a daughter Sebastiani asked to be recalled, and returned to Paris, heartbroken, to bury himself in military life once more. He fought through the Russian campaigns, was with the Emperor during the Hundred Days, and retired to live in England after the battle of Waterloo. In 1816 he returned to France to enter politics, becoming successively *Ministre de la Marine, Ministre des Affaires Etrangères,* Ambassador to Naples, and London, where he was succeeded by Guizot. His old age was embittered by the terrible death of his daughter, Fanny, Duchesse de Praslin, who was found hacked to pieces in her canopied bed in the Praslin house, in the Rue St. Honoré. She was said to be a passionate and nagging creature, and there is little doubt that her husband, the Duke, was responsible for her death. He had fallen under the sway of an apparently mousy young English governess, whom the Duchess accused of alienating not only her husband's love, but that of her children, too. The drama rocked France and almost ruined the already tottering government of Louis Philippe. Sebastiani had rushed to Paris to press the charges against his son-in-law. But the Duke refused to speak, and escaped trial by taking poison.

As a fiery septuagenarian, Sebastiani was still to be seen pacing up and down the olive yards of his Corsican estate. An American diplomat recalled seeing him, a dynamic figure, even then, sheltering from the heat under a yellow umbrella, muttering as he walked . . . alone with the huge sweep of his memories. *La Grande Armée,* the Mamelukes, Joséphine's dinner parties in the Rue Chantereine, to which, as *le Cupidon de l'Empire,* he was no doubt welcomed. Austerlitz, Waterloo, Constantinople, the secret life of the Seraglio he was one of the few to have penetrated. . . . And Aimée, the veiled figure he and Fanny came to know so well, so long ago. . . . An attack of apoplexy carried him off suddenly, one golden spring day. He had been seated at the luncheon table, and, suddenly, was no more. It was a perfect death. He had wished to be buried in the Invalides, among his peers, the other Marshals of France: the following August, with all the pomp and honors he commanded, his coffin was carried there. At that moment, a mysterious fire burst out; the banners and standards taken in battle from his defeated enemies went up in tongues of flame, thus conspiring, to the end, to surround him with an atmosphere of heroic drama.

At the moment when Sebastiani's path crossed that of the French Sultana, at the very moment of their joint triumph (though, it must be remarked, for different ends, his for his Emperor, hers for her son) all was turned to ashes. Just as, once before, Fate had stepped in, turning the wind against the British fleet, so, now, it stepped in again. Death struck, and all was changed. Fanny Sebastiani suddenly sickened and died. Her husband was broken. He blamed himself for bringing her to this Asiatic waste of dirt and disease, of burning suns and icy winds. Aimée, too, was desolate. She had welcomed Fanny like a sister. Fanny had brought back her girlhood in France, and had seemed to represent everything of *la douceur de France.* She had been the first, and only, French woman, besides Aimée, whom Selim and Mahmoud had known.

Her charm, and Sebastiani's strength, had confirmed all that Aimée had told them of her people. And now Fanny was dead. To Sebastiani, Constantinople was haunted, accursed. He fled.

Now, at last the Janissaries' hour had come, and they unleashed their long-pent fury in a rule of terror. In the name of nationalism, a wave of reaction set in. Playing on the dangerous French influence dominating the Sultan, they suppressed his Nizam-Djedid, seized the throne, deposed Selim, and proclaimed Mustapha as Sultan, his mother as Sultan Valideh. All this less than a month after Sebastiani's departure. Aimée, Mahmoud and Selim huddled together in captivity, went in hourly terror for their lives. Many of their entourage were killed outright, others disappeared or were imprisoned. Their officers of state, generals and governors of provinces were recalled, to be met with the bowstring. The Janissaries gave no quarter. Cruelty and reaction reigned once more.

When the news reached Paris, in spite of Sebastiani's advice, Bonaparte made his first open move towards annexing Turkey. He had always been perfectly cynical as to the protection he had extended, and he had never believed in the staying power of the pro-French faction. It had suited him to send Sebastiani; he could not have the English established there. Now, with reports of anarchy and terror coming in by every messenger and a sinister silence from Selim, he decided the time had come to disclose his plans. He was deaf to Sebastiani's pleas; deaf, we must suppose, to anything Joséphine may have said concerning the fate of her cousin. (Bonaparte was always able to be ruthless where family considerations did not coincide with his own policies.) In June he thundered off to Tilsit to meet the Tzar Alexander, where, embracing flamboyantly on an ornamental raft moored in midstream of the Niemen, the two demigods swore eternal friendship and concluded an agreement that the Ottoman Empire should belong to Russia. Such was their private understanding. Publicly, however, the treaty read otherwise; it provided for Russia's evacuation of the Danubian provinces. As Bonaparte saw it, this would clear the way for his ultimate conquest of Turkey, besides allaying the suspicions of the Porte as to his intentions. As Alexander saw it, the gesture would earn him French co-operation in his dreams of occupying all Turkey, from the Danube to Salonika. The two Emperors were delighted with themselves; each thought the other his dupe. Their standards floated over the pavilion on the raft; their aides-de-camps clanked their spurs and swords up and down the landing stage; at night, beside the long lines of horses picketed on the banks, the Cossacks broke into their wild dances. There were fireworks and military bands, and the junketings went on into the pale summer dawn.

While Mustapha and the Janissaries were liquidating their enemies, they had overlooked the one man who was to bring about their ruin. Baraiktar, Pasha of Rustchuk, a Bulgarian province on the Danube, was himself of Bulgarian origin, but a devoted servant of the Turkish Empire, and in sympathy with the French reforms. He was a Three-Tailed Bashaw by rank, a loyal supporter of the Sultan Selim by inclination. As soon as word reached him of Selim's deposition, he rallied his troops, and set out for Constantinople, leading an army of scowling Albanians. From the flat dun-colored banks of the Danube across Bulgaria to Turkey was a formidable march, especially in the torrid climate of midsummer, but Baraiktar pushed on, through the wild defiles of the Balkan mountains, beside the looped windings of the Yantra River, where it races yellow beneath Tirnovo, the ancient Bulgarian capital. On, by Kazanluk, where the Valley of the Roses melts into the mountains, always south, through those strange, secretive Slav villages, where Turkish domination rankled and Bulgarian patriotism smoldered for nearly five centuries. The avenging army marched on, till, come at last to the Turkish border country, the great mosques of Adrianople rose suddenly into sight. Turkish soil at last! Baraiktar found the konaks, or inns, full of rumors. The Sultan was dead! His French faction were impaled on the gates of the Seraglio; the Janissaries were in possession of the Divan. . . . Baraiktar pressed on, and reaching the outer walls of the Seraglio, surprised the guard, stormed the first courtyard, and was at the Gate of Felicity before Mustapha and his ministers were roused. But once the alarm was given, Mustapha's mother struck, serpent-quick. Her son's life was safe only if he represented the last of the Osmanlis. An old superstition held that both dynasty and empire stood, or fell, together. No one would touch Mustapha, were he the sole survivor of the Royal house. Selim and Mahmoud must die. She dispatched the guard to kill them where they languished in the Princes' Cage.

Selim, the gentle, the scholar, died like a lion. As the soldiers broke into his room, only one man stood beside him, Taiher Effendi, who flung himself between the Sultan and his assailants. But Selim knew his hour had come, and that it was Mahmoud who must be saved, to carry on the reforms he, Selim, had failed to achieve. Selim loved Mahmoud not only as a brother, but as the child of Aimée, *Naksh,* The Beautiful One, his Beautiful One. . . . Ordering Taiher to find Mahmoud and warn him, Selim drew his dagger and rushed on the guard, to fight a delaying action, and die of a hundred thrusts. But Mahmoud had been saved. Taiher reached him in time to help him escape onto the roof, by way of a chimney. Legend has it that Aimée succeeded in hiding her son in the disused stove of a bathhouse: in any case, his enemies found him gone. As they rushed after him, their

way was blocked by one of Aimée's devoted slaves, a Georgian woman
of formidable physique, known in the Harem as The Strong. She, too,
would defend Aimée's child with her life. She hurled a brazier of red-
hot coals at the guard, who fell back for another few, vital moments. By
now Baraiktar had battered down the Gate of Felicity and was raging
through the Seraglio calling for Sultan Selim, his master. But silence
met him everywhere. The courtyards were deserted, the kiosks empty,
the Harem silent; the Eunuchs, the cooks, the gardeners and the ministers—all had fled. At that moment, Mustapha's voice was heard.
"Hand over Sultan Selim to the Pasha of Rustchuk, if he wants the
pig's carcass," and he kicked his cousin's body across the threshold,
where it lay, terribly disfigured, under the blazing noonday sun.

Baraiktar flung himself down beside it, weeping bitterly, and vowing
vengeance: "Is it for the Pasha of Rustchuk to cry like a girl?" said his
captains. "Let us avenge our Sultan!" "Let us save Sultan Mahmoud!"
replied Baraiktar, and at that same moment Mahmoud himself appeared, blackened by soot, but in no way shaken by his ordeal. With
that majestic force which characterized him, even so young, he took
command. He told Baraiktar that he would avenge Selim himself, in
his own time, in his own way. And there sounds the first note of
implacable determination, of unhurried, calculated revenge which
Mahmoud was to nurture within him, unknown to all, save his mother,
for so many years, until at last it was unleashed in all its fury, crushing,
forever, the Janissaries and their way of government. In this aspect of
Mahmoud's nature we see Oriental cunning restrained by Western
discipline; the luxury of revenge was sublimated to long-term strategy.
Not for nothing had he studied French military tactics; not for nothing
had he hung on Sebastiani's words; absorbing from Ruffin, from his
mother, from the French artillery officers, all that he could, of the West.

He gave his orders coldly. There must be no more bloodshed; no
more dramatic gestures, by Baraiktar or anyone else, until he, Mahmoud,
commanded. His dynamic personality dominated the scene; his powerful voice rang through the courtyards. It was apparent that this was
no vitiated princeling, but a strong man. He led the way to the Hall of
the Sacred Mantle, where the Prophet's Standard, the Sanjak Sherif,
and other holy relics were kept. It was here that the new Sultans always prayed; here that Mahmoud now prayed alone, for some hours.
When he emerged, his mere presence silenced the throngs who had
crept out from their hiding places and now prostrated themselves in
terror and obedience. Mahmoud gave his orders, and Mustapha and
his mother were led away to their imprisonment. Baraiktar was created
Grand Vizier. That night the cannons of Top Kapou roared out a

Sultan's salute. Mahmoud was proclaimed Padishah of the Faithful, Allah's Vice Regent upon Earth.

In the shadow-filled mosques the people prayed, rocking backwards and forwards, prostrating themselves towards the East; in the *tekkées* of Scutari the Dervishes spun and howled in mystical frenzies. A new Sultan and a new time had come. It was Allah's will! They prayed for Mahmoud. Alone in the splendors of her Royal kiosk, Aimée prayed, too. She had never relinquished her Catholic faith; it had sustained her through so many trials. Now she was the Sultan Valideh; her son the Sultan; her enemies confounded; the future all before her. Thus we see the French convent girl, the trembling slave, who, so many years ago was carried from the Corsairs' *barque* to the Gate of Felicity, now mistress of those who believed they could enslave her. Once again, the words of Euphemia David must have rung in her ears. . . . *This son will reign gloriously, but the steps of his throne will be dyed with the blood of his predecessor.* . . . Surely it was God's will that she had been sent to Turkey, that Mahmoud had been preserved, to rule, and to reform. Perhaps, that night, she was the only one who prayed for Selim's soul.

At this point let us examine the impression which the young Sultan made on those around him. His energy and commanding air have been already noted; he is described as having a curious fixed stare, which he turned, like an unspoken question, upon any foreigners. Even the sight of a *Giaour*, among the crowds that cheered him as he passed, would produce this haunting gaze. It was as if he searched for civilization, for this magical, long-desired Western myth. He had what was described as a *severité mélancolique*. He was rather above middle height, powerfully built, with his father's livid pallor and jetty black beard. Prior to his accession he had remained unknown, unseen, living protected, rather than a prisoner, in the Princes' Cage, or his mother's apartments, known only to Selim's closest followers, or the French faction. Now it was seen with misgiving that he had many marks of the *Giaour* about him. He preferred a chair to cushions or a divan. He scorned to eat with his fingers, and used an elegant gold knife and fork. Worse still, he drank champagne at every occasion. (Indeed, after his death, which was wrongly attributed to drinking, by his enemies, his widow flung the whole contents of his cellar into the Bosphorus, in a gesture of grief and Moslem repudiation. The spectacle of thousands of bottles of fine French wines sinking off Seraglio Point, where once the unfaithful odalisques had perished, must have been edifying for those of the old school who had opposed such manifestations of infidel leanings.) When he rode, it was with a European saddle and in the style of the

French cavalry officers. Later, even more audacious, he wore a costume where an odd blend of tradition and innovation was apparent. The sable-lined brocades and glittering turbans of his youth gave way to a pair of pleated trousers, a topcoat cut like a uniform tunic, topped by a fez. The turban was condemned. His only mark of distinction was a heron's plume, or aigrette, attached to his fez by a gigantic diamond crescent. But he wore a sweeping green cloak, and his horses' trappings were still ablaze with jewels, and the Seraglio was still maintained in a style, which, even if it began to feel a slight pinch from Aimée's more thrifty French management, was, all the same, sumptuous. During his reign the numbers of odalisques declined, and while being in no way an ascetic, he showed a less Oriental approach to his pleasures and was positively domestic in his attitude towards his Armenian favorite. Besma, a simple creature, once a bathhouse attendant, by whom he had six children, and to whom he remained greatly devoted, over the years.

Like Selim before him, all things French found favor in his eyes; his reforms were spectacular, and disquieting, too. Once again, the people muttered. No more conservative nation than the Turks ever existed, and Mahmoud, in a gush of youthful enthusiasm, tried to sweep away all the old ills along with many time-honored customs. All must be shining new and Western, from knives and forks and fezzes to a system of taxation, or administrative changes. His enemies multiplied. In vain did Signor Donizetti, the new court musician, and brother of the celebrated composer, laud the Sultan's musical abilities, compose the *Sultan's March* and give Mahmoud lessons in counterpoint, dwelling on the special grace and melancholy of his songs. The Turks preferred their own cadences, those lovely minor airs, which unfold like an intricate arabesque, and seem suspended, languorous, on the air. Gérard de Nerval heard such a song in Egypt: "something pastoral, something of the dreaminess of a lover poured from these words so rich in vowels and cadenced like the song of birds. Perhaps, I thought, it is some shepherd's song from Trebizond or the Marmora. I seemed to hear doves cooing upon the tips of the yews: it was a song to be sung in blue valleys . . ."

Mahmoud concentrated largely on reforms of internal policy, aiming to set his house in order and complete the work Selim had left unfinished. Over the years he was responsible for such startling innovations as a system of quarantine which saved the city from a terrible outbreak of the plague in 1838. (That the plague had long been considered as endemic, rather than sporadic, in Constantinople, may have been due to the habit of barely covering the bodies, in their shallow graves.) He founded a school of medicine, and even sanctioned a treatise on anatomy, something which the conservative regarded as a piece of flagrant disobedience to the Koran, which is categoric on this point. *Even if the dead man had swallowed the most precious pearl, and that pearl not his,* the opening of the body was forbidden. Nor was Mahmoud any more approved when he ameliorated the lost of his Christian subjects, Syrian Christians, Orthodox Greek or Bulgarian minorities; and when he moved, though unsuccessfully, towards the suppression of the trade in Eunuch's, it was felt he had really gone too far. Next, he would be suppressing their Harems. He also constructed a theater at Pera, where he was often to be seen in the Imperial box. All things Western were welcome. When the nuns of a convent in France wrote asking if he would replace the carpets looted from their chapel by the Revolutionary mob, in exchange for their prayers, he and Aimée were very gratified. Christians turning to a Moslem Prince! It seems curious that French nuns should have conceived the idea of addressing the Sultan of Turkey, but it is not perhaps too wild a conjecture to think it was Aimée's old convent at Nantes (which had been a center of Terrorist manifestations), who received news of their former pupil's high estate and now appealed, circuitously, for her help. The ghost must have been overjoyed, and a pair of sumptuous carpets were dispatched, forthwith, in the Sultan's name.

Much later, Mahmoud was to proclaim the right of free worship in Turkey, and to establish the first Turkish gazette, but that was the work of the older monarch. Now he had to content himself with small-scale, though significant, moves. Once, overreaching himself in a touching gesture of imitation, he issued invitations for a ball at the Seraglio. But very few of the Turkish nobility would countenance their wives leaving the Harem to meet and mingle—let alone *dance*—with the Sultan's other guests. They preferred to brave the Imperial displeasure; so Signor Donizetti's fiddlers played, and the French dancing master Selim had originally appointed (no doubt at Aimée's suggestion) went round the waxed floor bowing and scraping before the ladies of the Seraglio. But it did not turn out the sort of ball they held at the Tuileries, such as Sebastiani and Fanny had so often described. . . . It was not a really successful evening. The conservative Turks could forgive the fez, could overlook such dubious experiments as schools or hospitals, but a ball . . . ! Dancing partners! The valse! They locked their harem doors, set the Eunuchs on guard and went to join the Janissaries, who were plotting in undertones.

If Aimée and her son imagined their enemies were vanquished, they were mistaken. Very soon, Mahmoud's policies were proved too indigestible for the country as a whole, and he was forced to be even more discreet. But the first signs of moderation were taken for weakness. Once more the Janissaries' kettle drums were heard; once more their enemies were strung up under the great plane tree which was their rallying point, and Aimée shuddered. Mustapha and his mother were the focal point for all their plans. Mahmoud could no longer afford to be merciful. He had seen Selim butchered; he had grown up in the shadow of the Princes' Cage. Violence was a tradition of his race. Only force could quell force, only terror could terrorize. He ordered the death of Mustapha and his mother, while all those women who were pregnant by Mustapha were to be thrown into the Bosphorus. It was in the accepted pattern; but it was Mahmoud's first act of violence. Alas! it was not to be the last. It came to be said of him and his sons, *"Mahmoud, lover of blood, Abd ül Aziz, lover of money, Abd ül Medjid, lover of women."*

Yet when we consider the antecedents and surroundings of the young Mahmoud, such action is seen to be more in the nature of self-defense. It was kill, or be killed, in the Seraglio. His ancestors, on both sides, had been a hot-blooded lot. In the great days of medieval Turkey, his forbears lived hard. The young princes who survived were often governing whole provinces at the age of fourteen; "victorious in battle, they were rewarded with voluptuous young slaves. They were fathers at the age of sixteen, and again, at sixty. The princes were gentle in the harem, ferocious in the camp, humble in the mosque and superb on the throne." How, then, expect Mahmoud to show clemency towards an unscrupulous enemy? Moreover, Aimée had brought him up to believe in his sacred mission, that ultimate goal of Westernizing the country. No doubt they both held that the ends justify the means.

Although despotic by nature, as Selim never was, Mahmoud was benevolent by intent. Yet to attain even a moderate degree of civilizing humanity, such as his attempted reform of the trade in slaves and Eunuchs, he was compelled to adopt the most autocratic, if not tyrannous, methods. On occasion, however, he could show remarkable patience. When one of his admirals had sentenced a malefactor to five hundred blows on the stomach, and killed him, by the hundredth, Mahmoud flew into a terrible rage, but, inviting the admiral to the Seraglio, merely ordered him to eat as many rich cakes. When, after seventy, the swooning admiral begged for mercy, Mahmoud replied that if a mere seventy *cakes* were unendurable, how could anyone be expected to endure five hundred *blows?*

It is probable that Aimée Dubucq de Rivery was often beside her son in his most ruthless actions. She had not lived twenty years in the Seraglio for nothing. The Koran could be interpreted comfortably as sanctioning the removal of rivals, saying, "If there be two Califs, kill one." She had perhaps grown, if not blunted, at least in agreement that he who struck first lived longest. Just as her Creole blood and those languorous charms with which so many of the island race were endowed may have helped her to adapt to the requirements of the Harem, so, too, the sultry background of Martinique, with an underlying menace beneath its tropic brilliance, may have given her an adaptability towards the sinistry of Turkish intrigues. It was not, perhaps, as alien to her as it would have been to an ordinary, convent-bred French girl, or one from an English schoolroom. Martinique was in her blood, with its centuries of dark spells, volcanic storms, and serpents darting from the surrounding luxuriance to strike down an unsuspecting victim. The parallel is there: Aimée, advancing through the savage luxuriance of the Seraglio; her cousin Joséphine showing an equal, though different, address in making her way through the jungle of revolutionary, court, and Bonaparte family life in France. Both were pliant and resourceful women.

Creoles are by nature given to display. Joséphine's extravagance bears this out. At the Seraglio Aimée was able to gratify such tastes to their full. Contemporary accounts speak of her elegance, the splendor of her jewels, and how the passion for precious stones was a salient feature of the whole nation. Many noblewomen, so festooned, and unable to attach so much as one more ornament to their person, used to adorn their slaves with their surplus jewels, thus admiring their possessions objectively. Sometimes, as a refinement of luxury, they would wear comparatively few jewels themselves, at great functions, weddings or such, but would be followed by a slave carrying a treasury of precious stones on a golden tray. Sharp-eyed Lady Craven speaks of a moment during the reign of Abd ül Hamid (about the time of Aimée's arrival in Turkey) when the nation's defenses were crumbling, "while the Porte delays building batteries upon the most important posts, under pretense of needing money . . . yet the jewelers cannot find diamonds enough to supply the demands of the Harem, for which they are paid in ready money." This was something which even Mahmoud could not hope to reform.

Lady Mary Wortley Montagu, describing her visit to a harem in 1717, wrote that her hostess wore "a girdle as broad as the broadest English ribbon, entirely covered with diamonds. Round her neck she wore three chains which reached to her knees; one of large pearls, at the bottom of which hung a fine colored emerald as big as a turkey egg; another consisting of two hundred emeralds closely joined . . . every one as large as a half-crown piece. . . . But her earrings eclipsed all the rest. They were two diamonds, shaped exactly like pears, as large as a big hazel nut. . . . She had four strings of pearls, the whitest and most perfect in the world, at least enough to make four necklaces, every one as large as the Duchess of Marlborough's." She goes on to speak of a gigantic ruby surrounded by twenty drops of clear diamonds, a head-

dress covered with "bodkins of emeralds and diamonds," large diamond
bracelets, "and had five rings on her fingers, except Mr. Pitts, the largest
I ever saw in my life. It is for jewelers to compute the value of these
things . . . but I am sure that no European Queen has half the quantity."

There were all sorts of lesser splendors, too. The Sultan's opium pills
were gilded, in one, two, or three layers of gilt, thus spacing or timing
the speed of their effect; which is possibly the origin of the phrase "gilding the pill." Luxury, as such, was considered all-desirable. When the
painted and gilded caïques were rowed up and down the Bosphorus,
dallying between the Sweet Waters of Asia and the ornate summer
houses, or *yalis,* along the shores, they were followed by a sparkling
shoal of jeweled fish attached by chains, so that they seemed to be
escorting the caïque, bobbing in its wake. These caïques were sumptuous affairs, less secretive than the hooded sleek gondolas of Venice,
and seemed to be made not so much for the assignation as the state
visit. They were piled with brocaded cushions, and over the stern,
Persian rugs, or a richly embroidered velvet carpet, in crimson, or
purple, the *hirame* trailed from the stern, out over the surface of the
water in a fan of splendor.

Some Sultans allowed their Harem considerable freedom; the ladies
were permitted to picnic at the Sweet Waters of Asia, heavily guarded
by the Eunuchs, or drive through the town, to the bazaars, though
this was a concession which was only granted during the middle and
latter part of the nineteenth century. In Aimée's day, the Seraglio remained sequestered. However, Selim, when Sultan, was, as we know,
very indulgent to Aimée's innovations, and by the time she became
Sultan Valideh, she had probably enjoyed more liberty than all the
other Seraglio women. She was deeply interested in every aspect of her
son's empire, not only in the political intrigues which were the passion
of other Seraglio mothers, but in its cultural and historic heritage, too.
It is known that Mahmoud went about his capital disguised, like Ha-
roun al Raschid, and like him, had for close friend his barber, who
kept him informed of the everyday life and opinions of his people. It
is probable that Aimée, too, made secret sorties about the city. Even
after twenty years she must have still seen it with something of a traveler's sense of wonder, and marveled at its dreamlike quality, the crumbling Byzantine splendors, the great subterranean cisterns, dank and
still, lying beneath the city's surging surface, and all the history and
legends of this place, where Crescent rose on Cross, where the Bazaar
had once stabled Justinian's two thousand horses, and where there were
any number of such strange-sounding, forgotten churches as St. Mary of
the Mongols, built by a Paleologue Princess to celebrate her safe return

after being sent as bride of an aged Mongol Khan, who died before the marriage was consummated.

Both mother and son had the adventurous strain of their ancestor Pierre Dubucq. It would not have suited either of them to be bound by the conventions of their rank. What interest, for either of them, to be escorted in state through the streets surrounded by Three-Tailed Bashaws and other Satraps? It is probable that Aimée, bundled in the heavy black *feridjie* worn by all Turkish women who ventured abroad, sometimes accompanied her son on these outings, mingling with the crowds along the slippery quays of the Fish Market, or crossed the bridge to Galata, among the throng where the peaked black lambskin caps of the Persians, the white skull caps of the Albanians, and the Turkomans' turbans were jostled together, all the hordes of the East, "with that dark dignity of bearing common to the men of the East," as one enraptured lady traveler puts it.

Everywhere, the Janissaries were apparent, slicing off heads, leaving the body to sprawl across the streets, head placed ignobly between the legs, nailing malefactors to their door by one ear, or setting off, down the Bosphorus, with a boatload of prisoners, to be executed as soon as they came to a suitable spot. (The Turks were prone to choose agreeable spots for their executions, as others might select harmonious surroundings for a picnic. With Arab fatalism the victims would embark, discussing the scenery their executioners chose for the fatal act.) At this time, the Janissaries' evil had reached a peak; and Mahmoud went about, in the streets and coffeehouses, noting it all, storing a horde of secret hatred, against the time when he could crush them forever.

The fearful risks which they ran, mother and son, on such incognito expeditions, must have brought them even closer. It was unthinkable for any Moslem woman of Court rank to go about unescorted, or in such dubious quarters. Mahmoud must have realized, even more, the remarkable nature of this enlightened, independent French woman who was his mother. We can imagine them, a humble-looking pair, mother and son, shambling past the impressive façade of the French Embassy, or Palace, as it was called, with its scarlet-coated kavass on guard (Janissaries, these, as most other officials about the city); past little booths full of honied confections, up and up, mounting the disreputable alleys leading to the heights, "that primrose path of Galata, winding upwards to depths of depravity," as an American social worker was to describe it, rather wildly, half a century later, when embroiled in the organization of homes of rescue for fallen women, or those misguided girls who arrived at Constantinople lured there by legends of Harem grandeurs. The missionary even went so far as to have all the trains and boats met by social workers wearing caps embroidered with their calling, and chosen for their linguistic abilities . . . but alas! the response was not encouraging. So many of the girls spoke another, more universal language, and did not seem to care about being saved.

Within the Seraglio Aimée, as Sultan Valideh, now reigned supreme. She had her own palace, entourage and revenues. Her son consulted her, and her alone, on every move. Besides affairs of state there was the organization of the Harem, with its etiquette and protocol; visits from the ladies of her Court; the supervision of the hospital, the library; the planning of new gardens, such as that which Melling, the French landscape painter had come to Turkey to design all along the Bosphorus. Now, the floral conceits of the Bostanji Bachi, or Head Gardener, were tempered by the introduction of a brother of the Head Gardener at Schönbrunn. Aimée's kiosk overlooked the Bosphorus, and was beside a little, hidden garden, shaded by cypress trees and planted with hyacinths, where she loved to walk in the cool of the evening, watching the golden sparks that flittered among the tombs in the dark groves of Scutari, across the water. Superstition held that they were departed souls, but they were more prosaically explained as being a phosphorescent glow induced by the agglomeration of bones. Another superstition held that the wheeling and dipping black birds that haunt the Bosphorus, neither sea gulls nor starlings, and which are never seen to rest, are damned souls condemned to wander, like Paolo and Francesca, "forever together on the unresting air. . . ."

Aimée cannot have had much time for such somber thoughts, however. The Sultan Valideh's hand was apparent throughout the Seraglio, from foreign policies to household accounts. There were many curious traditions which must be observed, too. At Ramadhan, when the month-long fasting drew to an end, and the beat of drums throbbed through the city, announcing the Night of Power, one of the Seven Holy Nights of the Moslem year, when the Sultan went in high state to pray in a mosque outside his palace, it was the Sultan Valideh who, custom decreed, must select and present him with a new bride, one of the latest recruits, a little creature fresh from the mountain valleys of Georgia perhaps, some luscious child who, it was expected, would not fail to produce a male heir.

Sometimes there were distractions of a more European nature: packets of the latest books from Paris; or the visit of a passing musician, recommended by Signor Donizetti's clever brother, Gaetano, whose operas were beginning to be remarked in the West. Or accounts (secondhand, and garbled, but entertaining, for all that) of Lord Byron's behavior, over at Pera, where he was, as usual, getting himself talked about while staying with the British Chargé d' Affaires. Once, a stately giraffe, or camel-leopard, arrived from Cairo, as a conciliatory gesture from Mohammed Pasha. This marvelous creature delighted the Sultan, and his Grand Vizier held levées, to which the whole Diplomatic Corps were invited, to watch the giraffe being put through his paces by Nubian grooms. But for the most part, Aimée's diversions were of a more homely character; a new Circassian dancing girl, or, perhaps, the compelling spectable of Babaluk frenzies, where, in a sort of cataleptic trance, the harem Negresses divined the future, a proceeding which must have recalled to her the voodoo paractices of the West Indies.

Most popular of all, among the Turks, was Karageuz, a puppet shadow-show full of robustly lewd antics, handed down from one generation to another. As Gérard de Nerval says, "The East does not share our ideas either of education or morality. It seeks to develop the senses: we endeavor to extinguish them." Whatever Aimée may have thought about such episodes as *Karageuz, the Martyr to Chastity*, she must not appear censorious, or even unappreciative.

One day there was the visit of some strolling players, which was to link Aimée's Oriental court with the Paris boulevards. All unsuspecting, she saw the great Debureau, many years before he became the idol of Paris, and his theater on the Boulevard du Temple was the rendezvous of such as Balzac, George Sand, and the Romantics. Debureau's luster has remained undimmed since his death in 1846. He has remained a symbol of all that was most brilliant in the tradition of pantomine. He was of Bohemian origin, born at Neu Kolin in 1796. He came of a straggling mountebank family who wandered about the world, thirsty in summer, shivering in winter, and always hungry. They dragged themselves from one little town to the next, across mountains and plains, wherever a few coppers could be earned, tumbling, wire-walking and juggling, competing with gypsies' tambourines and dancing bears. It was an inauspicious beginning for the greatest of all tragic clowns.

Around the year 1810 the Debureau family arrived in Constantinople and were, of course, commanded to appear before the Sultan. O! brilliant fortune! Their molting spangles were resewn, their tights washed, their act rehearsed to the point of exhaustion. But for an empty triumph. They were ushered through the sumptuous halls into a mirrored pavilion. Absolute silence reigned: it was completely deserted. It was, in Janin's words, "like the silence and desolation of the Théâtre Français when they play a piece by Monsieur Bonjour." The troupe were mystified. How could they divine that from behind slits in a brocaded curtain the Harem's élite were watching? As they hesitated, a turbaned Negro motioned them to begin their act. In silence, they spread out their threadbare strip of druggeting, pitiable against the Seraglio's Persian carpets. In silence they went through their act. In silence they pro-

ceeded to its climax, a human pyramid. Father stood on uncle, brother
supported cousin. Greatly daring, the young Debureau topped the
whole swaying edifice, balanced on a ladder. . . . "*Et voila!*" says Janin.
"*Voila! au sommet de son Art. O surprise! O recompense de
l'Artiste.* . . ." From the summit, Debureau could look down over the
curtain, into the forbidden paradise below. Here the Sultan's ladies
were gathered, "the voluptuous odalisques of the Seraglio, sacred Sultans of His Highness, those redoubtable Houris, whose very regard
could lead to death." His eyes met those of an unveiled odalisque.
Overcome, he crashed to the ground, bringing the whole performance
to an ignoble finish.

It must not be imagined that Mahmoud, for all his devotion to his
mother, was tied to her apron strings. Everything about him indicates
that she had brought him up to be a man of action, who spent a minimum of time in the ennervating confines of the Harem. The British
Ambassador may have opined that Mahmoud was an Oriental potentate
at his most despotic, but seen in perspective, with the knowledge of his
French blood, or rather, the manner in which his mother had deliberately fostered the Western strain, we see that it was this, rather than
Oriental despotism which gave such force to his character. Nor must we
overlook the influence of the British Ambassador, himself, Stratford
Canning, afterwards Lord Stratford de Redcliffe, the Great Elchi, or
Ambassador, as he was to become to the Turks. In the early years of
Mahmoud's reign, he was only a fledgling Minister of twenty-four (to
Mahmoud's twenty-five), yet between them, they might be said to have
given the final blow which brought Napoleon to a halt.

From the beginning, Mahmoud had followed Selim's precedent, and
made overtures to France: but these had gone unanswered; Napoleon
saw Turkey as a vassal rather than an ally, and was confident of obtaining it, in his own time. Meanwhile, he had other problems; his
divorce from Joséphine, and his plans for the Russian compaign. On
December 16, 1809, Napoleon repudiated Joséphine to marry Marie-
Louise. When the news reached Constantinople, Aimée and Mahmoud
were thunderstruck. They took it as a personal, family insult. Although
Aimée had never seen her cousin since they parted, as girls, in
Martinique, she had taught Mahmoud to revere the legend of brilliance
and charm which surrounded the Empress—his second cousin. Now
Mahmoud felt a chivalresque urge to defend her; moreover, it was
conclusive proof of Napoleon's perfidious nature. It was no longer possible to overlook many past treacheries, notably the Egyptian campaign
and the secret understandings behind the Treaty of Tilsit, which Mah-

moud had been unwilling to admit, for some time. From that moment, Mahmoud turned against Napoleon and his government implacably.

Overnight, the French Minister Latour-Maubourg found the Turkish Foreign Minister's attitude one of marked hostility. The Minister was acting on the Sultan's instructions, which, though categoric, were not explanatory, for Mahmoud showed a headstrong inclination to act on his own, without consulting his ministers, as the British Ambassador observed with misgiving. Overnight, as the French found nothing but hostility, so the British found gracious favor, the Ambassador (then Canning's predecessor, Robert Adair) being suddenly granted an audience and received with bewildering marks of esteem. Mahmoud, ever self-contained, gave no hint of the reasons behind his *volte-face*, but smiled, inscrutably, as news reached him of the French Minister's agitated dispatches sent off in feverish speed, one after the other, to advise Napoleon of the Sultan's change of heart. "The Porte has become *plus anglaise que les Anglais*"—"more English than the English"; he, the French Chargé d'Affaires, might as well leave, for all he could do to change matters, he wrote bitterly.

In a dispatch to the Foreign Office dated November, 1811, there are the following succinct headings: *Violent language held by the French Chargé d'Affaires in a note to the Sultan. . . . Mons. Maubourg fails in an attempt to open direct intercourse with His Highness.* And in July, heavily underlined, *The* CREDIT *of the French at Constantinople absolutely* GONE.

For the next two years Mahmoud continued to show marked coldness to France: once again he was looking westward for an ally—always the old atavistic longing for the West—but this time, it was towards England, Napoleon's arch-enemy, that he turned. Perhaps the English could provide as civilizing an influence, and prove more trustworthy allies. Thus Mahmoud; and Aimée, with Joséphine's divorce rankling, did not oppose the anti-French move. Besides, Stratford Canning was a man for whom Mahmoud felt an instinctive respect. Over the years their mutual respect was to grow into something akin to affection: though the period of Canning's greatest influence in Turkish affairs was only to come much later, when, as the Great Elchi, he ruled the Porte beside the Sultan Abd ül Mejid, Mahmoud's son.

While Napoleon dismissed Mahmoud's attitude as being of little importance, Stratford Canning saw a way to turn it to his country's advantage, and, to that end, he succeeded in persuading the Sultan to make peace with the Russians, with whom Turkey had been engaged in a long and costly war over the territories of Bessarabia, Moldavia, and the control of the Danube's Black Sea ports. The war had dragged on with considerable loss of life and prestige to Turkey. But now Mah-

moud had decided he would come to terms with his enemies. That he
chose such a moment, when Russia had the French knife at her throat,
seemed madness. It was obvious that by flinging all his weight against
Russia he could obtain victory, at last. But Mahmoud never acted on
impulse. He had his reasons. His country was not strong enough to win,
not humble enough to lose. The treaty could save lives—and face, too,
even with its humiliating terms (many of which were not incorporated,
or even demanded, at first). But behind all this reasoning we may conclude Mahmoud was also swayed by a long-cherished, private vengeance. He was settling an old score, on his own behalf, and on behalf of
his mother. If we read between the lines of history we can interpret his
action as being due, not only to Stratford Canning's persuasive powers,
but also to an Oriental sense of revenge, of cunning, to arrive, however
circuitously, at the downfall of one who had betrayed him, snubbed
all his advances and those of Selim, and humiliated his mother's cousin
Joséphine. At last, he, Mahmoud, the neglected Oriental, could meet
the great Frenchman on his own ground, and prove the decisive
factor in his fall. Revenge is sweet. Mahmoud was thoroughly Oriental
in this respect: he savored it to the full.

Dispatches to the Foreign Office about this time, speak of the Treaty's
ratification being prepared.

*Suspicion entertained by the Porte of Mr. Canning entirely done
away with.*

In a glow of mutual esteem and united aims, Sultan and Minister
were as one. On May 28, 1812, a month after Napoleon invaded Russia,
he signed the Treaty of Bucharest. This freed the Russian Army of
the Danube to march north, against Napoleon, now standing before
Moscow. It was a vital blow, and it came from a ghost: another message, but this time a deadly one, from the ghost of a Creole girl from
Martinique. The old Euphemia David had foreseen many strange
things; but life was to take an even more fantastic turn than anything
she had foretold the two children who came to visit her, their white
muslin dresses glimmering through the canebrakes in the summer
dusk. What even Talleyrand did not foresee was that when the Grand
Turk turned so inexplicably, so implacably, against Napoleon, it was
really only one little French girl avenging another.

Meanwhile, the Russian campaign had not been going according to
plan; there were the usual series of victories, yet Victory, that total victory to which Napoleon was accustomed, still eluded him. Too late he
realized how decisive the Sultan's support could be in the south, and, to
that end, sent a series of ingratiating overtures which remained unanswered. The prolonged silence was disquieting. He began ordering his
ministers to dispatch couriers "once or twice a week, to Constantinople

to carry the bulletins, and all possible news." And again: "Mere couriers do not have the same effect as officers. Send, therefore, some Polish officers. Have the Polish Confederation send an embassy of three members to Turkey, to act on behalf of the Confederation, to demand the guarantee of Turkey. You will realize the importance of this step." Now, at last, he saw the vital necessity of Turkish co-operation; of Turkish ships blocking the Crimea, and Turkish troops occupying Moldavia and Wallachia; in short, of keeping a large Russian force busy in the south. All this was in July, two months after Mahmoud had signed the Treaty of Bucharest with such secrecy. During all the rest of this fateful summer Mahmoud waited, for once displaying a truly Arab fatalism. He had done all he could. The rest was with Allah.

In August, the Russians were defeated at Smolensk; in September, at Borodino; the French still seemed invincible. In October, the humiliating terms of the Bucharest Treaty leaked out at the Porte, and when the people learned Bessarabia had been ceded to Russia, they turned against the Sultan. The Janissaries set fire to the city and it seemed that Mahmoud must be overthrown. In Moscow, Napoleon, too, had now heard of the Treaty, and realized its terrible implications for himself. Now his own words, *"le sabre est toujours battu par l'esprit"*—"the sword is always beaten by the mind"—were coming home to roost. It was Mahmoud, with the incisive French side of his nature, who had seen the way to deal the fatal blow, and by a stroke of the pen, turn the army of the Danube against the Grand Armée. In December, the French met disaster at Beresina. Napoleon fled to Paris: his men and horses perished in the retreat. It was all over. Aimée, looking out across the Golden Horn, must have wondered if Joséphine understood the message.

When news of the debacle reached London, where Stratford Canning was enjoying a prolonged holiday, he must have smiled, in his glacial way. It was the first of a long series of diplomatic triumphs. It may be recalled that while Canning's biographers claim it as his master-maneuver, the Duke of Wellington, in his memorandum on Napoleon's Russian campaign, claims the *coup de grâce* as being the work of his brother, the Marquis of Wellesley, then head of the Foreign Office (though a rather inert one, from whom Canning never received any instructions of worth). The Iron Duke described the Treaty of Bucharest as being a piece of strategy which gave his brother "the opportunity of rendering the world the most important service that ever fell to the lot of any individual to perform." Against this, David Morier, who was one of Canning's staff at the Porte, writes of the Foreign Office, "then asleep under the Marquis of Wellesley" and how Stratford Canning "without one word of instruction . . . or encouragement took

it upon himself to undertake the task . . . of effecting the peace between
the Porte and the Russian Government just in time to release Chicha-
gov's army. . . . *Quod ego attestor."*

But while the great statesmen and diplomats each claimed the master
stroke for themselves, they all overlooked the part played by a French
woman who remained faithful to the memories of her childhood.

Piece by piece, in fragments and snatches, the history of that faraway
moment is reconstructed, much of it, indeed almost all that centers
round Aimée Dubucq de Rivery, a matter of shadowy conjecture. The
walls of the Seraglio were high, dispatches were terse and did not dwell
on the more personal aspects or shades of influence round the Sultan's
throne. Even so, a thread is traced, through the great calfbound reports, stuffed away in the Foreign Office Archives or among the cliffs
of parchment in the Records Office. This was before the printed reports, or Blue Books, gave a spurious air of simplicity to the minutia
collected on each question where H.B.M. Foreign representatives were
concerned. Page after page of elegant flourishes, faded longhand by
some forgotten Embassy clerk . . . each dispatch opening dramatic
perspectives, however laconic the entry. Mahmoud's terrible struggle
with the Janissaries is summarized thus:

*Feb. 19, 1815. An attempt to reform the Janissaries. Disturbance in
consequence.*

*Feb. 25. Conflict in consequence of the perseverance of the Sultan
to reform the Janissaries.*

On March 10 a more sinister note sounds. *Atonement of the Janissaries for the late Acts of Violence against the Sultan.*

Mahmoud also seems to have made a good many gestures of purely
domestic *politesse* which are also scrupulously recorded in the files.
We read: *The Sultan's answer on the accouchement of the Duchess
of Cumberland,* or again, *The Sultan's answer to the Royal Letter on
the death of the Princess Charlotte.* Sometimes there are entries which
rouse wildest speculations and set one off on a further paper chase, bur-
rowing through the parchment cliffs.

*Arrival of a Confidential Person from Vienna, with disclosures relat-
ing to Bonaparte's marriage.* Or this, sandwiched between passages dealing with the Elgin marbles (referred to as Lord Elgin's Antiquities).

*Relative to a Dagger Intended for Constantinople, Messrs. Rundell
and Co., London.* But for what purpose, we wonder? Are we to suppose no worthy blade could be obtained in Turkey? Was violence afoot,
and could no member of the British Embassy risk purchasing a weapon
openly in the bazaars? Or was it intended as a present, best Sheffield
steel, a token of esteem to some Three-Tailed Bashaw?

For so much of the year 1812-1813, not only the French, but the British, too, were kept wholly in the dark as to the Sultan's real intentions, their only means of information being through their dragomans, or Embassy interpreters, who were Turks, and when their Sultan chose, singularly ill-informed. Mahmoud must have found a certain cynical satisfaction in appearing to comply with Canning's designs, while in reality following his own. If he had no counselors, neither did he seek confidence. Save for his mother, he always walked alone. One thing is clear: behind his acquiescence to the terms of the Treaty, behind his risk of internal anarchy, there seems to lie some purely personal motive. Why not? History is made by man, and man is made up of such impulses.

All through his life, a curiously malign fate seemed to stalk Mahmoud. His internal reforms were often balked by exterior causes; his armies decimated by overwhelming odds; and his country cynically used as a pawn in the game of international power politics. No sooner was the Russian threat removed, no sooner had Napoleon fallen, than the great pashas of his distant provinces banded together in defiance of his authority. In Egypt, Mohammed Ali, after butchering the Mamelukes, settled himself more firmly in his palace, and ruled there in defiance of the Sultan's orders. In Albania, Ali Pasha of Janina held the southestern provinces in thrall, and it was not until 1820 that Mahmoud was strong enough to crush him. None of his most cherished reforms could be achieved, he knew, unless he had, behind him, a strong and loyal army. It took him twenty years to build up such troops, for, at every step, there were the Janissaries to be reckoned with. But Mahmoud's invincible will, his growing sagacity, and above all, his quiet patience, held firm. He felt himself utterly alone, for although, when Canning was reappointed to the Porte in 1826, he proffered friendship, it was primarily a means of furthering British interests. The Great Elchi's real love for the Turkish people was only to grow, slowly, with the half-century he spent among them, culminating in the Crimean War of 1853. In the middle years of Mahmoud's reign there was still some mistrust, and many misunderstandings, which faded slowly, but did at last vanish in the glow of mutual respect and friendship.

Unhappy Mahmoud! He was born before his time; he chafed against the ignorance and prejudice of traditionalism; his enemies were quick to capitalize on his failures; even his progressive measures were regarded as the work of an iconoclast—an infidel. Alone together, mother and son went over the problems which beset them: it always came back to the same point: no reforms could be lasting, so long as the Janissaries remained to block the way: and as long as Mahmoud's army was inefficiently equipped, or harbored any Janissaries in its ranks, all hope of

real progress was out of the question. All then, hinged on the formation
of a new army, and like Selim before him, Mahmoud set about it,
laboriously. Step by step, mother and son continued to plan, in secret,
those various reforms which gained Mahmoud his title, and, at long
last, overcame the taunts of *Sultan Giaour* or *Infidel Padishah*. Between
them they had opened the windows. A bracing northern wind swept
in from Europe, stirring the falling leaves of the Seraglio courtyards,
rattling at the casements, imperatively. Before it, the phantoms faded;
at last even tradition was overcome.

But long before that day, Mahmoud had lost the guiding inspiration
of his life. In 1817 the little French girl from Martinique, *Naksh*, The
Beautiful One, The Powerful One, she who was to change the face of
Turkey, died in the Seraglio, where she had lived, since entering it
thirty-three years before. Just as the old fortuneteller had foreseen, great
triumphs and glories had been hers, and at the very moment Mahmoud's innovations seemed triumphant, when her happiness seemed
won, it was to fade, with her life.

On a winter night in 1817, five years after that snowy evening
when mother and son had learned of Napoleon's defeat, a boat crossed
the Golden Horn, and two men hurried to the Convent of Saint An-
toine, at Pera. It was a time of tempest; the winds howled round the
creaking wooden houses, rattling the shutters. No one was abroad:
only the five watchmen continued their rounds, striking their iron staves
on the stones as they walked, forever on guard for the outbreaks which
perpetually ravaged the city. The Superior of the Convent, Father
Chrysostome, was kneeling at prayer in his cell, when he was disturbed by a violent knocking on the doors. Two guards stood before
him, and bowing ceremoniously, presented a letter bearing the Imperial
*tughra*, or cypher. Escorted by the guards, Father Chrysostome went
down the steep descent to Galata, where a splendid caïque, with twelve
pairs of oars, was waiting. The caïque shot away from the shore, and
was lost in the blackness of the night. Arrived at the farther shore,
the priest was led through deserted gardens, and ushered into a room,
decorated with silken hangings, fine carpets and candelabra. It was,
for all its luxury, a lugubrious room. On the bed lay a dying woman,
attended by a Greek doctor. Beside the door two black slaves were
ranged. A few paces away stood a man whose bearing showed great
distinction, but who seemed overwhelmed with grief. "This man appeared to be about forty years of age; his height was above the ordinary; his brow high, and noble; his expression commanding. His beard
was black, and gave his face an impressive, grave beauty. His costume
was simple, but of a singular elegance. The sobs and lamentations,

which he was unable to control, told of his anguish." When Father Chrysostome entered the room, this man, whom all in the place obeyed, signaled the slaves to withdraw, the doctor, too. Approaching the bed, he bent over the dying woman. "My mother," he said, "you wished to die in the religion of your fathers. Let your wish be fulfilled." He motioned the priest forward, and stepped back into the shadows.

The priest listened to the woman's confession, her prayers and repentances; for more than an hour he prayed with her. Then, as she sank, he gave her Absolution. As the words of Extreme Unction sounded, the bearded man, sole witness of the scene, approached the bed, flung himself down beside it. The Padishah of the Faithful, "the Sultan Giaour" was calling upon Allah, in his loss.

Father Chrysostome was escorted back to the Convent by the same guards who had fetched him. Not a word was spoken. When he reached the Convent he found the Brothers waiting for him anxiously. In silence he went past them to spend the rest of the night before the altar, praying for the soul of Aimée Dubucq de Rivery, Sultan Valideh of Turkey.

Aimée died, as she had lived, in the Catholic faith. But she lies in one of the most splendid of all the Imperial Turbehs not far from Santa Sophia, in the high state befitting a Sultan's mother. The sunlight pierces the grilled windows, falling across the velvet catafalque; the trees in the little garden outside cast dappled shadows on the shimmering walls. Her epitaph is full of flowery phrases, and there is one oblique reference to her French blood. She is "Naksh, The Beautiful One, the Queen Mother, of noble foreign blood."

> Of her, Mahmoud, the Sultan of the World, was begotten,
> Of her, the Majestic Emperor of Shining Soul, was born . . .
> He, who opened the Gate of the Orient to a new light.

She, who may truly be said to have opened the Gate of the Orient to a new light, remains veiled, all her work attributed to her son; but then, perhaps, to achieve such a Prince had been life's work enough. Mahmoud, the son, had surrounded his mother's tomb with all the grandeur an Ottoman Sultan could devise. But Mahmoud the Reformer had one more tribute to pay.

At the first opportune moment, in 1826, nine years after Aimée's death, that Sultan whom she had taught French nursery rhymes, and so many other things, besides, crushed forever the Janissaries, so long her enemies, the butchers of Selim, the enemies of all that progress she had so ardently desired.

Mother and son had worked all their lives for this moment, and when at last it came, the mother was dead; but the son was ready. For years they had been compiling a list of the Janissaries' ringleaders. His new troops had been trained in secret, on the lines of a Western army. Thousands of muskets had been purchased in secrecy, too. So, when on that June morning, columns of smoke rising from Stamboul told the citizens of Pera that once again the Janissaries had mutinied, and were burning and looting the city, Mahmoud rode out to meet their challenge.

He went first to the Sultan Achmet mosque, where he raised Mohammed's sacred green banner, the Sandjuk Sherif, and standing beneath its fluttering silk, he denounced the Janissaries, and called on his people to destroy them. With pistols and daggers stuck in his belt he led his troops to the attack. The Janissaries knew their hour had struck, and fought desperately. The slaughter went on all day. Their barracks were fired. They were shot down and hunted out, their leaders hanged from the great plane tree outside their quarters in the Seraglio, where for so long they had strung up their own victims. From his house at Pera, Stratford Canning, newly returned to the Porte, watched the smoke rising ominously, and reflected on the monstrous abuses of power practiced by the Praetorian Guard, the Streltzi, and now the Janissaries, all of whom were to perish by their own corruption. His diary goes on to say that the sea of Marmora was mottled with dead bodies. *"The entrance to the Seraglio, the shore under the Sultan's window . . . are crowded with dead—many of them torn and in part devoured by the dogs."* No quarter was given. By nightfall five thousand had been killed. Next day, the formal abolition of the Corps was proclaimed in the Mosques. On June 22, Canning notes, *"All is as quiet here as the bowstring and saber can make it. . . . Executions and transportations go on incessantly. . . . Everything seems changed, or changing. . . ."* Canning was amazed to see how the Sultan's authority grew daily more assured. There was no murmur of counterrevolution. Mahmoud had proved himself master. His people were ready to follow him in his new policies. It had been a terrible tribute which Mahmoud the Reformer paid to Aimée Dubucq de Rivery, his mother; and it was a last triumphant message of victory sent by the ghost, to that Western world to which she had once belonged.

# THE JILTING OF GRANNY WEATHERALL

*Katherine Anne Porter*

KATHERINE ANNE PORTER (1890–    ) by common critical consent occupies a unique place among American writers. Despite a
remarkably slender output for one who has been putting pen to
paper since childhood, her rare, pure style and elegance of mind
have won readers all over the world, and prizes and honors as well.
*Flowering Judas, Pale Horse, Pale Rider* were early examples of her
work and, in between, other stories and essays have continued to
come, spaced too far apart for her admirers. *Ship of Fools* has been
one of the most popular and critically acclaimed novels of the decade.
Miss Porter was born in a small Texas town of ancestors who trace
back to American Revolutionary days. Withdrawn, reluctant, she
spins her skein to perfection before being satisfied.

SHE flicked her wrist neatly out of Doctor Harry's pudgy careful fingers and pulled the sheet up to her chin. The brat ought
to be in knee breeches. Doctoring around the country with spectacles on his nose! "Get along now, take your schoolbooks and go.
There's nothing wrong with me."

Doctor Harry spread a warm paw like a cushion on her forehead
where the forked green vein danced and made her eyelids twitch. "Now,
now, be a good girl, and we'll have you up in no time."

"That's no way to speak to a woman nearly eighty years old just
because she's down. I'd have you respect your elders, young man."

"Well, Missy, excuse me." Doctor Harry patted her cheek. "But I've
got to warn you, haven't I? You're a marvel, but you must be careful or
you're going to be good and sorry."

"Don't tell me what I'm going to be. I'm on my feet now, morally
speaking. It's Cornelia. I had to go to bed to get rid of her."

Her bones felt loose, and floated around in her skin, and Doctor
Harry floated like a balloon around the foot of the bed. He floated and
pulled down his waistcoat and swung his glasses on a cord. "Well, stay
where you are, it certainly can't hurt you."

"Get along and doctor your sick," said Granny Weatherall. "Leave a well woman alone. I'll call for you when I want you. . . . Where were you forty years ago when I pulled through milk-leg and double pneumonia? You weren't even born. Don't let Cornelia lead you on," she shouted, because Doctor Harry appeared to float up to the ceiling and out. "I pay my own bills, and I don't throw my money away on non-sense!"

She meant to wave good-by, but it was too much trouble. Her eyes closed of themselves, it was like a dark curtain drawn around the bed. The pillow rose and floated under her, pleasant as a hammock in a light wind. She listened to the leaves rustling outside the window. No, somebody was swishing newspapers: no, Cornelia and Doctor Harry were whispering together. She leaped broad awake, thinking they whispered in her ear.

"She was never like this, *never* like this!" "Well, what can we expect?" "Yes, eighty years old. . . ."

Well, and what if she was? She still had ears. It was like Cornelia to whisper around doors. She always kept things secret in such a public way. She was always being tactful and kind. Cornelia was dutiful; that was the trouble with her. Dutiful and good: "So good and dutiful," said Granny, "that I'd like to spank her." She saw herself spanking Cornelia and making a fine job of it.

"What'd you say, Mother?"

Granny felt her face tying up in hard knots.

"Can't a body think, I'd like to know?"

"I thought you might want something."

"I do. I want a lot of things. First off, go away and don't whisper."

She lay and drowsed, hoping in her sleep that the children would keep out and let her rest a minute. It had been a long day. Not that she was tired. It was always pleasant to snatch a minute now and then. There was always so much to be done, let me see: tomorrow.

Tomorrow was far away and there was nothing to trouble about. Things were finished somehow when the time came; thank God there was always a little margin over for peace: then a person could spread out the plan of life and tuck in the edges orderly. It was good to have everything clean and folded away, with the hair brushes and tonic bottles sitting straight on the white embroidered linen: the day started without fuss and the pantry shelves laid out with rows of jelly glasses and brown jugs and white stone-china jars with blue whirligigs and words painted on them: coffee, tea, sugar, ginger, cinnamon, allspice: and the bronze clock with the lion on top nicely dusted off. The dust that lion could collect in twenty-four hours! The box in the attic with all those letters tied up, well, she'd have to go through that tomorrow. All those letters—George's letters and John's letters and her letters to them both—lying around for the children to find afterwards made her uneasy. Yes, that would be tomorrow's business. No use to let them know how silly she had been once.

While she was rummaging around she found death in her mind and it felt clammy and unfamiliar. She had spent so much time preparing for death there was no need for bringing it up again. Let it take care of itself now. When she was sixty she had felt very old, finished, and went around making farewell trips to see her children and grandchildren, with a secret in her mind: This is the very last of your mother, children! Then she made her will and came down with a long fever. That was all just a notion like a lot of other things, but it was lucky too, for she had once for all got over the idea of dying for a long time. Now she couldn't be worried. She hoped she had better sense now. Her father had lived to be one hundred and two years old and had drunk a noggin of strong hot toddy on his last birthday. He told the reporters it was his daily habit, and he owed his long life to that. He had made quite a scandal and was very pleased about it. She believed she'd just plague Cornelia a little.

"Cornelia! Cornelia!" No footsteps, but a sudden hand on her cheek. "Bless you, where have you been?"

"Here, mother."

"Well, Cornelia, I want a noggin of hot toddy."

"Are you cold, darling?"

"I'm chilly, Cornelia. Lying in bed stops the circulation. I must have told you that a thousand times."

Well, she could just hear Cornelia telling her husband that Mother was getting a little childish and they'd have to humor her. The thing that most annoyed her was that Cornelia thought she was deaf, dumb, and blind. Little hasty glances and tiny gestures tossed around her and over her head saying, "Don't cross her, let her have her way, she's eighty years old," and she sitting there as if she lived in a thin glass cage. Sometimes Granny almost made up her mind to pack up and move back to her own house where nobody could remind her every minute that she was old. Wait, wait, Cornelia, till your own children whisper behind your back!

In her day she had kept a better house and had got more work done. She wasn't too old yet for Lydia to be driving eighty miles for advice when one of the children jumped the track, and Jimmy still dropped in and talked things over: "Now, Mammy, you've a good business head, I want to know what you think of this? . . ." Old. Cornelia couldn't change the furniture around without asking. Little things, little things! They had been so sweet when they were little. Granny wished the old days were back again with the children young and everything to be done over. It had been a hard pull, but not too much for her. When she thought of all the food she had cooked, and all the clothes she had cut and sewed, and all the gardens she had made—well, the children showed it. There they were, made out of her, and they couldn't get away from that. Sometimes she wanted to see John again and point to them and say, Well, I didn't do so badly, did I? But that would have to wait. That was for tomorrow. She used to think of him as a man, but now all the children were older than their father, and he would be a child beside her if she saw him now. It seemed strange and there was something wrong in the idea. Why, he couldn't possibly recognize her. She had fenced in a hundred acres once, digging the post holes herself and clamping the wires with just a negro boy to help. That changed a woman. John would be looking for a young woman with the peaked Spanish comb in her hair and the painted fan. Digging post holes changed a woman. Riding country roads in the winter when women had their babies was another thing: sitting up nights with sick horses and sick negroes and sick children and hardly ever losing one. John, I hardly ever lost one of them! John would see that in a minute, that would be something he could understand, she wouldn't have to explain anything!

It made her feel like rolling up her sleeves and putting the whole place to rights again. No matter if Cornelia was determined to be everywhere at once, there were a great many things left undone on this place. She would start tomorrow and do them. It was good to be strong enough for everything, even if all you made melted and changed and slipped under your hands, so that by the time you finished you almost forgot what you were working for. What was it I set out to do? she asked herself intently, but she could not remember. A fog rose over the valley, she saw it marching across the creek swallowing the trees and moving up the hill like an army of ghosts. Soon it would be at the near edge of the orchard, and then it was time to go in and light the lamps. Come in, children, don't stay out in the night air.

Lighting the lamps had been beautiful. The children huddled up to her and breathed like little calves waiting at the bars in the twilight. Their eyes followed the match and watched the flame rise and settle in a blue curve, then they moved away from her. The lamp was lit, they didn't have to be scared and hang on to mother anymore. Never, never, never more. God, for all my life I thank Thee. Without Thee, my God, I could never have done it. Hail, Mary, full of grace.

I want you to pick all the fruit this year and see that nothing is wasted. There's always someone who can use it. Don't let good things rot for want of using. You waste life when you waste good food. Don't let things get lost. It's bitter to lose things. Now, don't let me get to thinking, not when I am tired and taking a little nap before supper.

. . .

The pillow rose about her shoulders and pressed against her heart and the memory was being squeezed out of it: oh, push down the pillow, somebody: it would smother her if she tried to hold it. Such a fresh breeze blowing and such a green day with no threats in it. But he had not come, just the same. What does a woman do when she has put on the white veil and set out the white cake for a man and he doesn't come? She tried to remember. No, I swear he never harmed me but in that. He never harmed me but in that . . . and what if he did? There was the day, the day, but a whirl of dark smoke rose and covered it, crept up and over into the bright field where everything was planted so carefully in orderly rows. That was hell, she knew hell when she saw it. For sixty years she had prayed against remembering him and against losing her soul in the deep pit of hell, and now the two things were mingled in one and the thought of him was a smoky cloud from hell that moved and crept in her head when she had just got rid of Doctor Harry and was trying to rest a minute. Wounded vanity, Ellen, said a sharp voice in the top of her mind. Don't let your wounded vanity get the upper hand of you. Plenty of girls get jilted. You were jilted, weren't you? Then stand up to it. Her eyelids wavered and let in streamers of blue-gray light like tissue paper over her eyes. She must get up and pull the shades down or she'd never sleep. She was in bed again and the shades were not down. How could that happen? Better turn over, hide from the light, sleeping in the light gave you nightmares. "Mother, how do you feel now?" and a stinging wetness on her forehead. But I don't like having my face washed in cold water!

Hapsy? George? Lydia? Jimmy? No, Cornelia, and her features were swollen and full of little puddles. "They're coming, darling, they'll all be here soon." Go wash your face, child, you look funny.

Instead of obeying, Cornelia knelt down and put her head on the pillow. She seemed to be talking but there was no sound. "Well, are you tongue-tied? Whose birthday is it? Are you going to give a party?"

Cornelia's mouth moved urgently in strange shapes. "Don't do that, you bother me, daughter."

"Oh, no, Mother. Oh, no. . . ."

Nonsense. It was strange about children. They disputed your every word. "No what, Cornelia?"

"Here's Doctor Harry."

"I won't see that boy again. He just left five minutes ago."

"That was this morning, Mother. It's night now. Here's the nurse."

"This is Doctor Harry, Mrs. Weatherall. I never saw you look so young and happy!"

"Ah, I'll never be young again—but I'd be happy if they'd let me lie in peace and get rested."

She thought she spoke up loudly, but no one answered. A warm weight on her forehead, a warm bracelet on her wrist, and a breeze went on whispering, trying to tell her something. A shuffle of leaves in the everlasting hand of God, He blew on them and they danced and rattled. "Mother, don't mind, we're going to give you a little hypodermic." "Look here, daughter, how do ants get in this bed? I saw sugar ants yesterday." Did you send for Hapsy too?

It was Hapsy she really wanted. She had to go a long way back through a great many rooms to find Hapsy standing with a baby on her arm. She seemed to herself to be Hapsy also, and the baby on Hapsy's arm was Hapsy and himself and herself, all at once, and there was no surprise in the meeting. Then Hapsy melted from within and turned flimsy as gray gauze and the baby was a gauzy shadow, and Hapsy came up close and said, "I thought you'd never come," and looked at her very searchingly and said, "You haven't changed a bit!" They leaned forward to kiss, when Cornelia began whispering from a long way off, "Oh, is there anything you want to tell me? Is there anything I can do for you?"

Yes, she had changed her mind after sixty years and she would like to see George. I want you to find George. Find him and be sure to tell him I forgot him. I want him to know I had my husband just the same and my children and my house like any other woman. A good house too and a good husband that I loved and fine children out of him. Better than I hoped for even. Tell him I was given back everything he took away and more. Oh, no, oh, God, no, there was something else besides the house and the man and the children. Oh, surely they were not all? What was it? Something not given back. . . . Her breath crowded down under her ribs and grew into a monstrous frightening shape with cutting edges; it bored up into her head, and the agony was unbelievable: Yes, John, get the Doctor now, no more talk, my time has come.

When this one was born it should be the last. The last. It should have been born first, for it was the one she had truly wanted. Everything came in good time. Nothing left out, left over. She was strong, in three days she would be as well as ever. Better. A woman needed milk in her to have her full health.

"Mother, do you hear me?"

"I've been telling you—"

"Mother, Father Connolly's here."

"I went to Holy Communion only last week. Tell him I'm not so sinful as all that."

"Father just wants to speak to you."

He could speak as much as he pleased. It was like him to drop in and inquire about her soul as if it were a teething baby, and then stay on for a cup of tea and a round of cards and gossip. He always had a funny story of some sort, usually about an Irishman who made his little mistakes and confessed them, and the point lay in some absurd thing he would blurt out in the confessional showing his struggles between native piety and original sin. Granny felt easy about her soul. Cornelia, where are your manners? Give Father Connolly a chair. She had her secret comfortable understanding with a few favorite saints who cleared a straight road to God for her. All as surely signed and sealed as the papers for the new Forty Acres. Forever . . . heirs and assigns forever. Since the day the wedding cake was not cut, but thrown out and wasted. The whole bottom dropped out of the world, and there she was blind and sweating with nothing under her feet and the walls falling away. His hand had caught her under the breast, she had not fallen, there was the freshly polished floor with the green rug on it, just as before. He had cursed like a sailor's parrot and said, "I'll kill him for you." Don't lay a hand on him, for my sake leave something to God. "Now, Ellen, you must believe what I tell you. . . ."

So there was nothing, nothing to worry about any more, except sometimes in the night one of the children screamed in a nightmare, and they both hustled out shaking and hunting for the matches and calling, "There, wait a minute, here we are!" John, get the doctor now, Hapsy's time has come. But there was Hapsy standing by the bed in a white cap. "Cornelia, tell Hapsy to take off her cap. I can't see her plain."

Her eyes opened very wide and the room stood out like a picture she had seen somewhere. Dark colors with the shadows rising towards the ceiling in long angles. The tall black dresser gleamed with nothing on it but John's picture, enlarged from a little one, with John's eyes very black when they should have been blue. You never saw him, so how do you know how he looked? But the man insisted the copy was perfect, it was very rich and handsome. For a picture, yes, but it's not my husband. The table by the bed had a linen cover and a candle and a crucifix. The light was blue from Cornelia's silk lampshades. No sort of light at all, just frippery. You had to live forty years with kerosene lamps to appreciate honest electricity. She felt very strong and she saw Doctor Harry with a rosy nimbus around him.

"You look like a saint, Doctor Harry, and I vow that's as near as you'll ever come to it."

"She's saying something."

"I heard you, Cornelia. What's all this carrying-on?"

"Father Connolly's saying—"

Cornelia's voice staggered and bumped like a cart in a bad road. It rounded corners and turned back again and arrived nowhere. Granny stepped up in the cart very lightly and reached for the reins, but a man sat beside her and she knew him by his hands, driving the cart. She did not look in his face, for she knew without seeing, but looked instead down the road where the trees leaned over and bowed to each other and a thousand birds were singing a Mass. She felt like singing too, but she put her hand in the bosom of her dress and pulled out a rosary, and Father Connolly murmured Latin in a very solemn voice and tickled her feet. My God, will you stop that nonsense? I'm a married woman. What if he did run away and leave me to face the priest by myself? I found another a whole world better. I wouldn't have exchanged my husband for anybody except St. Michael himself, and you may tell him that for me with a thank you in the bargain.

Light flashed on her closed eyelids, and a deep roaring shook her. Cornelia, is that lightning? I hear thunder. There's going to be a storm. Close all the windows. Call the children in. . . . "Mother, here we are, all of us." "Is that you, Hapsy?" "Oh, no, I'm Lydia. We drove as fast as we could." Their faces drifted above her, drifted away. The rosary fell out of her hands and Lydia put it back. Jimmy tried to help, their hands fumbled together, and Granny closed two fingers around Jimmy's thumb. Beads wouldn't do, it must be something alive. She was so amazed her thoughts ran round and round. So, my dear Lord, this is my death and I wasn't even thinking about it. My children have come to see me die. But I can't, it's not time. Oh, I always hated surprises. I wanted to give Cornelia the amethyst set—Cornelia, you're to have the amethyst set, but Hapsy's to wear it when she wants, and, Doctor Harry, do shut up. Nobody sent for you. Oh, my dear Lord, do wait a minute. I meant to do something about the Forty Acres, Jimmy doesn't need it and Lydia will later on, with that worthless husband of hers. I meant to finish the altar cloth and send six bottles of wine to Sister Borgia for her dyspepsia. I want to send six bottles of wine to Sister Borgia, Father Connolly, now don't let me forget.

Cornelia's voice made short turns and tilted over and crashed. "Oh, Mother, oh, Mother, oh, Mother. . . ."

"I'm not going, Cornelia. I'm taken by surprise. I can't go."

You'll see Hapsy again. What about her? "I thought you'd never come." Granny made a long journey outward, looking for Hapsy. What if I don't find her? What then? Her heart sank down and down, there was no bottom to death, she couldn't come to the end of it. The blue light from Cornelia's lampshade drew into a tiny point in the center of her brain, it flickered and winked like an eye, quietly it fluttered and dwindled. Granny lay curled down within herself, amazed and watchful, staring at the point of light that was herself; her body was now only a deeper mass of shadow in an endless darkness and this darkness would curl around the light and swallow it up. God, give a sign!

For the second time there was no sign. Again no bridegroom and the priest in the house. She could not remember any other sorrow because this grief wiped them all away. Oh, no, there's nothing more cruel than this—I'll never forgive it. She stretched herself with a deep breath and blew out the light.

# OPERATION HEARTBREAK

## Duff Cooper

ALFRED DUFF COOPER (1890–1954) was a man of many
careers. Born in London, he received the classical start for a young
upper-class Englishman of Eton and Oxford. This in turn led to a
position in the Foreign Office, interrupted by World War I during
which he saw service in France as an officer in the Brigade of Guards.
Then followed many years as a member of Parliament and in highly
important government posts, climaxed by critical involvement as an
anti-Hitler leader in British politics. After the Second War, full
vindication came with his appointment to France as England's
ambassador. His books, though few, reflect his many areas of interest and are written with wit and charm. Among them is his
notable autobiography *Old Men Forget* which, among other things,
reports on his long and happy life with his wife, the famously beautiful Lady Diana Cooper. Another is the remarkable adventure story
that follows.

### PROLOGUE

IT was a long way from the capital to the coast, and they had been
obliged to leave very early in the morning. It had been cool then,
but now, although it was not yet midday, the three occupants of
the car were suffering from the heat.

The Military Attaché was also suffering from the wound which had
incapacitated him for further active service. It still caused him, at times,
acute pain. He would have thought it unmanly to say so, although it
would have secured him sympathy and forbearance. He preferred to
vent his misery by bullying his subordinates, being rude to his equals
and insolent to his superiors. He had recently arrived at his new post,
and was anxious to lose no time in becoming acquainted with his work.
He therefore resented bitterly having to spend a whole hot day attending the funeral of a brother officer whom he had never liked.

The Chaplain was equally unhappy. During a residence of several
years he had acquired the habits of the country, which did not include

long drives over bad roads in the heat of the day. He had put on weight recently, which he regretted, but he had no wish to lose it in the way he seemed likely to do in the next few hours. He was beginning to wonder in what state his collar would be when it came to conducting the service. Not that it would matter much what he looked like or said, he reflected bitterly, as nobody except his two companions would ever see him again or understand a word he was saying.

The third occupant of the car had been looking forward to the day's outing, and was determined to enjoy it. The Assistant Military Attaché was a very young officer, whose health had caused him to be sent abroad, in the hope that he might benefit from a dry climate. He was well aware of the growing discomfort of his elders, which afforded him a good deal of amusement.

"It's getting nice and warm," he said cheerfully, as the Chaplain for the third time mopped his brow. "I suggest we stop somewhere and have a drink."

The Chaplain and the Military Attaché hesitated. Each was determined to take the opposite line to the other and therefore waited for the other to speak first.

At last the Military Attaché said, "There's nothing fit to drink in this damned country, and there aren't any decent pubs."

The Chaplain pursed his lips. "I think that a glass of cold water would be very refreshing."

"As good a way of getting typhoid as any other, I suppose," grunted the Military Attaché.

"The ordinary water in this district is singularly pure," said the Chaplain. "If you won't take my word for it, you can doubtless obtain mineral water."

"Well, we should have to order something," said the Military Attaché. "It would hardly do if a great big British Embassy car drew up outside one of these miserable little inns, and three full-grown men, in their best clothes, jumped out and asked for three glasses of cold water for the good of the house. Remember, these people are neutrals, and we want 'em to remain so, and not to drive the whole country into the arms of the enemy. Use your imagination, Padre, if you've got any."

The Assistant Military Attaché felt that he could accept the argument as qualified assent. "May I tell the chauffeur to stop at the next likely place, sir? I've got a flask of whisky in my pocket, if you'd care for a whisky-and-soda. We can easily get soda-water, and personally I like the wine of the country."

Now, a whisky-and-soda was the one thing on earth that the Military Attaché most wanted, but all he said was: "Very well, you can do as you wish."

A few minutes later the three of them were sitting in the cool shade of a great tree with two bottles before them, a jug of water and a bowl of ice. The Assistant Military Attaché, who knew more of the language than either of the others, had slipped into the rôle of master of ceremonies. He first half filled the Military Attaché's glass with whisky from his flask and then poured in the mineral water. The Military Attaché saw that it was strong, but felt he needed it. He was in pain, but determined not to show it. He could sleep during the rest of the journey, and all he had to do at the end of it was to stand to attention.

The Assistant Military Attaché helped himself to wine and then, seeing that the Chaplain was gazing rather dejectedly at his glass of cold water, he leant over and poured some whisky into it, saying in reply to the feeble protest, "Come on, Padre, you know you like it, and it will kill those awful typhoid germs that Colonel Hamilton was talking about."

The Chaplain allowed himself to be persuaded. The Assistant Military Attaché looked at his watch.

"We're well up to time," he said, "and can afford to relax for at least a quarter of an hour."

Peace came to them as they sat there, stillness after speed, shadow after sunlight. Irritation and animosity were smoothed away. The Assistant Military Attaché was sensitive to atmosphere and felt that the moment was favourable for putting questions that he had long been wanting to ask.

"It's a strange business, this funeral that we're attending," he hazarded.

"It's much stranger than you suppose," replied Colonel Hamilton, sipping his whisky.

"He was in your regiment, sir, wasn't he?"

"I suppose so. There's nobody else of that name in the Army List."

"Was he only recently promoted?"

"You're thinking of the telegram I sent two days ago. As they're going to put a stone on his grave, I thought they'd better state his rank correctly. A month ago he was a captain, and one who had been passed over for promotion half a dozen times. He was out of a job, and so far as I could see had little chance of getting one. You saw the reply of the War Office to my telegram. 'Rank correctly stated as major'."

"It does seem a bit mysterious."

"It's as mysterious as be damned."

"Could it have been that he was employed by the Secret Service?"

"No, it couldn't. I don't know much about the Secret Service, and the less you talk about it, young man, the better. I dare say they trip up occasionally, but I can't believe they could be such fools as to employ this particular fellow."

"How about that packet that was found on the body? It was pretty decent of these people here to send it along to the Embassy without opening it."

"How do you know they hadn't opened it?"

"The seals were intact, sir," answered the Assistant Military Attaché confidently.

"Proves nothing," grunted the other, "but they'll know in London."

"Was he a good officer, sir?"

"I never thought so. He was not a fellow of whom I thought very highly. But I suppose there was no harm in him. *De mortuis nil nisi bunkum,* or whatever the old tag is. I'm talking too much. We ought to be on the road. That damned clergyman has gone to sleep. Wake him up and get a move on."

## I

NOBODY ever had fewer relations than Willie Maryngton. Neither his father nor his mother had brothers or sisters, and he himself was an only child. His mother died in giving birth to him on the 1st of January 1900, and his father, a professional soldier, was killed at Villers Cotterets in September, 1914. Willie's childhood was spent at the various military stations to which his father was posted, and his heart was given to the cavalry regiment in which his father served. The little boy could not tell that all the glamour which surrounded that regiment was part of the century he had missed, and that even in the war that was coming the cavalry was destined to play only a secondary rôle.

Willie was at a public school in 1914 when the war broke out, and for a few days he had wild plans of running away and joining the army as a drummer-boy. But news of his father's death, which arrived long after the event, had a sobering as well as a saddening effect, and he determined to concentrate henceforth all his abilities on making himself fit to receive a commission as early as possible. The Officers Training Corps then became for him more attractive than the playing-fields, and, although he had no natural bent for study, the mere name of the Army Class, when he attained to it, inspired him, so that he made up by hard work for what he lacked in ability.

His father had nominated a brother officer to act as the boy's guardian, and when he also fell, without having made any further provision for guardianship, his widow took on the responsibility of looking after Willie during the holidays. The loss of her husband, the care of her children and all the difficulties of war-time had embittered the middle-age of this in many ways admirable woman, leaving her with only one principle in life: the determination to do her duty. She was the daughter as well as the widow of an officer, and the noble ideal of service was the foundation of her character. She had three children; the eldest, Garnet, was three years older than Willie, went to a cheaper public school and was destined for the Royal Army Medical Corps. The youngest was a little girl of two who had been christened Felicity because she was born on the day when her father was promoted to the rank of major.

It was an austere household. There was little money to spare, and Mrs. Osborne, like many people by nature disinclined to spend, had enthusiastically accepted the Government's injunction to economise, and felt every time she saved a shilling a private thrill of pleasure as well as the satisfaction of performing a public duty.

Willie was no burden on the household. Both his father and his mother had had incomes of their own, and he would in due time inherit between two and three thousand pounds a year. Lawyers, whom he never saw, paid his school bills and also paid Mrs. Osborne liberally for his board and lodging in the holidays. She would render meticulous accounts of how the money was spent, and this effort at amateur book-keeping added to her cares, deepening the lines across her forehead and draining the colour from her fine eyes. Neither Willie nor the lawyers looked at the accounts she rendered, but she thought it her duty to render them, and whatever was her duty she would do. For duty was the watchword of this small house, situated between Aldershot and Camberley, and the only problem that could ever arise was to know where duty lay. That once known, the rest was simple.

There was, however, one member of the household to whom neither habits of austerity nor the call of duty made any appeal. If it be true that the criminal classes are largely recruited from the children of clergymen, it is equally easy to discover recalcitrants to the military tradition in officers' families, and even to find the sons of generals in the ranks of the pacifists. Horatio, Mrs. Osborne's second son, was nothing so serious, or so foolish, as a pacifist. He was one of those fortunate people to whom this world seems a vast park of amusement, and who dislike nobody except those who are bent on preventing others from enjoying themselves. To this disagreeable category soldiers, it seemed to Horry, evidently belonged. As a child he had hung about the barrack square and had heard the way in which non-commissioned officers spoke to private soldiers, and he hadn't liked it. He had seen the delinquents paraded for appearance before officers, when they must answer for the crimes of idleness, dirty buttons, unpunctuality, insobriety or absence without leave, and he had felt that those were his friends. He had once heard a drill-sergeant shout at a recruit, "Take that smile off your face," and the incident had made a deep impression on his childish mind. In later years he used to quote it to justify his hatred of militarism, saying that any system which discouraged smiling ought to be damned. There was nothing revolutionary in Horry's attitude; he only felt that soldiers, like schoolmasters—no doubt very good fellows in their way—were the natural enemies of those who, like himself, wanted to have fun.

Horry was younger than Garnet and older than Willie, who liked and looked up to both of them, with the respect that boys feel for immediate seniors. And they liked him. Everybody did. They were also, although he was quite unaware of it, impressed by the wealth that was coming to him, and the independence that it would bring. Garnet felt vaguely that a rich friend might be useful to him in his career. Horry thought what a good time Willie ought to have with his money, and hoped that he might sometimes be allowed to share in it.

Willie was distressed that Garnet should have chosen to go into the R.A.M.C. What he found difficult to understand was why such a big and powerful fellow as Garnet, bigger and more powerful than he would ever be, one who played football for his school and had won boxing competitions, should join a branch of the Service that was not actually engaged in fighting.

"I must say," he said one day to Garnet, greatly daring, "that I shouldn't care for your job—stuck somewhere well behind the lines, cutting people's legs off, with the supply of anaesthetics always running out."

It was difficult to provoke Garnet. Conscious of his own strength and satisfied with his own wisdom, he could take as much teasing as a large St. Bernard dog. He looked at Willie with mild contempt.

"Stuck well behind the lines!" he echoed. "That's all you know about it. Perhaps you'll be surprised to learn that the only man in the Army who has won two Victoria Crosses is a Medical Officer."

This came as news to Willie, but he wouldn't own it, Although he felt that the bottom had been knocked out of his argument.

"Yes," he said, a little flustered, "but decorations are all a matter of luck," quoting something he had heard his father say more than once. "All I meant was"—changing his ground—"that the medical profession is one thing and the military profession another, and I'd rather go in whole-heartedly for one or the other."

"Would you indeed?" replied Garnet calmly. "Well, I prefer to go in whole-heartedly for both."

This seemed to end the conversation, but Garnet, seeing that Willie

had nothing more to say and was feeling snubbed, crushed and crest-
fallen, went on, out of the kindness of his heart:

"And you see, my boy, one has got to think of the future. A day
comes when the Army doesn't want you any more. They turn you out
in the cold with a pension which you can't live on if you've got a wife
and brats. It'll be all right for you, no doubt, because you've got a bit of
money of your own. But lots of chaps find themselves right up against
it and don't know where to turn for a living. An officer of the R.A.M.C.,
on the other hand, is a member of a great profession which he has
been practising all his life. He has had lots of experience, tried all sorts
of climates and had a jolly good time. Then he buys a practice in
some nice part of the country and settles down to a happy old age, while
his pals, who've never been taught to do anything but fight the enemy,
are trying to become secretaries of golf clubs, and when they succeed
they add up the accounts wrong and go to prison for peculation."

This was a long speech for Garnet, but it was a matter to which he
had devoted much thought. While Willie was still considering the new
possibility of being obliged to leave the Army before he wanted to—he
had hitherto believed that soldiers remained soldiers until they died—
Garnet went on:

"And you know, Willie, my grandfather was in the R.A.M.C., which
is another reason for joining it—and a jolly good one, too. I've heard
tell that he was one of the most popular officers in India. He was known
all over the country. They called him the Deliverer of Bengal."

Garnet laughed.

Willie laughed, too, but he didn't know why. The nickname given to
Garnet's grandfather sounded very splendid to Willie—like the title of a
novel by G. A. Henty. But it must be funny if Garnet laughed, for he
did not laugh easily. Willie wondered whether it were something improper. Things usually were if he didn't understand them, but Garnet,
unlike Horry, was not amused by impropriety.

Willie took his problems to the latter for solution. The gynaecological
joke was explained, but Willie didn't think it funny, and when he
asked what Horry meant to do if he had to leave the Army before he
was a very old man, Horry answered:

"See here, little Willie" (an unkind nickname in those days, for it
meant to the British public the German Crown Prince), "the Army's
problem about me is not how long they are going to keep me, but how
they are going to get me into their clutches. That's what's worrying the
War Office and keeping General French awake at night. They'll have
to make this war last as long as the siege of Troy if they hope to get
Horry Osborne into the ranks."

"Into the ranks!" exclaimed Willie. "But don't you want to be an officer?"

"No, I do not," said Horry.

"But what else can one be," asked Willie, "except a barrister, or go into the Diplomatic Service? Surely you wouldn't be a doctor or a clergyman?"

"There are more professions in heaven and earth, little Willie," said Horry, looking very profound, "than are dreamt of in your philosophy."

So Willie's conversation with Horry ended, as had his conversation with Garnet, with a remark that he couldn't understand.

II

THE war went on and the boys grew up. Willie passed into Sandhurst at the earliest opportunity. His arrival there in August 1917 coincided with a prolongation of the course, which had formerly lasted nine months, and in future was to last a year. This was a cruel blow to him. It meant three further months away from the front. He had seriously thought of going through a course in a temporary officers' training corps, which would have lasted only four or six months. But it might have prevented him from getting a regular commission after the war, and the thought that his father had been at Sandhurst had clinched his decision, which he now regretted.

He did not distinguish himself at Sandhurst except by hard work and devotion to duty. He had hitherto had very little opportunity of riding, which he now took to with enthusiasm. He was not, and never became, a fine horseman, but he knew no fear, and the frequency of his falls became a legend. These, combined with his keen enjoyment of work and play, his easy good-nature and his guileless modesty, made him one of the most popular cadets of his year. The fact that he had plenty of money and no hesitation in spending it may have added a little gilding to his genuine charm.

He enjoyed that year. There are few more precious moments than those in which a boy feels for the first time the independence of manhood, when he can take decisions for himself, has no longer to ask permission or account for every action.

One anxiety only marred his happiness, and even made it difficult for him sometimes to share sincerely in the alternate rejoicing and gloom of his companions. When, in the autumn of 1917, orders were given for the church-bells to be rung in celebration of a British victory they brought no message of cheerfulness to Willie's heart, and when, in the following spring, the French and British armies were driven back, until it seemed that the retreat might turn into a rout, he could not suppress a secret thrill of satisfaction. That England could lose the war was not a possibility that ever entered into his calculations. When one of his companions suggested that this might happen he was not even angry, but looked upon that cadet ever after with indulgent pity, as someone who was not in possession of all his wits.

What Willie feared was not defeat but that the war should end before he crossed the Channel. It was not unnatural. During the four most formative years of his life he had had only one ambition. To go into battle with his regiment had been for him the summit of human desire. That regiment had seen comparatively little active service during the previous half-century. Willie had read its history again and again. Perhaps another fifty years would pass without a great war. He had seen somewhere a book called *The War to End War*. The title had sent a shiver of horror down his spine. And he had heard with deep dismay people talking about a League of Nations, which would make war impossible. So all the news that seemed good to others seemed bad to him, and whatever brought hope to most of the world brought him despair.

At the end of the following summer Willie left Sandhurst. He had acquitted himself with credit there, if without distinction, and he had made many friends. It was a proud day when he received his commission, and an anxious one when he presented himself to his regiment. Friends of his father ensured him a good reception among the senior officers; and among the junior ones he already had friends of his own.

The regiment had suffered casualties during the enemy offensive in the spring. There was a shortage of officers in France and every reason to suppose that Willie would find his way there within two or three months. Such leisure as he had from training was therefore devoted to the purchase of kit. No bride ever selected her trousseau with greater care and delight than Willie devoted to the buying of the drab little articles that compose an officer's kit. He never tired of consulting those with experience of such matters concerning the latest gadgets, and he was interested in the smallest details of such objects, from periscopes to writing-pads.

If only the news from the front had been less favourable he would have been the happiest of men. But he consoled himself with the thought—a thought which depressed so many others—that it was only the swing of the pendulum, that pendulum which had swung so often and so far since August 1914. There had been similar waves of optimism, like that which had followed the Battle of Cambrai only a year ago, when many had prophesied that the war would be over by Christmas, only to find that six months later the Allies were seriously thinking of abandoning Paris, and pessimists whispered that the war was lost.

These hopes and fears were for a while expelled by the exultation with which he received orders to be ready to go to France with the next draft. Earlier in the war officers had been granted a week or more "draft leave" before going overseas. This had now been abolished, but there were few if any duties imposed on those who were awaiting departure. Farewells to relatives—a tiresome obligation or a trying ordeal —filled the time of most young men in these circumstances. But no such obligation or ordeal awaited Willie. So that these were idle, happy and proud days for him. He frequented the military club to which he now belonged, and could not suppress a little swagger when he informed his acquaintances that he might be off "any day now." The departure of the draft was twice postponed, to his extreme annoyance, but at last the day was fixed, and Willie, who had promised to spend his last Saturday to Monday at Mrs. Osborne's, travelled down to Camberley on November 9th.

Horry was there on his arrival and greeted him with a cheer.

"Hail, little Willie. Come and kiss me. The war's over, and we're both safe."

"What rot you talk!" said Willie angrily. "I rang up barracks before I left. They had heard nothing. Everything was proceeding according to plan, and the draft is leaving on Wednesday. Instructions from the War Office were to carry on."

"Oh, I don't suppose your rotten old barracks has heard anything, nor the War Office either. It took them about a year to know the war had started, and they'll go on fighting it for a year after it's over, but everybody outside the War Office has heard that the Kaiser's chucked his hand in."

"You think you're very clever, Horry," said Willie, who was now flushed and heated, "but there was an officer at the club this morning, an old officer of my regiment, who did frightfully well in the Matabele war, and he's always been right about this war—Colonel Wright his name is, and he says the Kaiser's abdication will only make the Germans fight more doggedly, and he can speak German, and he thinks the Kaiser had only been a hindrance to Ludendorff and it's probably the German General Staff that have made him get out."

"All right, Willie," said Horry, seeing how deeply the other was feeling. "Three cheers for Colonel Wright, but I hope the old bastard's wrong this time. We'll drink his health in a glass of sherry, if Mum's got one, and hope for the worst."

Willie's wrath, which always went as quickly as it came, evaporated before Horry's smile, and at that moment Mrs. Osborne came into the room. She kissed the two boys with unusual warmth, and Willie noticed with surprise that there was colour in her cheeks and that her eyes were shining as they had not shone for four long years.

When Horry asked if there was any sherry in the house, she said that she had bought a bottle that afternoon and two bottles of claret.

"You'll be surprised," she added, for she saw they were, neither of them ever having seen her drink anything but water, or spend a shilling on the smallest luxury—"but Garnet may be coming to-night or to-morrow, and it will be the first family reunion we've had for so long."

Willie felt that he was not to be the hero of the evening, as he had expected, and he vaguely resented it. Knowing Mrs. Osborne's economy, he had taken his precautions, and he said, as gaily as he could:

"It's not only a family reunion, it's also the orphan's good-bye. I'm off to the war on Wednesday, and I've brought some champagne for you all to drink my health."

Mrs. Osborne gave him a quick look, and the light in her eyes went out for a moment.

"It was very sweet of you, Willie, to think of it," she said quietly. "We shall be very happy to drink your health, and happier still to think that the war is probably not going on much longer."

"Don't be too sure of that," said Willie, adding rather pompously, "There are, if I may say so, two schools of thought on the subject."

"One headed by Colonel Wright and the other by Colonel Wrong," sang Horry as he poured out the sherry.

Sunday was a day of rumours. There was nothing definite in the one newspaper which came to the house. Horry walked into Camberley while Willie played with Felicity, a beautiful, large-eyed, quiet child. Garnet arrived in the afternoon. He was careful not to commit himself, but said that there was no doubt at all that the Kaiser had abdicated and that the German delegates had gone to meet Foch in order to discuss the terms of an armistice.

"After all," said Willie, "an armistice doesn't necessarily mean peace. It's only a kind of an *ent'racte*.

"Quite," said Garnet, "but once the troops have stopped fighting I think it'll be very difficult to persuade them to begin again."

They drank champagne that evening, to which none of them was accustomed, and under its reassuring influence Mrs. Osborne lost her last fears that the war might continue, and Willie forgot his anxiety lest it should stop. Horry was in wonderful form, or at least they all thought he was, and they sat up later than they had ever done in that house.

Willie overslept the next morning, and when he came down found the dining-room empty. Mrs. Osborne was attending to household duties. Garnet and Horry had walked into the village to collect the news. Willie felt deeply depressed. Disconsolately he consumed the tepid remains of breakfast and strolled into the sitting-room, where he found Felicity engrossed in some obscure game with two battered dolls. She took no notice of him. He walked up and down for a minute or two and then he cried out:

"Oh, Felicity, I'm so unhappy."

She turned and looked at him very gravely. Then she nodded her head slowly and said:

"Yes, and I'm unhappy because you are."

The front door was opened and slammed to with a bang. The two young men dashed into the room. Mrs. Osborne followed them, breathless.

"It's all over!" shouted Horry. "No more doubts or rumours. Official announcement. The armistice will be signed this morning at 11 a.m."

"That is to say," added Garnet, looking at his wrist-watch, "in exactly forty-three minutes from now."

Mrs. Osborne's eyes were damp as she stretched out her hands and caught both her sons by an arm. Then she looked at Willie, and saw that his face was white and his lips were quivering.

"Run upstairs, Willie dear," she said quickly, "and see if I left my spectacles in your room."

Willie was through the door, up the stairs and into his room in a flash. He locked the door, threw himself on the bed and burst into tears.

As he lay there sobbing, two superficial sentiments almost made him forget his deeper sorrow. The first of these was shame that he, a grown man, holding the King's Commission, should have broken down and cried as he had never cried since he could remember. The other sentiment was one of profound gratitude to Mrs. Osborne, gratitude that made him love her, for having saved him from disgracing himself before the others. One could see that she was a soldier's daughter, he thought, by the rapidity with which she had appreciated the situation and given the right word of command. That was how he must act if ever he found himself in a critical situation in the war, and then he remembered again, with a fresh pang, that the war was over. But he could not lie there all day blubbing like a baby. It was nearly eleven o'clock. He must go downstairs and show a brave face, not a tear-stained one, if he could help it.

Having bathed his eyes and brushed his hair, he went downstairs, hearing the hall clock strike eleven as he went. He found them in the dining-room, where Horry was too busy struggling with the recalcitrant cork of a champagne bottle to pay any undue attention to his entry. The cork came out, followed by some of the contents of the bottle, which flowed over the table-cloth. Horry mopped up the spilt wine

with his fingers, which he then rubbed behind his ears, explaining to
his surprised companions that this was for luck. Then he filled the four
glasses.

"Here, Willie," he said, "have a glass of your own champagne, and
as you won't like to drink to peace, let's drink to the next war."

"No," said Mrs. Osborne; "that would be wicked. Let us drink to
the British Army," which they did, she adding softly to herself as the
glass touched her lips, "Alive and dead."

"We've forgotten Felicity," cried Horry. "If she never drinks champagne again in her life she must have some to-day."

They found her in the next room, still absorbed in her play. Horry
filled a liqueur glass and told her she must drink it all for luck. She
obeyed solemnly, and when asked if she liked it, she felt that the occasion called for something special, so she brought out an expression of
Horry's.

"Yes," she said, "damned good."

When the young men shouted with laughter, her large dark eyes
sparkled with success and mischief.

That afternoon Horry accompanied Willie to London. The sorrows
of youth, like the sorrows of childhood, although they may leave deep
wounds and lasting scars, can be quickly, if only temporarily, banished
by other distractions. Among the crowds that thronged the streets that
day, waving flags and cheering vociferously, there were few who waved
more enthusiastically or cheered louder than Willie, who had felt a
few hours earlier that there was nothing left to live for on earth.

By dinner-time they were both exhausted, and Horry said that if
Willie would pay the bill he would take him to the best restaurant in
London. Willie didn't mind what he paid, so they dined at Ornano's,
which did seem to Willie a very wonderful place indeed, and he was
glad to notice that even some of Horry's self-assurance deserted him
when the urbane head-waiter of historic fame approached them with
the menu. His attentions were mainly owing to the fact that the restaurant was almost empty, for they were dining at an unfashionably early
hour, and this was also why, Horry explained, none of the famous men
and beautiful women, whose presence he had promised, had yet arrived. Food was bad in those days and insufficient; sugar and butter
were almost unobtainable, but what was served to the young men,
seated on one of the corner sofas in a dim pink light, with music
gently playing, seemed to them delectable. The champagne was really
good, and so was the brandy, though it had not, as they imagined,
been bottled in the reign of Napoleon I.

They had had a long day and a great experience. They felt tired, but
very pleasantly so. The sophisticated atmosphere of the restaurant

made them feel suddenly older. The wine was able to have its soft, mellowing effect. Self-consciousness, the curse of English youth, fell from them, and they found words coming to them easily. Willie was able to pour forth all his sorrows, and the burden of them grew lighter for the telling. He even confessed that he had wept in his room that morning.

"I knew you had, old boy," said Horry. "We all knew, and we all thought the more of you. But don't you worry. You're not nineteen yet, and you'll be young for another twelve years. I'll bet there's another war in less time than that. You don't insist on a European war, do you? They're a damned sight too dangerous, in my opinion. You'd have much more fun smashing up the old Zulus or leading a cavalry charge against a pack of dancing Dervishes, like the 21st Lancers did at Omdurman. You see, you've got a vocation, Willie. I've always felt you had. You're a born soldier. You've never dreamt of being anything else—have you? Admit it!"

Willie, who was now enjoying himself enormously, gladly admitted it, and Horry went on:

"Now, if a man's got a vocation he always makes good. Somehow, sometime, his opportunity comes, and because it's the one thing he's been waiting for all his life, he's ready when it comes and he takes it. Your chance will come all right—and you'll take it—don't worry."

He paused a moment and lit a cigarette, while Willie, profoundly believing all that he had said, felt as though he had already distinguished himself in a war, and tried to look modest.

"You may not believe it," Horry went on, "but I've got a vocation too. But mine's a secret. I don't think I can tell you because, if you have a fault, it is that you're a bit old-fashioned, and you might be shocked."

"Oh, do tell me about your vocation, Horry," said Willie. "I long to hear, and I swear not to tell anybody."

"Let's have two more brandies first," said Horry, "one for you, to help you bear the shock, and one for me, because I like it."

The brandies were ordered, and they took some time to come, while Horry smoked reflectively and Willie wondered what Horry's vocation could possibly be.

"Well," said Horry at last, speaking with deliberation as he sipped his brandy, "it may surprise you, Willie, to learn that ever since I was ten years old I have had only one ambition in life, and that is to go on the stage."

Willie was shocked. Had he been in a less receptive mood the shock would have been greater, but to-night everything seemed strange and new; the world had changed since yesterday. His first thought was that Horry was making fun of him, as he had so often done before.

"You're pulling my leg?" he asked hopefully.

"I never was more serious in my life," was the reply.

"But, but," Willie stammered, "chaps like us can't be actors."

"What do you mean by chaps like us?" asked Horry scornfully.

"Damn it, Horry, I mean gentlemen." He could not have said it if he had been quite sober.

"There you are," exclaimed Horry. "I said you were old-fashioned. I might say you were a snob, but I know you're not. You're living in the past. Times have changed. They had changed even before the war, and they're going to change a jolly sight quicker after it. Not gentlemen, indeed! How about Sir Henry Irving and Sir Herbert Tree? And Charles Hawtrey was at Eton! And there's Gerald du Maurier, just got a commission in the Irish Guards. Since when have the Irish Guards given commissions to chaps who weren't gentlemen?"

This last argument, although the fact on which it was based was not strictly accurate, carried most weight with Willie. But he remembered hearing his father say that an officer, in a good regiment, who married an actress, would have to send in his papers. Yet it seemed to him easier for an actress to be a lady than for an actor to be a gentlemen. He had heard of people's daughters going on the stage, not without parental protest, but never of their sons doing so. However, he didn't want to quarrel to-night, or even to argue. He had always been fond of Horry, but never so fond as now, so that he allowed himself to be easily converted, and soon he was discussing with animation the kind of parts in which Horry would do best.

When they left the restaurant the Strand was quiet, although sounds of revelry came from the Mall, where the mob were burning a German cannon. The two young men walked home arm in arm, feeling happy and very superior to the roisterers. Horry was taking his call at the end of a triumphant first night, and Willie was galloping across the veld, at the head of his regiment, under a hail of assegais.

III

THE twenty-one years that passed between the two great wars seemed to many who lived through them to go quickly. The passage of time is measured by events, and when there are few events time passes unnoticed. It certainly flowed smoothly for Willie Maryngton. When he came to look back on it all, on the eve of the second world war, he was surprised to find how few events there were that stuck out in his memory.

He remembered very well leaving for the Continent two days after the Armistice. It was the journey to which he had been looking forward for years. How different it was from all that he had imagined! The thrill of war had been taken out of it, and there was nothing left but confusion, delay and discomfort. Inaccurate information awaited him at every turn. The troops were moving forward as fast as he was, and much faster than correct news of their movements travelled back.

He caught them up at last, and spent some months with the army of occupation. It was a depressing and disillusioning experience. Depressing because once again he found that the happiest hours spent by his brother officers were the least happy ones for him. These would occur at evening, in the mess, when the port was going round. Then would begin the endless discussions and reminiscences of the fighting. Sometimes these conversations were serious and even melancholy, but more often they were full of gaiety, for men remember more easily, and prefer to remember, the pleasanter incidents in their lives. The war was the great subject that they had in common, and it was inevitable that they should revert to it whenever good cheer and goodfellowship encouraged conversation. Nor could they be expected to know, or, if they had known, to care that the youngest and latest joined officer should suffer from their conversation. How often he felt that if only he had been present at one action all would have been different.

He was disappointed also in the enemy. All his youth he had pictured these formidable people as very fierce, very brutal, very evil, very brave. What he found was a herd of lumbering louts, subservient and clumsy, sometimes sullen and surly, but more often too anxious to please. Were these the same men, or any relation to those who had swept through Belgium almost to the gates of Paris in a few weeks, held up the Russian steam-roller, smashed the empire of the Czars and come near to defeating the Royal Navy in the North Sea? He could hardly believe it.

Nor was he satisfied with the spirit of his own men. He had thought to find in the regiment abroad a little less discipline, perhaps, but more enthusiasm and keenness than at home. So he had been led to expect by returning officers. But this, if it ever had been, was no longer the case. The men were restless and discontented, talking only of the return to civilian life, speculating on how soon it would come, and complaining of the delay. How could Willie at the age of nineteen understand that the morale of troops is better on the eve of battle than on the eve of demobilisation?

This first experience of being abroad with his regiment was not one upon which he looked back with any pleasure, and he was glad to return to England and to find himself quartered in a part of the country where good hunting was easily available. Horses henceforward filled his life. When he was not in the saddle he was talking or thinking about them. Those who do not know would be surprised to learn how large a part horses can come to play in the existence of a man, particularly of a young man, and above all of a young cavalry officer. In the days when horse cavalry still existed, the horse represented for such an one the centre both of his profession and of his recreation. It combined work and play. It could fill every hour of his activities during daylight, and prove an inexhaustible topic of conversation at night. Every day during the winter months, that his military duties permitted, he would hunt, his season beginning, indeed, long before winter with the first morning's cub-hunting. Point-to-points and steeplechases were the only other amusements in which he indulged. He bought a few jumpers and rode them in races with varying success but with unvarying enthusiasm, and he shocked himself once by saying in the heat of an argument that he would rather win the Grand National on his own horse than be awarded the Victoria Cross. He retracted this wild statement immediately, apologised and said that he must be drunk. But he wasn't, and there were those among his audience who agreed with him, to such a point can hippolatry stir the imaginations of young men.

The coming of spring meant for Willie the opening of flat racing, which in his opinion was an inferior sport. It meant also polo and the London season.

In the nineteen-twenties London was a gay city and England was a happy land. Those who had lived before the war made unfavourable comparisons with the past, but to the new generation, without previous experience, life as it was seemed agreeable enough. There had been a redistribution of wealth, but there was still plenty of it, and there was a boom of prosperity. The number of war casualties had been greater than ever before, but they were soon forgotten by the majority of the survivors, and the spectre of war was banished from men's minds.

All that the country had to offer in the way of enjoyment was laid before a young subaltern in a good regiment with an agreeable appearance and ample means. Willie helped himself generously to the good things that were offered him, but he did not fall into excess. Although he had no parents to guide him, their place was taken by the regiment, which he loved and honoured more than anything else in the world, and which therefore exercised over his conduct as strong an influence as any parents could have done. There were certain things which officers in that regiment did not do, and those things would never be done by Willie Maryngton.

He danced, he rode, he went racing and indulged in all the pleasures that became his age and circumstances. He was fond of dancing, but, out of the ball-room, he spent little of his time with girls. He found them difficult to talk to, and the regiment disapproved of men who were always hanging round women's petticoats.

He took a flat in Jermyn Street and joined another club, to which his father had belonged, and where the atmosphere was very different from that of the military club to which he belonged already. Most of the members were older men, but, although at first he was intimidated, he soon made many friends among them, for towards his elders he bore himself with a frank, unassuming manliness that quickly won for him sympathy and goodwill.

During these years, although it may be said that he had found his place in the world and was occupying it with confidence, he never forgot what he had missed, or ceased to regret it. A chance question from a neighbour at a dinner-party, "Where were you in the war?" a chance remark from an old member in the club, "You young fellows who've been through the war," would bring back a pang of the anguish he had felt when he was first told of the Armistice. And now that he was beginning to meet, as grown men, those who had been still at school on that day, he felt that they also had an advantage over him.

Hunting in the winter, polo in the summer and racing all the year round demanded an income larger than Willie's, and although he was not extravagant he came gradually to understand, as the years went on, that he was living beyond his means. It therefore came to him as a relief rather than a blow when he learnt that the regiment was to go to India. He was at the time facing a financial crisis. The prospect of cutting down his hunters, and perhaps having to give up polo altogether, was not a pleasant one. The news brought down upon him his creditors like a swarm of locusts. He was horrified to discover how much he owed. London tradesmen are very patient with rich young officers in good regiments, but their patience comes abruptly to an end when there is any question of the young gentlemen proceeding overseas for an indefinite period. Willie had to sell out capital in order to meet his liabilities, and discovered, as so many have before and since, that it is always the very worst moment to sell. Looking back on it all, Willie remembered only some very dull conversations with solicitors which had depressed him more than the knowledge that he had to face life in future on a reduced though still adequate income.

He almost lost sight of the Osbornes during these years. Mrs. Osborne wrote to him at regular intervals, giving him full information about each member of the family. Garnet was working in one of the large military hospitals; Horry, having done well at the Academy of Dramatic Art, was usually with some touring company in the provinces; Felicity was at school in Brussels. They all seemed very far away from the life that Willie was leading.

He saw Horry once before he left for India. He was having supper at the Savoy Grill with some brother officers after the theatre. Horry was there with a very pretty girl. Neither Horry nor his companion was in evening clothes, which slightly distressed Willie. But the girl was lovely, and one of his companions suggested that he should invite them both to join their party. Guilelessly Willie approached them and asked:

"Hallo, Horry! won't you both come over and sit with us?"

"No, we certainly won't," said Horry gruffly.

Willie was taken aback.

"Why not?" he asked.

"Because we think you'd bore us to death," said Horry.

The girl saw the hurt look on Willie's innocent face, and gave him a charming smile of compassion, which softened the blow.

Later, when he saw the two of them leaving the restaurant, he ran after them and asked Horry to lunch with him on the following day.

"No, I won't," said Horry, who seemed still unaccountably annoyed.

"Oh," said Willie, "that's too bad. I'm off to India at the end of the week, and you may never see me again."

"You're going to India?" cried Horry. "How was I to know? Of course I'll lunch with you to-morrow, bless you. Sorry I was cross. Name the time and place."

Willie suggested his club. Horry demurred.

"Wouldn't a restaurant be more fun? I tell you what, let's go to Or- nano's, where we dined together on Armistice night."

And so it was agreed.

It was with mixed feelings that Willie remembered the luncheon that took place on the following day. His first impression was that Ornano's had changed. It was no longer the magic haunt where il- lustrious beings consumed rare dishes and precious wines. It was a distinctly second-rate restaurant frequented by the riff-raff of Fleet Street and the Strand. The head-waiter of international renown had long ago soared to higher spheres, and the clientèle had deteriorated. Willie noticed a couple of bookmakers, whom he knew, drinking cham- pagne with two buxom blondes. He obscurely felt, although it would have been impossible for him to express the feeling in words, and he would have protested had he been charged with it, that this was a place to which he did not belong. What was worse, he felt that Horry did belong to it. Horry ordered a "gin and it" as though he were at home, and Willie felt he was being pompous when he said he would prefer a glass of sherry.

Horry was not unaware of the impression that Willie was receiving.

"This place has gone down a bit, but I still like it. You meet all sorts here, and the grub's good; but of course it's not the place it was in the days of Luigi."

"Why were you so cross with me last night?" asked Willie.

"It wasn't you, old boy; it was your friends. I know the type—more money than brains—stroll into the Savoy Grill half-tight and think they can pick up any girl they see there."

"No, no," Willie protested indignantly, "they're not like that at all. They're very good chaps; all in my regiment. I told them I knew you, and they said couldn't we all get together and have a jolly evening."

"Yes, and you probably told them I was on the stage, and they assumed she was, too, and they thought because she was an actress one of them might go home with her."

Willie indignantly denied the accusation.

"Look here," said Horry. "Supposing they'd met another fellow in the regiment, one of their own sort, out with his sister, and supposing she'd been a pretty girl, do you think they'd have suggested joining up?"

"Yes," said Willie, candidly, "I think they would."

"Well, I don't," retorted Horry, "and that's what made me so damned angry. Perhaps I was wrong, but you know what *esprit de corps* is— honour of the regiment and all that sort of twaddle. Well, we people on the stage feel about our profession as you do about yours, and however it may have been in the past, our morality in these days is just as good as anyone else's—better, perhaps, because we work harder. So it makes me mad with rage when people treat actresses as though they were all no better than they should be. And that was what I felt was happening last night. The girl I was with *is* an actress, as a matter of fact, and she happens to be an angel—happily married: her husband's playing lead in a first-rate show on tour, and she may be getting a West End job. I adore her, but I'm not in love with her. I've never even held her hand in the taxi. I kiss her on the cheek, you know, when we meet or say good-night, just as I would Mum or Felicity. So you can imagine what I feel when I think people are treating her like a tart."

"Yes, I think I can," said Willie, "but really you're wrong about the brutal and licentious soldiery. None of us were tight last night, and if you had come over to our table you would have had nothing to complain of; everybody would have treated her just like a lady."

"Just like a lady," echoed Horry, "but she is a lady, damn you! and much more of a lady than lots of the melancholy sisters of second-rate Army officers that I've met."

"Oh, for heaven's sake don't get angry again," said Willie. "You know jolly well that I didn't mean it that way. I meant they would treat her just the same as anybody else."

Horry recovered his good temper without difficulty, and they talked of other matters. There was no more quarrelling, but the conversation was not what it should have been between two foster-brothers on the eve of a long separation. They clung rather desperately to family matters, both feeling conscious of the lack of other topics. There were jokes about old Garnet, speculations on Felicity's future, slight anxieties about Mrs. Osborne's health. But when these subjects were exhausted and they tried to talk of themselves, they were both conscious that there was a mutual lack of interest. They had no friends in common. Horry cared nothing about the Army and as little about horses. Willie tried valiantly to discuss the theatre, but his interest in it was limited to musical comedy and revue. He hadn't seen the plays that Horry talked of, nor even heard the names which he mentioned with the greatest respect. So that they were both secretly glad when the meal was over, although they were both sincerely sorry to say good-bye.

## IV

THE happiest years of Willie's life were those that he spent in India. He had no doubt about it, when he reviewed the past. There he was able to recapture the nineteenth century, and enjoy life as he would have enjoyed it had he been born fifty years earlier. The days of the British Raj were already numbered, but a British cavalry officer could still be gloriously unconscious of the fact. On little more than his Army pay he could live like a prince, obedient servants at his beck and call, the best of everything the country could provide at his command, a string of polo ponies in the stable, and even an occasional shot at a tiger. Willie's reduced income was wealth in India, and although sometimes, sweltering in the sunshine, he would have given much for a cold, grey day in the shires, he was on the whole as happy as it is given to mankind to be.

But, because men can never be quite happy for long, he suffered during these years from one continual source of irritation and experienced one great sorrow. The irritation came from a brother officer, who was a few years senior to him and whom he had never liked. Hamilton was his name. He was not popular in the regiment, but he was indifferent to popularity. He was extremely efficient, and he was working for the Staff College examination. His efficiency was reluctantly admired, but his professional ambitions were regarded with suspicion. The general feeling was that a man who prepared himself for the Staff College would be obliged to waste in study precious hours that might be spent in playing or practising polo.

During their stay in India Hamilton became adjutant, a position which enabled him to inflict many minor annoyances on junior officers whom he didn't like. For some reason that would be hard to discover he had never liked Willie. Perhaps it was because everybody else liked him. Perhaps he secretly envied the popularity he affected to despise.

One of the reasons why Hamilton was not liked was that he had the courage to speak openly in favour of mechanisation, that fearful fate which hung like a shadow of doom over all cavalry regiments at this period.

"I'd as soon be a chauffeur," exclaimed Willie passionately one evening, "as have to drive a dirty tank about and dress like a navvy."

"Of course," replied Hamilton blandly, "if all you care about is wearing fancy dress, playing games on horseback, and occasionally showing off at the Military Tournament, you're perfectly right to take that view; but if you were interested in war, or ever hoped to take part in one, you'd be praying that your regiment might be mechanised before the next war comes."

This was a cruel thing to say to Willie, and only Hamilton knew how cruel it was. Willie grew very red, then very white. He longed to throw something or to strike a blow. With difficulty he controlled himself, muttered a monosyllabic expletive and stalked from the room.

The wound that had been inflicted took long to heal. Hamilton had won a Military Cross in the war and was no doubt entitled to sneer at Willie, who had seen no fighting. But Willie would wake up in the night and recall the incident. He would think of clever answers that he might have made, and groan with rage. He knew all the arguments that had ever been put forward for the retention of horse cavalry, but he had forgotten them when he needed them. Hamilton had had the best of it. He always did, he always would, because he was clever. He was a good soldier too, there was no denying it, but he couldn't really love the regiment, or be loyal to it, if he could speak of uniform as fancy dress, and if he wanted to see their horses taken away.

The misfortune that befell Willie in India was his first love affair. The opening act of this little drama was all that it should have been, and fitted perfectly into the nineteenth-century pattern of life. The heroine's father was the Colonel of an Indian Cavalry regiment—an old regiment with honourable traditions—and the father and grandfather of Colonel Summers had served in it. Daisy was a pretty girl of a very English type, who looked prettier in India than she would have done at home. She was fair and fluffy, with large blue eyes and a complexion like a wild rose, the delicacy of which had not yet been dimmed by the Indian sun, for she had only recently arrived from Europe. She had finished her education at the same school in Brussels as Felicity Osborne, and it was the discovery of this fact that first brought her to-

gether with Willie. It gave them a subject of conversation, and Willie
never found it easy to discover such subjects when he was brought into
contact with young ladies.

Daisy spoke with enthusiasm of Felicity. She had been the beauty
of the school and the favourite of the headmistress. Some of the girls
found her proud and reserved, but she and Daisy had always got on
well together, and had been the closest of friends. She was glad to talk
of her school life, for with her also subjects of conversation were not
always easy to find. So, at the various entertainments that the station
offered—polo-matches, picnics, cocktail parties and dances—Willie came
to be on the look out for Daisy and to spend with her the greater part
of his time. It was a happy day when he discovered that, not only was
she a friend of Felicity, but also that she took an interest in racing, and
was quite well informed about the branch of that sport which he himself preferred. Endless vistas of conversation now lay before them, for
the beauty of the turf as a conversational subject is that in racing, unlike art or philosophy, some important event has always just happened,
or is just about to happen, and the daily Press is full of reports and
speculations, which can be read and quoted.

Willie's admiration for Daisy increased rapidly and, being a simple
soul, he found it difficult not to talk of what was occupying his
thoughts. One evening before dinner, when the officers were smoking
on the veranda and the conversation was about horses, he remarked:

"That young Miss Summers knows an awful lot about racing, both
out here and at home."

"I suppose she gets her information from Coper Caffin," said Captain
Hamilton, and there was something in his tone that Willie didn't like.

"Why, is he a pal of hers?" he asked casually.

"They're inseparable," replied the other.

"Oh," said Willie, "I've never seen them together."

Then dinner was announced.

Caffin was a captain in the regiment which Daisy's father commanded. To Willie he seemed an old man. In fact, he was barely forty.
Willie was respectful to his seniors, and grateful if they were kind to
him, which Caffin had always been. He had an attractive Irish brogue,
and a full share of all those charming qualities that make Irishmen
popular. Hamilton said of him that he was more like a stage Irishman
than the genuine article. He was good looking, with light eyes and dark
curly hair beginning to go grey, and he was a superb horseman.

Not only could he ride a horse, but he could sell one; and there were
those who said that he was even more skilful in the latter activity than
the former. Buying and selling horses certainly occupied a great deal
of his time, and had earned him the nickname by which he was gen-

erally known. In the horse market honourable men accept a lower standard of integrity than elsewhere, but whether Coper Caffin always conformed even to that low standard was sometimes questioned; and there were young officers who long remembered with bitterness the deals they had done with him. Willie was not one of them. He had once bought a horse from Coper and he had paid a high price for it, but it had proved a good horse, and Willie was not one to complain of the price if he were satisfied with the purchase.

"Do you know Coper Caffin?" he asked Daisy the next time he met her.

"Oh yes," she answered. "He's sweet, don't you think so?"

"Sweet" was not the adjective that Willie would have chosen. "He's not a bad chap," he said, and added with greater conviction, "He's jolly good on a horse."

"Yes, he rides beautifully, doesn't he?" she agreed, and added, "And he's always been ever so sweet to me."

"You've known him some time, have you?"

"Oh yes, ever since I was a flapper. And he came to Brussels when I was at school there and took me out to lunch."

"What was he doing in Brussels?" Willie asked.

"Selling horses, I suppose. He's always selling horses. He's going to leave the Army soon and set up on his own in Ireland. He's got a lovely place there."

"Oh," said Willie dubiously. Nothing that he had heard of him previously had led him to believe that Coper Caffin belonged to the landed gentry.

Not long after this there was a dance to which Willie got permission from Daisy's mother to escort her, together with another young lady who was staying with them. The party was well planned, it was a beautiful evening, the heat was not excessive and dancing went on until late. When they at last decided to leave, the other young lady could not be found, and after a search which caused further delay they were informed that she had left earlier with somebody else. So they drove home together, Willie at the wheel and Daisy's pretty, tired head resting gently on his shoulder. When they reached the Colonel's bunga-low they got out of the car and without a word fell into one another's arms. There was a broad seat upon the veranda, on which they pro-longed their embrace. Those were moments Willie never forgot. It was the first time that he had held the yielding body of a young girl in his arms and felt soft lips pressed passionately to his.

"I think I've been in love with you for a long time," he said, "but I never really knew it until this evening. When did you know you were in love with me? It seems so wonderful."

That she was in love with him he had no doubt, else she would not have kissed him.

"You are so very sweet," was her answer, and her arms stretched out to him again.

When next they spoke he put another question.

"When shall we be married?"

Even in the dim light of very early dawn he could see she was surprised, but surely she would never have allowed him to kiss her so passionately unless she were prepared to marry him, and surely she would not have suspected him of being the kind of man who would treat a girl, a Colonel's daughter, in that way, unless he meant to make her his wife.

"Marry, marry, marry—oh, my sweet, it's very late at night to talk of marriage." She laughed a little indulgent laugh, as though she were talking to a child. "How do you know that you'll feel the same in the morning?"

"I'm not tight, if that's what you mean," said Willie. "You could see I wasn't by the way I drove the car. And as for to-morrow morning, it's that already. Look, the dawn is breaking. Could there be a better time of day to get engaged?"

Daisy was still bewildered. She was a child of her epoch, gay and shallow, not mercenary or scheming. She knew that she must get married. There were two younger sisters coming along, and two brothers at school, who were a heavy drain on the family resources, even while her father still drew full pay and lived in India. Willie, as she put it to herself, was very sweet—she had never met anyone sweeter. He was attractive, too; and yet she hesitated. He was so simple and so good —she had a curious unaccountable feeling that it would be rather a shame to marry him. She fell back on the excuse that one child gives to another.

"But what would our people say?"

"I haven't got any people," answered Willie—"not even an aunt or an uncle. I'll come and see your father to-morrow morning—this morning, I mean. Perhaps I should have done so before I asked you. I don't see why he should object"—and he added with some embarrassment, "I've got a little money, you know, as well as my pay."

"Oh, Daddy won't object. He'll be thankful to get rid of me, bless his heart. But are you sure, Willie, that you really want to marry me? You haven't known me very long, and one always hears about boys who marry the Colonel's daughter in India and spend the rest of their lives regretting it. Don't you think you might come to regret it, Willie?"

But as she asked the question she moved closer into his arms, thereby dissolving any doubts that he might have had. It was almost daylight when they separated, and they were engaged to be married.

Willie remembered vividly the interview he had with Colonel Summers on the following day. Military duties occupied the earlier hours of the morning, and midday is not a suitable time in India for paying calls, so that it was about sundown when he arrived, by appointment, at the Colonel's bungalow and was ushered into his presence. He had been feeling nervous, and had vaguely wondered whether he should not stand at attention, as in the orderly-room, and apply in official terms for permission to marry the Colonel's daughter. But he was immediately put at his ease.

"Help yourself to a glass of sherry, my dear fellow, and sit you down. It's been damned hot all day, hasn't it? But there's a breeze this evening. Now tell me what I can do for you."

Haltingly Willie told his story, confessing that he had already put the question to the young lady, and excusing himself for not having first obtained her father's consent. The Colonel did not pretend to be surprised. He had known well enough that there could be but one subject on which Lieutenant Maryngton would ask for a private talk with him. Nor did he pretend to hesitate. His wife had already given him all the information which a prudent father might demand of a prospective son-in-law.

"Well, my dear boy," he said, "I'll tell you frankly that, although I don't know you very well, you seem to be just the sort of young fellow whom I'd like my daughter to marry. You have my consent and my blessing, and I hope she'll make you a good wife. Let us shake hands on it, Willie."

They shook hands and finished their sherry, half bowing towards each other and half muttering something about good luck. Lighting his pipe and leaning back in his chair, the Colonel continued:

"It's a funny thing, but you probably know Daisy better than I do. I've hardly seen her, because I've been out here most of her life. Girls are very different from what they used to be. I suppose every father has said that—especially stuffy old colonels in the Indian Army. But tell me now, does Daisy ever talk to you about anything except ball-dancing and the moving pictures?"

Willie laughed. "Oh yes, sir; about hundreds of things. I think she's very clever. She's not highbrow, of course, but then I'm not quite what you'd call one of the intellectuals. She's awfully interested in horses, for one thing, and so am I."

"Yes," said the Colonel meditatively. "I've noticed that. I've noticed that." But he didn't seem particularly pleased about it.

That was a great evening for Willie. He was not sure afterwards

whether it was he or Daisy who had let out the news. They agreed
between them that it must have been her father. By dinner-time it was
all over the station. Wherever he went he was congratulated, and the
little bungalow which he shared with a brother officer was crowded
with friends who dropped in to drink his health.

One of the earliest callers was Coper Caffin.

"It's you that have broken my heart," he said, "for I would have
married the girl myself. But let the best man win has always been my
motto. Would you not like to give your bride a lovely hack as a
wedding present, for I think I know the animal?"

Willie laughed, and said he would be glad to inspect it. He thought
to himself that Coper was joking. He could not really have hoped to
marry Daisy. He was old enough to be her father.

Of the months that followed Willie's recollection was faint and hazy.
He was very happy, and the days slipped quickly away. He wrote his
good news to Mrs. Osborne and asked her to tell the others whose
addresses he no longer knew, and he also wrote to Felicity to tell her
that he was going to marry one of her school friends, and that they often
talked of her together and looked forward to seeing her when they
came home. Mrs. Osborne sent him her congratulations, together with
much family news, and a silver flask that had belonged to her husband.
He received no reply from Felicity.

To buy a suitable engagement ring he made a journey to Calcutta,
which he thought the most horrible place he had ever seen. Yet many of
his friends said they had great fun there, and arranged short visits as
often as they could. Daisy was pleased with the ring, and she seemed
pleased with him. They saw each other very often, and they never
quarrelled. Perhaps true lovers would have warned them that this was
a bad sign, for those are wrong who believe that there are more quarrels
after than before marriage. It was only when he looked back upon it all
afterwards that he understood there had been something missing. They
danced together, and rode together, and talked about dances and horses.
She refused to accept the mare that Caffin had wanted to sell him as a
wedding present, although she could give no good reason for doing so.
She said she had heard of a better one, and that in any case there was
no hurry. In spite of this continual companionship, Willie saw afterwards that they came no closer together. They knew no more of one
another's heart and mind, and even the rapturous caresses that had led
to their engagement were not repeated. There never seemed to be any
opportunity, or was it, as Willie sometimes thought, that Daisy deliberately avoided one? If it were so, he did not blame her, attributing reluctance, if it existed, to maiden modesty.

Of all the conversations that they had at this period he remembered only one distinctly. He had accompanied her home from a party, as on the other occasion, but this time it was in her father's car and there was a chauffeur in the front seat. None the less when they reached the bungalow she drew him into the dark shadow of the veranda, and laid her hands on his shoulders.

"Willie," she said, "I am very fond of you. I want you to believe that, and I want you to promise me something."

"Of course you're fond of me, or you wouldn't be marrying me, and of course I'll promise you anything the world," he said lightly, pressing forward to kiss her. But she still held him back.

"No, this is something serious. I want you to promise me, because I know that if you make a promise you will keep it always."

"Fire away," he said.

"I want you to promise that whatever I do you will always forgive me, and will believe that even if I hurt you I was sad to do it."

"Of course," he answered, "and you must promise me, too. I'm sure I'll be a rotten husband."

"No," she persisted. "You have got to say 'I promise that I will always forgive you, Daisy, and that even if you hurt me, I will believe that you were sad to do it.'"

Solemnly he said the words, she repeating them under her breath, her hands still resting on his shoulders. When he had finished she drew him close to her and held him in a long embrace.

A few days later she ran away with Coper Caffin.

## v

THE elopement gave military circles in India something to talk about for many days. Willie was at first more astonished than hurt. Men who have been seriously wounded are often unaware of the fact at the time, being conscious merely that they have received a blow. He was not proud, and therefore his pride did not suffer, as it would have with most young men. He felt vaguely sorry for Daisy, and he felt very sorry for her father, after he had seen him.

Their interview was one that he remembered. The Colonel, who had sent for him, was standing when he came into the room.

"Mr. Maryngton," he began almost sternly, "I have to apologise to you for the behaviour of my daughter and of an officer under my command. It is a hard thing for a man to feel ashamed both of his family and of his regiment."

"Oh, sir," interrupted Willie, who was moved by the older man's suffering, and who remembered the promise that he had made, "don't blame Daisy. She may have behaved foolishly, even wrongly, but I've forgiven her, for I know she's a good girl at heart. Captain Caffin's a rotter, but there are rotters in every regiment, and everyone knows that yours is one of the best in the Indian Army."

"Maryngton," said the Colonel, "you're a good fellow, a damned good fellow. I wish you'd married her. I fear you were too good for her." He blew his nose noisily. "Sit down for a minute and let's have a talk."

Willie sat down, feeling curiously at ease despite the other's embarrassment, and began to talk of how he had first heard the news and of the surprise he had felt.

"I can't blame Daisy," he went on, "for not marrying me if she didn't want to. In fact I think she was perfectly right. It must be wrong to marry someone you don't love. But what I can't understand is why she didn't tell me all about it. I should, of course, have agreed to call the engagement off. She knew me well enough to be sure that I wouldn't make any difficulties; and then—after an interval, of course —she could have got engaged to Caffin."

"My poor boy!" groaned the Colonel. "You don't understand the matter at all, nor all the wickedness of it. Caffin is a married man. He's been separated from his wife for many years, but they're not divorced and they can't be, because they're both Roman Catholics, or pretend to be."

Willie was horrified. "Do you mean to say they are going to live together without being married?"

The Colonel nodded.

"My God! what a swine the fellow must be," Willie exclamied. "I bet Daisy never knew he was married."

But the Colonel could not allow him even this cold comfort. "Her mother tells me," he said, "that she knew perfectly well."

Willie was neither strait-laced nor narrow-minded. Although he had lived a more chaste life than most of his contemporaries, it was due rather to lack of temperament than to high principles. He knew that many of his friends were the lovers of married women, and he thought none the worse of them, although he imagined they must feel very uncomfortable in the husband's presence. He knew that the marriage tie was looser than it used to be, and that conjugal infidelity was more easily condoned than in the past. He accepted the standards of his companions, and never worried his head about them; but young unmarried girls of his acquaintance still belonged, in his eyes, to a category set apart. Married women could do what they pleased, but that a young girl should commit adultery with a married man and bring shame on her family seemed to him an abominable thing.

It took him long to get over the shock. Perhaps it would be truer to say that he never got over it. Often he had to remind himself of the promise that he had made to Daisy. Sometimes he felt that she had obtained it under false pretences. She must have known then what she was meaning to do. He could still say to himself that he forgave her, but he could no longer have the same warm feeling towards her that he had had when he told her father so. He was afraid she must be a bad girl, after all, for she had run away with a married man, who was not only a terrible scoundrel but was also not quite a gentleman.

Willie felt that he must inform Mrs. Osborne of his misfortune and return the flask she had sent him as a wedding present. It was a difficult letter to write. Self-expression had never come easily to him, and to express himself on paper was far more difficult than to do so by word of mouth. He wrestled with his task for many days and nights, but when at last he had completed it, he felt a great relief, and in retrospect he always believed that the writing of this letter had helped him to understand his own feelings and to bear his sorrow. Too easily had he at first accepted the conventional opinion that a young man who has been jilted must be broken-hearted. Too tempting had he at moments found the obvious consolation that he had had a lucky escape. He had no desire to adopt an attitude, for he was naturally sincere, but the people who surrounded him, both men and women, were inclined to approach him on the one assumption or the other. The romantic pressed his hand and looked at him silently with sad eyes, while the worldly-wise almost gave him a congratulatory tap on the shoulder. And because he was not quite sure of his own feelings he found himself meeting the sad gaze with one equally melancholy, and responding to the congratulations by an intimation that he knew himself to be well out of a bad business.

He succeeded in telling Mrs. Osborne very simply that he was not broken-hearted, but that he was disappointed and unhappy; that he did not feel that he had had a lucky escape, but that he doubted whether his marriage to Daisy would have been a success. He had looked forward to being married and having a home of his own. He had thought it wonderful that a beautiful girl should love him, and for the first time he had had an interest in life outside horses and the regiment. But now, although he had forgiven Daisy, and was determined to retain no harsh feelings towards her, he felt sure that it was better for both of them that they had not married. This assurance comforted him, but did not make him happy. She had given him something that he had not possessed before, and now that it was gone, he missed it. He had come to look forward to life with a companion. Now the companion had vanished and he was feeling lonelier than he had felt before.

All this he succeeded in setting down in the letter which he eventually sent to Mrs. Osborne, but it took him a long time to do and, almost before the letter was despatched, he received one from England in a handwriting that was unknown to him.

Dearest Willie,
I'm so glad you didn't marry Daisy Summers. She was not the girl for you. I never liked her.

*Best love,*
Felicity.

Willie had not seen Felicity since she was a child, and he found it hard to believe that she was now the same age as, or perhaps a little older than, Daisy. The latter had always spoken of her as though they were great friends. This letter seemed hardly to confirm it. But Willie had noticed among Daisy's weaknesses a tendency to claim intimacy with people with whom it appeared, on closer enquiry, that she was barely acquainted. Willie had accumulated a good deal of leave by now. Curiosity aroused by this letter, the desire to see some of his foster-family again, and the growing sensation of loneliness, almost decided him to spend his leave in England, but the prospect of an extensive big-game shooting expedition, including invitations from ruling princes, proved more attractive.

He regretted this decision later. Before he set out on his expedition he received a long letter from Mrs. Osborne. It was kind and sympathetic, and Willie thought she seemed to understand him better now than she had done before. She gave him news of Garnet, whose duties had taken him to Malaya, and of Horry, who had made a success in a small but important part in the West End. Felicity was living with her in the old home, but went frequently to London, where she saw much of Horry. Mrs. Osborne was sending him back the flask and she hoped he would keep it always in memory of her. When he returned to his regiment three months later he found a letter from Horry informing him that she was dead.

VI

WHEN the regiment's tour of duty in India was over and they were expecting to return home, orders came that they were to proceed to Egypt, which caused much disappointment and discontent. The general rule was that regiments spent three years in Egypt, followed by five in India, and when, owing to political complications, the regiment had been ordered direct to India, they had innocently supposed that

they had escaped the first part of their exile. The War Office may overlook but it does not forget, nor was there any reason why one regiment
should have more favourable treatment than others, so in the normal
course of trooping the regiment went to Egypt, and spent three years
there, following upon the five they had spent in India.

Willie remembered very little of what happened during his time in
Egypt. He knew that he enjoyed it much less than he had enjoyed India. There was plenty of polo and plenty of racing, but both were of
a more professional character. In India, or the parts of it that he had
visited, the Army had seemed the centre of life, but here in Egypt it
was only an adjunct. In India the subject of politics was never mentioned in the mess. Everybody knew that there was a steady move towards the diminution of British power and prestige, and everybody regretted it. But there was little to be said and nothing to be done about
it. These things were controlled by politicians, who, it appeared, were
all determined to destroy the British Empire and to ruin the Army.
But here in Egypt politics were a common subject of conversation, and
everybody seemed to know something about them. It appeared also that
Lord Allenby, who was a great soldier, had been weak and had given
in to the natives, whereas Lord Lloyd, who was a politician, had been
strong and refused to give in. All this was very puzzling to Willie. In
India he had been able to feel separated by time as well as by space
from the modern world. In Egypt he was in the heart of it, and
he could not feel at home there.

He thought once or twice of returning to England on leave, but always some more attractive alternative presented itself. He visited the
Sudan and went on hunting trips into Kenya and Abyssinia. These
he enjoyed, but he disliked Cairo and Alexandria.

It was while he was in Egypt that he completed his thirtieth year,
and was promoted to the rank of captain. Neither event gave him
much satisfaction. To him thirty meant middle age, and although he
was pleased to be promoted, he knew that in other regiments there
were still to be found subalterns who had taken part in the fighting.
There were also thousands of civilians—he had often met them—who
had splendid war records, and had even temporarily commanded bat-
talions, and who now had abandoned their Army rank altogether. In the
presence of such people he felt needlessly ashamed, as though he
were assuming a rank to which he was not entitled.

When the time came for him to return to England he had an exaggerated idea in his own mind of the length of time he had been away.
He felt that he had left as a boy and that he was coming back as an old
man. He even wondered whether his friends would recognise him.
It was therefore a great surprise when, on the morning after his arrival,

the hall porter gave him a familiar nod when he walked into his club, and he had been there only a few minutes before an acquaintance greeted him casually with "Hallo, Willie! Haven't seen you about for quite a while. Been abroad or something?"

A club provides a wonderful home for the lonely, and an equally convenient escape from home for those who occasionally feel the need of it. There are the faithful old servants, who are always pleased to see members and who, unlike the servants at home, have neither complaints of their conditions, nor quarrels between themselves; or, if they have, the ordinary members never hear of them. There are all the daily newspapers, and the weekly ones, which are hardly worth purchase but merit a glance. The chairs are comfortable, there is never a crowd, and refreshment is easily and instantly obtainable. But above all there is the ease of intercourse—the conversation lightly begun and as lightly broken off the moment it becomes a burden, or even threatens to become one, to either party. Nor are subjects of conversation ever lacking. The news provides them, and, for such as Willie, the racing news, above all. They are varied by those very funny stories, which spring from an inexhaustible anonymous source, and which, for some mysterious reason, are very much funnier when told in the club than anywhere else.

Willie was happy in the society of men, especially men of his own sort, and he had been in the club hardly half an hour before he felt that he had never left it. After lunching there he spent much of the afternoon trying to discover at what theatre Horry was acting and, with the help of the hall-porter, he was at last successful. He bought a ticket and went there alone. The play proved to be an excellent comedy, and Willie, who had seen nothing of the sort for so long, thoroughly enjoyed it. It seemed to him that Horry, who had a good part, acted wonderfully well, and also that he had become younger and taller than Willie remembered him; but when they met afterwards he proved to have altered very little.

Willie had sent him a message saying that he would await him at the stage-door and inviting him to supper. Horry, as gay and enthusiastic as ever, threw his arms round Willie when they met, and was obviously delighted to see him.

"It couldn't be more fortunate," he exclaimed. "I promised to meet Felicity after the show; we shall find her at Rules, and you'll be able to swallow the majority of the family at one gulp. It's a pity Garnet's not here. He was home last year on leave, but he's gone back to the Far East, and I don't know when we shall see him again. Rules is quite close—we can walk there."

As they walked to the restaurant Willie talked of the play and was able, in all sincerity, to say how very much he had enjoyed it and how impressed he had been by Horry's performance. Horry was very pleased. All actors, indeed all artists, are made happy by praise, and Willie's praise was so genuine and so unqualified that it would have given pleasure to one much older and more hardened than Horry.

They were therefore both happy and smiling when they arrived. A tall, dark girl got up from a corner table and came towards them. She looked from Horry to his companion at first with curiosity and then with almost instant recognition. "It's Willie," she said, and taking his hand kissed him on the cheek, so gracefully and so naturally that he felt no embarrassment, but a thrill of happiness.

"How clever of you to recognise me," he said.

"You haven't changed a bit," she answered.

"Well, you certainly have," he told her. "You were a little girl with a pigtail when I saw you last. And then you were always away at school. I don't think I saw you at all during the last five or six years I was in England."

There followed, while they gave their orders, a discussion as to when exactly he had seen her last and how old she was at the time, and whether she had ever had a pigtail. Like all historical facts, these were curiously hard to establish, and Horry entered into the argument, holding strongly a view which differed from those of both the others.

"Anyhow," said Felicity, getting bored with the discussion, "all that matters is that I was a little child then and now I'm a grown-up woman —and you were a young man then and you're a young man still."

"How long does one remain a young man?" asked Willie.

"Until about sixty in my profession," said Horry, "and then they're middle-aged for an indefinite period until they suddenly turn into grand old men."

Felicity laughed. "I wish the girls could do the same."

"They damned well try to," said Horry, and then an argument started about the ages of actresses, into which Willie could not have entered even if he had known who the people were about whom they were talking, which he could not do, as all the ladies were referred to by their christian or more intimate names. It gave him an opportunity to look at Felicity. He had felt dazzled at first. He remembered suddenly that Daisy Summers had said she was beautiful, and yet, for some reason, he had not been prepared for her to be so. He had simply not thought about it. She seemed to him more beautiful than anyone he had ever seen. Her large dark eyes, her short curling hair, the grace of her gestures, the animation of her conversation, and the simplicity of her manner, the complete lack of any coquetry or apparent eagerness to please—all that she was made an impression upon him that he found difficult to understand. He felt for a moment that he wanted to laugh out loud, and then that he wanted to go away with Horry and drink a bottle of champagne, and then again all that he desired was to remain forever where he was, watching and listening and not having to talk. For a moment he wondered whether he was drunk. It was not till afterwards, when he was alone, that he knew he had fallen in love for the first time in his life.

One cause of his happiness that evening was the way in which they both treated him as one of the family. They were plainly pleased to see him, but showed him none of the consideration that is shown to a stranger. They talked without restraint about matters of which he was ignorant and people whom he didn't know. They felt no obligation to draw him into the conversation. This gave Willie a sensation that was new to him—the sensation of being at home.

He liked Rules. It was bohemian, but there was nothing modern about it. From there they took him on to a place in Covent Garden called the Late Joys or the Players Club. Here they drank beer and ate hot sausages and watched a variety entertainment. Most of the actors and the audience seemed acquainted with one another, and everybody joined in the choruses. The songs came from the music-halls of the last century, and to Willie, who had never seen anything of the kind before, everything seemed perfect. It was late when the brother and sister dropped him at Jermyn Street, where he had luckily found vacant the flat he had lived in before. They were both bound towards Chelsea.

"How about lunch to-morrow?" he asked Felicity.

"I can't to-morrow, Willie dear."

"May I ring you up in the morning?"

"There's no telephone where I'm staying, but we'll meet soon."

"And you, Horry?"

"I've got a matinée to-morrow, but you've got my telephone number. Give me a ring whenever you like and we'll fix up something. Good night, old Willie."

"Good night."

Willie felt a little sad that nothing had been arranged for the next day, but it was such a small regret that it could not cast a shadow over the great happiness in which he fell asleep that night.

VII

In spite of many efforts, Willie failed to see Felicity again before he left London. He heard that she had gone to Brighton, and he was obliged to join his regiment in a remote part of the country.

On the next occasion that he came to London she was still away, but he saw as much as he could of Horry, and turned the conversation in her direction as often as possible. He felt that, although he had known her so long, he knew her so little. He had no idea of who her friends might be, or how her life was spent, and he wanted most eagerly to find out.

He found Horry surprisingly unhelpful. He was, like many in his profession, extremely self-centred. Warm-hearted, sociable and very generous, he was always glad—unaffectedly glad—to see his friends, but never thought of them when he did not see them. He felt the same with regard to his sister. He was perhaps fonder of her than he was of anyone. There was nothing that he would not have done for her had she asked him. But when she was absent he never thought of her, and even when she was present he never questioned her about her plans or prospects.

"But what is her life?" asked Willie. "Who looks after her and takes her to parties?"

Horry could not have looked vaguer if he had been asked to solve a problem in algebra. These were questions that he had never asked himself.

"Well, you see," he said with much hesitation, "she was grown up before Mum died, and I think she used to go to gloomy parties in Aldershot and round about. Then people, friends of Mum, would ask her to stay in London. Then she got keen on acting and went to the Academy of Dramatic Art. Then she got a small part in some half-amateur, highbrow show, which led nowhere. She's got lots of friends, and she always seems perfectly happy." This he said almost defensively.

"But how about money?"

Horry's face cleared. Here was a question he could answer.

"Oh, she's all right for money. Mum left her everything that she could. Garnet was here at the time, and went into the whole thing very thoroughly. When everything was paid up and sold up and probated and executed and all the rest of it, he and I got a thousand quid each in ready, and young Felicity would have about five hundred a year safe for life in gilt-rimmed securities or whatever they're called. It's not the earth, but she won't starve, bless her heart, and if ever she wants a bit extra she's only got to ask her rich brother, the West End favourite with the big future in Hollywood."

It was true that Horry was making a name for himself on the stage and had already appeared successfully in pictures, but it was not the financial prospects of the Osborne family in which Willie was really interested.

"How about young men and all that?" he asked, trying very hard to make the question sound casual.

"Oh, she's got plenty," Horry answered. "I'm always seeing her with them at restaurants. Nobody I know, though, and she doesn't introduce them."

"What do they look like?" asked Willie.

"Not like you, Willie," Horry laughed. "No, not a bit. Flabby and floppy, coloured shirts and long hair, and I always hope they're going to pay the bill. Girls seem to like that sort nowadays. It puzzles me sometimes."

Willie's feelings were mixed. Relief predominated.

"Where does she live?" was the next question.

"She's sharing rooms at present with a girl friend, while she tries to find a flat. They're devilish hard to get these days. I've just seen one that I think will do for me, in Bloomsbury, very handy for the theatre," and then followed a long account of Horry's own future movements which interested him very much more than those of Felicity.

Before they separated, Willie made Horry promise to make a plan for his next visit to London, the date of which he already knew. Horry would get seats for a play, a popular success, which he knew that Felicity wanted to see, and Willie would take her. They would all meet for supper afterwards, when Horry would bring another girl to complete the party.

So Willie travelled north with the comfortable sensation of looking forward to a certain day. He needed comfort when he got there, for he learnt that the blow had fallen, and that the regiment was to be mechanised forthwith. To make the blow yet harder to bear there came the news that Hamilton, who had been away for two or three years, was returning as second-in-command.

It was at this time that the thought of leaving the Army first presented itself to Willie's mind, as a course that ought to be considered, and not as the abandonment of all that made life desirable. He had never taken any interest in machinery. He had never shared the interest which most of his contemporaries took in motor cars. He had found them useful for getting about and he had learnt to drive them, badly, but he had never tried to tinker with them when they went wrong. Even the little musketry and knowledge of machine-guns that a cavalry officer was obliged to master had proved a hard task for him, and he would not have liked to have had his knowledge tested.

Many of his friends who had joined when he had, and later, were now leaving the Army, and the news of mechanisation speeded up the dispersal. "You can't teach an old dog new tricks," one of them said to him, and the proverb, for some reason, stuck in his mind, and recurred to him as often as the possibility of leaving came up for review. But still he kept in his heart the ambition that he had had as a schoolboy and which had always remained with him. He was still young and active, and there were beginning to be rumours of war. The day might yet come when that ambition would be fulfilled and he would go into battle with his regiment.

The evening to which Willie had been looking forward arrived. Felicity came in her small car to pick him up at his club. He was standing in the window waiting for her. He felt proud to be called for by such a beautiful girl. They had a box at the theatre, which gave a sensation of comfort and intimacy. Between the acts Felicity took him to the bar, where she drank gin-and-orange, while he drink whisky-and-soda. He might not have approved of this in another girl, but she could do no wrong. He found no difficulty in talking to her. Conversation flowed easily. She told him that when she was a child he had been her hero. He trembled with pleasure, and asked her why.

"Oh, I don't know," she said. "I suppose because the others were brothers, and apart from them I didn't know anyone else."

His heart sank. He asked her whom Horry would be bringing to supper.

"I expect it will be Miriam Love," she answered. "They've been friends for a very long time. Horry does go off the rails occasionally—and so does she, if it comes to that—but they always come together again."

"What is she like, and what does she do?" asked Willie.

"She's very pretty. She's on the stage, but she hasn't got a part just now. She's married to a second-rate actor who does Shakespeare in the provinces."

"Does Horry love her?"

"Yes, I think he really does."

"Will they get married?"

"I don't think it has ever occurred to either of them. She's not divorced, so it wouldn't be possible at present. Oh, Willie, tell me about Daisy Summers. I'm so glad you didn't marry her. What happened?"

Willie told the little there was to tell, and Felicity listened sympathetically. He ended by saying how glad he had been to get her letter, and asked why she had written it.

"Oh, I don't know," she said. "I used often to think of you, and I was so sorry when I heard you were engaged to a girl of that sort."

"Did you think she was a bad girl?"

"Oh no, no—only silly, ordinary, and pointless."

They went on to the Savoy Grill, where they met Horry with Miriam Love. Willie recognised her at once as the girl who had been with Horry on that night, so many years ago, when he had invited them both to join him and his brother officers at supper. Ten years had made very little difference to her. He thought her better-looking than ever. He recalled that evening which they both remembered, and they laughed about how angry Horry had been.

"He still gets very angry about things that don't matter," said Miriam. "We had a terrible argument the other day about conscientious objectors. I said they ought to be shot, and that if they knew they were going to be there wouldn't be any. There aren't any in France or Germany. Horry got wild, said they were the bravest people in the country, and finally swore that if there were another war he'd be a conscientious objector himself."

"Oh, Horry!" said Willie. "How could you?"

"It was Miriam's fault," said Horry. "She's got a most irritating way of arguing. She can never keep anything in the abstract. If you say that the Chinese are very fine people, she says, 'Would you like to sleep with one?' If you say no, she says, 'There you are, you see,' and thinks she's won the argument. If you say yes, she says, 'Dirty beast!'"

It was a gay party. Everybody had plenty to say; Willie less than the others, but he did not feel out of it. When he suggested that they should go on to the Players Club it was already too late. Horry and Miriam went off together, and Willie was left with Felicity.

"Can't we go on somewhere else?" he asked.

"No," she answered decisively. "I'm tired. Jump into my car. I'll drop you. It's on my way."

He knew it would be useless to argue, but although he had enjoyed every minute of the evening, he was left with a feeling of failure. He thought it a pity that girls should own cars and should drive them. Especially at night. What were taxis for, anyway? He said good night almost crossly when she left him at his flat.

During the remainder of that summer Willie saw Felicity as often as he could. She seemed to have many engagements and never told him what they were. She never introduced him to her friends and, when he asked her to, said she did not think they would amuse him.

"You mean I shouldn't amuse them," he said.

"No," she answered, "but they wouldn't see your point, and you wouldn't see theirs."

She seemed always very pleased to see him, and although he did not tell her he was in love with her, she must have known it. When the holiday season came she disappeared without warning, and he heard that she had gone to Brittany. He himself paid visits in Scotland and Ireland, shooting and fishing, and thinking as little about Felicity or

about the future as he could. He had been hurt by her going away
without telling him, and he thought he would be wise to forget her. He
began to hope that he had succeeded in doing so.

During the winter it happened that he had to spend a Sunday
evening in London. He rang up Horry, and they arranged to dine
together at a little restaurant in Soho. When he arrived there Horry
was waiting for him at a table for three.

"Felicity's coming," he explained. "I told her she hadn't been asked,
but she insisted."

While they waited Willie asked after Miriam and enquired, with
assumed innocence, whether Horry still treated her only as his sister,
reminding him of what he had said years ago. He was not in the least
embarrassed, but answered frankly.

"No, that platonic, pedestal stuff didn't last long. It can't between
normal people. Her husband, about the worst ham-actor on the stage,
was unfaithful to her first, so she saw no reason why she should go on
being faithful to him. She's a grand girl, and has a heart of gold. I love
her."

"Why don't you get married?" asked Willie.

"The ham-actor, who's as nasty a piece of work off the stage as on it,
won't agree to a divorce. He's glad of a good excuse for not making
honest women of the girls he seduces. We're very happy as we are."

"Don't you want to have children?"

"I'm not at all sure that I do," said Horry, and became more serious.
"I have a good time myself and I enjoy life. I'm one of the lucky ones;
but I've no great admiration for this world, and I shouldn't think that
I was doing anybody a very good turn by bringing them into it."

Felicity arrived late. When the door of the restaurant was flung open
Willie knew it was her, and when she walked quickly in and sat down
without explanation or apology, he knew that he was more in love with
her than ever. How happy he felt to be with her, and with Horry once
again! How different their conversation was from that of his other
friends! And how infinitely more amusing! They drank Chianti and
talked until all the other diners had left, and most of the waiters.
Then they drank liqueurs, until the proprietor was obliged, very reluctantly, to tell them that it was long past closing time. They took a
taxi, and they dropped Horry first, and Willie insisted upon driving
Felicity back to Chelsea. He threw his arms round her and kissed her
passionately. She made no resistance. And when he told her that he
loved her better than the whole world, and that he had never loved
anyone else, she answered "Darling."

It was not a word that she used often. Too many of her contemporaries had robbed it of its beauty, and reduced it to the gutter by making it the commonest word in their vocabulary. But in her soft, deep voice it retained its own dark tenderness and sounded to him like a magic spell. It conveyed love and sympathy, and promised surrender.

"I've been so angry with you," he whispered—"I've tried so hard to forget you."

"Yes, I was afraid you were," she answered, very low.

"Why did you make no sign?" he asked, but she answered only "Darling."

When they came to the house where she was staying he asked whether he might come in. "No, my love," she laughed gently, "of course not. There are people there."

"Then you must have lunch with me to-morrow, for I have to leave in the afternoon."

"I can't to-morrow," she said, "but next time you're here."

They arranged when they would meet.

"I love you so," he said.

"I love you, too," she answered, and then firmly slipped out of his embrace and was gone.

VIII

In Willie's mind marriage remained the natural and logical sequel to love. If Felicity loved him she should be prepared to marry him, and yet he could hardly believe that she would. She had ideas on every subject that were so different from the ideas of other people. Under her influence his own views had broadened and undergone a far greater development than he suspected; yet, even so, she often said things that surprised him and expressed opinions that he could not accept. But she never shocked him. Sometimes he wondered why. The true reason probably was that she was always sincere and was incapable of indecency or vulgarity.

When he asked himself why he had not mentioned marriage during that memorable drive, he knew that it would have spoilt everything, but why it would have done so he found more difficult to explain.

He thought of little else during the days that followed. Out of his deep cogitations one conclusion emerged. He was sure that she would not marry him so long as he remained in the Army. He could not ask her to follow the drum. He could not picture her passing her life with the wives of his brother officers. They were nice women, whom he liked very much, and they were just like the women she had known as a child in her mother's house, but their ideas were not her ideas, nor their world her world. So he had to choose between his love and his regiment. It was a hard choice for him to make.

One evening he found himself alone with Hamilton. He had not come to like him, but long acquaintance had induced a certain intimacy, and his advice on any matter was worth having.

"I'm thinking of chucking the Army," Willie said suddenly. "Would you advise me to?"

Hamilton usually addressed Willie in a tone of superficially good-natured, but occasionally malicious, banter. Asked a serious question, however, about a serious and partly military subject, he immediately became serious himself, and sought to answer it to the best of his ability.

"There's a good deal to be said on both sides," he answered. "I know that you don't like mechanical warfare and you are finding it difficult to adapt yourself. It has robbed you of half your interest in soldiering. Much of your duty has now become a burden to you; once it was all a pleasure. And because you don't like it you are not going to be much good at it. At the same time, you are very fond of the regiment. I know that. I think you might miss it very much if you gave it up."

Touched by such good sense and such sympathy, Willie blurted out: "I'm thinking of getting married."

"Bravo!" said Hamilton. "That solves the problem," and then returning to his lighter tone, "Paterfamilias has no time for regimental duties."

"But is there going to be another war?" asked Willie. "I just missed the last one, you know, and I couldn't bear to miss the next one."

"I don't know whether there's going to be a war," said Hamilton, "but this I do know: if you leave the regiment now you'll go on the reserve of officers, and if a war comes along while you can still bear arms, you'll return to the regiment on the day of mobilisation—or a few days earlier."

"Can I count on that?" asked Willie. "Can I be quite certain that I shouldn't be pushed off into some other awful show, be made a Colonel of Pioneers or something?"

"You may be quite certain," said Hamilton gravely, "that you would rejoin the regiment as soon as war broke out. We should need every trained officer we could lay our hands on."

"That's a great relief to me," said Willie. "In fact it removes the chief obstacle that stood in my way. The only other thing is that I should have liked to have got my majority before I left."

Hamilton was silent. He had his own opinions as to Willie's qualifications for the rank of major. So after a moment or two Willie added:

"Well, I shall go on thinking it over. You won't tell anybody, will you?"

"I won't," said Hamilton, and he didn't.

When Willie next met Felicity he told her that he intended to leave the Army. She was very surprised.

"Oh, Willie," she said, "would you be wise to do that? It seems hard to imagine you out of the Army. It's so much a part of you. Would you be happy if you gave it up?"

"I should be happy if you would marry me," he said.

She gave him a quick look, uncertain if he were serious. She saw that he was.

"Oh, my poor love," she cried in deep concern, "I hope you will not think of that. I have no wish to marry. Whether I ever shall I cannot say, but certainly not now, not now. If that was why you wanted to leave the Army, pray do nothing of the sort."

"But why should you refuse to marry me?" he persisted obstinately. "You said you loved me a few nights ago."

"I do love you, I do indeed. But I can never see that that has much to do with it. So few married people love each other, and so many people who aren't married do."

"That's all cynical rot," said Willie. "Would you do away with marriage altogether?"

"Oh no, of course not, but I feel that it is not for me—not at present, anyway. I sometimes think that life is like a play—not a very original idea, because Shakespeare had it; but he said that each man in his time played many parts. I think most of them play only one. You're the soldier, just as Horry is the actor. I can't imagine either of you as anything else. I don't think I've been cast yet. I'm not the *jeune fille*— not the kind the audience expects, anyway—and, frankly, can you imagine me playing the married woman?"

"I don't know what I can imagine," said Willie ruefully. "I'm not imaginative—but I know that I'm madly in love with you and can never be happy unless you marry me."

"Please don't say that. Never is such a terrible word. You make me feel wicked and unhappy."

"Well, what am I to do?" asked Willie.

"I suppose that if I were a nice girl I should say 'Forget me,' but that's the last thing I want you to do. So go on loving me, my darling Willie, and I will go on loving you. And we'll have great fun, and not be too serious, and who knows what may happen in the end?"

Willie took these last, vague words as a kind of promise. He would say to himself afterwards, "She told me not to give up hope, but to wait." This was not quite what Felicity had meant.

## IX

TIME passed. Willie, hoping for promotion and lacking encouragement from Felicity, continually postponed a decision about leaving the Army. But his duties grew more irksome, and his desire to be in London whenever he wished increased. The regiment had lost its place in his mind, if not in his heart. He seldom thought of it. His first thoughts were of Felicity, his second of racing, so that he lived in two worlds and, together, they sufficed to fill his time. The regiment interfered with both. So that when he received yet another disappointment with regard to promotion, and when Felicity, to console him, said that captain was a more romantic rank than major, he decided to take the plunge and, not without many final searchings of heart, sent in his papers and became his own master for the first time in his life.

He went into partnership with a friend, and set up a small training-stable under National Hunt rules, partly in order to have something to answer when people asked him what he was doing, for in these days young Englishmen are ashamed to admit that they are doing nothing, and partly in order that when he went racing he might feel that he was attending to business and not wasting his time.

Felicity was sorry when he left the Army, although she had not tried to influence him in either direction. She had been brought up in the military tradition, and although she had moved into another sphere, she retained her respect and affection for the Army. Her opinions were not influenced in any way by the people who surrounded her.

Willie met Felicity by chance one day when she was with a tall young man, whose good looks were of a kind that he found particularly irritating. In the first place they were undeniable, and in the second place the young man, although his appearance and his clothes were unconventional, was not effeminate. His hair was long, and he wore a red sweater instead of a waistcoat, but there was something in his bearing that commanded respect. Felicity introduced them and said that her friend had just come back from Spain, and was returning there shortly.

"Have you been fighting in the civil war?" asked Willie.

"One mustn't say so, but as a matter of fact I have," the other answered.

Willie looked at him with envy. Here was a man, ten years younger than himself, perhaps, who had already taken part in war, and was continuing to do so. He surprised his friends at the club that evening by informing them that he was going off to Spain to take part in the fighting.

"On which side, Willie?" somebody asked him.

"Oh, I don't much mind about that," he said.

"Well, you see," it was explained to him, "either you have to join up with the Reds, burn down the churches and rape the nuns, or else you have to fight for Hitler and Mussolini and probably take your orders from a German officer."

"Is it as bad as that?" he asked.

"Worse, old boy. You're committing a legal offence by going there at all. Of course you'd assume a false name, but if you were caught, you being an officer on the reserve, you'd probably be cashiered. There would be headlines in the papers, and, oh golly, what a disgrace for the dear old regiment!"

Everybody knew Willie's weakness, and the theme was too good to be dropped.

"It wouldn't look well in the papers, I must say. 'Cavalry Captain caught in Convent,' 'British officer in crack regiment wins Order of Lenin,' 'Captain Maryngton embraced by Hitler.' It would break the poor old Colonel's heart."

Willie thought such jokes were not amusing, but they sufficed to destroy any intention he might have had of going to Spain. For the first time it was impressed upon him that it was far more difficult for a regular soldier than for a civilian to take part in a war.

Apart from the feeling of frustration that never altogether left him, these were not unhappy years for Willie. He was always occupied. His training-stable had ups and downs, and although over a long period the downs predominated, the ups were numerous and frequent enough to make life agreeable. He loved his club. He played all games of chance and enjoyed them, and the place where he had found so warm a welcome when he came back from India seemed likely to become his home for life.

What was lacking in this very masculine existence was provided by Felicity. His devotion to her never faltered, and she provided for him all that he demanded in the region of beauty and romance. She made no demands upon him. It was he who had always to arrange their meetings, and they were not as frequent as he would have liked. Often he felt that she was treating him badly, but he had only to be with her for five minutes to forget his grievance. Sometimes weeks or even months passed without their being alone together for a moment, and she seemed to be unaware of the fact. Sometimes she seemed to welcome and give back all his passion, at others she hardly allowed him to touch her hand. When he asked her to explain, or to give any reason for such strange alterations in her behaviour, she would say that she was sorry, she knew herself to be very tiresome, but he must take her as she was.

Willie went on living in Jermyn Street, where Felicity never visited him. It was one of her own unwritten laws. Nor did he invite her. There were still matters that he could not discuss with her, and favours that he could not ask. But despite the restrictions set upon their love-making, she made him happy. Her companionship was an unending pleasure, intensified by the thrill of desire. Sometimes, in the summer, they would take picnics into the country, spreading a cloth in some green, secluded spot and sleeping afterwards under the trees. Some-times they would go to the coast and bathe in the sea. Best of all, he thought, were the autumn and winter evenings when, having spent the day in the open air, hunting or racing, he would return to London and go to the club, where he would remain until the hall-porter came and murmured to him, confidentially, that there was a lady waiting for him outside. Then they would perhaps, if it were not too late, have some-thing to eat and drink before going to the theatre, and afterwards they would have supper either alone or with Horry, and Horry would usually bring a fourth. It was not always Miriam, and when there was a change Willie and Felicity would enjoy, afterwards, criticising the new favourite and speculating on Horry's degree of intimacy with her. Horry was earning a large salary now, his services were always in demand and he could pick and choose his parts. He had taken his flat in Bloomsbury, of which Willie approved, because it lay in the opposite direction to Chelsea, and there could therefore never be any occasion for Horry to drive Felicity home. She, on the other hand, after all these years, was still looking for a flat, and still sharing rooms with a friend, which Willie deplored, because it disposed of any argu-ment that he could use for crossing the threshold. It was a strange love affair, but Willie was beginning to become reconciled to it, as he was beginning to become reconciled to his existence. It seemed to be his fate, he sometimes thought, to be a soldier who never went to war, and a lover who never lay with his mistress.

## x

WHILE his life was thus jogging easily along there happened the great political event that was known as the Munich crisis. It made a disturb-ance in many people's lives. In Willie's it made a vast upheaval. Once again he felt as he had felt twenty years before and, while nearly all the world was hoping for peace, he prayed for war. Naturally he resented the settlement with great bitterness, and he was glad to find that there were others who felt as he did. His reasons were not their reasons, but this did not prevent him from applauding their denunciation of the shameful surrender. But when they said that the worst part of the policy was that it only meant we should have to fight the war later under less favourable conditions, he secretly hoped that they were right, and that it would come as soon as possible.

He was disappointed in the attitude of Felicity, who was for peace at any price, and they nearly quarrelled about it, as at that time so many good friends did. But he found an unexpected and fervent ally in Horry. It was unexpected, because he had always thought of Horry as a man who was opposed to any form of violence. He was, however, one who behind an easy-going, humorous approach to life hid a profound hatred of injustice and cruelty. He knew of the fate that had befallen some Jewish members of the German theatrical world, and he could not bear to think of Englishmen shaking the hand of the man who was responsible for such enormities. He was much more violent than Willie, and what he had to say about the paper signed by Hitler, which the Prime Minister waved triumphantly in the face of the applauding populace, was very savage.

In the days before the settlement, while Willie was eagerly awaiting his mobilisation orders, he had travelled up to where his regiment was stationed in order to be on the spot. The Colonel was abroad on leave, which shocked him, and Hamilton was in command. Hamilton refused to believe there would be a war, and told Willie not to get over-excited. He had been in Germany himself last summer and had talked to some German officers—very good chaps. He thought that if our politicians knew their business they could arrange for Germany to fight Russia. The officers he had met were pro-British, but very keen to have a go at the Reds. We ought to encourage them to do so and kill two birds with one stone.

Willie had asked whether the winner would not then turn on us, but Hamilton had replied that both sides would be exhausted.

"And then the looker-on, who will be us, and who, as usual, will have seen most of the game, who will have learnt a lot about modern warfare, without fighting, and will have built up his own armaments while the belligerents are destroying theirs, will be in a position to dictate to both sides. That's what's called statesmanship."

"I don't care what it's called," said Willie, "it sounds to me a dirty, tricky, cowardly business—the sort of thing that politicians would invent—and, what's more, I don't believe that any good will come of it. Well, you will know where I am if you want me."

"We shan't forget, Willie, and you may be sure that we shall send for you in the hour of danger."

Willie had felt that Hamilton was laughing at him, and hated him for it, but henceforth he had a very definite object in life and a great hope in his heart.

During the months that followed he thought of nothing but the coming war. He was now thirty-nine, and he had never bothered to take care of his health. Riding had kept him active, and he had detected in himself no symptoms of growing old. But he consulted a doctor and insisted upon a thorough examination. The doctor found little wrong with him, but suggested fewer cocktails and plainer food, and Willie followed his directions as scrupulously as though they were military orders.

He saw less of Felicity during this year. She refused to take life as seriously as he did, and preferred to accept the assurances given by Ministers and newspapers that there was nothing to worry about.

## XI

BEING on the reserve of officers, Willie did a short period of training with his regiment every year, and it so happened that he was actually with the regiment and under canvas in the month of September when the war broke out. Once again he experienced the same thrill of exultation that he had known just twenty-one years before when he was warned that he was to go with the next draft to France. He felt no older than he had done then, and on his knees he thanked heaven that his chance had not come too late. In the camp during those first days everything was in a state of feverish activity, for it was known that the regiment would be among the first to go.

Then came the shattering blow. One morning the Colonel sent for him.

"I've bad news, I fear, for you, Willie, but it's bad news for me, too. We're both in the same boat, or rather we're both out of it; neither of us is to go with the first contingent. Hamilton is taking the regiment abroad, and you and I have got to stay behind, look after what's left of it, and train on the young officers."

Willie's mouth went dry, he was unable to speak, and for one terrible moment he feared he was going to cry.

"Don't take it too hard," the Colonel went on. "It's worse for me than for you. In my case, if they don't let me go now it's a hundred to one they won't let me go at all. It means I'm on the shelf, finished for life."

Willie longed to say that the Colonel had fought in the last war, as the row of ribbons on his chest bore witness, that he was over fifty, a married man with children, and that he had much to console him for staying at home. He wanted to fall on his knees and beg to be allowed to go, but he knew that the decision did not rest with the Colonel, so that he could only stand there, still unable to speak.

"Don't take it too hard, Willie," the Colonel repeated, seeing that he was taking it very hard indeed. "I remember so well at the beginning of the last war, when some fool in high places had said, or was reported to have said, that it would all be over by Christmas, and lots of us were in despair because we thought we should never get out in time. But we all went in the long run, and it will be just the same again—heavy casualties in the first scrap, more officers wanted, none of the new boys ready to go. They'll be grateful enough for the old 'uns then, and there won't be too many of them. Meanwhile there will be plenty of work for us to do at home, and very important work too, and there's a job or two I want you to get on with immediately."

Willie was thankful that the Colonel then went on to explain to him a number of things that he wanted done which would necessitate a visit to the War Office and several days in London. He was, in fact, to act as second-in-command of the training unit that would remain behind. Although he found it difficult to follow all that the Colonel said, and was obliged to ask a number of questions, he was thankful to have these matters to discuss and not to be obliged to refer to the fearful blow which he had just received. If only he had been prepared for it, he felt that he could have borne it better. But in his crass stupidity, he told himself, it was the one thing that had never occurred to him. He knew perfectly well that when a regiment went abroad on active service some officers and men were left behind. But he had never thought that he would be among those officers. Some people, he told himself, were struck by lightning, some were eaten by sharks, some won the Calcutta sweepstake, but he had never believed that any of those fates would befall such an ordinary chap as him, Willie Maryngton. And he would never have thought that he would be the officer who was left behind. The Colonel had talked about the first scrap, but that was just the scrap that he wanted to be in. He had said something about heavy casualties. Willie minded little how heavy they were if he was in it, but how could he bear to sit at home hoping that his brother officers would be killed, so that he could take their place?

No reference was made in the mess that evening to the regiment's forthcoming departure, but Willie felt that it was generally known that he was not to go. Everybody was polite and kind to him as though he had just suffered some domestic tragedy, and, when he said that he was going to London next morning, nobody asked why.

When Willie went into his club on the following day he was surprised to find how many of the civilian members were already in uniform, and how many were expecting to go overseas almost immediately. At the time this made his position more painful, although subsequent experience taught him that these hopes of active service, if genuine, were too optimistic, and many of the most confident remained in uniform, and in the club, for the rest of the war.

He spent the greater part of the next day at the War Office, and was very far from having completed his mission at the end of it. The light was failing as he turned up Whitehall towards Trafalgar Square. He had almost bumped into a man who was walking rapidly in the opposite direction, when he saw that he was Horry, and they greeted one another.

"You're a bit off your beat here, Horry," he said. "Turn back with me and we'll have a drink at the Carlton bar."

"I'm sorry, old chap," said Horry, "but I'm in a hurry. Walk along with me in my direction for a bit."

Willie turned. As he did so he glanced curiously at Horry. There was something unusual in his appearance. Could he be sunburnt? No— he looked again, and then he saw what it was.

"Horry," he said quietly, "have you been playing in a matinée?"

"No, indeed. My show came off last week—and who ever heard of a matinée on a Friday?"

"Then, by God, Horry, I don't understand it," said Willie rather fiercely. "I thought perhaps you'd forgotten to take off your make-up. Are you aware, man, that your face is painted?"

He asked the question as though it were an accusation, and in order to add solemnity to it, he stopped, laid his hand on Horry's arm and looked straight into his eyes.

Horry threw back his head with his old gay laugh.

"Oh, my beloved Willie," he said. "Scotland Yard's just round the corner. Would you care to run me in for accosting? Come on, you old silly. I've got no time to lose."

"But explain, for God's sake explain," said Willie, as they walked on.

"It's very simple," said Horry. "I'm over forty, you know. I never thought I looked it, but it seems I do. They've turned me down at two of these damned recruiting places already, but there's one down here near Westminster Bridge. They haven't got the electricity working in it yet, but they keep it open till six, and by then the light's pretty bad. The chaps will be tired, they don't know me as you do, so they won't suspect anything, and I believe with this make-up I'll pull it off."

"Oh, Horry, how splendid! I thought that you'd be the last person to do a thing like this."

"I know." Horry looked almost ashamed of himself. "I'm not so keen on King and Country and all that stuff, but when I think about those blasted Nazis I just feel that I can't walk on to the stage and make an ass of myself as long as one of the bastards is left alive."

Willie was deeply moved, but all he could mutter was "Damned good show," and as they had reached the end of Whitehall he turned, rather abruptly, towards Storey's Gate and began walking back to his club across the park. His mind was full of admiration for Horry and of pity for himself. Here was a man two years older than he was, who, since leaving school, had never done a day's military training, and who might now be going to the war, while he, whose whole life had been devoted to the Army, who had made every possible effort to render himself an efficient officer, was forced to stay at home. The injustice of it rankled deeply.

He had broken off his conversation with Horry so suddenly that he had forgotten to ask him to telephone the result of his visit to the recruiting station. When he reached his club, therefore, he rang up and heard the jubilant voice of Horry at the other end of the line. All had gone well. The only doubt in the minds of the officials, so he assured Willie, was whether he was old enough to join the Army. He was to report on the following day.

Willie suggested that they should dine together, but Horry, after a moment's hesitation, feared it was impossible. Willie concluded that he was having a farewell dinner with Miriam, and keenly envied him. He asked for news of Felicity. He had tried to find her by telephone without success. Horry gave him a number. When he succeeded in getting it, after some difficulty, and asked for Miss Osborne, he was informed in a harsh female voice that "Osborne would be coming on duty at 10 p.m." He enquired who it was that he had the honour of speaking to, and learnt that it was the Superintendent of the Chelsea Branch of the Auxiliary Fire Service. He asked that Osborne might be requested to ring up his number when she arrived, and a grudging assent was given.

He was in the middle of a rubber of bridge after dinner when the call came through. Felicity's voice sounded tired on the telephone and not very friendly. After the usual greetings she said:

"I hope you're enjoying the war that you've been looking forward to for so long."

"Oh no, Felicity," he answered. "I am not enjoying it at all."

Her voice changed at once, and the warmth he loved so much came back into it.

"My poor Willie. I hate you to be unhappy. We'll lunch together to-morrow, and you shall tell me all about it."

She gave him the name of a restaurant in Chelsea, and told him the hour at which she would be there, warning him that her time was limited and that he must be punctual.

On the following day he waited for her at the restaurant for half an hour. Thinking there had been a mistake, he was about to leave, for it was not a restaurant which tempted him to have luncheon alone, and he was standing at the entrance, when she came running down the street. Breathlessly she explained that she had been unable to get away earlier, that her hours of duty were always being changed, that she would never have forgiven him if he hadn't waited, but that now all was well, as she was free for the afternoon.

He thought that she had never looked so lovely. The uniform—dark blue tunic and trousers and a small blue hat that could not contain her thick curling hair—became her admirably. She carried her gas mask slung over her shoulder and somehow conveyed a curious impression of efficiency. He was delighted with her.

"Tell me quickly," he said, "all about this Army you have joined, what your duties are and how you like it."

"It seemed," she said, "the best thing to do. One can't get into the Wrens, the Ats all hate it, and I can't bear the uniform of the Waafs, so here I am. I've got some friends in the same show. We can't have much to do until the bombing starts, then we shall have to go round putting out the fires and carting away the corpses. I'm only a driver. The one thing I can do is to drive a car, but I've only just learnt to clean one. Look!" She held out to him her beautiful hands, already dirtied and roughtened by labour.

He took one of them in his, pointed to the scratches on it, saying, "Honourable scars, honourable scars," then turned it over tenderly and kissed the palm.

"Even you," he murmured, "wounded already!"

He asked her whether she had heard about Horry. She had heard nothing, and when he told her she was not surprised.

"I thought he'd do something like that," she said, "but I wish he could have had a commission. He loves his comforts, and he has been used to them for so long."

"Perhaps he'll get one," said Willie. "Serve him right if he does, for then they won't let him go near the fighting."

He poured forth all his own unhappiness, and Felicity listened with large-eyed sympathy. She offered him such consolation as she could, but found little to say that he had not said to himself already. There was, of course, the very likely possibility of heavy casualties, against which Willie argued that young officers were being rapidly trained to fill the gaps.

Felicity maintained, rather feebly, the view that this war was not going to be like the last. Not only was there just as much important work to be done at home, but the people who stayed at home would be in as great danger as those at the front.

"Not the soldiers," said Willie bitterly. "You ought to see our air-raid shelters; we've been digging them all the summer, although the C.O. didn't believe in war. They're the best in the country and, what's more, it's an order to go down into them at the first alert. It's an offence to risk the life of one of His Majesty's valuable soldiers, even those who are too old to go out and fight for him. And what do you suppose we're spending our time doing now?" he added. "Camouflaging our barracks!"

"Well, you won't be safe when you come to London, anyhow, and I hope you'll come often because I see that I'm going to be terribly bored."

"I'll come as often as I can; you can count on that. But if you think that a bomb falling on my head in a London street is going to make up to me for not fighting with the regiment in France, you're wrong."

"My poor Willie," said Felicity sadly. "It seems to me that wars don't make people happy—not even the people who wanted them"—and she stretched her hand across the table and held his for a minute.

## XII

WILLIE was kept very busy that winter and the time passed quickly. If there were few casualties it was some consolation to him to know that there was so little fighting, and therefore that he was not missing much. He seldom came to London, and when he did he found it difficult to see Felicity, whose time also was occupied with small, tiresome duties, and who was intensely disliking her apparently unnecessary job, which increased the dreariness of the hard winter, the black-out and the uneventful war.

The only casualty that occurred in Willie's regiment was one that he least desired. The Colonel greeted him one morning in high spirits with the information that Hamilton had suffered some injury and was coming home.

"It seems," he said, "that he had a fall out riding. It has lamed him, and he's coming home for a bit, and I am to take his place. He'll take over here for the time being. He's fit for light duty."

"What was he riding a horse for?" grumbled Willie. "Why doesn't he stick to his dirty old tank? He can't fall off that."

That the Colonel should go out and that Hamilton should come home was a double-barrelled disaster for Willie, and made a bad beginning to the second six months of the war. Events of so much greater importance, however, followed that for a while Willie forgot his own grievances while the German armies swept through Denmark, Norway, Holland, Belgium and France. His reaction to these tremendous events was that of many Englishmen. After the dim frustration of the first eight months he felt a new enthusiasm and a kind of spiritual exaltation. For the first time in his life it occurred to him that defeat was possible, but it was a possibility that did not appal him. There could be no defeat unless the enemy landed, and if they landed there could be no defeat so long as there was one true Englishman alive. Then at last he would have the opportunity of fighting for his country and of dying for it, if need be.

On one of his visits to London at about the time of the fall of France he spent an evening with Felicity. She greeted him with the news that Horry had been killed in Boulogne. She had only just heard, but she was quite calm about it, although Willie knew that it meant even more to her than it did to him.

"Garnet told me this morning," she said. "He had had the telegram as being next of kin."

"It's too bad," said Willie.

"Too bad," she said.

"I sometimes think," he went on, "that we shall all be killed. I'd sooner be, if we're going to lose the War."

"Of course," she said quietly. "But it won't be so easy for women."

"Will they let you fight?" he asked.

"Can they stop us?" she answered. "We had a lecture yesterday about Molotov bombs. You throw them out of the window at a tank, and if you hit it the tank goes up in smoke. It sounds fun, but nobody has seen one yet."

Then they went on to talk of Horry, of how much they had loved him and how deeply they would miss him for the rest of their lives. It was a calm, sad evening. When they parted and Willie took her in his arms and kissed her cheek, he felt they had never been so close to one another before.

The important thing for Willie at this time was that the regiment, having suffered very lightly, was home again, and that he was with it. The Colonel was no longer there. He had had the final satisfaction of commanding during the retreat to Dunkirk, and had been transferred to some non-combatant job. Hamilton had been cured of his disability, promoted to the substantive rank of lieutenant-colonel and was in command. This slightly, but only slightly, mitigated Willie's happiness in being with his comrades again. He felt that the greater part of what was left of the Army was now in England, so that he was happy to be there too, and he secretly hoped that the enemy would invade.

The Battle of Britain damped his hopes, but he was uplifted by the glory of it, and cursed his fate that he had never learned to fly. His friends consoled him with the assurance that, judging by his prowess at the wheel of a car, he would certainly have destroyed any aeroplane he was in charge of, and himself with it. And even if he had survived he would have been permanently grounded long ago.

He still had his flat in London, and he went there as often as he could. He was there on the Sunday evening in September when the first serious bombing attack took place. Felicity was on duty that night. He was able to have only a few words with her on the telephone the following morning before he travelled back. When he pressed her for some account of her experiences she was reticent.

"Come on," he urged, "tell me more about it. What sort of time did you have?"

"Pretty bloody," she said, and he could get nothing more out of her, but he felt as he returned to the country that she had come closer to the war than he had.

As the days shortened and the frequency of bombing raids increased, the rumours of invasion began to be discredited, and in Willie's regiment they were replaced by whispers that the regiment would shortly be moving to the Middle East. Now, so it seemed to Willie, the great crisis of his life must come. When they had crossed the Channel without him, the blow had been severe, but they had been distant only a day's journey, or a few hours in the air, and he had always hugged to his heart the hope that any morning the summons to join them might arrive. But if they went to the Middle East, and it was said that troops now travelled round the Cape to get there—if they went to the Middle East without him, he felt that his fate would be sealed. Speculation on this subject occupied his mind day and night. Here at home he was treated like any other officer. He was senior captain and performed all the duties and received all the respect belonging to his rank. His health was excellent. He had worked conscientiously to make himself efficient. Conceit was the least of his failings, but he quite honestly believed that he was as good an officer as the majority. *But,* that terrible word which came at the end of all his optimistic reasonings, *but* he had been left behind a year ago when he was thirty-nine, he was now forty and soon he would be forty-one. The next youngest captain in the regiment was thirty-four. This captain was married with children, as so many of these young men were, while he himself was single, with no dependants in the world. That was a consideration that ought surely to be taken into account.

The men liked him—that he knew—and so did his brother officers. He was not brilliantly clever, but nor were they. He knew his job as well as they did, and had more experience. It was true that he had been away from the regiment for some years, but he had worked hard to catch up, and thought he had succeeded. Did they think that because he was a little older he was more likely to go sick? A doctor had assured him that a healthy man of forty was in every way as sound a proposition as a man of thirty. He had passed his medical examination with flying colours. Since he had rejoined he had not had a day's illness, which was more than most of them could say. *But, but* they had left him behind a year ago, why should they take him with them now?

Willie became so haunted by this obsession that he finally decided that he had better take some action that would put himself out of his agony. Between the decision and the action many days passed. At last one night, which was selected for no better reason than that he had had an extra glass of port after dinner, and that he found himself alone with Hamilton, the others having gone to the cinema, he boldly broached the subject.

"They say we may be going overseas again," he began.

"Do they?" said Hamilton, stretching for a newspaper.

"Oh, I'm not trying to extract confidential information about the movement of troops. I'm only interested in the movements of Captain Maryngton. I don't want to know whether the regiment is going or not, but what I do want to know—pretty damned desperately bad I want to know—is whether, if the regiment does go, I am likely to go with it."

Hamilton was silent.

"Look here, Colonel," Willie went on. "You've known me for a long time, and you must know what this thing means to me. I missed the last war by a few weeks, and all I have hoped for all my life is to see some fighting with the regiment. I had given up hope some years ago, when I left the Army. I thought there wouldn't be another war in my time, and then I thought I might get married. You were the only fellow I told, and I don't believe you ever repeated it, for which I'm damned grateful. Well, it didn't come off, and now I don't expect it ever will. I'm alone in the world, hale and hearty, just the sort of cannon-fodder they ought to be looking for—and, and, oh Hamilton, for God's sake tell me—have I got a chance?"

Hamilton replied, "Not an earthly."

Willie put his face in his hands, and Hamilton went on calmly:

"As you have asked me, it is better that you should know the truth. No officers under field rank, of your age, or anything like your age, are being sent abroad. You may have heard of exceptions. There are exceptions to every rule, but I can see no chance of your being one. It's bad luck, but that's how it is."

"I see," said Willie, "I see."

He got up slowly, left the room and walked upstairs to bed. As he went he thought he might have asked whether he had any chance of promotion. But he knew what the answer would have been.

The final calamity comes often almost as a relief after long anxiety, and Willie, although he assured himself that life no longer held any interest for him, slept better that night than he had done for some time. Next morning he felt very miserable, but told himself that he must bear sorrow with fortitude, and that at such a moment in the world's history there were more important things to think about than the fate of Willie Maryngton. There was still the regiment and there was still Felicity.

In a few days came confirmation of the rumours about the regiment's movements, and it was followed by definite orders to sail. Henceforth they all lived in a turmoil of preparation, where there was as much work for Willie to do as for anyone else. His heart was in the work and he threw himself into it with passion, resisting firmly any inclination to pause and think. Like a discarded suitor employed on the preparations for the wedding of his beloved, he tried to think only of the task in hand, and to forget what must be the end of it. But too soon the end arrived. There could be none of those festivities or farewell parties that used to celebrate the departure of troops. The demands of security insisted that to the public eye the regiment should be there one day, carrying on their normal functions and giving no sign of departure, and on the morrow they should have disappeared, leaving no trace behind. Willie travelled with them to the port of embarkation, and actually went on board the ship in which they were sailing. When he had shaken hands with some of his friends, and came over the side for the last time, he had a curious and most uncomfortable feeling in his chest, and he found himself foolishly wondering whether people's hearts really do break, whether it might not be more than a mere figure of speech.

XIII

WHEN he got back to London that evening an air-raid was in progress. There seemed to be one every night now. It was December 1940. There was no hope of getting a taxi at the station, so he left his kit there and walked through the deserted streets to his club. There were sounds of distant explosions, but the streets through which he walked were as quiet as they were empty. A gentle drizzle was falling. When he reached his destination he was damp and very tired. It was too late for dinner. He ordered some biscuits and a drink. Some members were playing billiards, others were watching them, and making unfavourable comments on their play. A friend came to sit by Willie and talked to him about racing. They had a drink together and then another one. Willie began to feel warm and at ease. The physical well-being spread from his senses to his mind. The regiment had gone but there were still good chaps in the club. The hall-porter came in to warn them that it was nearly closing time. He could not bear the thought of his lonely flat. Was there nowhere they could go on to? he asked. Somebody knew of somewhere—an underground night club, which was sure to be open. They had another drink, and three of them went on. It was far from being a first-class establishment. The jangling music, the tawdry decorations, the tired faces of the girls, brought back to Willie the mood of acute depression from which he had been escaping. Another drink only intensified his gloom. Two of the girls were sitting with them. They knew his companions and they had mutual friends of whom they talked. Willie tried to take part in the conversation, but whatever he said sounded stilted and dull. He wished that Horry were there. Horry always got on with everybody. He knew how to break the ice. Did either of these girls know Horry? Or had they known him, rather because he was dead, killed in the war. He was an actor but he got killed in the war. Funny thing. He would order another bottle so that they could all drink Horry's health—drink to his memory, rather—no good drinking his health now. Too late. How curious it was that even talking of Horry had helped to break the ice. He was getting on well with the girls now. They were nice girls too, and seemed sympathetic. He had no wish to go home with them, but he needed friends. Why shouldn't a man be friends with girls of that sort? He thought of Felicity and wondered where she was. He knew. She was driving round London, serving her country wherever the bombs were falling thickest. And the regiment was now at sea, going out to the war, hunted by submarines and enemy aircraft. And here was he, sitting half tight in a night club, talking to tarts. "But it is not my fault," he muttered to himself, "God knows it is not my fault."

Willie had eaten little all that day and, although he had forgotten it, he was very tired, so that the wine was too much for him and he had to be helped to bed.

When he awoke next morning to a dark December day and found himself in his bleak, ill-kept bachelor flat, with no very clear recollection as to how he had got there, he felt that he had reached the lowest rung on the ladder of depression. There was even a moment when he contemplated putting an end to his life, but he remembered having once heard his father say that to commit suicide was the act of a coward, and therefore, whatever fate might befall him, he knew he must face it rather than run away.

He was disturbed about his behaviour on the previous evening. He was not in the least ashamed of having been drunk, but he remembered talking about Horry, and he was afraid that he might have been maudlin and lachrymose, which he would have considered contemptible. For some time he lay on his back contemplating the misery of human life. Then he rang for breakfast and telephoned to Felicity.

"Willie speaking. Have I woken you up?"

"No, dear idiot, it's just struck eleven."

"What sort of a night did you have?"

"Pretty foul."

"Were you up very late?"

"No, the all clear went at 2.30. What were you doing?"

"Well, I stayed up pretty late, and I don't remember hearing the all clear."

"Tight again, I suppose."

"I don't see why you need say 'again'. It happens very seldom. And if it did happen last night, there was good cause for it."

"Why, what's the matter?"

"You know those chaps I was staying with, up in the north. They have all gone away and they've left me behind again."

"Oh, my darling!" she cried. "No wonder, no wonder. What can I do for you?"

"Can you dine with me to-night?"

"I can and will. I have two nights off. I get them every fortnight, you know. I had thought of going to rest in the country, but I hate the country at this time of year. So we'll dine together in that deep underground place in Berkeley Square where you can't hear the bombs, and we'll forget all about the war for once."

"You're an angel," said Willie. "I had just sent out for a pistol to shoot myself. I'll countermand the order and meet you there at eight. I shall be waiting with the largest and coldest martini ever manufactured."

Having eaten his breakfast and dressed, Willie set forth for his club, fortified in body and soul. He found one of his last night's companions, and eagerly asked him:

"Did I make a fool of myself last night?"

"Not more than usual, old boy."

"I was feeling a bit depressed and I was afraid I might have got maudlin."

"I think you asked one of those girls to be a sister to you, and you told the other she reminded you of your mother."

"I can't have said that," protested Willie, "because I never saw my mother."

"Oh, it may have been your grandmother, but you didn't make any suggestion to either of them that really interested them."

"No, I know I didn't. I was very tired and I hadn't had any dinner, so I got a bit muzzy, but I remember everything really. It was very good of you to see me home."

"Oh, I'm glad you remember that," said his friend—"but it happened to be George who saw you home, and he put you to bed. I felt it my duty to look after those poor girls."

The chaff that followed made no impression on Willie. His volatile spirits had risen at the thought of dining with Felicity, and looking forward to it made him happy for the rest of the day.

He was first at the rendezvous that evening. He usually was. He ordered double martinis, poured them both into one glass, and ordered another. Then he sat down to wait.

"Hullo Willie," he heard a voice say. He sprang up gladly to welcome Felicity, and found himself looking at someone whom for a moment he failed to recognise. Then he saw that it was Daisy Summers. They had not met since her elopement. She had changed so much that Willie forgave himself for his delay in recognising her. She had lost her prettiness, but she was still good looking, although her face was hard and lined.

"I am so glad to see you again, Daisy," he said. "I'm waiting for someone, but she's always late. Won't you sit down for a minute and have a drink?"

"That's very sweet of you, Willie," she said. "You always were very sweet." She sat down. "Your girl friend seems to have a healthy thirst, judging from your preparations. I'll have a whisky sour if I may."

"What's your life now, Daisy? Are you happy?"

"Yes, I'm pretty happy, thanks. I don't think anybody's very happy, do you? I've been working in the postal censorship since the beginning of the war. One feels one's doing something, but it isn't much."

"And er—your husband?"

"Oh," she laughed, "I suppose you mean the Coper. That didn't last long. I've been married since then. I heard from the old skunk the other day. He's living in Ireland, and says it's very nice to be a neutral."

"He's much too old to fight," said Willie. "They tell me that I am, and they won't let me go out."

"Poor old Willie! You always get the dirty end of the stick; I ought to have married you if I hadn't been a silly little fool, and a bitch. And you never have married, have you? Well, I expect you're wise." She looked at him reflectively for a moment—"We might go out together one evening."

"I'd love to," said Willie, but he didn't sound as though he meant it, so she shrugged her shoulders and said, "There's my boy. So long, Willie," and walked over to an overdressed young gentleman who was waiting impatiently at the door.

Willie sat down again and finished his cocktail. "Poor old Daisy!" he thought. "She was never a bad sort at heart. She was just fascinated by the Coper. I wonder how it would have turned out if we had married. She seemed to regret it just now. We might have had a lot of children. It would make one feel less useless if one had brought some decent people into the world. It would be interesting to discuss it with her. I might have been more welcoming about her suggestion that we should go out together. I'll go over and speak to her, if only to irritate that young puppy who's with her. Why isn't he in uniform?"

Willie strolled across to where Daisy and her friend were sitting.

"Daisy dear," he said, "you suggested our going out together but gave me no address except the Postal Censorship. What do I do? Ring up the Postmaster-General and say 'Please put me through to Daisy'—because I don't know your surname?"

"Silly Willie," she laughed, while the overdressed young man glared furiously. "We're not under the Postmaster-General but the Minister of Information. Here, give me your pencil," she said to the young man, who sulkily produced a gold one. She scribbled on the back of the menu. "Here you are," she said. "Name, address and telephone number. Mind you don't lose them, and mind you make use of them."

As Willie returned to his seat, Felicity arrived. "Who were you talking to?" she asked him.

"An old school friend of yours, Daisy Summers. Do you ever see her now?"

"Never, and I didn't see much of her then. She's made rather a hash of her life, I'm afraid."

"What has she done?"

"She didn't stay long with that Irishman she ran away with. I doubt if they were ever married, but they pretended to be. Then she did marry somebody quite nice, but it didn't go well, and they separated. Now they say she's being kept by that little Argentine."

"How dreadful!"

"Oh, I don't know. I dare say she's quite happy."

"I've promised to go out with her one night."

"Don't let her seduce you."

"Would you mind, Felicity, if she did?"

"Not if you promise to tell me all about it." This hurt Willie. She often hurt him without knowing it.

"Well," he said, "if you've quite finished that enormous cocktail and can still walk, we might go over to our table and have some dinner before closing time."

She had made no comment on the cocktail. This also had disappointed him. He would prepare things to amuse or please her and she would fail to notice them.

As they sat down at their table she said, "I think it's going to be a bad night. The moon's nearly full and there are no clouds. I'm glad I'm not on duty. By the way, have I seen you since the bombing of London started?"

This was the third unintended blow she dealt him. The dates on which he saw her were engraven on his heart, and the days between impatiently counted.

"Of course you have. We had luncheon together in October, and I saw you for a few minutes when I passed through London last month."

"Of course," she said absently, and he knew that she had no memory of those meetings. Then, as though recollecting herself, she turned to him impulsively. "But tell me about you. They've left you behind. Aren't they devils! I'm sure it's all the fault of that evil Hamilton. But I'm glad I've got you still here—darling. I know I'm selfish."

All Willie's irritation vanished, forgotten for ever, and he was the happy lover again. So he was able to talk about his disappointment calmly and to discuss the possibilities of invasion, which he had to admit were diminishing. He found that her sympathy really comforted him.

They heard faintly the sound of explosions from time to time, and the head-waiter whispered to Willie that a popular restaurant with a dancing-floor had been struck. He told Felicity, who said, "Lucky we didn't go there to-night."

"I wish you could get some more reasonable job," he said.

"By 'more reasonable' you mean safer. I'm beginning to wish so, too. I'm not very brave, you know. And I don't find that I get any braver. It's rather the other way round. I suppose nerves, like everything else, wear out."

"I heard of a job in the country, near where the regiment was, which might interest you."

"Oh no," she said at once, "I can't leave London. That would be running away. You may think it silly, but that's how I feel—and I think one's own feelings are the best guides one has as to what is right or wrong. I do lots of things that people think wrong, and I don't feel guilty, but if I left London I should be ashamed for the rest of my life."

"I don't believe you could do wrong," protested Willie, but she went on without listening to him.

"And I love London so. I think I love it more than England. If you had seen the people of London as I have this month—the ordinary, little, common, heroic people—so brave, so cheerful and so funny—with all their small treasures that they loved blown to smithereens, and making jokes about it, and sticking up their pathetic Union Jacks on heaps of rubble. And the great city itself, with its poor wounded face, so gaunt and ugly and grand and glorious—and old."

"Yes," said Willie doubtfully, "but I like the country better."

She looked at him, startled, as though she had forgotten he were there. Then she said, slowly: "My darling Willie. I would not have you any different."

"Thank you," he said. "I so often wish I were different."

"In what way?" she asked.

"Oh, I should like to be witty and brilliant, as I suppose your other friends are, whom you won't let me see."

"Talking of brilliance," she said, "old Garnet is home again. He's back from North Africa, where he had quite an exciting time. There's nothing brilliant about him. And, oh, Willie, he's grown so old. I can't bear people to grow old, can you? Of course he's more than fifteen years older than me, but he is my brother. I suppose it's the climate of the Far East. He wants so much to see you. I'll give you his telephone number. Write it down, don't lose it and don't get it mixed up with Daisy's, or there might be trouble."

She gave him the number, which he recorded in his pocket-book, and shortly afterwards they left. As they went up the stairs which led to the street she turned suddenly from the higher step and, bending down, kissed him on the lips.

The streets were quiet now and the moon was bright, but when they came to Jermyn Street they found policemen and firemen guarding the approach. Willie explained that he lived there and was going home. The policeman asked at which number he lived, and on being told said, "I fear you won't find much of that left, but you can go and have a look. You can't take the car through." Where had stood the substantial building in which he lived there was an empty space through which the moon, that should have cast a shadow on to the other side of the street, shone without hindrance. From what had been the basement smoke and dust were rising, together with the noise of men at work. Ambulances and fire-engines were standing by.

"Can I be of any help?" asked Willie of somebody who seemed to be in authority.

"No, thanks. The bomb fell an hour and a half ago. We have all the help we need."

"I lived there," said Willie, pointing to the void.

"You might very easily have died there to-night," said the stranger, and Willie, feeling there was no more to be said, returned to the car.

He explained to Felicity what had happened. He had lost everything he possessed in the world, for what he had left in the barracks, that the regiment had recently quitted, had arrived at his flat that day.

"And what are you going to do now, poor Willie?" she asked, smiling at him with amusement and love.

"I've got nowhere to sleep," he said weakly, standing by the door of the car.

"You had better come and sleep with me," she said. "Jump in."

Half dazed by the sudden event, and still further bewildered by her words, he obeyed her and sat silent by her side while the car sped westwards. It stopped at the entrance that he knew so well.

"Come in," she said. "There's nobody here tonight. I'll leave the car here. You can take it in the morning—but you must go early and send it back."

Willie hardly closed his eyes that night. He had no wish to sleep. He did not want to forget, even for a moment, that Felicity was lying in his arms, and that after all these years she had suddenly given herself to him with the sweetest simplicity and grace. But what did it mean? She had always said she loved him. Did she love him more now, and in a different way? She had always refused to marry him. Surely she would now consent? But what mattered most were the precious moments that were passing. Her head was resting lightly on his shoulder. She slept as silently as a child. He must not wake her. How tenderly he loved her now! Surely this precious night made up for all that he had lost in life.

Long before dawn he left her, very quietly. She turned with a little sigh on to her other side and was still asleep. He was glad that she had not woken. He would not have known what to say. He decided not to take the car, but to walk. He had plenty of time and plenty to think about. As he went down the King's Road, the lurid lamps of night became innocent primroses against the faint morning sky. He felt like a poor man who had suddenly inherited a vast fortune, in which he could hardly believe.

He went first to the site of his flat, in the vague hope of recovering some of his belongings. Any such hope was extinguished by one glance at the scene of devastation. He had then thought to go to his club, having forgotten that it would not be open at that hour. Nor did he like the prospect of arriving in an empty hotel bedroom with nothing but the clothes he wore. Suddenly he remembered that Felicity had given him Garnet's telephone number. Garnet was the type that would not mind being woken before his time. He turned into a telephone booth and rang the number. A voice answered immediately, "Colonel Osborne speaking."

"How like Garnet," thought Willie, "not to waste time saying 'hello'."

"This is Willie Maryngton," he said. "Did I wake you up?"

"No, I'm cooking my breakfast."

"Well, cook some more for me. I've been bombed out, and I'll come along as quick as legs or a taxi can take me."

"Very well."

## XIV

GARNET's faded eyes shone with pleasure as he opened the door of the flat to Willie.

"Right glad I am to see you," he said. "I suppose you got my number from Felicity. I feared she would forget to give it you."

Then Willie remembered that Garnet was Felicity's brother, and the thought made him feel a little wicked, but very grand.

"I never knew you were such an early bird," he said, for Garnet was fully dressed, and was laying tea and eggs, toast and marmalade, on the table, all of which he had plainly prepared himself, for there was no sign of a servant.

"I have to be," he answered—"I'm due at the hospital at nine, and I've patients to see before I go there. I was never so busy in my life."

"Everyone is except me," said Willie sadly. "How right you were to join the R.A.M.C. You've already been to the war, and now you're as useful as you ever were, serving the country every hour of the day, while I, younger than you, am no good for anything."

He was very hungry, and while they ate their breakfast he recounted to Garnet all his misfortunes.

Garnet listened sympathetically, and at the end said, "You're looking very tired. I'll prescribe for you. I have a small spare room. You're welcome to live in it as long as you like. Go there now and lie down on the bed and sleep. An old woman comes in the course of the morning to wash up and dust and break the crockery. She won't interfere with you. I'll leave her a note. When you wake the shops will be open. You can go and buy the things you most need. Except breakfast I have no meals here, and never know when or where I may get them, but I shall come back to sleep, and shall look forward to seeing you. Now I must hurry away."

It was too early, Willie thought, to telephone to Felicity, so he obediently lay down on the bed and slept until past midday. Then it was too late.

He was busy all day buying the things he needed. Every hour he telephoned to Felicity, but there was no reply. He came back to the flat soon after dinner to unpack his purchases, and having done so, was telephoning for the last time when Garnet returned.

"I was ringing up Felicity," he said, "but I can get no answer from her flat."

"She gets a couple of nights off now and then and usually goes away for a rest. She needs it. That work is a high strain on a girl."

"I am sure it is," said Willie. "I wish we could find her something less tiring and nerve-racking."

"Her health seems satisfactory. You look more tired than she does. What have you been doing all day?"

"Buying my trousseau. I thought it would be fun, but I didn't enjoy it. I suppose I should have made a list before I started. I seem to have got all the wrong things. Look at this beautiful dressing-gown, and I forgot to buy pyjamas and a brush and comb."

Garnet thought that Willie looked pathetic, helpless and strangely young.

"Come on now," he said. "We'll sit down and make a sensible list. I'm used to this sort of thing."

The next day was Saturday. Willie was due to stay with friends in the country, but he felt he could not leave London without having spoken to Felicity. He believed that she must be wanting to speak to him. She could not know that he was staying with Garnet, but she could have left him a message at the club. It was late in the afternoon when at last he heard her voice on the telephone. He had somehow vaguely expected that it would be altered, fraught with a new intensity, a more intimate affection, but she sounded as she had always done —cheerful and hurried. He told her that he was staying with Garnet, and she approved of the arrangement. He said he had been going away but would stay if she wanted to see him.

"Oh no," she answered. "I'll see you when you come back."

"Which day?"

"You'd better telephone next week."

He could not leave her so lightly.

"Felicity——" he said.

"What?"

"I'm so glad my flat was bombed."

"Yes, it must be fun to have the chance of buying everything new. I suppose the government will give you the money. Mind you buy some pretty new suits. I'm in a great hurry, have to go on duty, good-bye."

"Good-bye, my darling Felicity." She rang off.

Willie felt disappointed, but he did not know why. He had expected something different, but he could not say what. There were moments when he wondered whether the bomb that destroyed his flat had not also scattered his wits, and whether all that had happened afterwards had not been a dream.

It was many days before he saw Felicity again. Small things prevented them from meeting. When they did he came as soon as possible to the point.

"Now will you marry me?" he asked.

"No, my darling," she answered, "I won't."

"But surely what happened the other night has made a difference?"

"I see no reason why it should."

"But what is it that prevents you from marrying me?"

"It is too difficult to explain."

"Do you love somebody else more than me?"

She made no reply.

"Do you behave with lots of other people as you have behaved with me?"

"Willie, I refuse to be cross-questioned. You might make me angry, which I have no wish to be. You ought to know me better by now. You love me and you must try to understand me. I know it's hard. I am unreliable. I am wanton. I am ruled by my moods. I suppose that I am very selfish, and that alone would make me a bad wife. But I can't change and I don't want to. You must take me or leave me as I am."

"But have you no morals?"

"I suppose not. I know that some things are right and some are wrong. Sometimes I do wrong things and I am very sorry, but sometimes I do things which other people think are wrong and which don't seem wrong to me. I thought what we did the other night was not wrong. What did you think?"

"I don't know," said Willie, which was the truth. He had never asked himself the question, and now he wondered how he could have failed to do so.

"I haven't any religion," Felicity went on. "Perhaps I should be better if I had. Mother had none, you know. It was very curious that somebody so conscientious, so conventional and so very good should have been without it."

They went on to talk about the late Mrs. Osborne, and Willie got no farther in his quest, no nearer to his goal. Despairing of his hopes for marriage, he longed to enquire whether he could expect again what she had given him once. But he dared not ask her, for she still retained some quality cold, remote and virginal, which he trembled to offend.

They separated on that occasion without anything else of importance being said and with the briefest of caresses. The next time they dined he asked her whether her flat was occupied by others that evening. She said that it was. He asked her when it was likely to be empty again. She laughed.

"My poor darling," she said, "I know what you mean. But I can't arrange to make love as one fixes dates with dentists. Something will happen—all will be well."

Their relationship continued with little change. Willie took a furnished flat from a friend for the summer months. Sometimes his evenings with Felicity would end there, but not often. He never knew how it was to be.

In the autumn he was appointed to the post of instructor in an O.C.T.U. He was jubilant when he got the job, but it proved, in the end, another disappointment. The commandant was only a few years older than Willie, but those few precious years had enabled him to distinguish himself in the first war and earn a row of medals. Willie, on grounds of seniority, was second-in-command, and it just so happened that every one of the junior officers had been out to the war, and had either been wounded or become medically unfit. There was one who had been taken prisoner and had escaped.

Willie was determined not to be sensitive. He fought against it, but he was like a man with some physical blemish at which he feels that others must always be looking. He felt that these young officers must despise him—a dreary old dug-out who had never seen a shot fired in battle. And feeling so, he began to imagine things and to detect sneers where none were intended. He became suspicious and distrustful. He took unreasonable dislikes and began to find pleasure in exerting his authority and snubbing his juniors. He lost the happy gift of inspiring affection which he had unconsciously enjoyed all his life. He was no longer popular, and he knew it.

He came to look forward more and more to his visits to London. There at least he could find at the club the old companions, whom he knew so well, and upon whose good-fellowship he could rely. It never occurred to him that even here the standard had deteriorated; that the worthier members were either serving abroad or working too hard at home to have time for lounging.

Leave was difficult to come by. Although the work was not hard, not nearly so hard as Willie would have liked it to be, he was expected to be always on the spot and to take a sort of schoolmaster's interest in the welfare of the cadets. To go away, even when he had no duties to perform, was frowned upon as showing lack of enthusiasm.

Therefore he saw less of Felicity during this year, and the meetings he had with her were less satisfactory. The friend who had leased him the flat had now reoccupied it, so that he was obliged to stay at hotels, where she would seldom visit him. She also had found some new employment about the nature of which she was extremely reticent. It seemed to occupy more of her time than the previous one, and she was less certain as to when she would be free. Her reticence, combined with her obvious absorption in her work, irritated Willie. He was more easily irritated than he used to be.

Then came a break between two courses at the O.C.T.U. and it brought him a few days' leave, to which he had been looking forward very eagerly. He had made all the preparations for it that men do make when they have time to plan anticipated pleasure. He had made sure of having the rooms he wanted in the hotel he liked best, he had taken tickets for the theatre, he had hired a car for the night, and he had, of course, arranged with Felicity that she should go out with him. When he strode triumphant into his club at midday the hall-porter handed him a folded slip of paper on which was written: "Miss Osborne telephoned that she was very sorry she would be unable to dine with Captain Maryngton tonight."

Willie crumpled up the message and, tossing it aside, strode gloomily into the club. He felt that everybody must know, the hall-porter at least must, that he had been let down by a girl, and that he looked like a man waiting with a bunch of violets for someone who never comes. He wondered what he should do with the theatre-tickets as he scanned the welcoming faces of his club-mates, and found none with whom he would care to go to the play. Then he remembered Daisy Summers, and was glad to find that he still had her telephone number. He was pleased and surprised when she answered the call.

"It's Willie speaking," he said.

"Willie Maryngton?" she asked. "Come to life again after all these years?"

"It's not so long as you think, Daisy, only about a year. I'm up in London on leave. How about coming out with me, or would it wreck the work of the postal censorship?"

"Silly boy," she said, "the postal censorship wrecked me long ago, and now they try to do it without me—and a pretty good mess, I hear, they make of it."

"But will you come out to-night?"

"Of course I will."

"Shall we go to a play?"

"If there's anything worth seeing."

He mentioned the name of the play for which he had got seats.

"You'll never get in there," she said.

"I'll try—and I'm not so stupid as I used to be, so I'll pick you up at 6.30 and we'll have a good time."

Daisy was looking very pretty that evening, prettier than Willie remembered, and she was smartly dressed. She was impressed by Willie's efficiency in getting good seats for the most successful play in London, and he saw no need to tell her that he had got them three weeks before. After the theatre they went for dinner to a gay restaurant, where there was music and dancing and where Willie saw several of his friends. Felicity would never go to fashionable places of this kind, but Willie really preferred them. He and Daisy danced together, and drank champagne and he told himself he was having a very good time. They went on to a night club and it was late when he drove her home.

"Come in for a minute and have a drink," she said.

And he, knowing that it was not to have a drink, accepted the invitation.

He saw Felicity before his leave expired. She made no reference to having thrown him over, until he did. Then she said that she was very sorry, but that it had been quite impossible for her to go out with him that evening. She gave no reason.

"It was of no consequence," he said. "I got hold of Daisy Summers and we had quite a good time." He told her of the play, the restaurant and the night club.

"Did she seduce you?"

"That's a particularly catty way of putting it," he said.

"You know what I mean."

"Why should I tell you?"

"Because I want to know, and you know you can trust me."

"You said you wouldn't mind if she did, so long as I told you."

"I was wrong. I do mind. I am very sorry."

"But how do you know what happened?"

"I can't explain how I know," she answered with a tired sigh, "but I do. I think you will never be able to deceive me, Willie, and I hope you will never try."

Willie felt unhappy, not like Lothario, but like a little boy who has been caught doing something of which he is ashamed. He was also full of resentment.

"Why should you make such a fuss?" he protested. "I thought you attached little importance to such things and didn't think them wrong."

"Am I making a fuss?" she asked. "I'm sorry. I know very little about right and wrong, as I've always told you. And I can't see that right and wrong, good and evil, have anything to do with it. I just feel, as I have always felt, that Daisy is not the girl for you. You were very young when you got engaged to her, and you couldn't tell the difference, but you ought to be able to tell the difference now."

"You hate her, don't you?"

"Good heavens, no! How can you think so? I want her to be happy with her own friends, in her own way."

"I suppose you think I'm too good for her."

"No, not that either. She may be better than you, or me, for all I care. But she doesn't suit you, she doesn't become you, and I hate you to do what is unbecoming."

"I believe you are jealous of her," said Willie sullenly.

She smiled sadly. "Perhaps I am; you can think so if you like."

They parted coldly, as they had never parted before. At the last moment Willie felt inclined to throw himself on his knees and implore her forgiveness. But he was too angry to do so, and he felt strongly that there was no reason why he should. He could not live for ever on the scanty charity that Felicity dispensed to him according to her unpredictable moods. Daisy was a jolly good sort. He had no idea what Felicity meant by saying that she didn't become him. He had no wish to understand. Could it be that she was jealous? He would have like to think it, but he knew that it was not so.

XV

AFTER this the relationship between Willie and Felicity grew less happy. He would still try to see her whenever he came to London, but their evenings together were not as they once had been. The subjects of conversation were no longer the same. Felicity had taken an interest in the regiment, about which Willie had loved to talk. She had come to know intimately the lives and characters of men whom she had never seen, and would often surprise Willie by the accuracy with which she remembered details. She would enquire with real interest about the major's growing family or the subaltern's love affairs. But Willie did not care to talk about the men he was serving with now, or if he did, it was only to recount some remark by one of them, which he had interpreted as a hidden insult. His stories about his brother officers had in the past been full of fun and affection. Now they were laden with malice and dislike.

"Do you know who I met in the street this morning?" he said one evening to Felicity—"that dirty cad Hamilton."

"I know you don't like him," she answered, "but isn't 'dirty cad' a bit strong?"

"It's the luck some fellows have that maddens me. I heard he'd been wounded in Africa. It seems to have been pretty bad—his shoulder shattered to pieces, only a few months ago—and here I meet him swanking down Bond Street with his arm in a sling, quite the wounded hero, having just been appointed Military Attaché to one of the few neutral countries where life would be interesting in these days. Why can't they make me a Military Attaché?"

"Perhaps the fact that you can't speak a single word of any foreign language may have something to do with it."

"I'm told that that doesn't matter a bit. Foreigners respect you all the more if you can't speak their beastly language. I agree with the chap who said that anybody can understand English if spoken loud enough."

"Really, Willie, you do talk the most terrible nonsense at times."

Their evenings together seldom ended happily now. Felicity would gently loosen his arms when he threw them around her, and would turn away her face when he wanted to kiss her.

Because he was not happy in his work he was not good at it. He had no gift for teaching and no genuine interest in the progress of those he taught. One autumn evening when the talk had turned on to the fattening of turkeys for the Christmas market, he said, "That's what our work here is—grooming a lot of silly boys until we think they're fit to be sent out and get killed." It pleased him to watch the disapproval on the faces of the others, and he did not mind the silence that followed his remark.

He was not surprised therefore when, at the end of the year, his appointment was not renewed, and he found himself once more on the list of elderly officers awaiting employment.

It was now that Willie's friends began to notice a change in him. They found him less good company than he used to be. He had never been a wit or a brilliant conversationalist, but his good manners, his interest in whatever was being said and his happy smile, which came so easily, had made him someone who was welcome wherever he went. His manners were no longer so good, for the fountain from which they sprang, a kind heart, was drying up. He was losing his interest in his fellow beings and finding greater difficulty in smiling. Some thought it was due to an unhappy love affair, others that he was ill, or that he was drinking too much. In fact he was suffering from despair.

He went back to living with Garnet. It saved him the trouble of looking for something else. He disliked taking trouble about anything, and he argued that he might get a new appointment at any moment, so that it was wiser to incur no liabilities. Every morning he would wander to the club and spend most of the day there, doing nothing in particular. Sometimes he would go to a race meeting. More often he would follow the racing results on the tape. Garnet, who watched him with a professional eye, was unhappy about him. He detected symptoms that escaped the eyes of laymen.

"I'm worried about Willie," he said to Felicity. "He's letting himself go to pieces."

"What do you mean?" she asked.

"It is hard to explain, and still harder to understand, unless you have lived in the Far East, as I have. There they say it is the climate which has got you down. There, you know, the retiring age is fifty, and many a man is finished before he reaches it. A moment comes when something happens like the mainspring of a watch breaking. The façade remains the same, perhaps for a long time, and most people can see no difference. I used rather to fancy myself at being able to diagnose this particular disease, and Willie shows symptoms recently that have made me think of it."

"Oh, Garnet, what can we do to help him?"

"His state may of course be partly due to physical causes. I wanted him to go into hospital for a few days to be overhauled, but he wouldn't hear of it. He said the hospitals were now for fighting soldiers, and he would be ashamed to occupy one minute of a doctor's or a nurse's time."

"But what can we do to help him?" she repeated.

"A new job that would really interest him, or anything that would take him out of himself would be the best thing."

"Yes," she said, "but he is so hard to place. He isn't very clever, bless his heart, and he has no experience of anything except soldiering."

"We must think about it," said Garnet, as he left her. He was, as usual, in a hurry.

There is a district in London, near the heart of it, which has acquired, perhaps undeservedly, a bad reputation. Willie was walking through it one evening. He was returning from the club before dinner, because he had no appetite, and was thinking of going to bed. To his surprise he saw Felicity come out from a block of flats, to which is attached particular notoriety. He thought she looked taken aback when she saw him, but she only laughed when he asked her if that was where she was working now.

Two evenings later he was there again, designedly, at about the same hour. Again she came out of the same building, but this time she was not taken aback. She walked up to him and, standing still, said:

"You came here on purpose to spy on me."

He answered, "I came here to see if you were really working in that house."

"Have you nothing better than that to do?" she asked.

"No, by God, I haven't," he answered passionately, and all her wrath gave way to pity, for she felt as though she had torn the bandage off a festering wound.

She laid a hand on his arm.

"Come into this pub with me, Willie, and have a glass of beer."

He followed her meekly, and looking round at the unfamiliar precincts he said:

"I don't think I've ever been in an ordinary public-house in London before."

There was so much of the old, childish Willie in his naïve wonder that she was touched.

"I brought you in here," she said, "to give you a lecture, but you're really so touching that I don't think I can."

"Thank you, Felicity," he said.

"But listen to me, all the same. You know you are not as nice as you used to be."

"I know, I know."

"Do you really think that I'm running a brothel or working in one?"

"How could I think such a thing?"

"Then why did you come here this evening?"

"Perhaps it was just in the hope that I should see you."

"No, Willie, you know it wasn't. You suspected me. Perhaps you didn't define to yourself what it was that you suspected, but your mind is full of suspicion, hatred and darkness, and it is destroying your heart."

"I know, I know."

"You look ill."

"I feel it. I've felt rotten for days."

"You ought to be in bed."

"I stayed there yesterday, but it's so lonely in that grim little room. Garnet's out all day."

"Well, I'm going to take you there now, and put you to bed, and give you a hot drink and some aspirin. Old Garnet must have a look at you when he comes in. I think you've some fever," she said, holding his wrist.

She did as she had said, helping him to undress and to get into bed. He was very docile. Before she left him she bent over him and kissed his hot lips with her cool ones, and whispered to him that she loved him still, and that as soon as he was well all should be between them as it had been in the happiest days of the past. His arms held her close to him for a moment, but all he said was "Alas, alas!"

She scribbled a note to Garnet before she left the flat. He telephoned to her early next morning.

Willie had passed a bad night. He was suffering from pneumonia and had a high fever. But his constitution was good, his heart was sound, there were no complications, no cause for anxiety. Garnet had arranged for a good nurse to look after him. When Felicity went to see him that evening the nurse dissuaded her from going into his room. He was sleeping, and he needed all the sleep he could get. All efforts to bring down his temperature had failed. His condition was grave. He was no better on the following day. In the evening he fell into a torpor, and early the next morning he died.

### XVI

On that day Garnet went to have luncheon at the Service Club to which he belonged. He was sad and weary, having sat up half the night. He was overwhelmed with work, and felt that unless he relaxed for an hour and had a quiet meal instead of the glass of milk and sandwiches that he was accustomed to snatch at midday, he would become a casualty himself. That one of the first duties of a soldier was to take care of his own health was a maxim that he frequently impressed on others.

The large club dining-room was nearly full. In a corner he saw an old friend whom he had known in Penang. He was a Scotsman and now, so Garnet noticed, a Brigadier. He sank into the seat opposite, and the two old soldiers began to exchange grievances. Having disposed of the climate, they proceeded to condemn the long hours during which men were expected to work on this side of the world. Garnet explained that this was the first occasion for many months that he had been able to lunch at the club, and that he was only doing so today because he had felt on the verge of a breakdown.

"I was up half the night with a poor fellow who died early this morning, and when I got to the hospital there were a series of operations, so that I haven't even had time to certify his death."

"Do you have to nurse your patients as well as dose them?" asked the Brigadier.

"No, but this was a dear friend, who had been living in my flat,

Willie Maryngton. Did you ever know him?" Garnet mentioned his
regiment.

"I think I met him in India—a nice fellow—very sad."

"Yes indeed, and I suppose I shall have to make all the funeral arrangements."

"Can't you leave that to his relations?"

"The extraordinary thing is that he hasn't got any. I've known him
all my life. His father, who was killed in the last war, made my father
his guardian. My father was killed, and Willie was brought up with
us from the age of fourteen. He never had a single relation that he
knew of."

The Brigadier seemed interested and began to put questions.

"You say he died this morning? And you have not certified his
death? And he had neither kith nor kin?"

Garnet confirmed all these particulars, and the Brigadier went on
to make enquiries about Willie's activities during the war, about his
age and rank, and ended by asking:

"How many people have you informed of his death?"

"I telephoned to my sister this morning. We were both very fond
of him. The nursing sister and the charwoman, who looks after my
flat, are of course aware. But why all these questions? It's very kind of
you to take so much interest, but I don't quite understand."

"I am going to ask one more. Did he make a will? If so, where is
it? Who benefits by it, and who is the executor?"

"Yes, he made a will. I found it this morning. He left everything
to his regimental benevolent fund, and appointed as his executors the
firm of lawyers who have always acted for him."

"Osborne," said the Scotsman, solemnly, "do you believe in Providence?"

"No," said Garnet.

"Well, I do. I was brought up so to believe, and I have never lost
my faith. Providence is a great mystery, and I have seen many proofs
of it in my life. I am going to make three requests of you. First, that
you will not sign that certificate to-day. Second, that you will not mention Maryngton's death to another living soul. Third, that you will call
on me at my office this afternoon."

Garnet protested that he had no time to spare.

"You will have the time you would have given to registering the
death and making the funeral arrangements. You have known me for
many years and you know that I do not use words lightly. I tell you
that this is a matter of the very greatest importance."

His Scottish r's rolled impressively, and Garnet, although he felt
that he was dreaming, agreed to do as he was asked. Five o'clock

was the hour decided upon. The Brigadier drew a blank visiting-card from his pocket book, and wrote upon it. "That is the address," he said.

Garnet raised his eyebrows as he read it. "Well," he said, "I should have thought that that was the last place you would have chosen for your office."

"That," replied the Brigadier, "is precisely why I chose it."

They parted, and a few minutes later the Brigadier was entering that ill-famed building outside which Willie had waited a few days before. He took a lift to the third floor, where he let himself into one of the two flats. A slovenly-looking man, sitting in the passage, sprang smartly to attention.

"Fergusson," said the Brigadier, "a colonel, R.A.M.C., in uniform, will be calling at five o'clock. Show him straight in. I don't wish to be disturbed while he is with me."

"Sir," replied Fergusson.

The Brigadier went into his office, a small room with a large writing-table, sat down and rang the bell. Felicity appeared.

"I shall have a Colonel Osborne coming to see me about five," he said. "I don't wish any telephone calls put through while he is here, unless it is a matter of great importance."

"Colonel Osborne?" she repeated tentatively.

"Colonel Garnet Osborne, R.A.M.C."

"He is my brother."

"Is that so, Miss Osborne? Is that so? Another remarkable coincidence. Do you believe in Providence, Miss Osborne?"

"I don't know. I've never thought about it."

"There are worse things to think about. Your brother is an old friend of mine. We were together in Malaya. Have you all the documents ready and in order for Operation Z?"

"Yes, sir."

"Have you not thought of any better name for it? Z is a daft sort of a name for an operation."

"I haven't thought of another."

"Well, just go on thinking. Thank you."

She left the room.

When Garnet arrived he was shown straight into the Brigadier, who greeted him with the question:

"Did you know that your sister is my personal assistant?"

"My sister Felicity?" he asked in astonishment.

"She is Miss Osborne to me, but she tells me you are her brother, and I have no reason to doubt her veracity."

"Well, well! This is a strange day in my life," said Garnet.

"And you have not got to the end of it yet," replied the Brigadier. "Sit down."

He then proceeded to confirm all the particulars concerning Willie with which Garnet had supplied him at luncheon. He had a paper in his hand on which he had recorded them. He went through them in order to be sure they were correct.

"Thank you," he concluded when he came to the end of his questions. "You have given me some information—and now you are going to receive some in return.

"The purpose of this department, in which you find yourself, Colonel Osborne, is to deceive the enemy. Our methods of deception are, at certain times, extremely elaborate. The more important the military operations under contemplation the more elaborate are our preparations to ensure, not so much that the enemy shall be ignorant of what we intend to do, but rather that he shall have good reason to believe that we intend to do something quite different. I need not impress upon you the importance of secrecy, but I would say to you, what I say to all those who work with me, that there is only one way to keep a secret. There are not two ways. That way is not to whisper it to a living soul—neither to the wife of your bosom nor to the man you trust most upon earth. I know you for a loyal, trustworthy and discreet soldier, but for a million pounds I would not tell you what I am about to tell you, if I did not need your help.

"A military operation of immense magnitude is in course of preparation. That is a fact of which the enemy are probably aware. Its success must depend largely upon the enemy's ignorance of when and where it will be launched. Every security precaution has been taken to prevent that knowledge from reaching him. Those security precautions are not, I repeat, the business of this department. It is not our business to stop him getting correct information. It is our business to provide him, through sources which will carry conviction of their reliability, with information that is false.

"In a few days from now, Colonel Osborne, the dead body of a British officer will be washed ashore, on the coast of a neutral country, whose relations with the enemy are not quite so neutral as we might wish them to be. It will be found that he is carrying in a packet that is perfectly waterproof, which will be firmly strapped to his chest, under his jacket, documents of a highly confidential character —documents of such vital importance to the conduct of the war that no one will wonder that they should have been entrusted to a special mission and a special messenger. These documents, including a private letter from the Chief of the Imperial General Staff to the Gen-

OPERATION HEARTBREAK

eral Officer Commanding North Africa, although couched in the most, apparently, guarded language, will yet make perfectly plain to an intelligent reader exactly what the Allies are intending to do. You will appreciate the importance of such an operation; and you will also appreciate that its success or failure must depend entirely upon the convincing character of the evidence, that will prove the authenticity of these documents and will remove from the minds of those who are to study them any suspicion that a trick has been played upon them. The most important of all the links in that chain of evidence must be the dead body on which the documents are found.

"Now, Osborne, you are a medical man, and you must have discovered in your student days, when you were in need of material to work upon, what I have discovered only lately, the extraordinary importance that people attach to what becomes of the dead bodies of their distant relations. People, who can ill afford it, will travel from the north of Scotland to the south of England to assure themselves that the mortal remains of a distant cousin have been decently committed to the earth. You can hardly imagine the difficulty I have experienced. The old profession of body-snatching has no longer any practitioners, or I would have employed one. I have now secured the services of a gentleman in your line of business, a civilian, and our hopes rest upon what a pauper lunatic asylum may produce. But there must be difficulties. You may have heard, Osborne, that death is the great leveller, but even after death has done his damnedest there is apt to remain a very considerable difference between a pauper lunatic deceased from natural causes and a British officer, in the prime of life, fit to be entrusted with a most important mission."

"I see what you are getting at," interrupted Garnet. "You want me to agree to poor Maryngton's body being used for this purpose."

"Bide a while, bide a while," said the Brigadier, who had not completed his thesis. "You will appreciate the cosmic importance of this operation, upon which the lives of thousands of men must depend, and which may affect even the final issue of the war. This morning I was wrestling desperately with the problem of the pauper lunatic for whom an identity, a name, a background had to be created. Our enemies are extremely painstaking and thorough in their work. You may be quite certain that they have copies of the last published Army List, and I am sure that they have also, easily available, a complete register of all officers who have been killed since that publication, or whose names have appeared in the obituary columns. Their first action on being informed that the body of a dead British officer has been discovered will be to ascertain whether such a British officer was ever alive. If they fail to find the name of such an officer in the

Army List their suspicions will be aroused, and those suspicions, once aroused, may easily lead them to the true solution of the mystery. We should be forced to give to our unknown one of those names that are shared by hundreds, and should have to hope that, in despair of satisfying themselves as to the identity of the particular Major Smith or Brown in question, they would abandon the enquiry. But— I say again—we are dealing with a nation whose thoroughness in small matters of detail is unequalled, and it is my belief that within a few days the chief of their intelligence service would be informed that no officer of the name in question has ever served in the British Army. From that moment all the information contained in the documents, about which I told you, would be treated as information of doubtful value and of secondary importance. The result might well be that the whole operation would fail completely.

"While this grave problem is occupying my mind to-day, you sit yourself down before me and tell me of an officer who died this morning, whose death has not been registered, who has no relations, who was of an age and standing entirely suitable for such a mission and over the disposal of whose dead body you have control. Call it the long arm of coincidence, whatever that may mean, if you desire, but to me, Colonel Osborne," the Brigadier's voice grew hoarse with emotion, "it is the hand of Providence stretched out to aid His people in their dire need, and I ask you to give me your help, as God has given me His, in the fulfilment of my task."

He ceased and both sat silent. After a while Garnet said:

"What you are asking me to do is very extraordinary, and although I perfectly understand the terrible urgency, you must allow me to reflect." He paused—and then continued: "In the first place I should be acting quite illegally. I have no more right to conceal Maryngton's death than I have to dispose of his body."

"*Silent leges inter arma,*" replied the Brigadier. "I will give you my personal guarantee, written if you wish it, that will cover you from any legal consequences."

They sat again in silence for two or three minutes. When Garnet next spoke it was to ask:

"What should I actually have to do? And what am I going to say when Maryngton's friends, many of whom must have known that he was living with me, ask me what has become of him?"

The Brigadier was obviously relieved. He felt now that the other's mind was moving in the right direction.

"What you have to do is to lay out by the side of Maryngton's body to-night his uniform, omitting no detail of it. Don't forget his cap or his belt, and above all make sure that the identity disc is there. Put on the table his watch, his cheque-book and any small personal possessions that he always carried. At 2 a.m. some friends of mine will call upon you. There may be two of them, there may be three. You will show them which is Maryngton's room. Then you will go to bed and sleep soundly. You will, however, dream that Maryngton comes to you in the night and tells you that he is leaving England in the early morning. His mission is of a secret nature, and in case anything should go wrong he hands you his will, which you have already told me is in your possession. When you wake in the morning he will certainly have gone, and you will therefore believe your dream was a reality. It will probably be many days before you have to answer any enquiry. During those days you will repeat to yourself continually how he told you one night that he was leaving on a secret mission, how he gave you his will, and how he was gone on the following morning. You will come to believe this yourself, and it will be all that you know, all that you have to say to anyone who asks questions. One day you will read in the paper that Maryngton has died on active service. Then you will send his will to his lawyers; and that will be all."

Again Garnet sat in silence for several minutes.

"Does my sister know about this affair?" he asked.

"Miss Osborne is aware," said the Brigadier, "that an operation of this nature is in preparation."

"I would rather," said Garnet, "that she did not know that it was— that we were making use of—damn it, respect for the dead bodies of those we love is a very profound instinct in human nature. Willie Maryngton has been like a brother to us all our lives. I am sure it would distress her horribly."

The Brigadier looked grave and answered:

"You may be sure that I have already given very careful consideration to this part of the problem. Besides ourselves there are three other people, so far as we are aware, who know that Maryngton died of pneumonia this morning. I have decided that the best method of securing the discretion of the nurse and the servant is to say no more to them on the subject. To neither of them will the case present any peculiar or interesting feature. To impose secrecy upon them would merely stimulate their curiosity. If either of them reads the announcement of his death, which is unlikely, the fact that it is described as having taken place on active service will be accepted as part of the incomprehensible vocabulary of Whitehall.

"Now your sister is another matter. I have the greatest confidence in her reliability, but I cannot expect even her to keep a secret if she doesn't know it is a secret. She may have told someone of Maryngton's death already. If not, she is almost sure to do so."

"She's a strange girl," said Garnet; "she keeps her friends in separate compartments, isolated cells as it were. Since my brother was killed she and Willie had no mutual friends. I think it unlikely that she has told anybody. But I can make sure, which I promise to do. What is more, I can pretend to her that my conduct has not been strictly professional in allowing a friend to die in my own flat without calling in a second opinion, and failing to inform the authorities within twenty-four hours. On that ground I can ask her not to mention the matter, and then we can safely count on her silence."

"I don't like it, Osborne," said the Brigadier. "In affairs of this sort I like to have everything water-tight. The smallest leak may sink the ship—and what a ship it is! Think, man, the whole British Empire is on board!"

An ugly cloud of obstinacy crept into Garnet's eyes.

"I'm sorry," he said. "The whole business is hateful to me, and I just can't bear to bring my sister into it. Between ourselves, I once suspected that she was in love with Maryngton. I even hoped that they might marry. Can you imagine telling a girl what it is that you are intending to do with the dead body of a man who might have been her husband? It is a kind of sacrilege."

The Brigadier looked into Garnet's eyes, and he saw the obstinacy that lay there. He looked at his watch, and then he said,

"I'll not tell her. You have my word for it."

Garnet sighed.

"In that case I suppose I must consent," he said. "I can see no good reason for not doing so—except sentiment, or perhaps sentimentality —and I have never considered myself to be ruled by either. In any case, service must come first. You have given me my instructions. They are simple enough. They shall be carried out. Have you anything further to ask of me?"

"Lay out the uniform," said the Brigadier, "omitting no detail of it. Leave the small personal possessions on the table. Open the door when the bell rings. Dream as I told you, and believe that your dream is true."

They shook hands and Garnet turned to go.

"One more detail," said the Brigadier. "You have not by any chance got some spare major's badges among your equipment?"

"I doubt it," said Garnet.

"Very well. My friends will provide them. I have been thinking that the rank of captain is just one too low for an officer charged with such a very important mission. He appears as a captain in the last pre-war Army List. If he had been employed on important work since then he would have become a major by now, so I intend to make him one. These small details can prove of vast importance in this sort of work."

"Oh dear," said Garnet, "that was the promotion he was so anxious to obtain. Poor Willie! It is a heartbreaking business."

"Ay," said the Brigadier. "Operation Heatbreak would not be a bad name for it."

Felicity met Garnet in the passage. "Come into my room," she said. "I've got a cup of tea for you."

"It will be welcome," he answered. "I had a wretched night and I've been hard at it all day. Odd to find you here. You are, I must say, a very secretive girl."

"Now tell me all there is to tell about Willie. I felt that I couldn't bear to hear more this morning, when you told me he was dead, so I rang off in an abrupt and what must have appeared a callous way. But I can bear it now. Go on."

Garnet recounted the course of the short illness and explained that it was not uncommon for healthy men in middle-age to be carried off suddenly by a sharp attack of pneumonia.

"But I do think," he went on, "that there was something else, another contributory cause as it were, in Willie's case. I told you not long ago that I thought there was something wrong with him. In all illness, and especially in cases of this sort, the will of the patient plays a great part. There comes a moment when an effort is required. In this case that effort wasn't made. I am afraid that one of the reasons why Willie died was that he did not greatly wish to live."

"Ah!" Felicity gave a little cry, as though in sudden pain, but said no more.

After a pause Garnet went on to ask:

"Do you happen to have mentioned his death to anyone you've seen to-day, Felicity?"

"No," she answered. "I haven't seen anyone, for one thing, and there isn't anyone to whom I talk about Willie, for another."

"Well, I had rather that you kept it to yourself," he said, and went on to tell her the story he had invented about his alleged lapse from professional rectitude.

"I promise not to breathe a word," she said, but she looked at him with curiosity, asking herself whether such conduct was really unprofessional and, if so, whether Garnet could have been guilty of it.

"How about the funeral?" she asked.

"Oh, it seems there are some distant cousins in Yorkshire. The lawyers have communicated with them. They want him to be buried up there. It appears his forbears came from that part of the country. I couldn't object."

"He always told me he hadn't any cousins anywhere, but I'm glad they've been discovered. I hate funerals, and he would never have expected me to go to Yorkshire to attend one among people whom I don't know."

Hers was not an inquisitive nature, but it seemed strange to her that cousins who had remained unknown throughout his life should assert themselves within a few hours of his death.

Having finished his tea, Garnet rose to go.

"Good-bye, dear old Garnet," she said. "Now that you have found out where I work you might come and see me sometimes. I can always give you tea."

"I should like to come," he replied. "I am very busy, but I feel lonely sometimes."

"I suppose everybody does."

"Yes, I suppose so."

He went, and a few minutes later the bell summoned her to the Brigadier. She picked up her pad and pencil and went into his room.

"I had an interesting conversation with your brother," he said. "Did he tell you about it?"

"No."

"I told you that I met him in the Far East. We both know something about the pretty ways of the Japanese and we've been having a fine crack about them. Our Government will never resort to bacteriological warfare, you know, but I think it's just the sort of trick the Japs might play on us. So I was thinking that we might get it whispered around that we had something up our sleeve in that line more terrible than anything they would imagine. That might make them think twice before they used it."

"It might, on the other hand, make them use it immediately so as to be sure of getting their blow in first."

"Ay, but I think they've held off poison gas so far because they suspect we've got a deadlier brew than they have. Your brother is very knowledgeable in the matter of oriental diseases."

Felicity wondered why he was telling her all this. She had studied the Brigadier's methods, and she had noticed that when he volunteered information it was usually with a motive, and that the information itself was usually incorrect. Was he trying to deceive her, or had he perhaps some more subtle purpose?

"To change the subject," he went on, "to Operation Z, or Operation Heartbreak, as I'm thinking of calling it. I've received information from that doctor of whom I told you. He has to hand exactly what we were looking for. So the matter is now urgent. Time and tide—we depend on both of them, and neither will wait upon the other. There is not an hour to be lost. The Admiralty are standing by. They await only the pressure of a button to go ahead. And I am about to press that button. You have the wallet and the papers. I should like to have another look at them."

As Felicity went to her room to fetch them it occurred to her that the news which had come to the Brigadier from the doctor could not have been received that afternoon by telephone, for she had had control of all the calls that reached him, and it was strange, if time were precious, that he should have wasted so much of it in discussing remote possibilities with Garnet, and should have attached so much importance to the conversation.

She returned with the carefully constructed waterproof wallet and a thin sheaf of papers. The Brigadier slipped on a pair of gloves before he touched them. She smiled.

"You think, Miss Osborne, my precautions are a wee bit ridiculous. But it is always wiser to err on the side of prudence. I hope that in a few days these papers will be in the hands of a gentleman as prudent as I am, and better equipped. It may be that he will have them tested for finger-prints, and it may be that he has a photograph of my finger-prints on his writing-table. We are dealing with a very thorough people, Miss Osborne, a very thorough people.

"So this is the letter from the C.I.G.S.," he went on, carefully taking it out of the envelope. He read it slowly and chuckled. "He must have enjoyed putting in that joke about the Secretary of State. It just gives the hallmark of authenticity. He has made a very good job of it indeed."

He laid the papers on the table in front of him, and remained silent for three or four minutes, apparently lost in thought.

"A man setting out on a journey of this sort," he said at last, speaking very slowly, "would probably put into his wallet what was most precious and dear to him. A married man might put there the photographs of his wife and children. This is to be a single man." He paused again. "Do you think, Miss Osborne," he asked, "that you could draft a love-letter?"

"I can try," she replied, impassively.

"Do that," he said. "Meanwhile I must get on to the Admiralty and see the young men in our Operations Branch, who have a full night before them."

She rose to go.

"Make sure that there's no 'G.R.' in the corner of the paper you write on, nor 'For the service of His Majesty's Government' in the watermark."

"I will make sure," she said.

"And there is one more thing." He hesitated. "You must try to make that letter the kind a man would think worth keeping."

"I will try," she said, and left the room.

The Brigadier continued to look at the door after she had shut it. He had the habit of observing people closely. Was he mistaken or had he detected a light of revelation in her eyes, a kind of exultation in her manner, the air of one who goes with confidence to the performance of a grateful task?

He had no time to waste on speculation. His evening was fully occupied. He first had a long interview with two young men, who were members of his staff but not regular attendants at the office. Then there were a number of telephone conversations with the Admiralty and with other government departments. When he looked at his watch he was surprised to see how late it was. He rang the bell and Felicity came in with a sheet of paper in her hand.

"I am sorry I have detained you so long," he said—"all our preparations are now complete. Have you drafted the letter that I suggested?"

She handed him the paper she was carrying and said nothing. He put on his gloves before taking it and held it up to the light, examining it with a magnifying glass, and then, seemingly satisfied with his inspection, adjusted his spectacles and began to read:—

Darling, my darling, you are going away from me and I have never told you how much I love you. How sad, how heartbreaking it would be if you had never known. But this will tell you, and this you must take with you on your dark mission. It brings you my passionate and deathless love. Forgive me all the disappointment that I caused you. Remember now only the hours that I lay in your arms. I cannot have known how much I loved you until I knew that you must go away. I have been weak and wanton, as I warned you once that I should always be, but I have been in my own odd way, believe me, oh believe me, darling, I have been true. When we meet again you will understand everything and perhaps we shall be happy at last.

When he had finished reading it he did not look up.

"This should be signed with a Christian name," he said.

"Have you any suggestions?" she asked. There was a faint note of bitterness in her voice.

"An unusual one is likely to be more convincing than a common one. Your brother told me yours this afternoon. Have you any objection to making use of it? People show by the way they sign their own names that they are accustomed to doing so. Handwriting experts might be able to tell the difference."

"I will sign it 'Felicity'," she said.

"If the pen you have in your hand is the one with which you wrote the letter," he said, "you can sign it here," and he pointed to the chair on the other side of his table. She sat down and wrote and handed him back the letter. At the end of it she had written in her clear, bold hand "Felicity" and at the beginning "My Willie".

The Brigadier made sure that the ink was dry and then he crumpled the letter between his two hands so that she thought he was going to throw it into the waste-paper basket. He smoothed it out again very carefully, saying as he did so: "This is a letter which a man would have read many times. It should bear signs of usage." Then, still looking down at the letter and still smoothing it, he said:

"So you have guessed our secret. I gave your brother my word of honour that I would not tell you. I think I have kept my word."

"But why did he want me not to know?" she asked.

"He feared that it would cause you pain."

"He ought to have understood," she said, "that it is just what Willie would have wished more than anything in all the world."

## XVII

DAWN had not broken, but was about to do so, when the submarine came to the surface. The crew were thankful to breathe the cool, fresh air, and they were still more thankful to be rid of their cargo. The wrappings were removed, and the Lieutenant stood to attention and saluted as they laid the body of the officer in uniform as gently as possible on the face of the waters. A light breeze was blowing shoreward, and the tide was running in the same direction. So Willie went to the war at last, the insignia of field rank on his shoulders, and a letter from his beloved lying close to his quiet heart.

## EPILOGUE

EVERYTHING worked as had been intended. The neutral government behaved with the courtesy that is expected of neutral governments. After a certain delay, such as is inevitable in the movements of government departments, they informed the Ambassador, with regret, that the body of a British officer, whose identity appeared to be established, had been washed up by the sea, and that he was bearing a waterproof packet which they had the honour to forward intact. They would be glad to make any arrangements for the funeral that His Excellency might desire. They did not think it necessary to mention that the packet in question had been already opened with infinite care, and that before being closed again with care as infinite, every document in it had been photographed, and that those photographs were now lying under the eyes of the enemy, where the false information that they contained powerfully contributed to the success of one of the greatest surprises ever achieved in military history.

And so it was that the Military Attaché, the Assistant Military Attaché and the Chaplain found themselves travelling from the capital to the coast on that hot morning.

# *Part* V
# EDGE-OF-THE-SEAT
# DEPARTMENT

# THE SALT OF THE EARTH

*Rebecca West*

REBECCA WEST (1892–    ) was made a Commander in the Order of the British Empire in 1949. It was due recognition for a lifetime of distinguished writing. The range of her interests as a journalist has been extremely wide, but she has found time to produce several novels that have explored with compassion, perception and high intelligence the lives and minds of all kinds of people. Her impeccable prose has long been one of the ornaments of *The New Yorker,* in which appeared for the first time her articles on Lord Haw Haw which later developed into her book *The Meaning of Treason.* Among her less well-known pieces are the short novels she wrote several years ago, and which reveal her gift for characterization and prose portraiture. The following example is, in the truest sense, a collector's item.

ALICE Pemberton had not expected to enjoy the motordrive home, since because of it, the previous afternoon, she had received a bitter hurt. She had gone into the drawing-room to tell her mother that one of the young men who had been coming in for tennis so much of late, was very pleased indeed to give her a lift to Camelheath. With her invariable consideration she had been careful to mention the proposal nonchalantly, though she knew she would enjoy the drive through the spring countryside, and would find the society of the obviously admiring young man just such a gratification as a woman of forty needs from time to time. There could be no getting away from the fact that this meant her leaving her mother two days earlier than had been planned, and she was never one to take family duties lightly. But before she could well get the sentence out of her mouth there had flashed into her mother's eyes a look which nobody in the world could mistake for anything but an expression of intense, almost hilarious relief.

"It ought to be lovely for you!" Mrs. Anglesey had exclaimed. "You'll go through the New Forest, I expect. It'll be at its best with all the trees coming out."

"Very well, mother dear," Alice had said quietly, and had gone out of the dark drawing-room into the sunlit garden. Though she was reassured by the sight of the young man in white flannels, plainly eager to hear her decision, she could hardly still the trembling of her upper-lip.

"Not, my dear, that I shan't be terribly sorry to lose you!" her mother had called after her, but a second too late, a semi-tone too high pitched.

That night she lay awake for quite a long time wondering why it was that her mother had always had such a curious attitude to her. It was not that she did not care for her. Alice knew that quite well. When she had had diphtheria as a girl at school, when she had been operated on for appendicitis, the extremely passionate quality of her mother's anguish and relief had been as recognizable as the brilliance of lightning. Nevertheless she could not help seeing that in the ordinary intercourse of life Mrs. Anglesey felt her as a burden. She had sometimes suspected that her mother had hurried on her marriage to Jimmy not only because, as she had so often said at the time, long engagements dragged young romance past its proper time or ripening, but because she wanted her out of the house; and she had had to do more than suspect, she had often to record in black and white on the pages of her diary, that when her mother came to stay with her her visits were apt to be far briefer than those she paid to Madge or Leo.

"Of course there may be some reason for it," Alice pondered, determined to be broad-minded and generous. "I am the eldest of the three, I was born very soon after she married. Perhaps I came too soon, before she was reconciled to giving up all her pleasures for her babies, and she may have felt a grudge against me that she has never lived down."

But she could not help thinking that her mother ought to have lived it down if she had any sense of gratitude. For neither Madge nor Leo had done anything like as much for their mother as she had, and she had been willing to make even greater sacrifices, had they been accepted. Though she and Jimmy had loved each other so much she had been quite willing to face a long engagement, simply because she hated to imagine what home would be like without her. Since her father's death she had done what she could to replace his influence. She had kept Madge and Leo from getting out of hand as fatherless children notoriously do, she had tried to prevent her mother from giving way to that strain of fecklessness and untidiness which her most fervent admirers had to admit existed alongside her charm and vividness. Well, all that hadn't been appreciated. Alice remembered, and it was as if a pin had stuck into her, how Mrs. Anglesey had grown gay and gayer as the wedding-day approached, and at the actual ceremony had shone with a radiance quite unlike the melancholy conventionally ascribed to the bride's mother. She rolled over in bed, rubbing her face angrily against the sheets.

Anyway, even if her mother had not valued her properly then, she ought to have learned to do so, in the last few years of her age and mellowness. Hadn't she noticed what her daughter had done for her during this visit? Alice had put out of doors the horrible gipsyish old dressing-gowny tea gowns her mother had loved to shuffle about in for the evenings, and had bought her some nice old-lady dresses from quite a good shop in the proper colours, dove-grey and dark brown. She had gone over the housekeeping books and saved pounds by changing several of the shops, and had put an end to the custom by which cook had brought in the menu-book last thing at night and launched out into what proved simply to be shockingly familiar gossip. One can't get on those terms with one's servants. She had hired a car, too, and taken her mother round calling on all the nice people with whom she had lost touch, and when her mother had insisted on calling on the Duchess, and had settled down to chat as if they were two old cronies, she had been firm and just taken her home, for it does not do to presume on one's acquaintance with people like that. It had all been a lot of trouble, too, particularly when she was still feeling so weak. But it had all gone for nothing. And so, too, she suspected, had all she had done for Madge and Leo. They hardly ever seemed to realize any of her kindnesses to them, and sometimes they were quite rude. And Leo's wife, Evie, was almost worse.

But perhaps this was the price she had to pay for her perfect marriage. At least Jimmy adored her. "My dear husband!" she sighed, and presently went off to sleep, but not, as it appeared, to rest. For there began to hover about her a terror which she had met before in her sleep, and she stood helpless while it circled closer and closer, unable to move hand or foot, able only to shriek. Able to shriek, it appeared, not only in her dream, for she opened her eyes and found her mother leaning over her and trying to shake her, although she herself was shaking so that there was very little strength in her hands.

"Oh, mother darling!" said Alice. "These wretched nightmares! I wish I didn't have them so often!"

Mrs. Anglesey sat back, still shaking, her grey hair wild about her.

"Oh, my poor little girl," she gasped. "My poor little girl! What can it be that frightens you so?"

The immediate preludes to the motor-drive, therefore, were not auspicious. Alice had a headache when she woke in the morning, and on the young man's arrival her mother proved uncommonly tiresome. She insisted on getting up to say good-bye to her daughter, and when she presented herself on the front lawn Alice realized that a ruby velveteen morning gown, adorned with moulting marabout of a fawn shade that owed more to time than to the dyer, had somehow got back from the dust-bin to which she thought she had sent it. The young man was very nice about it, even affecting interest when Mrs. Anglesey insisted on telling him the story of the time when she met Edward the Seventh at Monte Carlo; and he dissembled what must have been his emotions when, after he had started his engine, a shriek from her made him stop again.

"Alice! Have you remembered to send them a telegram to say you're coming?"

"No. I don't want to. It'll be a lovely surprise for Jimmy. And I like walking in on servants unexpectedly. It does them good."

The engine birred again. There was another shriek.

"—and Alice!"

"Oh, mother dear!"

"Be sure you look in the kitchen for the copper pan. It's no use your laughing, my dear, it might be that—" she had her arm over the side of the car and they had to let her go on talking—"you know, Mr.— Mr.?—Mr. Acland, is it?—my daughter came here for a little sea air after she's been terribly ill, and my doctor says that though he didn't see her during one of the attacks he thinks it sounds like irritant poisoning. Anything gastric he says wouldn't have cured so soon. And we can't account for it any way except that I say it is one of the copper pans I gave her for her wedding that they've forgotten to have re-coppered. That's dreadfully dangerous, you know. The Duchess's sister Jane died of it somewhere abroad. So I tell Alice she must look most carefully when she gets home. Oh, my dear Mr. Acland, you don't know how ill she was, yellow as a guinea, and such vomiting and diarrhoea . . ."

These are not words one wants shouted to the winds as one drives off, looking one's best, beside a young man of twenty-three who believes one to be very nearly his contemporary, for a journey through the springtime. But the day went very well indeed. They got out of the town very soon and cut up through pine woods to the heathy hills, presently turning and looking their last on the Channel, were immense pillars of light and darkness marched and countermarched on a beaten silver floor against a backcloth of distant storm. Not long after they were in the New Forest, where the new grass blades were springing up like green fire through the dark, tough matting of heather, and in the same plantations the black ashes affirmed it was still winter, the elms went no farther than to show a few purple flowers, the oaks made their recurring confusion between spring and autumn and were ablaze with red young leaves, and the birches and hawthorns were comfortably emerald.

Up there, as the morning got along, they had their lunch, sitting by a stream that reflected a bank of primroses. Mr. Acland told Alice many things. Helping in his father's factory seemed rather grim after Oxford. It was terribly hard work, and no chance of success, only the hope of staving off failure. Life was awfully difficult just now, particularly if you were young. When, for example, was he likely to be able to afford to marry? And he would like to marry. Not that he knew anybody at the moment that he wanted to marry. There had been somebody . . . but that had proved to be a mistake. He supposed he wasn't quite like other people, but he wanted something more than mere prettiness. He wanted ideas . . . broadmindedness . . . sympathy. . . .

He kept his eyes on Alice as he spoke, and that was very natural, for she was very nearly a perfect specimen of her type, and time had done almost nothing to spoil her. A touch of silver gave her golden hair a peculiar etherealized burnish, and the oval of her chin was still firm. She had neither crowsfeet nor lines round her mouth, perhaps because she habitually wore an expression of child-like wonder, which kept her blue-grey eyes wide open and her lips parted. She did in actual fact look under thirty, and what was more than that, she looked benevolent, candid, trustworthy, all in terms of grace. Her acts of kindness, her own resolutions of honesty, her Spartan guardianship of secrets, would all, one felt confident, be transacted so that the whole of life would take a more romantic form for evermore. It was no wonder that Mr. Acland felt the liveliest satisfaction at her appearance.

His own, however, did not satisfy her nearly so well. She realized this when, speaking as earnestly as he had done, and encouraging him to seek for the perfect mate by relating her own story, she fixed her eyes on his face. Proudly yet modestly she described how she had lived all her life in Camelheath, and admitted that many people might pity her for this, since it would be idle to deny that it was quite the dullest town that could be found within fifty miles of London, but she claimed that nobody in the world could have lived a richer and fuller life than she had, thanks to the circumstance that when she was nineteen the leading solicitor in the town had sent for his nephew to come and be his junior partner, and that the boy had immediately fallen in love with her. "We have been married nineteen years, and we are as much in love as ever," she said. The sound of her own words made Jimmy's face appear before her, and she realized with an almost shuddering intensity how much she would rather be looking at him than at Mr. Acland. This was no vague, sentimental preference. There was some particular feature in Jimmy's face that gave her deep and delicious pleasure; yet she could not think what it was. Academically,

she acknowledged, Mr. Acland's broad-browed fairness was more likely
to earn points than Jimmy's retiring, quickly-smiling darkness, but that
was irrelevant to the intense joy he gave her by this quality which, just
for the moment, though she would have liked to tell the boy about it,
she could not name.

After she had told her story they got back into the car, feeling very
warm and intimate but a little solemn and silent; and about half-past
three they stopped in front of the Georgian house at Camelheath
which was her home.

"It's a very pretty house," said Mr. Acland.

"We've done a great deal to it," said Alice.

She rang. Though she always carried a key she hardly ever used
it, for she liked to keep Ethel on the alert about the door-opening; and
this technique had evidently paid, for Ethel confronted them before
a minute had passed.

"Why, it's the mistress! And looking so well, too! Why, I never did
expect to see you looking so well, ever again, mum! Well, the master
will be pleased . . ."

Cook, who had been waddling upstairs when the door opened,
leaned over the banisters and joined in.

"Well, mum, it's no need to ask if you're feeling better! I didn't
never see anybody so far gone come right up again! You're the proper
picture of health, now, you are, mum . . ."

She beamed at them while they ran on, regretting that Mr. Pemberton wouldn't be able to run over from his office that very minute,
because old Mr. Bates up at Stickyback Farm had died three days ago,
and he had had to go to his funeral this afternoon, assuring her that
Mr. Pemberton had missed her ever so, that when Ethel had taken him
up his blacks for him to change into after lunch he had said, "Well,
thank goodness, we'll be having your mistress with us very soon." Of
course the servants adored her. Well, so they might. She knew she
had an almost perfect manner with subordinates, and she really took
trouble over training them and thinking out devices for ridding them
of their little faults. She would never need to part with her servants,
if it was not for the curious vein of madness running through all
women of that class, which invariably came out sooner or later in some
wild attack of causeless rage. Well, there was some ground for hoping
that these two were superior to the rest of their kind. Cook had
been with her eighteen months, Ethel nearly three years. Perhaps at
last all her kindly efforts were going to be given their reward.

Graciously smiling, she dismissed them and took Mr. Acland into
the drawing-room. But he would not stay for tea. He had to admit,
with some nervous laughter and blushes, that his home was not quite

in the direction he had led her to suppose: that, in fact, he had made quite a preposterous detour to drop her at Camelheath, and that he would have to keep quite good time for the rest of his drive to get back for dinner.

"But it's been wonderful to see where you live," he said, looking round with admiration. Alice was leaning on the Adam mantelpiece, her brilliant fairness and her quiet, good beige suit harmonizing with the pale golden marble. On the fine Chippendale furniture, polished till amber light seemed to well up from the depths of the wood, were bowls of daffodils and early tulips; and between the mellow green brocade curtains a garden tidy to the last leaf showed spring flowers against the definite fine-grained darkness of hoed earth, a quaintly planned rose-garden here and there ruddy with new shoots, and orchard boughs rising frosted with blossom above black yew hedges.

"It's lovely, of course. But can you find people fit to be your friends in this little town?"

"I don't ask for very much, you know," said Alice bravely, "and I'm the centre of quite a little world here. Do you see that house over the fields, standing among the elms? My sister, Mrs. Walter Fletcher, lives there."

"It looks as if it was a lovely house, too."

"It might be. But poor Madge is a funny girl. She isn't a very good manager." She paused and sighed. "Then, as you drive out of town, you'll pass a big modern villa just by a fork in the road. That's where my little brother lives. At least he isn't little at all now, in fact he's the local doctor, as our father was before him. But I always think of him as my little brother. I had so much to do with him as a baby, you see, and then I haven't been able to see so much of him in later years. He made a marriage that from some points of view hasn't been a success." She looked into the distance for a minute and then said simply, "You know, I used to mind terribly not having any children. But I realize that if I had I wouldn't have been able to do a whole lot of things for others that badly needed doing."

"I'm sure that's true," said Mr. Acland gravely, "there aren't enough people like you to go round."

Soon after that he went. Alice was quite glad, for it would have been an anti-climax for him to have stayed any longer now that they had established this peculiarly deep and reticent sympathy. She walked out with him through the front garden, pausing sometimes to show him her collection of old-fashioned English herbs. "They have such lovely names," she said, "rosemary . . . thyme . . . musk . . . herb-of-grace . . . and dear old lavender. They give one the feeling of an age I believe I would have liked better than this horrid, hustling present day."

When they said good-bye he held her hand a minute longer than was necessary. "I wish you'd promise me not to do too many things for other people," he said. "I expect that's how you got ill."

"I'll try and be more sensible," she smiled.

As soon as she got back to the house she started on a tour of inspection. There was a pile of visiting-cards on the tray on the hall table —odd how many people had called while she was away—and lifted them to see if there was much dust underneath. But there was none there, nor anywhere in the drawing-room, nor in the dining-room, nor in the little library. Everywhere the flowers were fresh, and the water in the vases had been changed that morning, the ash trays had been emptied and polished, and the oak floors shone like brown glass. She went upstairs, running her hand along the fluting of the banisters. When she reached the landing she paused and examined her fingers, but they were still pink and clean.

There was nothing wrong in her bedroom, either. The billows of glazed chintz, biscuit-coloured and sprigged with rosebuds, had evidently just been put up again after a visit to the cleaner's. The silver toilet set on the dressing-table caught the afternoon sun with its brightness; and on the top of the tall-boy the pot-pourri bowl of blue and white porcelain shone with the proper clean milky radiance. She felt a great relief at getting back to her own house, so airy and light and spacious, so austerely empty of anything that was not carefully chosen and fine and mellow, after her mother's cluttered rooms. But she did not linger any longer, though this was perhaps her favourite room in the house, but opened the door into her husband's dressing-room. Perhaps Ethel had let herself be careless there.

Everything was all right there, too, however. There were too many books on the table beside the bed; its Sheraton legs quivered under the strain if one added the weight of a finger tip. She took an armful and put them back on the shelves on the wall, marvelling at the kind of book her quiet Jimmy liked to read: crude, violent tales about tramps, sailors before the mast, trappers of wild animals. But there was nothing else in the room that she could have wished different. The brushes and combs lay in front of his swinging mirror, gleaming and symmetrical; even the sock and handkerchief drawer was in perfect order; and the photograph frames along the mantelpiece almost gave her what she wanted, for it seemed impossible that Ethel could have got them quite as bright as this without neglecting some of her other duties. But as she turned away, her eye was caught by something about the largest photograph, the one standing in the middle of the mantelpiece, which showed her as a bride looking with wide eyes and parted lips over her sheaf of lilies. There was a hair running half across it, under the glass. She took up the frame and slipped out the photograph and then paused in surprise. There was no hair on the glass; but the photograph had been torn almost in two.

"Ethel!" she said angrily, and stretched her hand towards the bell. But she perceived that this damage must have been done long ago. Somebody had tried their best to repair by pasting the torn edges to a piece of paper beneath, and had made a very neat job of it. It had only become visible now because the paste had shrunk and hardened with age and the torn edges were gaping again. One of Ethel's predecessors must have done it during the frenzies of spring cleaning. "It must have been Lilian Hall," thought Alice bitterly. She could remember the names of all her many hated servants. What a pack they were! One could not trust any of them. She peered eagerly into her husband's wardrobe, for she knew that her careful supervision of his valeting had given him such confidence that he never looked at his clothes or shoes. But the suits hung sleekly pressed and completely buttoned from the hangers, and down at the bottom black shoes looked inky, brown shoes glowed with their cornelian tints.

When she saw the grey tweeds she felt a little startled for he always wore them at the office, until she remembered he had had to change to go to a funeral. The sight of his everyday suit brought him vividly before her, with his dark, thoroughly pleasant but not excessive good looks his slouch that seemed not so much slackness as a modest retreat from notice, the curious thrilling sense of expectation which, in spite of his quietness, he still gave her after their nineteen years of marriage. She put out her hand and stroked the suit affectionately, and then paused, puzzled because she had felt through the tweed something hard of an odd shape. It was lying along the bottom of his right hand inside breast pocket, and when she fished it out she saw that it was a cylindrical tube of very thick glass fitted with a screw-top, and two-thirds full of white powder.

"Why is Jimmy carrying medicine about with him? Can he be imagining he's ill again?" She wondered not for the first time, why she should be the only perfectly normal person, who never said she was ill except when she was ill, in a family of hypochondriacs. Then her heart contracted. "Perhaps he really is ill!" She remembered what her mother had suggested, that there might be a faulty cooking vessel in the kitchen which was tainting the food with mineral poison, and she hoped that poor Jimmy had not been keeping from her the news that he had had an attack like hers. To see what the medicine might be, she put her finger in the white powder, and sucked it; but though the haunting bitterness of its taste reminded her of something, she could not put a name to it. But she recognized the container. Old

Dr. Godstone, who had looked after the local practice during the period after her father had died and before her brother had been ready to take it over, had used these funny glass containers for some of his drugs. How like Jimmy to go on using something made up by that silly old man, which had probably lost whatever virtues it ever had through the lapse of time, instead of going along to Leo and having something really up-to-date made up! What would Jimmy do without her?

She went down the stairs humming with satisfaction and looked down on the top of Ethel's head in the hall, as she bent over her mistress's suitcase. Then it flashed over her why the house was so tidy. Mrs. Anglesey had rung up after all and warned them she was coming back. That had happened once before, shortly after Ethel had first come to her. She had come back and found the house a whirl-wind of plate-powder and blacking-brushes with the girl's attempts to catch up with her neglected work. What a talking-to she had given her! The silly girl had cried her eyes out, and would probably have left if her mother hadn't been so ill. Of course she had greatly improved since then, and no doubt she had allowed less to fall in arrears this time, but only some such warning would account for the exquisite order she found everywhere.

"Ethel!" she called, in a coolly humorous tone.

The girl's sleek head cocked up. "Yes, mum."

"The house is beautifully tidy."

"I'm so glad you found it right, mum."

"So tidy," said Alice, who had got down to the hall and was standing with her head lowered so that she could look searchingly into Ethel's doe eyes, while a whimsical little smile played round her lips, "that I was wondering if Mrs. Anglesey hadn't telephoned this morning to warn you I was coming back."

The girl grew pale and caught her breath for a second, then banged the suitcase down on the floor. "No, she didn't," she said. "The house has been this way all the time you've been away, and would have stayed so if you'd been away twice as long. And if you don't believe me you can call up the Post Office and see if there's been any but local calls put through here all day."

"Oh, very well, very well," said Alice, "but such things have been known to happen, haven't they, before now?"

The girl's eyes blazed. She picked up the suitcase and went up the stairs with it. As she went by her resentment was as tangible as a hot wind.

"What tempers they all have!" thought Alice. "And how tiresome it is just when I've got home! I wonder if anyone realizes just how

much it costs me to run this house in self-restraint and patience."
She sighed as it occured to her that her own household was only one
of her responsibilities, and looked at her wrist-watch. It was improbable that Jimmy would be in before five, she might just as well go
over and see how Madge and Leo were getting on, and what
new problems she would have to cope with in their households. "Ah,
if I only keep my health!" she said, looking at herself very gravely in
the glass over the hall table. It often struck her that there was something terrifying in the way the happiness of so many people, Jimmy,
Madge, Walter, and their two children, Leo, Evie, and their four,
all depended on her physically fragile self.

She liked the little walk across the fields to Madge's house; every
corner of the district was dear to her, for she was one of those people
who feel that they live in the nicest house in the nicest town in the
nicest county of the nicest country. But she was not so happy when
she was inside Madge's garden. If it looked as wild as this in the
spring, what would it be like in autumn? She knew Walter had turned
off one of the gardeners, but it shouldn't have been necessary to do
that, considering his income, if only Madge had been a better manager. It was really impossible to guess what she did with all her
money. And if one did have to turn away a gardener, surely one tried
to repair the damage by taking on as much of his work as possible.
But she wasn't in the least surprised to find Madge lying on the sofa
in the drawing-room, wearing an invalidish kind of tea-gown that
suggested she had been sticking in the house all day. She looked a very
bad pasty colour. It was really dreadful, the way she was letting herself go.

But she jumped up and kissed her sister with quite a show of animation. "Why, Alice, how marvellous you look! But I thought you
weren't coming back till Friday?"

"That's what I had planned, but a young man gave me a lift in
his car," answered Alice. "We had such a lovely drive across the New
Forest. It's been the most glorious day. Haven't you been out at all,
dear?"

"As it happens, I haven't."

"My dear, you ought to make some effort to get over the tendency
to lie about. It isn't good for you. You're a most dreadful colour . . ."

"Am I?" asked Madge, with a curious, distressed urgency. She sat
up on her cushions and stared at herself in a mirror on the other side
of the room.

"Yes, you are," said Alice, "most earthy and unwholesome. And
it's all because you don't take enough exercise. Look at me!" She laid
a finger against her perfect cheek. "I'm out in all weathers. Really,

dear, you must be careful. You know you're five years younger than me, and you look at least five years older."

"I dare say you're right," said Madge listlessly. "But you, dear? Are you quite better? You haven't had any more of those terrible attacks?"

"Not a trace of them. Mother's doctor thought they might have come from some pan in the kitchen that we hadn't had re-coppered. I'm going to look. I certainly hadn't a suspicion of a recurrence while I was away. But I did have another of those awful nightmares, you know I suppose it's all the worry that weighs down on me."

"What worry?" asked Madge, rather petulantly.

Alice smiled to herself, but the smile was a little sad. Didn't Madge really know even now how much of her happiness she owed to her sister's readiness to take on what most people would have pushed away as unnecessary worries? How Alice worked over her when she was a girl, always saying to her just as they went into the ballroom, "Now do hold yourself properly and try to hide those dreadful elbows," and keeping near her to see that she was behaving properly and saying the right things to her partners, and on the way home telling her all the things she had done wrong! And then, since Madge's marriage to Walter, Alice had been on hand day in, day out, always ready to point out faults in her housekeeping, to explain just why her parties had not been successful, to suggest where she was going wrong in bringing up her children. There was no use pretending it had always been an easy task. Madge had a childish intolerance of criticism, she sometimes became quite rude.

"Well, Madge," Alice began quietly, but Madge was asking, "How did you leave mother?"

"Oh, mother's all right," said Alice indulgently, "it's funny how she's quite happy muddling along."

"I don't see that she does much muddling," said Madge. "She knows how she likes to live, and she lives that way."

"Oh, my dear!" exclaimed Alice. "I call it a terrible muddle. Just think what I found her doing . . ." But Madge cut in quickly, "Here are the children coming in from their walk, and please, please, don't encourage Betty!"

"My dear, I think you're so wrong about Betty," Alice started to explain, but the children were with them. Little Godfrey ran straight to his mother; there was really something very morbid and effeminate about the way he always clung to her, and he ought to have been told to be polite and run and kiss his aunt instead of staring at her with great vacant eyes. But Betty went at once to Alice, who held out her arms. The child had a touch of her own brilliant fairness and neatness and decision, which was urgently needed in this dingy, feckless household. It was really very strange, the way that Madge did not seem to appreciate having such an attractive little girl. She supposed that it was just such an unreasonable aversion, probably springing from some odd pre-natal cause, as her own mother felt towards her. Every now and then she gave Betty a little smile, to show that there was a special understanding between them; but really she regretted having done it before long, for the poor child began to make confidences to her, which seemed to exasperate Madge. When Betty said that she had been sure her aunt would get better, because she had prayed for her every night, Madge had been visibly annoyed; and when Betty carried on the conversation along these lines to the point of describing a lecture on Indian missions that had been given at their local school and expressing a hope that she herself might become a missionary some day, Madge called sharply, "Annie, Annie!"

The nursemaid hurried in from the hall.

"Take the children straight up to the nursery," Madge told her, and leaned back on the cushions with her eyes shut until the din of protest had died, and she was alone with her sister again. "I asked you not to encourage Betty," she said. "I really don't see why you should come here and make my family talk the idiom of very old volumes of *The Quiver*."

"My dear, I never heard such nonsense," Alice objected. "If modern ideas have come to such a pass that a little girl of ten can't show a nice healthy interest in religion . . ."

"Betty's interest in religion isn't nice or healthy," said Madge. "It's sheer priggishness and exhibitionism."

"If you used shorter words and didn't try to be so scientific, and looked after your children in an old-fashioned way, it might be better. Must you have that untidy girl from the village as a nursemaid? I refused to let her come in and help Ethel last winter, she's so slatternly."

"We know she's not ideal. But we can't afford anyone better."

"But, my dear, why can't you? Your money seems just to run through your fingers. It isn't fair to Walter, and it's simply cruel to the children. They ought to have a nice, well-trained woman to look after them and teach them pretty manners."

She waited for any defence that might be forthcoming, but Madge had fallen into one of her sulky silences. "Well," said Alice at last, "you're a funny set, you new-fashioned mothers, I must say. Goodness knows what I shall find when I get to Leo's."

"Oh, are you going to Leo's?" said Madge. "I'll go down the avenue with you if you like." She was on her feet at once and moving towards the door, while Alice thought in amazement, "Why, I believe she's trying to get me out of the house, and I haven't been here for much more than half an hour! How queer and . . . petty!"

But she tried to conceal her feelings as they walked under the trees to the high road. "Nobody can say I am tactless," she thought, as she passed by the patches of rough grass and weeds without pointing them out to her sister. "And I'm not saying anything about how absurd it is that she should be wearing those trailing things that she has to hold up round her when she gets a breath of fresh air, instead of being out and about in sensible country clothes. I'll just give her a word about pulling herself together when we part." But when they came to the gate she forgot, for Madge let her skirts fall and put both her arms round her giving her a hug as if they were children again.

"Dear Alice, I'm so glad you are better," she said, and stood with her head on one side for a minute admiring her. "I love to see you looking so young and pretty. It was horrid when you were ill. You ought always to be well and happy."

"You're crushing my coat," said Alice; but she was pleased. "I think she is really grateful, though she's so odd and ungracious," she said to herself as she hurried along to Leo's house. "Well, it's encouraging."

She received no such encouragement when she arrived there. The front door was open, and when she passed into the hall she saw Colin, the eldest boy, walking up the staircase in the undisciplined manner of the bookish young, taking an immense time to mount from step to step because he had his nose deep in an open book.

"Colin!" she called.

He turned round, but did not answer the greeting. For a minute he stared blankly at her, his black forelock falling over his brows—heaven knew why Evie let her children go about with their hair that length—and his mouth stupidly open. Then a look of consternation spread over his face, he slammed the open book, and without saying a word rushed upstairs two steps at a time.

"Well, of all the manners!" breathed Alice. She heard her brother's short, dry, tired cough from the surgery, farther down the passage, and made a step in that direction. "Leo really ought to be told," she thought furiously. But just then her sister-in-law came to the top of the stairs. She stared down on Alice incredulously, turned and whispered, "Hush!" as if she were quelling a tumult in the shadows behind her, and then ran downstairs saying, "Well, Alice, this is a surprise! We thought you weren't to be with us till Friday!"

How hopelessly odd she was, how neurotic and unstable, the very last person to be a doctor's wife. She was trembling and breathless as if she had had a severe shock instead of merely receiving a visit from a sister-in-law. It was no wonder the children were such unattractive little savages.

"A young man gave me a lift in his motor-car," said Alice, trying to pass things off lightly, "and I thought I'd come along and see how you all were. How are you, Evie? That's right. And Leo? No symptoms, I hope?"

"None," said Evie, "absolutely none." She said everything with such odd over-emphasis that it really made one feel uncomfortable.

"Can I see him?" said Alice, moving towards the surgery.

"No, you can't," said Evie, stepping between her and the surgery door. "He's out. He's gone to Cadeford for a consultation."

There was a minute's silence.

"Has he, Evie?" asked Alice, raising her eyebrows and smiling.

Again there came the sound of Leo's high, dry, tired cough.

"I'll come some other day," said Alice, turning to the front door, "when I'm not in the way."

Evie put out a weak, shaking hand. "It's only that he's so busy . . ."

"Oh, my dear, I understand," said Alice. "It's a wife's duty to protect her husband. And anyway you of all people must know by this time that I'm not one of those people that bear grudges."

With a frank smile she held out her hand and after Evie had gripped and released it she let it rest for a minute on a half-inch of gaping seam in the other's jumper. "I wish you'd let me send you my little sewing-woman one day. Let me ring up and find out what day would be convenient. It would be a real pleasure if you'd let me treat you to that. I always think one feels much calmer and happier when one's really neat and tidy."

She found herself walking back to her house at a swinging pace. "I mustn't be angry with her," she kept on telling herself. "I know there's nothing the matter with the woman but jealousy, and it's a shame that Leo's children should be brought up as ill-mannered little gutter-snipes but I must remember that she can't help being what she is. It's only by chance that I was born what I am instead of like her." When a turn of the road brought her house in sight tears of relief stood in her eyes. There, in her beautiful, orderly spacious rooms, she could shut out all these awful people who loved quarrelling and unkindness. Already the afternoon sun was low over the fields, and it would soon be time to turn on the lights. She liked to think of that, because it had occurred to her once, when she had driven home later and seen from far off the rosy glow of her curtained windows, how fortunate, how right it was that her house could send brightness shining out into the dark, but that the dark could not come into her house and dim the brightness. In one's own home one was safe. She would take off her suit the minute she got in and put on a soft, lacy dressing-gown, and put eau de cologne on her forehead, and lie down on the couch in her bedroom till Jimmy came.

But when she got home she was waylaid by the cook. "Might I speak to you, mum?"

She followed her into the big, clean, airy, blue-and-white kitchen. "Well?" she said, looking round. "I'm sure you've nothing to grumble about in your kitchen, Cook! It's really a picture. Everything you could possibly want . . ."

"Yes, indeed, mum," said Cook. "But I was going to tell you we'd forgotten to say Mr. Robert Norman's coming to dinner with the master, and I wanted to ask you if I should cook something special for you, or if you'd have what they do."

"What are you giving them?"

"Artichoke soup, cod, saddle of mutton, and apple dumpling, and welsh rarebit."

"Oh, Cook," said Alice, "what a dreadful dinner! So dull and so heavy! After all the trouble I've taken working out menus with you, you really shouldn't give the master dinners like that just because you think I'm going to be out of the way."

"I wouldn't do no such thing," answered Cook, with her colour rising, "the master's eaten full as dainty every night you been away as when you was here. But Mr. Robert Norman likes to eat when he eats, and it was for him the master ordered this very dinner. I ain't nothing to do with it, 'cept cook it best I can."

"I can't think he really wanted this awful dinner," said Alice. "Are you sure you haven't made a mistake? Such things have been known to happen, you know, Cook. We're none of us perfect. Do you remember when just after you came you sent up a rice pudding at a dinner party when I ordered ice pudding? That was funny. Fortunately they were all very nice about it. Oh, don't be offended, Cook. We all make mistakes sometimes."

"We do, mum," said Cook. "And shall I cook you anything separate?"

"Well, I certainly won't be able to eat much of this terrible meal," smiled Alice. "But I'll try to get along on the cod and some of the apples out of the dumpling. And then before I go to bed I'll have my usual glass of hot chocolate malted milk."

"I've got a new brand of that for you," said Cook. " 'The Devon Dairymaid,' instead of Harrison & Cooper's. The man at the stores told me he had it, and I ordered a small tin to try."

"Oh, Cook, why did you do that? Haven't you a tin of the old sort left?"

"No, mum. It was all finished when you left. But it was twice you complained that the old kind tasted bitter."

"Yes, but I've tried this new kind when I was staying with Mrs. Anglesey, and it's horrid. It's just as dark as the other, but it has hardly any chocolate flavour, and you know I can only get down the malted milk if I don't taste it. I do think it's a pity you did that without asking me."

"Well, I'll get a tin of the old in the morning."

"Yes, but there's the new tin wasted, and every penny counts nowadays. And there's to-night. I'll have to do without one of the very few things I enjoy. But send it up just the same. Now do remember not to do this sort of thing. The times when you should show initiative you never do, giving people the same dreadful dinners I've taught you not to do, and then you go and make a perfectly unnecessary purchase like this. It's heartbreaking, Cook." She repeated, "Yes, it's simply heartbreaking;" but Cook made no answer, so she moved towards the door, but was plucked back by a recollection.

"Oh, by the way, Cook, are you sure that there's none of the copper pans that need re-coppering?"

"Quite sure, mum. We had the man to look at them only a few months ago. And anyway I'm cooking more and more in the fireproof and the aluminium."

"That can't be it, then. You know, Mrs. Anglesey's doctor thought that my attacks might have been not gastric at all, but due to irritant poisoning. And the only way we could think that I could have been poisoned was through some of the copper vessels having worn out. I can't think of any other way, can you, Cook?"

"No, mum, I can't. If you was a lady with a nagging tongue, always finding fault with everything, and making trouble where there's only kindness meant, then I suppose we might all be wanting to drop poison in your food. But you aren't like that, are you, mum?"

Alice's heart nearly stopped. Cook's face was bland but her tone was unmistakably insolent. What was the reason for this madness that afflicted one and all of the servant class?

"We'd better talk about this to-morrow, Cook," she said quietly, and left the kitchen. She supposed that they would both be going now, Ethel as well as Cook. How could they be so causelessly malevolent as to do this when she had just come home? The tears were rising in her eyes and she was going blindly towards the staircase when she heard an exclamation, and turned to see that the front door had opened and Jimmy was standing on the step outside, paralysed with amazement in the act of pulling off his gloves.

She ran to him and stretched her arms up his tallness. "Yes, I'm back two whole days too early! But a nice young man gave me a lift in his car!" Under her lips his face felt worn and cold; but clients' funerals were always trying. "Oh, my dear, I'm so much better!"

"I'm glad of that," said Jimmy. "I'm very glad of that."

"And, oh, I'm so pleased you've come in!" she cried. "It's been so horrid ever since I got back. Madge was horrid to me except for a little bit at the end, and Evie was horrid, and Colin was a hateful little beast, and Ethel was horrid, and now Cook's been horrid. Why does nobody but me want to be happy and live in peace?"

Jimmy put his arm round her shoulder and led her into the house, looking down on her tenderly as one might on a crippled child. "Poor little Alice," he said, "Poor little Alice."

## II

Ethel had lit the log-fire in the drawing-room, and it spat at them playfully while they crouched on the rug, Jimmy stretching out one hand to the warmth while Alice rubbed the other.

"It'll be a glorious blaze in a minute," said Alice, "and just as well, for you're simply icy, my darling. Was it too dreadful at the funeral?"

"No, not really," said Jimmy. "It wasn't too cold, or too harrowing, even. They'd all been expecting the old chap to go for ages so nobody felt it was a great shock."

"I like the younger son best, I hope he stays on at the farm, he's an awfully nice boy. Oh, Jimmy, the young man who brought me home was so nice. And it was miles out of his way really. He's coming to see us some day, you will like him. He was so sweet and patient with Mother, too. Just think, she would not let us get off this morning until she'd told him the whole of that interminable story about how she met King Edward at Monte Carlo."

"But perhaps he liked hearing it."

"Oh, my dear, who could? Who cares about such things nowadays. Besides, it's rather vulgar, I always think. But, darling, I do appreciate the way you turn a blind eye to my family's failings. I know perfectly well they're awful . . ."

"But, Alice, I don't think your family's awful."

"You chivalrous darling, you know it is. Anyway Madge and Evie were pretty awful this afternoon, I can tell you."

"What did they do?"

"Oh, Madge was lying on the sofa looking horribly pasty and un-wholesome. She hadn't put her foot outside the house all day. I can't understand why she's letting herself go. And then she's so silly about Betty. Just because the child's got a natural leaning to religion . . ."

"But, Alice, it's Madge's foot and Madge's house. If she doesn't want to put the one outside the other, surely it's her business. And surely Betty's her child and her business too?"

"But, Jimmy dear, Madge is my sister. You haven't any family feeling. You don't understand that I can't watch my sister doing everything wrong and just let her do it."

"Why not? She's thirty-five, darling. Time she learned to save her own soul."

"Nonsense, dear. You'd never have any civilization at all if you didn't have the people who knew best teaching all the others what to do."

"Oh, Alice, dear!"

"Well, it's true, darling. And that's why I won't give up going to Leo's house, however rude that woman is. Do you know what she did this evening? She looked me straight in the face and told me that Leo was out, when I could hear him coughing in the surgery! Did you ever hear of a wife being so jealous of her husband's sister? But I'm not going to give up. I've got a duty to that household. I must see the children get some sort of upbringing. That Colin's a perfect little savage."

Jimmy had got up and was standing above her, lighting his pipe. "Alice, Colin belongs to Leo and Evie, not to you."

"But, darling, you don't understand! If they can't look after him properly then I must do what I can," she answered absently. She loved the look of his face, lit red by the flame.

He sat down in the arm-chair and beckoned her to come and sit on his knee. "Alice, I wish you'd promise me something. It would really do a lot to make me happy. Will you do it?"

"I'll do anything for you, darling."

"Then promise me to leave Madge and Walter, and Leo and Evie alone for a bit. Don't visit them unless they ask you. Don't try to manage their affairs."

Alice stood up. "Jimmy, how absurd you are!" she exclaimed. "I've never heard you say anything so silly before! Anyone would think I was tactless or interfering."

"That's what I want you to promise."

She stared at him with eyes made immense by tears. "Jimmy, you don't think I'm tactless and interfering, do you? Because I couldn't bear to think you so completely misunderstood my character! As for being tactless, that is absurd, because if there is one good quality that I've got, it's tact. I've always been able to handle people without hurting their feelings. And as for interfering, I simply loathe it. But after all Madge and Leo are my sister and brother, and the trouble is that since they were babies they've depended on me for everything, and they'd never get anywhere if I didn't push them." She suddenly dropped on her knees and looked up into his face with an expression of panic. "They don't think I'm tactless and interfering, do they? Because I couldn't bear that, it would be so ungrateful of them! And you know I've thought of them, all my life long, far more than I've thought of myself."

Sobs began to shake her. "Oh, you poor child!" said Jimmy, and drew her close to him. "I know you have. But people are funny after they've grown up and married and got children. They like to be left alone."

"But they couldn't think that," said Alice, the tears running down her cheeks, "unless they'd stopped loving me."

"My dear, I'm sure they haven't. But I want you to make that promise all the same. Just humour them. Just let them be silly. To save your nerves."

"I'd rather do what was right than save my nerves."

"To please me, then," said Jimmy. He took her by the shoulders and smiled into her eyes, his dark, secret smile. "I might beat you if you didn't," he told her gravely.

He always made her laugh when he said that. "Silly!" she giggled, and he crushed her suddenly in his arms. "I promise!" she whispered in his ear, and disentangled herself just as Ethel brought in tea. "But all the same," she said, to cover her embarrassment because she knew her hair was rumpled, "I think they're preposterous if they are offended."

For tea there was a whole jarful of strawberry jam, which neither of them liked very much, and only a little cherry jam, which they both liked so well that the household supply rarely lasted thus late into the spring. It might have been thought there was enough of this for two, but she knew how thick he liked to pile it on his buttered toast, so she gave it all to him, and took the precaution of spreading it for him and putting it on his plate, so that he had no chance to be unselfish. Then, when the tea had been cleared away, she went and sat on his knee again and they were both silent, looking into the blazing wood.

"Lovely your hair is," he said at last. "You're a lovely child, and capable of being noble, even about cherry jam."

She leaned farther back, putting her face close to his. "Yet you haven't kissed me properly yet," she said.

"Haven't I?"

"No. You let me kiss you in the hall. But you haven't kissed me."

He murmured something under his breath and bent his lips towards her. But she twisted out of his grasp.

"Why did you say that under your breath?"

"What did I say?"

"You know perfectly well what you said. You said, 'Forgive me.' Why should I forgive you? Oh, Jimmy, what have you been doing?"

"Nothing. I didn't mean anything. They were just words that passed through my mind. Something I've been reading."

"Jimmy, really? Is that really true? You haven't been unfaithful to me?"

He shook his head. "No. I couldn't have done that, even if I'd wanted to. I've thought of you continually nearly all the time you've been away. No husband ever was haunted more steadily by the presence of his absent wife."

Her storm of suspicion weakened. "Is that true?" she asked piteously. "Are you sure? But then what did you want me to forgive you for?"

"I wanted you to forgive me for being me," he said, "and having to be what I am, and do what I have done." A smile passed over his lips. "Just as you might ask me to forgive you for being you."

She laughed happily at the idea, and settled down in his arms again, to receive his embrace. After his mouth had left hers she nodded her head wisely. "Yes, you love me. But how tired you are."

He muttered, lying quite relaxed, his head against her breast. "Yes, that's just it. I love you. But I'm so tired that I don't know what to do . . . I don't know how to carry on . . ."

"My poor darling, there's nothing worrying you in your business, is there?"

"Nothing." She could hardly hear his voice, he was evidently just dropping off to sleep.

"Well, everything else will be all right now I'm home."

"I hope so . . . I hope so . . ." She saw his hand drowsily groping for the table beside the chair, to touch wood.

They sat thus, with the twilight deepening on them to darkness, the firelight showing redder and more comforting. Sometimes they sighed in contentment, sometimes one or the other began to murmur a phrase of endearment, but did not finish it, sometimes they slept. Then all of a sudden, the room was flooded with light and Ethel was saying, "It's seven o'clock, and time you were dressing, because Mr. Norman do come early and no mistake. And I'd like you to have a look at the table, mum, to see if you think I did it right."

She spoke with the benignity of conscious pride, which they understood when they stood in the dining-room and saw the shining glory she had made.

"I put the tall daffies at the corner," Ethel told them expansively. "Nobody else done a table that way, that I ever see, but it gives you the good of them without you having to crane your necks to see who you're eating opposite. And I put the little dwarf daffies in the middle."

"My word, you've made a lovely thing of it, Ethel," said Jimmy. "The flowers aren't so many that the table looks crowded, but it's a grand show."

Alice said, "Wait a minute," moved a fork a little to the left, leaned over and shifted the linen centrepiece under the dwarf daffodils a fraction of an inch, then moved back and surveyed the table with great satisfaction. "Yes, that's very nice."

Jimmy sighed, very deeply. He seemed to be terribly over-tired.

Ethel, blossoming under the warmth of praise, continued, "There's so many daffodils out now that even old Wray can't be stingy about bringing them up to the house, though he'd do anything to keep all his flowers to hisself in the garden."

Alice said stiffly, "Well, Ethel, we've all of us so many faults that I don't think it becomes any of us to make fun of others."

There was a minute's silence, before Ethel swung round and went out of the room. "I say, I don't think you need have said that," said Jimmy. "She didn't mean to be ill-natured. She just said it as you or I might have said it." He had dropped into a chair and looked very white and lined.

"Nonsense, darling," said Alice, "you can't have servants talking against each other. But, oh, Jimmy, you do look tired. I wish this old man wasn't coming."

"Oh, I like old Norman. We get on awfully well together. He's been in a lot while you've been away. The nurse who looks after his imbecile child isn't well, and Mrs. Norman has to take charge in the evenings a good deal. So he's been glad to come along and have something to eat, and play a bit of two-handed bridge."

"Funny darlings you must have been together," said Alice. "Let's go and dress."

It was quite a successful dinner, Alice thought. She put on the new turquoise dress she had bought when she was staying with her mother, and the old man's eyes had brightened when he saw her. He was a gentleman farmer, the wealthiest and most important of his kind in the district, and there was some seignorial dignity about him, as well as the ashes of romantic charm, for, till he had been sobered by the tragic issue of his marriage, he had been a famous beau and blood. Even now that he was silver-haired, he made every woman he spoke to feel a little better-looking than she really was, and Alice found herself glowing as she entertained him, and forgetting to be sorry that she and Jimmy were not alone. But Mr. Norman seemed to tire very soon. His frosty grey eyes stopped sparkling and grew heavy, he talked less and less, and though they had started bridge he rose and left at twenty minutes to ten.

"What a handsome old thing he is, in his weather-beaten way," said Alice, when Jimmy came back from seeing him out. "But does he always leave so early?"

Jimmy went over to the fire and kicked a log down with his heel. "No, I've known him stay quite late."

"I expect that dreadful heavy dinner made him sleepy," said Alice. "I was sure when I heard what you'd ordered that it was a mistake."

Jimmy sat down in an arm-chair, and stared into the fire. "No, I don't think it was the dinner. But I think it was a pity you tried to teach him those new Culbertson rules. He's an old man, and he'd probably been out on horseback since eight o'clock this morning, and he just wanted to fiddle round with the cards a bit."

"Oh, my dear, he can't have found that a strain! And anyway, what's the use of doing anything if you don't do it well? Still I probably was wrong. But you forget, when you've been away, what clods the best of these people are."

"Yes, clods," said Jimmy, "without brains, without feelings, without sensitiveness. I think it was a pity too that you told him he ought to take his child to that brain surgeon at Geneva."

"Well, why shouldn't I? He's a wonderful man. Mother knows somebody who told her about the most marvellous cure . . ."

"I dare say," said Jimmy, "but you see Norman and his wife took the child there six years ago, and it wasn't any good."

"But why didn't he tell me so? What an extraordinary thing of him to do, to let me go on talking about it and never say a thing!"

"I expect he likes so little hearing the child talked about that when people start he just lets them say what they have to say and finish, and doesn't prolong it by getting up an argument."

"Well, if he feels like that even when people are trying to help him, I can't help it," said Alice, "but I must say I'm disappointed to think the old man's so ungracious."

"And I think it was a pity, too," said Jimmy, "that you told him so much of the ways you've reformed me since we were married, the way I naturally forget everything and lose everything unless you look after me. You see, he's thinking of handing over all his business to me, because he isn't satisfied with the firm of solicitors at Rosford that have handled his affairs up till now. The old partners are too old, and the young partners are too young, and he thinks I'm about right."

"Well, my dear, nothing I said can have made much difference. He can't have taken it as seriously as all that. And I did say I'd got you over all those things."

"Oh, I don't think he thought I really do lose and forget things more than most people," said Jimmy, "but I think he thought that a man whose wife talked about him like that couldn't be very good stuff."

"What a funny, old-fashioned point of view!" laughed Alice. "But I wish you'd dropped me a hint of all this. I might have said a few things that would just have turned the scales."

"I know. I was afraid of that," said Jimmy. "I think he might not have liked having his mind made up for him."

"If he's such a hopeless old crotchet as that," said Alice, "I wonder you want to have anything to do with him."

"Well, for one thing, I really do want some new business," said Jimmy. "It's odd how people don't come to me. It's almost as if one or other of us were unpopular in the county. And for another thing, I'm fond of old Norman and I'd like him to feel confidence in me for his own sake. It's worrying for an old man to have a wife thirty years younger than himself with a big estate and the responsibility of the child, and not feel that he's put some reliable person to look after her. I wanted to do that for him."

"Well, my dear, it's certain to come all right," said Alice. "We must just have him to dinner again, and I shall be specially nice to him. Are you coming to bed now, dear?"

"No, dear," said Jimmy, "not at once. I want to stay down here for five minutes and think something out."

He looked so boyish and pathetic, as he lay back in the chair with his long legs stretching out in front of him and his dark hair rumpled, and his perplexed eyes staring into the fire, that she had to bend over and kiss him as she passed. "Poor little boy!" she murmured in his ear. "You're sure you've got no special business worries? You will tell me if you have, won't you? If you've got into a muddle, it's quite likely I shall be able to think of some way out."

"Thank you, dear," said Jimmy, "there's nothing special. It's only that I'm living under a strain, and I've got to make up my mind to bear that strain."

"But what strain, darling?"

"Oh, just these difficult times, these difficult times."

She kissed the top of his head. "Poor little overwrought fellow!" she crooned, then straightened herself. "Don't be too long coming up to bed."

She enjoyed undressing in her own lovely room after having been away so long. Humming to herself she kicked off her satin shoes and peeled off her stockings, and stood on the rug in front of the fire, digging her bare toes into the clean, smooth, clipped lamb's pelt as she cast her several skins of silk. She liked the mountainous softness of her bed, with its fluffy apricot blankets and honey-coloured taffeta quilt, and the secret, sacred look the hangings gave the shadowed pillows, and the rosy, lacy nightgown they had spread out for her. In her mind's eye she saw her gaunt, voluble, wild-haired mother pacing her utilitarian room where there was a mahogany bed and a big round table with a reading lamp and many books on it, and she shuddered. "Will I ever get old?" she thought, "and stop matching my lovely room? I suppose I will some day, and quite soon too, for I am not young. It will be awful. But Jimmy will be nice to me, he will somehow spare me the worst of it. He always tries to spare me things, he is always kind. I thought he was a little fault-finding this evening, but that was only because he was tired. Oh, I am a lucky woman, I ought to be very kind to other people out of gratitude." Grave with this reflection she went into the bathroom, and as she lay in the warm waters a way she could be kind occurred to her. It was such a good plan that she longed to work it out at once, and a pricking urge to activity swept through her body, so that she had to jump out of the bath almost at once and rub herself with hot towels. Then she heard Jimmy go into the bedroom, and she flung on her dressing-gown and hurried in to tell him the news.

"Jimmy," she said, sitting down on the long stool in front of the dressing-table and brushing her hair with long, vigorous strokes, because her inspiration had filled her with vigour. "I've had an idea."

He had opened the dressing-room door, but he turned. "Well, it suits you, darling," he said, and came and stood by her, smiling as he watched her glowing face in the mirror, the flash of her arm as she passed the brush to and fro, and the changing lights in her hair.

"Listen," she explained, "I've been thinking over Madge. She can't go on as she's doing. I can't stand by and see my sister turning into a dowdy, middle-aged frump years before her time. Darling, do you realize she's a whole five years younger than I am? I must do something about it, and to-morrow morning I will. I'm going straight to Walter, and I'm going to suggest that he sends Madge for a month to that wonderful sanatorium near Dresden where they did Mrs. Lennox so much good. It's just what she wants. They give you massage and baths, and above all they won't let you be soft. They get you out of bed at seven o'clock and make you do exercises in the pine woods in a bathing dress, no matter how cold it is. She'll come back a different person. And while she's away I'll take on Betty and Godfrey—I am sure I could bring out Betty quite a lot, they don't understand her—and maybe I could look into the housekeeping books and see where the waste is, why there's always this air of pinching and scraping where there's ample money. Don't you think it's a grand idea?"

Jimmy sat down beside her on the stool. He took the hair-brush from her and laid it down on the dressing-table, then gripped both her hands with his. "Alice," he said. "Have you forgotten the promise you gave me this evening, in front of the fire? Didn't you give me your word you wouldn't interfere with Madge and Walter, or Leo and Evie any more?"

"But, heavens alive, this isn't interference!"

"My darling, what else is it?"

"It may be interference, strictly speaking, but you must admit that sometimes one just has to interfere. If Madge fell down in the road and there was a car coming along, surely you'd let me drag her out of the way?"

"Alice, won't you stop doing this thing if I tell you I'd rather you didn't?"

"No, I don't think I will. I hate the way you've suddenly started objecting to everything I do that's kind. And anyway I don't think it would be fair to Madge not to do it."

"Then," said Jimmy, "I'll have to tell you a whole lot of things that we all rather wanted to keep from you." He got up and walked to the fire and stood on the hearth, looking down on her intently. "Alice, you're all wrong about Madge and Walter. If you went to Walter to-morrow and told him that Madge ought to go to a sanatorium in Dresden, it would be monstrously cruel of you. Because he couldn't afford it."

"But, darling, it wouldn't cost much more than a hundred pounds."

"Walter hasn't got a hundred pounds."

"What do you mean, Jimmy? You must be mad. You know perfectly well they've at least three thousand pounds a year."

"They had, Alice. They haven't now. We live in bad times, and the worst of it is we've come straight to them out of times that were too good. About six years ago, when prices were rocketing, Walter sold out all his safe stuff, his gilt-edged, and bought things like steel and oil. They aren't worth a tenth of what they were. I tell you Walter hasn't got a hundred pounds. He owes quite a number of hundred pounds to the banks and the income-tax people."

"But, Jimmy, Walter must have been atrociously reckless. I do think when he had a wife and children he ought to have been more careful. I do think someone ought to speak to him . . ."

"Anyone who spoke to him would be a meddling fool that likes to kick a man when he's down. The whole world did what he did. It seemed the only sensible thing to do at the time. I'm sorry, Alice, but there isn't a single way of looking at the situation which affords one the slightest justification for feeling superior to Walter."

"Well, goodness knows, one wouldn't want that. Oh, I am sorry for them. But I do hope Madge is doing everything she can . . ."

"She's doing marvels. I've been over all the books. There isn't a woman living who could have been pluckier and more sensible. Madge is all right."

"I'm glad. Dear little Madge. But what I don't understand is why they didn't tell me? It seems a little cold and inconsiderate, when they know how fond I am of them. I can't help feeling just a weeny bit hurt . . ."

"They're hurt themselves, Alice. Walter's a proud man, and he cares for his family. He wanted to give them the best of everything, and leave them to carry on the life his stock have always lived, in the house where they've been for a couple of centuries. Now he can't give them anything but the bare necessities, they may not be able to go on living in that house. They're struggling nobly, but they may be beaten yet. While they're struggling they don't want anyone to talk to them about the tragedy, to suggest that if they had acted differently it needn't have happened, that they aren't taking it as sensibly as they might, that this and that little treat they give themselves when they're at breaking-point is an unjustifiable extravagance. That would just put the lid on their torture."

"Yes, but I obviously wouldn't be that someone. I only would have tried to help. Well, I am sorry!" She sighed and took up her hairbrush again.

Jimmy came back and sat beside her. He put his arm round her body, and kissed her ear, and she rested her cheek against his. He whispered to her and she said, "What, darling?" but then recoiled from him with annoyance, exclaiming. "No, of course I won't speak about it to them! I wouldn't care to, since they haven't chosen to tell me themselves."

"That's a good girl," said Jimmy.

Alice went on brushing her hair, and presently she smiled at the dark face she saw smiling at her in the mirror. "Aren't we lucky to have no worries?" she said. "Really, we couldn't be more at peace with ourselves and the world. But I suppose that's partly our own doing. We might have had lots of worries if we'd given way to them. I think I shall say something to Madge, you know. That's what she's doing, giving way to her troubles. Just because Walter's lost some money and she has to be careful, she needn't lie about on sofas looking dowdy and listless— Jimmy, Jimmy, what are you doing? Let go my wrist!"

"Alice, won't you please take it from me that there isn't any necessity to say anything at all to Madge, that she's one of the finest women who ever lived, and that she doesn't need any advice at all?"

"No, I can't take it from you, because I can see with my own eyes, and—Jimmy, you're hurting!"

He got up and went back to his place on the hearth-rug, and looked down on her again with that queer, intent look.

"Jimmy, what's the matter with you? Your eyes are blazing! And you haven't said you're sorry!"

He did not seem to hear. "Alice," he said, "have you ever read a fairy story where the princess lived in a beautiful palace, with a beautiful garden, and was warned by her fairy godmother that she could enjoy all this happiness for ever only if she didn't pick one particular flower, or eat one particular fruit? If she ignores that prohibition, she loses the whole thing. Our palace, our garden, our princess. It's quite an important story. You'll even find it in the Bible. And you sometimes find it coming true in real life."

"Jimmy, what are you talking about?"

"The point is that the fairy godmother's perfectly right, though there's no reason on the surface to show that she is. When the princess picks that flower or eats that fruit, the whole thing really does fall to pieces. If I ask you to take me as a fairy godmother, and ask you not to speak to Madge about being listless, will you remember and grant me this favour? Do it, do it, darling. Let's pretend we're people in a fairy-tale."

Alice turned her back on him and stared into the mirror, and presently saw him reflected just behind her. "Well," she began, but he said, "No. You needn't make any promise or half-promise. I can see from your face that you'd speak to Madge, if I went down on my knees, if the heavens opened. You couldn't possibly give up such a good opportunity of ordering somebody about, of making them feel inferior to you, of making their destiny seem so that if it worked out well they'd have to thank you for it, and not themselves."

"Jimmy!"

"Now listen. Madge doesn't lie on sofas and look dowdy because she's a sloven. She does it because she's ill. So ill that it's an effort for her to walk, to put on her clothes."

"Jimmy, you're dreaming! Madge has always made a fuss about little ailments, but she's as strong as a horse."

"Alice, Leo arranged for her to see a specialist six months ago, and I sneaked up to town to go with them. He said there wasn't any doubt. She's got pernicious anaemia."

"Oh, my dear, I know all about that. There's a wonderful new treatment for pernicious anaemia. I'll soon see to it that . . ."

"Alice, there isn't anything you can see to. There is a wonderful new treatment for pernicious anaemia, which cures everybody except two or three people out of every hundred. And the trouble is that Madge seems to be one of those two or three people. She's persevering with the treatment, and the tide may turn at any moment, but up till now she's been getting worse and worse. Do you understand? She's very, very ill."

Alice stood up. Her hairbrush slipped from her hand to the floor. "Oh, poor little Madge! My poor little Madge!" she whispered.

Jimmy gathered her into his arms. "I knew you'd feel pretty bad when you heard that," he said. "I've always known you really cared for her a lot. Cry if you want to, dear."

But she swallowed her tears and drew away from him briskly, saying, "But we ought to do something! What can we do for her?"

"Heavens alive, why should we have to do anything? Why must you always try to be omnipotent, and shove things about? Tragic things happen sometimes that we just have to submit to. We can't do anything in this particular case except stand by and be sorry for little Madge, and hope that the tide will turn, and give her as many presents and treats as we can. And above all we mustn't ever talk of it again. We mustn't even think of it, in case it shows in our talk, because Walter doesn't know."

"Walter doesn't know! But that's absurd. He ought to be told."

"Dear, he's having a hard struggle. Madge doesn't want him to be worried by knowing that she's dangerously ill. Particularly when the danger might pass and he'd have had the worry all for nothing. Besides, it's Madge's husband, and it's Madge's secret, and it's for Madge to decide whether he shall be told."

"But, really, Jimmy, I think you're wrong. Walter ought to be told. It's only fair to him. You know how irritable he is. I've often heard him say things to her lately that he wouldn't have said if he'd known how ill she was."

"Alice, I think I'll kill you if you don't promise not to tell Walter."

"Jimmy! What a queer, exaggerated thing to say! What's the matter with you to-night, Jimmy? I've never known you like this."

"Stop staring into that mirror. Put down that hairbrush. Turn round and look at me."

She wriggled round on the stool, her lip quivering. "It was your face I was looking at in the mirror, Jimmy."

"Listen," he said, "because I'm going to tell you the truth . . ."

"Don't tell me anything to-night. I'm tired and you're tired . . ."

"I'm going to tell you the truth about yourself, and I'm going to do it now, because it may be too late to-morrow. Alice, you're the salt of the earth. In all the twenty years I've known you I've never seen you fail once in honesty or courage or generosity. You wouldn't tell a lie if you were to gain a million pounds by it. You'd hold your hand in the fire to save a person or a principle you valued. You'd give away your last crust to anyone you felt as kin. I know perfectly well that now you've learned Madge is hard up you'll cover her with presents, even if it means you have to go without things yourself. And besides that, you've got a kind of touching, childish quality—a kind of—a kind of . . ."

"Jimmy, what's the matter with you? Why, you're almost crying! What's the . . ."

"Well, we'll leave that. The point is that nobody likes having salt rubbed into their wounds, even if it is the salt of the earth."

He bent over her like a boxer, peering at a recumbent adversary to see how his blow had told; but her blue gaze returned his steadily. "I'm afraid I'm not clever enough for all this," she said. "I haven't the vaguest notion of what you're driving at."

"I'm trying to tell you that you hurt people. You hurt them continually and intolerably. You find out everybody's vulnerable point and you shoot arrows at it, sharp, venomed arrows. They stick, and from time to time you give them a twist."

"Jimmy . . ."

"I know why you want to talk to Walter. You'll point out to him that he's been sharp to Madge several times lately, and that she's probably a dying woman. That'll harrow him. It'll add remorse to the agony he'll be filled with by the dread of losing her. It'll turn a simple, honourable grief to something shameful and humiliating. But it'll do worse than that. Walter's a man who lives on his temper. He can't find his way in action unless he lets himself go. When something happens he's quite incapable of thinking it out quietly. He has to swear and storm and stamp about, and at the end of all the fuss some definite plan has crystallized in his mind, and he can get on with it. Madge doesn't care when he snaps at her, she knows perfectly well that at the bottom of his heart he hasn't a thought except for her and the children. But if you pretend to him that what he did in temper was of deadly importance, then you break his mainspring. He'll go about cowed and broken, he won't be able to stand up to life. That's the worst of you, Alice. You find out what people live by, and you kill it."

Alice said gravely, "Jimmy, I don't understand this. Are you telling me that Madge and Walter have been talking against me? I've sometimes thought Madge wasn't quite loyal."

"Oh, stop talking nonsense."

"But you're being rude!"

"No loyalty can live near you. You are disloyalty itself. Of course we talk against you behind your back. We have to protect ourselves. You're out to kill your nearest and dearest. No, sit still. I've got a whole lot more to tell you. Do you want to know the real reason why you aren't welcome in Leo's house? You think it's because Evie's jealous of you. That is the most utter rubbish. The trouble about Evie, if there is any trouble about Evie, is that she's over-trained. She's had every instinctive naughtiness like jealousy educated out of her. If she thought your brother was fonder of you than of her she'd set her teeth and invite you to lunch, tea, and dinner, at her house for every day in the week. But she knows that Leo can't bear you. Oh, he loves you, as we all do, because we know that apart from this devilish cruelty you're an angel, and because you've got this queer power of seeming a pitiful child that one can't help loving. But you frighten Leo. You see, he came back from the war after he'd been gassed, and forgot it. He felt splendid, and he married Evie, and they had four children. Then he had to remember he'd been gassed. He had that attack of pneumonia, and that slow recovery. And every day when he was getting better you went and saw him, and you sat and looked at him with those round eyes and asked, with an air of prudence and helpfulness that meant damn-all, "But what are you going to do, Leo, if you have a breakdown and have to give up your practice?"

"Well," said Alice, "if a sister can't express her concern when her only brother's ill, I really don't know what we're coming to."

"Darling, don't you see what you were doing? You were up to your murderous tricks again. You were killing the thing by which he lived. He knows his number's up. He knows that one winter's day he'll get pneumonia, and then he'll die. And he doesn't want to die. He doesn't want to leave Evie. He adores her wit and her carelessness and her funny offhand way of treating everything as if it were a joke. People do, you know. Leo and Evie have a lot more friends than we have, you know. He doesn't want to leave his children either. And especially he doesn't want to leave Evie and the children deadly hard-up as he knows he will. So the only way he can get on from day to day is to forget that he's ill and going to die. But every time you come near him you remind him of it. 'How's the cough to-day?' you say. 'Oh, Leo, you ought to be careful.' My God, if you knew how often Evie's telephoned me, 'He's feeling low to-day, for God's sake keep her away . . .'"

"Jimmy," said Alice, "are you admitting to me that behind my back you've entered into a conspiracy against me with that woman?"

"But don't you understand that I'm telling you something real and true that you've got to listen to? This is something that you've done and mustn't go on doing. You've tortured Leo. Don't you realize that's why the eldest boy hates you so? Colin adores his father and he knows that every time you go to the house you leave him fit to cut his throat with depression. Naturally he gets black in the face when he sees you. But you're wrong when you hate him just as you're wrong when you like that abominable little pest Betty. She's becoming practically what they call a problem child. Just about her age children often start imitating some particular person in their surroundings, and somewhere in Betty's surroundings she seems to have found somebody who is an aggressive prig and public nuisance, who spends the whole of her forcible personality in proving everybody else her inferior. I can't think who it can be, of course. But anyway, she's almost driving the family mad. Will you try and realize in future when you try to stir up trouble against Colin that you do it because the boy comes between you and somebody you're trying to hurt, and when you encourage Betty it's because you scent she's going to be as cruel as yourself?"

Alice turned round on the stool and began to brush her hair again. "You're simply being rude," she said icily. "I think you'd better sleep in the dressing-room to-night."

"Oh, for God's sake listen to me and try to understand! Don't you realize that there's something wrong in this household and that we've got to alter it? Hasn't it struck you as odd that we've got no friends? People come here to formal dinner-parties and they ask us back, but they keep at arm's length. They're afraid of us. They're afraid of you. Look how you got old Norman on the hip to-night. Look how we can't keep our servants. And look how your own mother had to pack up and leave the town where she was born because she couldn't bear your tongue . . ."

"Oh, Jimmy, Jimmy, you mustn't say that!"

"It's true. You couldn't bear to admit her qualities, that she was brilliant and erratic and a marvellous story-teller. You built up a pretence that she was silly and untidy and garrulous. Didn't you tell me to-day what a shame it was that she'd made the young man who brought you here listen to the story of how she met Edward VII at Monte Carlo? Well, you're no fool. You ought to see that that's one of the funniest stories in the world, that she tells it superbly, and that the whelp whoever he was, was damn lucky to have the chance of hearing it. But you don't see that because you want to make her out senile and worthless. Well, she knew that perfectly. She went to Madge and Leo crying and said that she hated leaving them, but that you made her feel she ought to be either in her coffin or in a home for the aged . . ."

"Stop, Jimmy, stop! I know that's true!" She was crying now, with the deep, painful interminable sobs of a child, with their overtone of rebellion against wrong.

"Oh, my poor little girl, don't cry!" He had taken her into his arms, he was pulling out his big handkerchief. "You don't know how I've hated saying all this."

"But it's true about mother. I know that it's true about mother. She was so horrid to me."

"Horrid to you? But she was crazy with anxiety when—when you were ill, and she wrote again and again saying how much she wanted you to come down and have your convalescence with her. Don't think she doesn't love you. We all love you—only . . ."

"No. No. She doesn't love me. She was horrid to me last night. I did everything I could to be nice to her, I helped her in all sorts of little ways. But when I told her that I was going home two days earlier than I had meant, she was glad. She gave an awful look of relief that I'll never forget." She rubbed her weeping face against his coat-collar, but raised it to accuse him with miserable puzzled eyes. "Of course mother's always been horrid about me underneath, and of course we haven't any friends. People have always loved being nasty to me all my life. The girls at school gave me a most horrible time. And I've always minded it so because I do so like people to like me." Sobs choked her. "That young man—who brought me home in his car—he liked me."

"I'm glad of that," said Jimmy. "Poor little Alice, I'm glad of that."

For a minute her memory blotted out this hot room full of quarrelling, and built round her the fresh morning on the moors, with its background of sooty branches and sharp green buds, its music of birds singing high in blue shower-washed space, its foreground of forget-me-nots bending all one way under a glassy grey current. She remembered how gravely the boy's eyes had rested on her face, how gravely he had said good-bye. Then her face was contorted with a fresh spasm of weeping. "People are always so nice to me at first," she murmured, "but afterwards when I got to know them something hateful happens to them and they turn round and are cruel to me. But what I can't understand is why quite suddenly you've taken sides with them against me."

He gently pushed her away from him and took her face between his hands. "Alice, is that really all that I've been saying has meant to you? Haven't I made you feel the slightest suspicion that maybe you do things to people which they think horrid?"

"You've been talking a terrible lot of nonsense," said Alice. "What's the use of pretending that a dreadful boy like Colin, who sticks out his underlip when he sees you and looks awful and hasn't any manners, is a nice child, and that a charming little girl like Betty, who's always polite and clean and well-behaved, is for some obscure reason a little horror? And as for the rest, I think I understand only too well, thank you. For one thing it's perfectly plain that you've been listening to Evie. She's apparently made some wonderful story out of the simple fact that, being fond of my only brother, I've guessed that there's something wrong with his health, and shown a very natural anxiety. And as for Madge, I can see she's been disloyal. But sisters often are, and I never thought poor Madge was perfect, and I won't let it make a bit of difference. What worries me is that you should have listened to all these people when they were being spiteful about me."

"But, Alice, hasn't what I've said made any difference to you at all? Don't you feel that you've been doing some things that maybe, after what you've heard, you'd better stop doing?"

"No, I don't," said Alice. "It seems to me that what you've been attacking me about, thanks to all this nonsense you've been listening to, is just what you have to do when you're one of a family. I can't suddenly pretend that I haven't got any relations. Why, they'd be the first to be hurt. If I stopped going round to Evie's and helping her to clear up the messes she's always getting into, there'd be no end to her complaints."

"Sometimes," said Jimmy, "you don't strike me as a grown-up, wicked person at all. You strike me as a child who for some extraordinary reason wants to be punished and who goes on behaving worse and worse so that she'll compel somebody or other to punish her. Do you really mean to go on just the same?"

"Yes, I think so. If there's anything particularly you object to, I might . . ."

"Do you mean, for instance, to speak to Walter about Madge?"

She sat down on the stool again, and stretched behind her for the hairbrush with an enchanting gesture. "As a matter of fact, I do."

"Alice!"

"You see, I must." She squared her jaw and looked like an exquisitely beautiful, tear-stained little bull-dog.

"Why?"

"I happen to know something about Walter that makes it necessary."

"What's that?"

"Walter hasn't always been the husband to Madge that he ought to be."

"You mean he's been unfaithful to her? Ah, that little blonde slut at Cadeford."

"And he'd better be warned that this is no time for that sort of thing."

Jimmy whistled. "You could have a whole lot of fun out of that, couldn't you?" he said. "You might even get poor Walter into such a state of dither that he confessed everything to Madge, and that would kill her outright. She doesn't understand that sort of thing, God bless her. Really, this is a find of yours, Alice. With your peculiar gift there's no end to what you might be able to make of it."

He slid to the floor at her feet so suddenly, and in so limp a heap that she thought he had fainted, and was about to scream when he gripped her knees, laid his head on her lap, and spoke softly, "Alice, remember what I said to you. About the unreasonable requests in the fairy-tale, and how the threats came true. That if the flower was eaten, the fruit plucked, the castle falls to pieces. I'm going to make another of those unreasonable requests."

"My dear, I'm tired. This is my first night home, and I'd hoped for something rather different. What is it?"

He raised his head and his eyes implored her. "Let me sell the business. Let's sell this house. Let's go abroad. Let's stop bothering about Madge and Walter, and Leo and Evie, and just be ourselves. We wouldn't be rich, but with what Father left me, we'd have enough for comfort. Please, Alice. Please."

"Jimmy, I can't fathom you to-night. Do you really mean this?"

"I mean it more seriously than I've ever meant anything in my life."

"You seriously mean that for no reason you want us to sell all our beautiful things and give up my family and my friends, and wander about as if we'd done something awful and had to live abroad? Jimmy, I really think you're mad."

His head dropped back in her lap. It felt as heavy as a lump of lead, as if he were asleep. Then he looked up, and she saw with a kind of faint disgust, for she hated emotional displays in men, that the tears were thick on his lashes. "Forgive me, Alice," he said. "I think I've been mad, too, all evening. I've said cruel things to you, and they were useless as well as cruel. However, that's all over. You're a wonderful woman, Alice. You've got me right back where I was before you went away. As I was during your illness and before it. Perfectly sane." He jumped lightly to his feet and gave her a loud, almost a smacking kiss on the cheek. "Well, I'll go and undress now. The time's over for talk."

"I'm glad you're sensible again," she said, "and if I've irritated you by sticking to my point about Walter, do forgive me. But, you see, I am so fond of Madge."

"And just how fond I am of Madge," he answered, "is one of the things that you will probably never know."

The dressing-room door closed softly behind him. She sighed with relief that the scene was over, and went on with her hair, putting down her brush and using her comb. But she had to admit that she felt shattered by this curious breakdown of Jimmy's, this appearance of frenzy and unreason in a character that had seemed till now wholly free from them. When a coal fell from the fire, she started; and when behind the swaying red taffeta curtains there was a tap on one of the windows, she swung round and said aloud, "What's that?" and again there opened around her, an image of a lost paradise, of foregone security and peace, the sense of that blue cold noon on the clean heath. Then she remembered that the ivy had not yet been pruned this year, and that its dark arms often stretched as far as the window-panes, and she turned about again. But she felt uneasy and tearful, and was glad when Jimmy came in again, slim and well-made in the dark blue silk dressing-gown she had given him for Christmas, which he would wear only seldom, because he said it was too dandified for ordinary occasions.

He came and stood beside her, and she stopped combing her hair while she studied his reflection, and she uttered a faint exclamation of dismay.

"Anything the matter?" said Jimmy.

"No. Only when I was in the New Forest with that young man this morning, I looked at him and thought he was very good-looking, but that he hadn't something in his face which you have, and which I specially love. . . ."

"Yes?"

"And now I see what it is. It's your mouth."

"Well?"

"And yet your mouth's cruel. Your lips are full, but you hold them so that they're thin—it's a cruel mouth."

"Is it?" He bent down close to the glass. "It may be. It's hard to tell about oneself. I think I hate it when I have to be cruel, but maybe I don't. Probably one never gets into a position when one's forced to do something unless one really wants to do it."

"Jimmy . . ." she threw her comb down on the dressing-table. "I wish you wouldn't go on being so horrible and hateful and queer. I know I seem not to have any nerves, but I have, really. I'm frightened of lots of things. I have those nightmares, you know."

"What are your nightmares about?" he asked. "You've never told me what they actually were about."

"Why, I am standing in a room—now I come to think of it, it's this room—and something awful comes nearer and nearer to me, circling round me, drawing in on me, and I know that in the end it's going to destroy me utterly."

"And you can't stop it?"

"No. The funny thing is—now, that's something else I never re-membered before after I'd woken up—I could perfectly well stop this awful horror coming at me. Only for some reason I can't. I have to go on doing the very thing that brings it nearer."

Jimmy turned away from the mirror. "God, what a life this is," he said, "full of presciences that don't do us any good, full of self-consciousness that tortures us by telling us just what sort of hole we're in but never how to get out of it. It's nothing to cling on to, really."

"Jimmy, you're being odd again," she said. "Please don't. I can't stand it, my first night home." There ran before her mind's eye pictures of everything which had happened to her during this day which had risen so early to its peak, which was falling, in spite of all she could do, to such a dark, perplexing decline, and the memory of her first, slow, satisfied inspection of her home made her exclaim: "Oh, Jimmy, I found two things in your room that interested me."

He was at one of the windows now, staring out into the night between the red curtains, but now he strolled back to her. "What were they?"

"Well, you know that big photograph of me in my wedding dress? Just think, it's been torn nearly the whole way across!"

"No!"

"Yes, really. Whoever did it tried to cover it up by gumming the edges together, but now the gum's got old and it's cracked, and the tear shows again. I thought at first it was a hair under the glass. It must have been that dreadfully clumsy housemaid we once had called Lilian Hall."

"I wonder if it was."

"It would be Lilian, she ruined everything she touched. Then the other thing was the tube of white powder in your pocket."

"You found that too?"

"Yes. What is it?"

He dug down into his dressing-gown pocket and showed it to her on the palm of his hand.

"Yes, that's the thing," she said. "It looks like one of old Dr. Godstone's phials."

"That's just what it is," he said. "Once in his dispensary I picked it up, years ago, and he told me what it was. Then long after when he died and I was going through his effects I saw it and remembered the name on the label, and I slipped it in my pocket, though I never thought I'd need it then. Yet I suppose I must have known I would, really, or I would never have taken it."

"Well, there's no label on it now. What's it for?" said Alice.

"It's just something that sends people to sleep."

"But if you want anything of that sort, why don't you go down to Leo and get him to give you whatever's most thoroughly up-to-date? You know what old Dr. Godstone was. This is probably something that was used in the Ark."

"Oh, don't be too harsh on the old man. There's nothing wrong with this. It works quite all right if you give it in the right dose. If you give too little it's no good; and if you give too much that's bad, too. But if you give the right dose, there's no more trouble."

"Well, I suppose that's all right, provided you know the right dose."

"I do now," he said. He sighed deeply and stood for a second or two rolling it backwards and forwards on his palm, as though he would not be sorry to drop it; but he kept his eyes on it all the time. "I only found that out ten days ago. Saturday before last I felt restless all the morning. . . ."

"Oh, darling, I ought never to have left you," said Alice, "but I wrote you every Monday, Wednesday, and Friday, so you must have had a letter from me that morning."

"I had," said Jimmy. "Well, in the afternoon I got out the car and drove right across England to Bathwick. I'd never been there before in my life, I don't know anybody there. When I found myself driving past the Public Library I stopped and walked in, just as if I was a good Bathwick ratepayer, and consulted a book on drugs. And I got the proper dose."

"Well, it seems a casual way of taking medicine," said Alice, "but I suppose you'll be careful. Come in, Ethel." But it was Cook who came in with a glass and a steaming jug on a tray. She put it down on the dressing-table with a clatter, and her body was solid as masonry with grimness.

"Seeing as how there was unpleasantness about the new brand of chocolate," she said, ignoring Alice's absent smile, "I came up myself to explain that this is the old brand which I got through sending my sister's girl special down to the stores."

"Good gracious, is Minnie back from her place in London? I'm afraid they'll never keep her anywhere you know, she's so untidy. . . ."

"She's home on her holidays, while the family's gone to Italy," said Cook with quiet triumph and shut the door with a bang.

"What's all that about?" asked Jimmy. He was still rolling the phial of powder backwards and forwards across his palm, and looking at it as if it were a jewel.

"Oh, a fuss about nothing. She's a rude woman, and she'll have to go. It's only that she bought another brand of chocolate malted milk," said Alice, filling her glass from the jug, "and I like this. The sort she got was mawkish stuff, I could taste the malted milk through the chocolate, and I hate that. This is very strong, you can't taste anything but the chocolate."

"So if you hadn't made a row with Cook, you'd be drinking something with a milder flavour to-night?" said Jimmy. "By God, that's funny."

"Why?" asked Alice, and raised the glass to her lips. But she set it down again, because Jimmy was holding up his finger and jerking his head towards the door, "What's the matter?"

"Why has Cook gone down the passage to the spare rooms instead of going upstairs to her bedroom?"

"Has she?"

"Yes, I heard her."

"What an extraordinary thing. But these women," she tiptoed to the door, opened it softly, and stood for a minute on the darkened landing, peering down the passage and listening. But she heard nothing save the creaks and stirrings that are the voice of an old house at night, and presently she heard Cook's ponderous tread across the ceiling above her. She went back into the bedroom and said, "Jimmy, you're dreaming," and sat down at her dressing-table and drank her chocolate.

Jimmy did not answer her, and she turned and looked at him over the rim of her glass. He was standing on the rug in front of the fire, his hands shoved so deeply into the pockets of his dressing-gown that his shoulders were hunched up, and his tallness looked rangy and wolfish. He was watching her with eyes that stared like a fever patient's, and his teeth pulled in his lower lip and let it go, again and again, as if he were enduring agony.

"But you look so ill," she said, and set down her glass.

"Drink up that chocolate!" he told her, and she obeyed, then turned to him, her brows knit in annoyance, her lips parted, waiting for an explanation. But he said nothing, only came towards her and took the empty glass out of her hand with so curt a movement that she cried out in protest. It was a movement of a quality utterly unexpected in him, quite unlike any gesture she had ever seen him make throughout all the years they had been together. So might a burglar have snatched a ring from her finger. She stared at his back as he hurried out of the room, and put her hands to her head, trying to puzzle it out, when she heard the bathroom taps running.

"But what are you doing?" she asked as he came in with the clean glass in his hand and put it down, on the tray beside her, and poured into it what chocolate was left in the jug. "What are you doing?" she repeated, as he poured the chocolate back again out of the glass into the jug.

Her own voice sounded far away in her ears, but his voice sounded further away as he answered, "Just taking precautions that probably won't be successful, but I really don't care much about that."

She wanted to ask him to repeat what he had said, and say it more intelligibly, but then she thought she would rather tell him that she felt very ill. Sweat had come out on her forehead, snakes seemed to be sliding through her bowels, she wished she could either sit in a chair with a back to it or lie down, she was afraid she was going to slip down on the floor. She found it, however, difficult to speak. But Jimmy had seen for himself what was happening. She felt his hands slip under her armpits, and knew that he was carrying her over to the bed. With a great effort, for her lids were now very heavy, she opened her eyes and tried to see his face, and though everything shimmered glassy and wavered about her, she was sure that he was looking sorry for her, and as he laid her down and drew the blankets over her, she caught the words, heard indistinctly as through the surf of a tremendous sea, "Poor little Alice." She rolled over, cooling her damp forehead against the fresh linen pillow-slip, and moaning, because she knew that it meant something, if she could but collect her wits and think what it was, that now the taste of chocolate had gone, her mouth was full of haunting bitterness. But she was too tired, she could only mutter that she wanted some water.

# THE GENTLEMAN FROM PARIS

## *John Dickson Carr*

JOHN DICKSON CARR (1905–    ) was the son of a Congressman father who wished for him a political career in their native Pennsylvania. But the three fictional heroes of his boyhood—Sherlock Holmes, d'Artagnan and the Wizard of Oz—inspired in him a wish to write. He has carried their banner successfully through many long and prolific years with books of mystery and adventure that have made their author a leader in that field. He seems especially attracted by plots with some historical association. Following a long residence in England, Mr. Carr and his wife now live in Mamaroneck, New York, with their three children.

> Carlton House Hotel
> Broadway, New-York
> 14th April, 1849

**M**Y DEAR BROTHER:
Were my hand more steady, Maurice, or my soul less agitated, I should have written to you before this. *All is safe:* so much I tell you at once. For the rest, I seek sleep in vain; not merely because I find myself a stranger and a foreigner in New-York. Listen and judge.

We discussed, I think, the humiliation that a Frenchman must go to England ere he could take passage in a reliable ship for America. The *Britannia* steam-packet departed from Liverpool on the second of the month, and arrived here on the seventeenth. Do not smile, I implore you, when I tell you that my first visit on American soil was to Platt's Saloon, under Wallack's Theatre.

Great God, that voyage!

On my stomach I could hold not even champagne. For one of my height and breadth I was as weak as a child.

"Be good enough," I said to a fur-capped coachman, when I had struggled through the horde of Irish immigrants, "to drive me to some fashionable place of refreshment."

The coachman had no difficulty in understanding my English, which pleased me. And how extraordinary are these "saloons!"

The saloon of M. Platt was loud with the thump of hammers cracking ice, which is delivered in large blocks. Though the hand-coloured gas-globes, and the rose-paintings on the front of the bar-counter, were as fine as we could see at the Three Provincial Brothers in Paris, yet I confess that the place did not smell so agreeably. A number of gentlemen, wearing hats perhaps a trifle taller than is fashionable at home, lounged at the bar-counter and shouted. I attracted no attention until I called for a sherry cobbler.

One of the "bartenders," as they are called in New-York, gave me a sharp glance as he prepared the glass.

"Just arrived from the Old Country, I bet?" said he in no unfriendly tone.

Though it seemed strange to hear France mentioned in this way, I smiled and bowed assent.

"Italian, maybe?" said he.

This bartender, of course, could not know how deadly was the insult.

"Sir," I replied, "I am a Frenchman."

And now in truth he was pleased! His fat face opened and smiled like a distorted, gold-toothed flower.

"Is that so, now!" he exclaimed. "And what might your name be? Unless"—and here his face darkened with that sudden defensiveness and suspicion which, for no reason I can discern, will often strike into American hearts—"unless," said he, "you don't want to give it?"

"Not at all," I assured him earnestly. "I am Armand de Lafayette, at your service."

My dear brother, what an extraordinary effect!

It was silence. All sounds, even the faint whistling of the gas-jets, seemed to die away in that stone-flagged room. Every man along the line of the bar was looking at me. I was conscious only of faces, mostly with whiskers under the chin instead of down the cheekbones, turned on me in basilisk stare.

"Well, well, well!" almost sneered the bartender. "You wouldn't be no relation of the *Marquis* de Lafayette, would you?"

It was my turn to be astonished. Though our father has always forbidden us to mention the name of our late uncle, due to his republican sympathies, yet I knew he occupied small place in the history of France and it puzzled me to comprehend how these people had heard of him.

"The late Marquis de Lafayette," I was obliged to admit, "was my uncle."

"You better be careful, young feller," suddenly yelled a grimy little man with a pistol buckled under his long coat. "We don't like being diddled, we don't."

"Sir," I replied, taking my bundle of papers from my pocket and whacking them down on the bar-counter, "have the goodness to examine my credentials. Should you still doubt my identity, we can then debate the matter in any way which pleases you."

"This is furrin writing," shouted the bartender. "*I can't read it!*"

And then—how sweet was the musical sound on my ear!—I heard a voice addressing me in my own language.

"Perhaps, sir," said the voice, in excellent French and with great stateliness, "I may be able to render you some small service."

The newcomer, a slight man of dark complexion, drawn up under an old shabby cloak of military cut, stood a little way behind me. If I had met him on the boulevards, I might not have found him very prepossessing. He had a wild and wandering eye, with an even wilder shimmer of brandy. He was not very steady on his feet. And yet, Maurice, his manner! It was such that I instinctively raised my hat, and the stranger very gravely did the same.

"And to whom," said I, "have I the honour . . . ?"

"I am Thaddeus Perley, sir, at your service."

"Another furriner!" said the grimy little man, in disgust.

"I am indeed a foreigner," said M. Perley in English, with an accent like a knife. "A foreigner to this dram-shop. A foreigner to this neighbourhood. A foreigner to——" Here he paused, and his eyes acquired an almost frightening blaze of loathing. "Yet I never heard that the reading of French was so *very* singular an accomplishment."

Imperiously—and yet, it seemed to me, with a certain shrinking nervousness—M. Perley came closer and lifted the bundle of papers.

"Doubtless," he said loftily, "I should not be credited were I to translate these. But here," and he scanned several of the papers, "is a letter of introduction in English. It is addressed to President Zachary Taylor from the American minister at Paris."

Again, my brother, what an enormous silence! It was interrupted by a cry from the bartender, who had snatched the documents from M. Perley.

"Boys, this is no diddle," said he. "This gent is the real thing!"

"He ain't!" thundered the little grimy man, with incredulity.

"He is!" said the bartender. "I'll be a son of a roe (*i.e. biche*), if he ain't!"

Well, Maurice, you and I have seen how Paris mobs can change. Americans are even more emotional. In the wink of an eye hostility became frantic affection. My back was slapped, my hand wrung, my person jammed against the bar by a crowd fighting to order me more refreshment.

The name of Lafayette, again and again, rose like a holy diapason. In vain I asked why this should be so. They appeared to think I was joking, and roared with laughter. I thought of M. Thaddeus Perley, as one who could supply an explanation.

But in the first rush towards me M. Perley had been flung backwards. He fell sprawling in some wet stains of tobacco juice on the floor, and now I could not see him at all. For myself, I was weak from lack of food. A full beaker of whisky, which I was obliged to drink because all eyes were on me, made my head reel. Yet I felt compelled to raise my voice above the clamour.

"Gentlemen," I implored them, "will you hear me?"

"Silence for Lafayette!" said a big but very old man, with faded red whiskers. He had tears in his eyes, and he had been humming a catch called "Yankee Doodle." "Silence for Lafayette!"

"Believe me," said I, "I am full of gratitude for your hospitality. But I have business in New-York, business of immediate and desperate urgency. If you will allow me to pay my reckoning . . ."

"Your money's no good here, monseer," said the bartender. "You're going to get liquored-up good and proper."

"But I have no wish, believe me, to become liquored-up! It might well endanger my mission! In effect, I wish to go!"

"Wait a minute," said the little grimy man, with a cunning look. "What is this here business?"

You, Maurice, have called me quixotic. I deny this. You have also called me imprudent. Perhaps you are right; but what choice was left to me?

"Has any gentleman here," I asked, "heard of Madame Thevenet? Madame Thevenet, who lives at number 23 Thomas Street, near Hudson Street?"

I had not, of course, expected an affirmative reply. Yet, in addition to one or two snickers at mention of the street, several nodded their heads.

"Old miser woman?" asked a sportif character, who wore chequered trousers.

"I regret, sir, that you correctly describe her. Madame Thevenet is very rich. And I have come here," cried I, "to put right a damnable injustice!"

Struggle as I might, I could not free myself.

"How's that?" asked half a dozen.

"Madame Thevenet's daughter, Mademoiselle Claudine, lives in the worst of poverty at Paris. Madame herself has been brought here, under

some spell, by a devil of a woman calling herself . . . Gentlemen, I
implore you!"

"And I bet you," cried the little grimy man with the pistol, "you're
sweet on this daughter what's-her-name?" He seemed delighted. "Ain't
you, now?"

How, I ask of all Providence, could these people have surprised my
secret? Yet I felt obliged to tell the truth.

"I will not conceal from you," I said, "that I have in truth a high
regard for Mlle Claudine. But this lady, believe me, is engaged to a
friend of mine, an officer of artillery."

"Then what do you *get* out of it? Eh?" asked the grimy little man,
with another cunning look.

The question puzzled me. I could not reply. But the bartender with
the gold teeth leaned over.

"If you want to see the old Frenchie alive, monseer," said he, "you'd
better git." (*Sic,* Maurice.) "I hearn tell she had a stroke this morning."

But a dozen voices clamoured to keep me there, though this last
intelligence sent me into despair. Then up rose the big and very old
man with the faded whiskers: indeed, I had never realised how old,
because he seemed so hale.

"Which of you was with Washington?" said he, suddenly taking hold
of the fierce little man's neckcloth, and speaking with contempt. "Make
way for the nephew of Lafayette!"

They cheered me then, Maurice. They hurried me to the door, they
begged me to return, they promised they would await me. One glance
I sought—nor can I say why—for M. Thaddeus Perley. He was sitting
at a table by a pillar, under an open gas-jet; his face whiter than ever,
still wiping stains of tobacco-juice from his cloak.

Never have I seen a more mournful prospect than Thomas Street,
when my cab set me down there. Perhaps it was my state of mind;
for if Mme Thevenet had died without a sou left to her daughter:
you conceive it?

The houses of Thomas Street were faced with dingy yellow brick,
and a muddy sky hung over the chimney-pots. It had been warm all
day, yet I found my spirit intolerably oppressed. Though heaven knows
our Parisian streets are dirty enough, we do not allow pigs in them.
Except for these, nothing moved in the forsaken street save a blind
street-musician, with his dog and an instrument called a banjo; but
even he was silent too.

For some minutes, it seemed to me, I plied the knocker at number
23, with hideous noise. Nothing stirred. Finally, one part of the door
swung open a little, as for an eye. Whereupon I heard the shifting of
a floor-bolt, and both doors were swung open.

Need I say that facing me stood the woman whom we have agreed to call Mademoiselle Jezebel?

She said to me: "And then, M. Armand?"

"Madame Thevenet!" cried I. "She is still alive?"

"She is alive," replied my companion, looking up at me from under the lids of her greenish eyes. "But she is completely paralysed."

I have never denied, Maurice, that Mlle Jezebel has a certain attractiveness. She is not old or even middle-aged. Were it not that her complexion is as muddy as was the sky above us then, she would have been pretty.

"And as for Claudine," I said to her, "what daughter of madame. . . ."

"You have come too late M. Armand."

And well I remember that at this moment there rose up, in the mournful street outside, the tinkle of the banjo played by the street-musician. It moved closer, playing a popular catch whose words run something thus:

> Oh, I come from Alabama
> With my banjo on my knee;
> I depart for Louisiana
> My Susannah for to see.

Across the lips of mademoiselle flashed a smile of peculiar quality, like a razor-cut before the blood comes.

"Gold," she whispered. "Ninety thousand persons, one hears, have gone to seek it. Go to California, M. Armand. It is the only place you will find gold."

This tune, they say, is a merry tune. It did not seem so, as the dreary twanging faded away. Mlle Jezebel with her muddy blond hair parted in the middle and drawn over her ears after the best fashion, faced me implacably. Her greenish eyes were wide open. Her old brown taffeta dress, full at the bust, narrow at the waist, rustled its wide skirts as she glided a step forward.

"Have the kindness," I said, "to stand aside. I wish to enter."

Hitherto in my life I had seen her docile and meek.

"You are no relative," she said. "I will not allow you to enter."

"In that case, I regret, I must."

"If you had ever spoken one kind word to *me*," whispered mademoiselle, looking up from under her eyelids, and with her breast heaving, "one gesture of love—that is to say, of affection—you might have shared five million francs."

"Stand aside, I say!"

"As it is, you prefer a doll-faced consumptive at Paris. So be it!"

I was raging, Maurice; I confess it; yet I drew myself up with coldness.

"You refer, perhaps, to Claudine Thevenet?"

"And to whom else?"

"I might remind you, mademoiselle, that the lady is pledged to my good friend Lieutenant Delage. I have forgotten her."

"Have you?" asked our Jezebel, with her eyes on my face and a strange hungry look in them. Mlle Jezebel added, with more pleasure: "Well, she will die. Unless you can solve a mystery."

"A mystery?"

"I should not have said mystery, M. Armand. Because it is impossible of all solution. It is an Act of God!"

Up to this time the glass-fronted doors of the vestibule had stood open behind her, against a darkness of closed shutters in the house. There breathed out of it an odour of unswept carpets, a sourness of stale living. Someone was approaching, carrying a lighted candle.

"Who speaks," called a man's voice; shaky, but as French as Mlle Jezebel's. "Who speaks concerning an Act of God?"

I stepped across the threshold. Mademoiselle, who never left my side, immediately closed and locked the front doors. As the candle-glimmer moved still closer in gloom, I could have shouted for joy to see the man whom (as I correctly guessed) I had come to meet.

"You are M. Duroc, the lawyer!" I said. "You are my brother's friend!"

M. Duroc held the candle higher, to inspect me.

He was a big, heavy man who seemed to sag in all his flesh. In compensation for his bald head, the greyish-brown moustache flowed down and parted into two hairy fans of beard on either side of his chin. He looked at me through oval gold-rimmed spectacles; in a friendly way, but yet frightened. His voice was deep and gruff, clipping the syllables, despite his fright.

"And you——" *clip-clip*; the candle-holder trembled—"you are Armand de Lafayette. I had expected you by the steam-packet today. Well! You are here. On a fool's errand, I regret."

"But why?" (And I shouted it at him, Maurice.)

I looked at mademoiselle, who was faintly smiling.

"M. Duroc!" I protested. "You wrote to my brother. You said you had persuaded madame to repent of her harshness towards her daughter!"

"Was that your duty?" asked the Jezebel, looking full at M. Duroc with her greenish eyes. "Was that your right?"

"I am a man of law," said M. Duroc. The deep monosyllables rapped, in ghostly bursts, through his parted beard. He was perspiring. "I am correct. Very correct! And yet——"

"Who nursed her?" asked the Jezebel. "Who soothed her, fed her, wore her filthy clothes, calmed her tempers, endured her interminable abuse? *I* did!"

And yet, all the time she was speaking, this woman kept sidling and sliding against me, brushing my side, as though she would make sure of my presence there.

"Well!" said the lawyer. "It matters little now! This mystery . . ."

You may well believe that all these cryptic remarks, as well as reference to a mystery or an Act of God, had driven me almost frantic. I demanded to know what he meant.

"Last night," said M. Duroc, "a certain article disappeared."

"Well, well?"

"It disappeared," said M. Duroc, drawn up like a grenadier. "But it could not conceivably have disappeared. I myself swear this! Our only suggestions as to how it might have disappeared are a toy rabbit and a barometer."

"Sir," I said, "I do not wish to be discourteous. But——"

"Am I mad, you ask?"

I bowed. If any man can manage at once to look sagging and uncertain, yet stately and dignified, M. Duroc managed it then. And dignity won, I think.

"Sir," he replied, gesturing with the candle towards the rear of the house, "Madame Thevenet lies there in her bed. She is paralysed. She can move only her eyes or partially the lips, without speech. Do you wish to see her?"

"If I am permitted."

"Yes. That would be correct. Accompany me."

And I saw the poor old woman, Maurice. Call her harridan if you like.

It was a square room of good size, whose shutters had remained closed and locked for years. Can one smell rust? In that room, with faded green wall-paper, I felt I could.

One solitary candle did little more than dispel shadow. It burned atop the mantelpiece well opposite the foot of the bed; and a shaggy man, whom I afterwards learned to be a police-officer, sat in a green-upholstered arm-chair by an unlighted coal fireplace grate, picking his teeth with a knife.

"If you please, Dr. Harding!" M. Duroc called softly in English.

The long and lean American doctor, who had been bending over the bed so as to conceal from our sight the head and shoulders of Madame Thevenet, turned round. But his cadaverous body—in such fashion were madame's head and shoulders propped up against pillows —his cadaverous body, I say, still concealed her face.

"Has there been any change?" persisted M. Duroc in English.

"There has been no change," replied the dark-complexioned Dr. Harding, "except for the worse."

"Do you want her to be moved?"

"There has never been any necessity," said the physician, picking up his beaver hat from the bed. He spoke drily. "However, if you want to learn anything more about the toy rabbit or the barometer, I should hurry. The lady will die in a matter of hours, probably less."

And he stood to one side.

It was a heavy bed with four posts and a canopy. The bed-curtains, of some dullish-green material, were closely drawn on every side except the long side by which we saw Madame Thevenet in profile. Lean as a post, rigid, the strings of her cotton nightcap tightly tied under her chin, Madame Thevenet lay propped up there. But one eye rolled towards us, and it rolled horribly.

Up to this time the woman we call the Jezebel had said little. She chose this moment again to come brushing against my side. Her greenish eyes, lids half-closed, shone in the light of M. Duroc's candle. What she whispered was: "You don't really hate me, do you?"

Maurice, I make a pause here.

Since I wrote the sentence, I put down my pen, and pressed my hands over my eyes, and once more I thought. But let me try again.

I spent just two hours in the bedroom of Madame Thevenet. At the end of the time—oh, you shall hear why!—I rushed out of that bedroom, and out of number 23 Thomas Street, like the maniac I was.

The streets were full of people, of carriages, of omnibuses, at early evening. Knowing no place of refuge save the saloon from which I had come, I gave its address to a cab-driver. Since still I had swallowed no food, I may have been light-headed. Yet I wished to pour out my heart to the friends who had bidden me return there. And where were they now?

A new group, all new, lounged against the bar-counter under brighter gaslight and brighter paint. Of all those who smote me on the back and cheered, none remained save the ancient giant who had implied friendship with General Washington. *He*, alas, lay helplessly drunk with his head near a sawdust spitting-box. Nevertheless I was so moved that I took the liberty of thrusting a handful of bank-notes into his pocket. He alone remained.

Wait, there was another!

I do not believe he had remained there because of me. Yet M. Thaddeus Perley, still sitting alone at the little table by the pillar, with the open gas-jet above, stared vacantly at the empty glass in his hand.

He had named himself a foreigner; he was probably French. That was as well. For, as I lurched against the table, I was befuddled and all English had fled my wits.

"Sir," said I, "will you permit a madman to share your table?"

M. Perley gave a great start, as though roused out of thought. He was now sober: this I saw. Indeed, his shiver and haggard face were due to lack of stimulant rather than too much of it.

"Sir," he stammered, getting to his feet, "I shall be—I shall be honoured by your company." Automatically he opened his mouth to call for a waiter; his hand went to his pocket; he stopped.

"No, no, no!" said I. "If you insist, M. Perley, you may pay for the second bottle. The first is mine. I am sick at heart, and I would speak with a gentleman."

At these last words M. Perley's whole expression changed. He sat down, and gave me a grave courtly nod. His eyes, which were his most expressive feature, studied my face and my disarray.

"You are ill, M. de Lafayette," he said. "Have you so soon come to grief in this—this *civilized* country?"

"I have come to grief, yes. But not through civilization or the lack of it." And I banged my fist on the table. "I have come to grief, M. Perley, through miracles or magic. I have come to grief with a problem which no man's ingenuity can solve!"

M. Perley looked at me in a strange way. But someone had brought a bottle of brandy, with its accessories. M. Perley's trembling hand slopped a generous allowance into my glass, and an even more generous one into his own.

"That is very curious," he remarked, eyeing the glass. "A murder, was it?"

"No. But a valuable document has disappeared. The most thorough search by the police cannot find it."

Touch him anywhere, and he flinched. M. Perley, for some extraordinary reason, appeared to think I was mocking him.

"A document, you say?" His laugh was a trifle unearthly. "Come, now. Was it by any chance—a letter?"

"No, no! It was a will. Three large sheets of parchment, of the size you call foolscap. Listen!"

And as M. Perley added water to his brandy and gulped down about a third of it, I leaned across the table.

"Madame Thevenet, of whom you may have heard me speak in this café, was an invalid. But (until the early hours of this morning) she was not bedridden. She could move, and walk about her room, and so on. She had been lured away from Paris and her family by a green-eyed woman named the Jezebel.

"But a kindly lawyer of this city, M. Duroc, believed that madame suffered and had a bad conscience about her own daughter. Last night, despite the Jezebel, he persuaded madame at last to sign a will leaving all her money to this daughter.

"And the daughter, Claudine, is in mortal need of it! From my brother and myself, who have more than enough, she will not accept a sou. Her affianced, Lieutenant Delage, is as poor as she. But, unless she leaves France for Switzerland, she will die. I will not conceal from you that Claudine suffers from the dread disease we politely call consumption."

M. Perley stopped with his glass again half-way to his mouth.

He believed me now; I sensed it. Yet under the dark hair, tumbled on his forehead, his face had gone as white as his neat, mended shirt-frill.

"So very little a thing is money!" he whispered. "So very little a thing!"

And he lifted the glass and drained it.

"You do not think I am mocking you, sir?"

"No, no!" says M. Perley, shading his eyes with one hand. "I knew myself of one such case. She is dead. Pray continue."

"Last night, I repeat, Madame Thevenet changed her mind. When M. Duroc paid his weekly evening visit with the news that I should arrive to-day, madame fairly chattered with eagerness and a kind of terror. Death was approaching, she said; she had a presentiment."

As I spoke, Maurice, there returned to me the image of that shadowy, arsenic-green bedroom in the shuttered house; and what M. Duroc had told me.

"Madame," I continued, "cried out to M. Duroc that he must bolt the bedroom door. She feared the Jezebel, who lurked but said nothing. M. Duroc drew up to her bedside a portable writing-desk, with two good candles. For a long time madame spoke, pouring out contrition, self-abasement, the story of an unhappy marriage, all of which M. Duroc (sweating with embarrassment) was obliged to write down until it covered three large parchment sheets.

"But it was done, M. Perley!

"The will, in effect, left everything to her daughter, Claudine. It revoked a previous will by which all had been left (and this can be done in French law, as we both know) to Jezebel of the muddy complexion and the muddy yellow hair.

"Well, then! . . .

"M. Duroc sallies out into the street, where he finds two sober fellows who come in. Madame signs the will, M. Duroc sands it, and the two men from the street affix their signatures as witnesses. Then *they* are gone. M. Duroc folds the will lengthways, and prepares to put it into his carpet-bag. Now, M. Perley, mark what follows!

" 'No, no, no!' cries madame, with the shadow of her peaked nightcap wagging on the locked shutters beyond. 'I wish to keep it—for this one night!'

" 'For this one night, madame?' asks M. Duroc.

" 'I wish to press it against my heart,' says Madame Thevenet, 'I wish to read it once, twice, a thousand times! M. Duroc, what time is it?'

"Whereupon he takes out his gold repeater, and opens it. To his astonishment it is one o'clock in the morning. Yet he touches the spring of the repeater, and its pulse-beat rings one.

" 'M. Duroc,' pleads Madame Thevenet, 'remain here with me for the rest of the night!'

" 'Madame!' cries M. Duroc, shocked to the very fans of his beard. 'That would not be correct.'

" 'Yes, you are right,' says madame. And never, swears the lawyer, has he seen her less bleary of eye, more alive with wit and cunning, more the great lady of ruin, than there in that green and shadowy and foul-smelling room.

"Yet this very fact puts her in more and more terror of the Jezebel, who is never seen. She points to M. Duroc's carpet-bag.

" 'I think you have much work to do, dear sir?'

"M. Duroc groaned. 'The Good Lord knows that I have!'

" 'Outside the only door of this room,' says madame, 'there is a small dressing-room. Set up your writing-desk beside the door there, so that no one may enter without your knowledge. Do your work there; you shall have a lamp or many candles. Do it,' shrieks madame, 'for the sake of Claudine and for the sake of an old friendship!'

"Very naturally, M. Duroc hesitated.

" 'She will be hovering,' pleads Madame Thevenet, pressing the will against her breast. 'This I shall read and read and read, and sanctify with my tears. If I find I am falling asleep,' and here the old lady looked cunning, 'I shall hide it. But no matter! Even she cannot penetrate through locked shutters and a guarded door.'

"Well, in fine, the lawyer at length yielded.

"He set up his writing-desk against the very doorpost outside that door. When he last saw madame, before closing the door, he saw her in profile with the green bed-curtains drawn except on that side, propped up with a tall candle burning on a table at her right hand.

"Ah, that night! I think I see M. Duroc at his writing-desk, as he has told me, in an airless dressing-room where no clock ticked. I see him, at times, removing his oval spectacles to press his smarting eyes.

I see him returning to his legal papers, while his pen scratched through the wicked hours of the night.

"He heard nothing, or virtually nothing, until five o'clock in the morning. Then, which turned him cold and flabby, he heard a cry which he describes as being like that of a deaf-mute.

"The communicating door had not been bolted on Madame Thevenet's side, in case she needed help. M. Duroc rushed into the other room.

"On the table, at madame's right hand, the tall candle had burnt down to a flattish mass of wax over which still hovered a faint bluish flame. Madame herself lay rigid in her peaked nightcap. That revival of spirit last night, or remorse in her bitter heart, had brought on the last paralysis. Though M. Duroc tried to question her, she could move only her eyes.

"Then M. Duroc noticed that the will, which she had clutched as a doomed religious might clutch a crucifix, was not in her hand or on the bed.

"'Where is the will?' he shouted at her, as though she were deaf too. 'Where is the will?'

"Madame Thevenet's eyes fixed on him. Then they moved down, and looked steadily at a trumpery toy—a rabbit, perhaps four inches high, made of pink velours or the like—which lay on the bed. Again she looked at M. Duroc, as though to emphasize this. Then her eyes rolled, this time with dreadful effort, towards a large barometer, shaped like a warming-pan, which hung on the wall beside the door. Three times she did this before the bluish candle-flame flickered and went out."

And I, Armand de Lafayette, paused here in my recital to M. Perley.

Again I became aware that I was seated in a garish saloon, swilling brandy, amid loud talk that beat the air. There was a thumping noise from the theatre above our heads, and faint strains of music.

"The will," I said, "was not stolen. Not even the Jezebel could have melted through locked shutters or a guarded door. The will was not hidden, because no inch of the room remains unsearched. *Yet the will is gone!*"

I threw a glance across the table at M. Perley.

To me, I am sure, the brandy had given strength and steadied my nerves. With M. Perley I was not so sure. He was a little flushed. That slightly wild look, which I had observed before, had crept up especially into one eye, giving his whole face a somewhat lopsided appearance. Yet all his self-confidence had returned. He gave me a little crooked smile.

I struck the table.

"Do you honour me with your attention, M. Perley?"

"What song the Sirens sang," he said to me, "or what names Achilles assumed when he hid himself among women, although puzzling questions, are not beyond *all* conjecture."

"They are beyond *my* conjecture!" I cried. "And so is this!"

M. Perley extended his hand, spread the fingers, and examined them as one who owns the universe.

"It is some little time," he remarked, "since I have concerned myself with these trifles." His eyes retreated into a dream. "Yet I have given some trifling aid, in the past, to the Prefect of the Parisian police."

"You are a Frenchman! I knew it! And the police?" Seeing his lofty look, I added: "As an amateur, understood?"

"Understood!" Then his delicate hand—it would be unjust to call it claw-like—shot across the table and fastened on my arm. The strange eyes burned towards my face. "A little more detail!" he pleaded humbly. "A little more, I beg of you! This woman, for instance, you call the Jezebel?"

"It was she who met me at the house."

"And then?"

I described for him my meeting with the Jezebel, with M. Duroc, and our entrance to the sick-room, where the shaggy police-officer sat in the arm-chair and the saturnine doctor faced us from beside the bed.

"This woman," I exclaimed, with the room vividly before my eyes as I described it, "seems to have conceived for me (forgive me) a kind of passion. No doubt it was due to some idle compliments I once paid her at Paris.

"As I have explained, the Jezebel is *not* unattractive, even if she would only (again forgive me) wash her hair. Nevertheless, when once more she brushed my side and whispered, 'You don't really hate me, do you?' I felt little less than horror. It seemed to me that in some fashion I was responsible for the whole tragedy.

"While we stood beside the bed, M. Duroc the lawyer poured out the story I have recounted. There lay the poor paralytic, and confirmed it with her eyes. The toy rabbit, a detestable pink colour, lay in its same position on the bed. Behind me, hung against the wall by the door, was the large barometer.

"Apparently for my benefit, Madame Thevenet again went through her dumb-show with imploring eyes. She would look at the rabbit; next (as M. Duroc had not mentioned), she would roll her eyes all around her, for some desperate yet impenetrable reason, before fixing her gaze on the barometer.

"It meant . . . what?

"The lawyer spoke then. 'More light!' gulped out M. Duroc. 'If you must have closed shutters and windows, then let us at least have more light!'

"The Jezebel glided out to fetch candles. During M. Duroc's explanation he had several times mentioned my name. At first mention of it the shaggy police-officer jumped and put away his clasp-knife. He beckoned to the physician, Dr. Harding, who went over for a whispered conference.

"Whereupon the police-officer sprang up.

"'Mr. Lafayette!' And he swung my hand pompously. 'If I'd known it was you, Mr. Lafayette, I wouldn't 'a' sat there like a bump on a log.'

"'You are an officer of police, sir,' said I. 'Can *you* think of no explanation?'

"He shook his head.

"'These people are Frenchies, Mr. Lafayette, and you're an American,' he said, with somewhat conspicuous lack of logic. 'If they're telling the truth——'

"'Let us assume that!'

"'I can't tell you where the old lady's will is,' he stated positively. 'But I can tell you where it ain't. It ain't hidden in this room!'

"'But surely . . . !' I began in despair.

"At this moment the Jezebel, her brown taffeta dress rustling, glided back into the room with a handful of candles and a tin box of the new-style Lucifer matches. She lighted several candles, sticking them on any surface in their own grease.

"There were one or two fine pieces of furniture; but the mottled-marble tops were chipped and stained, the gilt sides cracked. There were a few mirrors, creating mimic spectral life. I saw a little more clearly the faded green paper of the walls, and what I perceived to be the partly open door of a cupboard. The floor was of bare boards.

"All this while I was conscious of two pairs of eyes: the imploring gaze of Madame Thevenet, and the amorous gaze of the Jezebel. One or the other I could have endured, but both together seemed to suffocate me.

"'Mr. Duroc here,' said the shaggy police-officer, clapping the distressed advocate on the shoulder, 'sent a messenger in a cab at half-past five this morning. And what time did we get here? I ask you and I tell you! Six o'clock!'

"Then he shook his finger at me, in a kind of pride and fury of efficiency.

"'Why, Mr. Lafayette, there's been fourteen men at this room from six this morning until just before you got here!'

"'To search for Madame Thevenet's will, you mean?'

The shaggy man nodded portentously, and folded his arms.

"'Floor's solid.' He stamped on the bare boards. 'Walls and ceiling? Nary a inch missed. We reckon we're remarkable smart; and we are.'

"'But Madame Thevenet,' I persisted, 'was not a complete invalid until this morning. She could move about. If she became afraid of'— the name of the Jezebel choked me—'if she became afraid, and *did* hide the will . . .'

"'Where'd she hide it? Tell me!'

"'In the furniture, then?'

"'Cabinet-makers in, Mr. Lafayette. No secret compartments.'

"'In one of the mirrors?'

"'Took the backs of 'em off. No will hid there.'

"'Up the chimney!' I cried.

"'Sent a chimney-sweep up there,' replied my companion in a ruminating way. Each time I guessed, he would leer at me in friendly and complacent challenge. 'Ye-es I reckon we're pretty smart. But we didn't find no will.'

"The pink rabbit also seemed to leer from the bed. I saw madame's eyes. Once again, as a desperate mind will fasten on trifles, I observed the strings of the nightcap beneath her scrawny chin. But I looked again at the toy rabbit.

"'Has it occurred to you,' I said triumphantly, 'to examine the bed and bedstead of Madame Thevenet herself?'

"My shaggy friend went to her bedside.

"'Poor old woman,' he said. He spoke as though she were already a corpse. Then he turned round. 'We lifted her out, just as gentle as a newborn babe (didn't we, ma'am?). No hollow bedposts! Nothing on the canopy! Nothing in the frame or the feather-beds or the curtains or the bedclothes!'

"Suddenly the shaggy police-officer became angry, as though he wished to be rid of the whole matter.

"'And it ain't in the toy rabbit,' he said, 'because you can see we slit it up, if you look close. And it ain't in that barometer there. It just—ain't here.'

"There was a silence as heavy as the dusty, hot air of this room.

"'It is here,' murmured M. Duroc in his gruff voice. 'It must be here!'

"The Jezebel stood there meekly, with downcast eyes.

"And I, in my turn, confess that I lost my head. I stalked over to the barometer, and tapped it. Its needle, which already indicated, 'Rain; cold,' moved still further towards that point.

"I was not insane enough to hit with my fist. But I crawled on the floor, in search of a secret hiding-place. I felt along the wall. The police-officer—who kept repeating that nobody must touch anything and he would take no responsibility until he went off duty at something o'clock—the police-officer I ignored.

"What at length gave me pause was the cupboard, already thoroughly searched. In the cupboard hung a few withered dresses and gowns, as though they had shrivelled with Madame Thevenet's body. But on the shelf of the cupboard . . .

"On the shelf stood a great number of perfume-bottles: even to-day, I fear, many of our countrymen think perfume a substitute for water and soap; and the state of madame's hands would have confirmed this. *But*, on the shelf, were a few dusty novels. There was a crumpled and begrimed copy of yesterday's New-York *Sun*. This newspaper did not contain a will; but it did contain a black beetle, which ran out across my hand.

"In a disgust past describing, I flung down the beetle and stamped on it. I closed the cupboard door, acknowledging defeat. Madame Thevenet's will was gone. And at the same second, in that dim green room —still badly lighted, with only a few more candles—two voices cried out.

"One was my own voice:

"'*In God's name, where is it?*'

"The other was the deep voice of M. Duroc:

"'*Look at that woman! She knows!*'

"And he meant the Jezebel.

"M. Duroc, with his beard-fans a-tremble, was pointing to a mirror; a little blurred, as these mirrors were. Our Jezebel had been looking into the mirror, her back turned to us. Now she dodged, as at a stone thrown.

"With good poise our Jezebel writhed this movement into a curtsy, turning to face us. But not before I also had seen that smile—like a razor-cut before the blood comes—as well as full knowledge, mocking knowledge, shining out of wide-open eyes in the mirror.

"'You spoke to me, M. Duroc?' She murmured the reply, also in French.

"'Listen to me!' the lawyer said formally. 'This will is *not* missing. It is in this room. You were not here last night. Something has made you guess. You know where it is.'

"'Are you unable to find it?' asked the Jezebel in surprise.

"'Stand back, young man!' M. Duroc said to me. 'I ask you something, mademoiselle, in the name of justice.'

"'Ask!' said the Jezebel.

"'If Claudine Thevenet inherits the money to which she is entitled, you will be well paid; yes, overpaid! You know Claudine. You know that!'

"'I know it.'

"'But if the new will be *not* found,' said M. Duroc, again, waving me back, 'then you inherit everything. And Claudine will die. For it will be assumed——'

"'Yes!' said the Jezebel, with one hand pressed against her breast. 'You yourself, M. Duroc, testify that all night a candle was burning at madame's bedside. Well! The poor woman, whom I loved and cherished, repented of her ingratitude towards me. She burnt this new will at the candle-flame; she crushed its ashes to powder and blew them away!'

"'Is that true?' cried M. Duroc.

"'They will assume it,' smiled the Jezebel, 'as you say.' She looked at me. 'And for you, M. Armand!'

"She glided closer. I can say that I saw her eyes uncovered; or, if you wish to put it so, her soul and flesh together.

"'I would give you everything on earth,' she said. 'I will not give you the doll-face in Paris.'

"'Listen to me!' I said to her, so agitated that I seized her shoulders. 'You are out of your senses! You cannot give Claudine to me! She will marry another man!'

"'And do you think that matters to me,' asked the Jezebel, with her green eyes full on mine, 'as long as you still love her?'

"There was a small crash as someone dropped a knife on the floor.

"We three, I think, had completely forgotten that we were not alone. There were two spectators, although they did not comprehend our speech.

"The saturnine Dr. Harding now occupied the green arm-chair. His long thin legs, in tight black trousers with strap under the boot-instep, were crossed and looked spidery; his high beaver hat glimmered on his head. The police-officer, who was picking his teeth with a knife when I first saw him, had now dropped the knife when he tried to trim his nails.

"But both men sensed the atmosphere. Both were alert, feeling out with the tentacles of their nerves. The police-officer shouted at me.

"'What's this gabble?' he said. 'What's a-gitting into your head?'

"Grotesquely, it was that word 'head' which gave me my inspiration.

"'The nightcap!' I exclaimed in English.

"'What nightcap?'

"For the nightcap of Madame Thevenet had a peak; it was large; it was tightly tied under her chin; it might well conceal a flat-pressed document which—but you understand. The police-officer, dull-witted as he appeared, grasped the meaning in a flash. And how I wished I had never spoken! For the fellow meant well, but he was not gentle.

"As I raced round the curtained sides of the bed, the police-officer was holding a candle in one hand and tearing off madame's night-cap with the other. He found no will there, no document at all; only straggly wisps of hair on a skull grown old before its time.

"Madame Thevenet had been a great lady, once. It must have been the last humiliation. Two tears overflowed her eyes and ran down her cheeks. She lay propped up there in a nearly sitting position; but some-thing seemed to wrench inside her.

"And she closed her eyes for ever. And the Jezebel laughed.

"That is the end of my story. That is why I rushed out of the house like a madman. The will has vanished as though by magic; or is it still there by magic? In any case, you find me at this table: grubby and dishevelled and much ashamed."

For a little time after I had finished my narrative to M. Perley in the saloon, it seemed to me that the bar-counter was a trifle quieter. But a faint stamping continued from the theatre above our heads. Then all was hushed, until a chorus rose to a tinkle of many banjos.

> *Oh, I come from Alabama*
> *With my banjo on my knee;*
> *I depart for Louisiana . . .*

Enough! The song soon died away, and M. Thaddeus Perley did not even hear it.

M. Perley sat looking downwards into an empty glass, so that I could not see his face.

"Sir," he remarked almost bitterly, "you are a man of good heart. I am glad to be of service in a problem so trifling as this."

"*Trifling!*"

His voice was a little husky, but not slurred. His hand slowly turned the glass round and round.

"Will you permit two questions?" asked M. Perley.

"Two questions? Ten thousand!"

"More than two will be unnecessary." Still M. Perley did not look up. "This toy rabbit, of which so much was made: I would know its exact position on the bed?"

"It was almost at the foot of the bed, and about the middle in a crossways direction."

"Ah, so I had imagined. Were the three sheets of parchment, forming the will, written upon two sides or upon only one?"

"I had not told you, M. Perley. But M. Duroc said: upon one side only."

M. Perley raised his head.

His face was now flushed and distorted with drink, his eyes grown wild. In his cups he was as proud as Satan, and as disdainful of others' intelligence; yet he spoke with dignity, and with careful clearness.

"It is ironic, M. de Lafayette, that I should tell you how to lay your hand on the missing will and elusive money; since, upon my word, I have never been able to perform a like service for myself." And he smiled, as at some secret joke. "Perhaps," he added, "it is the very simplicity of the thing which puts you at fault."

I could only look at him in bewilderment.

"Perhaps the mystery is a little *too* plain! A little *too* self-evident!"

"You mock me, sir! I will not . . ."

"Take me as I am," said M. Perley, whacking the foot of the glass on the table, "or leave me. Besides——" here his wandering eye encountered a list of steam-sailings pasted against the wall—"I——I leave to-morrow by the *Parnassus* for England, and then for France."

"I meant no offence, M. Perley! If you have knowledge, speak!"

"Madame Thevenet," he said, carefully pouring himself more brandy, "hid the will in the middle of the night. Does it puzzle you that she took such precautions to hide the will? But the element of the *outré* must always betray itself. The Jezebel *must not* find that will! Yet Madame Thevenet trusted nobody—not even the worthy physician who attended her. If Madame were to die of a stroke, the police would be there and must soon, she was sure, discover her simple device. Even if she were paralysed, it would ensure the presence of other persons in the room to act as unwitting guards.

"Your cardinal error," M. Perley continued dispassionately, "was one of ratiocination. You tell me that Madame Thevenet, to give you a hint, looked fixedly at some point near the foot of the bed. Why do you assume that she was looking at the toy rabbit?"

"Because," I replied hotly, "the toy rabbit was the only object she could have looked at!"

"Pardon me; but it was *not*. You several times informed me that the bed-curtains were closely drawn together on three sides. They were drawn on all but the 'long' side towards the door. Therefore the ideal reasoner, without having seen the room, may safely say that the curtains were drawn together at the foot of the bed?"

"Yes, true!"

"After looking fixedly at this point represented by the toy, Madame Thevenet then 'rolls her eyes all round her'—in your phrase. May we assume that she wishes the curtains to be drawn back, so that she may see something *beyond* the bed?"

"It is—possible, yes!"

"It is more than possible, as I shall demonstrate. Let us direct our attention, briefly, to the incongruous phenomenon of the barometer on another wall. The barometer indicates, 'Rain; cold.' "

Here M. Perley's thin shoulders drew together under the old military cloak.

"Well," he said, "the cold is on its way. Yet this day, for April, has been warm outside and indoors, oppressively hot?"

"Yes! Of course!"

"You yourself," continued M. Perley, inspecting his finger-nails, "told me what was directly opposite the foot of the bed. Let us suppose that the bed-curtains are drawn open. Madame Thevenet, in her nearly seated position, is looking *downwards*. What would she have seen?"

"The fireplace!" I cried. "The grate of the fireplace!"

"Already we have a link with the weather. And what, as you have specifically informed me, was in the grate of the fireplace?"

"An unlighted coal fire!"

"Exactly. And what is essential for the composition of such a fire? We need coal; we need wood; but primarily and above all, we need . . ."

"*Paper!*" I cried.

"In the cupboard of that room," said M. Perley, with his disdainful little smile, "was a very crumpled and begrimed (mark that; not dusty) copy of *yesterday's* New-York *Sun*. To light fires is the most common, and indeed the best, use for our daily press. That copy had been used to build yesterday's fire. But something else, during the night, was substituted for it. You yourself remarked the extraordinarily dirty state of Madame Thevenet's hands."

M. Perley swallowed the brandy, and his flush deepened.

"Sir," he said loudly, "you will find the will crumpled up, with ends most obviously protruding, under the coal and wood in the fireplace grate. Even had anyone taken the fire to pieces, he would have found only what appeared to be dirty blank paper, written side undermost, which could never be a valuable will. It was too self-evident to be seen. Now go!"

"Go?" I echoed stupidly.

M. Perley rose from his chair.

"Go, I say!" he shouted, with an even wilder eye. "The Jezebel could not light that fire. It was too warm, for one thing; and all day there were police-officers with instructions that an outsider must touch nothing. But now? *Madame Thevenet kept warning you that the fire must not be lighted, or the will would be destroyed!*"

"Will you await me here?" I called over my shoulder.

"Yes, yes! And perhaps there will be peace for the wretched girl with—with the lung trouble."

Even as I ran out of the door I saw him, grotesque and pitiful, slump across the table. Hope, rising and surging, seemed to sweep me along like the crack of the cabman's whip. But when I reached my destination, hope receded.

The shaggy police-officer was just descending the front steps.

"None of us coming back here, Mr. Lafayette!" he called cheerily. "Old Mrs. What's-her-name went and burnt that will at a candle last night—Here, what's o'clock?"

The front door was unlocked. I raced through that dark house, and burst into the rear bedroom.

The corpse still lay in the big, gloomy bed. Every candle had flickered almost down to its socket. The police-officer's clasp-knife, forgotten since he had dropped it, still lay on bare boards. But the Jezebel was there.

She knelt on the hearth, with the tin box of Lucifer matches she had brought there earlier. The match spurted, a bluish fire; I saw her eagerness; she held the match to the grate.

"A Lucifer," I said, "in the hand of a Jezebel!"

And I struck her away from the grate, so that she reeled against a chair and fell. Large coals, small coals rattled down in puffs of dust as I plunged my hands into the unlighted fire. Little sticks, sawed sticks; and I found it there: crumpled parchment-sheets, but incontestably madame's will.

"M. Duroc!" I called. "M. Duroc!"

You and I, my brother Maurice, have fought the Citizen-King with bayonets as we now fight the upstart Bonapartist; we need not be ashamed of tears. I confess, then, that the tears overran my eyes and blinded me. I scarcely saw M. Duroc as he hurried into the room.

Certainly I did not see the Jezebel stealthily pick up the police-officer's knife. I noticed nothing at all until she flew at me, and stabbed me in the back.

Peace, my brother: I have assured you all is well. At that time, faith, I was not much conscious of any hurt. I bade M. Duroc, who was trembling, wrench out the knife; I borrowed his roomy greatcoat to hide the blood; I must hurry, hurry, hurry back to that little table under the gas-jet.

I planned it all on my way back. M. Perley, apparently a stranger in this country, disliked it and was evidently very poor even in France. But *we* are not precisely paupers. Even with his intense pride, he could not refuse (for such a service) a sum which would comfort him for the rest of his life.

Back I plunged into the saloon, and hurried down it. Then I stopped. The little round table by the pillar, under the flaring gas-jet, was empty.

How long I stood there I cannot tell. The back of my shirt, which at first had seemed full of blood, now stuck to the borrowed great-coat. All of a sudden I caught sight of the fat-faced bartender with the gold teeth, who had been on service that afternoon and had re-turned now. As a mark of respect, he came out from behind the bar-counter to greet me.

"Where is the gentleman who was sitting at that table?"

I pointed to it. My voice, in truth, must have sounded so hoarse and strange that he mistook it for anger.

"Don't you worry about that, monseer!" said he reassuringly. "*That's* been tended to! We threw the drunken tramp out of here!"

"You threw . . ."

"Right bang in the gutter. Had to crawl along it before he could stand up." My bartender's face was pleased and vicious. "Ordered a bottle of best brandy, and couldn't pay for it." The face changed again. "Goddelmighty, monseer, what's wrong?"

"I ordered that brandy."

"He didn't say so, when the waiter brought me over. Just looked me up and down, crazy-like, and said a gentleman would give his I.O.U. Gentleman!"

"M. Perley," I said, restraining an impulse to kill that bartender, "is a friend of mine. He departs for France early tomorrow morning. Where is his hotel? Where can I find him?"

"Perley!" sneered my companion. "That ain't even his real name, I hearn tell. Gits high-and-mighty ideas from upper Broadway. But his real name's on the I.O.U."

A surge of hope, once more, almost blinded me. "Did you keep that I.O.U.?"

"Yes, I kepp it," growled the bartender, fishing in his pocket. "God knows why, but I kepp it."

And at last, Maurice, I triumphed!

True, I collapsed from my wound; and the fever would not let me remember that I must be at the dock when the *Parnassus* steampacket departed from New-York next morning. I must remain here, shut up in a hotel-room and unable to sleep at night, until I can take ship for home. But where I failed, you can succeed. He was to leave on the morrow by the *Parnassus* for England, and then for France— so he told me. You can find him—in six months at the most. In six months, I give you my word he will be out of misery for ever!

"*I.O.U.*," reads the little slip, "*for one bottle of your best brandy, forty-five cents. Signed Edgar A. Poe.*"

I remain, Maurice,
Your affectionate brother,
Armand

# CONFIDENCE TRICK

## John Wyndham

JOHN WYNDHAM is the pseudonym for a well-known author who, under his real name, has published several books and stories of a very different nature than *Confidence Trick*. Under the Wyndham pseudonym, he first published a successful novel called *The Day of the Triffids*, brought out by Doubleday in 1951.

"NEVER again," Henry Baider said to himself, once he had been condensed enough for the doors to close, "never again will I allow myself to be caught up in this."

It was a decision he had expressed before, and would probably, in spite of its face value, express another day. But in between he did do his best to assure that his infrequent visits to the City should not involve him in the rush hour. Today, however, already delayed by his business, he faced the alternatives of vexing his wife by delaying still further, or of allowing himself to be drawn into the flood that was being sucked down the Bank Station entrances. After looking unhappily at the moving mass and then at the unmoving bus queues, he had squared his shoulders. "After all, they do it twice a day and survive. Who am I—?" he said, and stepped stoutly forward.

The funny thing was that nobody else looked as if he or she thought it a subhuman, stockyard business. They just waited blank-eyed, and with more patience than you would find in a stockyard. They didn't complain, either.

Nobody got out at St. Paul's, though the increased pressure suggested that somebody had inexplicably got in. The doors attempted to close, drew back, presumably because some part of somebody was inexpertly stowed, tried again, and made it. The train drew heavily on. The girl in the green mackintosh on Henry's right said to the girl in the blue mackintosh who was jammed against her:

"D'you think you actually *know* when your ribs crack?" but on a philosophical note of fair comment rather than complaint.

Nobody got out at Chancery Lane, either. A lot of exhortation, shoving, and staggering achieved the impossible: somebody more was aboard. The train picked up speed slowly. It rattled on for a few seconds. Then there was a jolt, and all the lights went out.

Henry swore at his luck as the train drew up, but then, almost the instant it had stopped, it started to pull ahead again. Abruptly he discovered that he was no longer supported by the people round him, and flung out an arm to save himself. It struck something yielding. At that moment the lights came on again, to reveal that the object struck had been the girl in the green mackintosh.

"Who do you think you're—?" she began. Then her mouth stayed open, her voice failed, and her eyes grew rounder and wider.

At the same moment Henry had started to apologize, but his voice, too, cut out, and his eyes also bulged.

He looked up and down the coach that a moment ago had been jammed solid with people to the last inch. It now contained three others besides themselves. A middle-aged man who was opening his newspaper with an air of having been given his due at last; opposite him a woman, also middle-aged, and lost in contemplation; right away at the other end of the coach, in the last seat, sat a younger-looking man, apparently asleep.

"Well, really!" said the girl. "That Milly! Just wait till I see her in the morning. She knows I have to change at Holborn, too. Getting off and leaving me without a word!" She paused. "It *was* Holborn, wasn't it?" she added.

Henry was still looking dazedly about him. She took hold of his arm and shook it.

"It *was* Holborn, wasn't it?" she repeated, uncertainly.

Henry turned to look at her, but still with a vagueness in his manner. "Er—what was Holborn?" he asked.

"That last stop—where they all got out. It *must've* been Holborn, mustn't it?"

"I—er—I'm afraid I don't know this line well," Henry told her.

"I do. Like the back of my hand. Couldn't be anywhere but Holborn," she said, with self-convincing firmness.

Henry looked up the swaying coach, past the rows of strap-handles emptily aswing.

"I—er—didn't see any station," he said.

Her head in its red knitted cap tilted further back to look up at him. Her blue eyes were troubled, though not alarmed.

"Of course there was a station—or where would they all go to?"

"Yes—" said Henry. "Yes, of course."

There was a pause. The train continued to speed along, swaying more and jerking more now on its lightly loaded springs.

"The next'll be Tottenham Court Road," said the girl, though with a touch of uneasiness.

The train rattled. She stared at the black windows growing more pensive.

"Funny," she said, after a while. "Funny-peculiar, I mean."

"Look here," said Henry. "Suppose we go and have a word with those people up there. They might know something."

The girl glanced along. Her expression showed no great hopes of them, but: "All right," she said, and turned to lead the way.

Henry stopped opposite the middle-aged woman. She was dressed in a well-cut coat surmounted by a fur cape. An inch or two of veil fringed the round hat on her carefully dressed dark hair; her shoes, at the end of almost invisible nylon stockings, were black patent leather with elegant heels; both her gloved hands rested on the black leather bag on her lap as she sat in absent contemplation.

"I beg your pardon," said Henry, "but could you tell us the name of the last station—the one where all the other people got out?"

The lids rose slowly. The eyes regarded him through the fringe of veil. There was a pause during which she appeared to consider the several reasons which could have led such a person as Henry to address her, and to select the most becoming. Henry decided that no-longer-young was perhaps more apposite than middle-aged.

"No," she said, with a slight smile which did not touch the matter. "I'm afraid I didn't notice."

"It didn't strike you that there was anything—er—odd about it?" Henry suggested.

The lady's well-marked eyebrows rose slightly. The eyes pondered him on two or three levels.

"Odd?" she inquired.

"The way they all went so very quickly," he explained.

"Oh, was that unusual?" said the lady. "It seemed to me a very good thing; there were far too many of them."

"Quite," agreed Henry, "but what is puzzling us is how it happened."

The eyebrows rose a little higher.

"Really. I don't think I can be expected to—"

There was a harrumph noise, and a rustling of newspaper behind Henry. A voice said:

"Young man. It doesn't seem to me to be necessary for you to bother this lady with the matter. If you have any complaints, there are proper channels for them."

Henry turned. The speaker was a man with graying hair; he had a well-trimmed mustache set on a pinkly healthy face. He was perhaps fifty-five, and dressed City-comme-il-faut from black Homburg to dispatch case. At the moment he was glancing interrogatively toward the lady, and receiving a small, grateful smile in return. Then his eyes met Henry's. His manner changed slightly; evidently Henry was not quite the type that his back view had suggested.

"I am sorry," Henry told him, "but this young lady may have missed her station—besides, it does seem rather odd."

"I noticed Chancery Lane, so the rest must have got out at Holborn —that is obvious, surely," said the man.

"But they went so quickly."

"A good thing too. The people in charge must have found some new method of handling the traffic. They're always developing new ideas and techniques, you know—even under public ownership."

"But we've been going on for nearly ten minutes, nonstop, since then, and we've certainly not passed a station," Henry objected.

"Probably been rerouted. Technical reasons, I expect," said the man.

"Rerouted! On the underground!" protested Henry.

"My dear fellow, it's not my job to know how these things work— nor yours, I take it. We have to leave it to those who do. That's what they're there for, after all. Take it from me, they know what they're up to, even though it may seem 'odd,' as you call it, to us. God bless me, if we don't have faith in our expert authorities, where are we?"

Henry looked at the girl in the green mackintosh. She looked back at him. She shrugged slightly. They went and sat down, further up the coach. Henry glanced at his watch, offered her a cigarette, and they both lit up.

The train rattled along to a steady rhythm. Both of them watched the windows for the sight of a lighted platform, but they could see no more than their own reflections against outside blackness. When there was no more of the cigarette to hold, Henry dropped the remains on the floor and ground them out. He looked at his watch again, and then at the girl.

"More than twenty minutes," he said. "That's impossibility, raised several powers."

"It's going faster now, too," the girl observed. "And look at the way it's tilted."

Henry regarded the hanging straps. There could be no doubt that they were running down an appreciable incline. Glancing forward he saw that the other couple were now in quite animated conversation.

"Shall we try 'em again?" he suggested.

"—never more than fifteen minutes even in the rush hour. Absolutely never," the lady was saying as they came up. "I'm afraid my husband will be so worried about me."

"Well?" inquired Henry, of the man.

"Certainly very unusual," the other conceded.

"Unusual! Nearly half an hour at full bat without a station? It's absolutely impossible," said Henry.

The other regarded him coldly.

"It is clearly *not* impossible because it is being demonstrated now. Very likely this is some underground escape route from London that they constructed during the war, and we have been switched onto it in error. I have no doubt that the authorities will presently discover the mistake and bring us back."

"Taking them a long time," said the girl. "Due home before this, I am. And I got a date at the Pallay this evening."

"We'd better stop the train," said the lady. Her eyes were on the handle, with its notice that threatened five pounds' fine for improper use.

Henry and the other man looked at one another.

"Well, if this isn't an emergency, what is?" demanded the lady.

"Er—" said Henry.

"The authorities—" the other began.

"All right," she announced. "If you men are afraid to touch it, I'm not." She reached up, took a firm hold of the handle, and yanked it down.

Henry dropped into a seat quickly, pulling the girl down too, before the brakes should go on.

The brakes did not go on.

They sat waiting. Presently it became a fair bet that the brakes were not going to go on. The lady pushed the handle up impatiently, and pulled it down again. Nothing happened. She expressed her opinion of it.

"Cor! Listen to her! Did you ever?" said the girl beside Henry.

"Fluent. Have another cigarette," said Henry.

The train clattered and swayed along, the straps still hanging with a forward slant.

"Well," said the girl, after a time, "this properly dishes my date at the Pallay all right. Now that Doris'll get him. D'you think I could sue them?"

"I'm afraid not," Henry told her.

"You a lawyer?"

"Well, as a matter of fact, yes. Suppose we introduce ourselves. It looks as if we shall have to spend some time here, whatever they do. I'm Henry Baider."

"Mine's Norma Palmer," said the girl.

The City man said: "Robert Forkett," and nodded slightly to them.

"Barbara Branton—Mrs., of course," said the lady.

"What about him?" asked Norma, pointing to the man at the far end of the coach. "D'you think we ought to wake him and tell him?"

"I don't fancy it would help much," said Mr. Forkett. He turned to Henry. "I understood you to say you were a legal man, sir. Perhaps you can tell us just what our position is in this matter?"

"Well, speaking without my references," Henry told him, "I should say that in the matter of delay, no claim by us would lie. I think we shall find that the Company only undertakes to provide—"

Half an hour later he became aware of a weight pressing lightly against him. Looking round, he found that Norma had gone to sleep with her head on his shoulder. Mrs. Branton on the other side, had also dozed off. Mr. Forkett yawned, and apologized.

"Might as well all have a nap to pass the time, though," he suggested.

Henry looked at his watch once more. Practically an hour and a half now. Unless they had been going in a closed circle, they must have passed beneath several counties by this time. The thing remained incomprehensible.

To reach a cigarette he would have had to disturb the girl, so he remained as he was, looking at the blackness outside, swaying slightly to the train's motion, listening to the ti-tocketty-tock, ti-tocketty-tock, ti-tocketty-tock, of the hurrying wheels until his head drooped sideways and rested on the knitted cap on his shoulder.

The change of rhythm, the slight shuddering from the brakes, brought Henry awake; the rest stirred a moment later. Mr. Forkett yawned audibly. Norma opened her eyes, blinked at the unexpected scene, and discovered the situation of her head. She sat up. "Well, I never," she said, regarding Henry. He assured her it had been a pleasure. She began to pat her hair and correct herself according to her reflection in the still dark window opposite. Mrs. Branton reached under her cape, and consulted a small fob watch.

"Nearly midnight. My husband'll be quite frantic about me," she observed.

The sounds of slowing continued to descend the scale. Presently the windows ceased to be altogether black; a light, rather pinkish compared with the lamps inside, started to show, and gradually to grow stronger.

"That's better," said Norma. "I always hate it when it stops in the tunnel."

The light grew brighter still, the speed dwindled, and presently they were running into a station. They leaned forward to catch the name, but could see no plate on the wall. Mrs. Branton, on the other side, suddenly craned across.

"There!" she said. They turned quickly, but not soon enough.

"It was something Avenue, or Avenue something," she said.

"Well, we'll soon find out now," Mr. Forkett reassured them.

The train drew up, with a sigh from the braking system, but the doors did not open at once. There was a sound of echoing commotion further along the platform, out of which voices presently distinguished themselves calling: "All change!"—"End of the line!"—"All out here!"

"All very well—all change, indeed!" murmured Norma, getting up and moving toward the doors.

The others followed her. Quite suddenly the doors ran back. Norma gave one look at the figure standing on the platform.

"Ee-ow!" she yelped, and backed violently into Henry.

The figure wore little clothing. What there was seemed to be chiefly straps holding appurtenances, so that it was revealed as angularly male, in a rich mahogany red. Ethnologically, perhaps, the face might have been North American Indian, only instead of feathers it wore a pair of horns. Its right hand carried a trident; its left dangled a net.

"All out!" it said, moving a little aside.

Norma hesitated, and then scuttled past it. The others followed warily but more sedately, and joined her on the platform. The creature leaned into the open doorway, and they were able to observe his back view. The tail was waving with a slow, absent-minded kind of motion. The barb at the end of it looked viciously sharp.

"Er—" began Mr. Forkett. Then he changed his mind. He cast a speculative eye on each of his companions in turn, and pondered.

The creature caught sight of the sleeper at the other end of the car. He walked down and prodded him with his trident. There was some inaudible altercation. The creature prodded a few more times, and presently the man came out to join them, with the sleep not yet out of his eyes.

There was a shout higher up the platform, followed by a sound of running feet. A tough-looking young man came sprinting toward them. A net whistled after him and entangled him so that he fell and rolled over and over. A hearty shout of laughter came from the other end of the platform.

Henry glanced about. The dim rosy light was strong enough for him to see and read the station's name plate.

"Something Avenue!" he repeated under his breath. "Tch-tch!"

Mrs. Branton overheard him, and looked at it.

"Well, if that doesn't spell 'Avenues,' what does it spell?" she demanded.

Before he could reply a voice began to call: "This way out! This way out!" and the creature motioned them on, with its trident at the ready. The young man from the other end of the coach walked next to Henry. He was a large, forceful, intellectual-looking young man, but still not quite clear of the mists of sleep.

"What is all this nonsense about?" he said. "Collecting for the hospitals, or something? No excuse for it now we've got the Health Scheme."

"I don't think so," Henry told him. "In fact, I'm afraid it doesn't look too good." He indicated the station name plate. "Besides," he added, "those tails—I don't see how it could be done."

The young man studied the sinuous movements of one of the tails.

"But really—!" he protested.

Altogether, and exclusive of the staff, there were about a dozen people collected at the barrier. They were passed through one by one while an elderly demon in a small hutch checked them off on a list. Henry learned that the large young man was entered as Christopher Watts, physicist.

Beyond the barrier was an escalator of a somewhat antiquated type. It moved slowly enough for one to read the advertisements at the sides: preponderantly they offered specifics for burns, cuts, abrasions, and bruises, with here and there the recommendation of a particular tonic or pick-me-up.

At the top stood an ill-used looking demon with a tray of tin boxes suspended against his chest. He was saying monotonously: "All guaranteed. Best quality." Mr. Forkett, who was in front of Henry, caught sight of the card on the tray, and stopped abruptly. The lettering ran:

FIRST-AID KITS COMPLETE
each
£1    or    $1.50 (U.S.)

"That's an insult to the pound," Mr. Forkett announced indignantly. The demon looked at Mr. Forkett. He thrust his face forward aggressively. "So what?" he demanded.

Pressure of those behind pushed Mr. Forkett on, but he moved reluctantly, murmuring about the necessity for confidence, stability, and faith in sterling.

After crossing a hall, they passed into the open. There was a faint tang of sulphur in the air. Norma pulled on the hood of her mackintosh against the light drizzle of cinders. Trident-bearers shepherded them round to the right, into a wire-netted enclosure. Three or four demons followed in with them. The last paused to speak to the guard on the gate.

"Heaven's harps, is that celestial bus behind time again?" he asked resentfully.

"Is it ever *on* time nowadays?" the gate demon asked.

"Never used to have these holdups when the old man was running his ferry," grumbled the guard.

"Individual enterprise, that was," said the gate demon, with a shrug.

Henry joined the others who were surveying the scene. The view to the right was rugged and extensive, though smoky. Far away, at the end of the long valley, could be seen a brightly glowing area in which large bubbles formed, rose slowly, and took tantalizingly long to burst. To the left of it a geyser of flame whooshed up intermittently. At the back right a volcano smoked steadily while little streams of red-hot lava trickled down from its rim. In the middle distance the valley walls narrowed in two towering crags. The one on the left bore the illuminated sign: TRY HOOPER'S HIDEHARD. The other proclaimed: UNBURN IS THE ANSWER.

A little short of the right-hand crag, on the level valley floor, was a square encampment surrounded by several fences of barbed wire, and overlooked by a guard tower at each corner. Every now and then a string of flaming arrows would fly tracer-like into the compound from one of the towers, and the sound of howls mixed with demonic laughter would be borne faintly on the sulphurous breeze. From that point one was able to follow the road as it wound up and past them to the station entrance. A building opposite the station appeared to be a barracks where demons were queuing up to sharpen their tridents and touch up their tail barbs on a grindstone in the yard. The whole thing struck Henry as somewhat unconventional.

Almost opposite their netted enclosure was a kind of gibbet. It was occupied at the moment by a lady with nothing on who was hanging suspended upside down from chains round her ankles while a couple of junior demons swung on her hair. Mrs. Branton searched in her bag, and found a pair of spectacles.

"Dear me! Surely not—?" she murmured. She looked more carefully. "So difficult to tell that way up, and with the tears running into her hair. I'm afraid it is, though. Such a nice woman, I always thought, too."

She turned to the nearest demon. "Did she commit a murder, or something dreadful?" she asked.

He shook his head. "No," he said. "She just nagged at her husband so that he would find another woman and she would be able to divorce him for the alimony."

"Oh," said Mrs. Branton a little flatly. "Is that all? I mean, there must have been something more serious, surely?"

"No," said the guard.

Mrs. Branton remained thoughtful. "Does she have to do a lot of that?" she asked, with a trace of uneasiness.

"Wednesdays," said the guard. "She does other things other days."

"Pss-t!" a voice hissed suddenly in Henry's ear. One of the guard demons beckoned him aside.

"Want to buy a bit of the real stuff?" inquired the demon.

"What stuff?" Henry asked.

The demon brought his hand out of his pouch. He opened it and showed a metal tube which looked as if it might contain toothpaste. He leaned closer.

"The goods, this is. Best analgesic cream on the white market. Just rub it on every time before tortures—you'll not feel a thing."

"No, thank you. As a matter of fact, I think they'll probably find there's been a mistake in my case," Henry told him.

"Come off it, chum," said the demon. "Look. I'll take a couple of pounds—special to you, that is."

"No thanks," said Henry.

The demon frowned. "You'd better," he advised, shifting his tail into a threatening position.

"Well—one pound," said Henry.

The demon looked a little surprised. "Okay. It's yours," he said, and handed it over.

When Henry rejoined the group he found most of them watching three demons exuberantly chasing an extensive, pink, middle-aged man up the opposite mountainside. Mr. Forkett, however, was reviewing the situation.

"The accident," he said, raising his voice a little to contend with the increased lowing of sinners in the concentration camp, "the accident must have occurred between Chancery Lane and Holborn stations; that's fairly clear, I think. What is not at all clear to me, however, is why *I* am *here*. Undoubtedly there has been a departmental error in my case, which I hope will be rectified soon." He looked speculatively at the rest. Everyone became thoughtful.

"It'd have to be a *big* thing, wouldn't it?" asked Norma. "I mean they wouldn't send a person here for a little thing like a pair of nylons, would they?"

"Well, if it was only *one* pair of nylons—" Henry was beginning, but he was cut short by an exclamation from Mrs. Branton. Following her gaze, he saw a woman coming down the street in a magnificent fur coat.

"Perhaps this place has another side to it that we've not seen yet," she suggested, hopefully. "After all, where there are mink coats—"

"She doesn't look very pleased with it, though," Norma remarked, as the woman came closer.

"Live minks. Very sharp teeth," observed one of the demons helpfully.

There was a sudden, startling yelp behind them. They turned to observe the dark young man, Christopher Watts, in the act of twisting a demon's tail. The demon yelped again, and dropped the tube of analgesic cream it had been offering him. It attempted to stab with its trident.

"Oh no you don't!" said Mr. Watts, skilfully avoiding the thrust.

He caught the trident by the shaft, and wrenched it out of the demon's hand. "Now!" he said, with satisfaction. He dropped the trident, and laid hold of the tail with both hands. He swung the demon twice round his head, and let go. The demon flew over the wire-netting fence and landed in the road with a yell and a bump. The other demons deployed, and began to advance upon Mr. Watts, tridents leveled, nets swinging in their left hands.

Christopher Watts squared up to them, grimly watching them come on. Then, suddenly his expression changed. His frown gave place to a smile. He unclenched his fists and dropped his hands to his sides.

"Dear me, what nonsense all this is!" he said, and turned his back on the demons.

They stopped abruptly, and looked confused.

A surprising sense of revelation came over Henry. He saw quite clearly that the young man was right. It *was* nonsense. He laughed at the bewildered look on the demons' faces, and heard Norma beside him laughing too. Presently all the party was laughing at the discomfited demons, who looked first apprehensive and then sheepish.

Mr. Christopher Watts strode across to the side of the enclosure which faced up the valley. For some moments he regarded the smoky, luridly somber view. Then:

"I don't believe it!" he said, quietly.

An enormous bubble rose and burst in the fiery lake. There was a *woomph!* as the volcano sent up a mushroom cloud of smoke and cinders, and spilled better, brighter streams of lava down its sides. The ground trembled a little under their feet. Mr. Watts drew a deep breath.

"I DON'T BELIEVE IT!" he said, loudly.

There was a loud crack. The dizzy crag which bore the recommendation for UNBURN split off, and toppled slowly into the valley. Demons on the mountainside dropped their hunting and started to lope homeward with cries of panic. The ground shook violently. The fiery lake began to empty into a huge split which had opened in the valley floor. A tremendous gush of flame burst from the geyser. The mighty crag on the other side heeled over. There was a roaring and a crashing and a hissing of steam all around them, and through it Mr. Watts' voice bawled again:

"I DON'T BELIEVE IT!"

Suddenly, all was quiet, as if it had been switched off. All was black, too, with nothing whatever to be seen but the lighted windows of the train where it stood on the embankment behind them.

"Well," said Mr. Watts, on a note of cheerful satisfaction. "Well, that's that. Now let's go home again, shall we?" And by the light from the train windows he began to scramble up the embankment.

Henry and Norma moved to follow him. Mr. Forkett hesitated.

"What's the matter?" Henry asked him, looking back.

"I'm not sure. I feel it's not quite—not quite—"

"You can't very well stay here now," Henry pointed out.

"No—no, I suppose not," Mr. Forkett admitted, and, half reluctantly, he too began to climb the embankment.

Without any spoken agreement the five who had previously traveled together chose a coach to themselves. They had scarcely got aboard when the doors closed and the train began to move. Norma sighed with relief, and pushed her hood back as she sat down.

"Like being halfway home already," she said. "Thank you ever so, Mr. Watts. It's been a real lesson to me, it has, though. I'll never go near a stocking counter again, never—except when I'm going to buy some."

"I'll second that—the thanks part, I mean," said Henry. "I still feel that there was very likely some confusion between the legal and the common view in my particular case, but I'm extremely obliged to you for—er—cutting the red tape."

Mrs. Branton held out a gloved hand to Mr. Watts.

"Of course you'll realize that it was all a stupid mistake that I should be there, but I expect you've saved me hours and hours of dealing with ridiculous officials. I do hope you may be able to come and dine with us some time. I'm sure my husband will want to thank you."

There was a pause. It lengthened. Gradually the realization that Mr. Forkett was not taking his cue drew all their eyes upon him. He himself was gazing in a pensive way at the floor. Presently he looked up, first at them, and then at Christopher Watts.

"No," he said. "I am sorry, but I cannot agree. I am afraid I must continue to regard your action as antisocial, if not actually subversive."

Mr. Watts, who had been looking rather pleased with himself, showed first surprise, and then a frown.

"I beg your pardon?" he said, with genuine puzzlement.

"You've done a very serious thing," Mr. Forkett told him. "There simply cannot be any stability if we do not respect our institutions. You, young man, have destroyed one. We all had confidence in this affair—even you, to begin with—then you suddenly go and break it all up, an institution of considerable standing, too. No, I really cannot be expected to approve of that."

The rest of them stared at him.

"But Mr. Forkett," said Norma, "surely you wouldn't rather be back there, with all those demons and things?"

"My dear young lady, that is scarcely the point," Mr. Forkett reproved her. "As a responsible citizen I must strongly oppose anything that threatens to undermine public confidence. Therefore I must regard this young man's action as dangerous; verging, I repeat, upon the subversive."

"But if an institution is phony—" began Mr. Watts.

"That, too, sir, is beside the point. If enough people believe in an institution then it is important to those people—whether it is what you call phony or not."

"You prefer faith to truth?" said Mr. Watts, scornfully.

"You must have confidence, and if you have that, truth follows," said Mr. Forkett.

"As a scientist, I consider you quite immoral," said Mr. Watts.

"As a citizen, I consider you unscrupulous," said Mr. Forkett.

"Oh, dear!" said Norma.

Mr. Forkett pondered. Mr. Watts frowned.

"Something that is *real* isn't going to fall to bits just because I disbelieve in it," observed Mr. Watts.

"How can you tell? The Roman Empire was real enough once—as long as people believed in it," replied Mr. Forkett.

The argument continued for some little time, with Mr. Forkett growing more monumental and Mr. Watts more fundamental. Finally Mr. Forkett summed up his opinion:

"Frankly, your iconoclastic, revolutionary views seem to me to differ only in name from bolshevism."

Mr. Watts rose to his feet.

"The consolidation of society on faith, irrespective of scientific truth, is the method of a Stalin," he observed, and withdrew to the other end of the car.

"Really," said Norma. "I don't know how you can be so rude and ungrateful to him. When I think of them all with their toasting forks, and that poor woman hanging there without a stitch on, and upside down, too—"

"It was all quite appropriate to the time and place. He's a very danger-ous young man," said Mr. Forkett firmly.

Henry thought it time to change the conversation. The four of them chatted more generally as the train rattled on at a good speed, though not as fast as it had descended, but after a time the talk began to wilt. Glancing up the coach, Henry noticed that Mr. Watts had already gone to sleep again, and felt that there was no better way of spending the time.

He awoke to hear voices shouting: "Stand clear of the doors!" and to find that the carriage was full of people again. Almost as his eyes opened, Norma's elbow stuck into his ribs.

"Look!" she said.

The straphanger in front of them was interested in the racing part of his paper so that the front page faced them with the headline: RUSH-HOUR TUBE SMASH: 12 DEAD. Under it was a column of names. Henry leaned forward to read them. The holder of the paper lowered it to glare indignantly, but not before Henry had noticed his own name and those of the others.

Norma looked troubled.

"Don't know *how* I'm going to explain that at home," she said.

"You get my point?" inquired Mr. Forkett on Henry's other side. "Just think of the trouble there's going to be straightening this out—newspapers, coroners, heaven knows what. Not a safe fellow to have about. Quite antisocial."

"I don't know what my husband is going to think. He's such a jealous man," remarked Mrs. Branton, not without satisfaction.

The train stopped at St. Paul's, thinned somewhat, and then went on. Mr. Forkett and Norma prepared to get out. It occurred to Henry that he might as well get out, too. The train slowed.

"Don't know what they're going to say in the office, seeing me walk in. Still, it's been ever so int'resting, really. Ta-ta for now, everyone," said Norma, and wriggled into the departing crowd, with the skill of long practice.

A hand grasped Henry's arm as they stepped onto the platform.

"There he is," said Mr. Forkett. He nodded ahead. Henry saw the back view of Mr. Watts preceding them up the platform. "Can you spare a few minutes? Don't trust the fellow at all."

They followed up the escalator and round to the steps which brought them to the surface in front of the Royal Exchange.

There Mr. Watts paused and looked around him, seeming to con-sider. Then his attention fixed itself on the Bank of England. He strode forward in a forceful manner, and came to a stop facing the Bank, looking up at it. His lips moved.

The ground shook slightly underfoot. Three windows fell out of one of the Bank's upper stories. One statue, two urns, and a piece of balustrading swayed and toppled. Several people screamed.

Mr. Watts squared his shoulders, and took a deep breath.

"Good heavens! He's—" began Mr. Forkett, but the rest was lost as he sped from Henry's side.

"I—" announced Mr. Watts, at the top of his voice.

"DON'T—" he went on, to the accompaniment of an ominous trembling of the ground.

"BE—" but at that moment a strong push between his shoulder blades thrust him full in the path of a hurtling bus.

There was a shriek of brakes applied too late.

"That's 'im! I sore 'im do it!" screamed a woman, pointing at Mr. Forkett.

Henry caught up with him just as a policeman came running.

Mr. Forkett was regarding the façade of the Bank with pride.

"No telling what might have happened. A menace to society, that young man," he said. "They ought to give me a medal, but I'm afraid they're more likely to hang me—after all, tradition must be observed."

# THE BIRDS

## Daphne du Maurier

DAPHNE DU MAURIER (1907–   ) has lived in the very center of her own material. Granddaughter of the author of *Trilby*; daughter of Sir Gerald du Maurier, England's most celebrated and attractive actor-manager during the decades between the Wars, she is today Lady Browning, wife of Lieutenant General Sir Frederick Browning, an administrative executive of the Royal Household. The Cornish coast where she grew up as a child is the setting for the house in which she lives today, virtually the original of the one in her novel *Rebecca*. Strange, moody, romantic, intense—all these are the adjectives that belong to Miss du Maurier. A flair for horror and suspense is perhaps her special badge and finds full expression in the tale that follows.

O N December the third the wind changed overnight and it was winter. Until then the autumn had been mellow, soft. The earth was rich where the plow had turned it.

Nat Hocken, because of a wartime disability, had a pension and did not work full time at the farm. He worked three days a week, and they gave him the lighter jobs. Although he was married, with children, his was a solitary disposition; he liked best to work alone.

It pleased him when he was given a bank to build up, or a gate to mend, at the far end of the peninsula, where the sea surrounded the farmland on either side. Then, at midday, he would pause and eat the meat pie his wife had baked for him and, sitting on the cliff's edge, watch the birds.

In autumn great flocks of them came to the peninsula, restless, uneasy, spending themselves in motion; now wheeling, circling in the sky; now settling to feed on the rich, new-turned soil; but even when they fed, it was as though they did so without hunger, without desire.

Restlessness drove them to the skies again. Crying, whistling, calling, they skimmed the placid sea and left the shore.

Make haste, make speed, hurry and begone; yet where, and to what purpose? The restless urge of autumn, unsatisfying, sad, had put a spell upon them, and they must spill themselves of motion before winter came.

Perhaps, thought Nat, a message comes to the birds in autumn, like a warning. Winter is coming. Many of them will perish. And like people who, apprehensive of death before their time, drive themselves to work or folly, the birds do likewise; tomorrow we shall die.

The birds had been more restless than ever this fall of the year. Their agitation more remarked because the days were still.

As Mr. Trigg's tractor traced its path up and down the western hills, and Nat, hedging, saw it dip and turn, the whole machine and the man upon it were momentarily lost in the great cloud of wheeling, crying birds.

Nat remarked upon them to Mr. Trigg when the work was finished for the day.

"Yes," said the farmer, "there are more birds about than usual. I have a notion the weather will change. It will be a hard winter. That's why the birds are restless."

The farmer was right. That night the weather turned.

The bedroom in the cottage faced east. Nat woke just after two and heard the east wind, cold and dry. It sounded hollow in the chimney, and a loose slate rattled on the roof. Nat listened, and he could hear the sea roaring in the bay. He drew the blanket round him, leaned closer to the back of his wife, deep in sleep. Then he heard the tapping on the windowpane. It continued until, irritated by the sound, Nat got out of bed and went to the window. He opened it; and as he did so something brushed his hand, jabbing at his knuckles, grazing the skin. Then he saw the flutter of wings and the thing was gone again, over the roof, behind the cottage.

It was a bird. What kind of bird he could not tell. The wind must have driven it to shelter on the sill.

He shut the window and went back to bed, but feeling his knuckles wet, put his mouth to the scratch. The bird had drawn blood.

Frightened, he supposed, bewildered, seeking shelter, the bird had stabbed at him in the darkness. Once more he settled himself to sleep.

Presently the tapping came again—this time more forceful, more insistent. And now his wife woke at the sound, and turning in the bed, said to him, "See to the window, Nat; it's rattling."

"I've already been to it," he told her. "There's some bird there, trying to get in."

"Send it away," she said. "I can't sleep with that noise."

He went to the window for the second time, and now when he opened it, there was not one bird on the sill but half a dozen; they flew straight into his face.

He shouted, striking out at them with his arms, scattering them; like the first one, they flew over the roof and disappeared.

He let the window fall and latched it.

Suddenly a frightened cry came from the room across the passage where the children slept.

"It's Jill," said his wife, roused at the sound.

There came a second cry, this time from both children. Stumbling into their room, Nat felt the beating of wings about him in the darkness. The window was wide open. Through it came the birds, hitting first the ceiling and the walls, then swerving in midflight and turning to the children in their beds.

"It's all right. I'm here," shouted Nat, and the children flung themselves, screaming, upon him, while in the darkness the birds rose, and dived, and came for him again.

"What is it, Nat? What's happened?" his wife called. Swiftly he pushed the children through the door to the passage and shut it upon them, so that he was alone in their bedroom with the birds.

He seized a blanket from the nearest bed, and using it as a weapon, flung it to right and left about him.

He felt the thud of bodies, heard the fluttering of wings; but the birds were not yet defeated, for again and again they returned to the assault, jabbing his hands, his head, their little stabbing beaks sharp as pointed forks.

The blanket became a weapon of defense. He wound it about his head, and then in greater darkness, beat at the birds with his bare hands. He dared not stumble to the door and open it lest the birds follow him.

How long he fought with them in the darkness he could not tell; but at last the beating of the wings about him lessened, withdrew; and through the dense blanket he was aware of light.

He waited, listened; there was no sound except the fretful crying of one of the children from the bedroom beyond.

He took the blanket from his head and stared about him. The cold gray morning light exposed the room.

Dawn and the open window had called the living birds; the dead lay on the floor.

Sickened, Nat went to the window and stared out across his patch of garden to the fields.

It was bitter cold, and the ground had all the hard, black look of the frost that the east wind brings. The sea, fiercer now with turning tide, whitecapped and steep, broke harshly in the bay. Of the birds there was no sign.

Nat shut the window and the door of the small bedroom and went back across the passage to his own room.

His wife sat up in bed, one child asleep beside her; the smaller one in her arms, his face bandaged.

"He's sleeping now," she whispered. "Something must have cut him; there was blood at the corners of his eyes. Jill said it was the birds. She said she woke up and the birds were in the room."

His wife looked up at Nat, searching his face for confirmation. She looked terrified, bewildered. He did not want her to know that he also was shaken, dazed almost, by the events of the past few hours.

"There are birds in there," he said. "Dead birds, nearly fifty of them." He sat down on the bed beside his wife.

"It's the hard weather," he said. "It must be that; it's the hard weather. They aren't the birds, maybe, from around here. They've been driven down from upcountry."

"But Nat," whispered his wife, "it's only this night that the weather turned. They can't be hungry yet. There's food for them out there in the fields."

"It's the weather," repeated Nat. "I tell you, it's the weather."

His face, too, was drawn and tired, like hers. They stared at one another for a while without speaking.

Nat went to the window and looked out. The sky was hard and leaden, and the blown hills that had gleamed in the sun the day before looked dark and bare. Black winter had descended in a single night.

The children were awake now. Jill was chattering, and young Johnny was crying once again. Nat heard his wife's voice, soothing, comforting them as he went downstairs.

Presently they came down. He had breakfast ready for them.

"Did you drive away the birds?" asked Jill.

"Yes, they've all gone now," Nat said. "It was the east wind brought them in."

"I hope they won't come again," said Jill.

"I'll walk with you to the bus," Nat said to her.

Jill seemed to have forgotten her experience of the night before. She danced ahead of him, chasing the leaves, her face rosy under her pixy hood.

All the while Nat searched the hedgerows for the birds, glanced over them to the fields beyond, looked to the small wood above the farm where the rooks and jackdaws gathered; he saw none. Soon the bus came ambling up the hill.

Nat saw Jill onto the bus, then turned and walked back toward the farm. It was not his day for work, but he wanted to satisfy himself that all was well. He went to the back door of the farmhouse; he

heard Mrs. Trigg singing, the wireless making a background for her
song.

"Are you there, missus?" Nat called.

She came to the door, beaming, broad, a good-tempered woman.

"Hullo, Mr. Hocken," she said. "Can you tell me where this cold is
coming from? Is it Russia? I've never seen such a change. And it's
going on, the wireless says. Something to do with the Arctic Circle."

"We didn't turn on the wireless this morning," said Nat. "Fact is, we
had trouble in the night."

"Kiddies poorly?"

"No." He hardly knew how to explain. Now, in daylight, the battle
of the birds would sound absurd.

He tried to tell Mrs. Twigg what had happened, but he could see
from her eyes that she thought his story was the result of nightmare
following a heavy meal.

"Sure they were real birds?" she said, smiling.

"Mrs. Trigg," he said, "there are fifty dead birds—robins, wrens, and
such—lying now on the floor of the children's bedroom. They went for
me; they tried to go for young Johnny's eyes."

Mrs. Trigg stared at him doubtfully. "Well, now," she answered.
"I suppose the weather brought them; once in the bedroom they
wouldn't know where they were. Foreign birds maybe, from that
Arctic Circle."

"No," said Nat. "They were the birds you see about here every
day."

"Funny thing," said Mrs. Trigg. "No explaining it, really. You ought
to write up and ask the *Guardian*. They'd have some answer for it.
Well, I must be getting on."

Nat walked back along the lane to his cottage. He found his wife
in the kitchen with young Johnny.

"See anyone?" she asked.

"Mrs. Trigg," he answered. "I don't think she believed me. Anyway,
nothing wrong up there."

"You might take the birds away," she said. "I daren't go into the
room to make the beds until you do. I'm scared."

"Nothing to scare you now," said Nat. "They're dead, aren't they?"

He went up with a sack and dropped the stiff bodies into it, one
by one. Yes, there were fifty of them all told. Just the ordinary,
common birds of the hedgerow; nothing as large even as a thrush. It
must have been fright that made them act the way they did.

He took the sack out into the garden and was faced with a fresh
problem. The ground was frozen solid, yet no snow had fallen; nothing
had happened in the past hours but the coming of the east wind. It

was unnatural, queer. He could see the white-capped seas breaking in the bay. He decided to take the birds to the shore and bury them.

When he reached the beach below the headland, he could scarcely stand, the force of the east wind was so strong. It was low tide; he crunched his way over the shingle to the softer sand then, his back to the wind, opened up his sack.

He ground a pit in the sand with his heel, meaning to drop the birds into it; but as he did so, the force of the wind lifted them as though in flight again, and they were blown away from him along the beach, tossed like feathers, spread and scattered.

The tide will take them when it turns, he said to himself.

He looked out to sea and watched the crested breakers, combing green. They rose stiffly, curled, and broke again; and because it was ebb tide, the roar was distant, more remote, lacking the sound and thunder of the flood.

Then he saw them. The gulls. Out there, riding the seas.

What he had thought at first were the whitecaps of the waves were gulls. Hundreds, thousands, tens of thousands.

They rose and fell in the troughs of the seas, heads to the wind, like a mighty fleet at anchor, waiting on the tide.

Nat turned; leaving the beach, he climbed the steep path home.

Someone should know of this. Someone should be told. Something was happening, because of the east wind and the weather, that he did not understand.

As he drew near the cottage, his wife came to meet him at the door. She called to him, excited. "Nat," she said, "it's on the wireless. They've just read out a special news bulletin. It's not only here, it's everywhere. In London, all over the country. Something has happened to the birds. Come listen; they're repeating it."

Together they went into the kitchen to listen to the announcement.

"Statement from the Home Office, at eleven A.M. this morning. Reports from all over the country are coming in hourly about the vast quantity of birds flocking above towns, villages, and outlying districts, causing obstruction and damage and even attacking individuals. It is thought that the Arctic air stream at present covering The British Isles is causing birds to migrate south in immense numbers, and that intense hunger may drive these birds to attack human beings. Householders are warned to see to their windows, doors, and chimneys, and to take reasonable precautions for the safety of their children. A further statement will be issued later."

A kind of excitement seized Nat. He looked at his wife in triumph. "There you are," he said. "I've been telling myself all morning there's something wrong. And just now, down on the beach, I looked out to sea and there were gulls, thousands of them, riding on the sea, waiting."

"What are they waiting for, Nat?" she asked.

He stared at her. "I don't know," he said slowly.

He went over to the drawer where he kept his hammer and other tools.

"What are you going to do, Nat?"

"See to the windows and the chimneys, like they tell you to."

"You think they would break in with the windows shut? Those wrens and robins and such? Why, how could they?"

He did not answer. He was not thinking of the robins and the wrens. He was thinking of the gulls.

He went upstairs and worked there the rest of the morning, boarding the windows of the bedrooms, filling up the chimney bases.

"Dinner's ready." His wife called him from the kitchen.

"All right. Coming down."

When dinner was over and his wife was washing up, Nat switched on the one o'clock news. The same announcement was repeated, but the news bulletin enlarged upon it. "The flocks of birds have caused dislocation in all areas," said the announcer, "and in London the mass was so dense at ten o'clock this morning that it seemed like a vast black cloud. The birds settled on rooftops, on window ledges, and on chimneys. The species included blackbird, thrush, the common house sparrow, and as might be expected in the metropolis, a vast quantity of pigeons, starlings, and that frequenter of the London river, the black-headed gull. The sight was so unusual that traffic came to a standstill in many thoroughfares, work was abandoned in shops and offices, and the streets and pavements were crowded with people standing about to watch the birds."

The announcer's voice was smooth and suave; Nat had the impression that he treated the whole business as he would an elaborate joke. There would be others like him, hundreds of them, who did not know what it was to struggle in darkness with a flock of birds.

Nat switched off the wireless. He got up and started work on the kitchen windows. His wife watched him, young Johnny at her heels.

"What they ought to do," she said, "is to call the Army out and shoot the birds."

"Let them try," said Nat. "How'd they set about it?"

"I don't know. But something should be done. They ought to do something."

Nat thought to himself that "they" were no doubt considering the problem at that very moment, but whatever "they" decided to do in

London and the big cities would not help them here, nearly three hundred miles away.

"How are we off for food?" he asked.

"It's shopping day tomorrow, you know that. I don't keep uncooked food about. Butcher doesn't call till the day after. But I can bring back something when I go in tomorrow."

Nat did not want to scare her. He looked in the larder for himself and in the cupboard where she kept her tins.

They could hold out for a couple of days.

He went on hammering the boards across the kitchen windows. Candles. They were low on candles. That must be another thing she meant to buy tomorrow. Well, they must go early to bed tonight. That was, if—

He got up and went out the back door and stood in the garden, looking down toward the sea.

There had been no sun all day, and now, at barely three o'clock, a kind of darkness had already come; the sky was sullen, heavy, colorless like salt. He could hear the vicious sea drumming on the rocks.

He walked down the path halfway to the beach. And then he stopped. He could see the tide had turned. The gulls had risen. They were circling, hundreds of them, thousands of them, lifting their wings against the wind.

It was the gulls that made the darkening of the sky.

And they were silent. They just went on soaring and circling, rising, falling, trying their strength against the wind. Nat turned. He ran up the path back to the cottage.

"I'm going for Jill," he said to his wife.

"What's the matter?" she asked. "You've gone quite white."

"Keep Johnny inside," he said. "Keep the door shut. Light up now and draw the curtains."

"It's only gone three," she said.

"Never mind. Do what I tell you."

He looked inside the tool shed and took the hoe.

He started walking up the lane to the bus stop. Now and again he glanced back over his shoulder; and he could see the gulls had risen higher now, their circles were broader, they were spreading out in huge formation across the sky.

He hurried on. Although he knew the bus would not come before four o'clock, he had to hurry.

He waited at the top of the hill. There was half an hour still to go.

The east wind came whipping across the fields from the higher ground. In the distance he could see the clay hills, white and clean against the heavy pallor of the sky.

Something black rose from behind them, like a smudge at first, then widening, becoming deeper. The smudge became a cloud; and the cloud divided again into five other clouds, spreading north, east, south, and west; and then they were not clouds at all but birds.

He watched them travel across the sky, within two or three hundred feet of him. He knew, from their speed, that they were bound inland; they had no business with the people here on the peninsula. They were rooks, crows, jackdaws, magpies, jays, all birds that usually preyed upon the smaller species, but bound this afternoon on some other mission.

He went to the telephone call box, stepped inside, lifted the receiver. The exchange would pass the message on. "I'm speaking from the highway," he said, "by the bus stop. I want to report large formations of birds traveling upcountry. The gulls are also forming in the bay."

"All right," answered the voice, laconic, weary.

"You'll be sure and pass this message on to the proper quarter?"

"Yes. Yes." Impatient now, fed up. The buzzing note resumed.

She's another, thought Nat. She doesn't care.

The bus came lumbering up the hill. Jill climbed out.

"What's the hoe for, Dad?"

"I just brought it along," he said. "Come on now, let's get home. It's cold; no hanging about. See how fast you can run."

He could see the gulls now, still silent, circling the fields, coming in toward the land.

"Look, Dad; look over there. Look at all the gulls."

"Yes. Hurry now."

"Where are they flying to? Where are they going?"

"Upcountry, I dare say. Where it's warmer."

He seized her hand and dragged her after him along the lane.

"Don't go so fast. I can't keep up."

The gulls were copying the rooks and the crows. They were spreading out, in formation, across the sky. They headed, in bands of thousands, to the four compass points.

"Dad, what is it? What are the gulls doing?"

They were not intent upon their flight, as the crows, as the jackdaws, had been. They still circled overhead. Nor did they fly so high. It was as though they waited upon some signal; as though some decision had yet to be given.

"I wish the gulls would go away," Jill was crying. "I don't like them. They're coming closer to the lane."

He started running, swinging Jill after him. As they went past the farm turning he saw the farmer backing his car into the garage. Nat called to him.

"Can you give us a lift?" he said.

Mr. Trigg turned in the driver's seat and stared at them. Then a smile came to his cheerful, rubicund face. "It looks as though we're in for some fun," he said. "Have you seen the gulls? Jim and I are going to take a crack at them. Everyone's gone bird crazy, talking of nothing else. I hear you were troubled in the night. Want a gun?"

Nat shook his head.

The small car was packed, but there was room for Jill on the back seat.

"I don't want a gun," said Nat, "but I'd be obliged if you'd run Jill home. She's scared of the birds."

"Okay," said the farmer. "I'll take her home. Why don't you stop behind and join the shooting match? We'll make the feathers fly."

Jill climbed in, and turning the car, the driver sped up the lane. Nat followed after. Trigg must be crazy. What use was a gun against a sky of birds?

They were coming in now toward the farm, circling lower in the sky. The farm, then, was their target. Nat increased his pace toward his own cottage. He saw the farmer's car turn and come back along the lane. It drew up beside him with a jerk.

"The kid has run inside," said the farmer. "Your wife was watching for her. Well, what do you make of it? They're saying in town the Russians have done it. The Russians have poisoned the birds."

"How could they do that?" asked Nat.

"Don't ask me. You know how stories get around."

"Have you boarded your windows?" asked Nat.

"No. Lot of nonsense. I've had more to do today than to go round boarding up my windows."

"I'd board them now if I were you."

"Garn. You're windy. Like to come to our place to sleep?"

"No, thanks all the same."

"All right. See you in the morning. Give you a gull breakfast."

The farmer grinned and turned his car to the farm entrance. Nat hurried on. Past the little wood, past the old barn, and then across the stile to the remaining field. As he jumped the stile, he heard the whir of wings. A black-backed gull dived down at him from the sky. It missed, swerved in flight, and rose to dive again. In a moment it was joined by others—six, seven, a dozen.

Nat dropped his hoe. The hoe was useless. Covering his head with his arms, he ran toward the cottage.

They kept coming at him from the air—noiseless, silent, save for the beating wings. The terrible, fluttering wings. He could feel the blood on his hands, his wrists, upon his neck. If only he could keep them from his eyes. Nothing else mattered.

With each dive, with each attack, they became bolder. And they had no thought for themselves. When they dived low and missed, they crashed, bruised and broken, on the ground.

As Nat ran he stumbled, kicking their spent bodies in front of him.

He found the door and hammered upon it with his bleeding hands. "Let me in," he shouted. "It's Nat. Let me in."

Then he saw the gannet, poised for the dive, above him in the sky.

The gulls circled, retired, soared, one with another, against the wind.

Only the gannet remained. One single gannet, above him in the sky. Its wings folded suddenly to its body. It dropped like a stone.

Nat screamed; and the door opened.

He stumbled across the threshold, and his wife threw her weight against the door.

They heard the thud of the gannet as it fell.

His wife dressed his wounds. They were not deep. The backs of his hands had suffered most, and his wrists. Had he not worn a cap, the birds would have reached his head. As for the gannet—the gannet could have split his skull.

The children were crying, of course. They had seen the blood on their father's hands.

"It's all right now," he told them. "I'm not hurt."

His wife was ashen. "I saw them overhead," she whispered. "They began collecting just as Jill ran in with Mr. Trigg. I shut the door fast, and it jammed. That's why I couldn't open it at once when you came."

"Thank God the birds waited for me," he said. "Jill would have fallen at once. They're flying inland, thousands of them. Rooks, crows, all the bigger birds. I saw them from the bus stop. They're making for the towns."

"But what can they do, Nat?"

"They'll attack. Go for everyone out in the streets. Then they'll try the windows, the chimneys."

"Why don't the authorities do something? Why don't they get the Army, get machine guns?"

"There's been no time. Nobody's prepared. We'll hear what they have to say on the six o'clock news."

"I can hear the birds," Jill said. "Listen, Dad."

Nat listened. Muffled sounds came from the windows, from the door. Wings brushing the surface, sliding, scraping, seeking a way of entry.

The sound of many bodies pressed together, shuffling on the sills. Now and again came a thud, a crash, as some bird dived and fell.

Some of them will kill themselves that way, he thought, but not enough. Never enough.

"All right," he said aloud. "I've got boards over the windows, Jill. The birds can't get in."

He went and examined all the windows. He found wedges—pieces of old tin, strips of wood and metal—and fastened them at the sides of the windows to reinforce the boards.

His hammering helped to deafen the sound of the birds, the shuffling, the tapping, and—more ominous—the splinter of breaking glass.

"Turn on the wireless," he said.

He went upstairs to the bedrooms and reinforced the windows there. Now he could hear the birds on the roof—the scraping of claws, a sliding, jostling sound.

He decided the whole family must sleep in the kitchen and keep up the fire. He was afraid of the bedroom chimneys. The boards he had placed at their bases might give way. In the kitchen they would be safe because of the fire.

He would have to make a joke of it. Pretend to the children they were playing camp. If the worst happened and the birds forced an entry by way of the bedroom chimneys, it would be hours, days perhaps, before they could break down the doors. The birds would be imprisoned in the bedrooms. They could do no harm there. Crowded together, they would stifle and die. He began to bring the mattresses downstairs.

At sight of them, his wife's eyes widened in apprehension.

"All right," he said cheerfully. "We'll all sleep together in the kitchen tonight. More cozy, here by the fire. Then we won't be worried by those silly old birds tapping at the windows."

He made the children help him rearrange the furniture, and he took the precaution of moving the dresser against the windows.

We're safe enough now, he thought. We're snug and tight. We can hold out. It's just the food that worries me. Food and coal for the fire. We've enough for two or three days, not more. By that time—

No use thinking ahead as far as that. And they'd be given directions on the wireless.

And now, in the midst of many problems, he realized that only dance music was coming over the air. He knew the reason. The usual programs had been abandoned; this only happened at exceptional times.

At six o'clock the records ceased. The time signal was given. There was a pause, and then the announcer spoke. His voice was solemn, grave. Quite different from midday.

"This is London," he said. "A national emergency was proclaimed at four o'clock this afternoon. Measures are being taken to safeguard the lives and property of the population, but it must be understood that these are not easy to effect immediately, owing to the unforeseen and unparalleled nature of the present crisis. Every householder must take precautions about his own building. Where several people live together, as in flats and hotels, they must unite to do the utmost that they can to prevent entry. It is absolutely imperative that every individual stay indoors tonight.

"The birds, in vast numbers, are attacking anyone on sight, and have already begun an assault upon buildings; but these, with due care, should be impenetrable.

"The population is asked to remain calm.

"Owing to the exceptional nature of the emergency, there will be no further transmission from any broadcasting station until seven A.M. tomorrow."

They played "God Save the Queen." Nothing more happened.

Nat switched off the set. He looked at his wife. She stared back at him.

"We'll have supper early," suggested Nat. "Something for a treat —toasted cheese, eh? Something we all like."

He winked and nodded at his wife. He wanted the look of dread, of apprehension, to leave her face.

He helped with the supper, whistling, singing, making as much clatter as he could. It seemed to him that the shuffling and the tapping were not so intense as they had been at first, and presently he went up to the bedrooms and listened. He no longer heard the jostling for place upon the roof.

They've got reasoning powers, he thought. They know it's hard to break in here. They'll try elsewhere.

Supper passed without incident. Then, when they were clearing away, they heard a new sound, a familiar droning.

His wife looked up at him, her face alight.

"It's planes," she said. "They're sending out planes after the birds. That will get them. Isn't that gunfire? Can't you hear guns?"

It might be gunfire, out at sea. Nat could not tell. Big naval guns might have some effect upon the gulls out at sea, but the gulls were inland now. The guns couldn't shell the shore because of the population.

"It's good, isn't it," said his wife, "to hear the planes?"

Catching her enthusiasm, Jill jumped up and down with Johnny. "The planes will get the birds."

Just then they heard a crash about two miles distant. Followed by a second, then a third. The droning became more distant, passed away out to sea.

"What was that?" asked his wife.

"I don't know," answered Nat. He did not want to tell her that the sound they had heard was the crashing of aircraft.

It was, he had no doubt, a gamble on the part of the authorities to send out reconnaissance forces, but they might have known the gamble was suicidal. What could aircraft do against birds that flung themselves to death against propeller and fuselage but hurtle to the ground themselves?

"Where have the planes gone, Dad?" asked Jill.

"Back to base," he said. "Come on now, time to tuck down for bed."

There was no further drone of aircraft, and the naval guns had ceased. Waste of life and effort, Nat said to himself. We can't destroy enough of them that way. Cost too heavy. There's always gas. Maybe they'll try spraying with gas, mustard gas. We'll be warned first, of course, if they do. There's one thing, the best brains of the country will be on it tonight.

Upstairs in the bedrooms all was quiet. No more scraping and stabbing at the windows. A lull in battle. The wind hadn't dropped, though. Nat could still hear it roaring in the chimneys. And the sea breaking down on the shore.

Then he remembered the tide. The tide would be on the turn. Maybe the lull in battle was because of the tide. There was some law the birds obeyed, and it had to do with the east wind and the tide.

He glanced at his watch. Nearly eight o'clock. It must have gone high water an hour ago. That explained the lull. The birds attacked with the flood tide.

He reckoned the time limit in his head. They had six hours to go without attack. When the tide turned again, around 1:20 in the morning, the birds would come back.

He called softly to his wife and whispered to her that he would go out and see how they were faring at the farm, see if the telephone was still working there so that they might get news from the exchange.

"You're not to go," she said at once, "and leave me alone with the children. I can't stand it."

"All right," he said, "all right. I'll wait till morning. And we can get the wireless bulletin then, too, at seven. But when the tide ebbs again, I'll try for the farm; they may let us have bread and potatoes."

His mind was busy again, planning against emergency. They would not have milked, of course, this evening. The cows would be standing by the gate, waiting; the household would be inside, battened behind boards as they were here at the cottage.

That is, if they had had time to take precautions.

Softly, stealthily, he opened the back door and looked outside.

It was pitch-dark. The wind was blowing harder than ever, coming in steady gusts, icy, from the sea.

He kicked at the step. It was heaped with birds. These were the suicides, the divers, the ones with broken necks. Wherever he looked, he saw dead birds. The living had flown seaward with the turn of the tide. The gulls would be riding the seas now, as they had done in the forenoon.

In the far distance on the hill, something was burning. One of the aircraft that had crashed; the fire, fanned by the wind, had set light to a stack.

He looked at the bodies of the birds. He had a notion that if he stacked them, one upon the other, on the window sills, they would be added protection against the next attack.

Not much, perhaps, but something. The bodies would have to be clawed at, pecked and dragged aside before the living birds gained purchase on the sills and attacked the panes.

He set to work in the darkness. It was queer. He hated touching the dead birds, but he went on with his work. He noticed grimly that every windowpane was shattered. Only the boards had kept the birds from breaking in.

He stuffed the cracked panes with the bleeding bodies of the birds and felt his stomach turn. When he had finished, he went back into the cottage and barricaded the kitchen door, making it doubly secure.

His wife had made him cocoa; he drank it thirstily. He was very tired. "All right," he said, smiling, "don't worry. We'll get through."

He lay down on his mattress and closed his eyes.

He dreamed uneasily because, through his dreams, ran the dread of something forgotten. Some piece of work that he should have done. It was connected, in some way, with the burning aircraft.

It was his wife, shaking his shoulder, who awoke him finally.

"They've begun," she sobbed. "They've started this last hour. I can't listen to it any longer alone. There's something smells bad too, something burning."

Then he remembered. He had forgotten to make up the fire.

The fire was smoldering, nearly out. He got up swiftly and lighted the lamp.

The hammering had started at the windows and the door, but it was not that he minded now. It was the smell of singed feathers.

The smell filled the kitchen. He knew what it was at once. The birds were coming down the chimney, squeezing their way down to the kitchen range.

He got sticks and paper and put them on the embers, then reached for the can of kerosene.

"Stand back," he shouted to his wife. He threw some of the kerosene onto the fire.

The flame roared up the pipe, and down into the fire fell the scorched, blackened bodies of the birds.

The children waked, crying. "What is it?" asked Jill. "What's happened?"

Nat had no time to answer her. He was raking the bodies from the chimney, clawing them out onto the floor.

The flames would drive away the living birds from the chimney top. The lower joint was the difficulty though. It was choked with the smoldering, helpless bodies of the birds caught by fire.

He scarcely heeded the attack on the windows and the door. Let them beat their wings, break their backs, lose their lives, in the desperate attempt to force an entry into his home. They would not break in.

"Stop crying," he called to the children. "There's nothing to be afraid of. Stop crying."

He went on raking out the burning, smoldering bodies as they fell into the fire.

This'll fetch them, he said to himself. The draft and the flames together. We're all right as long as the chimney doesn't catch.

Amid the tearing at the window boards came the sudden homely striking of the kitchen clock. Three o'clock.

A little more than four hours to go. He could not be sure of the exact time of high water. He reckoned the tide would not turn much before half past seven.

He waited by the range. The flames were dying. But no more blackened bodies fell from the chimney. He thrust his poker up as far as it could go and found nothing.

The danger of the chimney's being choked up was over. It could not happen again, not if the fire was kept burning day and night.

I'll have to get more fuel from the farm tomorrow, he thought. I can do all that with the ebb tide. It can be worked; we can fetch what we need when the tide's turned. We've just got to adapt ourselves, that's all.

They drank tea and cocoa, ate slices of bread. Only half a loaf left, Nat noticed. Never mind, though; they'd get by.

If they could hang on like this until seven, when the first news bulletin came through, they would not have done too badly.

"Give us a smoke," he said to his wife. "It will clear away the smell of the scorched feathers."

"There's only two left in the packet," she said. "I was going to buy you some."

"I'll have one," he said.

He sat with one arm around his wife and one around Jill, with Johnny on his lap, the blankets heaped about them on the mattress.

"You can't help admiring the beggars," he said. "They've got persistency. You'd think they'd tire of the game, but not a bit of it."

Admiration was hard to sustain. The tapping went on and on; and a new, rasping note struck Nat's ear, as though a sharper beak than any hitherto had come to take over from its fellows.

He tried to remember the names of birds; he tried to think which species would go for this particular job.

It was not the tap of the woodpecker. That would be light and frequent. This was more serious; if it continued long, the wood would splinter as the glass had done.

Then he remembered the hawks. Could the hawks have taken over from the gulls? Were there buzzards now upon the sills, using talons as well as beaks? Hawks, buzzards, kestrels, falcons; he had forgotten the birds of prey. He had forgotten the gripping power of the birds of prey. Three hours to go; and while they waited, the sound of the splintering wood, the talons tearing at the wood.

Nat looked about him, seeing what furniture he could destory to fortify the door.

The windows were safe because of the dresser. He was not certain of the door. He went upstairs; but when he reached the landing, he paused and listened.

There was a soft patter on the floor of the children's bedroom. The birds had broken through.

The other bedroom was still clear. He brought out the furniture to pile at the head of the stairs should the door of the children's bedroom go.

"Come down, Nat. What are you doing?" called his wife.

"I won't be long," he shouted. "I'm just making everything shipshape up here."

He did not want her to come. He did not want her to hear the pattering in the children's bedroom, the brushing of those wings against the door.

After he suggested breakfast, he found himself watching the clock, gazing at the hands that went so slowly around the dial. If his theory was not correct, if the attack did not cease with the turn of the tide, he knew they were beaten. They could not continue through the long day without air, without rest, without fuel.

A crackling in his ears drove away the sudden, desperate desire for sleep.

"What is it? What now?" he said sharply.

"The wireless," said his wife. "I've been watching the clock. It's nearly seven."

The comfortable crackling of the wireless brought new life.

They waited. The kitchen clock struck seven.

The crackling continued. Nothing else. No chimes. No music.

They waited until a quarter past. No news bulletin came through.

"We heard wrong," he said. "They won't be broadcasting until eight o'clock."

They left the wireless switched on. Nat thought of the battery, wondered how much power was left in the battery. If it failed, they would not hear the instructions.

"It's getting light," whispered his wife. "I can't see it but I can feel it. And listen! The birds aren't hammering so loud now."

She was right. The rasping, tearing sound grew fainter every moment. So did the shuffling, the jostling for place upon the step, upon the sills. The tide was on the turn.

By eight there was no sound at all. Only the wind. And the crackling of the wireless. The children, lulled at last by the stillness, fell asleep.

At half past eight, Nat switched the wireless off.

"We'll miss the news," said his wife.

"There isn't going to be any news," said Nat. "We've got to depend upon ourselves."

He went to the door and slowly pulled away the barricades. He drew the bolts, and kicking the broken bodies from the step outside the door, breathed the cold air.

He had six working hours before him, and he knew he must reserve his strength to the utmost, not waste it in any way.

Food and light and fuel; these were the most necessary things. If he could get them, they could endure another night.

He stepped into the garden; and as he did so, he saw the living birds. The gulls had gone to ride the sea, as they had done before. They sought sea food and the buoyancy of the tide before they returned to the attack.

Not so the land birds. They waited, and watched.

Nat saw them on the hedgerows, on the soil, crowded in the trees, outside in the field—line upon line of birds, still, doing nothing. He went to the end of his small garden.

The birds did not move. They merely watched him.

I've got to get food, Nat said to himself. I've got to go to the farm to get food.

He went back to the cottage. He saw to the windows and the door. "I'm going to the farm," he said.

His wife clung to him. She had seen the living birds from the open door.

"Take us with you," she begged. "We can't stay here alone. I'd rather die than stay here alone."

"Come on, then," he said. "Bring baskets and Johnny's pram. We can load up the pram."

They dressed against the biting wind. His wife put Johnny in the pram, and Nat took Jill's hand.

"The birds," Jill whimpered. "They're all out there in the fields."

"They won't hurt us," he said. "Not in the light."

They started walking across the field toward the stile, and the birds did not move. They waited, their heads turned to the wind.

When they reached the turning to the farm, Nat stopped and told his wife to wait in the shelter of the hedge with the two children. "But I want to see Mrs. Trigg," she protested. "There are lots of things we can borrow if they went to market yesterday, and—"

"Wait here," Nat interrupted. "I'll be back in a moment."

The cows were lowing, moving restlessly in the yard, and he could see a gap in the fence where the sheep had knocked their way through to roam unchecked in the front garden before the farmhouse.

No smoke came from the chimneys. Nat was filled with misgiving. He did not want his wife or the children to go down to the farm.

He went down alone, pushing his way through the herd of lowing cows, who turned this way and that, distressed, their udders full.

He saw the car standing by the gate. Not put away in the garage.

All the windows of the farmhouse were smashed. There were many dead gulls lying in the yard and around the house.

The living birds perched on the group of trees behind the farm and on the roof of the house. They were quite still. They watched him. Jim's body lay in the yard. What was left of it. His gun was beside him.

The door of the house was shut and bolted, but it was easy to push up a smashed window and climb through.

Trigg's body was close to the telephone. He must have been trying to get through to the exchange when the birds got him. The receiver was off the hook, and the instrument was torn from the wall.

No sign of Mrs. Trigg. She would be upstairs. Was it any use going up? Sickened, Nat knew what he would find there.

Thank God, he said to himself, there were no children.

He forced himself to climb the stairs, but halfway up he turned and descended again. He could see Mrs. Trigg's legs protruding from the open bedroom door. Beside her were the bodies of black-backed gulls and an umbrella, broken. It's no use doing anything, Nat thought. I've only got five hours; less than that. The Triggs would understand. I must load up with what I can find.

He tramped back to his wife and children.

"I'm going to fill up the car with stuff," he said. "We'll take it home and return for a fresh load."

"What about the Triggs?" asked his wife.

"They must have gone to friends," he said.

"Shall I come and help you then?"

"No, there's a mess down there. Cows and sheep all over the place. Wait; I'll get the car. You can sit in the car."

Her eyes watched his all the time he was talking. He believed she understood. Otherwise she certainly would have insisted on helping him find the bread and groceries.

They made three journeys altogether, to and from the farm, before he was satisfied they had everything they needed. It was surprising, once he started thinking, how many things were necessary. Almost the most important of all was planking for the windows. He had to go around searching for timber. He wanted to renew the boards on all the windows at the cottage.

On the final journey he drove the car to the bus stop and got out and went to the telephone box.

He waited a few minutes, jangling the hook. No good, though. The line was dead. He climbed onto a bank and looked over the country-side, but there was no sign of life at all, nothing in the fields but the waiting, watching birds.

Some of them slept; he could see their beaks tucked into their feath-ers.

You'd think they'd be feeding, he said to himself, not just standing that way.

Then he remembered. They were gorged with food. They had eaten their fill during the night. That was why they did not move this morning.

He lifted his face to the sky. It was colorless, gray. The bare trees looked bent and blackened by the east wind.

The cold did not affect the living birds, waiting out there in the fields.

This is the time they ought to get them, Nat said to himself. They're a sitting target now. They must be doing this all over the country. Why don't our aircraft take off now and spray them with mustard gas? What are all our chaps doing? They must know; they must see for themselves.

He went back to the car and got into the driver's seat.

"Go quickly past that second gate," whispered his wife. "The post-man's lying there. I don't want Jill to see."

It was a quarter to one by the time they reached the cottage. Only an hour to go.

"Better have dinner," said Nat. "Hot up something for yourself and the children, some of that soup. I've no time to eat now. I've got to unload all this stuff from the car."

He got everything inside the cottage. It could be sorted later. Give them all something to do during the long hours ahead.

First he must see to the windows and the door.

He went around the cottage methodically, testing every window and the door. He climbed onto the roof also, and fixed boards across every chimney except the kitchen's.

The cold was so intense he could hardly bear it, but the job had to be done. Now and again he looked up, searching the sky for aircraft. None came. As he worked, he cursed the inefficiency of the authorities.

He paused, his work on the bedroom chimney finished, and looked out to sea. Something was moving out there. Something gray and white among the breakers.

"Good old Navy," he said. "They never let us down. They're coming down channel; they're turning into the bay."

He waited, straining his eyes toward the sea. He was wrong, though. The Navy was not there. It was the gulls rising from the sea. And the massed flocks in the fields, with ruffled feathers, rose in formation from the ground and, wing to wing, soared upward to the sky.

The tide had turned again.

Nat climbed down the ladder and went inside the cottage. The family were at dinner. It was a little after two.

He bolted the door, put up the barricade, and lighted the lamp.

"It's nighttime," said young Johnny.

His wife had switched on the wireless once again. The crackling sound came, but nothing else.

"I've been all round the dial," she said, "foreign stations and all. I can't get anything but the crackling."

"Maybe they have the same trouble," he said. "Maybe it's the same right through Europe."

They ate in silence.

The tapping began at the windows, at the door, the rustling, the jostling, the pushing for position on the sills. The first thud of the suicide gulls upon the step.

When he had finished dinner, Nat planned, he would put the supplies away, stack them neatly, get everything shipshape. The boards were strong against the windows and across the chimneys. The cottage was filled with stores, with fuel, with all they needed for the next few days.

His wife could help him, and the children too. They'd tire themselves out between now and a quarter to nine, when the tide would ebb; then he'd tuck them down on their mattresses, see that they slept good and sound until three in the morning.

He had a new scheme for the windows, which was to fix barbed wire in front of the boards. He had brought a great roll of it from the farm. The nuisance was, he'd have to work at this in the dark, when the lull came between nine and three. Pity he had not thought of it before. Sill, as long as the wife and kids slept—that was the main thing.

The smaller birds were at the windows now. He recognized the light tap-tapping of their beaks and the soft brush of their wings.

The hawks ignored the windows. They concentrated their attack upon the door.

Nat listened to the tearing sound of splintering wood, and wondered how many million years of memory were stored in those little brains, behind the stabbing beaks, the piercing eyes, now giving them this instinct to destroy mankind with all the deft precision of machines.

"I'll smoke that last cigarette," he said to his wife. "Stupid of me. It was the one thing I forgot to bring back from the farm."

He reached for it, switched on the crackling wireless.

He threw the empty packet onto the fire and watched it burn.

# THE SPECIALTY OF THE HOUSE

## *Stanley Ellin*

---

STANLEY ELLIN (1916– ) It is not often that a new writer's first story wins literary prizes and an international reputation. Such was the case with *The Specialty of the House*, which he proceeded to follow with a notable series of mystery stories. Mr. Ellin's success in one of the most congested of all literary markets is especially striking in view of his unlikely preparation for it. Dairy manager, steel-worker, teacher and soldier were some of the trades he pursued before trying to write. A compelling style and a strong communication of the strange and the eerie form the signature of his work. Today he lives with his wife in Brooklyn just across the river from Manhattan where he was born.

A ND this," said Laffler, "is Sbirro's." Costain saw a square brown stone façade identical with the others that extended from either side into the clammy darkness of the deserted street. From the barred windows of the basement at his feet, a glimmer of light showed behind heavy curtains.

"Lord," he observed, "it's a dismal hole, isn't it?"

"I beg you to understand," said Laffler stiffly, "that Sbirro's is the restaurant without pretensions. Besieged by these ghastly, neurotic times, it has refused to compromise. It is perhaps the last important establishment in this city lit by gas jets. Here you will find the same honest furnishings, the same magnificent Sheffield service, and possibly, in a far corner, the very same spider webs that were remarked by the patrons of a half century ago!"

"A doubtful recommendation," said Costain, "and hardly sanitary."

"When you enter," Laffler continued, "you leave the insanity of this year, this day, and this hour, and you find yourself for a brief span restored in spirit, not by opulence, but by dignity, which is the lost quality of our time."

Costain laughed uncomfortably. "You make it sound more like a cathedral than a restaurant," he said.

In the pale reflection of the street lamp overhead, Laffler peered at his companion's face. "I wonder," he said abruptly, "whether I have not made a mistake in extending this invitation to you."

Costain was hurt. Despite an impressive title and large salary, he was no more than clerk to this pompous little man, but he was impelled to make some display of his feelings. "If you wish," he said coldly, "I can make other plans for my evening with no trouble."

With his large, cowlike eyes turned up to Costain, the mist drifting into the ruddy, full moon of his face, Laffler seemed strangely ill at ease. Then "No, no," he said at last, "absolutely not. It's important that you dine at Sbirro's with me." He grasped Costain's arm firmly and led the way to the wrought-iron gate of the basement. "You see, you're the sole person in my office who seems to know anything at all about good food. And on my part, knowing about Sbirro's but not having some appreciative friend to share it, is like having a unique piece of art locked in a room where no one else can enjoy it."

Costain was considerably mollified by this. "I understand there are a great many people who relish that situation."

"I'm not one of that kind!" Laffler said sharply. "And having the secret of Sbirro's locked in myself for years has finally become unendurable." He fumbled at the side of the gate and from within could be heard the small, discordant jangle of an ancient pull bell. An interior door opened with a groan, and Costain found himself peering into a dark face whose only discernible feature was a row of gleaming teeth.

"Sair?" said the face.

"Mr. Laffler and a guest."

"Sair," the face said again, this time in what was clearly an invitation. It moved aside and Costain stumbled down a single step behind his host. The door and gate creaked behind him, and he stood blinking in a small foyer. It took him a moment to realize that the figure he now stared at was his own reflection in a gigantic pier glass that extended from floor to ceiling. "Atmosphere," he said under his breath and chuckled as he followed his guide to a seat.

He faced Laffler across a small table for two and peered curiously around the dining room. It was no size at all, but the half dozen guttering gas jets which provided the only illumination threw such a deceptive light that the walls flickered and faded into uncertain distance.

There were no more than eight or ten tables about, arranged to insure the maximum privacy. All were occupied, and the few waiters serving them moved with quiet efficiency. In the air was a soft clash and scrape of cutlery and a soothing murmur of talk. Costain nodded appreciatively.

Laffler breathed an audible sigh of gratification. "I knew you would share my enthusiasm," he said. "Have you noticed, by the way, that there are no women present?"

Costain raised inquiring eyebrows.

"Sbirro," said Laffler, "does not encourage members of the fair sex to enter the premises. And, I can tell you, his method is decidedly effective. I had the experience of seeing a woman get a taste of it not long ago. She sat at a table for not less than an hour waiting for service which was never forthcoming."

"Didn't she make a scene?"

"She did." Laffler smiled at the recollection. "She succeeded in annoying the customers, embarrassing her partner, and nothing more."

"And what about Mr. Sbirro?"

"He did not make an appearance. Whether he directed affairs from behind the scenes, or was not even present during the episode, I don't know. Whichever it was, he won a complete victory. The woman never reappeared nor, for that matter, did the witless gentleman who by bringing her was really the cause of the entire contretemps."

"A fair warning to all present," laughed Costain.

A waiter now appeared at the table. The chocolate-dark skin, the thin, beautifully molded nose and lips, the large liquid eyes, heavily lashed, and the silver white hair so heavy and silken that it lay on the skull like a cap, all marked him definitely as an East Indian. The man arranged the stiff table linen, filled two tumblers from a huge, cut glass picture, and set them in their proper places.

"Tell me," Laffler said eagerly, "is the special being served this evening?"

The waiter smiled regretfully and showed teeth as spectacular as those of the majordomo. "I am sorry, sair. There is no special this evening."

Laffler's face fell into lines of heavy disappointment. "After waiting so long. It's been a month already, and I hoped to show my friend here . . ."

"You understand the difficulties, sair."

"Of course, of course," Laffler looked at Costain sadly and shrugged. "You see, I had in mind to introduce you to the greatest treat that Sbirro's offers, but unfortunately it isn't on the menu this evening."

The waiter said: "Do you wish to be served now, sair?" and Laffler nodded. To Costain's surprise the waiter made his way off without waiting for any instructions.

"Have you ordered in advance?" he asked.

"Ah," said Laffler, "I really should have explained. Sbirro's offers no choice whatsoever. You will eat the same meal as everyone else in this room. Tomorrow evening you would eat an entirely different meal, but again without designating a single preference."

"Very unusual," said Costain, "and certainly unsatisfactory at times. What if one doesn't have a taste for the particular dish set before him?"

"On that score," said Laffler solemnly, "you need have no fears. I give you my word that no matter how exacting your tastes, you will relish every mouthful you eat in Sbirro's."

Costain looked doubtful, and Laffler smiled. "And consider the subtle advantages of the system," he said. "When you pick up the menu of a popular restaurant, you find yourself confronted with innumerable choices. You are forced to weigh, to evaluate, to make uneasy decisions which you may instantly regret. The effect of all this is a tension which, however slight, must make for discomfort.

"And consider the mechanics of the process. Instead of a hurly-burly of sweating cooks rushing about a kitchen in a frenzy to prepare a hundred varying items, we have a chef who stands serenely alone, bringing all his talents to bear on one task, with all assurance of a complete triumph!"

"Then you have seen the kitchen?"

"Unfortunately, no," said Laffler sadly. "The picture I offer is hypothetical, made of conversational fragments I have pieced together over the years. I must admit, though, that my desire to see the functioning of the kitchen here comes very close to being my sole obsession nowadays."

"But have you mentioned this to Sbirro?"

"A dozen times. He shrugs the suggestion away."

"Isn't that a rather curious foible on his part?"

"No, no," Laffler said hastily, "a master artist is never under the compulsion of petty courtesies. Still," he sighed, "I have never given up hope."

The waiter now reappeared bearing two soup bowls which he set in place with mathematical exactitude, and a small tureen from which he slowly ladled a measure of clear, thin broth. Costain dipped his spoon into the broth and tasted it with some curiosity. It was delicately flavored, bland to the verge of tastelessness. Costain frowned, tentatively reached for the salt and pepper cellars, and discovered there were none on the table. He looked up, saw Laffler's eyes on him, and although unwilling to compromise with his own tastes, he hesitated to act as a damper on Laffler's enthusiasm. Therefore he smiled and indicated the broth.

"Excellent," he said.

Laffler returned his smile. "You do not find it excellent at all," he said coolly. "You find it flat and badly in need of condiments. I know this," he continued as Costain's eyebrows shot upward, "because it was my own reaction many years ago, and because like yourself I found myself reaching for salt and pepper after the first mouthful. I also learned with surprise that condiments are not available in Sbirro's."

Costain was shocked. "Not even salt!" he exclaimed.

"Not even salt. The very fact that you require it for your soup stands as evidence that your taste is unduly jaded. I am confident that you will now make the same discovery that I did: by the time you have nearly finished your soup, your desire for salt will be nonexistent."

Laffler was right; before Costain had reached the bottom of his plate, he was relishing the nuances of the broth with steadily increasing delight. Laffler thrust aside his own empty bowl and rested his elbows on the table. "Do you agree with me now?"

"To my surprise," said Costain, "I do."

As the waiter busied himself clearing the table, Laffler lowered his voice significantly. "You will find," he said, "that the absence of condiments is but one of several noteworthy characteristics which mark Sbirro's. I may as well prepare you for these. For example, no alcoholic beverages of any sort are served here, nor for that matter any beverage except clear, cold water, the first and only drink necessary for a human being."

"Outside of mother's milk," suggested Costain dryly.

"I can answer that in like vein by pointing out that the average patron of Sbirro's has passed that primal stage of his development."

Costain laughed. "Granted," he said.

"Very well. There is also a ban on the use of tobacco in any form."

"But good heavens," said Costain, "doesn't that make Sbirro's more a teetotaler's retreat than a gourmet's sanctuary?"

"I fear," said Laffler solemnly, "that you confuse the words, *gourmet* and *gourmand*. The gourmand, through glutting himself, requires a wider and wider latitude of experience to stir his surfeited senses, but the very nature of the gourmet is simplicity. The ancient Greek in his coarse chiton savoring the ripe olive; the Japanese in his bare room contemplating the curve of a single flower stem—these are the true gourmets."

"But an occasional drop of brandy, or pipeful of tobacco," said Costain dubiously, "are hardly overindulgences."

"By alternating stimulant and narcotic," said Laffler, "you seesaw the delicate balance of your taste so violently that it loses its most precious quality: the appreciation of fine food. During my years as a patron of Sbirro's, I have proved this to my satisfaction."

"May I ask," said Costain, "why you regard the ban on these things as having such deep esthetic motives? What about such mundane reasons as the high cost of a liquor license, or the possibility that patrons would object to the smell of tobacco in such confined quarters?"

Laffler shook his head violently. "If and when you meet Sbirro," he said, "you will understand at once that he is not the man to make decisions on a mundane basis. As a matter of fact, it was Sbirro himself who first made me cognizant of what you call 'esthetic' motives."

"An amazing man," said Costain as the waiter prepared to serve the entree.

Laffler's next words were not spoken until he had savored and swallowed a large portion of meat. "I hesitate to use superlatives," he said, "but to my way of thinking, Sbirro represents man at the apex of his civilization!"

Costain cocked an eyebrow and applied himself to his roast which rested in a pool of stiff gravy ungarnished by green or vegetable. The thin steam rising from it carried to his nostrils a subtle, tantalizing odor which made his mouth water. He chewed a piece as slowly and thoroughly as if he were analyzing the intricacies of a Mozart symphony. The range of taste he discovered was really extraordinary, from the pungent nip of the crisp outer edge to the peculiarly flat yet soul-satisfying ooze of blood which the pressure of his jaws forced from the half-raw interior.

Upon swallowing he found himself ferociously hungry for another piece, and then another, and it was only with an effort that he prevented himself from wolfing down all his share of the meat and gravy without waiting to get the full voluptuous satisfaction from each mouthful. When he had scraped his platter clean, he realized that both he and Laffler had completed the entire course without exchanging a single word. He commented on this, and Laffler said: "Can you see any need for words in the presence of such food?"

Costain looked around at the shabby, dimly lit room, the quiet diners, with a new perception. "No," he said humbly, "I cannot. For any doubts I had I apologize unreservedly. In all your praise of Sbirro's there was not a single word of exaggeration."

"Ah," said Laffler delightedly. "And that is only part of the story. You heard me mention the special which unfortunately was not on the menu tonight. What you have just eaten is nothing when compared to the absolute delights of that special!"

"Good Lord!" cried Costain; "What is it? Nightingales' tongues? Filet of unicorn?"

"Neither," said Laffler, "It is lamb."

"Lamb?"

Laffler remained lost in thought for a minute. "If," he said at last, "I were to give you in my own unstinted words my opinion of this dish, you would judge me completely insane. That is how deeply the mere thought of it affects me. It is neither the fatty chop, nor the too solid leg; it is, instead, a select portion of the rarest sheep in existence and is named after the species—lamb Amirstan?"

Costain knit his brows. "Amirstan?"

"A fragment of desolation almost lost on the border which separates Afghanistan and Russia. From chance remarks dropped by Sbirro, I gather it is no more than a plateau which grazes the pitiful remnants of a flock of superb sheep. Sbirro, through some means or other, obtained rights to the traffic in this flock and is, therefore, the sole restauranteur ever to have lamb Amirstan on his bill of fare. I can tell you that the appearance of this dish is a rare occurrence indeed, and luck is the only guide in determining for the clientele the exact date when it will be served."

"But surely," said Costain, "Sbirro could provide some advance knowledge of this event."

"The objection to that is simply stated," said Laffler. "There exists in this city a huge number of professional gluttons. Should advance information slip out, it is quite likely that they will, out of curiosity, become familiar with the dish and thenceforth supplant the regular patrons at these tables."

"But you don't mean to say," objected Costain, "that these few people present are the only ones in the entire city, or for that matter, in the whole wide world, who know of the existence of Sbirro's!"

"Very nearly. There may be one or two regular patrons who, for some reason, are not present at the moment."

"That's incredible."

"It is done," said Laffler, the slighest shade of meance in his voice, "by every patron making it his solemn obligation to keep the secret. By accepting my invitation this evening, you automatically assume that obligation. I hope you can be trusted with it."

Costain flushed. "My position in your employ should vouch for me. I only question the wisdom of a policy which keeps such magnificent food away from so many who would enjoy it."

"Do you know the inevitable result of the policy *you* favor?" asked Laffler bitterly. "An influx of idiots who would nightly complain that they are never served roast duck with chocolate sauce. Is that picture tolerable to you?"

"No," admitted Costain, "I am forced to agree with you."

Laffler leaned back in his chair wearily and passed his hand over his eyes in an uncertain gesture. "I am a solitary man," he said quietly, "and not by choice alone. It may sound strange to you, it may border on eccentricity, but I feel to my depths that this restaurant, this warm heaven in a coldly insane world, is both family and friend to me."

And Costain, who to this moment had never viewed his companion as other than tyrannical employer or officious host, now felt an overwhelming pity twist inside his comfortably expanded stomach.

By the end of two weeks the invitations to join Laffler at Sbirro's had become something of a ritual. Every day, at a few minutes after five, Costain would step out into the office corridor and lock his cubicle behind him; he would drape his overcoat neatly over his left arm, and peer into the glass of the door to make sure his Homburg was set at the proper angle. At one time he would have followed this by lighting a cigarette, but under Laffler's prodding he had decided to give abstinence a fair trial. Then he would start down the corridor, and Laffler would fall in step at his elbow, clearing his throat. "Ah, Costain. No plans for this evening, I hope."

"No," Costain would say, "I'm foot-loose and fancy-free," or "At your service," or something equally inane. He wondered at times whether it would not be more tactful to vary the ritual with an occasional refusal, but the glow with which Laffler received his answer, and the rough friendliness of Laffler's grip on his arm, forestalled him.

Among the treacherous crags of the business world, reflected Costain, what better way to secure your footing than friendship with one's employer. Already, a secretary close to the workings of the inner office had commented publicly on Laffler's highly favorable opinion of Costain. That was all to the good.

And the food! The incomparable food at Sbirro's! For the first time in his life, Costain, ordinarily a lean and bony man, noted with gratification that he was certainly gaining weight; within two weeks his bones had disappeared under a layer of sleek, firm flesh, and here and there were even signs of incipient plumpness. It struck Costain one night, while surveying himself in his bath, that the rotund Laffler, himself, might have been a spare and bony man before discovering Sbirro's.

So there was obviously everything to be gained and nothing to be lost by accepting Laffler's invitations. Perhaps after testing the heralded wonders of lamb Amirstan and meeting Sbirro, who thus far had not made an appearance, a refusal or two might be in order. But certainly not until then.

That evening, two weeks to a day after his first visit to Sbirro's, Costain had both desires fulfilled: he dined on lamb Amirstan, and he met Sbirro. Both exceeded all his expectations.

When the waiter leaned over their table immediately after seating them and gravely announced: "Tonight is special, sair," Costain was shocked to find his heart pounding with expectation. On the table before him he saw Laffler's hands trembling violently. "But it isn't natural," he thought suddenly: "Two full grown men, presumably intelligent and in the full possession of their senses, as jumpy as a pair of cats waiting to have their meat flung to them!"

"This is it!" Laffler's voice startled him so that he almost leaped from his seat. "The culinary triumph of all times! And faced by it you are embarrassed by the very emotions it distills."

"How did you know that?" Costain asked faintly.

"How? Because a decade ago I underwent your embarrassment. Add to that your air of revulsion and it's easy to see how affronted you are by the knowledge that man has not yet forgotten how to slaver over his meat."

"And these others," whispered Costain, "do they all feel the same thing?"

"Judge for yourself."

Costain looked furtively around at the nearby tables. "You are right," he finally said. "At any rate, there's comfort in numbers."

Laffler inclined his head slightly to the side. "One of the numbers," he remarked, "appears to be in for a disappointment."

Costain followed the gesture. At the table indicated a gray-haired man sat conspicuously alone, and Costain frowned at the empty chair opposite him.

"Why, yes," he recalled, "that very stout, bald man, isn't it? I believe it's the first dinner he's missed here in two weeks."

"The entire decade more likely," said Laffler sympathetically. "Rain or shine, crisis or calamity, I don't think he's missed an evening at Sbirro's since the first time I dined here. Imagine his expression when he's told that on his very first defection, lamb Amirstan was the *plat du jour*."

Costain looked at the empty chair again with a dim discomfort. "His very first?" he murmured.

"Mr. Laffler! And friend! I am so pleased. So very, very pleased. No, do not stand; I will have a place made." Miraculously a seat appeared under the figure standing there at the table. "The lamb Amirstan will be an unqualified success, hurr? I myself have been stewing in the miserable kitchen all the day, prodding the foolish chef to do everything just so. The just so is the important part, hurr? But I see your friend does not know me. An introduction, perhaps?"

The words ran in a smooth, fluid eddy. They rippled, they purred, they hypnotized Costain so that he could do no more than stare. The mouth that uncoiled this sinuous monologue was alarmingly wide, with thin mobile lips that curled and twisted with every syllable. There was a flat nose with a straggling line of hair under it; wide-set eyes, almost oriental in appearance, that glittered in the unsteady flare of gaslight; and long, sleek hair that swept back from high on the unwrinkled forehead—hair so pale that it might have been bleached of all color. An amazing face surely, and the sight of it tortured Costain with the conviction that it was somehow familiar. His brain twitched and prodded but could not stir up any solid recollection.

Laffler's voice jerked Costain out of his study. "Mr. Sbirro. Mr. Costain, a good friend and associate." Costain rose and shook the proffered hand. It was warm and dry, flint-hard against his palm.

"I am so very pleased, Mr. Costain. So very, very pleased," purred the voice. "You like my little establishment, hurr? You have a great treat in store, I assure you."

Laffler chuckled. "Oh, Costain's been dining here regularly for two weeks," he said. "He's by way of becoming a great admirer of yours, Sbirro."

The eyes were turned on Costain. "A very great compliment. You compliment me with your presence and I return same with my food, hurr? But the lamb Amirstan is far superior to anything of your past experience, I assure you. All the trouble of obtaining it, all the difficulty of preparation, is truly merited."

Costain strove to put aside the exasperating problem of that face. "I have wondered," he said, "why with all these difficulties you mention, you even bother to present lamb Amirstan to the public. Surely your other dishes are excellent enough to uphold your reputation."

Sbirro smiled so broadly that his face became perfectly round. "Perhaps it is a matter of the psychology, hurr? Someone discovers a wonder and must share it with others. He must fill his cup to the brim, perhaps, by observing the so evident pleasure of those who explore it with him. Or," he shrugged, "perhaps it is just a matter of good business."

"Then in the light of all this," Costain persisted, "and considering all the conventions you have imposed on your customers, why do you open the restaurant to the public instead of operating it as a private club?"

The eyes abruptly glinted into Costain's, then turned away. "So perspicacious, hurr? Then I will tell you. Because there is more privacy in a public eating place than in the most exclusive club in existence! Here no one inquires of your affairs; no one desires to know the intimacies of your life. Here the business is eating. We are not curious about names and addresses or the reasons for the coming and going of our guests. We welcome you when you are here; we have no regrets when you are here no longer. That is the answer, hurr?"

Costain was startled by this vehemence. "I had no intention of prying," he stammered.

Sbirro ran the tip of his tongue over his thin lips. "No, no," he reassured, "you are not prying. Do not let me give you that impression. On the contrary, I invite your questions."

"Oh, come, Costain," said Laffler. "Don't let Sbirro intimidate you. I've known him for years and I guarantee that his bark is worse than his bite. Before you know it, he'll be showing you all the privileges of the house—outside of inviting you to visit his precious kitchen, of course."

"Ah," smiled Sbirro, "for that, Mr. Costain may have to wait a little while. For everything else I am at his beck and call."

Laffler slapped his hand jovially on the table. "What did I tell you!" he said. "Now let's have the truth, Sbirro. Has anyone, outside of your staff, ever stepped into the sanctum sanctorum?"

Sbirro looked up. "You see on the wall above you," he said earnestly, "the portrait of one to whom I did the honor. A very dear friend and a patron of most long standing, he is evidence that my kitchen is not inviolate."

Costain studied the picture and started with recognition. "Why," he said excitedly, "that's the famous writer—you know the one, Laffler— he used to do such wonderful short stories and cynical bits and then suddenly took himself off and disappeared in Mexico!"

"Of course!" cried Laffler, "and to think I've been sitting under his portrait for years without even realizing it!" He turned to Sbirro. "A dear friend, you say? His disappearance must have been a blow to you."

Sbirro's face lengthened. "It was, it was, I assure you. But think of it this way, gentlemen: he was probably greater in his death than in his life, hurr? A most tragic man, he often told me that his only happy hours were spent here at this very table. Pathetic, is it not? And to think the only favor I could ever show him was to let him witness the mysteries of my kitchen, which is, when all is said and done, no more than a plain, ordinary kitchen."

"You seem very certain of his death," commented Costain. "After all, no evidence has ever turned up to substantiate it."

Sbirro contemplated the picture. "None at all," he said softly. "Remarkable, hurr?"

With the arrival of the entree Sbirro leaped to his feet and set about serving them himself. With his eyes alight he lifted the casserole from the tray and sniffed at the fragrance from within with sensual relish. Then, taking great care not to lose a single drop of gravy, he filled two platters with chunks of dripping meat. As if exhausted by this task, he sat back in his chair, breathing heavily. "Gentlemen," he said, "to your good appetite."

Costain chewed his first mouthful with great deliberation and swallowed it. Then he looked at the empty tines of his fork with glazed eyes.

"Good God!" he breathed.

"It is good, hurr? Better than you imagined?"

Costain shook his head dazedly. "It is as impossible," he said slowly, "for the uninitiated to conceive the delights of lamb Amirstan as for mortal man to look into his own soul."

"Perhaps," Sbirro thrust his head so close that Costain could feel the warm, fetid breath tickle his nostrils, "perhaps you have just had a glimpse into your soul, hurr?"

Costain tried to draw back slightly without giving offense. "Perhaps," he laughed, "and a gratifying-picture it made: all fang and claw. But without intending any disrespect, I should hardly like to build my church on *lamb en casserole.*"

Sbirro rose and laid a hand gently on his shoulder. "So perspicacious," he said. "Sometimes when you have nothing to do, nothing, perhaps, but sit for a very little while in a dark room and think of this world—what it is and what it is going to be—then you must turn your thoughts a little to the significance of the Lamb in religion. It will be so interesting. And now," he bowed deeply to both men. "I have held you long enough from your dinner. I was most happy"— he nodded to Costain—"and I am sure we will meet again." The teeth gleamed, the eyes glittered, and Sbirro was gone down the aisle of tables.

Costain twisted around to stare after the retreating figure. "Have I offended him in some way?" he asked.

Laffler looked up from his plate. "Offended him? He loves that kind of talk. Lamb Amirstan is a ritual with him; get him started and he'll be back at you a dozen times worse than a priest making a conversion."

Costain turned to his meal with the face still hovering before him. "Interesting man," he reflected. "Very."

It took him a month to discover the tantalizing familiarity of that face, and when he did, he laughed aloud in his bed. Why, of course! Sbirro might have sat as the model for the Cheshire cat in *Alice!*

He passed this thought on to Laffler the very next evening as they pushed their way down the street to the restaurant against a chill, blustering wind. Laffler only looked blank.

"You may be right," he said, "but I'm not a fit judge. It's a far cry back to the days when I read the book. A far cry, indeed."

As if taking up his words, a piercing howl came ringing down the street and stopped both men short in their tracks. "Someone's in trouble there," said Laffler. "Look!"

Not far from the entrance to Sbirro's two figures could be seen struggling in the near darkness. They swayed back and forth and suddenly tumbled into a writhing heap on the sidewalk. The piteous howl went up again, and Laffler, despite his girth, ran toward it at a fair speed with Costain tagging cautiously behind.

Stretched out full length on the pavement was a slender figure with the dusky complexion and white hair of one of Sbirro's servitors. His fingers were futilely plucking at the huge hands which encircled his throat, and his knees pushed weakly up at the gigantic bulk of a man who brutally bore down with his full weight.

Laffler came up panting. "Stop this!" he shouted. "What's going on here?"

The pleading eyes almost bulging from their sockets turned toward Laffler. "Help, sair. This man—drunk—"

"Drunk am I, ya dirty—" Costain saw now that the man was a sailor in a badly soiled uniform. The air around him reeked with the stench of liquor. "Pick me pocket and then call me drunk, will ya!" He dug his finger in harder, and his victim groaned.

Laffler seized the sailor's shoulder. "Let go of him, do you hear! Let go of him at once!" he cried, and the next instant was sent careening into Costain, who staggered back under the force of the blow.

The attack on his own person sent Laffler into immediate and berserk action. Without a sound he leaped at the sailor, striking and kicking furiously at the unprotected face and flanks. Stunned at first, the man came to his feet with a rush and turned on Laffler. For a moment they stood locked together, and then as Costain joined the attack, all three went sprawling to the ground. Slowly Laffler and Costain got to their feet and looked down at the body before them.

"He's either out cold from liquor," said Costain, "or he struck his head going down. In any case, it's a job for the police."

"No, no, sair!" The waiter crawled weakly to his feet, and stood swaying. "No police, sair. Mr. Sbirro do not want such. You understand, sair." He caught hold of Costain with a pleading hand, and Costain looked at Laffler.

"Of course not," said Laffler. "We won't have to bother with the police. They'll pick him up soon enough, the murderous sot. But what in the world started all this?"

"That man, sair. He make most erratic way while walking, and with no meaning I push against him. Then he attack me, accusing me to rob him."

"As I thought." Laffler pushed the waiter gently along. "Now go on in and get yourself attended to."

The man seemed ready to burst into tears. "To you, sair, I owe my life. If there is anything I can do—"

Laffler turned into the areaway that led to Sbirro's door. "No, no, it was nothing. You go along, and if Sbirro has any questions send him to me. I'll straighten it out."

"My life, sair," were the last words they heard as the inner door closed behind them.

"There you are, Costain," said Laffler, as a few minutes later he drew his chair under the table: "civilized man in all his glory. Reeking with alcohol, strangling to death some miserable innocent who came too close."

Costain made an effort to gloss over the nerve-shattering memory of the episode. "It's the neurotic cat that takes to alcohol," he said. "Surely there's a reason for that sailor's condition."

"Reason? Of course there is. Plain atavistic savagery!" Laffler swept his arm in an all-embracing gesture. "Why do we all sit here at our meat? Not only to appease physical demands, but because our atavistic selves cry for release. Think back, Costain. Do you remember that I once described Sbirro as the epitome of civilization? Can you now see why? A brilliant man, he fully understands the nature of human beings. But unlike lesser men he bends all his efforts to the satisfaction of our innate natures without resultant harm to some innocent by-stander."

"When I think back on the wonders of lamb Amirstan," said Costain, "I quite understand what you're driving at. And, by the way, isn't it nearly due to appear on the bill of fare? It must have been over a month ago that it was last served."

The waiter, filling the tumblers, hesitated. "I am so sorry, sair. No special this evening."

"There's your answer," Laffler grunted, "and probably just my luck to miss out on it altogether the next time."

Costain stared at him. "Oh, come, that's impossible."

"No, blast it." Laffler drank off half his water at a gulp and the waiter immediately refilled the glass. "I'm off to South America for a surprise tour of inspection. One month, two months, Lord knows how long."

"Are things that bad down there?"

"They could be better." Laffler suddenly grinned. "Mustn't forget it takes very mundane dollars and cents to pay the tariff at Sbirro's."

"I haven't heard a word of this around the office."

"Wouldn't be a surprise tour if you had. Nobody knows about this except myself—and now you. I want to walk in on them completely unsuspected. Find out what flimflammery they're up to down there. As far as the office is concerned, I'm off on a jaunt somewhere. Maybe recuperating in some sanatorium from my hard work. Anyhow, the business will be in good hands. Yours, among them."

"Mine?" said Costain, surprised.

"When you go in tomorrow you'll find yourself in receipt of a promotion, even if I'm not there to hand it to you personally. Mind you, it has nothing to do with our friendship either; you've done fine work, and I'm immensely grateful for it."

Costain reddened under the praise. "You don't expect to be in tomorrow. Then you're leaving tonight?"

Laffler nodded. "I've been trying to wangle some reservations. If they come through, well, this will be in the nature of a farewell celebration."

"You know," said Costain slowly, "I devoutly hope that your reservations don't come through. I believe our dinners here have come to mean more to me than I ever dared imagine."

The waiter's voice broke in. "Do you wish to be served now, sair?" and they both started.

"Of course, of course," said Laffler sharply, "I didn't realize you were waiting."

"What bothers me," he told Costain as the waiter turned away, "is the thought of the lamb Amirstan I'm bound to miss. To tell you the truth, I've already put off my departure a week, hoping to hit a lucky night, and now I simply can't delay any more. I do hope that when you're sitting over your share of lamb Amirstan, you'll think of me with suitable regrets."

Costain laughed. "I will indeed," he said as he turned to his dinner.

Hardly had he cleared the plate when a waiter silently reached for it. It was not their usual waiter, he observed; it was none other than the victim of the assault.

"Well," Costain said, "how do you feel now? Still under the weather?"

The waiter paid no attention to him. Instead, with the air of a man under great strain, he turned to Laffler. "Sair," he whispered. "My life. I owe it to you. I can repay you!"

Laffler looked up in amazement, then shook his head firmly. "No," he said; "I want nothing from you, understand? You have repaid me sufficiently with your thanks. Now get on with your work and let's hear no more about it."

The waiter did not stir an inch, but his voice rose slighty. "By the body and blood of your God, sair, I will help you even if you do not want! *Do not go into the kitchen, sair.* I trade you my life for yours, sair, when I speak this. Tonight or any night of your life, do not go into the kitchen at Sbirro's!"

Laffler sat back, completely dumfounded. "Not go into the kitchen? Why shouldn't I go into the kitchen if Mr. Sbirro ever took it into his head to invite me there? What's all this about?"

A hard hand was laid on Costain's back, and another gripped the waiter's arm. The waiter remained frozen to the spot, his lips compressed, his eyes downcast.

"What is all *what* about, gentlemen?" purred the voice. "So opportune an arrival. In time as ever, I see, to answer all the questions, hurr?"

Laffler breathed a sigh of relief. "Ah, Sbirro, thank heaven you're here. This man is saying something about my not going into your kitchen. Do you know what he means?"

The teeth showed in a broad grin. "But of course. This good man was giving you advice in all amiability. It so happens that my too emotional chef heard some rumor that I might have a guest into his precious kitchen, and he flew into a fearful rage. Such a rage, gentlemen! He even threatened to give notice on the spot, and you can understand what that should mean to Sbirro's, hurr? Fortunately, I succeeded in showing him what a signal honor it is to have an esteemed patron and true connoisseur observe him at his work first hand, and now he is quite amenable. Quite, hurr?"

He released the waiter's arm. "You are at the wrong table," he said softly. "See that it does not happen again."

The waiter slipped off without daring to raise his eyes and Sbirro drew a chair to the table. He seated himself and brushed his hand lightly over his hair. "Now I am afraid that the cat is out of the bag, hurr? This invitation to you, Mr. Laffler, was to be a surprise; but the surprise is gone, and all that is left is the invitation."

Laffler mopped beads of perspiration from his forehead. "Are you serious?" he said huskily. "Do you mean that we are really to witness the preparation of your food tonight?"

Sbirro drew a sharp fingernail along the tablecloth, leaving a thin, straight line printed in the linen. "Ah," he said, "I am faced with a dilemma of great proportions." He studied the line soberly. "You Mr. Laffler, have been my guest for ten long years. But our friend here—"

Costain raised his hand in protest. "I understand perfectly. This invitation is solely to Mr. Laffler, and naturally my presence is embarrassing. As it happens, I have an early engagement for this evening and must be on my way anyhow. So you see there's no dilemma at all, really."

"No," said Laffler, "absolutely not. That wouldn't be fair at all. We've been sharing this until now, Costain, and I won't enjoy this experience half as much if you're not along. Surely Sbirro can make his conditions flexible, this one occasion."

They both looked at Sbirro who shrugged his shoulders regretfully.

Costain rose abruptly. "I'm not going to sit here, Laffler, and spoil your great adventure. And then too," he bantered, "think of that ferocious chef waiting to get his cleaver on you. I prefer not to be at the scene. I'll just say good-by," he went on, to cover Laffler's guilty silence, "and leave you to Sbirro. I'm sure he'll take pains to give you a good show." He held out his hand and Laffler squeezed it painfully hard.

"You're being very decent, Costain," he said. "I hope you'll continue to dine here until we meet again. It shouldn't be too long."

Sbirro made way for Costain to pass. "I will expect you," he said. "Au 'voir."

Costain stopped briefly in the dim foyer to adjust his scarf and fix his Homburg at the proper angle. When he turned away from the mirror, satisfied at last, he saw with a final glance that Laffler and Sbirro were already at the kitchen door; Sbirro holding the door invitingly wide with one hand, while the other rested, almost tenderly, on Laffler's meaty shoulders.

# THE END OF THE PARTY

## Graham Greene

GRAHAM GREENE (1904–  ) was raised in an English school of which his father was the headmaster. Upon leaving Oxford, he turned to journalism. The title of his first book, *The Man Within*, written by him in 1929, states the theme which has motivated his entire literary life. Whether in his thrillers, which he calls "entertainments" or his more sober investigations of man's mind and soul, one can always find not only a good story but also reflection and searching inquiry into why people are what they are. Out of his own wartime experience and his many journeys comes the wide tapestry of his backgrounds and characters, while out of his religious and psychological interests come deep understanding and excitement.

PETER MORTON woke with a start to face the first light. Through the window he could see a bare bough dropping across a frame of silver. Rain tapped against the glass. It was January the fifth.

He looked across a table, on which a night-light had guttered into a pool of water, at the other bed. Francis Morton was still asleep, and Peter lay down again with his eyes on his brother. It amused him to imagine that it was himself whom he watched, the same hair, the same eyes, the same lips and line of cheek. But the thought soon palled, and the mind went back to the fact which lent the day importance. It was the fifth of January. He could hardly believe that a year had passed since Mrs. Henne-Falcon had given her last children's party.

Francis turned suddenly upon his back and threw an arm across his face, blocking his mouth. Peter's heart began to beat fast, not with pleasure now but with uneasiness. He sat up and called across the table, "Wake up." Francis's shoulders shook and he waved a clenched fist in the air, but his eyes remained closed. To Peter Morton the whole room seemed suddenly to darken, and he had the impression of a great bird swooping. He cried again, "Wake up," and once more there was silver light and the touch of rain on the windows. Francis rubbed his eyes. "Did you call out?" he asked.

"You are having a bad dream," Peter said with confidence. Already experience had taught him how far their minds reflected each other. But he was the elder, by a matter of minutes, and that brief extra interval of light, while his brother struggled in pain and darkness, had given him self-reliance and an instinct of protection towards the other who was afraid of so many things.

"I dreamed that I was dead," Francis said.

"What was it like?" Peter asked with curiosity.

"I can't remember," Francis said, and his eyes turned with relief to the silver of day, as he allowed the fragmentary memories to fade.

"You dreamed of a big bird."

"Did I?" Francis accepted his brother's knowledge without question, and for a little the two lay silent in bed facing each other, the same green eyes, the same nose tilting at the tip, the same firm lips parted, and the same premature modeling of the chin. The fifth of January, Peter thought again, his mind drifting idly from the image of cakes to the prizes which might be won. Egg-and-spoon races, spearing apples in basins of water, blindman's buff.

"I don't want to go," Francis said suddenly. "I suppose Joyce will be there . . . Mabel Warren." Hateful to him, the thought of a party shared with those two. They were older than he. Joyce was eleven and Mabel Warren thirteen. Their long pigtails swung superciliously to a masculine stride. Their sex humiliated him, as they watched him fumble with his egg, from under lowered scornful lids. And last year . . . he turned his face away from Peter, his cheeks scarlet.

"What's the matter?" Peter asked.

"Oh, nothing. I don't think I'm well. I've got a cold. I oughtn't to go to the party."

Peter was puzzled. "But, Francis, is it a bad cold?"

"It will be a bad cold if I go to the party. Perhaps I shall die."

"Then you mustn't go," Peter said with decision, prepared to solve all difficulties with one plain sentence, and Francis let his nerves relax in a delicious relief, ready to leave everything to Peter. But though he was grateful he did not turn his face towards his brother. His cheeks still bore the badge of a shameful memory, of the game of hide-and-seek last year in the darkened house, and of how he had screamed when Mabel Warren put her hand suddenly upon his arm. He had not heard her coming. Girls were like that. Their shoes never squeaked. No boards whined under their tread. They slunk like cats on padded claws. When the nurse came in with hot water Francis lay tranquil, leaving everything to Peter. Peter said, "Nurse, Francis has got a cold."

The tall starched woman laid the towels across the cans and said, without turning, "The washing won't be back till tomorrow. You must lend him some of your handkerchiefs."

"But, Nurse," Peter asked, "hadn't he better stay in bed?"

"We'll take him for a good walk this morning," the nurse said. "Wind'll blow away the germs. Get up now, both of you," and she closed the door behind her.

"I'm sorry," Peter said, and then, worried at the sight of a face creased again by misery and foreboding, "Why don't you just stay in bed? I'll tell mother you felt too ill to get up." But such a rebellion of that destiny was not in Francis's power. Besides, if he stayed in and they would come up and tap his chest and put a thermometer in his mouth and look at his tongue, and they would discover that he was malingering. It was true that he felt ill, a sick empty sensation in his stomach and a rapidly beating heart, but he knew that the cause was only fear, fear of the party, fear of being made to hide by himself in the dark, uncompanioned by Peter and with no night-light to make a blessed breach.

"No, I'll get up," he said, and then with sudden desperation, "But won't go to Mrs. Henne-Falcon's party. I swear on the Bible I won't." Now surely all would be well, he thought. God would not allow him to break so solemn an oath. He would show him a way. There was all the morning before him now when the grass was still crisp with the early frost. Anything might happen. He might cut himself or break his leg or really catch a bad cold. God would manage somehow.

He had such confidence in God that when at breakfast his mother said, "I hear you have a cold, Francis," he made light of it. "We should have heard more about it," his mother said with irony, "if there was not a party this evening," and Francis smiled uneasily amazed and daunted by her ignorance of him. His happiness would have lasted longer if, out for a walk that morning, he had not met Joyce. He was along with his nurse, for Peter had to finish a rabbit-hutch in the woodshed. If Peter had been there he would have cared less; the nurse was Peter's nurse also, but now it was as though she were employed only for his sake, because he could not be trusted to go for a walk alone. Joyce was only two years older and she was by herself.

She came striding towards them, pigtails flapping. She glanced scornfully at Francis and spoke with ostentation to the nurse. "Hello, Nurse. Are you bringing Francis to the party this evening? Mabel and I are coming." And she was off again down the street in the direction of Mable Warren's home, consciously alone and self-sufficient in the long empty road. "Such a nice girl," the nurse said. And Francis was silent, feeling again the jump-jump of his heart, realizing how soon the hour of the party would arrive. God had done something for him, and the minutes flew.

They flew too quickly to plan any evasion, or even to prepare his heart for the coming ordeal. Panic nearly overcame him when, all ready, he found himself standing on the doorstep, with coat-collar turned up against a cold wind, and the nurse's electric torch making a short luminous trail through the darkness. Behind him were the lights of the hall and the sound of a servant laying the table for dinner, which his mother and father would eat alone. He was nearly overcome by a desire to run back into the house and call out to his mother that he would not go to the party, that he dared not go. They could not make him go. He could almost hear himself saying those final words, breaking down for ever, as he knew instinctively, the barrier of ignorance that saved his mind from his parents' knowledge. "I'm afraid of going. I won't go. I daren't go. They'll make me hide in the dark, and I'm afraid of the dark. I'll scream and scream and scream." He could see the expression of amazement on his mother's face, and then the cold confidence of a grown-up's retort. "Don't be silly. You must go. We've accepted Mrs. Henne-Falcon's invitation."

But they couldn't make him go; hesitating on the doorstep while the nurse's feet crunched across the frost-covered grass to the gate, he knew that. He would answer, "You can say I'm ill. I won't go. I'm afraid of the dark." And his mother, "Don't be silly. You know there's nothing to be afraid of in the dark." But he knew the falsity of that reasoning; he knew how they taught also that there was nothing to fear in death, and how fearfully they avoided the idea of it. But they couldn't make him go to the party. "I'll scream. I'll scream."

"Francis, come along." He heard the nurse's voice across the dimly phosphorescent lawn and saw the small yellow circle of her torch wheel from tree to shrub and back to tree again. "I'm coming," he called with despair, leaving the lighted doorway of the house; he couldn't bring himself to lay bare his last secrets and end reserve between his mother and himself, for there was still in the last resort a further appeal possible to Mrs. Henne-Falcon. He comforted himself with that, as he advanced steadily across the hall, very small, towards her enormous bulk. His heart beat unevenly, but he had control now over his voice, as he said with meticulous accent, "Good evening, Mrs. Henne-Falcon. It was very good of you to ask me to your party." With his strained face lifted towards the curve of her breasts, and his polite set speech, he was like an old withered man. For Francis mixed very little with other children. As a twin he was in many ways an only child. To address Peter was to speak to his own image in a mirror, an image a little altered by a flaw in the glass, so as to throw back less a likeness of what he was than of what he wished to be, what he would be without his unreasoning fear of darkness, footsteps of strangers, the flight of bats in dusk-filled gardens.

"Sweet child," said Mrs. Henne-Falcon absent-mindedly, before, with a wave of her arms, as though the children were a flock of chickens, she whirled them into her set programme of entertainment: egg-and-spoon races, three-legged races, the spearing of apples, games which held for Francis nothing worse than humiliation. And in the frequent intervals when nothing was required of him and he could stand alone in corners as far removed as possible from Mabel Warren's scornful gaze, he was able to plan how he might avoid the approaching terror of the dark. He knew there was nothing to fear until after tea, and not until he was sitting down in a pool of yellow radiance cast by the ten candles on Colin Henne-Falcon's birthday cake did he become fully conscious of the imminence of what he feared. Through the confusion of his brain, now assailed suddenly by a dozen contradictory plans, he heard Joyce's high voice down the table. "After tea we are going to play hide-and-seek in the dark."

"Oh, no," Peter said, watching Francis's troubled face with pity and an imperfect understanding, "don't let's. We play that every year."

"But it's on the programme," cried Mable Warren. "I saw it myself. I looked over Mrs. Henne-Falcon's shoulder. Five o'clock, tea. A quarter to six to half-past, hide-and-seek in the dark. It's all written down in the programme."

Peter did not argue, for if hide-and-seek had been inserted in Mrs. Henne-Falcon's programme, nothing which he could say could avert it. He asked for another piece of birthday cake and sipped his tea slowly. Perhaps it might be possible to delay the game for a quarter of an hour, allow Francis at least a few extra minutes to form a plan, but even in that Peter failed, for children were already leaving the table in twos and threes. It was his third failure, and again, the reflection of an image in another's mind, he saw a great bird darken his brother's face with its wings. But he upbraided himself silently for his folly, and finished his cake encouraged by the memory of that adult refrain, "There's nothing to fear in the dark." The last to leave the table, the brothers came together to the hall to meet the mustering and impatient eyes of Mrs. Henne-Falcon.

"And now," she said, "we will play hide-and-seek in the dark."

Peter watched his brother and saw, as he had expected, the lips tighten. Francis, he knew, had feared this moment from the beginning of the party, had tried to meet it with courage and had abandoned the attempt. He must have prayed desperately for cunning to evade the game, which was now welcomed with cries of excitement by all the other children. "Oh, do let's." "We must pick sides." "Is any of the house out of bounds?" "Where shall home be?"

"I think," said Francis Morton, approaching Mrs. Henne-Falcon, his eyes unwaveringly on her exuberant breasts, "it will be no use my playing. My nurse will be calling for me very soon."

"Oh, but your nurse can wait, Francis," said Mrs. Henne-Falcon absent-mindedly, while she clapped her hands together to summon to her side a few children who were already straying up the wide stair-case to upper floors. "Your mother will never mind."

That had been the limit of Francis's cunning. He had refused to believe that so well prepared an excuse could fail. All that he could say now, still in the precise tone which other children hated, thinking it a symbol of conceit, was, "I think I had better not play." He stood motionless, retaining, though afraid, unmoved features. But the knowledge of his terror, or the reflection of the terror itself, reached his brother's brain. For the moment, Peter Morton could have cried aloud with the fear of bright lights going out, leaving him alone in an island of dark surrounded by the gentle lapping of strange footsteps. Then he remembered that the fear was not his own, but his brother's. He said impulsively to Mrs. Henne-Falcon, "Please. I don't think Francis should play. The dark makes him jump so." They were the wrong words. Six children began to sing, "Cowardly, cowardly cus-tard," turning torturing faces with the vacancy of wide sunflowers to-wards Francis Morton.

Without looking at his brother, Francis said, "Of course I will play. I am not afraid. I only thought . . ." But he was already forgotten by his human tormentors and was able in loneliness to contemplate the approach of the spiritual, the more unbounded torture. The children scrambled round Mrs. Henne-Falcon, their shrill voices pecking at her with questions and suggestions. "Yes, anywhere in the house. We will turn out all the lights. Yes, you can hide in the cupboards. You must stay hidden as long as you can. There will be no home."

Peter, too, stood apart, ashamed of the clumsy manner in which he had tried to help his brother. Now he could feel, creeping in the corners of his brain, all Francis's resentment of his championship. Several children ran upstairs, and the lights on the top floor went out. Then darkness came down like the wings of a bat and settled on the landing. Others began to put out the lights at the edge of the hall till the children were all gathered round on hooded wings and waited for that, too, to be extinguished.

"You and Francis are on the hiding side," a tall girl said, and then the light was gone, and the carpet wavered under his feet with the balance of footfalls, like small cold draughts, creeping away into corners.

"Where's Francis?" he wondered. "If I join him he'll be less frightened of all these sounds." "These sounds" were the casing of silence. The squeak of a loose board, the cautious closing of a cupboard door, the whine of a finger drawn along polished wood.

Peter stood in the center of the dark deserted floor, not listening but waiting for the idea of his brother's whereabouts to enter his brain. But Francis crouched with fingers on his ears, eyes uselessly lowered, mind numbed against impressions, and only a sense of strain could cross the gap of dark. Then a voice called "Coming," and as though his brother's self-possession had been shattered by the sudden cry, Peter Morton jumped with fear. But it was not his own fear. What in his brother was a burning panic, admitting no ideas except those which added to the flame, was in him an altruistic emotion that left the reason unimpaired. "Where, if I were Francis, could I hide?" Such, roughly, was his thought. And because he was if not Francis himself, at least a mirror to him, the answer was immediate. "Between the oak bookcase on the left of the study door and the leather settee." Peter Morton was unsurprised by the softness of the response. Between the twins there could be no jargon of telepathy. They had been together in the womb, and they could not be parted.

Peter Morton tiptoed towards Francis's hiding place. Occasionally a board rattled, and because he feared to be caught by one of the soft questers through the dark, he bent and untied his laces. A tag struck the floor and the metallic sound set a host of cautious feet moving in his direction. But by that time he was in his stockings and could have laughed inwardly at the pursuit had not the noise of someone stumbling on his abandoned shoes made his heart trip in the reflection of another's surprise. No more boards revealed Peter Morton's progress. On stockinged feet he moved silently and unerringly towards his object. Instinct told him that he was near the wall, and, extending a hand, he laid the fingers across his brother's face.

Francis did not cry out, but the leap of his own heart revealed to Peter a proportion of Francis's terror. "It's all right," he whispered, feeling down the squatting figure until he captured a clenched hand. "It's only me. I'll stay with you." And grasping the other tightly, he listened to the cascade of whispers his utterance had caused to fall. A hand touched the bookcase close to Peter's head and he was aware of how Francis's fear continued in spite of his presence. It was less intense, more bearable, he hoped, but it remained. He knew that it was his brother's fear and not his own that he experienced. The dark to him was only an absence of light; the groping hand that of a familiar child. Patiently he waited to be found.

He did not speak again, for between Francis and himself touch was the most intimate communion. By way of joined hands thought could flow more swiftly than lips could shape themselves round words. He could experience the whole progress of his brother's emotion, from the leap of panic at the unexpected contact to the steady pulse of fear, which now went on and on with the regularity of a heart-beat. Peter Morton thought with intensity, "I am here. You needn't be afraid. The lights will go on again soon. That rustle, that movement is nothing to fear. Only Joyce, only Mabel Warren." He bombarded the drooping form with thoughts of safety, but he was conscious that the fear continued. "They are beginning to whisper together. They are tired of looking for us. The lights will go on soon. We shall have won. Don't be afraid. That was only someone on the stairs. I believe it's Mrs. Henne-Falcon. Listen. They are feeling for the lights." Feet moving on a carpet, hands brushing a wall, a curtain pulled apart, a clicking handle, the opening of a cupboard door. In the case above their heads a loose book shifted under a touch. "Only Joyce, only Mabel Warren, only Mrs. Henne-Falcon," a crescendo of reassuring thought before the chandelier burst, like a fruit tree, into bloom.

The voices of the children rose shrilly into the radiance. "Where's Peter?" "Have you looked upstairs?" "Where's Francis?" but they were silenced again by Mrs. Henne-Falcon's scream. But she was not the first to notice Francis Morton's stillness, where he had collapsed against the wall at the touch of his brother's hand. Peter continued to hold the clenched fingers in an arid and puzzled grief. It was not merely that his brother was dead. His brain, too young to realize the full paradox, yet wondered with an obscure self-pity why it was that the pulse of his brother's fear went on and on, when Francis was now where he had been always told there was no more terror and no more darkness.

# THE WAY UP TO HEAVEN

## *Roald Dahl*

ROALD DAHL (1916–   ) born in South Wales of Norwegian parents, was schooled in England, but at twenty-one was off to Tanganyika for the Shell Oil Company. The start of World War II found him still in Africa where he joined the RAF and flew fighter planes through many months of action in the Libyan desert, later in Greece and Syria. It was not until he was invalided out because of injuries that he started to put on paper some of the tales he had been narrating to friends. This embarked him on the career he now follows. Living at times in this country but more often abroad, he has achieved position among today's most successful short story writers. His subjects incline toward the macabre and the unpredictable.

ALL her life, Mrs. Foster had had an almost pathological fear of missing a train, a plane, a boat, or even a theatre curtain. In other respects, she was not a particularly nervous woman, but the mere thought of being late on occasions like these would throw her into such a state of nerves that she would begin to twitch. It was nothing much—just a tiny vellicating muscle in the corner of the left eye, like a secret wink—but the annoying thing was that it refused to disappear until an hour or so after the train or plane or whatever it was had been safely caught.

It is really extraordinary how in certain people a simple apprehension about a thing like catching a train can grow into a serious obsession. At least half an hour before it was time to leave the house for the station, Mrs. Foster would step out of the elevator all ready to go, with hat and coat and gloves, and then, being quite unable to sit down, she would flutter and fidget about from room to room until her husband, who must have been well aware of her state, finally emerged from his privacy and suggested in a cool dry voice that perhaps they had better get going now, had they not?

Mr. Foster may possibly have had a right to be irritated by this foolishness of his wife's, but he could have had no excuse for increasing her misery by keeping her waiting unnecessarily. Mind you, it is by no means certain that this is what he did, yet whenever they were to go somewhere, his timing was so accurate—just a minute or two late, you understand—and his manner so bland that it was hard to believe he wasn't purposely inflicting a nasty private little torture of his own on the unhappy lady. And one thing he must have known—that she would never dare to call out and tell him to hurry. He had disciplined her too well for that. He must also have known that if he was prepared to wait even beyond the last moment of safety, he could drive her nearly into hysterics. On one or two special occasions in the later years of their married life, it seemed almost as though he had *wanted* to miss the train simply in order to intensify the poor woman's suffering.

Assuming (though one cannot be sure) that the husband was guilty, what made his attitude doubly unreasonable was the fact that, with the exception of this one small irrepressible foible, Mrs. Foster was and always had been a good and loving wife. For over thirty years, she had served him loyally and well. There was no doubt about this. Even she, a very modest woman, was aware of it, and although she had for years refused to let herself believe that Mr. Foster would ever consciously torment her, there had been times recently when she had caught herself beginning to wonder.

Mr. Eugene Foster, who was nearly seventy years old, lived with his wife in a large six-story house on East Sixty-second Street, and they had four servants. It was a gloomy place, and few people came to visit them. But on this particular morning in January, the house had come alive and there was a great deal of bustling about. One maid was distributing bundles of dust sheets to every room, while another was draping them over the furniture. The butler was bringing down suitcases and putting them in the hall. The cook kept popping up from the kitchen to have a word with the butler, and Mrs. Foster herself, in an old-fashioned fur coat and with a black hat on the top of her head, was flying from room to room and pretending to supervise these operations. Actually, she was thinking of nothing at all except that she was going to miss her plane if her husband didn't come out of his study soon and get ready.

"What time is it, Walker?" she said to the butler as she passed him.

"It's ten minutes past nine, Madam."

"And has the car come?"

"Yes, Madam, it's waiting. I'm just going to put the luggage in now."

"It takes an hour to get to Idlewild," she said. "My plane leaves at eleven. I have to be there half an hour beforehand for the formalities. I shall be late. I just *know* I'm going to be late."

"I think you have plenty of time, Madam," the butler said kindly.

"I warned Mr. Foster that you must leave at nine fifteen. There's still another five minutes."

"Yes, Walker, I know, I know. But get the luggage in quickly, will you please?"

She began walking up and down the hall, and whenever the butler came by, she asked him the time. This, she kept telling herself, was the *one* plane she must not miss. It had taken months to persuade her husband to allow her to go. If she missed it, he might easily decide that she should cancel the whole thing. And the trouble was that he insisted on coming to the airport to see her off.

"Dear God," she said aloud, "I'm going to miss it. I know, I know, I *know* I'm going to miss it." The little muscle beside the left eye was twitching madly now. The eyes themselves were very close to tears.

"What time is it, Walker?"

"It's eighteen minutes past, Madam."

"Now I really *will* miss it!" she cried. "Oh, I wish he would come!"

This was an important journey for Mrs. Foster. She was going all alone to Paris to visit her daughter, her only child, who was married to a Frenchman. Mrs. Foster didn't care much for the Frenchman, but she was fond of her daughter, and, more than that, she had developed a great yearning to set eyes on her three grandchildren. She knew them only from the many photographs that she had received and that she kept putting up all over the house. They were beautiful, these children. She doted on them, and each time a new picture arrived, she would carry it away and sit with it for a long time, staring at it lovingly and searching the small faces for signs of that old satisfying blood likeness that meant so much. And now, lately, she had come more and more to feel that she did not really wish to live out her days in a place where she could not be near these children, and have them visit her, and take them for walks, and buy them presents, and watch them grow. She knew, of course, that it was wrong and in a way disloyal to have thoughts like these while her husband was still alive. She knew also that although he was no longer active in his many enterprises, he would never consent to leave New York and live in Paris. It was a miracle that he had ever agreed to let her fly over there alone for six weeks to visit them. But, oh, how she wished she could live there always, and be close to them!

"Walker, what time is it?"

"Twenty-two minutes past, Madam."

As he spoke, a door opened and Mr. Foster came into the hall. He stood for a moment, looking intently at his wife, and she looked back at him—at this diminutive but still quite dapper old man with the huge bearded face that bore such an astonishing resemblance to those old photographs of Andrew Carnegie.

"Well," he said, "I suppose perhaps we'd better get going fairly soon if you want to catch that plane."

"Yes, dear—*yes!* Everything's ready. The car's waiting."

"That's good," he said. With his head over to one side, he was watching her closely. He had a peculiar way of cocking the head and then moving it in a series of small, rapid jerks. Because of this and because he was clasping his hands up high in front of him, near the chest, he was somehow like a squirrel standing there—a quick clever old squirrel from the Park.

"Here's Walker with your coat, dear. Put it on."

"I'll be with you in a moment," he said. "I'm just going to wash my hands."

She waited for him, and the tall butler stood beside her, holding the coat and the hat.

"Walker, will I miss it?"

"No, Madam," the butler said. "I think you'll make it all right."

Then Mr. Foster appeared again, and the butler helped him on with his coat. Mrs. Foster hurried outside and got into the hired Cadillac. Her husband came after her, but he walked down the steps of the house slowly, pausing halfway to observe the sky and to sniff the cold morning air.

"It looks a bit foggy," he said as he sat down beside her in the car. "And it's always worse out there at the airport. I shouldn't be surprised if the flight's cancelled already."

"Don't say that, dear—*please.*"

They didn't speak again until the car had crossed over the river to Long Island.

"I arranged everything with the servants," Mr. Foster said. "They're all going off today. I gave them half pay for six weeks and told Walker I'd send him a telegram when we wanted them back."

"Yes," she said. "He told me."

"I'll move into the club tonight. It'll be a nice change staying at the club."

"Yes dear. I'll write to you."

"I'll call in at the house occasionally to see that everything's all right and to pick up the mail."

"But don't you really think Walker should stay there all the time to look after things?" she asked meekly.

"Nonsense. It's quite unnecessary. And anyway, I'd have to pay him full wages."

"Oh yes," she said. "Of course."

"What's more, you never know what people get up to when they're left alone in a house," Mr. Foster announced, and with that he took out a cigar and, after snipping off the end with a silver cutter, lit it with a gold lighter.

She sat still in the car with her hands clasped together tight under the rug.

"Will you write to me?" she asked.

"I'll see," he said. "But I doubt it. You know I don't hold with letter-writing unless there's something specific to say."

"Yes, dear, I know. So don't you bother."

They drove on, along Queens Boulevard, and as they approached the flat marshland on which Idlewild is built, the fog began to thicken and the car had to slow down.

"Oh dear!" cried Mrs. Foster. "I'm *sure* I'm going to miss it now! What time is it?"

"Stop fussing," the old man said. "It doesn't matter anyway. It's bound to be cancelled now. They never fly in this sort of weather. I don't know why you bothered to come out."

She couldn't be sure, but it seemed to her that there was suddenly a new note in his voice, and she turned to look at him. It was difficult to observe any change in his expression under all that hair. The mouth was what counted. She wished, as she had so often before, that she could see the mouth clearly. The eyes never showed anything except when he was in a rage.

"Of course," he went on, "if by any chance it *does* go, then I agree with you—you'll be certain to miss it now. Why don't you resign yourself to that?"

She turned away and peered through the window at the fog. It seemed to be getting thicker as they went along, and now she could only just make out the edge of the road and the margin of grassland beyond it. She knew that her husband was still looking at her. She glanced back at him again, and this time she noticed with a kind of horror that he was staring intently at the little place in the corner of her left eye where she could feel the muscle twitching.

"Won't you?" he said.

"Won't I what?"

"Be sure to miss it now if it goes. We can't drive fast in this muck."

He didn't speak to her any more after that. The car crawled on and on. The driver had a yellow lamp directed onto the edge of the road, and this helped him to keep going. Other lights, some white and some yellow, kept coming out of the fog toward them, and there was an especially bright one that followed close behind them all the time.

Suddenly, the driver stopped the car.

"There!" Mr. Foster cried. "We're stuck. I knew it."

"No, sir," the driver said, turning round. "We made it. This is the airport."

Without a word, Mrs. Foster jumped out and hurried through the main entrance into the building. There was a mass of people inside, mostly disconsolate passengers standing around the ticket counters. She pushed her way through and spoke to the clerk.

"Yes," he said. "Your flight is temporarily postponed. But please don't go away. We're expecting this weather to clear any moment."

She went back to her husband who was still sitting in the car and told him the news. "But don't you wait, dear," she said. "There's no sense in that."

"I won't," he answered. "So long as the driver can get me back. Can you get me back, driver?"

"I think so," the man said.

"Is the luggage out?"

"Yes, sir."

"Goodbye, dear," Mrs. Foster said, leaning into the car and giving her husband a small kiss on the coarse grey fur of his cheek.

"Goodbye," he answered. "Have a good trip."

The car drove off, and Mrs. Foster was left alone.

The rest of the day was a sort of nightmare for her. She sat for hour after hour on a bench, as close to the airline counter as possible, and every thirty minutes or so she would get up and ask the clerk if the situation had changed. She always received the same reply—that she must continue to wait, because the fog might blow away at any moment. It wasn't until after six in the evening that the loudspeakers finally announced that the flight had been postponed until eleven o'clock the next morning.

Mrs. Foster didn't quite know what to do when she heard this news. She stayed sitting on her bench for at least another half-hour, wondering, in a tired, hazy sort of way, where she might go to spend the night. She hated to leave the airport. She didn't wish to see her husband. She was terrified that in one way or another he would eventually manage to prevent her from getting to France. She would have liked to remain just where she was, sitting on the bench the whole night through. That would be the safest. But she was already exhausted, and it didn't take her long to realize that this was a ridiculous thing for an elderly lady to do. So in the end she went to a phone and called the house.

Her husband, who was on the point of leaving for the club, answered it himself. She told him the news, and asked whether the servants were still there.

"They've all gone," he said.

"In that case, dear, I'll just get myself a room somewhere for the night. And don't you bother yourself about it at all."

"That would be foolish," he said. "You've got a large house here at your disposal. Use it."

"But, dear, it's *empty*."

"Then I'll stay with you myself."

"There's no food in the house. There's nothing."

"Then eat before you come in. Don't be so stupid, woman. Everything you do, you seem to want to make a fuss about it."

"Yes," she said. "I'm sorry. I'll get myself a sandwich here, and then I'll come on in."

Outside, the fog had cleared a little, but it was still a long, slow drive in the taxi, and she didn't arrive back at the house on Sixty-second Street until fairly late.

Her husband emerged from his study when he heard her coming in. "Well," he said, standing by the study door, "how was Paris?"

"We leave at eleven in the morning," she answered. "It's definite."

"You mean if the fog clears."

"It's clearing now. There's a wind coming up."

"You look tired," he said. "You must have had an anxious day."

"It wasn't very comfortable. I think I'll go straight to bed."

"I've ordered a car for the morning," he said. "Nine o'clock."

"Oh, thank you, dear. And I certainly hope you're not going to bother to come all the way out again to see me off."

"No," he said slowly. "I don't think I will. But there's no reason why you shouldn't drop me at the club on your way."

She looked at him, and at that moment he seemed to be standing a long way off from her, beyond some borderline. He was suddenly so small and far away that she couldn't be sure what he was doing, or what he was thinking, or even what he was.

"The club is downtown," she said. "It isn't on the way to the airport."

"But you'll have plenty of time, my dear. Don't you want to drop me at the club?"

"Oh, yes—of course."

"That's good. Then I'll see you in the morning at nine."

She went up to her bedroom on the third floor, and she was so exhausted from her day that she fell asleep soon after she lay down.

Next morning, Mrs. Foster was up early, and by eight thirty she was downstairs and ready to leave.

Shortly after nine, her husband appeared. "Did you make any coffee?" he asked.

"No, dear. I thought you'd get a nice breakfast at the club. The car is here. It's been waiting. I'm all ready to go."

They were standing in the hall—they always seemed to be meeting in the hall nowadays—she with her hat and coat and purse, he in a curiously cut Edwardian jacket with high lapels.

"Your luggage?"

"It's at the airport."

"Ah yes," he said. "Of course. And if you're going to take me to the club first, I suppose we'd better get going fairly soon, hadn't we?"

"Yes!" she cried. "Oh, yes—*please!*"

"I'm just going to get a few cigars. I'll be right with you. You get in the car."

She turned and went out to where the chauffeur was standing, and he opened the car door for her as she approached.

"What time is it?" she asked him.

"About nine fifteen."

Mr. Foster came out five minutes later, and watching him as he walked slowly down the steps, she noticed that his legs were like goat's legs in those narrow stovepipe trousers that he wore. As on the day before, he paused halfway down to sniff the air and to examine the sky. The weather was still not quite clear, but there was a wisp of sun coming through the mist.

"Perhaps you'll be lucky this time," he said as he settled himself beside her in the car.

"Hurry, please," she said to the chauffeur. "Don't bother about the rug. I'll arrange the rug. Please get going. I'm late."

The man went back to his seat behind the wheel and started the engine.

"*Just* a moment!" Mr. Foster said suddenly. "Hold it a moment, chauffeur, will you?"

"What is it, dear?" She saw him searching the pockets of his overcoat.

"I had a little present I wanted you to take to Ellen," he said. "Now, where on earth is it? I'm sure I had it in my hand as I came down."

"I never saw you carrying anything. What sort of present?"

"A little box wrapped up in white paper. I forgot to give it to you yesterday. I don't want to forget it today."

"A little box!" Mrs. Foster cried. "I never saw any little box!" She began hunting frantically in the back of the car.

Her husband continued searching through the pockets of his coat. Then he unbuttoned the coat and felt around in his jacket. "Confound it," he said, "I must've left it in my bedroom. I won't be a moment."

"Oh, *please!*" she cried. "We haven't got time! *Please* leave it! You can mail it. It's only one of those silly combs anyway. You're always giving her combs."

"And what's wrong with combs, may I ask?" he said, furious that she should have forgotten herself for once.

"Nothing, dear, I'm sure. But . . ."

"Stay here!" he commanded. "I'm going to get it."

"Be quick, dear! Oh, *please* be quick!"

She sat still, waiting and waiting.

"Chauffeur, what time is it?"

The man had a wristwatch, which he consulted. "I make it nearly nine thirty."

"Can we get to the airport in an hour?"

"Just about."

At this point, Mrs. Foster suddenly spotted a corner of something white wedged down in the crack of the seat on the side where her husband had been sitting. She reached over and pulled out a small paper-wrapped box, and at the same time she couldn't help noticing that it was wedged down firm and deep, as though with the help of a pushing hand.

"Here it is!" she cried. "I've found it! Oh dear, and now he'll be up there forever searching for it! Chauffeur, quickly—run in and call him down, will you please?"

The chauffeur, a man with a small rebellious Irish mouth, didn't care very much for any of this, but he climbed out of the car and went up the steps to the front door of the house. Then he turned and came back. "Door's locked," he announced. "You got a key?"

"Yes—wait a minute." She began hunting madly in her purse. The little face was screwed up tight with anxiety, the lips pushed outward like a spout.

"Here it is! No—I'll go myself. It'll be quicker. I know where he'll be."

She hurried out of the car and up the steps to the front door, holding the key in one hand. She slid the key into the keyhole and was about to turn it—and then she stopped. Her head came up, and she stood there absolutely motionless, her whole body arrested right in the middle of all this hurry to turn the key and get into the house, and she waited —five, six, seven, eight, nine, ten seconds, she waited. The way she was standing there, with her head in the air and the body so tense, it seemed as though she were listening for the repetition of some sound that she had heard a moment before from a place far away inside the house.

Yes—quite obviously she was listening. Her whole attitude was a *listening* one. She appeared actually to be moving one of her ears closer and closer to the door. Now it was right up against the door, and for still another few seconds she remained in that position, head up, ear to door, hand on key, about to enter but not entering, trying instead, or so it seemed, to hear and to analyze these sounds that were coming faintly from this place deep within the house.

Then, all at once, she sprang to life again. She withdrew the key from the door and came running back down the steps.

"It's too late!" she cried to the chauffeur. "I can't wait for him, I simply can't. I'll miss the plane. Hurry now, driver, hurry! To the airport!"

The chauffeur, had he been watching her closely, might have noticed that her face had turned absolutely white and that the whole expression had suddenly altered. There was no longer that rather soft and silly look. A peculiar hardness had settled itself upon the features. The little mouth, usually so flabby, was now tight and thin, the eyes were bright, and the voice, when she spoke, carried a new note of authority.

"Hurry, driver, hurry!"

"Isn't your husband travelling with you?" the man asked, astonished.

"Certainly not! I was only going to drop him at the club. It won't matter. He'll understand. He'll get a cab. Don't sit there talking, man. *Get going!* I've got a plane to catch for Paris!"

With Mrs. Foster urging him from the back seat, the man drove fast all the way, and she caught her plane with a few minutes to spare. Soon she was high up over the Atlantic, reclining comfortably in her airplane chair, listening to the hum of the motors, heading for Paris at last. The new mood was still with her. She felt remarkably strong and, in a queer sort of way, wonderful. She was a trifle breathless with it all, but this was more from pure astonishment at what she had done than anything else, and as the plane flew farther and farther away from New York and East Sixty-second Street, a great sense of calmness began to settle upon her. By the time she reached Paris, she was just as strong and cool and calm as she could wish.

She met her grandchildren, and they were even more beautiful in the flesh than in their photographs. They were like angels, she told herself, so beautiful they were. And every day she took them for walks, and fed them cakes, and bought them presents, and told them charming stories.

Once a week, on Tuesdays, she wrote a letter to her husband—a nice, chatty letter—full of news and gossip, which always ended with the words "Now be sure to take your meals regularly, dear, although this is something I'm afraid you may not be doing when I'm not with you."

When the six weeks were up, everybody was sad that she had to return to America, to her husband. Everybody, that is, except her. Surprisingly, she didn't seem to mind as much as one might have expected, and when she kissed them all goodbye, there was something in her manner and in the things she said that appeared to hint at the possibility of a return in the not too distant future.

However, like the faithful wife she was, she did not overstay her time. Exactly six weeks after she had arrived, she sent a cable to her husband and caught the plane back to New York.

Arriving at Idlewild, Mrs. Foster was interested to observe that there was no car to meet her. It is possible that she might even have been a little amused. But she was extremely calm and did not overtip the porter who helped her into a taxi with her baggage.

New York was colder than Paris, and there were lumps of dirty snow lying in the gutters of the streets. The taxi drew up before the house on Sixty-second Street, and Mrs. Foster persuaded the driver to carry her two large cases to the top of the steps. Then she paid him off and rang the bell. She waited, but there was no answer. Just to make sure, she rang again, and she could hear it tinkling shrilly far away in the pantry, at the back of the house. But still no one came.

So she took out her own key and opened the door herself.

The first thing she saw as she entered was a great pile of mail lying on the floor where it had fallen after being slipped through the letter hole. The place was dark and cold. A dust sheet was still draped over the grandfather clock. In spite of the cold, the atmosphere was peculiarly oppressive, and there was a faint but curious odor in the air that she had never smelled before.

She walked quickly across the hall and disappeared for a moment around the corner to the left, at the back. There was something deliberate and purposeful about this action; she had the air of a woman who is off to investigate a rumor or to confirm a suspicion. And when she returned a few seconds later, there was a little glimmer of satisfaction on her face.

She paused in the center of the hall, as though wondering what to do next. Then, suddenly, she turned and went across into her husband's study. On the desk she found his address book, and after hunting through it for a while she picked up the phone and dialled a number.

"Hello," she said. "Listen—this is Nine East Sixty-second Street . . . Yes, that's right. Could you send someone round as soon as possible, do you think? Yes, it seems to be stuck between the second and third floors. At least, that's where the indicator's pointing . . . Right away? Oh, that's very kind of you. You see, my legs aren't any too good for walking up a lot of stairs. Thank you so much. Goodbye."

She replaced the receiver and sat there at her husband's desk, patiently waiting for the man who would be coming soon to repair the elevator.

# Part VI
# THE WORLD TODAY

# THE GIRL FROM CALIFORNIA

## *John O'Hara*

JOHN O'HARA (1905– ) one of the literary greats of our era, has reached the peak of his talent at a time when many of his famous contemporaries have been dropping by the wayside. His novels and short stories alike are distinguished by his fantastic ear for American speech and a capacity to depict an era and a milieu with camera-like clarity. Every story he writes has been researched with infinite care. Son of a doctor and the eldest of eight children, O'Hara was born in Pottsville, Pennsylvania. After graduation from Niagara Prep School, he worked as a ship steward, railway clerk, gas-meter reader, amusement park guard, soda clerk, and press agent. For a time he was secretary to the late Heywood Broun. Increasingly important writing on newspapers and magazines was climaxed in 1934 with the publication of his first novel, *Appointment in Samara,* an immediate success. From that day to this, there has been no question of John O'Hara's place in American literature.

THE limousine stopped and the driver paid the toll and waited for his change. The attendant in the toll booth looked at the couple in the back of the car and smiled. "Hyuh, Vince. Hello Barbara," he said.

"Hyuh, fella," said Vincent Merino.

"Hello," said Barbara Wade Merino.

"Going to Trenton, Vince?" said the attendant.

"That's right."

"I knew you was from Trenton. Good luck, Vince. So long Barbara," said the attendant.

"Thanks, fella," said Vincent Merino. The car moved along. "He knew I was from Trenton."

"Jesus, I'm glad to get out of that tunnel," said his wife. "I get the worst claustrophobia in a tunnel."

"Well, with me it's the opposite. I hate to ride in an airplane."

"I know," said Barbara. "Jack Spratt could eat no fat, his wife could eat no lean."

"We're gonna both of us eat plenty of fat where we're headed for. Today you forget about the calories. *And don't be nervous.* Take it easy. My fathernmother are no more different than your fathernmother. My mother aint even Italian."

"I know. You told me."

He tried to distract her. "You see them broken-down shacks and all? That used to be a pig farm, and you know something? The guy that owned it ran for President of the United States."

"Who cares?"

"Well, your mothernfather are always talking about America, the land of opportunity. Now you can tell them you seen a pig farm on the Jersey meadows, and the owner run for President the United States. I never heard of that in California."

"Thanks for trying to take my mind off it, but I wish today was over. What else will we do besides eat?"

"I don't know. Maybe the old man will make the load. If he's as nervous as you are, he could easily make the load. He could be starting right now. I hope not, though. He starts hitting the grappa, by the time we get there he could be passed out."

"How long does it take for us to get there?"

"About an hour and a half, I guess."

"Maybe I could go to sleep."

"You mean now?"

"Yes. You got any objections?"

"No, no objections if it'll calm you down."

"You sound disappointed."

"Not exactly, but if you go to sleep you're not gonna see New Jersey. I just thought, I know a hell of a lot about California, but you never saw New Jersey except from ten thousand feet up."

"On the train from Washington last year, when I was making those personal appearances."

"Yeah. The only reason why you took the train was because the whole East was fogged in. A hell of a lot you saw that time. All right, go to sleep if it'll relax you."

She put her hand on his cheek. "You can show me New Jersey on the way back."

"Sure. That's when *I'll* want to sleep."

"I wish we were both in bed right now," she said.

"Cut that out, Barbara. You're taking an unfair advantage."

"Oh, go to hell," she said, and turned her back and pulled the robe over her shoulder.

In a little while she fell asleep. She was always able to fall asleep. On the set, when she was making a picture, she could finish a take and go to her portable dressing-room and sack right out. Or if they were home and had had a fight, she would slam the bedroom door and in five minutes' time she would be sound asleep. "With Bobbie it's a form of escape," her sister said. "She's very fortunate in that respect."

"I'm built like a cow, so it's only natural," Barbara would say.

"Don't knock the build," Vincent had said. "It gets you two hundred gees a picture. And me. It got you me. You'd of been one of them boy types I wouldn't of looked at you. I wouldn't of *looked* at you."

The smell of a cigarette or the sound of the radio would wake her up, so he postponed a smoke and sat in silence as the car sped along the Turnpike . . . Then he realized that he had been asleep, too. He looked out on both sides but failed to recognize his surroundings. From his watch he made a quick calculation; they were ten, fifteen—more or less—minutes from the Trenton exit. He put his hand on his wife's hip and shook gently.

"Bobbie. Barbara. Get with it, kid."

"Huh? Huh? What? Where are we? Oh. Hello. Are we there yet?"

"I figured we're not far from it."

"Ask him. The driver," she said.

Vincent pressed the switch that lowered the division. "How much longer we got, driver?"

"We'll be in Trenton in five minutes, Mr. Merino. Then it's up to you."

"Thanks," said Vincent. "How about a little coffee?"

"All right," she said. "I'll do it." She poured coffee from a vacuum bottle. She put a lump of sugar in his cup and drank hers black and unsweetened. He gave her a lighted cigarette.

"Well, we're almost there," he said.

"Is the fellow from *Life* going to be there?"

"I don't know for sure. I doubt it. As soon as I told them it wasn't gonna be every Italian in Mercer County they lost interest."

She looked at herself in her vanity mirror. "Thank God for that, at least. Anyway they make a habit of sending a photographer and bossing everybody around, and that's the last you ever hear of it."

"I know. I don't even know for sure if my brother's coming from Hazleton. Both of my sisters will be there, that's for sure. But I bet their husbands have to work. My other brother Pat, him and another fella from Villanova. You couldn't *keep* them away."

"I hope I get them all straight."

"Pat's the college boy and he looks something like me. My eldest sister is France. Frances. My younger sister is Kitty. She's about the same age as you."

"Frances is the older one and Kitty's the younger one. And Pat's the college boy, and resembles you. What about your brothers-in-law? What are their names?"

"Take my advice and don't find out their names. That way my sisters won't get jealous, if you don't know their husbands' names. Anyway, I bet they won't be there."

"Who else?"

"The priest. Father Burke. And maybe Walter Appolino and his wife. He's a senator. State senator. If he wants us to pose for a picture, why, we better."

"What's the priest gonna be there for?"

"Well, maybe he won't come, being's we got married by a justice of the peace."

"Are they all going to make a stink about that? Because if they do, I'm going to turn right around and go back to New York. I don't have to take anything from them."

"You won't have to. Kitty's husband aint a Catholic and her kids aren't being raised Catholic. I aint worried about that, so don't you be. The only trouble I predict is if my old man makes the load, and Pat starts trying to make a pass at you. I'll give the son of a bitch a punch in the mouth if he does."

"Listen to who's talking."

"Right. Exactly. Listen to who's talking is right. He patterns himself after me because just because he happens to be Vince Merino's brother. Well, hands off Vince Merino's wife, Pasquale Merino, if you don't want to go back to Villanova minus a couple teeth. And don't you encourage him. Don't stand too close to him. He don't need any encouragement in that direction."

"Is there any of your old girl friends going to be there?"

"Not unless my brother Ed comes from Hazleton. I used to date her before Ed did."

"Did you score with her? I don't have to ask, I guess."

"Well, if you don't have to ask, why ask? What's the use of asking a question that you know the answer beforehand? Sure I scored, but not after she started dating Ed. Only Ed don't believe that. I don't think Ed'll be there."

"She probably throws it up to him that she could have married you."

"Hey, you're pretty smart. That's what she does do. And is she ever wrong? I wouldn't of married her even if I'd of kept on living in Trenton."

"Why not?"

"Because she thought she owned me, and she didn't."

"I own you, don't I?"

"Well, I guess so, but that was my own free will. I wanted to own you, so I let you own me. But I never wanted to own her. What the hell? I did own her and I never even wanted to. She was all right for then, but I never intended to be stuck in Trenton all my life. I hope they don't come. I hope there's only my two parents, and my sisters without their stupid husbands, and my kid brother if he behaves himself. Oh, Walter Appolino. Walter is more used to meeting celebrities, like he goes to New York all the time and every time he goes to the Stork Club. Walter was the first guy I ever knew that went to the Stork Club, when I was sixteen or seventeen years of age."

"Large deal."

"Come off it, Bobbie. When you were sixteen who did *you* know that went to the Stork Club?"

"When I was sixteen—well, *seven*teen—I was going there myself."

"Yeah, I guess so." Vincent now gave his full attention to the task of directing the driver through the streets of Trenton. In time they stopped at a detached white frame house which had a front porch, a front and back yard, and a one-car garage in the rear. "This is it," he said. "Is it worse or better than you expected?"

"Frankly, better."

He smiled. "My old man's a bricklayer at Roebling's. I bet he makes better than your old man."

"I didn't say he didn't. That's your mother in the doorway?"

"Yeah, that's Mom. Hey, Mom, wuddia say?" He got out of the car and embraced his mother. Barbara followed him. "Three guesses who this is."

"How do you do, Mrs. Merino?" said Barbara.

"I'm pleased to meet you, Barbara." Mrs. Merino shook hands with her daughter-in-law. "Come on in and be introduced to the others."

"Who all's here, Mom?" said Vincent. "Did Pop make his load?"

"What kind of talk is that? No, he didn't make any load. Is that the way you talk about your father?"

"Forget it. Who else is inside?"

"The Appolinos. Walter and Gertrude Appolino. He's the state senator. Senator Appolino, but a great friend of ours. And his wife. And my two daughters. Vince's two sisters, Frances and Catherine. Both married. Barbara, do you want to go upstairs and freshen up first, or will I introduce you to the others?"

There was no need to reply; all the others came out on the porch and Mrs. Merino made the introductions. As soon as all the names were mentioned there was a sudden, blank silence.

"All right, everybody stand here like a bunch of dummies," said Vincent. "Let's go inside or we'll have the whole neighborhood standing around." Two girls and a boy in their early teens came forward with autograph books and held them out to Barbara and Vincent.

"Put 'To my old friend Johnny DiScalso,' " said the boy.

"The hell I will," said Vincent. "Who are you? Pete DiScalso's kid?"

"Yeah."

"Your old man arrested me for driving without a license. You're lucky I sign my name for you. Who are you, girl?"

"Mary Murphy."

"Which Murphy? Your old man sell washing machines?"

"He used to but not any more."

"Is this your sister?"

"Yeah, I'm her sister. Monica Murphy. Our father used to sell washing machines but now he don't any more."

"Leo Murphy, Vince," said Senator Appolino. "I got him fixed up as an attendant over in the State House. Very good man, Vince, you know what I mean."

"Oh, sure. Leo's all right. Give my regards to your father, girls."

"Thanks, Vince," said the senator. "All right, girls, run along now. And, Vince?"

"What?"

"Forgive and forget. Put 'To my old friend Johnny DiScalso.' I'd appreciate it, you know?"

"Votes?" said Vincent.

"Sixteen guaranteed, sometimes more," said the senator. "And, Barbara, you, if you don't mind? Just something personal for Johnny? 'To my friend,' or something like that? Appreciate it. Appreciate it very much, Barbara."

"All right," said Barbara.

"Fine. Fine," said the senator. "Vince, I'm sorry Gert and I have to go to a colored funeral, but we'll be back later and your parents said it'd be all right if I brought a few friends back with us. Okay?"

"I don't know how long we'll *be* here, Walt."

"Yeah, but I'd appreciate it very *much,* Vince. I kind of promised these people, you know what I mean?"

"How many, Walt?"

"Under forty or fifty. They just want to say hello and like shake hands with you and Barbara. Ten minutes of your time, that's all, and a couple pictures for the papers. Ten minutes, fifteen minutes."

"If we're still here, Walt," said Vincent.

"Yeah. Well, I'd appreciate it, Vince. I really would. I more or less promised them, and I sure would hate to disappoint them. It'd look funny, you know, you coming back to the old home town and didn't see anybody. You know what some people would say, and I wouldn't want them saying that about Vince Merino and his lovely bride Barbara. I'm not gonna say goodbye, folks. We'll be back before you know it."

The senator and his wife departed, and the group on the front porch went inside to the parlor. "Pop, wud you tell Walt?" said Vincent after the women went upstairs.

"Huh. I didn't tell him, he told me. Right away he seen it in the paper you and Barbara was in New York, would you be coming to Trenton? Your mother told him yes. Here he is."

"You need him?"

"Well, I don't *need* him. Maybe he needs me as much as I need him but you got that crazy brother Pat, you never know what he's gonna do, so it's no use antagonizing Walt."

"Yeah. Where is Pat?"

"He'll be here, him and his roommate with his second-hand, third-hand Jag. The roommate keeps the car in Philly. They'll end up with a broken neck, the two of them. Well, it won't be long till the army gets him. He won't be staying at Villanova much longer."

"Why don't you knock a little sense into him?"

"Wait'll you see him and you'll know why. You didn't see him since he filled out. He could take you or me or maybe the two of us."

"Huh. How's Ed?"

"Ed? Oh, him and Karen are like cats and dogs. She was here in Trenton a couple weeks ago but she never came near us. She was here for two weeks last summer and never came around. They're all washed up. Ed was here in March or April, sometime, and he stayed drunk for two days. Your mother and I couldn't get anything out of him, but you can put two and two together."

"Well, give me some *good* news. Are France and Kitty all right?"

"Oh, I guess they're all right. Kitty was fooling around with some married man till your mother and France, and Father Burke got into it. Harry was responsible for that, but that don't give Kitty grounds to fool around with a married man."

"But France is all right?"

"Yeah. Well, you'd never know it now that France was a pretty girl when she was around sixteen."

"No."

"You got a good-looking girl for a wife. She even looks better in real life. You gonna have kids?"

"Well, not for a while."

"Yeah, I see what you mean. She put on weight you might have a hard time getting it off again. I don't blame you. Save your money and then have the kids. What is she? Twenty-three or four?"

"She's twenty-four."

"Well, maybe she could have one the year after next and then a wait a while."

"How are *you*, Pop?"

"Oh, hell, I'm all right, I guess. Why? Do I look as if I wasn't?"

"You look all right. How old are you now?"

"I'm a day older than I was this time yesterday. How old do you think I am?"

"I don't know. Around fifty?"

"Well, close. I'm forty-eight. I was bothered with this hernia last year, you remember when I was operated? I was made foreman, so I don't have as much heavy work."

"You still like your booze?"

"Huh. You wouldn't of had the nerve to ask me that five years ago. I don't drink no more. A little beer and a little wine, but no hard stuff. I cut out the hard stuff. Monday mornings I used to start getting dizzy up on the scaffolding, so I quit everything but a little wine and beer. But Ed's making up for it, and so's Pat. They'll scrape him up off the road one of these days. He's a wise guy, you can't tell him anything that he don't know all the answers. Is that your Chrysler outside?"

"Hired."

"What are you driving now?"

"I got an Austin-Healey, but I had it for two years and I'm thinking of getting something else. I only put about fourteen thousand miles on it, being away so much making pictures overseas."

"What happens with Barbara when you go away like that?"

"Well, the only time since we were married, she was in the same picture."

"Yeah, but I see where you're going to Portugal and she won't be there. What do you do then?"

"I don't know. It never happened since we were married."

Vince's father pointed a finger at him. "Start a baby. Take my advice and start a baby right away. Maybe it'll keep you straight. I don't know her, but I know you. The only thing that'll keep you straight is maybe if you have a baby started. Maybe. Forget the money, Vince. Forget it."

"Pop?"

"What?"

"How are you and Mom getting along?"

"What kind of a question is that to ask me? Who the hell do you think you are?"

"Oh-ho-ho. I touched a sore spot. Accidentally I touched a sore spot. Are you fooling around with somebody, Pop?"

"Did she say something to you?"

"When would she have a chance to say something to me?"

"Over the phone she could have."

"No, she didn't say nothing. But you took it so big, as soon as I asked you how you were getting along. I knew if it wasn't the booze it's either a woman or money. And you were never stingy. I'll give you that."

Andrew Merino's blue Tyrolean eyes showed trouble. He put his hand on his son's knee. "You're a man now, Vince, but some things you're still not old enough. I don't want to talk about it."

"Who is she? She older, younger? Married?"

"When I tell you this, it's the God's honest truth. I was never in bed with her."

"Oh, Pop. Come off it. You're a pretty good-looking guy."

"Oh, hell, I was as bad as you or Pat back in my twenties."

"Does Mom know the woman?"

"Don't say it that way, Vince. That sounds as if there was something, and there aint. I have a cup of coffee with her."

"At her house?"

"I never been inside her house."

"Does she feel for you?"

Andrew Merino hesitated, then nodded. "But she won't see me after work. She's in the office."

"Then what's Mom's beef?"

"Huh. Wait till you're married that long. We were twenty years of age when we got married. You'll find out."

"I come here to show my wife a typical Italian family, my folks. My Italian father and my Irish mother by the name of Merino. Mr. and Mrs. Andrew Merino, Trenton, New Jersey. And you wanta know something? The old lady give me a look when I got out of the car, and right away, *right away* I got the whole picture. You hung back and didn't hardly say anything. Then I thought to myself, Pop had this operation a year ago."

"No, it aint the operation, Vince."

"Oh, you don't have to tell me now, but that's what I thought. Five years ago you wouldn't of let Walt Appolino be the take-charge guy, not in your house. You sure you don't have a guilty conscience, Pop?"

"I got a guilty conscience for my thoughts. But what do you want, Vince? Do you want me to tell my own son that I don't love his mother? That's my guilty conscience, but I don't have to tell that in confession."

"You go to confession?"

"No."

"You don't, hey?"

"No, and that's why your mother thinks there's something going on.

I been two years without making my Easter duty. She says to me, next Sunday's the last chance to make your Easter duty. I tell her to mind her own business. Then she's positive I'm going to bed with Violet Constantino."

"Oh, Violet Constantino. Johnny's wife. That's who it is? She used to be a good-looking woman."

"She didn't only used to be. But Violet don't have to make her Easter duty. She's a Methodist, so your mother can't keep tabs on her that way."

"Pop, you gotta get this thing straightened out."

"I know. I know, Vince. To tell you the truth, I was hoping I could talk to you about it. I can't talk to nobody else."

"What does Johnny Constantino think of the whole thing?"

"Johnny Constantino," said Andrew Merino. He shook his head. "Him and I go bowling every Wednesday night."

"That don't answer my question, Pop."

"It wasn't suppose to. I was just thinking, him and I go bowling every Wednesday night, plus I give him a ride home from lodge meeting once a month. And I wonder. We been friends all our life, from boyhood, then I reach the age of forty-six and all of a sudden I fall in love with Violet, his wife for twenty years. I don't get anywhere with her, a cup of coffee in the morning, and 'How are you?'"

"Wuddia mean you never been inside her house?"

"I never been inside of their house. The two women don't get along. When do you remember me or your mother being inside the Constantinos'? Never."

"Well, they always lived the other side of town somewhere."

"If they lived over there next door it would be the same."

"Why don't Mom like her?"

"Well, the last couple years you can figure it out why. But before that your mother didn't like any woman that had a job. Violet had a diploma from commercial school and she could always get a job in an office. The best your mother could ever get was waitress or extra saleslady at Christmas. It wasn't her fault. She didn't have the education. But she used to say Violet was high-hatting her. But if it wasn't that she'd of found some other excuse. She don't like Johnny, either. Your mother don't like many people outside of her own family. The Appolinos and Father Burke. But she don't like ordinary people. I'm surprised those Murphy kids and Johnny DiScalso had the nerve to come here today. She chases any kids that run across our lawn."

"Not when I was a kid."

"Oh, not when you was a kid. You know why. She wanted all the kids playing in our yard. That way she'd know where you were. And

France. And Kitty. And Ed. But the minute they all grew up, no more kids playing on the front lawn. No more kids in the back yard. It's a wonder France or Kitty ever got a husband. 'Go down and tell them it's time to go home,' she used to say, when one of the girls had a boy friend. Eleven o'clock! Those girls were brought up strict. They might as well of had Father Burke living in the house. You didn't see any of that, but I saw plenty. And what could I do? Give her any opposition and she'd say, all right, if I wanted to be responsible. You remember young Audrey Detmer?"

"On Bergen Street?"

"Got knocked up when she was fifteen and they had five boys that she didn't know which one was the father. 'You want another Audrey Detmer in your own family?' she used to say. Your mother. Well, we almost did, with Kitty. Kitty's first was six months after she got married."

"Listen, Pop, I could of told you a few things about Kitty."

"I wouldn't of been surprised. Well, here they come down. You want a shot of something, or a cocktail? What kind of a cocktail does Barbara drink?"

"She can't handle it. She'll drink a little vino, and that's all I want."

Andrew Merino grinned. "You still got the weak stomach?"

"For liquor."

"Well, you can get drunk on wine, but you don't get Irish-drunk like Ed and Pat."

"Yeah? What about you and your grappa?"

"I never drank it because I liked it, Vince. I only drank it for the effect."

"To forget about Mom, huh?"

"Now, now, you don't have to say that," said Andrew Merino.

"What don't he have to say?" said his wife.

"I was talking to *him*, Kate. I wasn't talking to you," said Andrew Merino.

"All right, have your secrets," said Kate Merino. "I guess we're gonna have to start eating without Pat and his friend. Barbara, you sit anywhere you want to."

"She's suppose to sit next to me," said Andrew Merino.

"Well, she don't have to if she don't want to."

"The place of honor is on my right."

"I was gonna have her sit next to Walt, but he had to go to some funeral," said Kate Merino.

"Yeah. I wish it was his," said Andrew Merino. "Sit here, Barbara. You like Italian food?"

"I love it."

"You got any real Italian restaurants out in Hollywood?"

"Oh, sure. Lots of them."

"Well, my wife is Irish but she knows how to cook Italian food, so dig in. You know what that is, don't you? Thatsa leetla beeta Eye-talian prawn? You like da prawn?"

"Oh, cut the dialect, Pop," said Kitty.

"I no talka the dialect. Me speaka da perfect English, yes-no, Barbara?"

"Sure. Perfect."

"Lay off, Pop," said Vince.

The meal proceeded, and since they were all good eaters, the conversation was incidental to the enjoyment of the food. "I want to help you with the dishes, Mrs. Merino," said Barbara.

"No, we'll leave them till later, but thanks for making the offer," said Kate Merino.

"Would you smoke a cigar, Vince? I got some cigars," said Andrew Merino.

"No thanks, Pop. Maybe Barbara would like one."

"Don't give them that kind of an impression," said Barbara. "But I'll have a cigarette if you'll give me one."

"I ate so much I don't want to get up from the table. I don't want to move," said Vince, lighting his wife's cigarette. He passed his case along to the others, and they lit their own.

"Boy, solid gold," said France. "Can I read what it says inside?"

"From the studio. I know it by heart. 'To Vincent Merino for the Oscar he earned and will some day get. 1958.' That's when everybody said I was gonna get the Oscar."

"It shows what the studio thought of you, and that's what counts," said his mother.

"You're so *right* it's what counts," said Vince.

"We all sat here that night watching the TV," said France. "We were just as nervous as you were, if not more so. They put the TV camera on you, and you sure were nervous."

"Who did you go to that with, sweetie?" said Barbara.

"Renee Remy, who else? Who did you?"

"I don't remember."

"Brad Hicks," said France. "The TV director."

"Figures," said Vince.

"Well, I didn't know you then."

"Was that the front door?" said Kate Merino. "That'll be Pat, just when we're all finished eating."

Kitty Merino got up and went to the hall door. They all watched her, and she held her hand to her mouth and whispered to them: "It's *Karen.*"

"Oh, Christ," said Andrew Merino.

"Anybody home?" Karen's voice called out.

"We're all back here, Karen," said Kitty. "Come on back."

"Is that you, Karen?" called Kate Merino. "We're in the dining-room." Then, to the others: "Now don't anybody say anything, then maybe she won't stay. Just be polite."

Karen appeared in the hall doorway. "Hello, everybody. A regular family gathering, eh? Hello, Mrs. Merino. Pop. Kitty. France. Oh, hello, Vince."

"Hello, Karen," said Vince. "Ed with you?"

"No, he had to work but he sends everybody regards."

"Introduce you to my wife. Barbara, this is Karen, my brother Ed's wife."

"Hello, Karen," said Barbara, extending a hand.

"Well, naturally I recognize you, but I'm pleased to meet you personally."

"Did you have your lunch, Karen?" said Kate Merino. "We're keeping stuff warm for Pat and a friend of his, but the way it looks I don't think they're gonna be here."

"Oh, I ate over an hour ago, thanks. At my family's."

"How's your mother?" said Kate Merino.

"She seems better."

"Karen's mother had a serious operation for cancer," said Kate.

"They think they got it all," said Karen.

"We called up when she was in the hospital," said France.

"She told me, yes. She appreciated it."

"How's Ed?" said Vince.

"Oh, just the same."

"I wish he would of come with you. I didn't see Ed since you moved to Hazleton."

"Is it that long? Well, you'd still recognize him."

"Will you have a drink of something, Karen?" said Andrew Merino.

"No thanks. Ed takes care of that department," said Karen.

"Is Ed lushing it up?" said Vince.

"Now, Vincent!" said his mother.

"Yes, speak to him, even if he is the big movie star," said Karen. "Ed's your own brother."

"I just asked a simple question."

"Yeah. Simple," said Karen. "You ever been to Trenton before, Barbara?"

"No, only passed through it on the train."

"Yeah, that's what they say about Trenton," said Karen. "What part of the country did you originate?"

"Well, I was born in Montana, but my parents moved to L. A. when I was two years old."

"I had an uncle worked in Montana. Did you ever hear of Missoula, Montana? It sounds like you ought to use it cooking, but there is such a place."

"I heard of it, but I left there when I was two years old."

"Azusa. You got some funny names in California, too. Is there such a place as Azusa, or did they just make that up for a gag?"

"It's real," said Barbara.

"They got just as funny names around Hazleton, where I live. Did you ever hear of Wilkes-Barre? And they used to have a place called Maw Chunk. M, a, u, c, h, c, h, u, n, k. I don't pronounce it right but then they changed it to Jim Thorpe. From Maw Chunk to Jim Thorpe."

"Let's go sit in the front parlor," said Kate Merino. "It's nicer in there."

"What's wrong with here? I like sitting around the table," said Vince.

"The dirty dishes. Come on, everybody. Andy, bring two chairs for the Appolinos."

"Oh, is Walt coming?" said Karen.

"Walt and Gert. They were here early and then they had to go to a funeral," said Andrew Merino.

"What did you think of Walt, Barbara? Quite the big shot around here, so he thinks."

"He seemed all right."

"Who else was here? Father Burke?" said Karen. "He's usually here, too."

"Is that suppose to be some kind of a crack, Karen?" said Vince.

"You haven't changed."

"No, neither have you," said Vince. "You always came in this house with a chip on your shoulder."

"Take it easy, everybody," said Andrew Merino.

"Goodbye, everybody," said Karen.

"Goodbye? You just got here," said Kate Merino.

"I know where I'm not wanted," said Karen. She looked at everyone in the room, individually, except Vince, then went back in the hall and out the front door.

"Huh," said Vince.

"I wonder when she came down from Hazleton," said Kitty. "I bet she's been here a week or more."

"What possessed her to come over here today, if that's as long as she was going to stay," said Kate Merino. "To see Vince and Barbara, I know, but common politeness she should have stayed longer."

"Well, common politeness or whatever you want to call it, Bobbie and I gotta be going," said Vince.

"So soon?" said Kate Merino.

"Mom, I didn't give any time how long we'd stay. I got an interview at five o'clock at the hotel, and Bobbie has to do a TV tape."

"Well, this wasn't much of a visit, but I guess it's better than none. I don't know what we'll tell Walt," said Kate Merino.

"Vince didn't make Walt any promises," said Andrew Merino.

"I didn't make anybody any promises. I wasn't sure we could get here at all," said Vince.

"I wish I would of thought to bring my camera," said Kitty.

The chauffeur was asleep in the car, and a dozen women and children were standing quietly on the sidewalk when Vincent and Barbara left the house. As though by some tacit agreement the family all stood on the porch to wave farewell.

"Back to New York, Mr. Merino?" said the chauffeur.

"But fast," said Vince. "Go to the end of this street and turn right, then the first left and that'll put us on U.S.1. After that you look for Turnpike signs." He pressed the button that raised the division.

"If you got anything to say, save it till later," said Vince. "I don't want to talk about them."

"Well, now you know something."

"What?"

"You used to say to me, why didn't we go visit my folks. It was only thirty miles."

"You knew it was gonna be like this?"

"It could have been a lot worse," said Barbara. "You showed good sense leaving. They hate us, they all hate us. Either way, they hate us. If we're nice, they hate us just as much as if we treat them like dirt."

"All but Pop."

"Yeah, I guess he was all right, but he didn't fit in with the rest of them."

"Pop didn't? How didn't he fit in?"

"Don't ask me how. I just felt sorry for him," said Barbara. She took his hand. "What are you smiling at?"

"That Pat. Wait till he gets there and we're halfway to New York."

"Families," she said. "They're just like everybody else. They don't like us. Well, I didn't use to like Ava Gardner before I was in pictures. Or Lana Turner. Who did they think they are?"

"And now they're you, huh?"

"Sure."

"You want to go to sleep?"

"Wait till we get out of the built-up section. They're liable to think I'm drunk."

"I'd like to see the look on Walt's face, with his fifty politicians."

"Erase them from your mind, honey. It's the best way," she said.

# DUMB KID

## Jerome Weidman

---

JEROME WEIDMAN (1913–   ) came to New York the easy way by being born there a year before the start of World War I. A large part of his work as a uniformly top-ranking novelist, short story writer, satirist and playwright amounts to an unsentimental valentine to the city of his birth. With deadly accuracy he writes of its people; the tone and flavor of their speech, their ways of thinking and acting uptown and down—a distinction that is often of driving importance to his characters. He is a demon for work as is evidenced by his prodigious output in almost every branch of literary endeavor except the sonnet. *Dumb Kid* is an example of his skill at depicting human beings in a simple yet significant moment of their lives.

H E was bent down, behind the counter on which the cash register stood, when he heard the door open. For a moment he remained there, his back bent, his hands on the shoe boxes he had been arranging, wondering who it might be.

It couldn't be Mr. Lazarus. It was only a little after eight, and Mr. Lazarus never came in before nine-thirty. "Myself, I'm here in the morning half-past nine, ten," he had said. "You got plenty time to open up around nine. It's a business neighborhood. Nobody buys shoes early in the morning when they're rushing to get to work on time."

But Dave opened the store at eight. He wanted to show Mr. Lazarus that he wasn't lazy. In that hour he could straighten up the stockroom in the back and run the vacuum cleaner over the rug and arrange all the boxes that had been left over from the day before.

Maybe it was a customer. That would be fine! Not only would he have the store all arranged and ready for business when the boss came in, but he'd actually have a sale on the register, too! He hoped it *was* a customer.

The door slammed shut and he straightened up.

A girl in a bright-colored dress, without a hat, was standing in the doorway.

"Oh!" she exclaimed, and then smiled. "You scared me. You're not hiding, are you?"

"N-no," he stammered, and felt his face grow warm. "I—I was just straightening things up a little."

She smiled again and came further into the store. He watched her face, fascinated by the way she smiled, her teeth slightly parted and gleaming behind soft red lips. She looked around quickly and then back at him.

"It's pretty early, isn't it?" she said.

"It is, a little," he started to say, then remembered that she might be a customer. "But we're open for business," he added brightly.

She seemed not to hear him, moving her head around, looking into every corner of the store. The smile had gone out of her face, but her mouth was still open, as though she had forgotten to close it when she stopped smiling. Her hair was blonde and a little out of place because she wasn't wearing a hat, but he thought that somehow it seemed right that way. It made her look vague and soft, as though he were not looking at her directly, but only seeing her reflection in a body of water.

Suddenly she turned back to him, and the pleasant smile was on her face again. "I want to get a pair of shoes," she said in a friendly voice.

A customer!

"Certainly!" he said, smiling back at her and coming out briskly from behind the counter. "Won't you have a seat?"

She sat down, crossing her legs, and drew her skirt down over her knees.

He slipped onto a stool in front of her and reached for her shoe. "Let's just take a look at the size," he said, trying to sound like Mr. Lazarus.

She raised her foot a little toward him, and he slid the shoe off gently. There was a small hole in her stocking over the big toe. He could feel himself blushing and he looked at her quickly, but she did not seem to be embarrassed. She swung her leg gently while he looked inside the shoe.

"Five and a half," he said and stood up. "Anything special you wanted to see? I mean, an opera pump, an oxford—?"

She frowned slightly and looked undecided. "Oh—I don't know," she said. "Let's see something to match my dress."

He went to the shelves and pulled out a box. Suede, with a single strap and a neat buckle. No—a little too conservative for a young girl like that. Maybe, though. She looked quiet and reserved. She might want a conservative shoe. He took down another box. The same, but with a patent leather bow. A little more dressy. She was looking at him and their eyes met. She smiled. He blushed and looked away.

"I don't know if this is what you want," he said, coming toward her and avoiding her eyes. "But let's just try it on to see if the size is right."

"Oh, no!" she cried, releasing a peal of tinkly laughter, when he held the shoe out to her. "I want something a little more—well *you* know, something a little—"

"Oh, sure!" he said quickly. "I just wanted you to look at it, that's all." What a fool he was! A young, pretty girl—and him showing her a dead-looking shoe like that! "How about this one?" He held up the shoe with the patent leather bow.

She looked at it dubiously, the full red lips pouting.

"Just slip it on for size," he said hurriedly. Gosh, he hoped he didn't lose a customer just because he was too dumb to bring out the kind of shoe she wanted! "Just try it on, and if it fits, I'll show you some real nice stuff. Just try it on," he urged.

She held out the foot with the torn stocking and he felt his face grow warm again as he slid the shoe onto it. He kept his eyes on the shoe and swore at himself for being nervous. She must think he was a dumb kid who didn't know what it was all about!

"How is it?" he asked, patting the sides of the shoe.

"It *feels* okay," she said, "but—"

"All right," he said, reaching for the shoe again. "Now that we know the *size* is right, I'll show you something you'll like."

She wriggled her toes as he slipped the shoe off and he almost dropped the shoe. She smiled at him and he turned away quickly to hide his embarrassment. What the devil was wrong with him?

If he didn't pull himself together, she'd be sure to get disgusted and walk out. And not only wouldn't he have a *sale* on the register when Mr. Lazarus came in, but he wouldn't even have the store cleaned up!

"Say!" he heard her laugh behind him. "All I'm getting is *one* pair."

He looked at the boxes he had been unconsciously pulling down from the shelves and smiled foolishly.

"I was just—" he began.

"Here, wait a minute," she said kindly. "Let's see what you've got." She stood up and walked toward him, moving unevenly because she was wearing only one shoe.

"You take them down," she said, "and I'll look at them. All right?"

"All right," he said, relieved, and began to pull out boxes. She stood at his side, their shoulders touching, facing the wide wall of closely packed shoe boxes. He pulled out a box, opened it, held it in front of her. She looked at it quizzically for a moment, then shook her head and said, "No." Or she would smile and nod and say, "Maybe this one," and put the opened box aside. After a time she said, "Whew! This ought to be enough. Now let's see."

Both of them surveyed the litter of boxes and covers and tissue paper.

"Gee," she said, looking up at him with a smile of apology, "I certainly messed up the place for you, didn't I?"

"That's all right," he laughed happily. "As long as you get something you like." He meant it, too, he assured himself, a little surprised, and wasn't just saying it because she was a customer.

She picked up several boxes an hobbled back to her seat. "You want to bring the others?" she asked over her shoulder, smiling at him.

"You bet," he said and carried across the store the rest of the boxes she had set apart.

He wanted to help her try them on, but she was working too quickly, taking shoes from the boxes, slipping them on, kicking them off, trying on new ones. He sat on the stool in front of her and watched her turn the half-dozen pairs of shoes into a hopeless jumble of boxes and covers and paper. For a moment he thought of the work he'd have, straightening them all out again. He glanced at the clock. It was twenty to nine. He'd never be able to get the store arranged before Mr. Lazarus came in. But that didn't matter. He'd have a sale on the register!

And, anyway, for a girl like that, so neat looking and soft and pretty, a girl that—that—he couldn't think of a word to describe the warm glow that spread through him when he looked at her—for a girl like that he'd clean up *any* mess. Even if she *didn't* buy! But no. She wasn't just looking. She really meant to buy. He could tell by the serious way in which she looked at the shoes she slipped on, matching them against the color of her dress.

He stole a glance at her. Their eyes met again and he blushed.

"Say," she said, smiling at him, "which of these two do you like best?"

She was holding her foot straight out, looking at the shoe on it, with her head cocked to one side. In her hand she held up another one.

"Oh, I don't know," he said, pretending to examine both of them closely. The one on her foot was neat and simple. He thought it looked well on her. The one in her hand had a large ribbon on the instep. It was a little too—too—well, not just exactly right for a nice, quiet-looking girl like that. "Of course, it's all a matter of taste," he said in Mr. Lazarus' best manner. "But, personally, I prefer the—"

"I like *this* one better," she said with sudden decision.

She kicked off the shoe on her foot and slipped on the one she had been holding. She gave the large ribbon an adjusting pat and

stuck her leg straight out, twisting her head and wriggling her foot
back and forth at the end of the leg to get a better view.

"Yes," she said finally, "I think that looks about the best of the
bunch. Don't you?"

"*I* think so," he said, looking at the shoe critically. Funny how it
didn't look so good when she held it in her hand, but the minute
she put it on it seemed perfect, as though it had been made for her.
"It looks fine on you, all right."

"Good," she said. "I'll take them."

"Shall I wrap them up, or will you wear them?" he asked, trying
to hide the excitement in his voice. He had made a sale!

"I'll wear them," she said quickly, and slipped on the second shoe.

He stood up, a little out of breath, but smiling and victorious. "That'll
be three ninety-five," he said.

She looked at him for a moment and then said quietly, "I haven't
got any money."

He gasped stupidly, the sound escaping from him as though he had
been violently struck. His mouth hung open and he stared at her in
amazement, without comprehension.

"Come on, come on," she said, and her voice was suddenly hard.
"Snap out of it!"

He continued to stare at her, openmouthed, trying to bring back
into focus the soft face, the gleaming teeth, the full, smiling lips.

She stood up and faced him with a cold, calculating half-grin.

"Well?" she said, and cast a meaningful glance toward the curtained doorway of the stockroom in the rear of the store.

"Oh!" he said, as though he had suddenly remembered something,
and stepped back, away from her. He shook his head quickly. "Oh,
no," he said.

"Oh, well," she said with a tired shrug, twisting her lips into thin
angry lines, and sat down. She lifted one leg across her knee to get
nearer to the shoe and began to undo the large ribbon bow.

For another moment he stared at her, then he said quickly, "It's
all right—you don't have to take them off."

At once her face brightened into a pinched, knowing smile and
she looked up at him. But he took several steps away from her. She
shrugged again and re-tied the ribbon hurriedly. Then she stood up
and walked toward the door with a faint swagger, looking back at him
derisively over her shoulder.

He continued to stare at the door for a few moments after it had
closed. His eyes were still unblinking with a look of astonished dis-

belief as he took his thin wallet from his hip pocket and counted out four dollar bills.

The bell of the cash register shook him from his trance.

"Gee whiz," he exclaimed, softly, as he dropped the bills in and took out a nickel.

# A & P

## *John Updike*

---

JOHN UPDIKE (1932–   ) has achieved great distinction as a novelist, poet and writer of short stories. He was born in a small town in Pennsylvania, attended Harvard where he contributed to the famed *Lampoon,* and then went on to Oxford. For two years he was a member of the staff of *The New Yorker* and his prose and verse still occasionally adorn its pages. Mr. Updike's style is subtle, haunting and entirely his own. In recent years he has lived in Massachusetts with his wife and two children.

I N walks these three girls in nothing but bathing suits. I'm in the third checkout slot with my back to the door, so I don't see them until they're over by the bread. The one that caught my eye first was the one in the plaid green two-piece. She was a chunky kid, with a good tan and a sweet broad soft-looking can with those two crescents of white just under it, where the sun never seems to hit, at the top of the backs of her legs. I stood there with my hand on a box of HiHo crackers trying to remember if I rang it up or not. I ring it up again and the customer starts giving me hell. She's one of these cash-register-watchers, a witch about fifty with rouge on her cheekbones and no eyebrows, and I know it made her day to trip me up. She'd been watching cash registers for fifty years and probably never seen a mistake before.

By the time I got her feathers smoothed and her goodies into a bag—she gives me a little snort in passing, if she'd been born at the right time they would have burned her over in Salem—by the time I get her on her way the girls had circled around the bread and were coming back, without a pushcart, back my way along the counters, in the aisle between the checkouts and the Special bins. They didn't even have shoes on. There was this chunky one, with the two-piece—it was bright green and the seams on the bra were still sharp and her belly was still pretty pale so I guessed she just got it (the suit)—there was this one, with one of those chubby berry-faces, the lips all bunched together under her nose, this one, and a tall one, with black hair that hadn't quite frizzed right, and one of these sunburns right across under the eyes, and a chin that was too long—you know, the kind of girl other girls think is very "striking" and "attractive" but never quite makes it, as they very well know, which is why they like her so much—and then the third one, that wasn't quite so tall. She was the queen. She kind of led them, the other two peeking around and making their shoulders round. She didn't look around, not this queen, she just walked straight on slowly, on these long white prima-donna legs. She came down a little hard on her heels, as if she didn't walk in her bare feet that much, putting down her heels and then letting the weight move along to her toes as if she was testing the floor with every step, putting a little deliberate extra action into it. You never know for sure how girls' minds work (do you really think it's a mind in there or just a little buzz like a bee in a glass jar?) but you got the idea she had talked the other two into coming in here with her, and now she was showing them how to do it, walk slow and hold yourself straight.

She had on a kind of dirty-pink—beige maybe, I don't know—bathing suit with a little nubble all over it and, what got me, the straps were down. They were off her shoulders looped loose around the cool tops of her arms, and I guess as a result the suit had slipped a little on her, so all around the top of the cloth there was this shining rim. If it hadn't been there you wouldn't have known there could have been anything whiter than those shoulders. With the straps pushed off, there was nothing between the top of the suit and the top of her head except just *her*, this clean bare plane of the top of her chest down from the shoulder bones like a dented sheet of metal tilted in the light. I mean, it was more than pretty.

She had sort of oaky hair that the sun and salt had bleached, done up in a bun that was unravelling, and a kind of prim face. Walking into the A & P with your straps down, I suppose it's the only kind of face you *can* have. She held her head so high her neck, coming up out of those white shoulders, looked kind of stretched, but I didn't mind. The longer her neck was, the more of her there was.

She must have felt in the corner of her eye me and over my shoulder Stokesie in the second slot watching, but she didn't tip. Not this queen. She kept her eyes moving across the racks, and stopped, and turned so slow it made my stomach rub the inside of my apron, and buzzed to the other two, who kind of huddled against her for relief, and then they all three of them went up the cat-and-dog-food-break-fast - cereal - macaroni - rice - raisins - seasonings - spreads - spaghetti - soft-drinks-crackers-and-cookies aisle. From the third slot I look straight up this aisle to the meat counter, and I watched them all the way. The fat one with the tan sort of fumbled with the cookies, but on second thought she put the package back. The sheep pushing their carts down the aisle—the girls were walking against the usual traffic (not that we have one-way signs or anything)—were pretty hilarious. You could see them, when Queenie's white shoulders dawned on them, kind of jerk, or hop, or hiccup, but their eyes snapped back to their own baskets and on they pushed. I bet you could set off dynamite in an A & P and the people would by and large keep reaching and checking oatmeal off their lists and muttering "Let me see, there was a third thing, began with A, asparagus, no, ah, yes, apple-sauce!" or whatever it is they do mutter. But there was no doubt, this jiggled them. A few houseslaves in pin curlers even looked around after pushing their carts past to make sure what they had seen was correct.

You know, it's one thing to have a girl in a bathing suit down on the beach, where what with the glare nobody can look at each other much anyway, and another thing in the cool of the A & P, under the fluorescent lights, against all those stacked packages, with her feet paddling along naked over our checker-board green-and-cream rubber-tile floor.

"Oh Daddy," Stokesie said beside me. "I feel so faint."

"Darling," I said. "Hold me tight." Stokesie's married, with two babies chalked up on his fuselage already, but as far as I can tell that's the only difference. He's twenty-two, and I was nineteen this April.

"Is it done?" he asks, the responsible married man finding his voice. I forgot to say he thinks he's going to be manager some sunny day, maybe in 1990 when it's called the Great Alexandrov and Petrooshki Tea Company or something.

What he meant was, our town is five miles from a beach, with a big summer colony out on the Point, but we're right in the middle of town, and the women generally put on a shirt or shorts or something before they get out of the car into the street. And anyway these are usually women with six children and varicose veins mapping their legs and nobody, including them, could care less. As I say, we're right in the middle of town, and if you stand at our front doors you can see two banks and the Congregational church and the newspaper store and three real-estate offices and about twenty-seven old freeloaders tearing up Central Street because the sewer broke again. It's not as if we're on the Cape; we're north of Boston and there's people in this town haven't seen the ocean for twenty years.

The girls had reached the meat counter and were asking McMahon something. He pointed, they pointed, and they shuffled out of sight behind a pyramid of Diet Delight peaches. All that was left for us to see was old McMahon patting his mouth and looking after them sizing up their joints. Poor kids, I began to feel sorry for them, they couldn't help it.

Now here comes the sad part of the story, at least my family says it's sad, but I don't think it's so sad myself. The store's pretty empty, it being Thursday afternoon, so there was nothing much to do except lean on the register and wait for the girls to show up again. The whole store was like a pinball machine and I didn't know which tunnel they'd come out of. After a while they come around out of the far aisle, around the light bulbs, records at discount of the Carribbean Six or Tony Martin Sings or some such gunk you wonder they waste the wax on, sixpacks of candy bars, and plastic toys done up in cellophane that fall apart when a kid looks at them anyway. Around they come, Queenie still leading the way, and holding a little gray jar in her hand. Slots Three through Seven are unmanned and I could see her wondering between Stokes and me, but Stokesie with his usual luck draws an old party in baggy gray pants who stumbles up with four giant cans of pineapple juice (what do these bums *do* with all that pineapple juice? I've often asked myself) so the girls come to me. Queenie puts down the jar and I take it into my fingers icy cold. Kingfish Fancy Herring Snacks in Pure Sour Cream: 49¢. Now her hands are empty, not a ring or a bracelet, bare as God made them, and I wonder where the money's coming from. Still with that prim look she lifts a folded dollar bill out of the hollow at the center of her nubbled pink top. The jar went heavy in my hand. Really, I thought that was so cute.

Then everybody's luck begins to run out. Lengel comes in from haggling with a truck full of cabbages on the lot and is about to scuttle into that door marked MANAGER behind which he hides all day when the girls touch his eye. Lengel's pretty dreary, teaches Sunday school and the rest, but he doesn't miss that much. He comes over and says, "Girls, this isn't the beach."

Queenie blushes, though maybe it's just a brush of sunburn I was noticing for the first time, now that she was so close. "My mother asked me to pick up a jar of herring snacks." Her voice kind of startled me, the way voices do when you see the people first, coming out so flat and dumb yet kind of tony, too, the way it ticked over "pick up" and "snacks." All of a sudden I slid right down her voice into her living room. Her father and the other men were standing around in ice-cream coats and bow ties and the women were in sandals picking up herring snacks on toothpicks off a big glass plate and they were all holding drinks the color of water with olives and sprigs of mint in them. When my parents have somebody over they get lemonade and if it's a real racy affair Schlitz in tall glasses with "They'll Do It Every Time" cartoons stencilled on.

"That's all right," Lengel said. "But this isn't the beach." His repeating this struck me as funny, as if it had just occurred to him, and he had been thinking all these years the A & P was a great big dune and he was the head lifeguard. He didn't like my smiling—as I say he doesn't miss much—but he concentrates on giving the girls that sad Sunday-school-superintendent stare.

Queenie's blush is no sunburn now, and the plump one in plaid, that I liked better from the back—a really sweet can—pipes up, "We weren't doing any shopping. We just came in for the one thing."

"That makes no difference," Lengel tells her, and I could see from the way his eyes went that he hadn't noticed she was wearing a two-piece before. "We want you decently dressed when you come in here."

"We *are* decent," Queenie says suddenly, her lower lip pushing, getting sore now that she remembers her place, a place from which the crowd that runs the A & P must look pretty crummy. Fancy Herring Snacks flashed in her very blue eyes.

"Girls, I don't want to argue with you. After this come in here with your shoulders covered. It's our policy." He turns his back. That's policy for you. Policy is what the kingpins want. What the others want is juvenile delinquency.

All this while, the customers had been showing up with their carts but, you know, sheep, seeing a scene, they had all bunched up on Stokesie, who shook open a paper bag as gently as peeling a peach, not wanting to miss a word. I could feel in the silence everybody getting nervous, most of all Lengel, who asks me, "Sammy, have you rung up their purchase?"

I thought and said "No" but it wasn't about that I was thinking. I go through the punches, 4, 9, GROC, TOT—it's more complicated than you think, and after you do it often enough, it begins to make a little song, that you hear words to, in my case "Hello (*bing*) there, you (*gung*) hap-py pee-pul (*splat*)!"—the *splat* being the drawer flying out. I uncrease the bill, tenderly as you may imagine, it just having come from between the two smoothest scoops of vanilla I had ever known were there, and pass a half and a penny into her narrow pink palm, and nestle the herrings in a bag and twist its neck and hand it over, all the time thinking.

The girls, and who'd blame them, are in a hurry to get out, so I say "I quit" to Lengel quick enough for them to hear, hoping they'll stop and watch me, their unsuspected hero. They keep right on going, into the electric eye; the door flies open and they flicker across the lot to their car, Queenie and Plaid and Big Tall Goony-Goony (not that as raw material she was so bad), leaving me with Lengel and a kink in his eyebrow.

"Did you say something, Sammy?"

"I said I quit."

"I thought you did."

"You didn't have to embarrass them."

"It was they who were embarrassing us."

I started to say something that came out "Fiddle-de-doo." It's a saying of my grandmother's, and I know she would have been pleased.

"I don't think you know what you're saying," Lengel said.

"I know you don't," I said. "But I do." I pull the bow at the back of my apron and start shrugging it off my shoulders. A couple customers that had been heading for my slot begin to knock against each other, like scared pigs in a chute.

Lengel sighs and begins to look very patient and old and gray. He's been a friend of my parents for years. "Sammy, you don't want to do this to your Mom and Dad," he tells me. It's true, I don't. But it seems to me that once you begin a gesture it's fatal not to go through with it. I fold the apron, "Sammy" stitched in red on the pocket, and put it on the counter, and drop the bow tie on top of it. The bow tie is theirs, if you've ever wondered. "You'll feel this for the rest of your life," Lengel says, and I know that's true, too, but remembering how he made that pretty girl blush makes me so scrunchy inside I punch the No Sale tab and the machine whirs "pee-pul" and the drawer splats out. One advantage to this scene taking place in summer, I can follow this up with a clean exit, there's no fumbling around getting your coat and galoshes, I just saunter into the electric eye in my white shirt that my mother ironed the night before, and the door heaves itself open, and outside the sunshine is skating around on the asphalt.

I look around for my girls, but they're gone, of course. There wasn't anybody but some young married screaming with her children about some candy they didn't get by the door of a powder-blue Falcon station wagon. Looking back in the big windows, over the bags of peat moss and aluminum lawn furniture stacked on the pavement, I could see Lengel in my place in the slot, checking the sheep through. His face was dark gray and his back stiff, as if he'd just had an injection of iron, and my stomach kind of fell as I felt how hard the world was going to be to me hereafter.

# Part VII
# EXIT LAUGHING

# MY GRANDMOTHER AND THE DIRTY ENGLISH

## *Aubrey Menen*

---

AUBREY MENEN (1912–    ), was born in England of a high caste Indian father and an Irish mother and was educated in London. He has spent many years in India and today lives in Italy. His activities have been widespread and include dramatic criticism in London, several successful novels, and a wartime career as the most influential radio commentator in India. His mixed ancestry, added to a rare gift for gentle but trenchant humor, has made him a unique and highly readable observer of today's world. The past engages him as much as the present, and the following is a delightful reminiscence of his boyhood.

My grandmother, like Michelangelo, had *terribilità*. She had a driving will; she would not be balked and whatever she did was designed to strike the spectator with awe. She was also something of a stick. She rarely spoke to anyone who was not of her own social station and she received them formally: that is to say, with her breasts completely bare. Even in her time women were growing lax about this custom in Malabar. But my grandmother insisted on it. She thought that married women who wore blouses and pretty *saris* were Jezebels; in her view, a wife who dressed herself above her waist could only be aiming at adultery.

When I was twelve she demanded that I be brought and shown to her. I was incontinently taken half across the earth, from London to South beyond the town of Calicut. My mother came with me.

The last part of the journey was made by dugout canoe (there being no railways and no good roads near our family estate) and in this we were poled on a moonlit night up the Ponnani River. The river was lined with palm trees and crocodiles.

My mother taking fright at these beasts, I sang to keep them away from the boat. I sang a song I had been taught at school called "Drake's Drum." This had been written in the reign of Queen Victoria and told how, if the Spaniards should embark on the unlikely project of attacking nineteenth century England, Drake would come back to life and drum them up the Channel "as he drummed them long ago." I had been taught many songs of similar sentiments but this was the noisiest. I sang it with a will because my young heart (especially in such very foreign parts) glowed with the sentiment. The crocodiles yawned and, like the Spaniards in the Victorian age, showed no signs of attacking.

This singing marked a stage in my life. Shortly afterwards I lost my innocence. My grandmother took me in hand and I never thought the English were perfect again.

When our boat journey was done, servants with flaming torches led us along narrow paths between tall trees, and finally conducted us to a house. This house was large and smelt of paint. It was (my father said) not my ancestral roof.

When my grandmother had heard that my mother intended to make the visit as well as myself, she had given orders for a special house to be put in repair for my mother's accommodation. It was on the furthest confines of the family property. This was her solution of a difficult problem. My mother was ritually unclean, and therefore whenever she entered my family house, she would defile it. The house would have to be purified and so would every caste Hindu in it. It followed logically that if my mother stayed in the house, it would be permanently in a state of defilement and permanently in a state of being ritually cleaned. Since this ceremony involved drums and conch shells, my mother's visit foreshadowed a prolonged uproar. All this was avoided by my grandmother's decision to put her up in a separate building.

I cannot say that my grandmother was ever rude to my mother. She never referred to her by name but always as 'the Englishwoman.' This was not necessarily an insulting expression, but my mother had Irish blood and what with this, and the house, and some other pin-pricks, her temper rose. She ordered a quantity of medical stores from Calicut, and when they arrived she set up a free dispensary on the verandah, to which the peasants flocked. It was an admirably devised answer. My grandmother had shut the door in my mother's face: she now had the galling experience of seeing my mother industriously cleaning up the doorstep. As my mother well knew, each drop of iodine that she dispensed stung not only the grateful patient, but also my grandmother's conscience.

My grandmother brooded on this for a while and then sent my mother a bag of golden sovereigns. My mother, taking this to be a bribe at the worst, or at the best, a tip, sent it back. But she was wrong. It was a peace offering. It was sent again next day, accompanied by the family goldsmith who sat, slept and ate on the verandah for one week while he made the sovereigns (with tweezers and a charcoal fire) into a great gold collar which my mother still, on occasions, wears.

When, fourteen years before my trip, my father had written from England to say that he was getting married to a white woman, my grandmother had been far from giving the union her blessing. But it would be wrong to say that she had objected to it. If an American boy of twenty-two wrote home from foreign parts to say that he had taken to cannibalism, his parents would not object. They would be so revolted that a mere objection would never meet the case. So with my grandmother.

She had never met the English but she knew all about them. She knew they were tall, fair, given to strong drink, good soldiers and that they had conquered her native country. She also knew that they were incurably dirty in their personal habits. She respected them but wished they would keep their distance. It was very much the way that a Roman matron looked upon the Goths.

My eldest uncle had been to England for two years and he spoke up for the English. He said that while the Hindus were undoubtedly the most civilised race on earth and had been civilised a thousand years before the English, nevertheless, the English were now the masters of the Hindus. My grandmother's reply to this was that the English were masters of the Hindus only because 'nobody would listen to *us*.' By this she meant that our family along with others of the same caste had strongly objected to Vasco da Gama being allowed to land in Calicut. They had, in fact, done their best to get him and his sailors massacred. But the country was not behind them and he escaped. Everything, my grandmother argued (and not without some reason) had started with that.

But her chief complaint was that the English were so dirty, and this was rather a poser for my uncle. When my grandmother asked if, like decent people, they took a minimum of two baths a day, my uncle, who could not lie to his mother without committing a disgraceful sin, said that, well, no: but a few took one bath and the habit was spreading. He could go no further than that. But he added that my grandmother should remember that England had a cold climate. This she loyally did, and when she discussed the matter with me, she was able to treat the matter lightly, as one does the disgusting but rational liking of the Eskimos for eating blubber.

As for the question of eating, she did not have the expected prejudices. She did not think it strange that the English ate ham and beef. The outcaste hill-tribes (called *Todas*) who made the family straw mats and cleaned the latrines, ate anything. She was not disturbed either, about their religion, because my uncle assured her that they had practically none. Their manners, however, she abominated. If she did not mind them eating meat, she considered their way of eating it beyond the pale of decent society. In my family home, each person eats his meal separately, preferably in a secluded corner. The thought that English people could sit opposite each other and watch each other thrust food into their mouths, masticate, and swallow it, made her wonder if there was anything that human beings would not do, when left to their own devices.

She was not surprised to hear, after this, that in England a woman could have more than one husband, particularly (and this was the crowning paradox) if she had been a widow. To the day of her death my grandmother could never understand how people could call themselves civilised and yet allow widows to marry again. For her the very foundation-stone of society was that a child should have one father, and obey him. Nobody ever dared her wrath sufficiently to explain the position of women in English society. She was intensely proud of the standards of her house and she permitted no lewd talk to define them—certainly never in her presence.

With this background, then, my grandmother's peace offering of a bag of sovereigns was a considerable victory for my mother, particularly since the gold collar which the goldsmith had been told to make from them was the characteristic jewellery of a Malabar bride.

The way was now open for me. I could go and see her. I had waited about three weeks.

I had many meetings with her. I used to visit her in considerable state. The distance from our home—the isolation wing, so to speak—to the main family mansion was too far for walking in the Malabar sun. I used to go by palanquin. It was a hammock of red cloth with rather worn embroidery of gold thread, and it was swung on a black pole which had silver ornaments at either end. Four virtually naked men, two in front and two behind, carried the palanquin at a swift trot. There was considerable art in this. If the four men trotted just as they pleased, the hammock would swing in a growing arc until it tipped the passenger out on to the road. To prevent this, the men trotted in a complicated system that I never really understood: watching them and trying to trace it out was as difficult as trying to determine the order in which a horse puts its hoofs down. They kept their rhythm by chanting. I used to fall asleep on the way, listening to them. It must have presented an interesting spectacle—a red palanquin, the sweating men, and a sleeping schoolboy wearing an English blazer with its pocket sewn with a badge gained by infantile prowess at some sport that I do not now remember.

The family house was vast and cool and in my view, unfurnished. But to my grandmother's eye it was very elegant. There was nothing but the floor to sit on. She disliked chairs and thought them vulgar. What use were they, except for ostentation? She approved of beds but insisted that the mattress be made of taut string—nothing else was considered clean. She also had a taste for handsome brassbound boxes. So beds, boxes and oil-lamps were the sole furniture of the innumerable rooms of the house. There were no tables and no table-cloths. In my grandmother's house, if anybody dared eat in any fashion but off a fresh plantain-leaf, his next meal would have been served in the kitchen, where the servants were allowed to eat without ceremony.

My grandmother usually received me sitting by her favourite box in her boudoir. She made an unforgettable picture. She had great black eyes, a shock of white hair and lips as lush and curved as a girl of eighteen. The skin of her bosom, bare as I have said, was quite smooth. I used to sit on the floor in front of her in my school blazer and since my father had never taught me Malayalam, (wishing me to be brought up like any other English schoolboy), we talked through one of my uncles.

The things my grandmother told me were a puzzle at the time. But I have come to understand them better. Much as she looked down on the English, I think that had she met some of them, had she overcome her well-bred fastidiousness and actually mixed with them, she would have found she and they had much in common. Her riding passion, like theirs, was racial pride. She believed—and this made her character—that she belonged to the cleverest family of the cleverest people on earth. According to Lord Russell, this was also the firm faith of Mrs. Beatrice Webb, who used to repeat it to herself in moments when, otherwise, she might have felt inferior, such as when she made her entry into a distinguished party. Though my grandmother never went to parties I'm sure that she, too, repeated the formula as a stiffener of her already formidable morale.

She felt that she was born of a superior race and she had all the marks of it. For instance, she deplored the plumbing of every other nation but her own. She would often say to me, through my uncle: "Never take a bath in one of those contraptions in which you sit in dirty water like a buffalo. Always bathe in running water. If you have servants to pour it over you, that's best. But otherwise you must stand under a tap or pour the water over yourself. A really nice person does not even glance at his own bath water much less sit in it" Here she would laugh to herself, while my uncle translated; not an unkind laugh, but a pitying one, as she thought of the backwardness of the white man's bathroom.

Another mark—and I have met it in many nations—was that she
believed that English sexual morals permitted and encouraged all sorts
of abominations from which a civilised person shrank. She spoke to me
with great freedom on this point: I was after all at puberty. I
could not always follow the drift of her remarks, but I did gather that
she felt strongly on one point. Why, if the English wanted their offspring to grow up decently and not lewdly, did they omit to marry
them off when they were children? There was something sinister in the
neglect. A child should grow up knowing quite well that all that side
of his life was settled according to the best available advice and in the
best possible manner for his welfare. When he was eighteen or twenty
the marriage would be consummated. Till then, he did not have to
worry his head about women—or if he did worry, he knew he was
morally slipping.

History, I have discovered, is on my grandmother's side. The great
majority of civilised peoples have always agreed with her. Romance and
love and such things were, in antiquity, things for slaves. Respectable
families arranged their marriages as my grandmother arranged those of
her offspring. To take a single example, my grandmother and Brutus
would fully have understood each other. She felt hurt that she had
not been consulted over my father's marriage: while among the many
sidelights that we have on that honourable man who assassinated Julius
Caesar is a letter in which he complains at being left out of the bargain-
ing that went on during the betrothal of 'my dear little Attica,' who
was nine years old.

But a grandson was a grandson, even although her permission had
not been sought to bring him into the world, and she set about being
a mother as well as a grandmother to me. She knew that soon I would
go back among the heathen to finish my education and she wanted me
to go back knowing who and what I was. On one of my visits she gave
me a small book in which was written all my duties and privileges
as a member of my class. The book was written on dried palm-leaves,
strung together with a cord between two covers of wood. It began with
a prayer to God thanking Him for creating us—our caste, that is—so
much superior in every respect to the great majority of other human
beings.

My grandmother explained what followed several times and with
much emphasis, for she wanted to imprint it on my memory. Our family
belongs to the caste—or class—called Nayars. The Nayars of Malabar
are as old as Indian history and therefore, it can be assumed, a good
deal older. My grandmother told me that traditionally we had two obligations to society. We were warriors when there was fighting to do: and

when there was not, we had the duty, on certain holy days, of carrying flowers to the temple.

I remember that I thought this very romantic at the time and could not understand why my grandmother took it so prosaically: to me, warriors, flowers and temples conjured up a picture of some Oriental Round Table. But my grandmother was right. Our caste is a commonplace: it exists everywhere. In England it is scattered all over the countryside. The men are what is called 'Army' and the women take not only flowers, but fruit to the temple on the occasion of the Harvest Festival. It is curious, and inexplicable, that the combination of these two activities, whether in the Shires or in the coconut groves of Malabar, produces the most ferocious snobs.

My grandmother explained to me that as a Nayar, I should always be very careful to keep my dignity when dealing with Brahmins: Brahmins are priests. The priests who have the cure of souls of my family are treated as domestic chaplains. Since their temples are on our property my grandmother had several 'livings,' so to speak at her disposal, this side of religious affairs always being left in the hands of the older women. Priests were therefore expected to make themselves agreeable, in return for which they were regularly fed. They were expected to mind their own business, which was to perform the weekly ceremonies and to direct their preaching at the lower orders, particularly the servants. The Anglican Settlement in England was much more elaborate but reduced to what it meant to the average priest-in-the-vestry, it came much to the same thing, and provides one more reason why I wish my grandmother had visited the country of my birth.

But my grandmother was quite ignorant of these striking resemblances and begged me when moving among the English to remember myself. "They will look up to you, as a Nayar, to set an example," she used to say. "They know that you have two thousand years of advantage over them and they will be willing to learn. Show them this book. They will be very interested. It was written when they still went about naked. And I will give you some trinkets which you can hand out as gifts: some amulets which we use and some things made of sandalwood, which is very rare in England so I am told, and much sought after. They will help you make friends. But remember, it is your *example* which will count more than anything."

She gave me all the things she promised and as she had foretold, they were much admired. Some of them, I believe, are still in my school museum. She also gave me her blessing, which was what I had been brought across the world to get.

I thought over her advice but I was in some confusion. My headmaster, wishing me good by and good-luck when I had set out on my trip had said much the same thing. "Let them see," he had said, "by your example that you have been trained in an *English* school. Wherever you go, it is for *you* to set the tone." He did not give me any sandalwood, but I was very impressed. I was also very greatly impressed with what my grandmother had said.

In my dilemma I remembered that I had another grandmother. She had been born, as I have said, in Killarney, but had come to England to live—briefly enough, for she had died before I was born. I asked my mother about her. She told me many things but one stood out in my mind above all others.

"My mother," she said, "was never really happy among the English. She longed to go back to Killarney. Sometimes when things had become unbearably tiresome, she would heave a long, deep sigh, shake her head and gently close her eyes."

# EVELYN WAUGH RUNS A FAIR

## Edward R. F. Sheehan

EDWARD R. F. SHEEHAN (1930– ) is a New Englander who after graduating from Boston College saw several years of service as a foreign correspondent for the *Boston Globe*. Events carried him into some exciting fields such as the Suez crisis and the Hungarian uprising. More recently he has been press officer at our embassies in Cairo and Beirut, and has traveled widely through Asia and Africa. So far his writing has been limited to lively and informed journalistic articles but a novel may be expected from him soon.

SINCE I was educated systematically in the suspicion of the Lion and of Lloyd George, the idea of actually visiting England had always frightened me a little. When I eventually managed to outgrow my misgivings, it was for a curious if not contradictory reason: I enjoyed reading Aldous Huxley, Graham Greene, and Evelyn Waugh and wanted to meet them. My pilgrimage was inopportune, for when I reached London I found that Huxley was in California and Greene in Cuba. The only member of my triumvirate geographically accessible was Waugh and he, so everyone said, was Olympian in his aloofness.

Nor did I feel that my credentials would very much impress Waugh. I was a struggling young writer with not much money, attempting to install myself as a foreign correspondent for a group of New England newspapers. I rented a room in an establishment called the Hester House, off Russell Square. I had no friends in London. It was a cold, humid, rainy summer.

There were no alternatives: I had to try my luck with Waugh. He supposedly never even acknowledged requests for interviews, but wouldn't brevity displease him least? I scrawled out a one-line postcard asking whether we might not meet when he next came up to London, and sent it off to Stinchcombe, Gloucestershire, where he was then living.

I was astonished at the promptness of his reply to a proposal so casual. His letter had two enclosures: an engraved invitation card and a large printed poster. The invitation read:

MR. & MRS. EVELYN WAUGH

request the honour of your company at a Garden Fete in aid of St. Dominic's Church, Dursley, to be held (weather permitting) on Saturday, August 14th, 3 p.m.–7 p.m. at Piers Court, Stinchcombe, Dursley

*

Refreshments–Children's Sports–Stalls, Etc.

*

Admission 1/-; Children 6d. Donations gratefully accepted from those unable to be present.

*

A small but interesting collection of Paintings, mostly Victorian narrative pictures, and of rare books, never previously exhibited, will be on view in the house 4 p.m.–7 p.m. (wet or fine). Admission 1/-.

The poster said much the same as the invitation, but the letter was in a class by itself:

Piers Court, Stinchcombe
Nr Dursley, Glos.
August 6th

Dear Sir,

Thank you for your kind interest in me.

I suggest you change your plans slightly and come here on the fourteenth for the fete. You would find material for an article on a typically English rural event and you could be of great help to us.

We need men of resource to manage traffic, detect thieves, "bark" at side shows, spend money, and judge children's sports. Also in the morning to help erect booths.

Have you any accomplishments other than writing—conjuring, ventriloquism, contortionism—that you would be willing to display? Can you draw lightning portraits? We can offer you a bed on the night of the fete and the remains of the refreshment tent. There will not be much luncheon or dinner for us that day. Plenty of wine, however, for willing helpers.

Perhaps you play the trumpet? The Stinchcombe Silver Band would welcome a solo while they rest.

Have you a motorcar or do you wish to be met at Stroud?

Yours faithfully,
Evelyn Waugh

Please post attached poster in Grosvenor Square.

I replied by accepting Waugh's invitation and apologized for my lack of experience in ventriloquism, contortionism, and the other lively arts. I volunteered, however, to recite selections from *Finnegans Wake* standing on my head and afterwards to organize the hopscotch.

"It is good of you to come and help at our fete," Waugh wrote by return post. "I presume you are in robust health, in which case you can be of great service on the morning of Saturday erecting booths, carrying pictures, etc. Therefore if it is convenient I suggest your coming Friday evening."

Waugh seemed to be more in search of a stevedore than in need of a house guest, but his invitation, whatever its motive, did represent the chance to pass an entire weekend with a novelist whose writings I revered. Besides, I was weary of the stale kippers and garrulous landlady at the ghastly Hester House.

An indulgent drama critic on one of the London newspapers had advised me I might soon grow equally weary of what he called Waugh's "snobbery." One aspires to many things in the course of a lifetime, and during that rainy British summer I rather fancied I aspired to snobbery. I obediently mounted the poster in Grosvenor Square and then went to Paddington Station and took a train to Goucestershire.

## THE MAN IN THE
## RED SMOKING JACKET

I CANNOT remember very much about Waugh's gardener, who met me at Stroud Station, but I do remember the ride in the twilight to Waugh's house in Stinchcombe. The deep valleys of Gloucestershire meet at Stroud, and then the town climbs the abrupt Cotswold hills. When we reached the high grassy ridge of the Cotswold, stretching before us was the wide valley of the Severn River. The sun had set; some horses were grazing near the road, their dark silhouettes outlined against a backwash of purple light.

It was nearly dark by the time we turned into the drive. There, looming before us, was Waugh's Georgian manor. The gardener left me alone on the front doorstep and drove off. I rang the bell more than once and waited. Finally I tried the door and found it locked. I began to feel—to borrow a phrase from Malcolm Muggeridge—like a letter delivered to the wrong address. Just then the door opened and I found confronting me a rather round, rubicund man in a red smoking jacket.

"Mr. Sheehan, I should imagine?" Evelyn Waugh put an oversized cigar back into his mouth and extended his hand. A sharp-nosed but attractive woman came out of the drawing-room and Waugh introduced her as Laura, his wife. Before I could exchange pleasantries with her, Waugh had picked up my luggage and started up the stairs. "Come along," he said, "I'll show you your room. I say, your bag is rather heavy, perhaps you'd better lend a hand. What have you got inside?"

Nothing unusual, I indicated, beyond some books and a carton or two of cigarettes.

"Cigarettes," he repeated. "Cigarettes! Well, here we are. This is your room. Unlike your overheated American homes, we have no central heating in this house, so I imagine you will have to get along without it. Now, do you want some supper?"

"No, I had something a little after six," I said. "I mean, I thought you would have dined already."

"My dear fellow, dine at six o'clock? We never dine at six o'clock here. We'll be waiting for you downstairs, where you can have something to eat when you are ready to join us. *Six o'clock!*"

My chamber, the master guest-room, was large, old-fashioned, and comfortable. The bed was lavishly canopied, the canopy generously tasseled. In a corner of the room stood an enormous Victorian washstand, an impressive monstrosity elaborately decorated with metal work and mosaic. In the adjoining bathroom was a more conventional basin with a gaping hole in it. As if not to be outdone, this basin had pasted onto it a testimonial which proclaimed: *"This willful destruction of property was perpetrated by Lady Genevieve Fennington-Cawley."*

There was a knock at the door. I opened it to find a lean, red-headed young man of about fifteen. "Oh hello. I'm Auberon Waugh. Should the housekeeper heat hot water or will you draw your bath cold? Also do you prefer your fish boiled or broiled?"

"Well, if you don't mind I'll take my bath cold and my fish boiled," I said with some uncertainty, fearful lest taking them any other way might have bordered on the savage.


## HIS VIEW OF HOLLYWOOD

THE Waughs and the eldest of their six children were waiting in the drawing-room. They may not have eaten at six, but they had eaten, and I picked at my fish self-consciously while they quietly surveyed me.

Waugh sat opposite me, on the edge of the divan, nursing a brandy. Contemplating him, I tried to imagine him in his youth, for in the back of my mind was the description, made by one of his earlier Boswells of a radiant young man of sensuous mouth, splendid eyes large and set far apart, and "hyacinthine locks of hair." I thought that if age had not faded such features neither had she disciplined them. His reddish hair he still has in abundance, but mere ruddiness has replaced radiance in his face. Most remarkable now are surely his eyes, which alternately dart, distend, and wander far, far from under the arched eyebrows which so sparsely frame them. The plump unity of his features, the large head resting on a short, comfortable frame, somehow combine to give him an almost elfish look.

The remarkable eyes came out of their faraway gaze and focused sharply on me.

"Where are you from?" Waugh asked.

"From Boston," I said.

"I have been there."

"The politics are interesting there." I was trying to make conversation.

"You like politics?" he asked, apparently intrigued.

"I love politics," I said, plunging forward.

"I loathe politics," he rejoined. "Please change the subject."

Throwing out the first thought that came to me, I told him about an American woman I met in Florence who could talk of nothing but her dog. Hoping to get him started off on any kind of tangent, I asked him why middle-aged women talked so much of dogs.

"Why old boy," Waugh said, "it's obviously to keep you from talking about politics!"

The remark did not put me at my ease, but at least it meant Waugh was shifting into second gear. He now let out the clutch on one of his favorite subjects. "You Americans," he said. "What an extraordinary breed you are! And by the way, what extraordinary questions you ask. While on my lecture tour in your country, the inquiry most often directed at me was whether or not I slept in the nude."

"In America it's sex or money," I conceded, expressing surprise that in his case it was not the size of his royalties they asked about.

"On the contrary," he said, "the problem was not their avarice but mine. They could not meet my price. In Hollywood, I was offered $125,000 for the cinema rights to *Brideshead Revisited,* but even that was not enough for what they wanted in return. I did not see how they could cast the same man as nineteen years old in one frame and then as thirty-two in another—unless of course they took a nineteen-year old and waited thirteen years to finish the film. Your Hollywood people are not as patient as I, so there we were, high and dry."

Waugh was no more indulgent about the state of England than he was about the state of Beverly Hills. As the evening progressed many of the kingdom's greatest names, best known novelists, newest plays,

and nearly all the practices and preferences peculiar to its modern
epoch became victims of his exquisite disdain.

". . . Oh yes, she showed up *here* once. We got rid of *her* in a
hurry, didn't we? . . . You remember, old girl," he addressed his wife,
"when he cornered me that Saturday afternoon in White's—don't ask
me how he got in—waving the manuscript of his new play in my face
like a regimental flag. I had to be left in peace, so I glanced at a few
pages and then told him that either one of us was illiterate or gobble-
degook had become a language. The play ran three seasons in New
York. . . ."

Waugh's judgments produced occasional chuckles among the children
and uncritical silence from Mrs. Waugh, a woman of few words who
seemed to accept those of her husband with a serenity that bordered on
adoration. The conversation eventually drifted to the fete, and I asked
Waugh why of all people he, who so valued his privacy, should be
opening his home to the public. "Why dear boy," he said, "because St.
Dominic's Church is in financial need and because the parish is part
of our simple way of life here." Rising, he went to the corner of the
room and pulled down a wall map of Piers Court, which he beckoned
me to examine. At first I thought it unusual that an estate of only some
few acres should require mapping out; but as he murmured again
"way of life," I thought I understood.

Waugh's new reverie was interrupted by Virginia, his teen-aged,
red-haired daughter. "Where are we going to put Teddy tomorrow?" she
asked. They had already begun calling me Teddy.

"I think we'll put Teddy in the car-park," said Waugh. "Teddy will
do splendidly in the car-park. We have the special headpiece for him."

"Headpiece?" interjected Auberon. "Papa, you're not going to make
Teddy wear *that*."

"Yes, the headpiece," Waugh replied cryptically. Little I said from
then on raised a shadow of interest in Waugh's face—his family seemed
amused at the magnitude of my inability to stir him from his daydreams
—until I mentioned Graham Greene's letter in the Manchester *Guardian*.

"What letter in the *Guardian*?" Waugh came quickly back to life.

"Greene has written to the Cardinal Archbishop of Paris," I explained, "protesting the denial of a Church burial to Colette, and the
*Guardian* has a story about it on the back page."

"Why, the man is mad," Waugh exclaimed. "The man is mad. I love
Graham, but he is mad. I remember once when he came down here
from London for a visit. The family were all away. Graham and I were
both working and we met only at meals. Then I discovered that for
hours Graham would disappear from the house. When I finally asked

him what he was doing, he explained that he could not write another word until a certain combination of numbers—I think it was 987, something like that—appeared to him by accident. He was spending all his time by the roadside waiting for those numbers to pass on a license plate. He could not write another line until he saw them. Well, it is a poor country road, and there are not many motorcars. Graham had a long wait."

We retired for the night on that note. Tomorrow was the fete and there was a long day's work ahead. "There will be a great deal to do in the car-park, Teddy. And with your headpiece you will be the paragon of the day."

## THE SEVEN MINOR VIRTUES

Saturday dawned a morning of alternating showers and sunshine. Waugh said he had a whole convent of Poor Clares praying it would be fine for the fete, and throughout the morning it was nip and tuck. Until the very hour of the fete—three o'clock—we were not to know who would gain the day, the Poor Clares or the Powers of Darkness.

The Waugh family were having breakfast as I entered the dining-room, smoking a cigarette. "Now come here, Teddy, sit down and have something, and get rid of that blasted cigarette!" Waugh leaped out of his chair, seized the lighted cigarette from my mouth, opened the window, and threw it out.

We ate a substantial country breakfast of fruit, bread, sausage, ham and eggs, and tea, served by the Waughs' matronly cook. Then I asked Auberon, a good-natured lad, if he would show me around the "park." This mellow, rambling, tree-girt house was enhanced without by a manicured front lawn, a miniature mock Greek temple, and classic statuettes in various poses. In the rear, there were hen coops, lamb coops, and pig pens. A rolling side stretch of luxuriant grass rising into a hillock was to serve as the car-park for the afternoon.

Bron (Auberon) took me first to the Greek temple diagonally facing the front of the house, a garden Acropolis with the torsos, stumps, and heads of Ionic columns deposited about in contrived Romantic decadence. But the temple was not nearly as intriguing as the mystery of "The Edifice" (so Bron called it) toward the rear of the house. The Edifice was a complex of pillared, classical walls about five feet high, an ornate obstacle course without roof, pediment, or apparent purpose. Surmounting the walls were seven small statues. "What do the statues represent?" I asked Bron. "They are the seven virtues," he said. "Oh? Temperance? Chastity—?" "No," he answered cryptically, "they are the seven minor virtues." To this day I do not know the identity of the seven minor virtues, for when I re-entered the house and asked Waugh, he mumbled something about my limbering up for the car-park and placed a broom in my hand.

Mrs. Waugh was already running around in faded blue jeans. This was not out of character, for she was the day-to-day manager of the physical establishment.

I had Victorian books to rearrange for exhibit in the library, ladders to climb, rugs to roll up, and electric lights to move. Waugh allowed electricity at Piers Court, but no radio. He finally installed a telephone, but most of the time refused to answer it. He does not own a gramophone, for he claims he cannot understand music, not even the classics. As for television, he said he had never heard of it. For Waugh, progress means something more than sitting-room electronics and bathroom plastics. It means a whole new nineteenth century.

Nowhere among Waugh's possessions was the nineteenth century more affectionately enshrined than in his collection of Victorian-epoch narrative pictures, some tragic, some satirical, some otherworldly, each telling a story of its own. "The Prince and His Friends"—a caricature by Max Beerbohm of King Edward VII and his entourage—was one of these. Three paintings respectively depicted travel during the last three centuries. A journey aboard a Victorian railway carriage was benevolently joyful, but fierce highwaymen were shown as still at large during the eighteenth century, and representing the twentieth were the hysterical passengers of a crash-bound modern airship. "They are all doomed," chuckled Waugh, and lit up another cigar.

Despite all the shifting around the exhibition required of Waugh's treasures, he was never in any doubt about where to put what. He seemed to have predestined the position of each object as he would a character in one of his novels—each occupying its proper place, some ordained to attract great attention, others to play supporting or only incidental roles. Waugh assigned a protagonist's prominence to the monstrosity—the Victorian washstand. "Get Bron to help you, and place it on the landing of the stairs," he decreed. Negotiating the marble monument around banisters to its place of honor was no easy task, and Waugh's directions hardly helped.

"Watch the corner, Teddy!—wouldn't want to stick you with a re-plastering bill. Ah, that's it. Splendid!"

The rarest collector's item of the day, however, was not exhibited and Waugh's decision to conceal it from public view struck me as unworthy of his comic genius. I refer to The Commode, an immense armchair repositorium upholstered completely in leopard skin. Only the great perforation amidships betrayed this specimen for what it was.

Toward midday the heavy work was done. Waugh poured himself a gin and bitters. Then Bron, rather out of breath, broke in on us.

"Papa," he said, "there's the nicest young American down at the gate. He's all by himself and it's still hours before the fete. What shall we do with him?" The gate had been locked until the appointed hour, a young sentinel posted before it.

Waugh poured himself another gin. "Teddy," he turned to me, "go down with Bron to the gate and look this fellow over. If he's acceptable, invite him to luncheon. If he's not, get rid of him."

On the way down the path, Bron and I devised the signal system to be implemented when I had decided whether or not the stranger was up to snuff. We decided I would engage him in a brief discussion of Waugh's works (something I hadn't dare do with Waugh) and if I mentioned *Vile Bodies* Bron was to invite him in.

The stranger at the gate turned out to be a young fellow with horn-rimmed spectacles from the American Embassy in London, an articulate chap called Conley. Conley was a Waugh worshiper who not only had read everything his idol had written but had left London that morning at an impossible hour because there was only one train. "I didn't want to miss the opportunity of meeting him for the first time," he said. "I'm sorry to be so premature."

"Don't worry," I replied, "I don't think he'll consider you a vile body."

Bron carried the motion. "I say, won't you come to luncheon?" Three other early birds, all old ladies, we left behind to reflect on the large notice posted at the gate:

NO ADMITTANCE ON BUSINESS

Waugh was waiting for us in front of the house. No sooner had I introduced him to Conley than Father Collins of St. Dominic's, Dursley, came up the drive in his car. Father Collins opened his door, and several glass jars of peppermints fell with a crash to the ground. The infant Waughs, a few of their countryside chums, Bron, and Mr. Conley bent down to clean them up.

"Don't bother," Waugh counseled Conley. "We have plenty of child labor here. Besides, your services will be put to better use in the scullery."

"But the broken glass is mixed in with the sweets," Conley observed.

"That is no reason for throwing them away," Waugh retorted, "and any casualties will be for a worthy cause."

At a quarter to three it was raining again, and all the outdoor games seemed doomed. Waugh's resignation bordered on mysticism. "The Poor Clares are praying for good weather," he said, "and it will be fine." The weather was as good as his word, for at five minutes to three, when he told everyone to "man your battle stations" it had rained for the last time that day.

"All ready, Teddy? Then follow me. We must dress you up in your headpiece first."

I followed Waugh to the room that sheltered the leopard-skin commode, the only place downstairs not rearranged for the fete. From a wooden cabinet Waugh extracted a gleaming metal object. "Teddy, this is your headpiece," he said. "How formidable you will look in the car-park!" The headpiece was a German helmet of Franco-Prussian War vintage, complete with spike. How it sparkled in the new sunlight that now illumined the room, how it bathed me in reflected glory as only a brass hat can! And the spike! It looked as long and sharp as a bayonet.

"No thank you," I said.

"Why what on earth do you mean?"

I told Waugh he would have to impale me on that spike before he would ever get me to wear it publicly on my head.

"My dear boy," he protested, "do you realize what this means? You are trying to deprive the fete of one of its prime attractions—a unicorn in the car-park."

But Waugh was not beaten. In the moist green grass of the car-park, that afternoon, a unicorn grazed. It wore horn-rimmed spectacles and attracted much attention. Conley made a good unicorn.

## THE BABY AUSTIN'S BURDEN

The fete was on. With Conley replacing me in the car-park, I was temporarily at large. The visitors swarmed over the grounds of Piers Court; they queued into the house and then came popping out of it like tweed peas from a Georgian pod. Waugh did not at first mingle with them. Not that they were all unworthy of that honor, for a lot of distinguished and dashing people had come down from London and not a few members of the "old" nobility were there.

The Lord of the Manor of Stinchcombe was enthroned in the Greek temple, attired, not in the loud country tweeds he is famous for, but in a bourgeois dark gray suit. There was a great deal of activity outside the house. When Waugh eventually caught sight of me in the crowd, he beckoned to me, told me the sideshows required my services, and assigned me to peddling home-made muffins to the younger set. Laura Waugh was operating the cardboard roulette wheel and Father Collins supervised the secondhand bookstall, where a book on the Pope lay alongside *The India-rubber Man,* by Edgar Wallace. Virginia was reading palms and Bron ran a stall where the maladjusted were allowed, for a penny a throw, to vent their hatred of human society by heaving rocks at old chinaware.

Music was provided by the Stinchcombe Silver Band, inadvertently syncopated by Pepsi-Cola being popped open all over the lot. An ensemble resplendently dressed in blue and red, the Silver Band puffed its way through an unfamiliar repertoire in which each member seemed to be applying his own private theory of melody. A mysterious tent labeled "The Holy Friar" intrigued me terribly, but so busy was I marketing my muffins and so long was the queue outside I could not get into it.

Waugh was so pleased that he descended into the crowd and parked himself on the front doorstep. An enormous woman waddled up to him.

"How old is this house?" she demanded.

"Madam," Waugh said quietly, "the part you're looking at is Georgian, and it's 150 years old."

"Well," she snorted, "I have a Georgian house that's 300 years old!"

Next came Douglas Woodruff, editor of the distinguished Catholic London *Tablet,* and himself not an unimpressive human monument.

"What do you think of the new Greene letter?" Waugh inquired.

"What's this?" asked Woodruff, puzzled. "*What* Greene letter?"

"You mean you haven't heard?" Waugh said condescendingly. "I thought *everybody* had." Beating out a man like Woodruff with a morsel of this kind was enough to put Waugh in his finest fettle that weekend.

At about 4:30, the crush of visitors on the lawns and those queuing up to get inside the house had reached its peak. Suddenly, past the constable at the gate whose duty it was to detour all vehicles to the car-park, up the path scattering minor poets and dowager duchesses, past the Holy Friar's tent and to the very door of the mansion came a chauffeur-driven Baby Austin. The door swung open, and as though a mouse had brought forth a mountain, out stepped a gentleman with a pink, boiled face and long hair. He wore a bright yellow shirt, a suede jacket, pearl-gray trousers, and sneakers. In one hand he held an anthology of poetry almost the size of an encyclopedia and over his other arm he carried a bright leather bag of Polyphemic dimensions.

"Good heavens," Waugh murmured, "it's Quentin Davenport!"

The new arrival surveyed the premises, muttered something to himself, consulted his book of verse, and delved into his leather bag. Then he came in for a landing on the front doorstep, where he was stopped abruptly by Waugh.

"Look here, old boy, you can't come into this house until I see what's inside that bag."

"Damned cheek," fumed the visitor. "Leave my bag out of this."

"You have your choice, sir," Waugh said. "Open up the bag or stay out of the house."

Still protesting, the newcomer opened the bag and Waugh rummaged around inside it.

"What's inside?" I asked.

"A bottle of whiskey and some dirty handkerchiefs," Waugh revealed.

The bag incident did not do a great deal to improve the newcomer's humor, and once within the house he began to consult his bottle as frequently as his verse. To everyone who inquired after his identity, Waugh would only reply:

"His name is Davenport. He belongs to an old Catholic family and was sent down from the University for writing a blasphemous poem."

Mr. Davenport could not find very much in Waugh's house that he liked, and he made no effort to keep his opinions to himself. He was not impressed with the library, nor with Waugh's rare illuminated books, the fruit of twenty years of collecting. Repton's architectural masterpiece *Brighton Pavilion,* Pyne's *Royal Residences,* some volumes on the Crystal Palace at Hyde Park, the illuminated Victorian psalters, the chromolithographic folios of the mid-nineteenth century— all of these Waugh had described as depicting "a great turning point in the history of industrial design and domestic decoration."

"Balderdash," said Mr. Davenport. "Ho! Ho! Look at that one! Rare, he says. I've seen six like it in Charing Cross!" *The Shakespeare Gallery* (some engravings done in 1805 by Boydell), Bickman's eighteenth-century, copper-engraved *Universal Penman,* four high pedestals cut down to pilaster size, and an elephant-foot wastebasket, Mr. Davenport reviled as "rubbish and rot of imperial capacity."

In the drawing-room hung a painting labeled "An Afternoon on the River," by Augustus Egg, R.A., the first patron of the pre-Raphaelites. Hearing some of the visitors speculate on whether it was an early Egg or a late Egg, Mr. Davenport quivered his nostrils and assured them "it is obviously a poached Egg, left too long lying about."

When the car-park began to disgorge the motorcars and people began to head back to London, I went into the room of the leopard-skin commode, where I found Conley having a drink with Waugh. I reminded Conley there were no more trains to London that night and that if he wanted to ask for a lift back only a few cars remained.

Whereupon Waugh grabbed him by the arm and said, "Come along, Mr. Conley!" Before Conley knew what had happened, Waugh had dragged him out of Piers Court and down the rolling front lawn. From a distance I could see an Austin trundling down the path. Waugh, planting himself firmly in the middle of the path, raised his hand. The vehicle screeched to a halt. Waugh flung open the rear door and a spirited discussion followed between Waugh and the owner of the motorcar. Even from the front lawn it was apparent that Conley did not want to get into the car, and it seemed that the occupant was as reluctant about accepting Conley's company. Waugh settled the dispute by stuffing Conley into the Austin, patting the roof as one might pat the head of a stray dog one wants off the premises, and sent it on its way.

"What did you do with Mr. Conley?" I asked Waugh as he came back up the path.

"I put him in the motorcar with that horrible pansy going to Bath," Waugh said.

"But Bath is not in the direction of London."

"I know."

Champagne was served that evening before supper. I helped Waugh bring the bottles and crystal glasses into the dining-room. I loosened one of the corks and left the bottle on the table. Soon there was an explosion, and for an instant I thought Conley had returned to murder Waugh for putting him in the car with Mr. Davenport. But it was only the champagne cork. The champagne began to fizzle over onto the table and cumbersomely I tried to stop it with the palm of my hand.

"Pour it, you silly ass!" Waugh shouted.

Wiping up the spilled champagne, I remembered a similar embarrassment Waugh himself was said to have experienced when he accidentally splashed port on a superior officer during his wartime sojourn in Yugoslavia (a mission from which he returned insisting Tito is a woman). "People who can't be careful shouldn't drink," complained the officer. "I do not intend," Waugh replied, "to abandon the habit of a lifetime to appease your temporary displeasure."

But no such rejoinder occurred to me, and still flustered, I forgot to stop smoking when we sat down to dinner. Waugh's eyes popped out of his head. Before I could marshal my presence of mind, he took the cigarette out of my hand and crushed it.

"Papa," Virginia complained presently, "I caught Teddy talking politics with Mrs. Potter."

"You did?" Waugh asked. "Who is Mrs. Potter?"

"Why Papa, you remember. She's the Archbishop of Westminster's sister. Mummy relieved her of three shillings twopence at the roulette."

"Oh yes. I recall talking to her before she went into the Holy

Friar's tent. She was still unaware of the nature of our Holy Friar, and I believe she thought we had hired a bogus monk to hear unauthorized confessions."

"I never did get inside that tent," I said. "Who *was* the Holy Friar?"

"The Holy Friar was an old frying pan, perforated in the center and suspended on a string," Waugh revealed.

"Evelyn," Mrs. Waugh interjected, "I feel badly about Mr. Conley. I feel dreadfully guilty about the way you put poor Conley into the motorcar with Mr. Davenport." Everybody began to feel badly about Conley.

"Teddy, will you go to early or late church tomorrow?" Waugh asked. Then he smiled mischievously. "Mr. Davenport belongs to an old Catholic family, and was sent down from the University for writing a blasphemous poem. I wonder what will happen to Conley. . . ."

I awoke the next morning, not on my own initiative, but because Waugh was standing below my open window calling, "*Teddy for early church*," through a megaphone. I understand he has since been neglecting this instrument in favor of a Victorian ear trumpet, which he brandishes at literary luncheons.

For the ride to church, Waugh did not have a horse-drawn victoria, but he did have the next best thing: a Ford station wagon so old even his family complained about it. With Mrs. Waugh driving—and her cigar-flourishing husband managing to make the dowdy back seat more aristocratic simply by sitting on it—we were soon on our way to hear one of Father Collins' earnest sermons and to collect the Sunday morning papers for the reviews of the fete. (Waugh was disappointed; the rural editions did not carry any.) When we returned to Piers Court, Waugh showed me a letter from a back issue of the *Times* which observed that "one refrains from smoking at meals as a matter of elementary courtesy."

## ABROAD

WAUGH and his wife drove me to the station that afternoon. We were a good twenty-five minutes early for my train and they waited with me. This gave Waugh the opportunity to examine my somewhat weather-beaten gray hat, which lay atop my luggage. He was nearly as critical of my hat as Mr. Davenport had been of his house.

"You puzzle me, Teddy. You refused to appear in our car-park in a handsome headpiece but you are prepared to walk the streets of London in this hat. Most extraordinary."

"What would you have me wear?" I asked.

"Buy a bowler."

It was his parting shot, for when the train came and he helped me with my luggage, he said simply, "It's been great fun. You must write to us. I hope you can come again sometime." I thought I detected a trace of whimsical affection in his good-by.

As I catnapped in the train, the kaleidoscope of the weekend passed before me as the panorama of a man's life is said to pass before him at the moment of his death. I saw Victorian washstands, boiled fish, and the poached Egg. Chromolithographic folios and the leopard-skin commode. Spilled champagne, anonymous statues, and elephant-foot wastebaskets.

But I never saw Waugh again. And to my two or three letters came the same reply printed on a postcard: "Mr. Evelyn Waugh is abroad. His letters are not being forwarded. They will be dealt with on his return."

The postcards were addressed in his own hand.

# NO LEGS NO JOKES NO CHANCE

## *Helene Hanff*

HELENE HANFF is a young Philadelphian who yearned from childhood for a playwright's career on Broadway, but has not yet achieved
it. Her efforts, however, have never faltered, and along the way she
has won contests, lost jobs, and had a variety of experiences in
the theatre. Now living in New York, she has turned out a merry
book about all of this. The chapter from it which follows finds her
in the very middle of a great moment in show-business history.

I n the memoirs of both Lawrence Langner and the late Theresa
Helburn, co-producers at the Theatre Guild for forty years, quite
a lot of space is devoted to the story of a certain Theatre Guild
event. Neither account reads the way I remember it happening.

It's a matter of veiwpoint. Terry and Lawrence *were* the Theatre
Guild; the rest of us just worked there. To say that we saw things differently from the way Terry and Lawrence saw them is only to point
out that Alice's version of the Mad Tea Party would differ considerably
from the March Hare's or the Mad Hatter's version.

Let us go back to December 1942, to the morning after the opening
of a ponderous Theatre Guild flop called "The Russian People."

Despite the fact that we'd waited up till 4:00 A.M. for the notices,
Joe—my boss—and I were at work in the press department at 10:00 A.M.
as usual, composing ads and "pulling quotes" that would fool the public
into thinking the show was a hit. (Joe was the Theatre Guild press
agent. I was his assistant.)

Pulling quotes works like this. Suppose Atkinson wrote: "For the
fourth time this season the Theatre Guild has wasted a superb production on a dull and empty play." You pulled out the two good words
and printed at the top of your ad: "'Superb Production!'—Atkinson;
*Times*." This sort of thing takes practice, but we'd had a lot of practice. Not to beat about the bush, "The Russian People"—a lugubrious
bore about the Nazis and the Russian front—was the Theatre Guild's
sixteenth straight flop. Looming up ahead, according to the brochure

we had sent to Guild subscribers in nineteen cities throughout the country, was a new American Folk Opera. (Like "Porgy and Bess," we assured everybody.) It was to be based on a flop the Guild had produced back around 1930; and it was to have not only a murder committed on-stage, but a bona-fide operatic ballet. It was budgeted at $100,000.

The rumor that reached us the morning after "The Russian People" opened put an end to our worries about where the money was coming from to produce the new Folk Opera. Rumor had it that after six-teen flops the Guild was bankrupt, that Terry and Lawrence were selling the Guild Theatre and Building, and that the Theatre Guild would go out of existence.

People from Casting and Production and the Executive Offices wandered morosely up to the Press Department all day to indulge in the usual bitter castigation of the management. (Our garret was ideal for this since it was the one place where Terry and Lawrence could be counted on not to set foot, especially in December. Like all top-floor garrets, ours was freezing cold.)

This would not be happening, everybody said, if the two Theatre Guild producers weren't amateurs, dilettantes, and raving, staring crazy. They'd sell season tickets all over the country, so the talk ran, for "Six Forthcoming Guild Productions" when they had only four plays under option and disagreed violently about three of them. And then, after every flop, the two of them would embark on Economy Drives which consisted in cutting the number of towels issued weekly to each office and threatening to take the water cooler out of the Casting De-partment because too many strangers were drinking our water.

And so on and on and on. It was an old refrain with lots and lots of verses. But this day the tone was especially bitter. Not just because January is a very cold month to be thrown out of work in, but because nobody was anxious to see the Theatre Guild close down. I'd worked there only a year and a half, through eight flops, but most of the others could remember the great days of the Guild: the Shaw openings, the Lunt openings, the five-hour O'Neill drama which the Guild doorman was said to have referred to innocently throughout its run as "Strange Intercourse."

Joe and I made up the ads in a thick gloom. We checked the second-night press list, phoned in the house-seats, and sent a lavish assortment of balcony tickets to the USO. Then Joe went downstairs to get Law-rence's okay on the ads, and I went down to get Terry's.

She was in her office, in an armchair, having tea. Terry was about four-feet-eleven, with white hair rinsed a deep cerulean blue, and a cheerful little bulldog face. Reaching for the ads and reviews in my hands, she said:

"Well, dear, we seem to be having a run of bad luck!"

She read the ads carefully, glancing at a review now and then to
check a quote and murmuring: "I don't know what the Boys want!"
Finally she said they were fine, and handed them back to me.
As I reached the door, she said:

"I notice Lawrence was first on the program, dear. That's twice
in a row, isn't it?" (If the program for one show read "Produced by
Lawrence Langner and Theresa Helburn," the program for the next
show had to read, "Produced by Theresa Helburn and Lawrence
Langner.") I said I was sure Mr. Langner hadn't been first twice in a
row because Joe was always careful to rotate and always had me check
the last program before he made up the new one.

"All right," she said agreeably. "Just remind him: I'm first on the new
show."

My gloom evaporated. "The Russian People" hadn't been the one-
flop-too-many after all. We were going to do another one.

We read about it a few days later in one of the gossip columns. Joe
came in with the afternoon papers and said disconsolately:

"Terry scooped her own Press Department again."

She was always scooping us. She would never tell us anything about
a new production for fear we'd tell somebody. (In the theatre, everything is a secret.) Then she'd confide it to some columnist. Between
acts of "The Russian People" she had told a columnist—in strictest
confidence—that the composer and librettist had finished the new Theatre Guild operetta, and that it was to be called "Away We Go." She
hadn't told him, though, what we were going to use for money. We
knew they were holding backers' auditions nightly and we had heard
they had a promise of $30,000 from somebody. But that's all I heard
about money until Black Friday after the show opened in New Haven.

The new year set in; "The Russian People" closed, and the
management plunged on with "Away We Go." By the end of January
the cast was set. It included two old friends from earlier Theatre
Guild flops; the male lead went to the young man who had played
the juvenile in "Yesterday's Magic"; and the role of the singing
comedienne went to the ingénue from "Papa Is All." (She had never
sung before, and both were unknown, of course.) The leading comic
was an actor very well known in the Yiddish Art Theatre but he hadn't
done much in English. The ingénue lead went to a young lady who
had appeared on Broadway only once in a small part but who had sung
a lot of operetta, summers. Add an Armenian director and a Russian
ballerina, and our new American Folk Opera was all set.

During February, actors and technicians drifted into our office with

Progress Reports. This was, they told us, the damnedest musical comedy anybody had ever thought up for a sophisticated Broadway audience. It was so pure you could put it on at a church social. It opened with a middle-aged farm woman sitting on a bare stage churning butter, and from then on it got cleaner. They did not feel a lot of arty dancing in long dresses was likely to improve things much.

The purity complained of was obvious on the day of the dress-parade. As the girls walked across the stage in their bright, period farm costumes, not an ankle or upper arm was visible. I don't even remember seeing a neck. As I went back upstairs to the Press Department, I heard Lawrence suggest to the costumer that the dresses might be cut a little lower here and there without spoiling the authenticity.

Joe went up to New Haven early in March, a few days before the opening. He was very worried. Not about the show. Joe, like the good press agent he was, believed that by the time "Away We Go" opened in New York it was going to be the greatest thing since "Hamlet." What worried him was that some drama editor or some columnist's secretary like Winchell's Rose (she must have had a last name but I never heard her called anything but Winchell's Rose) would sneak up to look at the show before it was Ready. As of now, Joe did not feel it was Ready.

"Away We Go" opened in New Haven to mild but approving notices. Pleasant, pretty musical, they said. Since none of us expected any dancing in the streets over this epic, the reviews cheered us. But about midafternoon that day, a columnist phoned, leaving word for Joe to call him the minute he got back from New Haven. It was very important. He didn't sound as if it were anything pleasant.

Joe got back on Friday, full of enthusiasm. The show, he assured us, was great. It had a few weak spots but they would all be fixed by the Boston opening. A few wiseacres *had* come up from New York and said the show was corn and wouldn't last a week on Broadway. But Terry and Lawrence were not worried, Joe said. They knew they had a hit.

Lois, Joe's secretary, gave him the columnist's message and Joe returned the call. He listened for a few minutes. Then he hung up. Then he told us the news. According to the columnist, Winchell's Rose had gone up to New Haven, seen the show, and wired Winchell her report. The wire read:

NO LEGS   NO JOKES   NO CHANCE

Winchell, said the columnist, had shown the wire to our principal backer, who was at this moment rumored to be pulling his $30,000 out of the show.

Joe called New Haven. Terry and Lawrence had heard about the wire, but they didn't mention the $30,000, and neither did he. They merely said calmly that the show would open in Boston on schedule.

A few days later, we learned they had sold the Guild Theatre and Guild Building to a radio network.

The Boston notices were fair, though not nearly as good as Boston had given some of our other flops. Joe phoned to tell us the whole second act had been thrown out and everybody was working around the clock on the new second act. With the new second act, Joe felt, it would really be a great show.

For the next week, Lois and I were busy mimeographing, folding, sealing, stamping, and mailing 10,000 press releases to Guild subscribers about the New York opening of "Away We Go." We had 8,000 mimeographed when Joe came back from Boston and told us we'd have to throw them all away and start over. There had been a title change.

Nobody, it seemed, liked the title, "Away We Go." The composer had wanted to change it to "Yessirree," but Joe was thankful to report he'd been talked out of that. The title finally agreed on, thanks largely to Lawrence's wife who came from out that way, was "Oklahoma."

It sounds fine to you; you're used to it. But try to imagine you're working in a theatre and somebody tells you your new musical is to be called New Jersey. Or Maine. To us, "Oklahoma" was the name of a state.

We had folded several hundred new releases when the call came through from Boston. We heard Joe say, "Yes, Terry," and then he looked at us.

"They want," Joe said in a faraway voice, "an exclamation point after 'Oklahoma'."

Which is how it happened that far, far into the night Lois and I, bundled in our winter coats, sat in the outer office putting 30,000 exclamation points on 10,000 press releases, while Joe, in the inner office, bundled in his overcoat, phoned all over town, hunting down and waking up various printing firms and sign painters involved in the change. We were bundled in our coats because the heat had been turned off by an economy-minded management now happily engaged in spending several thousand dollars to alter house-boards, playbills, posters, ads, and souvenir booklets—to put an exclamation point after "Oklahoma."

"Oklahoma!" was to open on March 31. We were not sold out on opening night, Guild subscribers having dwindled to a handful after sixteen flops. And when I woke that morning (with a cold) it was snowing. That evening, by the time I had fought my way home through the sleet, my guilt about not going to the opening had given way to self-preservation. I had dinner and went to bed. In bed I reached for the wet newspaper I'd brought home, and turned to the theatre page. Our big opening night ad leaped out at me: "OKLAHOMA!"

Slowly—surely—with that foggy, open-mouthed bewilderment you were bound to feel sooner or later if you worked at the Theatre Guild long enough—I saw that Terry and Lawrence were right. About the exclamation point. I did not allow myself to speculate on the insane possibility that they might also be right about such brain waves as an operatic ballet instead of a chorus line—a clean, cornfed musical with no legs and no jokes—and a cast full of people like Alfred Drake and Celeste Holm and Bambi Lynn and Joan McCracken and Diana Adams that nobody had ever heard of.

I switched off the bed lamp, thinking how typical it was of the Guild that the notices would be coming out on April Fool's Day, and as I drifted off to sleep I said a silent good luck to Alfred Drake, the juvenile from "Yesterday's Magic," who was at that precise moment walking out on the stage of the St. James Theatre singing. "Oh, what a beautiful morning!"

# GET YOUR GRANDFATHER OFF THE TRACK

## *Ralph Schoenstein*

RALPH SCHOENSTEIN (1933– ) A bright new light in the deserted field of truly humorous writing is provided by this young writer whose first book *The Block* was called by writer Jerome Weidman "a piece of pure enchantment." Born and raised literally on the sidewalks of New York, Mr. Schoenstein glories in his native heath and finds his material there. His only absence from it was caused by the U. S. Army, a two year hitch as a buck private in Japan where, as he says, he served his officers well day and night "with cheeseburgers, club sandwiches, and occasionally a ham on rye. As long as the mustard held out I served my country well." But not a man for matters martial, he is now well satisfied to be living again in New York with his wife and child, turning out for a newspaper syndicate some of the funniest columns being written today.

THE Block was clever outdoors, but indoors our imaginations approached genius. Whenever darkness, bad weather, or an enemy drove us from the street, we often went to apartment 6A to play indoor variations of almost every outdoor sport. My family's apartment was an ideal YMHA. Most of the old West Side apartments not only had big rooms with thick walls and high ceilings, but also long foyers that invited bowling, sprinting, punchball, and pitching.

I wonder if the builders of modern New York realize that their new apartments make lousy gyms. Walk into a bedroom of a new Manhattan apartment and you'll find no space for basketball, a ceiling too low for volleyball, a floor too thin for track, and walls too fragile for punchball. But 6A of 210 West 78th Street was as spacious and solid as Stillman's Gym (and often smelled the same way). It didn't even have the problem of wall-to-wall carpeting. When The Block went there for its Olympic games, we just removed the scatter rugs and the gym was ready for action.

With the possible exception of water polo, there was no outdoor sport we couldn't play in some manner in my bedroom. We played baseball with a toy bat and ping-pong ball—a game in which a drive hit off the wall was a double, one off the mirror a triple, one off the ceiling a home run, and one out the window a trip downstairs for the batter. We played badminton by stringing a cord across the room and using ping-pong paddles so the shuttlecock wouldn't fly too fast. If you want to play bedroom badminton with regulation rackets, you need the world's best reflexes and a catcher's mask.

Using that same cord, we were able to play volleyball with a pair of my socks. (If your family is interested in this game, use the heaviest woolen socks you can find; silk socks make a lifeless volleyball.) We also used ping-pong paddles to play ping-pong on a long mahogany table my mother had foolishly put in my room because she served big lunches and dinners there. Mother was grateful for our ping-pong games because they gave her fascinating conversation when guests sat at this table. "See that nick on the edge of the table?" she would proudly tell a friend. "My son has a marvelous forehand smash. And perhaps you're wondering about those black marks on the ceiling, the spots on the wall, and the chips in the door. Well, the score was tied and Joel was at bat . . ."

Our most important indoor sport was basketball, which we played with a spaldeen and two inverted lamp shades I hung with friction tape over the doorways at opposite ends of my room. One doorway led to the kitchen, the other to my parents' bedroom. These basketball games were furious battles in which as many as six of us—two teams of three—could simultaneously be destroying my room. The smell of sweat was oppressive, but I never opened the window wide for fear that one of us might fly out during an inspired attempt to steal the ball. If my mother hadn't been such a good housekeeper, bedroom basketball wouldn't have been so dangerous: she waxed the floor so well that we were constantly diving into it. When his ceiling first came alive with the thunder of stamping feet and the thumping of falling bodies, Mr. Tishman in 5A must have been hard pressed to picture the scene above.

During bedroom basketball, I spun wildly about the court, desperately trying to save both the game and the furniture. And all the time I spun, I kept hoping that when Maurey made his speedy lay-up shot, he wouldn't follow through into my parents' bedroom to be congratulated by my naked mother. I remember that we once tried closing the door under the basket, but this solution gave us a new problem. On a Maurey-like lay-up, Bobby slipped and punched his right arm through the door, which was glass painted to look like wood. Naturally, my mother was upset about Bobby's accident because he'd bled on her best scatter rug before he could skid back into the game. Mother always preferred that any destruction be confined to The Block rather than the apartment.

Miniature basketball with lampshades and a spaldeen wasn't the only indoor variety we played, for my father had given me not only a regulation cowhide basketball but also a regulation iron hoop and net, the kind we saw at Madison Square Garden, the kind country boys put on their garages. Always anxious to be professional sportsmen, we were forever trying to hang that heavy iron hoop in my bedroom; but it wouldn't hold still for tape and my mother wouldn't hold still for nails. For a while, we tied it to chairs and stood them on my bed. This goal had the necessary height but no backboard (unless you could count a big wall mirror) and therefore no rebounds (unless you could count my mother's rebound when a ball hit that mirror). A second problem was that our glass door couldn't resist a flying basketball anymore than it could resist Bobby's arm. In desperation, we finally took the hoop, net, and ball to the courtyard below my window, where we played for several minutes before the superintendent chased us. It was just as well that we couldn't play longer: in a wild courtyard game, a cowhide basketball would quickly have been worn to shreds by stone and concrete, had it not first been confiscated by a maid waiting for her laundry.

My favorite indoor sport was the track meet. When The Block gathered in my apartment for the 78th Street Olympiad, their dedication to sport was so great that they sometimes came in sneakers, sweat shirts, and sweat pants. On summer nights, we stripped down to undershorts, socks, and skin—a sight that would have charmed any mother. Once the Olympiad had begun, even if we weren't undressed, mother never went to the kitchen through my bedroom, possibly because it was soon smelling like a stockyard. In this room, we were able to stage almost every event of a collegiate track meet; only the javelin and discus throws presented unconquerable challenges. The broad jump was the easiest to stage. "My apartment was just *made* for broad jumping," Mother used to boast to her friends. "Ralph's room is a natural pit." It was nice that mother was proud of my room, but she did exaggerate a bit: you couldn't call the room a natural pit because it lacked sawdust, something Mr. Tishman of 5A always wanted to buy for us. Living in 5A of 210 must have been like living in the basement of Madison Square Garden.

The high hurdles also were easy to stage. We put two chairs about ten feet apart in my room and raced from the pantry to the finish line, which was either the door or far wall of my parents' bedroom, depending on the kind of race we wanted and the position of my parents. None of us sailed over these chairs all the time, but when we missed, it wasn't by much. We could have run *low* hurdles with a stool and a piano bench, but The Block always sought the greatest challenges. To be a champion hurdler was my boyhood dream, so instead of walking

around bushes, sofas, and low fences, I hurdled them. I hurdled with
such zeal that I once fractured both arms when I almost cleared a fence
on one of the Broadway islands. The top crossbar of this hurdle should
have fallen when my foot hit it; but since this bar was attached iron,
I did the falling. I suddenly found myself sprawled on the trolley
tracks like one of Bernie's mice. For the next few weeks, I was a basketball referee and a track timer.

The indoor high jump was as challenging as the hurdles. From my
bedroom window to the opposite wall, I ran a cord that could be raised
or lowered by a device so ingenious that I can't remember it. We did
our high-jumping by running to this cord from an angle, springing over
it in contorted leaps, dives, and sprawls, and landing on my bed, which
we had to use because Mr. Tishman never got us that sawdust. We
could have done pole-vaulting with the same equipment but we were
afraid the ceiling would interfere with Eddie's head. My mother would
have been very upset had Eddie cracked open his head on this clean
white ceiling (although bloodstains above would have caused the most
fascinating of all dinner conversations). Eddie had claimed he could
pole-vault twelve feet. He probably could have, but only in the right
apartment. You just can't go pole-vaulting in *any* bedroom, unless it
happens to be in Versailles or the Vatican. Had we been able to hold
our meets in the Vatican, we not only could have pole-vaulted but our
mile run also would have been much less awkward.

Nevertheless, in spite of our small, waxed, winding, and cluttered
track, the mile was still my favorite event because I was fast and because
it gave me a chance to use my stop watch. I'd been clever enough to
figure that a mile was eighty-three times around my apartment. (There
might have been seventy-two laps to this 6A mile. I can't check it
because I'm now living at another track.) Bobby held The Block record
for this waxed mile: he sprinted, slipped, skidded, stumbled, and staggered through it in about nine minutes. He would have made much
better time had he not kept running into my grandfather on the pantry
turn.

There were only two indoor sports we didn't play in my apartment.
One was blind man's bluff, which we sometimes played at Eddie's because my mother was always trying to throw it out of the bedroom
Olympiad. To elude the desperate lunges of the blindfolded blind man,
the rest of The Block jumped on beds, bureaus, tables, chairs, and
each other. When my mother went out and we played blind man's bluff
in my bedroom, we had a dilemma: if we removed the good furniture
to prevent breakage, we removed places of refuge; and if we left all the
refuge in the room, some of it soon looked like refuse. When my mother
came back and we moved the game to Eddie's, it was even harder to

avoid getting tagged because his bedroom was smaller and had less furniture. At Eddie's, the champion of this game was Bernie, who rarely became the blind man. It's hard to tag someone when he's hanging out the window.

The other indoor sport we sometimes played outside my apartment was regulation, non-courtyard basketball. Every so often, when we were tired of running into walls, doors, parents, and each other, we went to the gym of a Presbyterian church on 73rd Street off Broadway. When we played there, we never revealed our real names because they didn't sound especially Presbyterian. If you must crash a church, the least you should be is Christian. We would have played in one of the local synagogues if there'd been a basketball court in any of them. (One of the basic problems of modern American Judaism is the lack of basketball courts in synagogues.) But in spite of the fact that we shot baskets as Christians, we weren't unaware of our own religion. On Yom Kippur, Judaism's solemn day of atonement, we always stayed out of school and atoned by playing grim games of stickball. While we atoned, we picked up one more street enemy: a bearded rabbi from 229 who tried to chase us from stickball to synagogue.

In addition to indoor variations of outdoor games, we also played war games designed for both the indoors and outdoors—in fact, for a little of each. Since most of our war games required us to lean out of windows, they were really semi-indoor (or semi-outdoor) games. I'd like to say we held them because of patriotic fervor, but it would be a lie; our basic motive was less noble. Although partly inspired by a desire to help our country, a much greater desire was to harass some of its citizens whom we considered more important enemies than the Germans or Japanese. Most of our retaliation was wreaked from my living-room windows in the form of water bombs, marbles, and buckshot. A water bomb was a piece of typing paper intricately folded into a container with a small hole into which we poured water. When this bomb hit the sidewalk six floors below, it exploded with a bang audible on Amsterdam and a splatter that moistened the terrified enemy. A water bomb was more effective when dropped *in front* of the enemy. True, he was better moistened when one fell on his head; but the direct hit lost in noise what it gained in saturation. Although marbles were primarily used for daylight bombing during World War II, they and paper containers could also be used for nonmilitary purposes; but buckshot had only one use for us because there wasn't much to hunt on 78th Street. All the mice we found were already dead and the doormen we wanted to shoot were never in season.

I remember that early in the war, Barry and I once spent a whole afternoon dropping water bombs, marbles, and buckshot just in front of and/or on top of doormen, superintendents, landladies, and sundry nonbelligerents who were moving along the sidewalk below. (We always tried to bomb walking landladies because it was more sporting to hit moving targets.) Leaning out the living-room window and crying, "Bombs away!" we were neither delinquents nor imbeciles: we were Navy daredevils destroying Japanese ships from F4F Wildcats in the Battle of Midway. Barry and I, who kept better wall maps of the war than George Marshall, attacked the 78th Street units of the Japanese fleet with bombing techniques we learned from bubble-gum cards, for, about 1942, warfare replaced ballplayers in certain patriotic brands of bubble gum.

Such home-front bombing was the least we could do to help the war effort. If an enemy ship ever stopped sailing and looked up at the window of 6A, Lieutenant Barry and I were hidden behind the blackout shades that all windows had to protect Americans from another enemy. The Japanese fleet almost always chose to run rather than counterattack. But during one engagement, while we sang "Praise the Lord and Pass the Ammunition" and wished Billy Mitchell could have seen our style, a battleship I supposedly sank with a marble steamed up to the bomb bay and threatened to take my mother prisoner. A week later, while Barry and I were fighting the Battle of the Coral Sea, Bobby got some marbles, leaned from his bedroom window, and brilliantly opened a second front: one of his purey bombs cracked the skylight of Tony's Italian Kitchen and sprinkled glass in a vat of minestrone. Not only had Bobby made the greatest direct hit of the war, but he'd also dropped the only bomb on a real enemy. We never had a chance to attack any Germans or Japanese on our street; so when Bobby destroyed that Italian soup, he struck a blow at the belly of the Axis.

Eddie felt our weapons were too simple and Bernie, who was pretty simple himself, felt our strategy was bad. When Eddie fought from my living room, he found water bombs, marbles, and buckshot ineffective, so he used either stick matches or "cherry bombs," which were lead weights with caps that exploded when dropped. Bernie was the only Block member who wasn't a Navy ace, Hop Harrigan, or Colin Kelly: he was Paul Muni spreading sabotage behind the enemy lines. A born saboteur, Bernie had become Paul Muni after seeing *The Commandos Strike at Dawn*. Thereafter, the coins he put on trolley tracks were land mines for tanks and the dissected mice were Germans he'd blown up. Although he mined Broadway with explosives of all denominations, the only thing Major Bernie Muni was ever able to sabotage was the United States Treasury.

Not all our war games were destructive. The Block was also interested in such peaceful facets of war as communications and logistics. If one of us in the sixth-floor bomb bay wanted to send a message to one of us in the concrete battlefield, he sometimes sent it by a parachute that was a skate key tied to an adult's handkerchief. I never sent more than three or four such messages during any one campaign because my father had only a certain number of handkerchiefs. I didn't want him to get suspicious when he went to his bureau for a fresh parachute to blow his nose.

Another way to send messages from the bomb bay to the battlefield was to use two Dixie cups connected by a taut string that carried voices. Barry and I were forever trying to set up this private telephone between his bedroom and my living room, but neither of us could throw a Dixie cup across the street into the other's window. Eddie was glad we couldn't connect an inter-building phone because he didn't want anything more than Nina hanging over the infield. (A fly ball deflected by a telephone line would have been a maddening Hindu.) We sent more than messages from the bomb bay to the battlefield: we also liked to drop an occasional roll of toilet paper out the window and let it unwind down the street while we held the other end. This war game was neither destructive nor useful. There was no possible military purpose in such tumbling tissue—unless you wanted to make a gaudy surrender. In fact, it should be called a *post*war game because its only use was for parades. If any hero marched home to 78th Street, we were ready.

In both war and peace, we played most of the traditional store games in our apartments. We schemed, argued, and cheated at Monopoly, Electric Baseball, Parcheesi, and Ward Cuff Football; and we also conceived versions of our own. For example, Maurey and I invented a basketball game that was played with index cards, checkers, rubber bands, and dice. We were constantly changing the rules, but only because the game never quite worked. The time it came closest to working we found ourselves shooting crap.

Not all our indoor fun was from playing sports: we also were zealous spectators at many collegiate and professional basketball games in Madison Square Garden. No excitement in my bedroom was greater than the frenzy generated by the games of City College. And imagine how frenzied they would have been if they hadn't been fixed. When we didn't see a game, we often heard it on the radio. Bert Lee, Ward Wilson, and Marty Glickman brought us basketball and Ranger hockey while Red Barber and Connie Desmond described Dodger baseball. Broadcasts of ball games played outside New York weren't live but the filtering of a Western Union ticker through Red Barber's mellow imagination. There were no cracks of bats or roaring crowds; just the clicking ticker and Barber's honeyed purrs: "Up now is Dixie Walker—one reason Mr. Durocher is currently occupying the catbird seat . . .

(CLICKS) . . . Cooper's first pitch is a slow curve that just misses outside . . . (CLICKS) . . . Both Coopers inform the plate umpire of his
error on that call . . . (FIVE-SECOND SILENCE) . . . Now big Mort's
ready again . . . (CLICKS) . . . shakes off one sign from little brother
. . . pumps with that grand motion . . . delivers . . . and Walker
swings and lines it high and deep to right center . . . (CLICKS) . . .
Moore's racing back to the wall . . . but that one is out of the pea
patch to tie the game . . . Oh, doctor. Mr. Walker laid the heavy
hickory to a hanging fastball and sent it on a formidable journey . . .
(CLICKS) . . . Friends, let the old redhead tell you about a treat instead
of a treatment . . ."

Ball games may have sounded like stock market reports (especially
during a line failure when Barber had to stall by reading batting
averages), but boxing matches from Madison Square Garden were
charged with drama. Since they always began at ten o'clock, until our
teens we had to hear them undercover—through the earphones of crystal
radios beneath our blankets. Most of us built crystal sets so we could
secretly hear sports events after our bedtimes, when our mothers thought
we were asleep. It was hard to tune one of these crude little radios
even above the blankets because the cat's whisker required delicate
adjustment, as did the selector on the copper coil wound around the
cardboard center of toilet paper. But even though a sportscast through
earphones and between sheets often sounded like a phone call from
Calcutta, we happily tolerated the inconstant voice of Don Dunphy
when it brought us the action of a big fight. There were Friday nights
when I fought sleep as hard as Joe Louis fought a challenger so I could
hear him remain heavyweight champion of the world.

In those dark days before television, The Block needed radio not
only for sportscasts but also for adventure and a pal called Uncle Don.
Our favorite art form was the fifteen-minute heroic serial, about ten of
which were broadcast consecutively every weekday afternoon. If we
didn't play in the street or my apartment after school, we heard some or
all of these programs. Most had noisy beginnings that occasionally gave
my grandfather indigestion because I sometimes insisted on listening at
dinner. "Captain Midnight" had a hysterical announcer paging the
captain like Johnny calling for Philip Morris, after which came twelve
tolls of Big Ben. "Superman" began with a rifle shot, speeding train,
and hurricane; "Terry and the Pirates" with Chinese chaos; and "Dick
Tracy" with a panicky announcer making a staccato cry for the great
detective, after which someone with a machine gun tried to put the
announcer out of his misery. These serials were narcotics; if you made
the mistake of hearing any installment, you were hooked. Then you
could break the habit only after the story's last installment when you

had a few seconds to turn off the radio before the next story began and you again were hanging from the cliff.

We liked these programs more for their prizes than their thrills. (We had enough adventure of our own.) If you sent the top of an Ovaltine jar to Captain Midnight, he sent you a decoder which could decode secret messages known only to those spies whose mothers didn't mind uncovered jars of Ovaltine. The Captain's daily secret message usually ordered you to tune in tomorrow so you could receive another secret message to keep listening. The most useful prize came from the Lone Ranger: for a Cheerios box top, he sent you a magic weather ring that turned purple whenever it rained. This prize was especially helpful to Bernie. Whenever he was walking along the street and wanted to know if it was raining, all he had to do was look at his magic ring. Jack Armstrong's prize was almost as useful: for a Wheaties box top and a quarter, he sent you a pedometer, which you attached to your leg to see how far you walked. Because Barry and I received our pedometers the same day, we had a contest to see who could walk the most miles. The contest lasted only a few exhausting days because Barry was disqualified when I caught him running around the block. He never knew that I strapped my pedometer to my grandfather whenever he left the house.

After the terrifying adventures of Hop Harrigan, Superman, Batman, Dick Tracy, Mandrake the Magician, Terry, Captain Midnight, the Green Hornet, and Jack Armstrong, we needed the happy change of pace that was Uncle Don. A relentlessly jolly father image, Uncle Don generated thirty minutes of dinnertime sunshine. He began each broadcast with a bubbling rendition of his theme song, ever-conscious of the meaning of its words:

> Hibbadeegits hotsah rainbow ree,
> Sibonya skipadee hi lo dee.
> Hoaneecoatdoak with an alakazon,
> Sing this song with your Uncle Don!

Then he entertained us nephews with songs, stories, jokes, doggerel, and the *Journal-American* funnies. Once a year, Uncle Don said your name because he always congratulated kids on their birthdays; and sometimes he also gave you a hint about where to find a present that was hidden for you. I remember birthdays when he had me crawling around the apartment in search of a hidden present that my mother had foolishly told him about. "Ralphie Schoenstein," he'd say, "if you'll look behind the big sofa in . . ." and I'd hit the floor for some gleeful destruction. Nothing was more fun than getting Uncle Don's permission to tear apart your living room.

Throughout the war and until the Marshall Plan, Uncle Don merrily told stories, invented nonsense, read funnies, sang songs, and talked to animals after daily flights to Manhattan in his "puddle jumper." He might have gone on to talk to frogs on television had he not lost track of the second hand of his studio clock. The moment he thought he was off the air, he mumbled into a live microphone, "That should take care of the little bastards." All over New York, New Jersey, and southern New England, nephews and nieces stopped crawling around the living room floor, raised their little faces in bewilderment, and asked their mommies to define a new word.

Although I had my best times with The Block, I must confess that I also had many wonderful experiences not shared with Eddie, Bobby, Dickie, Maurey, Barry, Bernie, and Joel. On certain special days, I left them to do things that any boy would consider more memorable than throwing toilet paper from windows, fracturing arms on trolley tracks, watching for the matron while Eddie bombarded girls, dissecting mice, or dodging steaming cataracts. Because my father was a prominent and gregarious city editor, I sometimes left 78th Street to mix with the men who ran New York. I remember celebrating I Am an American Day in Central Park with Mayor William O'Dwyer, a good friend of Dad's whom I called Uncle Bill. Afterwards, I rode to Gracie Mansion in Uncle Bill's limousine behind a motorcycle policeman. All the way I savored the delicious thought that this cop leading me to the mayor's home might once have attacked a certain game of stickball.

But whenever I spent a Sunday afternoon at Gracie Mansion, I felt bad, for its huge lawn was ideal for touch football; and I felt guilty because I was lounging by the East River when I should have been across town at the Hudson helping The Block to goad parkmen into a spiked charge. I dislike dropping impressive names (except, of course, Eddie's), but during my rich and public boyhood, I also went to the circus with Mayor Fiorello LaGuardia and I made a bar mitzvah speech to a congregation that included Jimmy Walker, probably the only Mayor of New York who ever sat in the front row of a synagogue. (The speech he later made at my party was considerably wittier, possibly because it was in English.) Don't think I was merely a mayor-mixer. I also went to Yankee Stadium with Governor Dewey for a Joe Louis fight, after which Dad and I rode in Dewey's car while the sirens of his police escort screamed through Harlem. It must have been during that ride that he started to lose the Presidency.

One would think that a police-escorted ride with the Governor of

New York would be the biggest thrill a boy could have; but it didn't give me the kick I got the day I hit a spaldeen three sewers to score Eddie from the blue Buick with the game's winning run. No matter what VIP took me to what big event, when I was away from 78th Street, I was a displaced member of The Block. When Uncle Bill visited our apartment, there was a good chance that I'd leave him after a while for some quiet broad jumping with Maurey. When I went to the circus with Mayor LaGuardia, my major interest was in buying a whistle for the referee to use in bedroom basketball. And when Jimmy Walker gave me the boxing gloves that Joe Louis had worn to hold a world's championship, it was no time before Eddie was using them to slam Bobby into my grandfather.

# HOW TO TALK TO A MAN

## Jean Kerr

JEAN KERR (1924–    ), as everyone knows who has read her books, is married to drama critic Walter Kerr. Together with their five sons they inhabit a suburban house so large and unlikely that she calls it the "Kerr-Hilton" and flees from it to sit in parked cars to work in peace on her prose and an occasional play. She writes about all this in her own lucid and merry way without a trace of cuteness or you-can-do-it-too-ness. Nobody in the world can do it better than Mrs. Kerr.

OF course, I have no statistics, and nobody ever tells me anything. But I suspect one reason marriages break up is that some wives, after spending a full hour in rich, deeply shared silence with the beloved, are apt to remark, "In heaven's name, *say* something, will you?"

The problem stems quite naturally from the fact that women speak because they wish to speak, whereas a man speaks only when driven to speech by something outside himself—like, for instance, he can't find any clean socks, or he has just read in a headline that Herbert Hoover foresees no depression in 1960. A wife who really feels cheerful and chatty early in the morning (a circumstance that can be explained only by a faulty metabolism) can always inveigle her husband into conversation by using a little imagination and by learning to snap up cues. She might say, "Speaking of clean socks reminds me, did you read John Hutchens' review of *The Mackerel Plaza?*" Now he's on the spot. He has to say something, even if it is only to comment on the total absence of any connection between his socks and *The Mackerel Plaza.*

I have a rather engaging little trick for stirring my own husband into statement. I just quote a few lines from the balcony scene of *Romeo and Juliet.*

"He speaks," I say in mock lyrical tones, "but he says nothing. What of that? His eye discourses. I will answer *it.*" Thus prodded, he is apt to say things he will have to retract later, but there are risks to everything.

Actually, if you had wanted a husband who would be a stimulating conversationalist, you should have married a mechanic or even a gardener—certainly not an author or a professional man or, last of all, a lecturer. When we got married, my husband was a lecturer and professor of drama and I used to imagine the stimulating, intellectual conversation we were going to have at breakfast. Like this:

ME: That play last night was interesting, didn't you think?
HIM: Very. Of course, the author is still heavily in debt to Chekhov —the despairing protagonist, the shackling environment, the complete stasis in the third act and, of course, the total absence of climax.
ME: Yes, he has an almost kinetic sense of atmosphere, but he never licked the story line.
HIM: Licked it? He should have joined it.

(Appreciative chuckles all around.)

This, however, is a transcript of the actual conversation:

HIM: (Despairingly) I'll bet this is diet bread.
ME: What's the matter with diet bread?
HIM: (After a pause) Everything. Why don't we eat things other people eat?
ME: Such as—
HIM: (Passionately) Those flat sticky things with ham inside them. Or muffins. Why don't we ever have muffins?
ME: (Evenly) Very well, dear, we'll have muffins.
HIM: (Suspiciously) Oh, I know you. You'll get diet muffins.

We really should have our own radio show.
It's interesting to observe the phenomenon that will cause a husband who hasn't opened his yap in weeks suddenly to find the gift of speech. Just order a new coat that differs in any way at all from the last five coats you have owned and watch Big Chief Still Waters blossom into Alistair Cooke, a veritable fount of articulation. "Yes, I know it's the new style, but we haven't got a space ship yet. Oh, I see, all the fullness in the back is *supposed* to make you look as if you're standing in a head wind! Well, never mind. It'll be economical, anyway—in the summer you can take it to the beach and use it as a cabana." Etc.
There is a cure for this. Just take him with you when you go to Bonwit Teller's. Once you deposit him on that chaste Empire sofa in Misses's Suits, his whole attitude will change—not to mention his pulse, temperature, and rate of breathing. Precisely what causes men to go into

shock in Bonwit's I can't imagine. My husband keeps looking from right to left in a state of ashen panic, as though he feared at any moment one of those elegant salesladies was going to snatch him and set his hair. But at any rate he brings a more judicious attitude to the subject of high style. "Yeah, yeah," he mutters at my first reappearance from the depths of the dressing room, "it looks great, let's get out of here."

Some men do most of their talking at the movies ("Good Lord, I knew I was in for *Moby Dick,* but you didn't say there was going to be forty minutes of cartoons!"). My father is a man like that. The most he has spoken in thirty years was on a certain unfortunate occasion when my mother (who can't remember the titles of movies) took him for the second time in three weeks to see Bob Hope in *Son of Paleface.*

But let's get down to cases:

## How to Talk to a Man When He's Snoring

When I speak of snoring I do not refer to the simple, rhythmic snorp-bleet, snorp-bleet to which every loyal, understanding wife should adjust. I am here talking of snoring which has the range and crescendo of a musical composition—where you can actually detect a verse, two choruses, and a release. I used to give my husband a gentle shove and whisper, "Honey, turn over—you're snoring." The result was that he turned over and in two minutes was snoring louder than before, while I lay awake for hours planning a separation and wondering what we were going to do about the children and all those monogrammed towels.

Then I learned the trick, which is to get the snorer interested. Don't make statements. Ask questions. Shake him and say, "Darling, what are you trying to say?" Eventually, after a few incoherent "huh, huhs" and "what, whats," he'll ask, "What do you mean, what am I trying to say?" After a few more equally pointless questions and answers he will be so cross that it will be at least fourteen minutes before he'll be able to snore again, giving you ample time to get to sleep first.

## How to Talk to a Man in a Fashionable Restaurant

I once read an interview with the Duchess of Windsor in which she said that she and the Duke hated to eat in public restaurants because they had to converse so animatedly and affect such feverish interest in each other—lest rumors start that they were estranged—that she never could enjoy a bite of her dinner. It ought to be (but somehow it isn't) helpful to tell yourself that you're not the Duchess of Windsor and that nobody is even the tiniest bit interested in whether you and your husband have spoken since 1943. The point is that in a restaurant (like

Sardi's, for instance) where you are surrounded by the tinkling laughter of beautiful models engaged in vivacious conversation with movie actors, you do feel somehow that you can't just sit there, specters at the feast, looking like two people who have just learned that their 1958 income-tax return was being investigated. Of course there are lots of things on your mind that you could say ("Well, you saw that Chris got D in Health Habits again," or, "The man came about the drier and he says we need a whole new unit"), but this doesn't seem to be the time or the place.

A couple I know have solved the problem beautifully. She just tells him the story of The Three Bears, a narrative which is admirable for the purpose because of its many rising inflections. And he helps her out by occasionally interjecting a remark like "By George, you mean she ate every last bite of the baby bear's porridge?" Do try it some time. Anybody overhearing you will conclude that you are discussing a new television spectacular—either that, or you're both a little bit dotty. If you should be concerned about this aspect of the matter, or if you should happen to intercept a stunned glance from the waiter, you can always drop in a covering remark like "Red Buttons—*there's* your Baby Bear!"

## How to Talk to a Man When He's Taking a Shower

Here you have a captive audience and an ideal opportunity to tell a husband a number of things that you don't want him to hear. (Later on you can say, "Of course I told you, you just don't listen!") There is no limit to the amount of unwelcome information you can get off your chest at one clip in these circumstances: "The man from Macy's was here and I took thirty dollars out of your wallet," and "Betty called, she and George are going to drop in," and "The children are going to be in a Humpty-Dumpty play tonight—Col is playing Humpty and John is one of the king's men and we both have to go."

## How to Talk to a Man on the Telephone, Long Distance

When a man calls you from Tulsa, he invariably makes the mistake of calling either from a public bar or from his mother's living room. Neither setting is exactly conducive to a free exchange of ideas. There, within earshot of his fellow revelers or his mother, he can hardly say the one thing you want to hear, which is that he misses you terribly, it's been a nightmare, a nightmare! and he's never going to make a trip alone again. For that matter, you can't tell him you miss him either, because the children are there with you and they become downright alarmed at any hint that their parents have preserved this degrading adolescent attachment so far into senility. So, if you're not careful, it's going to be a total loss of five dollars and eighty-five cents.

Don't, whatever you do, launch into that foolish litany of last-minute health bulletins: "Yes, I'm fine, yes, Chris is fine, yes, Gilbert is fine, etc." Let it be understood in advance that if one of the children should be rushed to the hospital for an emergency appendectomy, you'll mention it.

### How to Talk to a Man before a Party

There are two occasions when a wife absolutely expects that a loyal husband will cleave to her side: when she's having a baby and when she's having a party. (It's interesting to note that the announcements on both occasions always seem to imply that these are joint projects, but, when it comes right down to it, who has that baby and who has that party? You do.) No one expects a husband to go out in the kitchen and stuff eggs, but he might try being a moral support during that horrible, hollow half hour before the first guest arrives. There you are, wandering aimlessly about from ash tray to ash tray, suddenly as much a stranger in your own home as if you were on Person to Person showing Ed Murrow around. And one of the reasons you can't rely on your husband for a comforting remark is that this is precisely the moment he chooses to lay a few asphalt tiles on the floor of the rumpus room.

If you should stand on your rights and say, "Don't you disappear anywhere at all, just stay right here!" he will eventually lighten the tension by muttering, "Great Scott, you forgot limes!" What he should say, of course, is something soothing, like "Darling, you look charming in that dress. It reminds me of the night we met, do you remember? You were dancing with Hugh, and I came in with Connie and Leo . . ."

The last time we had a party I suggested this constructive line of conversation to my husband. He claimed that he'd once said something very similar, and what I said was "In heaven's name, stop chattering about the night we met and go get some ice."

### How to Talk to a Man after You've Told Him That If He Doesn't Stop Fiddling with That Old Toaster He Is Going to Blow a Fuse, and He Does.

There is no way. Just light a candle and count ten or your blessings, whichever is greater.

# HELL CREEK CROSSING

## William Faulkner

WILLIAM FAULKNER (1897–1962) was not only one of the greatest writers of his time, but as fine a gentleman as the editors of this anthology ever met. He gave his friendship sparingly, but once it was given, it was for life. Faulkner was not only born in Mississippi, but spent most of his life there. "Yoknapatawpha County" was the name he gave to his home territory when he began writing about its characters, customs, and legends. Quickly enough recognized by discerning critics, Faulkner's unyielding obscurities and involved technique baffled the general public, and to make ends meet he had to turn to a series of incongruous and uncongenial jobs. With *Sanctuary,* however, he won his first large audience, and he could at last afford to center his life on the career he sought. Settling down in an old mansion in Oxford, Mississippi, he devoted his mornings to writing, and the rest of the day to huntin', ridin', and to expert consideration of his favorite Bourbon brews. In 1950 William Faulkner won the Nobel Prize for Literature. What follows below is a choice episode from *The Reivers,* his final, and in many ways, his most entertaining book.

So I learned at the tender age of eleven that a man is not the victim of his fate or destiny at all, nor even of circumstances, but simply of his appetites. And not just his own appetites, but those of his friends too if he is not careful.

Of course there was circumstance in it too: That a year ago (this was 1905) my grandfather had bought the second automobile in Jefferson, and two days ago my mother's father had died suddenly in Bay St. Louis, 300 miles away, and that thirty-odd years ago Boon Hogganbeck had been born and had been a member (retainer, man Friday) of our family or us ever since—a big man, whose grandmother had been a Chickasaw squaw, over six feet tall with a face like a gigantic walnut, of whom my grandfather was already saying that at any moment now I would outgrow. Nor do I forget Ned either, who was older than Boon and should certainly have known better, who had been born a slave in my great-grandfather's backyard and had never let any of us forget or evade it. The fact that when my grandfather and grandmother and father and mother left by train that Saturday morning to attend Grandfather Lessep's funeral, to be gone at least four days, and my grandfather left the key to the garage door where Boon could get his hand on it was merely coincidental too. The fact remains that what started Ned and Boon and me for Memphis in grandfather's automobile that Saturday afternoon was simply our appetites: I, an eleven-year-old boy who for four days would be free of check of father and mother and vulnerable to the seduction of a cross-country motor trip to anywhere, even by Boon Hogganbeck; and Boon Hogganbeck, who loved—found a year ago that he did automobiles as other people love symphonies or gambling or making money; and Ned, who, as he told Boon himself when we found him stowed away in the back of the car with the spare gasoline can and axe and a lantern and shovel, would like a trip too and deserved one in grandfather's automobile as much or even more than either of us, since I was merely grandfather's grandson and Boon wasn't any kin to him at all.

That was about sundown. I mean, when we—Boon and I—discovered that Ned too already dressed in his black Sunday suit and hat and the boiled white collarless shirt held at the neck by a brass stud shaped like the head of a small venomous snake, and the small worn handbag which had belonged to my great-grandfather and which contained a Bible and a pint flask containing about two tablespoons of whisky, was hidden beneath the tarpaulin in the back of the car, where he had lain concealed all the time Boon (me steering) was manhandling the automobile by simple brute force through the mudhole at Hurricane Creek five miles from Jefferson. But we were ten miles farther on now, within a mile or so of Ballenbaugh's, where we would spend the night —too far now for Boon to make him get out and walk back to town, which Ned knew.

So it was full dark when we reached Ballenbaugh's; Boon had long since stopped and got out and lit the coal-oil headlights. In the old Chickasaw days it was known as Wyott's Crossing. Then Ballenbaugh, a deserter from the Confederate Army, came and dispossessed it and turned it into a clearinghouse for horse and cattle thieves (some said murderers too), a place of unsavory repute which honest people, and even people who merely wanted to keep what they had, avoided; this until the summer of 1886, when a Baptist minister named Hiram Hightower—also a giant of a man, as tall and almost as big as Ballenbaugh himself, who on Sunday from 1861 to 1865 had been one of Forrest's company chaplains and on the other six days one of his hardest and most outrageous troopers—rode into Ballenbaugh's armed with a Bible and his bare hands and converted the entire settlement with his fists, one at a time when he could, two or three at a time when he had to. So when Boon and Ned and I approached it in this May dusk of 1905, Ballenbaugh was accomplishing his third avatar in the person of a fifty-year-old maiden: his only child: a prim fleshless severe iron-gray woman who farmed a quarter section of good bottom cotton- and corn-land and conducted a small store with a loft above it containing a row of shuck mattresses each with its neat perfectly clean sheets and pillow cases and blankets for the accommodation of fox- and coon-hunters and fishermen, who (it was said) returned the second time not for the hunting and fishing but for the table Miss Ballenbaugh set.

She heard us too. Nor were we the first; she told us that we were the thirteenth automobile to pass there in the last two years, five of them in the last forty days; she had already lost two hens and would probably have to begin keeping everything penned up, even the hounds. She and the cook and a Negro man were already on the front gallery, shading their eyes against the ghostly flicker of our headlights as we drove up. She not only knew Boon of old, she recognized the automobile first; already even after only thirteen of them, her eye for individual cars was that good.

"So you really did make it to Jefferson, after all," she said.

"In a year?" Boon said. "Lord, Miss Ballenbaugh, this automobile has been a hundred times farther than Jefferson since then. A thousand times. You might as well give up: you got to get used to automobiles like everybody else." That was when she told us about the thirteen cars in two years, and the two hens.

"At least they got a ride on an automobile for a little piece anyway," she said. "Which is more than I can say."

"You mean to say you aint never rode in one?" Boon said. "Here, Ned," he said, "jump out of there and get them grips out too. Loosh, let Miss Ballenbaugh set up in front where she can see out."

"Wait," Miss Ballenbaugh said. "I must tell Alice about supper."

"Supper can wait," Boon said. "I bet Alice aint never had a car ride neither. Come on, Alice. Who's that with you? Your husband?"

"I aint studying no husband," the cook said. "And I wouldn't be studying Ephum even if I was."

"Bring him on anyway," Boon said. The cook and the man came and got in too, into the back seat with the gasoline can and the folded tarpaulin. Ned and I stood in the lamplight from the open door and watched the automobile, the red tail lamp, move on up the road, then stop and back and turn and come back past us, Boon blowing the horn now, Miss Ballenbaugh sitting erect and a little tense in the front seat, Alice and Ephum in the back seat waving to us as they passed.

"Whooee, boy," Ephum shouted at Ned. "Git a horse."

"Showing off," Ned said; he meant Boon. "He better be sho proud Boss Priest aint and standing here too. He'd show him off." The car stopped and backed and turned again and came back to us and stopped. After a moment Miss Ballenbaugh said,

"Well." Then she moved; she said briskly: "All right, Alice." So we had supper. And I knew why the hunters and fishermen came back. Then Ned went off with Ephum and I made my manners to Miss Ballenbaugh and, Boon carrying the lamp, we went upstairs to the loft above the store.

"Didn't you bring nothing?" Boon said. "Not even a clean handkerchief?"

"I wont need anything," I said.

"Well, you cant sleep like that. Look at them clean sheets. At least take off your shoes and pants. And your maw would make you brush your teeth too."

"No she wouldn't," I said. "She couldn't. I aint got anything to brush them with."

"That wouldn't stop her, and you know it. If you couldn't find something, you'd make something to do it with or know the reason why."

"All right," I said. I was already on my mattress. "Good night." He stood with his hand up to blow out the lamp.

"You all right?" he said.

"Shut up," I said.

"Say the word. We'll go back home. Not now but in the morning."

"Did you wait this long to get scared?" I said.

"Good night," he said. He blew out the lamp and got on his mattress. Then there was all the spring darkness: the big bass-talking frogs from the sloughs, the sound that the woods makes, the big woods, the wilderness with the wild things: coons and rabbits and mink and muskrats and the big owls and the big snakes—moccasins and rattlers— and maybe even the trees breathing and the river itself breathing, not to mention the ghosts—the old Chickasaws who named the land before the white men ever saw it, and the white men afterward—Wyott and old Sutpen and Major de Spain's hunters and the flatboats full of cotton and then the wagon trains and the brawling teamsters and the line of brigands and murderers which produced Miss Ballenbaugh; suddenly I realised what the noise was that Boon was making.

"What are you laughing at?" I said.

"I'm thinking about Hell Creek bottom. We'll hit it about eleven oclock tomorrow morning."

"I thought you said we'll have trouble there."

"You damn right we will," Boon said. "It'll take that axe and shovel and bob wire and block and tackle and all the fence rails and me and

you and Ned all three. That's who I'm laughing at: Ned. By the time
we are through Hell Creek tomorrow, he's going to wish he hadn't
busted what he calls his manners nor et nor done nothing else under that
tarpollyon until he felt Memphis itself under them wheels."

Then he waked me early. And everybody else within a half mile,
though it still took some time to get Ned up from where he had slept
in Ephum's house, to the kitchen to eat his breakfast (and even longer
than that to get him out of the kitchen again with a woman in it).
We ate breakfast—and after that breakfast if I had been a hunter or a
fisherman I wouldn't have felt like walking anywhere for a while—
and Boon gave Miss Ballenbaugh another ride in the automobile, but
without Alice and Ephum this time, though Ephum was on hand. Then
we—Boon—filled the gasoline tank and the radiator, not because they
needed it but I think because Miss Ballenbaugh and Ephum were
there watching, and started. The sun was just rising as we crossed the
Iron Bridge over the river (and the ghost of that steamboat too; I had
forgot that last night) into foreign country, another county; by night
it would even be another state, and Memphis.

"Providing we get through Hell Creek," Boon said.

"Maybe if you'd just stop talking about it," I said.

"Sure," Boon said. "Hell Creek bottom dont care whether you talk
about it or not. It dont have to give a durn. You'll see." Then he said,
"Well, there it is." It was only a little after ten; we had made excellent
time following the ridges, the roads dry and dusty between the sprouting fields, the land vacant and peaceful with Sunday, the people already
in their Sunday clothes idle on the front galleries, the children and dogs
already running toward the fence or road to watch us pass; then in the
surreys and buggies and wagons and horse- and mule-back, anywhere
from one to three on the horse but not on the mule (a little after
nine we passed another automobile; Boon said it was a Ford; he had an
eye for automobiles like Miss Ballenbaugh's), on the way to the small
white churches in the spring groves.

A wide valley lay before us, the road descending from the plateau
toward a band of willow and cypress which marked the creek. It didn't
look very bad to me, nowhere near as wide as the river bottom we had
already crossed, and we could even see the dusty gash of the road
mounting to the opposite plateau beyond it. But Boon had already
started to curse, driving even faster down the hill almost as if he were
eager, anxious to reach and join battle with it, as if it were something
sentient, not merely inimical but unredeemable, like a human enemy,
another man. "Look at it," he said. "Innocent as a new-laid egg. You
can even see the road beyond it like it was laughing at us, like it was

saying If you could just get here you could durn near see Memphis; except just see if you can get here."

"If it's all that bad, why dont we go around it?" Ned said. "That's what I would do if it was me setting there where you is."

"Because Hell Creek bottom aint got no around," Boon said violently. "Go one way and you'd wind up in Alabama; go the other way and you'll fall off in the Missippi River."

"I seen the Missippi River at Memphis once," Ned said. "Now you mention it, I done already seen Memphis too. But I aint never seen Alabama. Maybe I'd like a trip there."

"You aint never visited Hell Creek bottom before neither," Boon said. "Providing what you hid under that tarpollyon for yesterday is education. Why do you reckon the only two automobiles we have seen between now and Jefferson was this one and that Ford? Because there aint no other automobiles in Missippi below Hell Creek, that's why."

"Miss Ballenbaugh counted thirteen passed her house in the last two years," I said.

"Two of them was this one," Boon said. "And even them other eleven she never counted crossing Hell Creek, did she?"

"Maybe it depends on who's doing the driving," Ned said. "Hee hee hee."

Boon stopped the car, quickly. He turned his head. "All right. Jump out. You want to visit Alabama. You done already made yourself fifteen minutes late running your mouth."

"Why you got to snatch a man up just for passing the day with you?" Ned said. But Boon wasn't listening to him. I don't think he was really speaking to Ned. He was already out of the car; he opened the toolbox Grandfather had had made on the running board to hold the block and tackle and axe and spade and the lantern, taking everything out but the lantern and tumbling them into the back seat with Ned.

"So we wont waste any time," he said, speaking rapidly, but quite composed, calm, without hysteria or even urgency, closing the box and getting back under the wheel. "Let's hit it. What're we waiting for?"

Still it didn't look bad to me—just another country road crossing another swampy creek, the road no longer dry but not really wet yet, the holes and boggy places already filled for our convenience by previous pioneers with brush tops and limbs, and sections of it even corduroyed with poles laid crossways in the mud (oh yes, I realised suddenly that the road—for lack of any closer term—had stopped being not really wet yet too) so perhaps Boon himself was responsible; he himself had populated the stagnant cypress- and willow-arched mosquito-whined gloom with the wraiths of stuck automobiles and sweating and cursing people. Then I thought we had struck it, except for that fact that I not only couldn't see any rise of drier ground which would indicate we were reaching, approaching the other side of the swamp, I couldn't even see the creek itself ahead yet, let alone a bridge. Again the automobile lurched, canted, and hung as it did yesterday at Hurricane Creek: again Boon was already removing his shoes and socks and rolling up his pants. "All right," he said to Ned over his shoulder, "get out."

"I dont know how," Ned said, not moving. "I aint learned about automobiles yet. I'll just be in your way. I'll set here with Lucius so you can have plenty of room."

"Hee hee hee," Boon said in savage and vicious mimicry. "You wanted a trip. Now you got one. Get out."

"I got my Sunday clothes on," Ned said.

"So have I," Boon said. "If I aint scared of a pair of britches, you needn't be."

"You can talk," Ned said. "You got Mr. Maury. I has to work for my money. When my clothes gets ruint or wore out, I has to buy new ones myself."

"You never bought a garment of clothes or shoes or a hat neither in your life," Boon said. "You got one pigeon-tailed coat I know of that old Lucius McCaslin himself wore, let alone General Compson's and Major de Spain's and Boss's too. You can roll your britches up and take off your shoes or not, that's your business. But you're going to get out of this automobile."

"Let Lucius get out," Ned said. "He's younger than me and stouter too for his size."

"He's got to steer it," Boon said.

"I'll steer it, if that's all you needs," Ned said. "I been what you calls steering horses and mules and oxen all my life and I reckon gee and haw with that steering wheel aint no different from gee and haw with a pair of lines or a goad." Then to me: "Jump out, boy, and help Mr Boon. Better take your shoes and stockings—"

"Are you going to get out, or do I pick you up with one hand and snatch this automobile out from under you with the other?" Boon said. Ned moved then, fast enough when he finally accepted the fact that he had to, only grunting a little as he took off his shoes and rolled up his pants and removed his coat. When I looked back at Boon, he was already dragging two poles, sapling-sized tree trunks, out of the weeds and briers.

"Aint you going to use the block and tackle yet?" I said.

"Hell no," Boon said. "When the time comes for that, you wont need to ask nobody's permission about it. You'll already know it." *So it's the bridge* I thought. *Maybe there's not even a bridge at all and that's what's wrong.* And Boon read my mind there too. "Don't worry about the bridge. We aint even come to the bridge yet."

I would learn what he meant by that too, but not now. Ned lowered one foot gingerly into the water. "This water got dirt in it," he said. "If there's one thing I hates, it's dirt betwixt my nekkid toes."

"That's because your circulation aint warmed up yet," Boon said. "Take a-holt of this pole. You said you aint acquainted with automobiles yet. That's one complaint you wont never have to make again for the rest of your life. All right"—to me—"ease her ahead now and whenever she bites, keep her going." Which we did, Boon and Ned levering their poles forward under the back axle, pinching us forward for another lurch of two or three or sometimes five feet, until the car hung spinning again, the whirling back wheels coating them both from knee to crown as if they had been swung at with one of the spray nozzles which house painters use now. "See what I mean?" Boon said, spitting, giving another terrific wrench and heave which sent us lurching forward, "about getting acquainted with automobiles? Exactly like horses and mules: dont never stand directly behind one that's got one hind foot already lifted."

Then I saw the bridge. We had come up onto a patch of earth so (comparatively) dry that Boon and Ned, almost indistinguishable now with mud, had to trot with their poles and even then couldn't keep up, Boon hollering, panting, "Go on! Keep going!" until I saw the bridge a hundred yards ahead and then saw what was still between us and the bridge and I knew what he meant. I stopped the car. The road (the passage, whatever you would call it now) in front of us had not altered so much as it had transmogrified, exchanged mediums, elements. It now resembled a big receptacle of milk-infused coffee from which protruded here and there a few forlorn impotent hopeless odds and ends of sticks and brush and logs and an occasional hump of actual earth which looked startlingly like it had been deliberately thrown up by a plow. Then I saw something else, and understood what Boon had been telling me by indirection about Hell Creek bottom for over a year now, and what he had been reiterating with a kind of haunted bemused obsession ever since we left Jefferson yesterday. Standing hitched to a tree just off the road (canal) were two mules in plow gear—that is, in bridles and collars and hames, the trace chains looped over the hames and the plowlines coiled into neat hanks and hanging from the hames also; leaning against another tree nearby was a heavy double-winged plow—a middlebuster—caked, wings shank and the beam itself, with more of the same mud which was rapidly

encasing Boon and Ned, a doubletree, likewise mud-caked, leaning
against the plow; and in the immediate background a new two-room
paintless shotgun cabin on the gallery of which a man sat tilted in a
splint chair, barefoot, his galluses down about his waist and his (likewise muddy) brogan shoes against the wall beside the chair. And I
knew that this, and not Hurricane Creek, was where (Boon said) he
and Mr Wordwin had had to borrow the shovel last year, which (Boon
said) Mr Wordwin had forgot to return, and which (the shovel) Mr
Wordwin might as well have forgot to borrow also for all the good it
did them.

Ned had seen it too. He had already had one hard look at the mudhole. Now he looked at the already geared-up mules standing there
swishing and slapping at mosquitoes while they waited for us. "Now,
that's what I calls convenient—" he said.

"Shut up," Boon said in a fierce murmur. "Not a word. Dont make
a sound." He spoke in a tense controlled fury, propping his muddy
pole against the car and hauling out the block and tackle and the
barbed wire and the axe and spade. He said Son of a bitch three times.
Then he said to me: "You too."

"Me?" I said.

"But look at them mules," Ned said. "He even got a log chain already hooked to that doubletree—"

"Didn't you hear me say shut up?" Boon said in that fierce, quite
courteous murmur. "If I didn't speak plain enough, excuse me. What
I'm trying to say is, shut up."

"Only, what in the world do he want with the middlebuster?" Ned
said. "And it muddy clean up to the handles too. Like he been— You
mean to say he gets in here with that team and works this place like
a patch just to keep it boggy?" Boon had the spade, axe and block
and tackle all three in his hands. For a second I thought he would
strike Ned with any one or maybe all three of them. I said quickly:

"What do you want me—"

"Yes," Boon said. "It will take all of us. I—me and Mr Wordwin
had a little trouble with him here last year; we got to get through this
time—"

"How much did you have to pay him last year to get drug out?"
Ned said.

"Two dollars," Boon said. "—so you better take off your whole pants,
take off your shirt too; it'll be all right here—"

"Two dollars?" Ned said. "This sho beats cotton. He can farm right
here setting in the shade without even moving. What I wants Boss
to get me is a well-travelled mudhole."

"Fine," Boon said. "You can learn how on this one." He gave Ned the block and tackle and the piece of barbed wire. "Take it yonder to that willow, the big one, and get a good holt with it." Ned payed out the rope and carried the head block to the tree. I took off my pants and shoes and stepped down into the mud. It felt good, cool. Maybe it felt that way to Boon too. Or maybe his—Ned's too—was just release, freedom from having to waste any time now trying not to get muddy. Anyway, from now on he simply ignored the mud, squatting in it, saying Son of a bitch quietly and steadily while he fumbled the other piece of barbed wire into a loop on the front of the car to hook the block in. "Here," he told me, "you be dragging up some of that brush over yonder," reading my mind again too: "I dont know where it came from neither. Maybe he stacks it up there him-self to keep handy for folks so they can find out good how bad they owe him two dollars."

So I dragged up the brush—branches, tops—into the mud in front of the car, while Boon and Ned took up the slack in the tackle and got ready, Ned and I on the take-up rope of the tackle, Boon at the back of the car with his prize pole again. "You got the easy job," he told us. "All you got to do is grab and hold when I heave. All right," he said, "Let's go."

There was something dreamlike about it. Not night-marish: just dreamlike—the peaceful, quiet, remote, sylvan, almost primeval setting of ooze and slime and jungle growth and heat in which the very mules themselves, peacefully swishing and stamping at the teeming infini-tesimal invisible myriad life which was the actual air we moved and breathed in, were not only unalien but in fact curiously appropriate, being themselves biological dead ends and hence already obsolete before they were born; the automobile: the expensive useless mechnanical toy rated in power and strength by the dozens of horses, yet held help-less and impotent in the almost infantile clutch of a few inches of the temporary confederation of two mild and pacific elements—earth and water—which the frailest integers and units of motion as produced by the ancient unmechanical methods, had coped with for countless gen-erations without really having noticed it; the three of us, three forked identical and now unrecognisable mud-colored creatures engaged in a life-and-death struggle with it, the progress—if any—of which had to be computed in dreadful and glacier-like inches. And all the while, the man sat in his tilted chair on the gallery watching us while Ned and I strained for every inch we could get on the rope which by now was too slippery with mud to grip with the hands, and at the rear of the car Boon strove like a demon, titanic, ramming his pole beneath the automobile and lifting and heaving it forward; at one time he dropped, flung away the pole and, stooping, grasped the car with his

hands and actually ran it forward for a foot or two as though it were a
wheelbarrow. No man could stand it. No man should ever have to. I
said so at last. I stopped pulling, I said, panted: "No. We cant do it.
We just cant." And Boon, in an expiring voice as faint and gentle as
the whisper of love:

"Then get out of the way or I'll run it over you."

"No," I said. I stumbled, slipping and plunging, back to him. "No,"
I said. "You'll kill yourself."

"I aint tired," Boon said in that light dry voice. "I'm just getting
started good. But you and Ned can take a rest. While you're getting
your breath, suppose you drag up some more of that brush—"

"No," I said, "no! Here he comes! Do you want him to see it?"
Because we could see him as well as hear—the suck and plop of the
mules' feet as they picked their delicate way along the edge of the
mudhole, the almost musical jangle of the looped chains, the man riding one and leading the other, his shoes tied together by the laces
looped over one of the hames, the doubletree balanced in front of
him as the old buffalo hunters in the pictures carried their guns—a
gaunt man, older than we—I anyway—had assumed.

"Morning, boys," he said. "Looks like you're about ready for me now.
Howdy, Jefferson," he said to Boon. "Looks like you did get through
last summer, after all."

"Looks like it," Boon said. He had changed, instantaneous and
complete, like a turned page: the poker player who has just seen the
second deuce fall to a hand across the table. "We might a got through
this time too if you folks didn't raise such heavy mud up here."

"Dont hold that against us," the man said. "Mud's one of our best
crops up thisaway."

"At two dollars a mudhole, it ought to be your best," Ned said. The
man blinked at Ned a moment.

"I dont know but what you're right," he said. "Here. You take this
doubletree; you look like a boy that knows which end of a mule to
hook to."

"Get down and do it yourself," Boon said. "Why else are we paying
you two dollars to be the hired expert? You done it last year."

"That was last year," the man said. "Dabbling around in this water
hooking log chains to them things undermined my system to where
I come down with rheumatism if I so much as spit on myself." So
he didn't stir. He just brought the mules up and turned them side
by side while Boon and Ned hooked the trace chains to the single-
trees and then Boon squatted in the mud to make the log chain fast
to the car.

"What do you want me to hook it to?" he said.

"I dont care myself," the man said. "Hook up to any part of it you want out of this mudhole. If you want all of it to come out at the same time, I'd say hook to the axle. But first I'd put all them spades and ropes back in the automobile. You wont need them no more, at least here." So Ned and I did that, and Boon hooked up and we all three stood clear and watched. He was an expert of course, but by now the mules were experts too, breaking the automobile free of the mud, keeping the strain balanced on the doubletree as delicately as wire walkers, getting the automobile into motion and keeping it there with no more guidance than a word now and then from the man who rode the near mule, and an occasional touch from the peeled switch he carried; on to where the ground was more earth than water.

"All right, Ned," Boon said. "Unhook him."

"Not yet," the man said. "There's another hole just this side of the bridge that I'm throwing in free. You aint been acquainted here for a year now." He said to Ned: "What we call the reserve patch up this-away."

"You means the Christmas middle," Ned said.

"Maybe I do," the man said. "What is it?"

Ned told him. "It's how we done at McCaslin back before the Surrender when old L.Q.C. was alive, and how the Edmonds boy still does. Every spring a middle is streaked off in the best ground on the place, and every stalk of cotton betwixt that middle and the edge of the field belongs to the Christmas fund, not for the boss but for every McCaslin nigger to have a Christmas share of it. That's what a Christmas middle is. Likely you mudfarming folks up here never heard of it." The man looked at Ned awhile. After a while Ned said, "Hee hee hee."

"That's better," the man said. "I thought for a minute me and you was about to misunderstand one another." He said to Boon: "Maybe somebody better guide it."

"Yes," Boon said. "All right," he told me. So I got under the wheel, mud and all. But we didn't move yet. The man said, "I forgot to mention it, so maybe I better. Prices have doubled around here since last year."

"Why?" Boon said. "It's the same car, the same mudhole; be damned if I dont believe it's even the same mud."

"That was last year. There's more business now. So much more that I cant afford not to go up."

"All right, goddammit," Boon said. "Go on." So we moved, ignominious, at the pace of the mules, on, into the next mudhole without stopping, on and out again. The bridge was just ahead now; beyond it, we could see the road all the way to the edge of the bottom and safety.

"You're all right now," the man said. "Until you come back." Boon was unhooking the log chain while Ned freed the traces and handed the doubletree back up to the man on the mule.

"We aint coming back this way," Boon said.

"I wouldn't neither," the man said. Boon went back to the last puddle and washed some of the mud from his hands and came back and took four dollars from his wallet. The man didn't move.

"It's six dollars," he said.

"Last year it was two dollars," Boon said. "You said it's double now. Double two is four. All right. Here's four dollars."

"I charge a dollar a passenger," the man said. "There was two of you last year. That was two dollars. The price is doubled now. There's three of you. That's six dollars. Maybe you'd rather walk back to Jefferson than pay two dollars, but maybe that boy and that nigger wouldn't."

"And maybe I aint gone up neither," Boon said. "Suppose I dont pay you six dollars. Suppose in fact I dont pay you nothing."

"You can do that too," the man said. "These mules has had a hard day, but I reckon there's still enough git in them to drag that thing back where they got it from."

But Boon had already quit, given up, surrendered. "God damn it," he said, "this boy aint nothing but a child! Sholy for just a little child—"

"Walking back to Jefferson might be lighter for him," the man said, "but it wont be no shorter."

"All right," Boon said, "but look at the other one! When he gets that mud washed off, he aint even white!"

The man looked at distance awhile. Then he looked at Boon. "Son," he said, "both these mules is color-blind."